D0977206

THE ARCHIVIST

ALSO BY REX PICKETT

Sideways

Vertical

Sideways 3: Chile

THE ARCHIVIST

a novel

REX PICKETT

Published in 2021 by Blackstone Publishing
Cover and book design by Kathryn Galloway English

Printed in the United States of America

First edition: 2021
ISBN 978-1-5385-1964-6
Fiction / Mystery & Detective

Version 1

CIP data for this book is available
from the Library of Congress

Blackstone Publishing
31 Mistletoe Rd.
Ashland, OR 97520

www.BlackstonePublishing.com

For Kate

Would you rather love the more, and suffer the more; or love the less, and suffer the less? That is, I think, finally, the only real question.

–Julian Barnes, *The Only Story*

PART I

THE FIRES OUTSIDE

From: San Diego Union-Tribune,
December 17, 2017

LA JOLLA, Calif.—San Diego police have identified the drowning victim at Black's Beach as Nadia Fontaine, an archivist employed at Regents University's Memorial Library. Discovered in the early-morning hours on Thursday, the victim was said to have been surfing at night in dangerous conditions. A distinguished member of the Society of American Archivists, Ms. Fontaine was most recently archiving the papers of Pulitzer Prize–winning author Raymond West.

CHAPTER 1

A Hard Rain's Got to Fall

8/3/18

All alone. Blissfully. I'm driving down the coast to San Diego to start a new job at Regents University. I'll be working as a project archivist on the Raymond West Collection, West being a celebrated writer whose work I'm vaguely familiar with.

The coast of California is beautiful, but the state is on fire!

Emily Snow was twenty-seven years old. She drove a three-year-old Mini Cooper S, shaded blue, her favorite color. She loved shifting the gears. Senna, the legendary Brazilian Formula One racer, who died tragically, was one of her heroes. She thought about him. She thought about many things as she drove down the coast of California, after a too brief sojourn in San Francisco and a stint as a cataloger at the Pacific Film Archive, to her new assignment in San Diego as a true archivist in manuscript processing. Prior to Pacific Film Archive, she had worked as a project archivist at the Harry Ransom Center on the campus of the University of Texas at Austin, immersed in its incredible collections of famous authors like Ian McEwan, Anne Sexton, and Nobel laureates Kazuo Ishiguro and Gabriel García Márquez, part of whose collection she had been privileged to work on. An archivist's dream. She adored Austin for its countercultural irreverence, but it was a city she was glad to say goodbye to when things went sour with a young musician by night / tech guy by day named Louis. Emily, no stranger to exploratory relationships, believed in fidelity, commitment. Now, her only commitment was to herself, and the uncertain life that unfolded before her. Like the ocean that stretched dark and white-capped blue to a milky pink horizon whose setting sun seemed to have touched off fires on the far side of the world. A sense of liberation suffused her. She had no ties to the past. All she wanted was to somehow make a difference on this planet going to hell.

Hell. California was on fire. Years of drought had laid a thick carpet of tinder. A superbloom had arisen out of a winter of unseasonably heavy rains. All it took were the Diablo winds in the north and the infamous Santa Anas of the east to galvanize the pyromaniacs into action and rip the power lines from their moorings and set the state ablaze. Fires had galloped west through Napa and Sonoma, hurtled surreally in the middle of the night over six lanes of asphalt and torched neighborhoods in Santa Rosa. Winds clocked at over sixty miles per hour drove currents of ash down the coast and caused many of the terrified inhabitants of San Francisco to don masks. The skies to the east were tarnished a brownish red color, as if some malignant force in the heavens had unleashed a virulent poison upon its planet.

Emily was driving away from the blackened ruins of one fire into the rotating cyclonic maw of another that was now burning through the Santa Barbara hillsides when her cell rang.

"Hi, Mom," she said, finger-wrestling with her earbuds, not wanting to get cited for her third cell violation in the past year. "How are you?"

"Are you in San Diego yet?" Her voice had the querulous intonation of a mother worried for an only daughter.

"No, not yet,"—she glanced out the window at the dark-blue ocean on the stunning Big Sur Drive—"but I'm making my way down the coast now."

"That's good. How are you feeling?" her mother asked.

"I'm fine. How are you?"

"I'm okay, Em. It's not fun in here," she replied, referring to the assisted-living facility she had moved to after suffering a cracked hip.

"I'm going to get you out to San Diego, Mom."

"Oh, I hope so," she said in a hopeful, higher octave. "Are you nervous?"

"About the new job?"

"Being all alone."

"No, I prefer it. For now."

Their conversation ground to an awkward halt. Emily was afraid to offer more, as if it would continue to deepen a line of questioning that she found uncomfortable. A private woman, she didn't like to have to hide her true self, but she wasn't fond of exposing it either. Maybe that's what had happened with Louis. She wouldn't let him in. She wouldn't let him in all the way. She longed for intensity, but only if it would be reciprocated. She feared he would take that big step inside and consume her like the fires ravaging the desiccated California forests. And in consuming her, he would colonize a part of her that she hoped never to cede. "What happened with Louis, dear?" was exactly the question she didn't want to have to address. There was no confabulating it away.

"I'll let you know when I get there, Mom."

"Drive safely."

Emily clicked her phone to the magnetized car mount. Absently, she played with a music app and tapped around until she located a station that played '80s rock. OMD, the Cure . . . From a decade before she was born, but the finest in pop music in her opinion, when music still had soul. The skies were darkening now, bleeding crimson. The charnel odor of ash stung her nostrils with the twin traces of death and rebirth. She had recently read an apocalyptic book titled *The Sixth Extinction* and believed that this is what the planet would look like when rats the size of Labradors, the author doomfully theorized, roamed the earth seeking the last vestiges of humankind. She wondered if the fires could climb over the hills and burn all the cars on Coast Highway 1 and leave nothing but a swath of gray all the way to the ocean, where the waves relentlessly battered the rocky shoreline. The sublime beauty and the horror that was California. Emily Katherine Snow, a girl raised in a small town in Massachusetts, who dreamed expansively when she was young, but now would be remembered by few if the fires incinerated her.

Emily was still floating in the same cloud of fatalism when she wheeled into the parking lot of a marine-themed restaurant in Morro Bay, a tourist town at the southern end of the Big Sur drive that boasted a wharf and a gigantic rock that jutted out of the shoreline like a granitic pustule.

She perused the laminated menu that a young waiter offered her. Debating a cold craft beer, she worried that it would make her sleepy during the stretch of miles facing her ahead.

"Fires are something, aren't they?" the waiter remarked.

Emily smiled without showing her teeth and nodded, not looking to attract men.

"They're saying they could make it all the way to Morro Bay."

"Morro Bay?"

"Where you're sitting." He smiled, exposing a mouth of brilliant white.

"Oh. I've been on the road." She looked off, not wanting to encourage him, if encouragement is what he had in mind. Emily wished she could read men better. She knew she was attractive to them, even if she deliberately wore off-putting black brow-line glasses and styled her chestnut-brown hair in a short, ragged, unkempt shag, as if she had cut it herself with a pair of scissors and a pocket mirror. As if, if you thought about it, she were an escapee from a lunatic asylum. She wore a poker-faced countenance and a mannish fashion statement of fleece vests over button-up shirts that made you question whether she was brilliant or crazy. Or both. She aspired to the misimpression. It was another way to armor herself.

"What's that you're reading?" he inquired, reaching to turn the book so he could make out its title. She let him. "Raymond West. *Lessons in Reality*." He turned the book back so that it faced her again. "Never heard of him."

"It won the Pulitzer. And some other prominent literary awards."

"Ah. Got to check him out someday."

As he walked away, Emily followed his retreating figure with wary eyes, her antennae vibrating. Men were the furthest thing from her mind.

Even though the restaurant was perched at the edge of a vast ocean, she was served an uninspired meal of overcooked fish and limp vegetables. She ate ravenously, her nose buried in *Lessons in Reality*. West's prose melted on the page. She could never write like that.

The Santa Ana winds had kicked up when she left the restaurant. She unfolded the collar to her fleece jacket so that it protected her neck as she walked back to her car. A tumbleweed hurtled across the street, reminding Emily of a scene out of a Sergio Leone film where a triad of desperate men faced off with drawn guns in a clichéd Mexican standoff. Overhead, gulls seeking cover cawed invisibly from the now dark and desolate wharf gloomily spangled with fog-blurred lights.

Back in her car, Emily realized she was facing another five brutal freeway hours before she got to Del Mar, an unincorporated beach hamlet north of San Diego where the apartment the library helped her secure was waiting. She reset her Google Maps app and turned the engine over on her car.

The wind buffeted her Mini as the route headed inland. Through the windshield, the fires raged in the foothills to the east of the 101 freeway, growing closer with the high-velocity easterly winds. Even though the fires were in the distance, they were advancing apocalyptically now, slanting and leaping, racing raggedly across the low-elevation mountains like an unapologetic force. *Leaping like dragons' tongues*, Emily almost said out loud to herself, recalling a lyrical phrase from a short story she had recently listened to on a podcast. "Love goes where it will; the arrow can only follow," she mouthed from some distant star in her literary memory. The fires, to her, seemed analogous to that unpredictable and uncontainable life force.

Raymond West's Pulitzer winner was also an audiobook, and she was listening to it now as the conflagrations lit up her driver's-side window. West had elected to narrate his own words. His voice had, Emily thought, a slight accent, but she couldn't place it. It was a gravelly, modulated voice—a man who was no stranger to smoke and drink, she thought. Or was she inflecting his voice with her imagination? She tried to marry his voice to the author's photo on the dust jacket, to paint an image of the man in three-dimensionality. With his shoulder-length hair, angular face, and rascally smile, he reminded her of the playwright Sam Shepard circa the late seventies.

In an adrenalized, coffee-fueled daze, she blasted through Santa Barbara, where the fires incandesced the night sky with infernos of violent orange. In contrast, West's voice drawled on, enunciating every word, bringing the dialogue to life with a thespian's flair. *Lessons in Reality* was deep, emotional, and soul baring, charting in hypnotic prose the interior landscape of a young man who yearned for experience but who was suicidally beset by fear of failure.

Los Angeles was looming below her now, dotted with pinpoints of lights that stretched to seeming infinity. The coffee had grown cold in her thermos. Her cell hadn't rung. Louis had texted her when she was at the restaurant, and she had impetuously decided to place a block on all his future texts. She had an image of her hand carving the air and creating a tabula rasa, starting over from a blank page. West's sonorous voice kept her awake. She marveled at his grasp of language. At times she shuddered in cringe-worthy respect at how personal he could be. The passages where he described the main character's various romances, his many—often self-destructive—amorous encounters. Hearing their accounting in his own voice, she felt an eerie sense of heightened closeness to him, as if he were narrating directly to her and no one else. Her absorption grew and helped the miles fly past.

Emily paused the audiobook and drank in Greater Los Angeles in all its blazing neon ugliness. The ten-lane freeway was bounded by garishly lit car dealerships, furniture warehouses, cheerless stucco apartment complexes, franchise restaurants, commercial office compounds with their mirrored fenestration and sepulchral cinderblock architecture. She couldn't imagine how anyone could work, let alone live, here. Emily briefly dated an LA screenwriter she met online. They traded emails and texts for weeks, and then, maddened with desire and almost ready to profess her undying love, she flew out to meet him. Within minutes the magic dissipated. He had said he worked in television, but that turned out to be a fiction when Emily pinned him down to specifics. Her impression of the entertainment business from this intense young man named Vince was that it was a world of desperate carapace-shelled pseudoartists who viciously competed in the concrete-and-glass megalopolis of a sun-drenched hell, cannibalizing one another for connections and an ephemeral moment in the spotlight. As much as Emily loved movies and some select TV shows—mostly British sketch comedies of the past—the people who created them seemed born like vermin to battle its cruel hierarchy to success. Women in particular, she gleaned from Vince, braved an even harsher truth in Hollywood, and always had. Like LA, not for her. She'd felt ashamed that she had let her imagination run riot with this wannabe screenwriter, booked a hotel room in Venice Beach, bivouacked miserably for two days after the magic had evaporated, and flew back to Austin and the emollience of Harry Ransom's vast library, content to be an archivist.

For a gleeful moment, Emily fatalistically fantasized about the fires burning through LA and torching it to the ground. There, Hollywood, take that!

At an off-ramp gas station, the howling Santa Ana winds whipped Emily's hair until it smarted her cheeks. She was reminded of a novella by Raymond Chandler titled *Red Wind.* Its premise was how the Santa Anas elicit the worst in the inhabitants of Los Angeles. The hot, dry winds—like the Föhn winds of Germany, which drive people to madness and suicide—activate the darkest impulses in the deepest recesses of the psyches of some Southern Californians and make them manifest in the most depraved way. Chandler, she reasoned, as she tried to fight off drowsiness, presaged the wave of pyromaniacs who crawled out of the weed-fissured cracks when the winds howled out of the canyons hot and ferocious.

From West LA to San Clemente, the drive was an alienating blur of one car dealership and corporate office edifice after another, a neon emblem of what late-stage capitalist America had devolved to. Long Beach, with its oil refineries scaffolded in webs of lights, loomed like something out of one of those dystopian movies that were fashionable of late, and which Emily loathed. No doubt they used Long Beach for locations for the worst the planet had to offer, Emily chuckled to herself. It resembled a lost civilization in ruin, one whose people had long since abandoned it for more Edenic lands, taking their plundered oil riches with them.

From Long Beach to San Clemente, cinderblock-hideous corporate headquarters gave way to more cheerless housing for people who could only afford to live close to the deafening freeway, the aortic lifeline to everything that epitomized Southern California. Emily's own feelings of loneliness—the boyfriend who cheated on her; her mother recovering from her hip fracture and all alone in assisted living in Massachusetts; no siblings; no friends other than Professor Mark Erickson from UT Austin, who had mentored her—was mirrored in this depopulated world of stark desolation. She wondered if she would one day find someone who got her for who she was, who would take the time—unlike Louis, unlike the narcissistic screenwriter—to get to know her deep down, in her soul. Maybe that's why she had chosen the archival profession. It demanded of one, Emily cynically thought, a kind of solitariness that would prove a bulwark to the inevitable disappointment of intimate relationships.

Blackness rushed up at her from the ocean when she sped past San Clemente. Stars feebly twinkled in the night sky. Known as the Camp Pendleton drive, it was an untrammeled twenty-mile stretch of freeway owned by the federal government and controlled by the military. It was the only section of the freeway that prevented Los Angeles and San Diego from becoming one uninterrupted, overdeveloped coastline. San Diegans in particular, someone had told her, prayed it would never be commercialized; they reveled xenophobically in this lacuna between them and evil Los Angeles to the north. To Emily, the blackness that yawned at her was a welcome reprieve from nearly two hundred miles of soul-destroying freeway "scenery" she had carved her way through, hands hooked tight on the steering wheel, head bent forward, foot moving from the accelerator to the brake and back again as the traffic thickened and thinned with frustrating regularity.

Following the electronic voice of Google Maps, she bent off at the Del Mar Heights exit twenty miles north of San Diego and angled west. She coasted down a steep hill until she came to the Coast Highway. As she waited at the red light, she noticed there were no cars. The emptiness was welcoming. She had to execute a U-turn to get to the condo complex where she had rented a place for three months—the time the university had allotted her to finish up the Raymond West Collection.

Emily pulled into her designated spot, switched off the engine, and climbed out of her Mini Cooper, her ears buzzing from the long drive as if she had conch shells over them. She inhaled deeply—the air smelled of ash mixed with the brine of the nearby ocean and a beach heaped, she imagined, with decaying kelp. Fires had broken out in nearby Temecula, northeast of San Diego, but she didn't fear them here, where the surf pounded the cliffs and vast subdivisions separated her from the infernal madness.

Emily wrestled a bag out of the back seat and opened the unlocked door to her building. She found herself on the third of four floors of an eighteen-unit complex contoured like a horseshoe and facing the black void of the ocean. The quiet was so pronounced that she could distinctly make out the placid sighing of breaking waves. A half moon, bathed in amber, hung suspended in the night sky, the eye of some mythological animal. A peace pervaded Emily as she found her unit, number 11. The exhausting drive, the heavy feeling of loneliness and uncertainty, briefly vacated her. She had a job, she reminded herself. An apartment by the beach. While California burned and half the planet ravened for food, Emily had found an oasis of serenity.

Squatting down, she felt for the keys the landlord had left under the mat, relieved when her fingers closed around them. She opened the sliding glass door to her unit and turned sideways with the bulk of her bag to enter. Something alive brushed the inside of her left calf. Her heart raced. She groped for the light switch and snapped it on. An overhead light flickered to a pale blue. She dropped her bag and searched, terrified, for the animal that had darted in between her legs. Fearing a raccoon, she tiptoed around the small, sparsely furnished two-bedroom apartment as if it were booby-trapped. Raccoons scared her. One had bit her when she was young, and she had been obligated to endure a painful series of rabies injections.

She switched on the kitchen light. In the corner she noticed a black, furry object withdrawing into itself, its iridescent emerald eyes glowing around a pair of black pupils that drilled into Emily's heart. Emily bent down to the cowering animal, calmed when she recognized it was a cat. He recoiled at Emily's tentative touch.

"Here, kitty; here, kitty," she whispered. She extended a hand and scratched the top of the cat's head and petted her. Him? Yes, a *him*, she quickly determined. His fur was thick and satiny. He wore no collar, but possibly was microchipped for identification because he didn't act like a feral. Without protestation, Emily scooped him up and walked him outside, set him down gently, and slid the door shut. The meowing began immediately, at first plaintive, then more gutturally animalistic, beckoning her to let him back in. Until it faded into the pounding surf with a plangency that played at her emotions.

Emily plopped down on the black Naugahyde couch. She raked a hand through her hair and combed it off her face. It felt greasy and unwashed from the drive. She threw her feet up on the oblong coffee table and took in her short-term rental. Off the living room was a small dining area with a table and four chairs. Around a wall must have been the kitchen, but she was too tired to get up and check it out. A large-screen TV reflected her looking at it blankly. White walls flowed down to a white-tiled floor, half of it covered with a brown sisal rug. On one wall hung an expressionist Air France poster of Chile, a country as far away as Emily's imagination could transit. The long drive had narcotized her. She felt dead to the world. Until . . .

The black cat meowed again. His silhouette could be glimpsed behind the shroud of the white venetian blind. Emily had to chuckle at the blatancy of the premonitory symbolism of a black cat greeting her arrival in a new city, with a new job. She didn't subscribe to superstitions. What did she believe in, she wondered, all twenty-seven years of her, all alone, hunkered down for the next three months in a city where she was an outsider?

CHAPTER 2

Entropy

8/4/18

Predictably, I dreamed of fires. And moving from one house to another. I had no money. Roommates who were douchebags. The world was falling apart. I felt lost and alone, desperate and savage like an animal, and I remember that I desired a home I could call mine. I awoke to this apartment, a job, the sound of the ocean. Maybe dreams, in their compensatory function, make us appreciate what we have.

Emily awakened bathed in blinding sunlight. The room was white—too white. White walls, white ceiling, beige carpeting. For a moment she panicked, thinking she was in an institution, her thoughts briefly stampeded until the bracing light of consciousness reined them in.

Emily showered and shampooed the grunge out of her hair, threw on a pair of burgundy corduroys and a faded black long-sleeve T-shirt, and slipped into the kitchen. The refrigerator was as cavernously barren as when she had opened it before going to bed.

Dying of thirst, Emily powered up her laptop. The internet connection worked—thank God!—and she went online, typed in her address, and asked Google for nearby stores. The postapocalyptic dream still lingered in the penumbra of her befogged brain, and she tried to shake free of its ragged remnants. She needed coffee; she needed food; she needed not to feel anxious.

Emily climbed sleepily into her car, found the freeway a mile away, rode one exit north, and pulled into the Flower Hill shopping mall. She intuited her way to Swell Coffee, a local third-wave coffee house, and ordered an Ethiopian pour-over and a croissant. While she waited for her order, she surveyed the large, airy room with narrowed eyes. The customers constituted a cross section of youth she associated with Southern California. They were casually dressed, some in sandals, all of them either staring at cells or bent over laptops, even those who were seated across from each other.

"I guess the fires are still burning," Emily remarked, if only to hear her voice, as the young male barista slid her cup of coffee on a saucer toward her. A second dish rattled next to it with her heated croissant.

"Yeah, it's terrible for the horses," he lamented.

"What horses?" Emily asked.

No one was waiting behind her, so the barista produced his tablet and played Emily a news clip that showed startled Arabians bolting from their stables as smoke billowed in the skies behind them. In panicked herds, some of the horses galloped off in zigzagging patterns, while others tragically returned to their stables, where, the barista informed her, they burned to death in a kind of frenzied, unconscious self-immolation, their home their chamber of death.

"That's terrible," Emily remarked, prying her eyes away. The alarming video reminded her of her dream, that entropy seemed disconcertingly ubiquitous now. Who would bring order to the chaos? And those horses, rearing and bucking beneath a canopy of flames—she realized she had inadvertently brought a hand to her mouth to stifle her dismay.

Emily took her coffee and pastry and sat down at an unoccupied table. Like everyone else, she stared into her phone. There were the usual email advertisements and announcements from her past places of employment. Fastidious like so many archivists, she preferred to keep her inbox clear because she hated it when emails stared back at her like the black cat who had stolen into her apartment, seeking attention. The one from Louis she filed in a folder without reading. Seeing his email caused his profile photo to pop up and haunt her too-vivid imagination, degrading it with anger. She promised herself to delete it when she had time.

When she glanced up, a man a few years older than her was staring at her furrowed brow. She instinctively glanced away. A female colleague at Harry Ransom had warned her that Southern California men were strange. Because the city, with its vast network of cobwebbed freeways, was structured around the automobile, it fostered a personality of alienation that made men more socially awkward. Smart women like Emily tended to generalize that asocial men were tougher to understand, that their desires were often singularly focused, their libidos refracted through a distorted lens from too many miles spent alone on the road. It was a city of loners, and Emily was determined to be the most alone of all in the three months she was going to spend here.

Using her cell to locate nearby stores, Emily spent the afternoon on the crisscrossing freeways, stocking up on food and supplies. She wandered around in a high-ceilinged Bed Bath & Beyond, bought blackout curtains and some culinary improvements like a decent tea kettle and the best chef's knife she could afford. At Jimbo's, a natural foods grocery chain, she filled two bags with staples. She drove freeways under fitful skies that bled blue through the orange from the fires that were ravaging the inland mountains and canyons.

Back in her apartment, she distributed her purchases among the cabinets and refrigerator. She popped open the cage-and-cork-secured half liter of ale from Societe, a local craft brewery that had been recommended online, poured a glass, and went to work on the blackout curtains with a tool kit the apartment owner had thoughtfully supplied. She unpacked and stocked the bathroom shelves with shampoo, conditioner, lavender-scented soap, some makeup, Q-tips, a toothbrush, and the remainder of her essentials. One suitcase of clothes was stacked onto open shelving, dresses hung on plastic hangers. She traveled light. As in her dream, she was always on the verge of departure. Maybe she didn't want a home. Maybe she wanted to be a roustabout, a project archivist the rest of her life, moving itinerantly from job to job and never settling down. Yes, that's who she would be.

Before dark, she changed into a pair of sweatpants and a black T-shirt with white lettering that read "I Love Baudelaire" and walked down the steps of the apartment complex to a short alley that led through a quiet neighborhood of seaside homes. Within blocks she came to the bluff that fronted the Pacific. Santa Ana winds gusted from her back and groomed the incoming waves, blowing spray back off their feathering lips. Emily took up surfing the few months she spent in the Bay Area and found that she liked it. She enjoyed the solitariness of it, the fact that you didn't—unlike tennis—need a partner. She loved being with nature, even if the invisible creatures that teemed beneath conjured the mythic ogres of Jung's collective unconscious. The adrenaline rush of her first wave was addictive, and she was hooked. She would have to buy a new board and a wet suit, she decided, as she drank in the view. La Jolla Cove hooked out into the sea's heart from the south. To the north, the coastline gently curved westward and the hills were painted like a watercolor.

Emily leaped down to where the train tracks were laid along the cliff's edge and headed south. She couldn't believe how close the tracks ran along the vertical face of the friable bluff. Two or three more storm-lashed winters and these tracks would have to be put out of commission, she thought to herself.

Two teenage surfers outfitted in black wet suits and cradling small tri-fins under their arms approached her along the tracks. They both nodded at her, and she nodded back as they trod wordlessly past. Emily pulled a pair of wireless earbuds out of her sweatpants pocket and plugged her ears with them. Enlivened by the scenic view, her legs leaped in front of her, and she took off running, a mixtape filling her ears.

As she jogged along the bluff, she could feel a smile draw a line in her face. The way those surfers, a decade younger, had ogled her made her realize she was still a woman to be reckoned with. With her shock of spiky hair, luminous sky-blue eyes, slender but feminine figure that showed muscle where it was meant to, she knew she was beautiful, but she made a deliberate effort to conceal it. Louis had complimented her many times on her looks, usually—she winced in remembering—when they were naked and entangled in twisted, sodden sheets, his desire for her inflamed.

Fuck you, Louis. I really believed you showed promise. That's why I gave my heart to you. And then you trampled on it, extinguished it like the butt of a cigarette you had finished smoking halfway down. I had to live with that other woman's face in your text messages, her words in your emails, your words to her, the same words you said to me. I've never been so betrayed in all my life. I could have had almost anyone, but I fell for you because I believed in you. I will always love someone who can conjure magic through a talent for an art. But your words were sacred and inviolable to me. To read them written to someone else—what a fucking betrayal!

Emily halted her racing thoughts when she noticed a woman approaching, jerking a panting cocker spaniel on a leash. She didn't want the woman to think she was mad. Hurt had brought tears to her eyes, and she wiped them with a swipe of her hand. It occurred to her that with the earbuds visible in her ears the woman might assume she was talking on the phone. The woman smiled as she passed and said hi. Emily smiled a reply as she slowed to a walk, her heart beating, still, after these weeks since her breakup, trying to expunge the image and voice of Louis from her imagination.

She was about to start up again, because she wasn't finished with her diatribe, when she felt the dirt beneath her sneakers tremble. Mere feet from the railroad tracks, she turned abruptly and saw a train looming up. She backed away toward the cliff, but there was little room between the tracks and the abyss. The train's horn blared, and it shattered the silence in a deafening, shrill cry of warning. As it hurtled past, Emily tried to capture the faces in the upper deck, but they cascaded in a blur as the force of the train's passing buffeted her. She turned away from the dust that was kicked up and shielded her eyes with the back of her hand. In those few thunderous seconds of the train streaking past, she felt like it had taken Louis and all those despairing feelings and sucked them out of her head. The loud clacking of the train's wheels as it retreated around the bend at Torrey Pines Beach was the ellipsis that Emily needed. In that percussive, cathartic moment the Amtrak Surfliner mysteriously delivered, she resolved to be alone until she found the one who would get her on every layered, geological level where she believed her mind, heart, and body's want of exaltation had swept her. This is why she had decided to go into the archival profession. She could sink deep into others' lives, plumb their dark seafloors, anonymous to the world, alone with their narratives, a voyeur to their lives, preserving their words and images and films and the other items that constituted the documentation of a life.

The heart-racing rush of the train so perilously close to her had yanked the shroud of pain from her blackened heart, coloring it red. She pulsed with life suddenly. Maybe one day, she thought madly to herself, something she wrote would be immortalized by an archivist who cared for her legacy the same as she hoped to do for the works in her care.

The path along the train tracks, bristling with sharp rocks, wound down to the beach. The rusted iron rails angled inland over a trestle and a saltmarsh lagoon where frost-white egrets reflected the light of the sinking sun.

Emily removed her sneakers and rolled up her sweatpants and skirted the water's edge. A spent wave spumed above her ankles. The water felt warm enough to slip into, but she wasn't wearing her swimsuit. Surfers bobbed on the golden water, silhouetted by the milky-blue sky. To Emily they looked like the remaining survivors of an ancient order brought to near extinction by some cataclysm, oblivious to the planet's end while they waited for the ocean to pump in the next set of waves.

The water surging at her ankles promoted in Emily the idea that she was half in the ocean and half on the earth and that this duality somehow made her different from everyone else, sui generis. As she strolled aimlessly south, the cliffs of Torrey Pines State Reserve rose up, their sandy-brown, washboard faces colored orange by the grand spotlight of a lowering sun. The tops of the cliffs were ridged with rare Torrey pine trees and what looked in the dying light from the shore's edge like a vast fortress set imperially to ward off the advances of an imagined foe.

A set of waves advanced on the shore. The surfers sprang to life, windmilling their arms in hopes of getting out to where the new break line had been drawn by an unpredicted increase in the swell. The waves exploded phosphorescent white in the bewitched blue waters. Here and there a scream of pure exultation could be heard faintly through the thunder of the breaking waves as a black, wet-suited surfer streaked across its translucent face, barely ahead of the whitewater, where a wipeout and a beatdown awaited.

Emily stopped and tented her forehead with a bare hand. The waves were rising off the ocean's surface, higher than the beach where she had begun her walk, and peeling off in two directions, an avalanche of white-water tumbling shoreward.

The water fell quiet as the set died. The sea flattened, and the evening-glass surfers resumed their positions on their boards, shaking the water from their hair, exhilarated from the ocean's inexorable swells and the sublime beauty of nature.

A surfer rode in on the whitewater, hands planted on the nose of his board, his back arched, and his head erect. He picked up his board and splashed through the shallows in the direction of Emily.

"What beach is this?" Emily called out.

"Black's," replied the surfer, without breaking stride.

She charted his retreat in the fading light, but she wasn't looking at him; she was staring at something in her mind. *Black's*. The name sounded familiar. Emily suddenly remembered the article she had come across in the *Union-Tribune* when researching her predecessor, Nadia Fontaine. Fontaine had died in a drowning accident—right here at Black's Beach. There was no accompanying photo, only a short article about a Regents University archivist who had drowned last November.

Whitewater surged over Emily's ankles, wresting her from a developing image of the drowned woman who had unwittingly brought her to San Diego. Was it some weird frequency illusion that had brought her here?

Emily turned to go back. Over the craggy cliffs a spectacular blue supermoon rose, as if hoisted by invisible pulleys and wires. Closer to the earth than other moons, it loomed like a cosmic eye detached from its socket in the galaxies and fallen to earth. Emily imagined that it had descended to scrutinize her, to study her, to watch over her like a benevolent force. It seemed almost at arm's reach because she could make out the topography of the celestial orb, its mountains and valleys, ravines and moraines, or whatever was blue veined on the moon's orbed face.

In the semidarkness surfers sloshed out of the water and slipped silently past Emily. In their wet suits they looked like mermen of some long-ago past before humankind had evolved completely into terrestrial creatures. She didn't fear them. The moon was watching over her.

Another train, this one hurtling south, came rumbling down the tracks as Emily walked along the dirt pathway on the bluff's razor-thin edge. Now that it was night, its single revolving headlight shone brightly, and she threw up a forearm to shield her eyes. She stopped to let it pass. Mere feet away, it surged by with tremendous force. This time she could make out the faces of its passengers illuminated by the train compartment's lights.

Back at her apartment, Emily bent down to pet the black cat, who had curled himself up on the mat at the entrance to her unit. She stroked his thick, lustrous fur, and he purred contentedly and raised his pensive eyes to her beseechingly.

"All right, you," Emily whispered. She picked him up with one arm and carried him inside. The stray displayed no resistance, no feral aggression, hung limply in her hands. Emily set him down. She opened a can of tuna she had bought for herself and forked a small portion onto a salad plate and set it on the floor. From that moment forward, until someone claimed him, the cat was hers. She poured a glass of Societe IPA, smoothed the hair out of her face, and sat down at the dining room table, alone but exhilarated from the run. The cat looked up at her, licking his whiskers contentedly. He ambled shyly over toward Emily and leaped up onto the table. Emily reached out a hand. She decided to name him Onyx in honor of the color of his fur, and for the mood that she had been in when she gave notice at the Pacific Film Archive and landed this project-archivist assignment in San Diego, a city she had never visited before. "Huh, Onyx, you think I'll find it here?" she asked him.

CHAPTER 3

In the Beginning Was the Word

8/5/18

In Del Mar now. I befriended a stray cat I'm naming Onyx. I know it's prosaic, but I don't care. He can stay as long as he doesn't sink his fangs into me. I'm speaking this into my Voice Memos app. One day, when I find the time, I'll transcribe these.

When I raise my head, I can see the Pacific Ocean above the rooftops of the apartments. The sky is still painted with the cinders of the fires. According to the news, they continue to burn all up and down California.

My soul doesn't belong here.

Emily greedily ate a mix of yogurt and granola for breakfast. With the coffee gear she purchased, she ground the right amount of beans and produced a perfect pour-over. Onyx was curled up on the couch, sleeping, with the gimlet eye of a wary cat. Emily tried to rescue her dream from the torn pennants of awakening and reassemble it, but she couldn't find it behind the frayed skein of other things that were now occupying her mind.

Emily hated Sundays. Her parents used to make her go to church, but she never paid attention to what the pastor said. She wasn't even sure what denomination of Christian they were. They did it ritualistically because they thought it was the right thing to do at the time. But by the time she turned ten, her father was tired of the pastor knocking on their door and asking for donations, so they stopped going. Sundays became a day of play in the summer, but as an only child it was often one of loneliness in the frigid winters of Massachusetts. She burrowed into books as her parents entertained friends on the floor beneath her. Now and then she was trotted down and bombarded with the usual questions about what she wanted to be when she grew up. Because she was fascinated with books, she often replied, "Librarian," then scampered back upstairs.

Emily didn't know what she wanted to pursue professionally when she enrolled at Oberlin College, nor where a degree in English would land her. It wasn't as if she had decided on a vocation, set her heart on a goal, and wasn't going to waver in her pursuit. Her parents, like all parents, wanted her to map out her life, achieve her goals, settle down, and be happy. She knew she loved literature, and she was drawn to universities, particularly the libraries. Citadels of intellect she characterized and worshiped them. She was enamored of wandering the aisles of these libraries between sessions, when the students were gone. Her first real boyfriend was an anthropology graduate student she met in the stacks of a library. Emily found something sexy about meeting him there all alone, instead of in a bar, or—God forbid!—lurking on some online dating app. The first time, they had talked intensely for hours. Then she searched for him and was disappointed when she didn't see him gathering another bundle of books to take to a table where he was working on his thesis. She had fantasies of him—a tall, slender man with a ghostly, handsome face—ravishing her in the unisex private bathroom. The first time they made love was at his graduate student apartment. Once, though, she had confided her fantasy, and he made it a reality. They made a game out of it, pretended to meet, sweated up a storm in the small room, replete with disheveled clothes and whispered dirty talk, emerging red-faced and blushing when one of the facilities guys pushed a trash bin past. The affair ended when he finished his thesis and enrolled in a PhD program at a university in Oregon. Maybe it was the whole cycle of enchantment, reawakened sexual desire, and disappointment that ended it for Emily. She got bored with men easily. Their shortcomings always emerged through the palimpsest of the initial infatuation. But ever since, even though she had never duplicated the temerity of that encounter, libraries remained bewitched by a mesmeric aura of quiet romance that existed nowhere else in the world.

Emily climbed into her Mini and turned on an audiobook of Chilean poet Pablo Neruda's work. On short jaunts, she liked listening to poems. Neruda's metaphorical use of nature to express the yearnings of his soul called to her, even though she was aware that he had recently become politically incorrect. *Fuck that*, she cried out in her head.

She drove south on the Coast Highway in the direction of Regents University to get a first look at her new place of employment. As she reached the bottom of the hill, the Los Peñasquitos Lagoon blew open her view to the low, rolling hills to the east. Smoke mushroomed in the blue skies and flooded it with gray. Emily had read that the fires were less than 10 percent contained and were burning, news reports fatalized, out of control. Government cutbacks had forced layoffs of firefighter personnel, and now that the entire state was a patchwork of raging conflagrations, many fires were left to burn without waging a battle to contain them. In Emily's imagination, she glimpsed the beginnings of a dystopian America in those unmanageable fires. Her generation, she thought, would be facing an overpopulated world that would degenerate into savagery as precious resources were plundered and depleted.

Regents University was a complex of six colleges sprawled over a hilltop north of La Jolla. Eucalyptus trees sprouted up from its undulating grounds and rose high into the ash-cloaked sky. The campus buildings were constructed of concrete in a stingray-hued gray that reminded one of a vast Stonehenge, structures that would last centuries, perhaps outlive mankind. On first view they were both imperial and ugly. They inspired the urge to splash them with color and mar them with graffiti, to infuse life into them. But the longer one stared at them, the more they made sense. Unlike brick, concrete could withstand earthquakes, which, given that Regents was close to the infamous San Andreas fault line, was certainly taken into consideration when the blueprints of the original design were drafted. Then too, if those fires raging in the small eastern towns of Ramona and Mount Julian were to jump the freeways, fueled by fresh Santa Ana winds that could stream their embers for miles, the soaring eucalyptus trees would be torched like giant matchsticks, but the buildings, colored charcoal by the conflagrations, would remain standing, immutable, and students and faculty could resume studies on a scorched landscape, their classrooms and materials undamaged.

As Emily weaved her way through the campus arteries, she passed a verdant soccer field that was devoid of activity. Regents was on a quarter system, and the fall quarter wasn't due to begin for another six weeks. Parking spaces were plentiful. Sidewalks were desolate. A skateboarder streaking past through a stop sign startled Emily, and she braked violently to avoid him. No, it was a *she*! She lowered the volume on her audiobook, intimidated a little now by the vast university sprawl.

Emily parked on the street in a "B"-designated space (students and staff) and crawled out of her Mini, straightening her legs to a blinding sky. Rising sentinel-like before her was the signature campus building: Memorial Library. Where Special Collections & Archives was located—her new home for the next three months. A hexagonal, eight-story monstrosity with massive concrete pillars that corbelled out into a pedestal holding it all in place, Memorial Library bulged to its widest at the fifth floor, then tapered tentlike back in to the eighth. The edifice's wraparound windows had a mirrored cast and reflected the surroundings: campus, towering eucalypti, the heavens. The sky burned orange on the windows and flared in blinding fulgurations as the aspect changed. It looked like what screenwriters and production designers might imagine a spaceship to look like if an alien race had decided to colonize this hilltop in La Jolla. Some said it resembled a giant jeweled ring raised aloft by the colossal concrete pillars that jutted at acute angles. It was a formidable structure, the tallest on campus, by far the largest in terms of square footage, and the one most trafficked. You could study four years here and graduate from this university and not remember much, but you would remember Memorial Library the way you might a life-changing dream.

As Emily approached the library from the concrete plaza, the edificial colossus seemed to gather itself up higher and higher until she was standing directly beneath it, her head bent back at an angle of ninety degrees, her eyes reaching all the way up into the ash-occluded skies. Nothing could bring this library down, Emily thought to herself. Its books and papers, and all the items in Special Collections, would be here for seeming eternity. It suffused Emily with a feeling there might actually be order in chaos, an antidote to impermanence, seeming immortalization of that which was deemed important by Helena Blackwell, the director of Special Collections, and the woman who had hired a nervous Emily over a Skype conference call—hell, handpicked her on a recommendation by Professor Erickson at Harry Ransom Center, an avuncular man who had sung Emily's praises—and didn't so much interview her as outright offer her the job. The project archivist position at UCLA Film & Television Archive, though intriguing, didn't interest her, because of her antipathy for LA. Emily was more interested in literature than she was in film preservation anyway. The Harry Ransom Center had an open door for her whenever she wanted to return—she was already that well respected and liked there. At the callow age of twenty-seven she was considered a consummate, if a little unseasoned, professional archivist.

Emily lowered her head and took the steps down to the main floor. Above the sliding doors were four window panels, designed by acclaimed artist John Baldessari, with the words READ WRITE THINK DREAM etched in the tint so that they glowed white from the interior light. Emily wondered if these words meant the same thing to her generation, and the one rushing inexorably after that, as they did to her.

The automatic doors peeled away to allow Emily inside the cavernous Memorial Library. An elderly woman sat alone in front of a computer monitor at the information desk. Otherwise, the library's main floor was vacant. The quiet was sepulchral.

Emily approached the desk, and the woman looked up and smiled with eyes in two nests of loose, gray skin magnified by her bifocals. "I start work here tomorrow," Emily blurted out.

"Oh. What department?" she asked, adjusting her glasses.

"Special Collections and Archives," Emily replied.

"Oh, Helena Blackwell. You're going to enjoy working for her. She's an institution."

Emily smiled and extended her hand. "I'm Emily Snow."

"Deborah. Nice to meet you." Deborah took her hand and shook it briefly.

Emily glanced around. "It's quiet."

"Fall quarter doesn't start until mid-September."

Emily nodded. Two student workers, bent at the waist, pushed carts laden with haphazardly strewn piles of books toward a service elevator. Perspiration mottled their coal-gray uniforms. The elevator doors clanged open, and they disappeared from view.

"I think I'm going to explore a little," Emily said.

"Go up to the eighth floor. Views are amazing."

"Okay. I will."

Deborah flung out an arm as if she'd made the exact same gesture many times and pointed to the elevators. "Welcome to Regents."

Emily smiled, turned, and headed in the direction Deborah had indicated. She rode a swiftly rising elevator car eight floors up without a single stop, each passing floor marked by a piercing *ding* that caused Emily to cover her ears. The *dinging* was possessed of that sharp, piercing tone that sometimes schemed to plunge her into a heightened state of anxiety. At an early age, Emily had been diagnosed with the newly named disorder misophonia, a selective sound sensitivity affliction. A dog barking uncontrollably, a TV with its volume on loud in an apartment complex across a street, someone slurping soup—these discrete sounds, and annoying others like them, could drive Emily to distraction, to frustration and paroxysms of rage, to, she once pessimistically foredoomed in her dorm at Oberlin, full-blown madness. At times, relief seemed out of reach. Thank God for the invention of headphones and earbuds and cellphones that could pump music and podcasts and audiobooks into her sensitive ears to block out a world that seemed hellbent on tormenting sufferers like her. "Read, write, think, dream," Emily intoned to herself as she held her hands over her ears until the elevator finally clanked to a stop at the eighth floor. She made a mental note to take the stairs next time.

The elevator doors sprang open, retreating into the foot-thick concrete walls with a shuddering bang. Emily stepped out of the elevator car. Murky darkness gave way to a gush of sunlight, which suffused the space through the floor-to-ceiling windows in a spectacular orange glow that garlanded the eighth floor. Emily drank in the auric light. A sign greeting guests to the eighth floor admonished them it was an ultraquiet floor: no talking, no cellphone use, even typing on laptops was discouraged. Emily smiled; a sanctuary, she thought. *This is where I'll come when the anger builds*. Although sometimes these ultraquiet places were the worst—one guy sniffling incessantly could trigger the worst of fantasies, catapult her into a homicidal fury. Living with misophonia was not easy, which was why, she psychoanalyzed, she had an affinity for the claustral quiet of libraries.

Emily aimlessly weaved through the chairs and shelves of books to the nearest window, which dreamed west toward the ocean, over the tops of the trees and the somber campus buildings that dotted the grounds. Wooden desks lined the windows in an enfilade of study nooks, all empty. To the north, the outlines of the hills of Ramona and Escondido were rimmed red-orange with fires. Columns of smoke plumed upward, mushrooming spectacularly into the sky. Bulky-winged planes unloaded fire retardant on the obstreperous blaze to halt its progress, but the fires, in defiance, seemed to be broadening their destructive path. Devastating conflagrations aside, it was a magnificent view, she thought.

Emily drifted over to a public computer that greeted everyone who stepped off the elevator. She moved the mouse in a tight circle, and the screen bloomed to life. In a search box she typed the name Raymond West. A lengthy list of titles with their call numbers materialized on the screen. She traced them with her finger until she found West's legacy work, *Lessons in Reality*. She typed the call number down on her cell and went in search of the book.

On a middle shelf in a center aisle, Emily found the blue, clothbound copy of *Lessons in Reality* wedged between other books by Raymond West. They occupied nearly an entire row. She slipped out the Pulitzer winner that she had been chipping away at in both print and audio and carried it to a south-facing desk, luxuriating in the eighth-floor view for a moment before she settled into the chair. Despite the fires, despite the intense feelings of loneliness that had seized her on the drive down from San Francisco, a peace enveloped her now. In the clock-ticking quiet, the crackle of the book's pages sounded abnormally loud when she opened it and leafed through them. The novel looked and sounded like a living thing, beating heart and all.

The explosive burst of a power drill caused Emily to look up from her book. At the east end of the floor, a worker stood on a ladder, drilling screws into a bracket mounted on the ceiling. One, two more shattering eruptions of noise, and then he stepped down. Emily, momentarily unnerved by the shrill din, calmed, but a faint echo lingered.

Emily knew early on that she wanted to be close to the intellectual milieu of the university. Growing up in the small town of White River Junction, Vermont, she feared that if she strayed too far from the university and academic life, she would be jettisoned into an unforgiving world where aesthetics were subsumed by the dog-eat-dog Serengeti of bloodthirsty survival. Later she had unearthed in therapy that her misophonia drew her magnetically to these oases of serenity. Here on the eighth floor, she could read in quiet, eat in quiet, think in quiet. If someone started repetitively tapping a pencil on the desk or clicking the plunger on a ballpoint pen—sounds that drove Emily into fear or flight—she could slip her Bose QuietComfort headphones over her ears and let herself drift off to a world that was inviolably hers, and hers alone. Fortunately, the drilling had stopped.

She bowed her head to the book, but she wasn't focusing on the words. Louis had not been particularly sensitive to her misophonia issues, and near the end, the symptoms of Emily's affliction had erupted into arguments. He couldn't have known the rage that was seething inside her when he slurped his coffee. She experienced moments where she fantasized marching across the room of their small apartment, snatching the cup out of his hand, and tossing it out the window. Surely he would then know what it was like to suffer from this disorder. Then too, she had come to realize, he had ample reason to believe she wasn't suffering from an affliction that had only been recently classified but might indeed be crazy.

This was why Emily loved the peace of libraries, the quiet of reading, the relative tranquility of her profession. If it immured her in a world of fantasy, then so be it. Who wouldn't want to be so engrossed in her work that a day fled by like a bird gliding close to the water, striping the blue with effortlessly flapping wings? As her thoughts drifted, she wondered if she would ever find a man who could tolerate her misophonia, someone, in essence, who would love her for who she was, love that she was born different. Or was Emily fated to go through life increasingly alone until she ended up one day on a Pacific Northwest shore where the crashing surf relentlessly battering the gigantic rocks drowned out all sounds and made the world tolerable?

Emily closed West's legacy work, passages of dense lyricism haunting her mind. She picked the book up with both hands and ran her fingers caressingly along the spine. When she looked up from the well of her thoughts, where ideas flitted like coruscating minnows and deeper creatures pursued her and seemed likely to never go away, the sun was setting and the sky was shaded aubergine. The eucalypti were bent westward from the force of the fiercely gusting Santa Ana winds that Emily couldn't hear from inside the immense concrete cocoon of Memorial Library. The world around her was now a panoramic diorama, as if she were the one in the snow globe of the library staring out.

Emily glanced back down at *Lessons in Reality*. She leafed to the page where she had left off the night before. It was a graphic lovemaking scene. Reading it made her blush. The power of his words, the passion in his voice. How could a man feel like this, so strongly about a woman? She wondered what it would be like to meet him, how she would feel. To meet the man who bared his soul expressively in his work, in novel after novel, in the one play he wrote, and books of poetry that reminded her of Neruda's lyrical excursions into the oceanic depths of the turbulently erotic.

The quiet of the library's eighth floor entombed her. She didn't want to leave. The first night at her new apartment she had awakened to the sound of water running upstairs. A yipping pug across the concrete balcony that led to the upper floor had already made her begin to despise its owner, an obese man with a face wearily road-mapped with burst capillaries from a misspent life, she imagined, of alcohol and other addictive abuses. When he had insouciantly waved and smiled, her own returned smile masked a growing anger that was expressed by the internal scream, *Shut your fucking dog up, or I'll call Animal Control!* Fortunately for Emily, she still had the requisite sense of decorum to prevent her from acting out her fantasies.

Emily raised her eyes and gazed out the window. The sky was darkening, the vivid purples coloring violet and the lights of the surrounding campus buildings burning now like the fires off in the distance of Mount Palomar and Ramona. She planted both hands on the desk and pushed herself to her feet.

She replaced West's novel back where she had found it and rode the elevator down with her index fingers jammed in her ears. She could still hear the *bing bing* of the floor indicator as the elevator dropped past each floor to the ground level, but it was barely audible now and didn't annoy her as much.

Memorial Library was closing up. Emily smiled and waved at Deborah peering intently into her computer monitor. It occurred to Emily at that moment that Deborah was the only person she knew in San Diego. But that would all change tomorrow, when she would meet the entire staff of Special Collections & Archives.

The sliding glass doors parted for Emily when she broke the sensors' invisible detection beam. Winds howled upon her exit. For a moment she was buffeted ferociously by them, and they nearly pitched her to the concrete. She stopped, leaned into the bracingly cold winds, regained her balance, unknotted the sweater from around her waist, and hastily pulled it on. Her glasses came off, and she had to retrieve them from the sweater and replace them on the bridge of her nose. Above and behind her, READ WRITE THINK DREAM was now etched in a rainbow of colors. She hugged her chest against the cold. During the day, the Santa Anas were scorchingly hot dry winds, but at night they turned arctic, originating as they did from high desert elevations where snow dotted the hilltops and knifed into you like myriad shards of ice.

Emily was all alone on a campus of six colleges that boasted an enrollment of thirty-five thousand undergraduates and equally that many employed to service all those needy students. It was larger in population than many cities in the US. And she was still all alone as she hurried back to her car. On the concrete terrace of the library's faux third floor, the winds broke her stride and slashed at her, unimpeded, shifting and funneling tornado-like, forcing her to lean into them to maintain her footing. Scraps of paper trash, handbills and the like, skittered across the concrete in swirling fits and starts, pushed by the strong winds. She tucked her hair behind her ears, but it kept coming loose and whipping her face in slaps like swells bashing a seawall. Emily smiled to herself. It felt wild and freeing.

Unlike Austin, San Diego shut down early. The three-mile drive back to Del Mar was enveloped in a satiny darkness. Out her driver's-side window grinned the ocean, waves exploding phosphorescently in the night, fissuring the black sea with moving white lines. To her right, in the far distance, Emily could make out the fires tearing across the mountains in coronas of orange flames flaring uncontrollably in the night sky, a giant luminescent centipede crawling on its crests, raining embers across the landscape. Between the high surf and the fires, Emily suffered the impression she was in the veritable eye of an apocalypse that was closing in on her from two sides.

Back in her apartment, Emily switched on the TV but kept the sound muted. Like most sane people, she hated commercials, had come of age despising appointment viewing. She picked at a take-out salad she had hastily assembled at Jimbo's and sipped a beer. Onyx, settling in like he had lived there forever, purred on the couch next to her. He liked his whiskers stroked, and Emily obliged him absent-mindedly as she perused the Archivist's Code of Ethics, which she kept in her wallet, folded up like a love letter from a breakup she had never reconciled. Before every new job, she reread its tenets, the guiding principles of her chosen profession. She read,

> The Society of American Archivists is a membership organization comprising individuals and organizations dedicated to the selection, care, preservation, and administration of historical and documentary records of enduring value for the benefit of current and future generations.

"Enduring value," she said out loud to herself. It was one of the questions that haunted many archivists.

Her eyes felt tired. She folded up the code of ethics, set it on the table, and straightened to her feet. Startled, Onyx woke, sat up on his haunches, and yawned, revealing his fangs.

"Tomorrow, I begin on the Raymond West Papers, Onyx." Onyx looked at her with the unblinking eyes of an owl, sentient it seemed to Emily, a person who, in her frequent aloneness, anthropomorphized the animals in her life. She had made her first friend in San Diego.

CHAPTER 4

In Dreams Begin Responsibilities

8/6/18

Monday, August 6. Dismaying dreams last night of records boxes opened and precious documents everywhere. I tried hurriedly to gather them together, but I noticed that doors were open and the Santa Anas were blowing in, scattering the papers all over, lifting them up into the rafters of the ceiling, hurtling them out open windows into the out-of-doors, where I would never be able to retrieve them . . .

I woke in a panic to my alarm. Time to get ready.

Emily didn't know why she set her alarm late. It was cold when she stumbled sleepily into the kitchen and filled exactly twelve ounces of water into her electric, variable-temperature kettle. She pushed the tangled hair out of her face and blinked back the dream that was still playing havoc with her obsession to remember it in exacting detail. The shower revived her, but everything was moving fast now. A needy Onyx, head bent ceilingward, meowed hungrily. She measured out recently roasted beans from Indonesia and ground them in the conical burr grinder she had unpacked the night before. She dumped the ground coffee into a filter fitted into a porcelain dripper and started to pour over tiny dollops of precisely heated 199-degree water.

Another alarm went off, this one reminding her to pick up the pace.

"Shit," Emily cursed herself, hating to be hurried. She poured the remainder of the water over the freshly ground coffee, quickly opened a tin of cat food for Onyx, and forked a few oily lumps in a bowl for him.

It was all about what to wear. Nervous, Emily had laid out an ensemble the night before. For her first day she didn't want to show up too outré or too hipster—her literary hero quotation T-shirts, Doc Martens, and faded jeans—she would wait for that. On the other hand, she had no intention of highlighting her diaphanous beauty with too much makeup and a sexy dress. She decided on a knee-skimming black skirt, a white button-up blouse, and a V-necked sweater vest. She applied a little foundation and the faintest brush of mascara and traced her full lips with gloss, knowing that it would be gone by noon. She posed with hands on hips and studied her appearance in the mirror. Her black glasses made her look studious, a little too stern. Contacts no doubt made her look prettier, more open. She raised and lowered her glasses, then decided on the forbidding seriousness of them. She was going in on the first day with a purpose, a conviction. The glasses semaphored that. Done.

Emily threw her cosmetics into her purse in case she felt in need of freshening up, marched into the kitchen, knelt to pet Onyx and, while glancing anxiously at her watch, said out loud to him, "I hope you don't get lonely. But I can't let you outside. I'll be back around five thirty." Onyx was preoccupied with his food and ate in silence. Emily smiled at her new friend.

She straightened, grabbed her purse, rooted around in it frantically for her car keys, realizing she was late now and already ideating excuses, collected her thermos of Indonesian pour-over, and slipped out the sliding glass door.

In her Mini, she mounted her cell on the dash, tapped in the work address for Memorial Library she had inputted the day before and went, "Shit. Are you fucking kidding me?" It was only a five-mile commute, but her Google map displayed a blood-red aorta of cars all the way to Regents University.

Emily eased into the flow of cars on Coast Highway and headed south. At the top of the descent, she could make out the traffic ahead of her. Cars were necklaced like a vast string of automotive pearls, dazzling under the reflection of a burning early-morning sun. They inched along until they reached ocean level, where one lane trifurcated and the congestion mercifully eased.

Emily, who once harbored vivid fantasies of being a Formula One driver on the European Grand Prix circuit, pressed the accelerator to the floor and weaved in and out of the cars climbing the hill through verdant Torrey Pines State Reserve. She was cruising along at sixty miles per hour now, starting a new job and feeling free, a professional "roamie," as her mentor at Harry Ransom had colorfully characterized her, and Emily liked that. She owed nobody anything, wasn't yoked to the earth with a husband and children, saddled with debt, or obsessed with the need for a man in her life.

It was 9:15, and she was expected to be at work at 9:00. Parking in the Jameson structure wasn't too bad since fall quarter had yet to begin and she located a space without too much trouble. Purse in hand, she raced down the concrete steps and headed in the direction of the library, its eight-story hexagonal mass of concrete and glass almost preternaturally indomitable against the soot-polluted, yellow sky.

She careered left as she entered the library and walked briskly in the direction of Special Collections & Archives. The musty odor of books greeted her nostrils. She weaved around a pair of display cases featuring an exhibit of pen-and-ink drawings of Torrey pines drawn by a gifted, reclusive Japanese artist. She didn't have time to enjoy them.

With a full exhalation, Emily stopped at the reference desk. The young woman looked up at her.

"Hi, I'm Emily Snow. I'm the new project archivist. Where do I go?"

"Hi, Emily. I think they're waiting for you." She gestured through a glass door.

"Thank you." Emily felt nervous suddenly. Her underarms felt tacky from perspiration when she raised her arms over her head to stretch and breathe out her mounting anxiety. She worried that she had overthought what she was wearing as she walked into Special Collections & Archives. She worried that she had spent too much time alone the past week.

Helena Blackwell came out of her office to greet Emily. She was a woman in her late sixties, her face fissured from experience, worry, and the pressure of a job title that had exacted its toll on her physiognomy. A loose, plum-colored sweater fell away over a beige-colored linen skirt, and her neck was ringed with fake pearls that jangled when she moved. She thrust out her hand. There was something disconcerting about her tea-stained overbite, but she seemed affable on the surface.

"You must be Emily," Helena said in a high, ringing voice.

Emily took Helena's hand in hers. It felt sandpapery beneath a film of lotion. She could feel herself pressing a smile to her face. "Yes. Sorry I'm late. I'm five miles from here, but it took half an hour," she excused herself breathlessly.

Helena smiled. "Don't worry, Emily. Now you know."

"Yes."

"Wait until the quarter starts, you'd better give yourself an extra fifteen minutes." She shifted gears. "It's good to have you here safely and on board this exciting project." Her words were as rehearsed as Emily's.

"I'm looking forward to it, Ms. Blackwell."

"Helena. We're all on a first name basis here."

"Okay."

"Good." Helena cracked another practiced smile. "Well, it's great to meet you in person finally."

"Likewise. Yes."

"How was the drive down from . . . ?"

"San Francisco. Beautiful. Except for the fires."

"Oh, aren't they terrible," Helena exclaimed. "Five years ago we had to evacuate as a precautionary measure. Can you imagine?"

"No," replied Emily.

"I guess you can't stop nature," chortled Helena. "Those poor horses." She shuddered to evince her empathy.

For a brief moment, the herd of magnificent animals, their manes on fire, galloped through Emily's imagination.

"Everyone's dying to meet you," Helena said, changing the subject. She shifted her somewhat cumbrous body in the direction of the entrance to Special Collections, beckoning Emily to follow. "Come."

Emily noticed that Helena walked with a balky gait, as if favoring a bad hip. But she moved with a purpose, charging down a gray, low-pile-carpeted corridor, talking to a trailing Emily as her words seemed to boomerang off an invisible wall in front of her and land back where Emily was striding to keep up.

They walked down the passageway under unflattering overhead fluorescent lights reflecting off the white walls and the fog-gray partitions, making Emily squint and want to put her sunglasses back on.

Helena stopped at the entrance to one of the cubicles in the open-plan department. She extended an arm to Emily and smiled, the lines in her face now showing like the cracks in a dry riverbed. "This is your desk."

Emily stepped in past the welcoming arm of Helena. She reconnoitered the rectangular space. The cubical was spartanly furnished. A computer stood sentinel on a cream-shaded desk flanked by filing cabinets on both sides. An ergonomic black office chair was angled to one side. Above the computer, attached to the wall, was a brown corkboard with colored pushpins. It was empty except for a single framed five-by-seven-inch black-and-white picture of a woman with short-cropped hair and the intensely beautiful countenance of a lynx. Emily could feel the sweat developing in her underarms and realized she was more nervous than she was letting on.

"That's a pretty skirt," Helena remarked.

"Thank you."

"So, this is where you and West will be for the next three months." Helena referred to Raymond West by his last name, as if it were code for his project, and he had ceased to be a real person.

"I understand he's on the faculty here," Emily remarked, trying to make small talk.

"Yes," replied Helena.

"I would love to meet him sometime."

"That won't be necessary," Helena reproved. "Excuse me a second." Helena disappeared from view, as if sucked away by the force of a pressing obligation.

Emily sat down in the office chair and set her purse on the laminated wood desk. She heard footsteps down the hall, a door opening, indistinguishable voices. She stared at the photo of the inscrutable-looking woman on the corkboard. Upon closer inspection it appeared to be scissored from the dust jacket of a book. Her eyes looked plaintive as they stared dolefully at the photographer. The right side of her face was cast ominously in shadow, otherworldly looking, presaging some future doom.

Voices of two women pulled Emily away from the photo and back into another forced smile as she swiveled in her chair to meet the approaching footsteps. Helena stood in the entryway to Emily's cubicle next to a woman who was both taller and thinner than Helena. Considerably thinner, as if she suffered from an eating disorder. She was professionally attired in a black pantsuit with a light-blue crepe button-up shirt. Her straight black hair was styled in an asymmetrical bob and streaked with coffee highlights. Emily thought the hairdo looked severe, pretentious, like someone who had been talked into it by an overly creative hairdresser.

"This is Jean," Helena introduced. "Your supervisor. Jean, Emily."

Jean bent forward into the room and shot out an arm as if it were something she did on a regular basis. "Hi. Nice to meet you."

Emily rose from her office chair and shook Jean's hand perfunctorily. "Nice to meet you."

Helena turned to Jean. "Emily worked with Professor Erickson at Harry Ransom."

"Yes. I think I knew that." Jean pretended not to be impressed. "The Henry Miller Collection."

"Arthur Miller," Emily corrected. "The playwright."

"I know Arthur Miller's a playwright," Jean retorted through a strained smile and pursed lips. A current of tension streamed between the two of them. Emily sensed a micromanager—her worst nightmare. Jean sensed an individualist—her bête noire.

Perhaps conscious of the imminent tension, Helena threw open her arms and proclaimed insouciantly, "Well, we're all here."

Defused by her sudden ebullience, Emily and Jean were at a sudden loss for words.

Jean backed away and said to Helena. "So, ten o'clock for a coffee get-together and to get Emily up to speed?" Helena nodded. Jean turned to Emily. "Look forward to working with you. I'm just over there." She motioned with her index finger as if inscribing a question mark in the humidity-free air. As if drawn by some inaudible message, she slipped away.

"Jean'll come get you at ten," Helena said to Emily.

"All right."

Helena left. Emily glanced to where Jean had pointed. A head-high partition separated the two of them, hardly affording Emily any privacy. She leaned back in her office chair and took in her new surroundings. Soon, she imagined, it would be piled with records and document boxes of Raymond West, and the work would begin. Jean would no doubt be a frequent, if unwelcome, presence on this job, Emily thought distastefully as she fixed her gazed again on the unidentified woman's photo. She had meant to ask Helena or Jean about it.

Emily glanced at her watch and switched on the computer. The home screen opened with the names of two drives that she would need to access. She would also need someone to help her set it up with her own email account because it looked like it had been wiped clean. Emily drifted to other thoughts. She checked email on her cell, but her inbox was empty.

Minutes before 10:00 a.m., Jean reappeared. "Are you ready, Emily?"

Emily nodded and rose from her chair. She picked up her purse by the strap, slung it over her shoulder, and followed Jean out into the hallway. She lengthened her stride to keep up with Jean's brisk, officious pace. They went back out the way Emily had come in but veered across an open space with metal shelving laden with books. Picture windows, tinted amber, looked out onto the entrance to the library.

They came to a door with a vertical rectangular glass inset affording a view inside. Jean pushed open the door for Emily and gestured inside with a motion of her head. Her asymmetrical bob shifted and obscured half her face. Up close, Emily noticed that Jean's eyebrows were thickly colored black and waxed to a sheen like the fenders of a guy's coveted car.

The conference room, which served as an all-purpose meeting place for staff of Special Collections & Archives, consisted of a banana-shaped table festooned with a dozen office chairs, upholstered in worn blue fabric. The overhead fluorescent light didn't flatter anyone. At the head of the table, facing Emily as she came in, sat Helena, wearing that manufactured smile on her face that Emily suspected could easily morph into a downturned expression of contempt. Next to her was a man in his sixties, professorial-looking in a yellow oxford shirt and a brown wool coat. Opposite him was a woman Emily's age. She had pinkish hair and a silver stud piercing over one eyebrow.

Seated next to her was a young man in his early thirties. He was wearing a black T-shirt untucked over a pair of faded black jeans. On the chest of the shirt was stenciled the colorful red logo of Gordon and Smith Surfboards. Another man—in his forties, with thinning hair, and engrossed in his cell phone—was attired in a pink Burberry sweater over brown khakis. In the center of the table stood a carafe of coffee surrounded by a stack of Styrofoam cups and paper plates piled with cookies and brownies.

Helena stood and opened her arms to the room as if preparing to catch a beachball that had been tossed to her. "Hi, Emily, welcome to Special Collections. Let me introduce you to everyone." Helena rested a hand on the older man's shoulder. "Next to me here is our head librarian, David Verlander."

Verlander raised his hand, wriggled five parted fingers, and smiled warmly. "Hi, Emily," he said in a pipe-tobacco voice. "We've heard so much about you."

"David worked at Harry Ransom back in the day, didn't you, David?" Helena enthused. Verlander pushed his lips out and nodded as if receding wistfully into memory. "You two should catch up over coffee." Helena extended an arm to the young woman with the eyebrow piercing. "This is Chloe, our other archivist."

"Hi, Emily." Chloe tilted her head to one side and smiled.

"Nice to meet you," Emily said, wearying of all the introductions.

Helena swept her arm across the table. "This is Joel. He's our digital archivist, as well as our film preservationist." Joel pushed his sun-bleached brown locks out of his face and gave her the surfer's shaka sign. This made Emily grin with embarrassment. "When he's not calling in sick to go to surfing."

"These offshore Santa Anas . . ." Joel joked. Everyone laughed. "Nice to have you here, Emily. Are you a surfer?"

"I started recently," Emily said in a cheery voice.

"Really? Well, let's you and me have a paddle. I'll show you some moves."

"And this is Jeffrey," Helena interrupted, motioning to the man in the pink sweater. "He's from Human Resources." Everyone laughed again.

"Hi, Emily," Jeffrey said in an affectedly effeminate voice. "I *don't* surf."

"And, of course, Jean you've already met, our supervising archivist."

"Yes," said Emily, glancing at Jean out of respect.

Joel stood and pulled out a chair next to him for Emily. "Sit down. Get comfortable."

Emily folded herself into the hard chair, and Joel plopped down next to her. By the way he avoided looking at her, Emily could tell he was attracted to her, and she instinctively adjusted the collar on her shirt and fingered the buttons close to her neck to make sure they were fastened. He wore a subtle, masculine cologne that she didn't find offensive. And unlike Jean, he wasn't chewing gum, one of Emily's more acute misophonia triggers.

Helena stared ominously at her watch. "Elizabeth was expecting to join us. I'm guessing she got held up in traffic."

Joel sensed Emily's confusion at the mention of a first name. He whispered over his shoulder to Emily, "Elizabeth West. Raymond West's wife."

Emily raised her chin in recognition of Joel's explanation.

"Let's get started, shall we." Helena swiveled her head. "Jean, could you update us all, and especially Emily, on where we are currently with the West Papers?"

Verlander looked up from his cell, and a smile broke from his mouth like a sun through clouds. "I have a sotto voce announcement." He paused for dramatic effect.

"David," said Helena in a singsong voice that suggested they were old friends, or that she had had a longstanding crush on the head librarian that had never come to fruition.

"A little bird just texted me," teased Verlander, "that our boy West has gone up to twelve-to-one in the UK on the Nobel." His eyes crinkled at the corners with impish delight.

Emily swept her gaze quizzically around the room. She was aware that her arms were pressed to her sides, fearing pit stains from nerves and anxiety on this, her first day in a new department, with a whole new cast of dramatis personae she was trying to suss out.

"I don't think our new project archivist knows what you're referring to, David," prodded Helena.

Verlander trained his avuncular gaze on Emily. "I'm sorry, Emily. Raymond West has been unofficially short-listed for the Nobel. I say *unofficially* because they lay odds on this in the UK. If he won . . ."

"Shh," shushed Helena, drawing a bejeweled index finger to her lips.

"It would be epic for this library," blurted out Joel.

"Epic," echoed Verlander, in a croaking voice that resonated with deeper meaning.

"You're all making me nervous," joked Emily. Everyone laughed when she reached for a brownie on the plate in the center of the table as if they all understood the pacifying qualities of a sweet. She took a dainty bite and set it on a napkin, popped open her thermos and took a satisfying sip of her Indonesian pour-over. She closed it with a snap, and that seemed to signal someone to begin.

Helena stirred. "Well, it'd be something if he were to be the world's laureate of literature, wouldn't it?" She raised an index finger to her lips. "But not a word about it when Elizabeth comes. She's superstitious about this stuff." She glanced at her oversized wristwatch again, widened her eyes, then spoke as if to the timepiece. "Okay, shall we get started here?" Helena placed her hands on the table. "Jean, where are we now with the West Collection?"

Jean spread open a manila folder and leafed through the documents inside. Emily cocked her ear and listened closely. "We're eighty-five percent through processing the bulk of the collection, the container list is coming along, but we have"—Jean looked up—"the new addition to the collection. I don't know how big that is."

"I don't think it's too extensive," Helena interjected. She turned to Joel. "And where are we with the digitization?"

Joel brought a fist to his mouth and cleared his throat. "I've got most of the photos digitized, but there's still the matter of the born-digital items—diskettes, floppies, one hard drive—that were never, apparently, printed out," he elucidated. "Not a ton, because he's a pretty analog guy, but they should be made manifest."

"Let's not worry about those for now," Helena interjected.

"It won't be a complete collection," Joel objected. "A percentage of it will be . . . out there," he pointed to an imaginary overhead cloud.

"I think what we need here is enough of the collection to be initially available to the public, and to roll out the rest as necessary," voiced Helen. "Mindful of the restrictions, of course." She turned to Jean for affirmation.

"More product, less process," chirped Jean, as if she had plagiarized the words from a lecture she had attended at a recent conference. It was quickly dawning on Emily that Jean was Helena's designated toady.

"What're in the digital files of the archive?" Verlander inquired of Joel.

"I don't know," said Joel, shrugging. "I haven't had a chance to look at them." He glanced over his shoulder at Emily. "I assumed, with our new hotshot project archivist, she would be the one responsible—"

"I'm not inclined to authorize the digital files of the collection to be processed at this time," Helena chopped him off with an acerbic finality.

Accompanied by the shuffling of feet, a figure loomed in the rectangular pane of glass separating the room from the corridor. Everyone stopped talking and, as if drawn by a powerful magnet, swung their gazes in the direction of the noise. A faint knock rapped on the door. On cue, Joel leaped to his feet and opened it. Elizabeth West stepped inside. She was a magnificent fifty-year-old woman with the strikingly lavish looks that both genetics and money had vouchsafed her. She was elegantly dressed in black silk pants and a beautiful blue linen shirt that flowed to midthigh. A diamond the size of a shooting marble stood like a miniature temple on a gold band. She didn't walk into the room; she floated in, on a cloud of privilege.

"Elizabeth!" Helena exclaimed, rising awkwardly to her feet in an effusion of flummery.

"Sit down, Helena," said Elizabeth in an unruffled voice of authority inflected with a vague British accent that life in Southern California had sought to erase. "Sorry I'm late. I was on the phone all morning with the estate attorney."

Helena gestured to Jean with a surreptitious hand signal, and Jean straightened from her chair and led Elizabeth to the end of the conference table opposite Helena and politely drew out a seat for her.

"Thank you, Jean." Elizabeth unburdened herself of her Birkin bag and toured the assembly with her glinting blue eyes. Thick but professionally applied makeup transformed her face into an otherworldly beauty born of artifice. No one in the room could afford the clothes she wore or the jewelry that scintillated on her perfectly manicured hands and encircled her wrists. Palpable wealth was in the room, Emily realized, and the tone of everyone's voices had been stripped of its casualness and lowered deferentially.

"Elizabeth," Verlander said, nodding.

"David."

"You're looking . . . well," he finished, choosing his words carefully.

Helena chuckled nervously through the grotesqueness of a disorganized expression. The crosscurrents of tension in the room were not clearly identifiable to Emily, but it felt as if piano wires were pulled taut in overlapping configurations and struggling for harmony.

"Elizabeth. You remember Joel. Our digital archivist and film preservationist," Helena introduced.

"Hi, Mrs. West," Joel said, their universes unfamiliar except here at the library.

"And, of course, Chloe, who worked on some of your husband's collection," Helena continued the introductions, a smile frozen on her face, a hand opening in Chloe's direction.

Elizabeth smiled at Chloe without showing her teeth.

Helena unfolded an arm toward Emily as Elizabeth unknotted a silk scarf tied around her neck and tucked it in her purse, exposing a black pearl choker that haunted her neck. "And this is our new project archivist, Emily Snow. She's going to be taking over Raymond's collection."

Elizabeth, sitting erect in her chair, presented her head to Emily the way a lion might to a vast veldt in Africa to surveil future prey. After a long, unblinking, unnerving stare, she finally said, "I like your glasses."

"Thank you," said Emily. Triggered by the manner in which Elizabeth appeared to be sizing her up, Emily felt a low voltage current of apprehension suffuse her for a moment, and her pulse quickened.

"It's nice to finally meet you." Elizabeth smiled warmly. "Welcome aboard." She paused and studied Emily for another probing moment, as if her eyes possessed the power of clairvoyance. "To entrust my husband's work to you is a fragile, and fraught, passing of the baton. I hope you don't bobble it, to complete the metaphor."

"You have my word that I will treat his papers with the utmost punctiliousness," Emily assured her.

"*Punctiliousness*," Elizabeth hooted gleefully. "Raymond would appreciate your command of polysyllabics, young lady."

Emily's face colored red. Jean tensed, sensing a minor seismic shift in admiration from the woman who, as it turned out, paid all their salaries, endowed Verlander's and Helena's positions, and could buy a Ferrari with her Amex Black Card. By her mere presence, she commanded the room and was the de facto font of all its energy.

"We were just talking about the progress on the collection, getting Emily up to speed on where we are, how much time we have left before the . . ." Helena paused and threw her head at Verlander. "But I know David's going to make a big announcement at the Town Hall meeting, so I don't want to steal his thunder."

"It wouldn't be the first time," Verlander quipped.

"Emily, as I might have told you, interned at Harry Ransom," Helena bragged to Elizabeth about her new project archivist, annoying Emily each time she referenced her past employment.

"Harry Ransom," intoned Elizabeth. "We almost assigned his papers there. Of course, with Márquez, one of Raymond's favorite authors, it was a tough decision."

"Professional jealousy," Verlander joked, his eyes on Emily.

"I think Ray knows when he's in the shadow of superior talents," Elizabeth qualified.

"Why did you decide to bring it to Regents?" Emily ventured, fishing for a tone of amiability in a room fraught with tension.

"This is my husband's alma mater. This is where he grew up. This is where he teaches. La Jolla is our home." She raised her eyes to a point in space only she could visualize. "And there were other considerations having to do with the trust that will be unveiled over time," she closed enigmatically.

"Well, it's an honor to have him here, I'm sure. And a privilege for me to be asked to work on the collection. And if he wins—"

Verlander audibly cleared his throat, interrupting Emily.

"Wins?" Elizabeth inquired.

"More . . . accolades," Emily finished vaguely, satisfying Verlander.

"Yes, I know the Nobel's on everybody's mind," a perceptive Elizabeth said. "But let's not jinx it. The important thing is the collection and"—she faced Helena—"the future of the library."

"Of course," reassured Helena, kowtowing to Elizabeth. "We can't predict these things."

"So, where are we?" Elizabeth said, jump-starting the meeting.

Helena raised her eyebrows at Jean, cuing her to begin.

Jean began nervously. "Well, we're pretty far along with your husband's papers. The finding aid is coming along—"

Elizabeth cut Jean short. "Do we have an ETA on when it will be all finished up?"

"We understand there's a new addition to the collection, which could change things in terms of the planned opening."

Elizabeth surreptitiously traded looks with Helena. Wordlessly, they brokered who would offer the explanation. Helena spoke up. "We had some boxes go back to the estate to be curated. But they'll be ready to be picked up . . . tomorrow?" she smiled at Elizabeth.

"Yes," reassured Elizabeth.

"Once we get them, we'll have a better idea. Emily, do you want to interject anything here?"

"I won't know until I see those document boxes and sort through what's in them," Emily said.

"We're going to be assigning you a student assistant," Jean said.

"That will be helpful." Everyone waited on Emily. "I'll also be curious to see how my predecessor processed and arranged this. If it's in a similar fashion to how I work, this could go fast."

Smiles broke out all around as the tension in the room seemed to ease at Emily's words. Joel took another bite of a brownie. Jean sipped from a Styrofoam cup with the tab of a tea bag dangling over the side.

"Okay, then." Elizabeth appeared ready to leave.

Emily adjusted her glasses. "I have a question." Everyone directed their attention to Emily. "Just out of curiosity, did my predecessor leave the project before she drowned, or . . . ?"

The convocation fell silent. The buzzing of the overhead fluorescent bulbs gave audible presence to the electrical current now suffusing the conference room. If there once had been a concerted team spirit, there now was a welter of crosscurrents and fragile divisions regarding West. Emily glanced from colleague to colleague. Jean's head was bent forward, and she was engaged in meaningless note-taking. Verlander's gnomish face was expressionless, his eyes unnaturally wide. He fingered a meerschaum pipe in his front coat pocket, eager to light it. Helena's face had gone slack in a look of dread that had transformed it beyond easy recognition. Joel scratched his forehead, as if promoting an ellipsis to the next topic of the meeting. Chloe absently rolled her tongue around in her mouth, squeegeeing Emily's question from the air, where it trembled like a tuning fork still vibrating. Jeffrey absorbed the uncomfortable pause in the meeting with a sanguinity born of ostensible ignorance. Elizabeth stiffened, as if she were a mannequin in a window display of a store where she didn't belong.

Emily, twisting in the wind, waited, crucified by the silence.

"She was let go, yes," Helena finally spoke, her words as sharp and cold as icicles falling into the void. "There were . . . improprieties we would rather not get into."

"I see," said Emily, not wanting to contaminate the room with a pressing follow-up question on the precise nature of the "improprieties."

"Well," said Jean, in a lilting tone intended to steer the mood back to the professional. "I'll show Emily the stacks where the West Collection is and bring up the boxes yet to be processed. Joel can get her set up on her computer. I'll have Jorge in Security make her a key card."

"Good," said Helena, exhaling audibly.

Elizabeth West seemed to have traveled somewhere else, where the winds were more favonian. She manufactured a smile and threw it across the length of the conference table at Helena. "Still coming by tomorrow?"

"Of course," replied Helena.

Elizabeth stood. Proud. Regal. A lioness whose scars were made invisible by sartorial affluence. She directed a warm smile at Verlander. "Let's not bruit about the Nobel, David. Besides, Ray is too young. He has many more years to win it."

"Of course." Verlander smiled abashedly. Even though he was the head librarian of the university, the top dog of this Brutalist edifice of learning and archival immortalization the power clearly resided with Elizabeth West. She could shift fortunes, both personal and professional, with a stroke of the pen. And that was now patently obvious to an intimidated and visibly shell-shocked Emily.

"Emily," Elizabeth said in leaving, "it was nice to meet you." She extended a hand and Emily took it. Was it her imagination, or did Elizabeth pull her ever so slightly toward her, demanding a kind of privileged privacy, as if wanting to whisper a secret? "I'm sure my husband's papers will be in good hands." One of which she gripped firmly for emphasis.

"They will be well cared for," Emily reassured her again.

Parting goodbyes murmured through the room as Elizabeth extricated herself from the well-wishings and departed, leaving in her wake a vacuum of outsized privilege for all to inhale deeply. The focus was drawn magnetically toward Helena, for reasons Emily had yet to ascertain. Everyone, even Verlander, it seemed, waited on her postmortem. She propped her elbows on the table, interlocked her fingers, and rested her head thoughtfully on the tepee fashioned by her hands. She conjured a smile and then cast Emily a reproving look. "We must do everything to make Elizabeth proud."

"Of course." Emily's heart was still hammering away.

Helena rose on her balky hip, a ship listing, battered by overhead swells. With her back turned to everyone, she said, "Your predecessor was a fine archivist. But she set us back. Months!" Picking up her purse, she bent at the waist, gazed down at Emily, and smiled to calm the waters that had stormed up within her. "But then you couldn't have known." She lifted her gaze to the entire room. "Carry on, everyone."

As Helena went out the door, everyone gathered their belongings and got up from their chairs. Verlander, wanting to mollify the tension, suggested to Emily in parting that they meet for coffee and reminisce about Harry Ransom. Chloe—glued to her cell, thumbs leaping to respond to a mosaic of texts—said goodbye with a backward glance. Jean made a casual appointment with Emily for that afternoon to give her a tour of the stacks. Jeffrey, pleased that there were no overtly politically incorrect moments, slithered out as silently as a snake, vanishing before anyone could notice.

"What was all that about my predecessor?" a still unnerved Emily inquired of Joel once the room had emptied of its hostility.

"There was bad blood between the two of them," he said obliquely.

Emily reared back her head in response. "Bad blood?"

"Some other time." Joel glanced at his diver's watch. "Would you like to get lunch?"

"Okay, I guess."

Emily walked alongside Joel on the concrete pathway that led to the Barnes Center. Mirrored windows bounding the walkway reflected the apocalyptic orange skies, momentarily blinding them. Emily could sense Joel's physical presence next to her—the curly locks, the strong shoulders—and she instinctively distanced herself a little, leaving some professional space between them.

"These fires are something, aren't they?" commented Joel, throwing his head eastward, in the direction of the unseen conflagrations.

"All the way down the coast, you could see them."

"The spine of California on fire," Joel lyricized. "You drive all alone?"

"Yes. I prefer driving alone."

Joel led her on concrete walkways, around a plaza, pointed out the bookstore, and then directed her to a casual restaurant on the second floor of the cavernous Barnes Center, a hub of restaurants and shops for the six colleges, devoid of students now, like a plague-evacuated city.

Tasmania was a high-ceilinged café with tall windows that let light filter in at column-like diagonals. They ordered at the counter. Emily decided on the vegetarian chili, and Joel opted for a lamb burger, medium rare.

"Are you vegan?" Joel asked as they made their way to an empty table, Joel carrying a card with a handwritten number held in small metal stand.

"No. I'm not vegan."

"'Cause I don't want to gross you out."

Emily chuckled as they pulled up chairs and plopped themselves down.

"I dated a girl who was vegan. When I ate meat, it was as if I was personally responsible for the slaughter of innocent animals."

"I imagine that didn't last." Emily suppressed a laugh.

Joel shook his head. "Nope."

Emily looked around. "Who eats here?" Emily asked.

Joel looked where Emily's gaze had strayed. "Everyone. Faculty. Staff. Grad students. Undergrads prefer the fast-food joints on the first floor. Cheaper."

Emily turned back to Joel. Their eyes swept each other's and deliberately avoided locking.

"So, my . . . predecessor?" Emily ventured cautiously.

Joel reorganized his expression by drawing a hand across his face. He shrugged an answer.

"Did you know her?" she asked.

"Of course. She was my colleague."

Emily nodded. "Then why all the hugger-muggery?"

"What?" Joel was engulfed with laughter.

"Hugger-muggery. It was in a le Carré novel, I think."

"You like le Carré?"

Emily nodded. "Some of his stuff. I like literary mysteries."

Their order came. A young woman with blue-streaked hair set a plate in front of Joel and a bowl with a square of cornbread in front of Emily, took the placeholder with the number, and wordlessly walked away.

"Why all the hugger-muggery?" Emily persisted.

Joel, startled, seemed to have forgotten the question. "As Helena said, there were *improprieties*," he replied, sinking his teeth into his lamb burger.

"Care to elaborate?"

Joel shook his head.

"She drowned, right?" Emily turned to him with her spoon full of chili frozen at her lips. "That's tragic. And no one talks about it?"

Joel lifted his hands and exhaled before dropping them back to the seat cushion.

"What were the circumstances?"

Joel turned to her. "Emily. We just met. I don't know you at all." He looked away. "It was a surfing accident, okay?"

Emily studied his face. He seemed gripped by a narrative that had begun to unfold, but one that was being held back by a levee of circumspection.

"So, you surf?" he deliberately changed the subject.

Emily nodded. "Just started. I took it up in San Francisco. I needed something to . . ."

"Sunset Beach?"

Emily nodded, glad that he didn't pry.

"That's a gnarly wave."

"Tell me about it." Emily rolled up her left sleeve and presented her forearm to Joel. A large welt where a surgeon's needle had stitched back together a nasty gash gleamed red in Joel's eyes.

"Skeg?" asked Joel, fascinated.

Emily nodded.

"That's kind of hot." He held up his hands in surrender as if to explain he wasn't hitting on her.

She rolled her sleeve back down and rebuttoned it at the cuff. "Twelve stitches."

Joel raised his right leg and locked it into a horizontal position. He rolled back one pant leg of his faded jeans until it was above the knee and displayed a tanned leg with a carpet of fine blond hairs. He twisted his leg to the side to reveal a scar of his own marring the flank of his calf. It was a strip of smooth, bright red where the hairs didn't flourish.

"Wow." Emily wanted to joke *That's pretty hot, too,* but feared he might get the wrong idea over what was, for her, scar-comparing and nothing more.

"Surfing can damage you," Joel agreed. "I've had two shoulder surgeries and a microdiscectomy." He rolled his pant leg back down and tucked his leg under the table.

"All surfing injuries?" asked Emily, sipping her chili.

"I can't stay out of the water when it's overhead. It's an obsession."

"Yeah, Louis was the same way."

"Louis is your boyfriend?"

"Was." Emily glanced down and away. There were no eyes for another man right now, especially a colleague.

As if to demonstrate his sensitivity, or calculating that another time would be more propitious, Joel nodded acknowledgment. "Would you like to go surfing sometime?" he ventured, presuming he had solid ground on that mutual interest.

Emily smiled. "I would." She frowned. "I don't have a board, though. Left it in San Fran."

Joel smirked. "I've got a quiver, Ms. Archivist." Emily fought off an embarrassed smile. "I might even have a wet suit that'll fit you."

"Cool."

"And if these Santa Anas keep blowing, Black's is going to be going off."

Emily's thoughts went to something else—that afternoon on the beach. "Is that the hot local break?"

"One of them. How's your chili?"

"Good," Emily said, taking another slurp.

On the walk back to the library, it was impossible to miss the fires billowing smoke high into the afternoon sky. A film of ash had rained down on the concrete, thick enough that you could make out the ghostly footprints of invisible pedestrians who had left traces of their comings and goings.

Back in Special Collections, Jean materialized to claim an impatient Emily at her desk. "Come on, I'll show you where West is living."

Emily tore her eyes away from the framed photo on the wall that had drawn her infinite curiosity and spun out of her desk chair.

Down a hallway, they came to a halt at a locked door. Jean swiped a key card on a black card reader, a buzzer sounded, and she pushed the door open with broken sticks for arms. Jean threw Emily a backward look. "The stacks are strictly off limits." With an admonitory gesture, she pointed to the ceiling with her index finger as they walked in single file.

Emily glanced up and took note of the security cameras in the ceiling's corners as she continued to follow a purposefully striding Jean. They passed ten-foot-high metal shelving lined with gray document boxes, all neatly categorized by white identification labels inked with handwritten codes. They pressed on through passageways of literary and Nobel-winning prominence, rounding a corner and continuing until they came to a stop at a midpoint of shelving. In the low light, Jean indicated a region of boxes with an impassive flourish of her right arm.

"This is the West Collection," she said tonelessly. "Seventy-seven linear feet," she added in the same monotone, as if underwhelmed or just not caring.

Emily, awestruck, whistled under her breath as she gazed up at the rows of document boxes that were evenly and meticulously stacked together on the six levels of shelves. "And he's only fifty-one."

"Is he?" Jean said with no change in her expression, not fishing for an answer.

Emily ran her tongue over her upper teeth, mesmerized by all the work that seventy-seven linear feet represented for a writer. An unemotional Jean didn't seem to appreciate the impressive oeuvre as much as Emily. To her, they were inanimate document boxes, donor items that had been processed and stored for future researchers and curious fans. Emily could almost imagine her supervisor clapping dirt off her hands when the project was completed, as if they contained nothing more than income tax records in a government office. Gazing at all the boxes, Emily's heart started pounding, witnessing for the first time the mountain she was tasked to climb. "Published his first novel when he was twenty-three." Emily spoke more to herself, realizing now that Jean was more a career supervisor and not a true archivist in the romantic sense she idealistically held herself to be. "Won the PEN/Faulkner," she added softly, admiringly, as if to dig a needle into her new boss and subtly let her know who was now the new master of this esteemed collection, this prized acquisition.

"Didn't know that," replied Jean, darting a look at Emily with a sharp turn of her head.

"Can't wait to get a look at some of those early manuscripts," Emily enthused.

Jean ignored Emily's girlish excitement. "Nicola will help you bring up the ones that haven't been processed. Okay?"

"Okay." Emily was still admiring all the boxes, transfixed by their resonant value in a way that Jean was oblivious of. Where Emily saw the repository of an artist's soul, Jean saw drawers in a morgue, more interested in the progress of the library's renovation and the university's chance to show itself off to the world.

"Shall we go?" suggested Jean.

Emily pried her eyes away from the collection. "Okay."

Together they walked out of the closed stacks and back to the warren of cubicles, where they peeled off to their separate offices.

A moment later, the head of security, Jorge, wearing grey khakis and a pale green short-sleeve shirt, loomed in the entrance to Emily's cubicle. He was a large man, but unlike Joel he was all flesh and folds of flesh. Even his youthful face moved like Jell-O when he spoke or when his features transformed under the spell of a joke that caused him to laugh incongruously loud, pinching his eyes shut. "Are you ready to get your key card?" he asked Emily.

Emily stood from her chair. "You're Jorge?"

"Yes. Come with me." Jorge swerved his large body toward the entrance, then angled it sideways so he wouldn't knock down the movable partition.

Emily followed Jorge out of Special Collections. His footsteps thundered in front of her.

"How do you like San Diego so far?" Jorge asked amiably, physically unable to give her a full backward glance.

"I just got here," Emily answered. "It's kind of . . . all freeways, isn't it?"

Jorge found the description too oblique to directly respond, so he shifted the topic. "I know you're on this special project and might be working late to get it done, so I wanted to let you know that if you need an escort to your car or anything, you call us in Security. Deal?"

"Deal. Have there been any problems?" Emily caught up with him and paced now by his side in a hurried gait as they moved past the circulation desk and a bank of computers manned by students at their summer jobs.

"We've had some complaints of a creep stalking some of the staff in Special Collections, but the police are investigating. I'm sure they'll figure out who it is and get a restraining order," he finished hopefully. "I just don't want you walking alone back to the parking structure if you feel uncomfortable."

Emily flexed her biceps. "I'm going to a gym. And I'm a runner too."

"Ms. Snow," Jorge said, stopping at a windowless door and towering over her. "The campus is pretty safe overall, but it's open to the public. All kinds of creeps come and go here. I know."

Emily dropped her arm. "Okay."

Jorge swung open the door and held it so that Emily could enter in front of him. "This is where *I* live."

Inside the small room were two desks positioned perpendicular to each other against the walls. On each desk stood three oversized monitors. Static black-and-white images displayed rooms and corridors and elevator stairwells, offices, and the stacks where Jean had taken Emily on an abbreviated tour.

Jorge chivalrously pulled out a roll-away chair and beckoned Emily to sit. "Ma'am."

Emily sat down in the chair. Compared to Special Collections, temperature-controlled for preservation purposes, it was warm in the room and her face felt flushed as Jorge plopped himself down next to her. Wordlessly, he took a blank white plastic, wallet-sized card and inserted it into a reader connected to the computer. He placed his sausage-thick fingers on the keyboard and tapped in some letters and numbers. He sat back a moment and blinked his eyes to focus on the tiny crimson dot that flashed on the card reader. When it turned green, he removed the card and held it up in front of Emily. She raised a hand to get it, but he kept it inches out of her reach.

"This is your personal key card, Ms. Snow. Don't lose it; don't break it; don't give it to anyone else to use. You have access to the department between seven thirty a.m. and seven thirty p.m. Before and after those times, your card will not work. Understood?"

"Okay."

Jorge slid the card into Emily's waiting fingers. "If you're the first one in in the morning—and I doubt you will be, because Jean usually gets here before anybody—you'll need to disarm the alarm. I can show you that tomorrow. And the same is true if you leave after seven thirty. Otherwise all hell will break loose."

"You've got a lot of cameras in the library," Emily remarked, sweeping an index finger across the bank of monitors.

"Eight floors, Ms. Snow. And when the students come with those expensive laptops . . . watch out."

Emily rose to her feet. She held her key card up. "Thanks, Jorge."

"You're welcome." Emily started for the door, but Jorge stopped her. "Remember, we're here for you."

"Thank you, Jorge. I appreciate that."

Back in her cubicle, Emily switched on her computer. The monitor came to life on a marine-themed screensaver. On the home screen, under

"Computer," two network drives connected to the library's main servers were listed. One was her own personal drive, denoted simply by her name. The other was titled "Library Private (Panopticon)." She deduced that this was the drive where all the collections were cataloged and indexed and where the finding aids of all the collections could be found. Emily stared at the file folders, briefly acquainting herself with them, then her eyes drifted to the wall where the photo of the woman with the intense eyes still gazed down at her.

Hearing a noise, she spun around in her chair and was startled by a presence in the entryway to her cubicle. She exhaled with relief when she realized it was Joel and not Jean or Helena.

"Jean wanted me to help you set up your email account," he said.

"Okay," Emily said.

Joel grabbed the back of an extra chair. "Do you mind?"

"No." Emily rolled back from the computer monitor and let Joel slide into the empty space. He placed one hand on the mouse and deftly moved the cursor around the screen. A form document page came up. Emily didn't pay attention. Joel set both hands on the keyboard and quickly typed in some letters.

"We all use our first initial, last name, and the university extension." He slid back in his chair. "You just need to pick a password." He flared open his hand, inviting her to resume her position at the desk.

Emily rolled back into place, hunched forward, went through the password protocol business, leaned back in her chair.

"What password did you choose?" Joel asked, deadpan.

Emily threw him a smirking backward glance.

"Just kidding." Joel straightened to his feet. "Welcome to the world of West," he said, throwing out his arms. "Now we can IM. Black's this weekend?"

"Let's see how the week pans out," Emily parried. "But, yeah, I'd like to get out in the water." She pointed a finger at the picture on the otherwise empty bulletin board above her computer. "Who is she?"

Joel turned his head in the direction she was pointing. "Clarice somebody. Obscure Brazilian writer. Strange name. Blanking."

"Left by my predecessor?" Emily asked.

Staring fixedly at the photo, Joel nodded. "I guess they didn't take it down when they cleared out her office." He blinked in memory. "She liked her writing. Thought it was dark and passionate. I found it impenetrable."

"Nadia Fontaine was her name, right?"

"Yes," Joel muttered.

"Sounds like a stage name."

Joel smiled a laugh. "She was also a writer."

"What'd she write?"

Joel threw a furtive glance to the entrance that opened to the main hallway. "I'll tell you some other time." He looked at his watch too obviously.

"She didn't like being an archivist?" Emily said with a puzzled look.

"Everybody wants to be something else," Joel mused philosophically. "No, I think she loved her work." He lowered his voice. "Just not the office politics, the bureaucratic side." He jerked a thumb toward the cubicle divider and lowered his voice to a whisper. "And the micromanager with her fucking productivity apps tyrannizing our existences."

Emily smiled wryly. Then she grew thoughtful. "Super sad about her drowning."

Joel's shoulders slumped, and he nodded almost imperceptibly. "I sincerely don't want to talk about it." He collected himself from his reverie. "I'll leave you to your work," he said, somewhat evasively. "Let me know about surfing. I'm just down the hall." He pointed. Smiled. Left.

Emily watched him leave, worried that she had put up her guard too protectively with Joel and that he was already turning a cold shoulder to her, but she wanted to keep their nascent relationship on a professional course. She turned back to the picture on the wall. Clarice . . . ? Short-cropped hair. That countenance of a lynx.

Emily spent what was left of the afternoon familiarizing herself with the software, with how some of the other archives were organized. She perused a few of the finding aids to get a feel for their style. When five o'clock came, Emily gathered up her purse and thermos. Not wanting to be haunted by a writer whom her predecessor admired, she decided to take the picture down from the wall. She started to hide it away in one of the filing cabinets, but then it didn't feel right being there either, so she slid it into her purse and walked outside. She paused at the reference desk to say goodbye to Chloe.

"What did you think of Elizabeth West?" Chloe asked. "Pretty intense, huh?"

Emily didn't say anything in reply. "What are you doing on reference desk?"

"We all have to pull a shift. Even Helena."

"Seriously?"

"You won't. You're special. A project archivist."

"Are you shitting me?" said Emily.

"The way Helena talked you up . . . no. There's an urgency to finish up this project."

"I gathered. I'm excited. I've become a fan of his writing. Do you think I'll ever get a chance to meet him?" Emily asked, in a voice she hoped didn't sound too girlishly excited.

Chloe stiffened. "He used to come in now and then, but I haven't seen him in a while."

"To research something . . . ?"

"I think because she had questions about the collection."

"*She* being my predecessor?" Emily wanted Chloe to clarify.

Chloe nodded, then turned to her computer without elaborating.

"Nadia Fontaine?"

Chloe nodded once, kept her eyes averted.

"Is it forbidden to talk about her?"

Chloe shrugged.

"Something I should know?" Emily gave her a few seconds to respond. When she didn't, she said, "Okay, well, see you tomorrow, Chloe."

Emily hurried across the plaza. As evening closed in, the Santa Anas had gained in velocity again, and a sudden, cyclonic gust knocked her sideways. It struck her hard enough that her purse fell to the concrete as she struggled to regain her balance. Her purse's contents spilled and fanned out in all directions, a cylinder of lipstick rolling away from her. Deborah, the woman from the information desk, materialized suddenly and was squatting to help Emily retrieve her possessions.

"No, I'm fine, I don't need any help." Emily was obsessively chary of anyone rummaging through her personal belongings.

"Okay." She glanced at the sky. "This wind is something, isn't it?" remarked Deborah, straightening from the anarchic sprawl of the purse's contents.

"Yeah." Emily looked at her expressionlessly, hoping she would move on. The small framed photo of the unknown woman was in her hand, but the glass was now spiderwebbed with hairline fractures.

Deborah—one hand clutching her sun hat, the circular brim whipping violently—took the hint and made off through a visible wind of whooshing debris.

Emily drove back to Del Mar along the now familiar Coast Highway. Propelled by the strong winds, unmoored tumbleweeds kangarooed wildly across Torrey Pines Golf Course toward the cliffs in the distance. At the bottom of the hill, the inlets of the Los Peñasquitos Lagoon rippled in a watery moiré pattern. White herons hunkered down, wings drawn to their sides, their swanlike necks knifing through the wind. The westward sky was an explosion of angry blood red, as ash from the fires, thrown high into the air, blanketed the sinking sun in an angry occlusion of color. The offshore winds held up the shoulder-high swells, and Emily imagined Joel chasing those mythical waves and thought of those blond hairs freckling the back of his hands as he set up her computer for her. She briefly thought of Louis and his last, desperate text to her, "Come back to me, unchanged." She would never go back to wanting someone. She realized that relationship was about her needing someone to want her, needing someone to awaken a passion in her who, as it turned out, was nothing more than a washboard floodplain of desiccated silt. *Come back to me, unchanged.* She snorted out loud. *What the fuck does that mean?*

As she climbed the hill in the molasses-slow commuter traffic, it looked like the sun had sparked more fires on the other side of the earth. *Shit,* Emily thought. She needed to get some groceries. She was starving. The chili had been five hours ago, and her stomach was rumbling in protest.

She turned right on Del Mar Heights and climbed a steep hill. She downshifted her Mini into second and weaved impatiently through more slow-moving traffic following Google Maps.

She bought a few extra supplies at Jimbo's and then stopped next door to pick up a take-out dinner at Urban Plates, one of those casual, cafeteria/healthy-style franchises that were proliferating in Southern California.

Onyx met Emily at the sliding glass door entrance with a raised head and a staccato burst of meows. Emily set her bags on the floor and squatted down to pet Onyx, who had followed her into the kitchen. A pang of guilt pricked her when she noticed that both his food and water bowls were empty. She rushed to fill one with water. Then, before putting her groceries away, she opened a tin of cat food and scooped it into the other bowl. The pungent scent of fish was too intoxicating, and Onyx lost interest in Emily as she unloaded her purchases into the refrigerator and cabinets.

Weary from all the driving, she plopped down on the couch, popped open the top of the Styrofoam container, and brandished a fork at the chimichurri grass-fed steak and beet-salad side. She poured a glass of Societe pale ale from a half-liter bottle. It was bracingly cold and pleasantly astringent in her mouth. She ate hurriedly as she opened her laptop and waited for it to come to life. Her screensaver displayed a photo of the stacks at Harry Ransom, a capacious room, empty of human beings, with endless shelves of boxes and books and blue shafts of diagonal light. To Emily, it was heaven.

When she was finished eating, she rummaged in her purse for the photo she had taken down from the wall in her office. With careful fingers she surgically removed the broken shards of glass from the frame. She typed "Clarice" and "Brazilian" into Google as Onyx leaped up onto the couch and nestled next to her. He yawned so wide that his fangs hung in the air for a moment before he closed his mouth. His tongue ran across his sated lips as sleep pursued him. Emily's hand found the top of his head and scratched him behind the ears. On her screen, a checkerboard of mostly black-and-white photos featuring an interesting-looking middle-aged woman filled her screen: Clarice Lispector. Emily had never heard of her. Most of the pictures were notable for their tortured, chain-smoking depictions of the serious-faced author. On the woman's Wikipedia page Emily learned Lispector was a Ukrainian Jew whose parents had moved to Brazil when she was barely a year old. Her oeuvre of half a dozen books was written in Portuguese. She was widely considered to be one of the foremost writers in all of Latin American literature before her untimely death in 1977 at the age of fifty-six. Emily navigated over to

Amazon and downloaded Lispector's *Collected Stories* to her e-reader. She now suddenly desired to know what her predecessor saw in the work of this unfamiliar writer that had prompted her to personalize her office wall with her presence.

As Onyx slumbered, Emily desultorily rehashed the day in her head. She had met a lot of new people, absorbed a weft of nebulous politics. With the care of an archivist, she removed the picture from the frame. She set the picture of Lispector aside—that fey-like face, those haunted eyes, a cigarette burning between bejeweled fingers in many of the photos, an artist plagued all her life by inner torment. Turning her attention to the frame, Emily discovered something odd lodged in the corner of the cardboard backing. At first glance, it appeared to be an ancient Memorial Library catalog card, typewritten and punched with a single hole for securing it in the filing drawer. Emily drew it closer to her eyes. On the lined, pale yellow card it read *Le Rêve d'un Flagellant.* With her smattering of French, Emily didn't need Google to translate. "The dream of a flagellant," she whispered. Something naughty stirred in her. The author was a Maurice de Vindas, too obscure for even Emily to recognize. Typed on the card was the barest abstract describing the book, which didn't tell Emily much of anything other than where it could presumably be found in the library. She flipped the card over. Her eyes widened. On it, in block letters, was written "MR—YNF—Find!!!" *The fuck?* Emily, who possessed a heightened intuitive, interpretive sense of things, was jarred by the size of the letters. She could feel anger in their sharp and hurried strokes, emotion, desperation—what Emily likened to a message in a bottle, scribbled hastily by a doomed castaway.

Baffled, slightly unnerved, Emily set it down on the coffee table, her eyes fixed on it. The beer was making her feel drowsy. "The dream of a flagellant," she spoke to herself as she rose slowly, so as not to wake Onyx, and headed toward the bedroom.

CHAPTER 5

The Raymond West Collection

8/7/18

I dreamt the fires were nearing the ocean, where they would be extinguished by the cold waters. The boxes that constituted the seventy-seven linear feet of the Raymond West Papers were bobbing on the ocean's surface, dispersed anarchically out to the horizon, an archivist's recurring nightmare for sure. They were all on fire. I was shouting to everyone that we had to save them, that the entire collection of a major writer was going down like an armada of small ships under siege by an enemy known as the Big Lie.

I woke to Onyx meowing. When I opened the door, he leapt spring-loaded onto the bed as if the poor devil had been crying all night at the threshold to my bedroom. It wasn't yet light outside. When I checked my cell, it read 5:55. I crawled back in bed and petted a shivering Onyx. He calmed at my touch, bent his head up, and looked at me with sad and quizzical eyes. I petted him until the fear bled out of his quivering muscles and a peace invaded him. Never have I felt such grief or compassion for a living creature. Not even in a man! I vowed then and there to always leave my door open, and if he awakened me in the middle of the night by cannonballing onto my head, then so be it, for it would be a small annoyance compared to his tolerating that inexpressibly terrible fear of being abandoned all alone.

Maybe I was projecting, because for some stupid reason tears formed in my eyes.

Emily finished the journal entry and tapped Save Voice Memo and marked it with the date. In front of the mirror, she hurriedly fixed herself up, applying as little mascara and lip gloss as she deemed necessary. She blow-dried her hair and combed it with her fingers until it produced that messy look she liked. Today was going to be a day of moving boxes, so she wore her tight, slate-gray corduroys and a black long-sleeve, scoop-neck T-shirt. She slung a sweater through the straps of her purse. She filled Onyx's bowls and bent to pet him. "I'm sorry I'm going to be gone all day, but at least you're not homeless."

Dramatic columns of pyrocumuli produced from the fire tornadoes detonated in the eastern sky as Emily headed south on Coast Highway. She estimated that the complex of conflagrations ravaging inland San Diego had burned closer to the university now, resurrecting the dream and all its kaleidoscopically vivid imagery. Chuckling, she threw an anxious look to the ocean to see if there were any document boxes drifting out to the horizon, but all she glimpsed were black wet-suited surfers bobbing beyond the break, randomly scattered men and women on an abandoned chessboard.

The strong winds whipped her hair as she made her way to the library, its impressive Brutalist countenance rising up and up and up as she approached, its mirrored windows reflecting a blinding, nuclear-incandescent light. A glance at her watch made her lengthen her already hurried stride. She admonished herself to turn out the lights at a more decent hour, immerse herself in that meditation app she had downloaded and never used, and set her alarm a half hour earlier, but the library catalog card and the cryptic handwritten note had kept her staring at the ceiling in puzzled contemplation.

Jean was waiting at the threshold of her cubicle when Emily arrived. Her arms were stapled across her chest. Her expression was frozen like a human rivet in a rictus of disapprobation. She glanced, annoyed, from her watch to Emily and back to her watch, as if words were superfluous.

"I'm sorry," spluttered Emily. "I'm still getting used to the traffic. Hard to imagine that it takes half an hour to go five miles."

Jean cocked her head dismissively, as if to say, *Excuses don't work with me.*

Emily didn't say anything, preferring to keep her distance until she better understood her new de facto nemesis.

Jean invited Emily's gaze to the shared office. When Emily looked in, she noticed a young man sitting in her cubicle. He stood up and extended his hand. "Hi, I'm Nicola." He had short black hair and a teenaged face stippled sporadically with bright-red acne. Sinewy slender in a tight white T-shirt and matching black jeans offset by a pale linen coat that suggested to Emily that he hailed from wealth.

"Nicola's your student assistant," Jean elaborated. "I've already taken him down into the stacks and shown him the boxes that are marked to bring up."

Emily noticed half a dozen boxes that had already been hauled up to her cubicle. She winced to herself when she saw them. "Thank you, Jean, but I can handle the boxes, if you don't mind. I prefer them brought up in a certain order."

Jean shook her hair out of her face, an affectation of hers that was beginning to annoy Emily. Her features remained expressionless. "We've got a series of deadlines."

"I'm well aware of the urgent nature of this project, Jean. Thank you."

Nicola's eyes ping-ponged between the two of them.

Jean wore a dismissive smile. "Carry on, then." She slipped away like a fish darting under a rock.

Emily faced Nicola. She took his hand finally. "It's nice to meet you."

"Nice to meet you, Ms. Snow."

"You can call me Emily."

"Okay," Nicola said with a nervous laugh. "Do you want me to bring up the rest of the boxes?"

Emily's temper ignited and her nostrils flared. "No. In fact, we're going to take these boxes back, and begin all over."

"Okay." Nicola was flustered. "These were the ones she said to bring . . ."

"I know I'm only the project archivist and will be gone in three months, but you take your instructions from me, okay?" Emily could feel her jaw jutting forward a little, and for a moment she felt like Reese Witherspoon in the movie *Election*.

Emily and Nicola walked side by side back into the stacks. As Nicola brought back the six boxes, Emily briefly assayed the contents of the others.

She knew the tedious part would be the manuscripts, and she wanted to get that underway before poring over the boxes with the diskettes and hard drives, as well as the ones overflowing with photographs and other memorabilia. She also hoped to get a visual sense of the scope of his archive in the event she had to retrace her archival steps to any of the boxes to cross-reference an item. Looking up at all the boxes, she still couldn't believe the magnitude of the collection. Sure, Dickens had died when he was fifty-seven, and—my God!—look at all the novels he had penned! But the sheer size of West thrilled through Emily in an emotive way that a few archivists still understood. She wanted to take a picture of it and post it somewhere to show West's fans how prolific their favorite author was, how excited she was to be its caretaker, but selfies and social media postings weren't her style. She had already witnessed two colleagues' careers suffer irremediably because of irresponsible postings. To Emily, the internet was a dark road to infinity, potholed with links. A necessary tool, not a pathway to a life.

Nicola returned, out of breath, gulping air. "Jean wanted to know why I was taking the boxes back."

"Tell her to go fuck herself." Emily smiled to show she was kidding. "What'd you tell her?"

"That I was doing as instructed."

Emily nodded. "Good." A rising tide of animosity was growing in her toward her supervisor. She didn't like being micromanaged; she didn't like being told how to do her job. Turning to Nicola, she indicated the boxes she wanted.

He dollied the boxes back up to Emily's cubicle, trailing her. He excused himself, as he had a prior engagement. It was a part-time job, and his hours were flexible. "I'll be in tomorrow at nine," he promised, waving goodbye and hooking his arm through the strap of a rucksack stuffed with books. "Nice to meet you." He glanced around. "It looks like a big job."

"It is. But we'll get through it."

"Goodbye," he said softly and then raced off.

Emily sat down in her chair. She didn't look up when Jean materialized in the threshold of her door.

"What's with the boxes?" she asked sharply.

"I have my own system, Jean," Emily said. "If I hear differently from

Helena, I'll be sure to alter the course of my strategy," she added testily, quickly setting the departmental boundaries. Emily thrust a smile at Jean to show she wasn't going to take any shit.

Before Jean could plant her own stake in the sand, Helena appeared behind her. For a moment, Emily sensed a fractious triangulation of power, but Helena just smiled and chirped, "I'm glad we're all so collegial already." No one said anything. "Emily, would you like to have lunch with me at the Faculty Club? Chef Christoph is doing his skirt steak. If you're not a vegetarian."

Emily shook her head no. "I'd love to."

Jean, feigning that she wasn't miffed, said, "Have a nice lunch," then smiled and returned to her cubicle to answer her phone.

"Stop by in ten minutes?" Helena suggested.

"Okay," Emily said.

Helena wheeled away from the door and thundered back down the hall.

Chloe popped her head over the partition that divided her cubicle from Emily's. "Lunch at the Faculty Club with Helena. She's never asked me." Chloe rolled her eyes to the ceiling. "Thank God."

Emily smiled a laugh and made a mental note that the partitions were far from soundproof.

Ten minutes later, on the dot, Emily appeared at Helena's door. She knocked on the glass rectangle inset with a shatterproof crosshatching of wire.

"Come in," she heard Helena call out.

Emily opened the door, but she had to push it with effort to force herself inside. A stack of books toppled to the floor. Inside Helena's office, Emily was presented with a sight that offended her aesthetics. The small room was littered with tottering towers of folders and papers and books and boxes. Because she was the director of Special Collections, no one dared reprove Helena for lack of organization and order. Indeed, the room was such a veritable disturbance of *dis*organization that one even vaguely critical remark could potentially upset the whole domino chain of rationalizations, and the years of accumulation, that held the room together. Surely, Emily believed, there had to be a proverbial method to her madness, a comfort in her hoarder's neglect.

"Don't mind the mess," Helena excused the room with a practiced phrase. "I know where all the bodies are buried!" she chortled.

Emily gaped in stupefaction at the room. Professor Erickson at Harry Ransom would have been appalled at this eyesore.

Helena collected her purse and stood up from her chair. They sauntered out of the library together, nearly half a century in age apart. Helena knew all the staff and she waved to some of them without breaking stride. Outside, they both changed into sunglasses to shield their eyes. They climbed a short flight of stairs and walked across the concrete plaza that was the faux third floor of the library in the blinding, bright sunlight.

"Do you believe these fires?" commented Helena.

"No," said Emily. "Positively apocalyptic."

"Dries out my sinuses," complained Helena. And with a handkerchief, she blew her nose. "So, you're getting settled in?" she asked Emily without looking at her.

"Yes."

"Good."

The Faculty Club was a short walk across campus in the direction of the ocean. Walking briskly, they wound together on asphalt paths that led sinuously to the centrally located single-story structure. Inside was a high-ceilinged, expansive room furnished with tables festooned with chairs. Occupying one entire side was a cafeteria-style station where the lunch for that Tuesday steamed away in stainless steel containers bobbing in baths of simmering water. Emily assembled a salad while Helena heaped her plate with Chef Christoph's skirt steak and a tangle of green beans.

"No steak?" Helena asked Emily, as she steered her across the floor to an empty table.

"No. A salad's fine."

Emily sat down across from Helena at a window table. Helena's eyes surveyed the room. "I bet I know everybody in here," Helena boasted.

"How long have you been here?" asked Emily.

"Ages. Once it was just me in an office. Me and David Verlander. He's a nice man, isn't he?"

"Yes," agreed Emily. "Seems so."

"There used to be only two colleges. Now there are six. Soon to be eight. Can you believe that?"

"San Diego's a beautiful city in which to get an education," Emily said, growing increasingly uncomfortable in the director's presence.

"Do you think you'd like to stay?"

Was Helena floating a job offer? "I don't know," said Emily.

"Are you sure you don't want to try any of this skirt steak?" Helena offered.

"No thanks."

A white-haired man in his seventies came over and traded greetings with Helena. "And this is our new project archivist, Emily," introduced Helena, beaming.

The bespectacled professor smiled down at Emily. "And what are you working on, Emily?"

"The Raymond West Papers."

"Ah. Our resident literary celebrity."

"We're getting that finished up finally," said Helena.

"Good to hear, Helena. Well, I'll leave you two ladies to business." He moseyed off.

Helena bent her head across the table to Emily. "That's Professor Wright. He's chair of the Lit Department. West is about to be appointed chair—when Professor Wright moves up to dean of Humanities."

"Won't all the bureaucracy of being chair interfere with his writing?" Emily inquired.

"Elizabeth wants it," she answered oddly.

Emily almost asked, *He's doing it for his wife?* but held her tongue. The university's politics were only nebulously adumbrated, but Emily assumed that Helena was hip deep in all of them.

Triggered by a thought, Helena leaned forward and fixed Emily with an admonitory look. "You realize this project is top priority." Emily nodded affirmatively. "If you have any issues with West—anything—you come directly to me. Is that understood?"

Emily nodded that she understood. Helena's words vibrated authoritatively in the air. Her eyes loomed unnaturally large in her oversized glasses. Emily understood the reason for the invitation now, and she found it a little disquieting. Perhaps this was a rite of passage for all new hires.

Helena finally withdrew her gaze from Emily, wiped her mouth with a cloth napkin, whiplashed into a smile, and announced, "We're going to Elizabeth's residence after this lunch."

Emily lifted her eyes to her inquiringly, dumbfounded. "The Wests'?"

"We have a new addition to his collection, remember?" Emily raised her eyebrows in recollection. "I'm going personally to pick it up. And I thought you might like to come." A lilt of excitement lifted her voice.

"Uh, sure," Emily said haltingly, sensing that it wasn't a question but a privileged invitation that you didn't turn down.

After lunch they headed back in the direction of the library and climbed into Helena's Lexus, which was parked in one of the "A" spots, designated for faculty and high-level staff. The motor purred at the push of a button. Helena steered them out of the labyrinthine campus roads with practiced knowledge and down onto La Jolla Shores Drive. As they rounded the first corner, the town of La Jolla emerged majestically into view. It was situated on a high knoll overlooking an outcropping that jutted into the Pacific, nestled around a cove where protected sea lions, marine fowl and even crustaceans lived in temperate waters at the doorsteps of the rich.

"Do you live in La Jolla, Ms. Black–I mean Helena?" Emily asked.

"Oh, God no." She swung the wheel to the left on the sharply curving road that descended into La Jolla. "The traffic is terrible. Especially in the summer. Now, if you're like the Wests, who don't have to go anywhere, it's fabulous."

As they coasted down the hill in a car whose engine was so silent it was hard to tell if it was running, Helena flung out an arm.

"This is Scripps Institution of Oceanography. We have an annex here. Fortunately for you, all of West is in the main library."

Emily gazed out the window at the pier that ran a short distance into the water. Research boats bobbed in the gentle swells, moored to its pilings. The sapphire-blue waters scintillated in the bright sunlight. With the orange, fire-blemished skies, La Jolla was awash in gold, windows on its tallest buildings glinting in the glare of the sun.

"Raymond Chandler lived in the La Valencia Hotel for a while, didn't he?" remarked Emily.

"Did he? David would know. He wrote a book on Chandler."

Emily swung her head to Helena. “Really?”

“Yes. I didn’t read it. I tried to. It went over my head.”

“I’ll check it out,” said Emily, struggling for conversation, uncomfortable in the director’s presence.

They drove in silence through downtown La Jolla, its narrow streets lined with a mélange of boutique clothing stores and fast-food eateries incongruously situated next to luxury-car dealerships. To Emily, it looked like the wealthy occasionally liked to slum it at Jack in the Box, while next door the lavishments of their caprices—clothing boutiques and the like—reassured them they still lived in a rarefied neighborhood, barricaded from any portents of a coming socialist revolution.

Off La Jolla Boulevard, Helena turned onto a shaded street colonnaded by mature pines. In the distance sparkled the Pacific Ocean, a flat deep-blue expanse flecked with whitecaps, which met a jaundice-tainted sky in a perfect horizontal line. In a world that was all hers, seemingly oblivious to Emily, Helena coasted toward it, her eyes roaming the quaint homes that retained a feel of a fairy-tale La Jolla, as if descending to a chimerical realm that ended where the surf crashed against the rocks, sending up spray over the few homes that jealously hugged the precious California coast. To Emily, a daughter of atheists, and an antideist herself, the solemnity of this final leg to the Wests felt like going to church. When Emily glanced over, Helena had the resentful gaze of someone who would never be rich.

Helena wheeled into a circular drive as if she had executed the turn many times before and settled in behind a sleek, two-door black Mercedes. She turned to Emily. “We’re not here to talk about the past,” she cautioned enigmatically. “Only the future.” Their eyes met behind the opacity of dark sunglasses and came to a wordless accord. “You realize Elizabeth West is probably the richest woman in San Diego.” Palm fronds chattered in the intermitted gusts of the Santa Anas as if to underscore her words, whose ominousness lingered in the cool air-conditioned car.

“I didn’t know,” Emily managed.

“She’s the only person who intimidates me,” she confided. “Let’s go.”

Helena opened her door and swung out of the car, Emily following suit. Helena’s heels clicked on the flagstone walkway that led to an eave hung over two massive doors. Helena pressed a button that rang a chime inside that evoked in Emily the image of an enchanted world. The waves exploding against the cliffs only intensified her vision of the world that awaited inside.

"Who is it?" a woman's voice inquired over an intercom.

"Helena," Helena spoke into a discreetly tiny speaker. "For Elizabeth."

Looking into a compact held close to her face, Helena hurriedly finger-combed her hair. She reached into her purse to fetch her lip gloss, but the door opened before she could find it. Greeting them was a beautiful, slender Indian woman flowing in a pale lavender shirtwaist. Gold hoop earrings glittered beneath her moonless-night hair.

"Hi, Helena," trilled the young woman, extending her hand.

Helena took her hand as if it bore the fragility of a small, injured bird and shook it lightly. She stepped aside and turned to Emily. "Sushma, this is Emily. She's our new archivist."

Sushma smiled and they traded hellos.

"Sushma's Elizabeth's über-assistant," Helena said to Emily. "Without her, Elizabeth would be at a great loss."

Sushma produced a humble smile at the flattering comment and pushed open the door wider. The great room mushroomed into view, much as the drawing back of a curtain might reveal a massive seascape by Turner. "Come on in," Sushma beckoned in a honeyed voice. Helena and Emily followed her inside. Sushma craned her head over a delicate shoulder. "I'll let her know you're here. Have a seat in the living room, and I'll be with you in a minute."

The foyer was paved with inlaid blue mosaic tiles that looked precious enough to be eaten on and not stepped over. The walls were the palest of blue, replete with ghostly images of feathering waves, as if a graphic artist had taken the sky and lightened it almost to white in an ukiyo-e style. The vaulted beam ceilings gave a cavernous majesty to the room. Helena stepped out of her shoes, looked at Emily, and then pointed at her feet. Emily nodded and squatted down to untie her black leather tennis shoes that she now felt chagrined about having worn. When she stood, she was taller than Helena, whose heels abnormally magnified her height. It felt strange to suddenly find her so diminutive, given her stature at the university.

Helena wandered on the walkway, stopping to admire the Melanesian artifacts adorning the entryway wall. Weathered, hand-carved masks and other talismanic objects celebrating the rituals of some South Pacific tribe were mounted in antique frames. It represented a small gallery of priceless art that greeted the guests in an impressive but tasteful display of the collector's opulence.

Past the entryway, two steps above the great room, Helena grasped the wrought iron balustrade to steady herself and imbibe the spectacular view. "Would you look at that," she effused about the large picture windows that showcased the Pacific, which floated ethereally above an immaculately landscaped backyard and a white, weathered palisade that sloped toward the ocean before it dropped off into infinity.

Emily directed her attention to where Helena was staring trancelike, moving her head back and forth in quiet awe. The roar of crashing waves was now unmuffled, and it gave Emily the sense that Elizabeth West had deliberately wanted to marry the décor of her house with the ebb and surge of the sea.

"Stunning, isn't it?" whispered Helena.

"I don't think I'll get here on my salary," Emily quipped.

"Neither of us will ever get here, my dear," Helena said with barely disguised resignation to her own station in life.

Emily pointed to a large painting mounted on the far wall. "Is that an O'Keeffe?"

Helena gazed at the wall. "I can't believe she bought it," exclaimed Helena. "*Sky above Clouds*. Yes, Georgia O'Keeffe." She stepped down into the great room and, captivated by the painting, moved toward it as if it were a large magnet whose attraction she was powerless to resist.

Emily descended noiselessly into the great room on a pair of polished bamboo steps, but her eyes were on the ocean and the spray that the waves threw up like watery fangs before dropping below the sandstone cliffs.

"It's one of a series," Helena spoke to the painting. "I believe The Art Institute of Chicago has one."

"It would have cost millions," said Emily, turning her attention to the painting. The O'Keeffe was created on a dramatically large canvas that dominated the entire wall. It was, as the title described, an image painted above the clouds in a photo-realist style. But the clouds—a hundred or so—were shaped and contoured like biscuits spread apart in a vast, celestial pan, the lapis lazuli of the sky differentiating each and every one of them in a grid-like pattern.

Helena turned away from the painting. "She bought it for Raymond because the clouds look like the keys on a typewriter. And the horizon in the distance makes Elizabeth see the page on which his next masterpiece will be composed."

Emily was taken aback by Helena's eloquent explanation, deprecatingly surmising that she was echoing something Mrs. West had once said. "It sounds like they have a close marriage," remarked Emily.

"Yes. They do." She tore her eyes away from the painting and turned to Emily. "Shall we sit?" Helena beckoned Emily to the large, oyster-gray sectional that framed the center of the room. Emily sat down. The couch was so immense that when her rear reached the backrest, her legs wouldn't fold to the floor. She elected to perch on the edge. "You can take your sunglasses off," Helena chided.

Emily removed her sunglasses and set them on a glass-top table with a blue-oxidized brass frame that was the size of a small car. Oversized books on art and architecture decorated its surface and kept it from appearing barren. Amid the artfully arranged collection, Emily noticed a cookbook. She picked it up and leafed through it, as Helena studied her with watchful eyes. The book was *Arzak Secrets* by the eponymous chef of the world-famous Arzak restaurant outside San Sebastián, Spain. Leafing absently through it, Emily looked up from the colorful pictures of the sumptuous dishes. "Mrs. West likes to cook?"

Helena shook her head sharply. "It's Raymond's passion."

Emily nodded. With both hands, she set the book back down on the table with the care of an archivist.

Sushma returned and leaned over the balustrade. "She's on a call. She'll be with you in a few minutes. Can I offer anyone some tea?"

"Do you have that Himalaya one?" inquired Helena. "That was so lovely."

"I believe we do." She turned to Emily with that gleaming smile of perfectly white teeth. "Emily?"

"I'll have the same, thank you."

Sushma evaporated as quickly as she had appeared, her figure silently receding.

Emily dreamed her gaze upward toward the picture windows, where, if you closed your eyes, the thunderous waves seemed to crash against the glass. "An extraordinary home."

"Yes," said Helena, glancing at her watch, venturing a backward look as if she had heard the footsteps of someone approaching, visibly anxious in Elizabeth's house.

"How long have you and Mrs. West known each other?" asked Emily.

"We go way back to the beginning of Special Collections. I took an early interest in her husband's work." In lowered tones, she added, "Of course, I didn't have her trust fund."

Emily sensed that ripple of rancor, born of envy, rising in Helena, and she suppressed her urge to ask more questions. It was enough to know they had a history.

Sushma floated down into the great room and set two lightly clattering china saucers with cups of hot water nested in them. Muslin bags of the vaunted Himalayan tea rested on the lips of the saucers. "I hope you like it. It's my favorite. The top leaves only." She ran her thumb over her fingertips as if to underscore its rarity. "Give it a few minutes to steep," she murmured.

"Thank you, Sushma," said Helena.

Emily dipped her tea bag into the teacup and watched the hot water bleed a warm golden shade as she stirred in some honey from an accompanying tiny saucer with a delicate spoon. The tea whorled clockwise with mystery.

The sudden advance of hurried footsteps startled Helena and Emily, and their teacups rattled in their saucers when they automatically set them down. Elizabeth materialized like a woman comfortable in her affluence. She reminded Emily of Catherine Deneuve this afternoon, as beautifully regal as she was in Buñuel's *Belle de Jour*, as if levitating above them on a floor different from the one everybody else came in on. The epitome of aplomb, she was a woman holding fast to what remained of her youth. She was comfortably but elegantly attired in black silk slacks and a billowy burgundy shirt that floated to midthigh. Her auburn hair framed her face with two complementary waves, as if created by whoever created the ocean. Jewelry dangled and gleamed from both wrists and a neck exposed to the sun. Her engagement ring refracted the sun, scintillating superciliously like a warning light. She eased onto the edge of the far side of the sectional, her back to the ocean, her warm smile radiating from a natural, seemingly ageless beauty. Midnight-blue eyes appeared bright and thinking as if she were always phasing in and out of something important or pressing.

"I love your shirt, Elizabeth," Helena gushed.

"Thank you." She spoke in a lower octave, as if half of her were, or yearned to be, somewhere else.

"You remember Emily," Helena said.

"Of course." Elizabeth turned to Emily. "How are you?"

"Fine," replied Emily, feeling nervous again in her presence.

"How is San Diego treating you?" Elizabeth spoke to a thought in the distance without making eye contact with Emily.

"I love being near the ocean," Emily said, just as another wave thundered against the cliffs.

"She was admiring your O'Keeffe." Helena raised her head to the painting.

"Yes." Elizabeth threw the massive canvas a perfunctory look. "My husband can see it when he comes in. Because it looks like a typewriter, it reminds him that he should never forget his calling." She chortled, as if roused to life by something unspoken. "God forbid." Helena gave Emily an imperceptible knowing nod. Elizabeth interlaced her fingers and covered her mouth with the small globe she had made. "I think only writing makes him truly happy. When he's not writing, he feels like he's dead," she finished in what felt like a rare flush of honesty and heartfelt emotion.

"Does he still write on a manual typewriter?" Emily asked.

Elizabeth nodded, blushing in confessing he did.

"That's so cool," the millennial in Emily effused.

"And sometimes in longhand when it's pulsing through him, when he needs the tactile connection between pen and paper more than the mechanical, rhythmic clacking of keys," Elizabeth elaborated in phraseology that made Emily realize the woman's devotion to her husband's life and work was all-encompassing.

"Did you ever want to be a writer?" Emily ventured.

Helena darted a look at Emily, as if warning it wasn't appropriate to get too personal with Elizabeth, but Elizabeth's flash of a smile eased Helena's anxiety. "I've dabbled," Elizabeth admitted. "But when you're living with the Great One"—she twirled an index finger and fashioned an imaginary dirt devil in the air—"it's hard to pick up pen and paper without judgmental eyes paralyzing you." She cast her eyes down and spoke in lowered tones. "Besides, I can't go where my husband goes in his writing. And if you can't go where he goes, you're never going to be one of the remembered." Her words hung in the air with the weight of solemnity and ineffable years. Who could ever know what it was like to live with a famous author?

"What's Mr. West working on now?" Emily asked, youthfully eager for all the information she could mine.

"Oh . . ." A jaded lilt crept into Elizabeth's voice as she raised her head. "He accepted an offer to adapt one of his novels for the cinema. He's never written a screenplay before. He's having a hell of a time with it. He's not used to listening to punitively meddling voices, especially when they're so . . . so contradictory to his vision. He prefers the theater when he's not working on a novel."

Emily's brief brush with a Hollywood writer stirred some commentary in her, but she held back, sensing that she was monopolizing Helena's time with Elizabeth and overstepping her bounds.

"How's the tea?" Elizabeth spoke to the oceanic view.

"Lovely," said Helena, relieved that the subject had shifted from Elizabeth's husband and his mythical reputation.

"Like perfumed earth," complimented Emily.

From her trance, Elizabeth smiled, but her thoughts were suddenly far away, as if her mind had become unmoored and drifted out to sea.

"It's a beautiful house you have," Emily said.

"Yes. But soon it will be like the lost city of Atlantis." And as she fatalistically augured the future of her home another set of waves beat against the cliffs, sending fingers of seawater high over the lawn and the low palisade that was all that remained between the three of them and a watery blue void, lending more meaning to Elizabeth's doomful prediction. "Which is why we're moving."

"You're moving?" Helena asked, taken aback, her eyes torn with anxiety. "To the house in London?"

"No. God no. I love London, but the British drive Raymond crazy with all their carousing and socializing. He gets no work done there. No, we're building a new house on the top of Mount Soledad." She pointed eastward and up to an empyreal realm beyond the walls of this, in her society-ascendant view, nautical-themed relic of old La Jolla.

Elizabeth's revelation transformed the features of Helena's face into a relieved glow. Emily knew that Elizabeth was a major donor to the university, and to the library in particular, but she didn't know to what extent. She was intuiting now that it was more than substantial, that Helena had worked indefatigably to cultivate this relationship to where it was now burnished to a delicate, if fragilely held-together, perfection. "When will it be done?" Helena enthused. "It sounds lovely."

"Oh, it's a big project," Elizabeth in an exasperated tone. "We had to tear down the hideous structure that was there. We're installing a small museum."

"Your Impressionism collection?" Helena wondered.

"Yes," Elizabeth qualified with modesty. "I should take you up some time. The views are extraordinary. And, of course, we'll have a grand housewarming when it's all finished." She smiled at the visualization of its completion.

Helena beamed a radiance her soul didn't own. Glancing back and forth between the two of them, Emily surmised that Helena was perhaps not always on the guest list for Elizabeth's events, and that when she *was* invited it made her feel special. In every way—money, house, husband—Helena was envious of Elizabeth. However, her envy never bore the ashes of bitterness, only the second-class status of sycophancy. She needed Elizabeth. And, perhaps, she felt proudly, Elizabeth needed her. After all, Helena was the griffin hovering over her husband's legacy and she, too, had a purpose in this money-and-fame configuration.

"I want to create new memories," Elizabeth said dreamily. "New memories in a new house." She painted the great room with roving eyes, as if abandoned by the *old memories* she had alluded to, but reluctant to elaborate.

"Many memorable, and enduring, books were written here," Emily said.

"Oh, no." Elizabeth directed her gaze to Emily, across the now disorganized expression of Helena. "He writes everything at Isla Negra."

Emily's brow corrugated questioningly. "Isla Negra?"

"It's a little beach cottage he keeps up in Del Mar. He lived there when he was attending Regents. I bought it for him as a wedding present. We were young." She gazed off to the amplitude of the ocean view and went through the rhythms of remembering. "His words revolutionized me," she said with a quiet conviction in her voice. "I had to have him, you see." She smiled wistfully at the memory.

Emily felt uncomfortable that Elizabeth had opened up to her personally. All she could offer in reply was, "Named after Pablo Neruda's seaside home in Valparaíso?"

"Yes. I gave him the space to write. The opportunity. Because, you see, every writer needs someone to fall in love with him, someone who believes that aspiring to be a writer of enduring fiction is a noble ambition. In a day when books are dying," she lamented.

A door opened and closed. Elizabeth's leonine head lurched up and her chin jutted forward. "Speaking of the devil."

Simultaneously, Helena and Emily turned. In the foyer, crisscrossed by shafts of light streaming in through the skylights, appeared a tall, rangy man in his early fifties. He had shoulder-length, coffee brown hair, flecked with gray at the temples. Clad in faded jeans and black T-shirt, he was hitching forward on halting steps. Emily recognized Raymond West from his dust jacket photo on *Lessons in Reality*, and though age was beginning to claim him, she still thought, with his angular, lined face, and aquiline nose, the resemblance to the playwright Sam Shepard was striking. His cheeks were sandpapery unkempt with a day's growth of beard. He stopped in a column of shadow and smiled without showing his teeth when he spotted the three women in the recessed great room all looking up at him from their tea.

"What is this, the meeting of the La Jolla bluestockings?" Raymond quipped in his husky baritone, a voice Emily had grown familiar with as that of the narrator of *Lessons in Reality*.

Helena feigned a hyena-like laugh. Elizabeth rose from the sectional and made a move toward her husband that was merely gestural. "Dear, you remember Helena, of course."

Raymond raised his sunglasses to the top of his head, revealing his twinkling blue eyes, and peered into the blinding sunlight. "Of course. How are you, Helena?"

"I'm fine." A nervous, crooked smile creased her face.

"And who's this?" Raymond inquired, tenting his eyes with a flattened hand as he squinted painfully into the afternoon sun that poured in through the picture windows.

Emily started to introduce herself, but Elizabeth chopped her off. "This is Emily Snow. She's your new archivist."

A resigned exhalation was audible through his nose. He manufactured a smile, again without parting his lips. "I would come down and greet your properly, Ms. Snow, but"—he lowered a hand to his right hip and squeezed it—"I'm still recovering from an accident. I snapped my femur."

"I'm sorry," offered Emily, wincing.

The room fell momentarily silent. "The physical therapy is doing wonders, though, isn't it, dear?" asked Elizabeth, more as a statement than a question.

Raymond tilted his head to one side and shrugged his shoulders.

"I'm honored to be finishing up your papers," Emily said.

"She comes highly recommended from the Harry Ransom Center," Elizabeth elaborated.

"Ah, Márquez. You should find some wonderful letters from him in my archive. I feel honored," he said in a genuine tone. He gathered some momentum and started off, hurting to move on the injured leg. "Well, carry on. I'm going to pack it in. I'm tired."

"Did you have a good day writing, Ray?" Elizabeth said in her sonorous voice.

Raymond paused in a band of sunlight. It was then that Emily noticed he was clutching a wooden cane in his right hand. "Adapting your own novel is like eviscerating your soul. I see why they farm it out to hacks and why we end up so often with forgettable films from sometimes enduring works. To do it to your own work takes a certain form of literary masochism that I didn't know was a requirement for the assignment until it was too late. Now, if I give it over to them, they'll turn it into something unrecognizable, I fear. I'm trapped in a purgatorial fate. I understand why Chandler nearly drank himself to death just over there." He crooked his cane in a vaguely southerly direction.

"What novel of yours are you adapting?" Emily asked.

"*A Time of Uncertainty*," he answered.

"That's one of my favorites," gushed Emily across the broad expanse of the room, thrilled that it was one of the first books of his she had read when she was offered the job. Helena looked pale and undone, as if Emily had violated some unspoken pact not to interact with Raymond West.

"I'm sure—if it's ever made—they'll change it to something generic like *Happiness Blues*," Raymond laughed sardonically.

Uneasy laughter erupted from the three women.

"I'm off, ladies." Raymond leaned on his cane and hobbled off in a hitching gait, the thudding of the cane against the travertine floor marking his slow progress down an arched hallway.

"He's looking better," Helena observed.

"He suffered a horse-riding accident a while back, didn't he?" said Emily.

Helena and Elizabeth looked at Emily with raised eyebrows.

"I did my research," Emily admitted.

"Yes," said Elizabeth. "It was an appalling break." She shook her head at the awful memory. She directed her attention to Emily. "Don't take anything he says about Hollywood seriously. He loves the movies. He took the assignment because he was stuck on something else. I think it's good for him. He likes to ride the train up to LA and take those Hollywood meetings. He knows movies and TV are eclipsing literature, his first love. But he wouldn't turn down an Oscar."

Emily, chastened by Helena's stare, didn't say anything, though questions galore were swirling in her head. It was thrilling to meet the man whose papers she would be working on. Her heart pumped blood to her face and she couldn't help but feel adrenalized by his presence, however fleeting. She realized she was in awe of the man as he slipped away through the checkerboard of shadows and sunlight. It surged through her all at once that it might be her only chance to ever speak to him. As new as she was to the profession, Emily knew that archivists were usually anonymous in the processing of a donor's papers.

Elizabeth waited until Raymond had disappeared out of earshot before she turned back to Emily. Another set of waves lashed the cliffs, thundered against the windows and caused them to shudder as if they might shatter. "I hope our curator has done a thorough job of organizing my husband's items." She interwove her elegant fingers again and telescoped her head forward. "As you seem to be familiar with my husband's work, you know he writes in a personal style. Sometimes *too* personal for my taste, but then, he's the artist." Her eyes narrowed into two dark lines, and she leaned forward, her face stamped with concern. "If you come across anything of an even slightly compromising nature, you'll let Helena know."

"Of course." Emily nodded up and down to reassure her.

Elizabeth rested back against the giant cushion and smiled up at the sky, a calm suffusing her.

Sushma reappeared at the balustrade as if summoned by telepathy. "The gentleman from the university is here."

"Thank you, Sushma." Elizabeth turned to Helena and Emily as she rose from the sectional. "Well, I think that's an afternoon."

Emily and Helena straightened to their feet. Elizabeth now seemed icily distant, as if she had retreated to a world where Emily and Helena didn't belong but had been vouchsafed a visit because, of necessity, sometimes the paths of the rich intersect with those they must conduct business with.

"I love the new look of the house, Elizabeth," said a walking Helena, now moving toward the entrance with an unwillingness to leave. "Sad that you're moving."

Elizabeth ushered them to the door. "It's a change we both wanted. Soon we'll be at the top of the hill, and when the next glacier calves off from Antarctica and the seas rise another ten feet, we'll be safe." She spoke the apocalyptic words with the conviction of a woman who believed it, but with a solemnity of someone who, with all her wealth, couldn't prevent its inexorability.

Jim, a scruffy-bearded guy from Facilities, was outside, lugging boxes from the garage to a waiting Regents University van. Sweat mottled his slate-gray uniform and beaded his sunburned forehead. The ocean threw up spray between the homes almost in his face as if mocking him and the one-bedroom apartment he occupied twenty miles inland.

"I think that's it, Helena," Jim said, wiping his brow with a blue kerchief. He surveyed the neighborhood with the scheming expression of a petty criminal who was casing it for a future robbery. "It's beautiful down here."

"Yes. It is. Thanks, Jim." Helena turned to Emily as if addressing both of them. "Her student assistant will be down at the loading dock to bring these up."

"Good deal." He wheeled on squeaking tennis shoes, circled around to the front of the van, fired up its coughing motor, and drove away on squealing tires, leaving behind a world he wished would one day soon be submerged in seawater.

Helena was quiet for the first leg of the drive back to Regents. Emily debated making small talk, but she sensed Helena was depressed. Depressed that she, too, was leaving the home by the sea in a neighborhood where the wealthy congregated, a community and a lavish way of life that her salary would never afford her? Unsettled that Emily had engaged Raymond in ebullient conversation, however brief, when she had been tacitly forbidden?

Staring forward over the steering wheel, driving faster than when they had come from the university, Helena suddenly broke into a sharp burst of words, "I'm glad you got to meet Raymond, but you do realize he's technically a donor and you're staff?"

"Of course." Dismayed, Emily interpreted her tone to clearly convey that Helena was cementing the hierarchical structure, that the delicate fabric that webbed the relationship between Helena and Elizabeth was not to be encroached upon, that the lines were strictly demarcated.

Helena jutted her jaw forward almost on the top of the steering wheel. "If I were a trained archivist, if I weren't busy with my town-and-gown events and all the hobnobbing I have to do to keep this institution running," she turned to Emily with a venomous gaze, "I would finish the collection myself."

Her nerves rattled by Helena's bizarrely transported voice, Emily fixed her gaze on the anachronistic dashboard compass mount. It rotated like a squid's eye, a meaningless direction device, out of touch with modern technology, thought Emily. What she had to say in response would only foment ill will with this intransigent woman who, it seemed, could whipsaw from the friendly to the patronizing as her fickle moods dictated.

"I want this to go smoothly," Helena muttered in a vaguely assuaging tone.

Emily watched the ball in the compass spin to the northeast and tremble in the black bubble.

"You're going to hear about this Friday at David's town hall presentation, but I'm going to let you in on the secret." Helena paused for dramatic effect. "Elizabeth is giving the library twenty-five million dollars." She drew out the syllables and widened her eyes a little more with each note of emphasis.

"Wow." Emily sucked in her breath, but in a way that Helena could hear, as if to underscore its import.

"We have to do this in an entirely professional, and timely, fashion."

"I understand," said Emily, in an annoyed voice. "I was just being friendly."

"I know. But I would rather you not get personally involved." She whipped her head to Emily with daggers in her eyes and resentment in her voice. "On any level."

As they rode in a clock-ticking silence up the hill past Scripps the skies were marbled orange and crimson. "I guess there's been no break in the fires," observed Emily inanely, in a blatant effort to change the topic and palliate the tension that still throbbed in the car.

Helena said nothing, her silence further defining the hierarchical strata of power, Emily deduced. Helena drove on, forehead furrowed in thought, eyes storming behind her lightly tinted sunglasses. Anxiety seized Emily, and the Lexus suddenly felt claustrophobic.

Helena pulled up at the turnaround toward the "A" parking spaces, the ones reserved for faculty and upper-level staff. Through the car's windows, Memorial Library broadened against the sky, now more imposing than ever, the mushrooming clouds in the eastward distance seeming to spew out of its massive hexagonal head.

Helena spoke over her right shoulder, "I'm going to drop you off here. I've got some errands to run."

"Okay, that's fine." Emily pushed down on the lever handle, and the open door allowed in hot, dry air. A hand tight on her forearm prevented her momentarily from exiting.

"I have a lot of faith in you. That's why I wanted to introduce you to Elizabeth. So you would know what's at stake." Helena forced a smile.

Emily nodded, stepped out of the car and closed the door quietly, ensuring that it was latched shut for fear that one false move might ignite the tinder of annoyance that had found its way to Helena's earlier sanguine demeanor.

Emily strode across the vast concrete plaza to the stairs that led down to the main floor of the library. The blistering Santa Anas caused her to lower her head. An attractive man turned to look at her as he passed. Emily hardened her expression and did not return the look. Men gawked at her all the time, and though it often gave her a little thrill of femininity, she trained herself to avert the stares. To her, men were clouded in complications, usually not deep enough for her, bumbling, clumsy, not worth the inevitable disentangling. Her mother always flattered her that she would be the one to dictate the terms when it came to men, but Emily was skeptical. Was Helena concerned that Raymond might find his new archivist attractive to the point of kindling desire? It was a wild conjecture flitting through Emily's mind as she entered Memorial Library, still trying to process the afternoon at Elizabeth's and the Raymond West sighting.

A bright-faced Nicola hauled up the boxes from the new addition from the loading dock into Emily's cubicle. Perspiration beaded his forehead. He forearmed it off his brow, inhaled, and caught his breath, winded from the trek. He plopped the last two boxes down on the shelving that formed one wall of Emily's temporary office. Emily was glad to see the West boxes erecting a makeshift wall and beginning to occlude the view of the corridor and her passing colleagues. Her whole being cried out for privacy.

Emily swiveled away from her desk and smiled at Nicola. "Thank you, Nicola."

Nicola shifted uncomfortably in place. "What next?"

"We're going to go through all the boxes," Emily said. "For starters, I want you to help me arrange the items into separate piles."

"Okay."

"We're going to organize them into manuscripts, correspondence, memorabilia, and miscellaneous. If you have any questions, ask me, okay?"

"All right," said Nicola.

Jean poked her head into the entryway. "Am I bothering you?"

"No." Emily turned to Nicola. "Why don't you take a coffee break. Jean and I have some business."

Nicola tossed a friendly smile at Jean and slipped sideways past her out of Emily's cubicle.

Jean grabbed the back of an extra office chair, bent forward, and asked, "Do you mind?"

"No," Emily said, but she automatically stiffened.

Jean sat down in the office chair and, using her feet as paddles, rowed it on its wheeled legs so that it was next to Emily at her desk. "I heard you went with Helena to Elizabeth's," she said with a tremor of envy in her voice.

"Yes."

"What's the house like?"

"You've never been?" asked Emily.

Jean reached for Emily's computer mouse and inched closer to the computer. She shook her head no, as if it were obvious that a visit to Elizabeth West's was an anomaly, if not a privileged honor bestowed on a few. "I heard it's beautiful," she said, as she navigated the cursor over Emily's home page.

Emily drifted off for a moment in her imagination, uneasy about Jean commandeering her computer's controls. Somehow she could still hear, and feel, the ocean pounding in her heart from the seaside mansion. "It's another world," she finally said. "I come from a modest background. My uncle had a house on the Cape, but I've never been to a place where the walls were a museum and the views so stunning."

"That's nice that Helena took you down there," Jean said through pursed, thin lips.

"I guess." Emily bowed her head. "I even got to meet Raymond West."

Jean gave Emily a sharp backward glance and an expression of searching surprise. "Really?"

"Yeah. It must have been a bad accident he suffered because he was still hobbling along on a cane, poor guy," said Emily.

Jean blinked wordlessly in response. She clicked the mouse and motioned with her head for Emily to concentrate on the monitor. "This is Panopticon," she started, in that clipped voice of hers. Emily inched forward next to Jean and peered at the screen. Jean clicked on the Panopticon folder and a directory unfurled like a rope ladder might if the rungs were file folders. Listed under each directory entry were codes for file names. "This is the West Collection here. This is where you will live." She clicked on a folder with the code RW Coll. "Here you'll find everything your predecessor had done to date."

Emily nodded. "Okay." She was growing exasperated at everyone referring to Nadia Fontaine, an archivist at the library for nearly a decade—as well as a fellow in the Society of American Archivists, Joel had informed her—as "your predecessor." As if the mere vocalization of her name would resurrect an ignominious past that no one dared revisit. Or as if there were a mandate from on high that her memory was to be permanently expunged. *Eerie*, thought Emily.

"Did my . . . *predecessor*," Emily began with a sly tinge of sarcasm, "keep a personal file on the West Papers?"

"If she did, I didn't find one when we cleared out her desk drawers," Jean replied curtly.

"Because it would speed up the process enormously," Emily said.

"She did a lot of things that were unconventional." Jean stood bolt upright from the chair. "I trust that you'll know how to proceed from here. If you have any questions, let me know." She crossed the cubicle to the entrance, stopped, and made a half turn. "When you get a feel for the scope of the collection, I'd like a summation of your game plan."

"Okay. But as you can see"—Emily swept her hands across the brown cardboard boxes that Nicola had brought up from the loading dock and neatly stacked—"there's a whole new accession."

"It's not a new accession," Jean corrected her. "Recurated. You'll find"—she stabbed a finger at the computer monitor—"that much of it has already been processed."

"Why did it leave Special Collections and go back to the Wests if it had already been processed?" inquired Emily.

"I don't know," snapped Jean.

"Okay," said Emily. "Noted for now."

Jean gestured to the wall above the computer with an upward tilt of her head. "What happened to the picture?"

"I took it down. Tabula rasa." Jean frowned at the lexicological arcana that Emily was already becoming infamous for. "A clean slate," Emily defined.

Jean flashed a smile that appeared and disappeared almost imperceptibly. Superciliously, she pirouetted on the balls of her feet and walked down the corridor back to her corner cubicle, her restive manner discomfiting to Emily.

Emily swung around in her chair and faced the computer. She studied the file names in the West Collection without exploring any of them in detail. She wanted to get a feel for the scope of what was there and how it was organized.

A little while later, Nicola returned with a sheepish smile, but it was close to five o'clock and she released him to whatever world he retreated to.

When he was gone, Emily lifted the top off the first box that had been ferried up from the Wests' home in La Jolla. Lifting out the items, she came across bundles of letters fastened together with elastic bands. To Emily's trained eye, the rubber bands appeared brand new. It suggested to her that the correspondence had been combed over. It also crossed her mind that the collection might have been recently expurgated. It didn't surprise her that the letters from West, the ones that had been donated to the collection, were typewritten. If West still wrote on a typewriter and in cursive in notebooks, it made sense that his correspondence would not be printed out from computer-generated email files—or were they on a disk somewhere? Surely he engaged in email correspondence. Caressing one of the letters, she ran her finger over the inked indentations produced by the hammering keystrokes. Email and texts, Emily shook her head to herself. The bêtes noires of the archivist. So much potentially treasured correspondence lost, orbiting out there in cyberspace somewhere. There were new software programs being developed to catch up with this grievous content loss, but Emily realized that future archivists would only be able to preserve a fraction of it for posterity.

Snooping around, Emily found some correspondence between Raymond West and a theater director in New York from the '90s. West had written a play that had been workshopped at the La Jolla Playhouse and migrated its way to Off Broadway. It won a raft of Obies and the Drama Desk Award for Outstanding Play. Emily made a note to herself to check to see which institution housed the play director's papers, because that's where she would find Raymond's side of the correspondence. Perhaps, if he didn't have an archive, she could get them to donate Raymond's letters.

As she grew more absorbed in her reading, Emily was oblivious to the footsteps that padded down the hall and the lights that switched off in the other cubicles, darkening the overall space by degrees. The first interoffice IM from Joel—"Are we up for surfing this weekend?"—had gone unanswered. Her immersion became all-consuming. Soon she was poring over Raymond's early handwritten journals, scribbled in lined, bound notebooks with the haste and imprudence of youth. They were personal, soul baring, self-lacerating about his early, hitching stabs at writing—he, the potential future Nobel laureate waxing insecure. She shook her head, gasping out loud at an entry where he described in excruciating self-flagellating detail his inability to ever love, to ever find the great passion in his life. Emily cross-referenced the handwritten journal entry and was relieved at first to learn that it was before he met Elizabeth. Or was it?

A voice startled her. "Ms. Snow, it's almost seven-thirty," admonished Jorge. "Alarm's going to go off if you go out that door after that."

Emily set the journal on top of a stack that had piled up on the desk, marking hours that had gone by like minutes. "Have you been spying on me?" she teased.

"There are no cameras in the cubicles. That would be an invasion of privacy."

"You might see what women do when they're all alone," Emily brazenly said. "We cry a lot."

A crooked smile disorganized Jorge's face. Embarrassed, he looked down, shuffled his feet, silence enveloping his large frame.

Emily quickly collected her belongings and followed Jorge into the main lobby. Night had fallen. Open until 10:00 p.m., the main library, now in the chrysalis of summer, was eerily quiet. The immense floors bloomed larger in the absence of students. Diffuse fluorescent lighting gave the library a morgue-like feel. Cocooned in their warmth, libraries were where Emily felt most comfortable. Without a library she would feel untethered somehow. She viewed her life belonging to a string of libraries, among books, lost in the papers of famous or obscure writers. She often joked that she would like to be buried in one.

"Would you like me to walk you to your car?" Jorge offered, arm extended to the sliding door entrance.

"Huh?" said Emily, still lost in the labyrinth of her free-associating thoughts.

"Or call for an escort?"

"No, I'm fine," said Emily. "I need to check on something."

"Okay. You have our number, so text us if you want an escort."

"Okay. Thanks, Jorge."

Jorge smiled, turned and trudged back to Security and the monitors that would catch him his next laptop thief. Emily watched him walk off and started toward the elevator. In her hand she clutched the superannuated catalog card she had found wedged in the backing of the picture frame on her predecessor's bulletin board. She studied it closely. The reference numbers indicated that it was on the top floor, the eighth. She pressed the button for the elevator. The doors banged open, and she heard that irritating *bing bing* tintinnabulation and recoiled. She turned away from the maw of the elevator car and pushed down on the latch of the nearby heavy door that led into the stairwell. This will be good exercise, she rationalized to herself, not wanting to admit that the piercing high-frequency bells had recrudesced her misophonia and the anxiety it engendered.

She started up the winding, spiral stairway in the cylinder of concrete, her shoes clomping on the giant metal steps. Halfway up, she stopped to catch her breath and raised her head. For a moment, she thought she was in that Hitchcock movie where a woman is thrown off the top floor and pinwheels to her death. *Vertigo*? Acrophobic since she was a child—particularly to any activity that had to do with flying or climbing—she fixed her eyes on her feet. Every floor comprised three short flights of stairs, each floor marked by a giant red number painted on the exit door. Emily climbed, spiraling upward in a steep ascent, pushing the boundaries of her own vertigo. Her calves and thighs burned. Perspiration ran in rivulets from her armpits and trickled down the sides of her torso. She wanted to rip off her sweater vest, but she was afraid of stopping for fear that her eyes would accidentally glimpse the yawning opening that plummeted to the bottom floor and she would faint.

When there were no more steps to climb, she had reached the eighth floor. Winded, but wanting desperately to overcome her fear, Emily gripped the balustrade, ventured a glance down the stairwell shaft, a fifteen-foot-wide cylinder around which the steps spiraled all the way to the concrete floor below. Feeling dizzy, she reared back, looked sharply away, fumbled anxiously for the lever handle on the door with the big red 8, and pressed down, ejecting herself from the terrifying stairwell out to the top floor, hand clutched to her heart, hyperventilating. The door slammed shut with such thunderous force that a startled Emily leaped back. A sepulchral quiet followed. The eighth floor was awash in overhead fluorescent lights that glowed through soft yellow diffuser panels.

Faint noises drew Emily's attention, and she drifted instinctually in that direction. At the west end of the vast rectangular space, she spotted two men from Facilities indiscriminately stripping books off shelves and stacking them on carts in disorderly piles, as if preparing for a demolition. She wondered what they were doing. The violent way they treated the books appalled her. She considered introducing herself and simply asking why they were carting the books away, but they seemed engrossed in their work. She glanced at the catalog card in her hand and an anxiety rose up in her that maybe the book she was about to search for had already been yanked out of circulation.

Emily moved hurriedly along the inner perimeter, glancing at the alphabetically sequenced letters and numbers that were posted at the head of each row of shelves. She stopped when she came to PC (French authors), under which she found a sequence of numbers, in which the corresponding numbers on her catalog card matched, sandwiched somewhere in between.

She ducked into the narrow aisle, claustrophobically hemmed in by two banks of metal shelving that held row upon row of books, clothbound and identified by typewritten labels taped to the bottom of their spines, books yet to be removed by the Facilities crew. Emily traced a finger across the individual labels, paying close attention to the call numbers, homing in on her prey. Well-read for her age, she recognized some authors and titles as she crabbed in a left-to-right progression, bending her knees and then squatting as she descended the ladder of rows.

On the bottom row in the midpoint of the aisle, Emily found the book that matched the card catalog card: *Le Rêve d'un Flagellant* by Maurice de Vindas. She gently pushed back the two neighboring books and pulled the de Vindas out from its exposed spine like an antiquarian bookseller might. Squatting low to the floor, she flipped open the cover. She barely had time to be shocked by the frontispiece of a man with a half-naked woman bent over his knee, when something slipped out of the title page spread and fell to the linoleum like a windblown feather. Emily quickly retrieved it. Lined notebook paper torn from its original binding and folded into eighths, met her inquisitive eyes. She slowly unfolded it. It opened outward like a carefully handcrafted origami flower. Her heart pounded furiously; she could feel its hot pulse course and jump behind her breast. The missive was handwritten in a difficult-to-decipher scrawl. Emily had only gotten as far as the salutation—"My Raymond"—when she heard the approach of leather heels clicking on the linoleum. Instinctively, she wadded up the handwritten letter up and plunged it into her sweater vest pocket clenched in her fist, slammed the book closed, and looked up, sucking in her breath when she recognized the round, amiable face of David Verlander.

"Ms. Snow. Didn't know you were fluent in French."

Emily rose on quaking legs. "I was looking for a book," she replied breathlessly.

Verlander reached out and took hold of the book in her hand, as if this were common among Special Collections colleagues. In that instant she realized an excuse—hell, a lie!—would be preferable to preventing him from snatching it from her, so she released it to his hand. He looked at the binding through the bottom of his bifocals, leafed through it briefly, then closed it with a snap and said in impeccably accented French, "Maurice de Vindas. *Le Rêve d'un Flagellant.*" He handed the book back to her. "An obscure, interesting . . . rarity of erotica."

Emily blushed crimson. "I have a friend, she's, um—"

Verlander waved her off, tacitly admitting that he was the one responsible for the awkward moment. "Harry Ransom, as you might know, has quite a collection of the . . . blue literature."

Emily looked down and laughed nervously. "I've heard rumors."

Another cart loaded with hastily piled books, like rubble from a construction site, rumbled past. The Facilities worker seemed unaware of their presence in the aisle.

"Where are they taking all the books?" Emily inquired.

"They're making way for the eighth-floor renovation." Verlander gave the empty shelving a pensive backward glance. He returned his gaze to her. "You'll hear all about it at the town hall meeting on Monday. You're coming?"

"I'm planning to," replied Emily, her hand closing around the letter concealed in her pocket, gripping tighter and tighter.

Verlander pointed at the book, now safely back in her possession. "Another week and you would have had trouble finding that exquisite little treatise of transgression." Emily exhaled a short laugh through her nostrils. "How is it going with West?"

"I'm just getting underway. I was organizing his journals and glanced at some of them. Prolific. A cornucopia for scholars of his work."

"Yes. There are some writers like Fitzgerald, who had it from birth." He gazed off, lost in reflection. "And then there are writers like me, who slaved and slaved and never found it. I don't think you can teach writing. You either have it or you don't. It's a gift, don't you agree?"

"Yeah, I think so." Emily shrugged.

"And not everyone can take their rightful place at the bottom of the ocean and submerge themselves in those dark depths day after day and, with only the kindling of words, create masterpieces like these." He pointed an index finger at the Vindas.

"I'm sure my friend will . . . find it interesting," Emily said.

Verlander smiled at her thinly disguised white lie. "Have you tried your hand at the dark art?"

At first Emily thought he was alluding to something in the book, and she stammered . . . unable to form words.

"Writing," he elucidated.

"Oh," exclaimed Emily, relieved. "No. God, no." She colored red again.

"I tried to write once, but the thought of waking every morning and going to a desk all alone scared me. I feel drawn to a library, to archival materials, to records. This is where I belong."

Verlander smiled in silent understanding. "I know what you mean. You're a dyed-in-the-wool archivist. Coming down?"

Emily shook her head, afraid of what he would think if she told him she couldn't accompany him on the elevator. "I'm going to hang out."

"If you have any questions about the West Collection, my door is open if you ever need to chat. I'm familiar with his work—less so with the man himself. He's a very private person. *Gregarious* would not describe him."

"I got a chance to meet him today," a still-nervous Emily blustered.

"Oh?" Verlander, who had already started to take a step away in the direction of the elevator, stopped and turned. "How is he?"

"I guess he had a bad accident."

"Yeah, that was a . . . rough deal." He played with his moustache. "For everyone." A bleak smile deepened his wrinkles. "Enjoy your book." he said, winking.

Verlander wandered off. His leather-soled shoes reverberated, then receded. Emily peeled away in the direction of the desks lining the windows. She sat down and propped her elbows on a table in the middle. Twenty desks were arrayed in her line of sight, all unoccupied. She telescoped her head to the window and absently studied the view. The tall trees swayed in the blustery Santa Anas, but she couldn't hear the rustling of their leaves and the creaking of their branches through the soundproof glass. With the raging fires, and embers raining from the sky, it was an apocalyptic world outside, but she was safe in its center, enwombed in Memorial Library's concrete mass.

Emily opened the cover on *Le Rêve d'un Flagellant*. The frontispiece stared back at her like a depraved fantasy dislodged from her unconscious and catapulted up to her in an unbidden dream. It was a reproduction of a woodcut of a portly man in a suit, brandishing a riding crop above a woman bent over a chair. Scantily clad in naughty lace, her netted stockings hiked to midthigh, her frozen backward glance of excitement and fear seemed to be enticing, or challenging, the man to strike her.

Emily drew a hand to her mouth and gasped. Not because she found the prurient image offensive, but worried that Verlander had seen this image when he glanced in the book. Did he now think she was into kinky sex? lived a double life? was a member of some secret society that explored the penumbras of erotic pleasure? The library suddenly didn't feel secure anymore. Surely he wouldn't report to Helena that he had stumbled across Emily on the eighth floor after hours, truffle hunting for out-of-print, first edition erotica. She convinced herself he was more discreet than that. But Emily knew that gossip could move like the current of a flash flood. The overhead lights flickered off, and a little pang of fear seized her. The library was preparing to close.

The Santa Anas lashed at her as she made her way in a racing stride across the desolate plaza to the parking structure. It had been another long day. She was glad to get back to her apartment, where Onyx plaintively meowed his hunger and the depth of his solitude. He greeted her by flipping over on his back, paddling his forepaws and begging for some play. She stroked his whiskers and talked to him. "I'm a bad girl, Onyx."

CHAPTER 6

Forbidden Realms

My Raymond,

Fuck. Can I still call you My Raymond? I can't think of you any other way. No one has ever truly belonged to me. I didn't feel people really did belong to each other, like a thing, an object to hang your coat on. I can't stand ownership. And I've been trapped my whole adult life. So have you, I think, but in a different way. Your snare is bigger than mine. It would take something far greater than me, greater than our love, to pry it open and free you at last. I realize that now. But you belong to me, more than anyone has ever truly belonged to anyone. And I, your Nadia, your "Eavesdropping Angel," belong to you. I always have since the moment I opened that first black Moleskine notebook of yours and read your words, your private journals. I am alone tonight with my intemperate, raging, annihilated heart. And I knew you and knew you belonged to me from the beginning of fucking Time itself.

Perhaps your snare, your prison is home to you now and you don't even feel the pain of us being apart. At least until you catch a glimpse of me in a photo or when someone whispers, "Nadia." And all I want to shout is HOW COULD YOU FUCKING LEAVE ME?! How can you abandon what we created together? You know what I'm talking about. I wrote it too, you know! Transcribed it from your Moleskines!

Was your inspiration, wasn't I? The mistress wrote through tears. I was not your amanuensis!

But of course, you had to give it up, didn't you? And never will you breathe life into it, into me, again, will you? Will you?

If you go down to Black's Beach sometime in the dark, when the moon is bright and the tide is high, perhaps the wind will whisper my name and carry me on the dark waves far, far away. I can hear the surf roaring right now.

Don't forget me, my Raymond. I am lost forever in the deep waters without you. You follow me everywhere. And I'll miss you. Every. Single. Fucking. Day. Of. My. Life.

Your Nadia . . . forevermore

Emily slowly set the crumpled sheet of the letter down. She glanced at her cell: 12:11 a.m. Absently, she stroked Onyx, who was slumbering peacefully, albeit with the gimlet eye of a cat who never truly sleeps. Maybe he sensed her unease at the eerily phantomlike words of her dead predecessor because he rotated his head in her direction and looked at her quizzically. If only a cat could know what Emily now felt she knew. Maybe, thought Emily, if only she were a cat and could be oblivious of what she had just read. The curse of abstract thought, beyond the quotidian desiderata of sustenance, propagation, and sleep. Oh, to be blissfully unaware in that limited animal consciousness!

Engrossed in a pandemonium of kaleidoscopic thoughts orbiting her brain, the palimpsest of a past taking form like a photo developing in a darkroom, Emily rose from the couch, rousing Onyx to a fang-baring yawn. She found a half-drunk bottle of beer in the refrigerator, twisted the cap off, and took a sip. She turned to the north-facing window, to the black sea and colorless sky in the distance, a panorama of emptiness. She slid open the window to allow in a wave of fresh, ocean-scented air. Her apartment had turned claustrophobic all of a sudden, as if other lives had entered it in a ghostly, unwanted occupation. Del Mar had fallen asleep, and with it, the ambient noise of traffic had quieted to the occasional rise and fall of a lone car speeding past. The unceasing Pacific heaved waves inexorably up onto the shore in a muffled dream. Emily gazed into the blackness, inhaling the pungent brackish air. Okay. Nadia Fontaine, a celebrated archivist, drowned—the reason she, Emily, was in San Diego now as a project archivist to finish up her work—and Raymond West had had an affair with her. That was now almost certain, from the evidence of the letter alone. Okay, Emily almost spoke out loud, this was not unprecedented. She had read case studies in countless archivists' journals for fuck's sake. Yes, it was a dangerous crossing of the ethical line for an archivist, but love goes where it will; the arrow can only follow. (Who wrote that? Emily ransacked the books in her brain, still unable to place it.) That's why there existed a tacit understanding in the archival world about such amorous liaisons. What if the donor and the archivist had a falling out and the archivist was aggrieved to the point of venting his or her misery by retaliating against the collection? Destroying or stealing incriminating documents in a jealous rage. Unethical. Illegal. Immediate dismissal. A career in tatters at the very least, if discovered. And no professional archivist, unless insane, would ever destroy anything that involved preservation of the historical and cultural record. And what if the archivist decided to end it and the donor retaliated by demanding his or her papers back? Calamitous.

Emily bent at the waist, nausea invading her stomach like a backed-up toilet. She crossed the living room, threw open the sliding glass door and burst onto the walkway, into the fresh sea air. Clutching the railing with both hands, she breathed in and out in heaving gulps, as if her lungs were a pair of giant bellows. The unmuted volume of the crashing surf battering the reefs filled the condominium complex with an oceanic roar, as if she were standing all alone in the center row of an amphitheater. But she wasn't hearing the surf anymore. She was hearing the disembodied anguished cry of a woman she had never met, the voice of a woman from the afterlife, as it were, preternaturally crying out. *Eavesdropping angel*—in quotation marks. Was that Raymond's pet name for her? That would make almost any woman archivist's heart swell with a heady mixture of pride and a feeling of uniqueness. Hell, capsize her on the shoals of impossible romance. Emily shook her head. The inscrutable reference to a collaboration of an undefined nature. *How can you abandon what we created together?* A book? Was this the book that Raymond was blocked on? The reason he had taken the Hollywood screenwriting job? Her thoughts ran away from her like skittering cockroaches alarmed by light. Almost too much to take in at once, questions converged on Emily from all sides, pressed in on her, took hold inside her soul like mythological Eve biting the apple in slow motion and ushering in the advent of original sin.

What a letter! And why secrete it in a book on a floor where the books were fast disappearing? Did she mean to send it to him and then not send it? And why not an email? Surely, if their relationship had reached this intense height of clandestine passion and ensuing pain, they had communicated through other methods as well. Or did Nadia Fontaine mean for someone else to find it? Was it a cry into the moonless night wilderness whose only rationale was, like so much of literature and poetry and art, an attempted catharsis of all that she was suffering? To be forsaken by a lover . . . in the white-hot cauldron of something they were collaborating on?

Wind chimes tinkling from the nearby porch of another unit broke Emily's freefall into the void of her thoughts. Gaining velocity from the mountains, the Santa Anas tore over the roofs, and the wind chimes rustled and shattered the silence again, this time like a warning. *Beware, girl!* She wished she hadn't zeroed in on the damn chimes, because now they were nettling her and she would never be able to get rid of them. Another gust of wind. A palm frond directly above her bent to its force and scratched the rooftop like the nails of a giant hand. Now it was doing it every ten seconds or so. How had she not heard it before? Why was its sound now grating and awful and omnipresent in her consciousness, when moments before, she had been inviolably in her thoughts, ruminating on the anguished letter? Her senses were heightened, she decided. The antianxiety medication awaited in the medicine chest, but she didn't like resorting to the pills, because they made her feel foggy on waking, requiring an extra cup of coffee to rev up her brain to the RPMs needed to efficiently perform the job she was hired to do.

Another wild buffet of wind, and this time Emily heard the chimes and the scratching monster thumb of the swaying palm frond above her and couldn't face the imminent terror of the moonless sky and the out-of-doors anymore. An irrational rage was suffocating her. When a pair of man's eyes peered out at her from the dim orifice of a nearby window, she fled into her unit. Fortunately, the sliding glass door was nearly soundproof. But, even then, because she was focused on those discrete, intolerable noises, she could still faintly hear them. And now any vestige of their repetitive and maddening nature was sending her into a psychodramatic tailspin.

Wanting to close off the noises that were clinging to her like a spiderweb on her face, Emily shut down her computer and careened into the bedroom on slippery stockinged feet, the tortured last words of Nadia Fontaine replaying in her mind like some elegy of wounded injustice, irremediable and final, an exhortation to the truth.

In the bedroom, she climbed out of her work clothes and into the loose, warm softness of her pajamas. Then, alerted by faint meowing, she leaped up from the bed, remembering her intention not to close the bedroom door and shut out an affectionate and needy Onyx. As soon as she turned the latch on the door and opened it, Onyx darted in and hopped up onto the bed, a baby jaguar with his sleek and muscular gait. Emily crawled under the covers and stroked the little guy's fur and spoke to him soothingly. Faintly, as if in dream now, she could still hear the tinkling of the wind chimes, but it didn't chafe with the same obstinate insistence as before. She fumbled in the dark for the pair of memory foam earplugs that had been her salvation time and time again, rolled them into hard little bullets between her thumb and forefinger, planted them in her ears, and held them in until they expanded and shut out the world of cacophonous noise.

Emily closed her eyes, but her predecessor's letter hovered numinously over her, its handwritten scrawl clawing at her soul with its pleading cry. She wanted to listen to her meditation app, but she couldn't without taking out the earplugs, and the last thing she wanted was to let those unwanted sounds sluice in and set off her anxiety. And if she fell asleep with headphones on or earbuds in, she would almost certainly awake in the middle of the night and have to begin the process of getting ready for bed all over again. She found comfort in stroking Onyx. If only his purring could be heard, but even that pacific sound was now silenced. Emily was in a bathysphere of her own making. She prayed she would wake to the abating of the Santa Ana winds, and to a plan going forward on the letter she had stumbled across, as an archivist is wont to do, but was now wishing she hadn't.

CHAPTER 7

The Waters of Black's

8/10/18

I dreamt of feeling exalted by an all-consuming passion. The oceans teemed with vivid, colorful marine life. Forests where I gallivanted were inhabited by creatures illustrated by a great fabulist of another century. On a windswept beach, a man I could not identify took me in his arms and raised me to the moon. I felt safe, wanted, needed, until he started to walk me, against my will, into the cold, dark waters. I awoke with my hand clutching my chest, breathing in gasps. Bright sunlight flooded this white-walled apartment. When I looked at my cell, I realized the alarm was ringing!

Emily drove along the ocean, an anonymous link in the chain of automobiles made up of all the commuters converging on the university and the surrounding medical and research institutions that employed, it seemed, half of San Diego. Her eyes flitted from the traffic to the dash clock. Late again. She banged frustratedly on the steering wheel. Changing lanes would only put her in another slow-crawling row of commuter hell. Instead, she inserted her AirPods and turned on Neruda, prompted by what Elizabeth had told her about Raymond writing at his self-dubbed Isla Negra in Del Mar.

After a parking cluster-fuck due to one of Regents' many summer campus events, Emily, motivated by her tardiness, half-ran across the concrete plaza, the Santa Anas stinging her eyes. Running late, she hadn't had time to apply any makeup. On the drive she had applied some lip gloss and a touch of mascara, nearly rear-ending the car ahead of her in the attempt.

At last inside the campus oasis that was Memorial Library, Emily raced to her cubicle and slapped her purse onto her desk, ready for work. Nicola was sitting in an office chair, patiently waiting for her. He looked up from his cell on which he was distractedly thumb-tapping a video game.

"Hi, Emily."

"Hi, Nicola. Has Jean been in?"

He nodded with widened eyes to insinuate that wires of tension had begun to form in the department surrounding her tardiness.

A moment later, alerted by their voices, rabbit-eared Jean appeared in the entryway to Emily's cubicle. She tapped the face of her oversized watch while glowering wordlessly. How was Emily to explain the chasm that had widened with the discovery of the framed photo, the cryptic catalog card that led her to the BDSM erotica of *Le Rêve d'un Flagellant*, the tortured letter of her predecessor—to Raymond West!—and how she had hardly slept. Emily feared that even thinking these thoughts might cause them to flash across her forehead like an electronic message board.

"I'm sorry. I'll try to get up earlier," Emily apologized.

"This is a tremendously high-profile project," Jean reprimanded her in front of Nicola, whose doe-like eyes were cast to the floor.

"Fully aware, Jean."

Jean bore into Emily with admonitory eyes. Her face assumed malignant features. Then she feigned a smile and disappeared back to her cubicle.

"TGIF," whispered Nicola, when Jean was out of earshot.

Emily met Nicola's eyes and laughed in spite of herself. "How do you get here so fast?"

"I bike."

Emily looked at him quizzically.

"There's a wide bike lane across the freeway and I fly by the traffic," he smiled triumphantly. "And there's a bike rack right outside. But coming from Del Mar? I wouldn't recommend it. Triathletes train on that hill."

"Plus, I would arrive in such a state of dishabille that I wouldn't be presentable," Emily joked. She glanced around her cubicle. "I see you've brought all the boxes up."

Nicola, still puzzling over *dishabille*, leaned back in his chair and rolled it away from a wall-facing table. The West boxes from the reaccession were neatly stacked and awaiting inspection. Emily looked intently at them with a different perspective. "And these are all the boxes from the loading dock?"

"Yes. Did you want me to help you go through them?" Nicola asked.

Emily raised a fist to her mouth and delved into her mind. Nicola watched and waited. She clambered out of her thoughts, still absorbed in the letter and the mysterious way she had found it. For Christ's sake, she was sitting in her chair! Only nine months ago Nadia would have been in this very spot, inhabiting the anguish poured out in the letter. And a few weeks later she would turn up dead on a beach, drowned.

Emily shook her head, her mind still far away. "No, Nicola, I need to be alone with this." She turned to him and smiled to show that it was nothing personal. "Why don't you take the day off," she suggested. "I need to hunker down here and familiarize myself with this project."

"Okay. Sure?"

Emily nodded, avoiding his gaze, preoccupied.

A little wounded, Nicola gathered up his backpack. "Text me if you need me."

Emily smiled absently at him as he left. She swung her desk chair to her computer and switched it on. She waited for it to boot up, then she clicked on the Panopticon drive and navigated to the Raymond West Collection. From her purse she produced an oversized Moleskine and christened a personal file for her own records. Without the advantage of her predecessor's personal West file, she would have to start over from the beginning.

Emily devoted the morning to carefully combing through the West boxes and organizing the items into separate piles. Manuscripts, correspondence, memorabilia, and the born-digital items—CD-ROMs, 3.5-inch floppies, thumb drives—which would have to be separately assayed.

The temperature was a chilly, constant fifty-eight degrees in Special Collections for preservation purposes. Outside it was in the nineties, arid winds still blowing ash toward the ocean, but in her cubicle it was freezing. The cold penetrated the fabric of her clothes and seeped into her bones. When she heard unwanted sounds, they seemed shriller when transmitted through the cold, humidity-free air. Emily paused and climbed into her fleece zip-up vest.

As she pored back over the items in the West reaccession, Emily fretted over what she might find, Nadia's letter still weighing on her mind. Was she already searching for something? She was possessed suddenly by a desire to read the correspondence that came spilling out of the boxes, and now and then she stopped to inspect a letter addressed to Raymond West. If Emily fantasized that she would find anything from her predecessor, she was disappointed. Whatever correspondence they had shared either never made it into West's archive or had been scrubbed clean—*The reason the boxes had been returned to the Wests?* she wondered. She leaned back in her chair. An incipient fear seized her, but she shook it off.

The afternoon wore on. Emily cross-checked items in the new addition. Many of them had already been identified by her predecessor and were listed in the extensive finding aid. In fact, Emily realized, there didn't seem to be anything new. She wondered suspiciously why they had been taken off the premises in the first place. Had the Wests' curator gone back through West's papers and performed a more thorough purging of items they deemed inappropriate for the collection?

Voices drifted through and over the shoji-thin cubicle dividers. When a coworker was on the phone, she could clearly hear them. Even if they spoke in undertones, she could still distinctly make out their whispery voices intimating details of their lives—embarrassing to a private person like Emily. She didn't talk on the phone much anymore. It was mostly texting and email, and she refused to participate on social media. She wanted to be a ghost among her fellow millennials. In truth, she dreamed of a simple life, that of a Luddite, only embracing objects and pursuits that were palpable and real.

Taking a break, Emily googled *Le Rêve d'un Flagellant*. She clicked Images, and the screen blossomed with ink woodcuts in a cornucopia of erotica. Emily narrowed her eyes at the screen, hypnotized. "NSFW," she incanted, a finger on the mouse clicker, poised to evacuate. For some reason the quaintly pornographic images made her think about her own love life and the few men she had been romantically involved with. There had been some experimentation, there had been men who had wanted things that she didn't feel comfortable giving them, and she wondered for a moment if she had been missing out, if another world in the demimonde of sexual exploration awaited her one day.

Emily's thoughts drifted back to Nadia and to the cataclysmic letter—its finality, its wailing woundedness. She had to have been having an affair with Raymond West, if that's whom the letter was truly addressed to. But how perilous! Given who Raymond's wife was and her deep, entangled roots with the university. Emily's speculations ran riot. Had Raymond broken off the affair because he feared it compromised him? After all, he was now rumored to have been tapped for chair of the Literature Department. Emily bounced her pen against her lips, realizing she was of two minds. The erotic photos blurred out of focus. When she heard knuckles rapping on the entrance to her cubicle, she tensed and instinctively threw her hand to her monitor to shield the pornographic images from view. With her other hand she frantically groped for the power button.

It was Chloe and her round, smiling face. "Hi. Am I disturbing you?"

"Hi, Chloe," said Emily, as her monitor imploded to black. Had Chloe seen what was on the screen? wondered Emily. If she had, her features betrayed nothing.

"Would you like to grab lunch? Some of us here in the department are going over to Rubio's."

Emily held up her lunch box in its nylon sack. "I brought my own."

"Bring it along and eat with us."

"I'd love to, Chloe, but some other time. I'm immersed in something right now."

"I can see." She raised her eyebrows, annoying Emily by not elaborating. "Some other time then."

"Okay, Chloe."

Chloe turned and disappeared from the entryway. Did coworkers come and go unannounced like this? Emily waited until the footsteps had retreated. Afraid that Chloe would walk past again with her coworkers on their way to lunch, Emily took out her lunch box and set it on the table. Then she remembered it was forbidden to eat in Special Collections, so she left it unopened.

Special Collections cleared out for lunch. The tapping of keyboards, footsteps, and closing doors had mercifully quieted. From her purse, Emily brought out Nadia's letter. Reading it over in the ensuing silence, she found the words haunted her even more profoundly than before. She could almost divine Nadia's voice in the anguished exhortation.

> *How can you give up on what we created together? You know what I'm talking about. I wrote it too, you know! Transcribed it beautifully from your Moleskines! . . . I was not your amanuensis!*

"I was not your amanuensis." Was she his muse? Whatever it was they were working on, she didn't want to be solely considered his "muse." She obviously had her heart invested in the project too. Joel had informed Emily that Nadia was a published author. Had she and Raymond been collaborating on a book? Was that possible? And if so, where was the work? To Emily, the Raymond West Papers had suddenly taken on a whole new dimension.

Forsaking lunch, Emily switched her computer back on. She conducted a search for *Nadia Fontaine Archivist Drowning* and then stopped when the web page thumbnails and links blossomed on her screen. Was her computer linked to a main server? Did other people—someone in IT?—have access to her online roaming? She lowered her chin to her chest and brooded on the possibility. Not on her private drive, at least she didn't think so.

An interoffice IM slid in on the top right of the screen like a warning banner. It was from "Jbeery." Joel! She exhaled in relief. It read: "Are we on for Black's Sat.?"

Emily placed her fingers on the keyboard and typed in the reply box: "What time?"

"7:00."

"A.M.?!?!"

"Morning glass."

Jesus. Emily closed her eyes. She buttoned the last button on her shirt because the cold was streaming down the front. "Okay. Where do you want to meet?"

Joel sent her a link to a Google Maps location and Emily replied, "Okay."

"How's West?"

"It's a . . . bigger project than I thought."

"I can imagine," Joel fired back.

"Hey, question: I was given access to two drives, my own personal and, of course, Panopticon, where all the collections live. What happened to the C: drive?"

A minute crept past before Joel answered. "What C: drive?"

"Dark archives."

"Dark Storage?"

"Dark storage. Dark archives. What's the diff," Emily furiously typed.

Another minute crawled past. The next text box that appeared on Emily's screen read: "I don't know." Emily decided not to press the issue, thinking through its repercussions. Before she could reply, Joel IM'd back: "Have you talked to Jean about it?"

Emily typed: "No. And probably wouldn't. If I thought I should have access I would go to the director."

"I wouldn't advise going to Helena," typed Joel cryptically. The screen went still. Emily leaned back in her chair. What was Joel thinking on the other end?

Emily's introspection was broken by the sound of voices and footsteps. She closed the instant messaging window from her screen and debated whether she should have brought up her predecessor's personal file—that all-important, invaluable, roadmap to any collection. She wondered whom she could trust. One thing was abundantly clear: she could never show Nadia's letter to anyone.

Over the tattered remnants of the day, Emily buried herself in the new boxes. She familiarized herself with West's papers, delving deeper and deeper into his collection. She put Nadia's letter on the back burner. She didn't share it with anyone, not even Joel. Nights were spent in quiet contemplation. Her mother called frequently with a litany of complaints. Emily tried to console her that she would visit once the West project was completed and would see about getting her moved to a place she liked better. Regents Special Collections & Archives thrummed all around her. She took her lunches alone and kept a professional arm's length from her colleagues. In the evenings she jogged along the bluff as the pelicans soared overhead. She followed where it sloped down to the beach and sprinted along the water's edge to get her heart pumping, then climbed the twisting path back up the cliff to where the train tracks ran. Sweating and panting, she walked the final half mile back to her apartment. Nadia's tortured letter surfaced unbidden—hard as she tried, she couldn't put it out of her mind.

Saturday morning, Emily's alarm awakened her at 6:00 a.m. Even crepuscular Onyx was startled. He arched his back, yawned, and motivated himself to move. Emily's laptop still sprawled on the bed. With nothing to do Friday night, she had fallen asleep reading web articles in local papers on Nadia Fontaine and her tragic accidental drowning. She learned a few details from the scant few obituaries, one in particular: she was married when she died.

The sky was still dark as Emily weaved her way down a deserted Coast Highway in the direction of La Jolla. To the east, a band of salmon-hued light announced the imminent rising of the early-morning sun. Emily hadn't showered, hadn't even had time for her morning journal ritual. Over her bathing suit she'd climbed into a pair of sweatpants and layered a hoodie over a T-shirt with a quote stenciled on it: "You are the knife that I twist into my heart—F. Kafka." It was a quote from one of his letters to Milena Jesenská, his Czech translator, the woman to whom he had famously poured out his anguished soul. If nothing else, thought Emily, it was a unique conversation starter. If the guy didn't know Kafka, purge with prejudice. If he knew Kafka, but not Milena or the collection *Letters to Milena*, it might pique his interest—and hers. Huge points if he knew Milena. Love everlasting if he had read *Letters to Milena*. She hadn't found him yet, but the road map to her heart was in plain sight.

Emily sped past Torrey Pines Golf Course where silver-haired men were warming up on the driving range in preparation for their tee times. She swung the wheel this way and that, winding around the slate-gray buildings of the university, and turned sharply onto La Jolla Farms Road and into a conspicuously wealthy neighborhood, judging by the Spanish-style mansions that lined the wide streets. In the foggy light of early dawn, she made out a figure standing next to a forest green Honda Element.

Emily pulled up next to the waiting figure and rolled down her window. "Hi, Joel."

"I didn't recognize you without your glasses."

"I'm not going to wear my glasses to surf," Emily said. "I put in my contacts."

"Excellent." He turned and threw an arm out. "Find a place to park."

Emily parallel parked close by. She locked up her car and walked in the morning silence back to where Joel was waiting. A few other surfers were unstrapping their boards from the tops of their cars and making their way to the entrance of a private road.

When Emily got to Joel's car, he had the hatch of his Element open. In the seatless back compartment were what looked to be half a dozen surfboards stacked on one another. Joel was lifting one out. He measured it against Emily's five-foot-six height.

"Do you feel comfortable on a short board? Because I've got something a little longer."

"Whatever you think is best, Joel."

"Let's go with the short one. It'll be lighter." He leaned the board against the side of his car and rummaged through a large pail stuffed with wet suits. He plucked one out, unfurled it, and held the curved figure of the customized woman's suit up against Emily. "Hmm."

"These for your girlfriend?" Emily asked.

"I don't have a girlfriend," Joel said in a neutral tone.

"Former girlfriend?"

"I'll tell you some other time. Good news is, I have a wet suit for you. Three-mil full."

"Sweet." Emily held out her arm and slung the wet suit over it. The arid Santa Anas were already drying out her contacts, and she blinked her eyelids rapidly to keep them lubricated.

Joel found a board that he thought was right for the current conditions, mumbling something about a surf website report that predicted the waves to be in the four-to-six-foot range. He locked up his van and directed Emily with a nod toward the private road that led down to Black's Beach. Emily felt a twin shiver of fear and excitement as she trudged alongside him.

They came to a swinging metal barricade secured by a chain that was coiled around a steel post and held in place by a brass Yale lock. It was easy to step around it.

"Only the residents and a few select people have a key to this," Joel noted, pointing to the lock and chain. "The one percent. Alas, that's not us."

Emily giggled. "How long of a walk is it?"

"Half a mile. Unfortunately, it's all uphill coming back, when you're all surfed out." Joel raked his eyes appraisingly over Emily's figure and focused on her athletic soccer thighs. "You look like you're in pretty good shape."

Emily smiled silently and cast her eyes away.

They slithered around the barricade through a narrow opening on the side and started down a single-lane asphalt road. It was growing lighter now, and the flora in the canyon they were descending into gleamed with dew. An owl hooted from somewhere in the dense vegetation, as if warning the world of surfers encroaching on his territory.

"Is this where you usually surf?" Emily asked, making small talk as they walked down the steep incline.

"Here. La Jolla Shores. PB Point. But because of the walk, you only get serious surfers here," Joel explained. He threw her a backward look. "Do you think you might move down here if you like it?"

"I don't know. I find San Diego kind of alienating."

Joel nodded thoughtfully. "It takes time to build a network of friends here, that's for sure."

"And a cultural wasteland to boot," she added, feeling feisty.

"There is the university," said Joel defensively. "And La Jolla Playhouse puts on some pretty awesome theater."

"Yeah. I've heard." All week, Emily had been dying to pump Joel for more information about Nadia, especially the details of her death, but it was early in the morning and he seemed to have his mind focused on surfing, not work. He was tall and strong and monosyllabic in his answers, and she was still feeling him out.

Around the corner, out of view, they could hear a set rolling in. The breaking waves cracked like whips in the early-morning quiet. The shrieking cries of surfers exulting in their rides pierced the stillness.

"Sounds bigger than Surfline projected," Joel remarked.

"How can you tell?"

"I've been surfing since I was eight. Parents used to drop me off at PB Pier every day in the summer with my older brother and then come collect us at dusk. You learn to tell just by the sound how big the waves are. I know exactly what the water temperature is as soon as I step in."

"So, you've surfed all your life?" Emily asked. Joel nodded. "Did you ever want to go pro?"

Joel shook his head and smirked. "Those guys are freaks. Besides, I discovered books and films, and that's what I really wanted to devote my life to. Still do." He trailed off, pervaded by a palpable sadness.

Halfway down the winding road, the ocean broadened into view through the vee of the canyon. The surface of the water was a quivering mirror of cobalt blue. Where it met the sky, it sketched a horizontal line of demarcation that would have fooled explorers of old into believing that the world was flat and they were destined to fall off a watery precipice.

Joel directed Emily down a sandy pathway to the beach. Half a dozen surfers bobbed in the water, infinitesimally tiny compared to the immensity of the world they faced. Joel set his board down on the sand, and Emily plopped hers next to his. He wordlessly handed her a bar of wax. Emily took it and knelt. The sand felt cold and damp as it extruded between her toes underfoot. A set loomed on the horizon as they waxed their boards. Both of them looked up as the swells came out of the early-morning gloaming and traveled toward them. The offshore Santa Ana winds barreled down the private road and slammed against the waves in apparent defiance, seemingly obstinately determined upon their never reaching the shore. In that perfect surfer's wind-and-wave confrontation, where the two forces were locked in combat, Nature produced pristine waves that were held up longer than normal, grooming them to perfection. Eventually, the laws and forces of physics brought the waves crashing down, but not until they were held on display for a few extra seconds of oceanic beauty before giving up their long journey to someone in a black rubber suit screaming his head off.

Joel tucked his bar of wax into a back pocket of his wet suit and turned to Emily, who was mimicking his preparations. "Are you going to be okay out there?"

"Yeah, I think so." Emily felt a surge of apprehension as the last wave of the set—an overhead eight-footer—detonated on the outside of the break, jettisoning two surfers left and right on the edging whitewater. The remaining surfers, caught inside, pushed down on the front of their boards and duck-dived under the wave, hoping there wouldn't be a rogue fifth wave in the set that would separate them from their boards.

They leashed their boards to their ankles, securing them with Velcro, and Joel led Emily toward the water. He pointed to a narrow band of rough water left of where the waves appeared to be breaking. "There's a rip channel out here. We're going to ride it out and then paddle into the break," Joel instructed.

"Gotcha." Emily set her board on the surface of the shallow water, one hand planted on its deck to guide it through the spent whitewater of the once prodigious waves. Joel splashed his board down next to hers, and they floated them out through the rip current, a channel of mottled water that flowed back out to the sea.

When they had waded to waist-high water, they maneuvered onto their boards and started paddling. Emily noticed that Joel was keeping a close eye on her. A set of waves formed in the distance. The first one broke in a cracking roar of spent energy. Now that they were out in the open ocean, flat to the water, the sheer force and height of the waves was both more palpable and intimidating. The sound was louder, deafening even, and as they paddled into deeper waters, it evoked a constellation of helplessness, fear, and adrenalized excitement.

"Just remember," called out Joel, one hand cupped to the side of his mouth, "if you wipe out, you've got your board as a flotation device. The waves are your friend. They're going to bring you in."

When they had paddled out far enough to where the waves were breaking, they turned their boards and pointed them north. Emily had lettered in both soccer and swimming in high school and had superior upper body strength for a woman her size, but she hadn't been out in the water in a while and her shoulder muscles were already burning. Together, they stroked their way into the lineup. Joel waved to someone he knew. They were in a lull, and the ocean was ominously quiet, slyly disguising its true, raw power. They sat up on their boards and soaked in the view. The dark faces of the early-morning cliffs towered over the sand and yawned back at them impassively, imperially. The eastward sky was colored a blood orange, the wildfires burning uncontained. A squadron of fewer than a dozen pelicans glided in formation low across the water, their preying eyes seeking swarming bait balls of minnows. Emily followed their flight with an awestruck admiration. They lent a kind of primeval quality to the morning, something pristine and from another age—until the puerile cry of a surfer on the far side of the lineup destroyed the silence with a shrill whistle directed at Emily.

"Apparently he's never seen a woman before," joked Joel, who paddled toward a different section of the lineup, Emily in tow.

Emily watched him paddle ahead of her. His shoulder muscles rippled with every stroke. His buttocks stood up like twin hillocks, sheeny in the black wet suit. Not bad for a digital archivist, she thought to herself, then looked quickly away when he threw her a backward glance to make sure she was okay.

They glided into a deeper part of the lineup and sat on their boards again, bobbing in the cold water, waiting out the lull.

"One time I was out here all by myself. First thing in the morning. Right out there"—Joel pointed with an outstretched arm—"a whale spouted. It was fucking intense."

"What'd you do?" Emily inquired.

"Paddled in. That was too heavy for me." He shook his head at the memory. "This is a submarine canyon, so the waves come out of deeper water, which is why it's a great break. It's also why you've got to be on the lookout for . . . whatever." Joel trailed off.

"Great whites?" asked Emily.

Joel shrugged. "We're not on their menu. But sometimes they mistake us for animals who are."

Emily glanced anxiously down at the semitransparent water, wishing now it wasn't so lucent. She couldn't make out the bottom. Craning her neck, she turned to look at the magnificent cliffs. A red sun was hoisting itself into the sky, winched aloft by invisible forces. It looked like the bloodshot eye of a benevolent, prehistoric monster, putting Earth on trial with its Cyclopean gaze.

The water was suddenly a flurry of activity as everyone in the lineup started madly paddling toward the horizon where a set of waves was forming, drawn up by the shallow sandbars. Surfers were jockeying for position. Joel swung his board around and windmilled his arms furiously. The wave rose up like a giant clam opening, and soon he had disappeared from view. Emily caught a glimpse of him standing and could make out his head as he was slung to the right. Four more waves were rising right behind it, each one bigger and breaking farther out from shore. Emily started paddling. She crested the next swell and saw three more she had to clear or else be pummeled. She paddled hard. Her heart beat with trepidation and the thrill of danger. She popped through the lip of the next approaching wave and slapped the water on the other side with the bottom of her board hard enough it briefly knocked the wind out of her. Two more loomed up, higher and farther out, and Emily clawed the water with her arms to get over them. The other surfers were screaming jubilantly. The waves cracked like thunderclaps when they broke.

Then the ocean quieted again. Outside the break, Emily had found a moment of solitude, so far out to sea that it scared her. All the other surfers had caught waves and were now making their way back out to the new lineup in deeper water. The small head of a marine creature broke the surface and looked at Emily in benign curiosity with its dark-shaded eyes and whiskered snout. It startled Emily at first, but she quickly realized it wasn't a shark.

Joel glided up next to her. "Sea lion," he said nonchalantly. "Tons of them. They're friendly."

Emily laughed nervously. The sea lion slipped back into the mystery of his world. "Did you catch a good one?" asked Emily.

"Yeah. Bigger than I thought. You okay? Feeling comfortable?"

"Yeah. Fine."

"That set was bigger than I thought," said Joel.

Remembering the articles on Nadia's death, Emily thought about her predecessor surfing out here at night. She couldn't imagine it. Not even on a full moon, when surfers say the ocean is surfable. The woman possessed temerity—or a death wish or something. Her board, according to the news reports, had struck her head and her leash had wrapped around her neck, garroted her, and snapped her hyoid bone. Emily shuddered at the image that suddenly flared luridly in her mind.

"You ever surf at night on a full moon?" she asked Joel, as other surfers cruised back into the lineup, shaking water from their hair and whooping to one another.

"Why do you ask?"

"Just wondering?"

"I have. Yes. It's got to be a complete full moon. You've got the waves all to yourself. But it's pretty spooky."

Emily snorted a nervous laugh. Joel playfully splashed some water on her.

"Nice out here, isn't it?" he asked.

"Yeah."

"Good to get out of that mausoleum with all those dead writers," Joel said.

Emily nodded toward the horizon. Joel turned his board around, saw another set rolling in, flattened on his board, and started paddling into position.

"All right, it's your turn, Emily. Follow me."

Joel paddled in a northeasterly direction to where the main peak of the first wave was rising. Emily trailed. She spun her board around and, head arrowed forward, started paddling.

"Go," Joel urged. "Paddle hard!"

Emily felt the resistance of the water give way as the wave grew under her like a powerful, uncontrollable force, like lovemaking at its most intensely passionate. Soon she had stopped paddling and was being swept forward by the power of the wave alone. Instinctively, she leaped to her feet, stood shakily, like a giant bird just born from its egg and hobbling uncertainly on spindly feet. She leaned left, and her board turned into the face of the wave, now disintegrating into whitewater behind her. She threw out her arms like an aerialist for balance. A scream, originating deep down in her gut, shrieked from her, and for a brief second she experienced a liberation the likes of which she had never felt before. The wave was tall. Its watery lip towered above her head. If she reached her hand up, she could touch it. In that moment she had taken wing in solitary flight.

Then, as if conspiring against her, the wave crossed an irregularity in the sandbar and started to section in front of her. She should have straightened her board and rode it in on her belly, but she tried to surf through it and the whitewater engulfed her in a foam whorl, catapulting her from the board. She heard a muffled tear and feared that her Velcro leash had detached and she was now weightlessly alone in the tumult of the wave. The cascading tons of water drove her relentlessly to the bottom. She kept her eyes closed tight so she didn't get water in her contacts. Pushed to the seafloor, her hands scraped hard, packed sand. Her lungs were expanded with air she needed to exhale. For a moment she found herself in a spinning vertigo and wasn't sure which way was up or down. She pushed off the bottom with her feet and propelled herself upward, gaining equilibrium. Like the sea lion, she broke the ocean's surface, but unlike the sea lion, she now hyperventilated for precious air. Out of her peripheral vision she could see Joel paddling frantically toward her. But another wave was breaking, and it closed him off from view. Emily took a deep breath and dove down under the wave, remembering Joel's advice that the waves were her friend. As it rumbled over, it twirled her around and around. She had wiped out before, but never in surf this massive, this powerful. Without her board as a floatation device, she was beholden to the inexorable forces of the ocean and its fickle, sometimes fatal, consequences. She shot to the surface again. Blew air like the tiniest of baby whales, gulped oxygen again with both nose and mouth, and dived before the next wave thrashed her. She was tiring. The three-wave beatdown was exacting its toll. Where was Joel? In her closed-eye blindness she glimpsed images that made her panic for a moment, thinking she was sliding to the precipice of drowning. An abyss yawned, and her world went black. For a brief moment she felt liberated from all the constraints and stresses of being human. This was the experience of death in rehearsal, a surrender to galactic nothingness.

But something, someone, wanted her back, and she rose upward again. This time a muscular arm was hooked under hers. When she broke the surface of the water, she could make out Joel in her blurred vision, his board alongside her, his face wearing a dark expression of concern.

"Joel!" Emily cried, or tried to cry, shooting out an arm.

"Come on, hang on to me, you're fine," he shouted to a gasping Emily, her lungs now swamped with seawater. Another wall of whitewater tumbled toward them, but Joel held on to her tightly. More water flooded her lungs. Emily was struggling now, coughing up brackish water, but Joel wouldn't let go. He held her with one arm hooked around her neck and paddled with the other. The orange-lit shore approached and mercifully the distance between them closed. The water shallowed, and their feet touched the sand. They slogged through waist-deep water, the whitewater of spent waves rolling shoreward past them gently now.

When Emily finally staggered into ankle-deep water she collapsed to her knees. Head bent forward, she coughed up two lungfuls of water. Joel had a hand planted on her back and was slapping her lightly. "You'll be all right."

Emily looked up at him with a stricken expression.

"Pretty bad wipeout, huh?"

Emily nodded, in between vomiting up more seawater. When her lungs were clear and she was breathing normally again, she raked the wet hair out of her face and turned to Joel. "For a few seconds I was flying. Then I just lost it."

"I shouldn't have taken you out on a day this big," said Joel. "I'm sorry. You must hate me."

"No, it's okay. I thought I could handle it. It was my fault. Go on, go back out if you want. I'll rest here."

"You sure?"

Emily nodded. Something thrilled through her and she smiled. "It was pretty awesome while it lasted."

Joel smiled, stood up and retrieved her board, which was ebbing and surging at the tide's edge.

Emily clambered out of the water and took her board from Joel. He retrieved his and paddled back out. Emily sat on the sand next to her board, arms wrapped around her knees. When she looked out at the exploding waves, she almost couldn't believe she had been out that far. Maybe she should have told Joel she hadn't been surfing that long. Maybe she didn't want to miss out on the excitement of catching a wave taller than she was, even if it meant imperiling herself in the ocean's depths. Maybe she subconsciously wanted to test the same waters as her predecessor.

Joel surfed past noon as Emily rested on the shore. Safely out of the water, the peace of Black's Beach, mixed with the sonorous breaking of the waves, pervaded her and delivered a suffusion of calm. The sun was climbing higher in the sky, its red coloring to yellow, whitening the sand and warming her body. She unzipped her wet suit and set her hand on her board. She could feel the wax growing malleable from the heat of the sun. She debated going out again, but the waves, ceaselessly pouring in, terrified her.

Restless, Emily wandered aimlessly down the beach. Overhead, paragliders dangling by nylon cords cruised along the ridge of the vertical cliff that rose high above. The paragliders evoked Julian Barnes's *Levels of Life*, particularly the chapters on early aeronauts and their often mortal experiments with hot-air ballooning. What to make of those intrepid men, and sometimes women, who adventured up high into the sky and soared at the mercy of fickle winds, many of them, tempting fate on a dream, plunging to their deaths in cold oceans. What was it with these adrenaline junkies? Flying? Mountaineering? Speeding around a racetrack at over two hundred miles per hour? Surfing at night under a full moon? Emily preferred holding her fate in her own hands, not placing it in those of others, or in contraptions or machines, and not putting it at the mercy of Nature's mercurial forces.

Emily woke from a nap when Joel splashed back in an excited trot and stood dripping before her. "Awesome session," he announced, exhilarated. "Whew!"

Emily nodded, then straightened to her feet, clapping sand off her hands and wet suit.

"Feeling better?" Joel asked in a tone of solicitude.

"Yeah," Emily said.

"Let's get some coffee."

They hiked back up the private road. Under the hot, overhead sun the canyon vegetation was now glowing a vivid green. Awakened birds were chattering flirtatiously. The asphalt felt warm under their bare feet.

After they had stowed the boards away and changed back into their clothes, Joel asked Emily to follow him in her car. She obliged. They caravanned down Torrey Pines Road and meandered through La Jolla. Joel looped onto La Jolla Boulevard and Emily followed. They headed in the direction of Bird Rock, the first beach hamlet south of La Jolla. Joel pulled into an angled parking space and Emily braked to a halt next to him. Together they skipped across the street and went into the al fresco Bird Rock Coffee Roasters. An early afternoon zephyr wafted in through the large open-air windows. The emporium smelled of pulled shots of espresso.

"I know you told me you like good coffee," Joel remembered.

"Yes."

"Well, this is the best in San Diego."

"Okay," Emily trilled. "We shall see."

Emily ordered a Panamanian Geisha pour-over, and Joel opted for a cappuccino. When their orders were ready, they sat on the open window's planked, communal sitting ledge and faced the traffic.

Emily sipped her coffee. She could feel Joel's gaze on her. "This is good. Exquisite." Joel smiled. She turned to him. "Better than roasteries in San Francisco."

"Yeah. Totally. Glad you like it. I hear there's a new location opening near you."

"Cool." Emily narrowed her eyes in thought. "Raymond Chandler lived around here somewhere, didn't he?"

"Yeah, as a matter of fact"—Joel pointed in a northwesterly direction—"right over there. On the cliff. With his wife, Cissy."

"You know Chandler's work?"

"I've read every word. He wrote *The Long Goodbye* there. Took him five years. Have you read his collected letters?"

Emily shook her head.

"Fucking brilliant." Joel slurped his cappuccino.

Emily stiffened at the slurping, one of her misophonia triggers, and tried to quell her mounting agitation.

"Do you like Chandler?"

Emily nodded. "Who doesn't? His command of the language. His sardonic metaphors. 'She wore enough makeup to paint a steamer yacht.'"

Joel laughed. Emily could sense that he liked her. She looked down into her coffee, afraid to meet his eyes.

Joel held up his phone. "Are you on Facebook?"

"No." Emily shook her head in mock disgust.

"Twitter? Instagram?"

"Fuck no." Emily spoke over her coffee to the passing traffic. "I don't do social media."

"A true loner, aren't you?"

Emily smiled, but his innocent question picked at a wound that hadn't fully healed.

"Number where I can text you?"

"Where do you live, Joel?" she asked, deliberately ignoring his request, fearing it would let Joel too far into her world.

Joel was fond of gesticulating answers before he verbally delivered them. This time he pointed south, down La Jolla Boulevard. "PB"

"You went to Regents?"

Joel nodded. "Yep."

"English Lit?"

"Comparative. Minor in Vis Arts. Film."

"You make films?" she asked.

"I've made a few shorts. Yeah."

"Did you ever want to go to Hollywood and try to make it?"

A perceptible cloud of regret scudded across Joel's face. He shrugged. "I suppose. Like a lot of people. I hate LA, though. Insane traffic. You grow up in San Diego and you get used to no traffic jams." He chuckled. "Until recently." He turned to Emily. "Maybe with digital, Hollywood will migrate down here, and then I'll give it another shot."

Lassitude was drawing over both of them. Patrons came and went. The sun had arced across the sky and had become an orange disk on its downward trajectory. A flock of seagulls flew over the rooftops where Raymond Chandler once toiled on a manual typewriter to compose his masterpiece. Emily dreamed her gaze toward the squawking gulls, envying their freedom. She and Joel traded film and literary likes and dislikes, and she discovered they had a fair amount in common. He was shocked she had read—and liked—Bukowski. She was surprised he had read Anaïs Nin's unexpurgated diaries. They both loved the film *The Unbearable Lightness of Being*, their sensibilities dovetailing at tragic romances and books and films created by artists unafraid of brutal honesty.

"Why does everyone refer to my predecessor by her job title and not her name?" Emily finally blurted out, apropos of nothing, except the fact that ever since she had read the letter her mind had never left Nadia.

Joel swayed his head from side to side, debating whether to answer or not. "Helena and Nadia clashed over something, and the bad blood contaminated the department. In an indeterminate, complicated way," he mumbled.

"She was found drowned where I just almost drowned, wasn't she?" Emily asked pointedly.

"Yeah," Joel replied, his eyes on the sidewalk, as if he didn't want to talk about it. A silence fell. Cars roared past in a steady stream. People scolded their dogs and jerked on their leashes. Joel looked up and broke the silence, "Would you like to get the most awesome seafood tacos in all of San Diego and watch one of my short films?"

"Sure," said Emily. "But I can't stay too long."

"That's cool."

Joel scrambled off the window's ledge. "I'm just around the corner on Sapphire."

"Okay, I'll follow you," said Emily, jumping down to the sidewalk.

Emily followed Joel's Element about a mile south. She pulled in behind him at Oscar's Mexican Seafood. It was a small, turquoise-painted, wood-framed shack annexed to a vape and marijuana paraphernalia store on one side and a dive bar on the other. Joel ordered their special-of-the-day tacos, but Emily refused to let him pay. They caravanned a few more blocks until they came to a generic two-story stucco apartment complex in need of a paint job, a wood-lettered name nailed to the façade: Paradise Palms, the two *P*s designed in the shape of palm trees.

Emily shadowed Joel up the concrete steps to his second-floor apartment in the fading light. Inside, Emily found a guy's apartment that looked like it hadn't been upgraded since his college days. Bookcases were composed of cinderblocks and one-by-eight boards—but he did have a lot of books, thought Emily, in a more positive appraisal. The coffee table was not her taste: a lacquered scrap of whorled driftwood decorated with two iridescent abalone shells employed as marijuana ashtrays; a recent copy of *American Archivist*, a semiannual Society of American Archivists journal; and old, archival issues of *Film Comment*, a once vibrant periodical for cineastes. On one of the bookshelves, Emily spotted a wind-up 16 mm movie camera mounted on a block of wood. As Joel disappeared into the kitchen, she drifted over to investigate.

"Would you like something to drink?" Joel called out from the kitchen. "A beer?"

"Cool," said Emily with a backward glance. "As long as it's not in a can."

"Snob," Joel shot back.

Emily lifted the movie camera with two hands and held it like a wounded songbird. Joel noticed her admiring it when he returned. Turning it over in her hands, Emily looked up at him. "Is this Bolex yours? It's so cool."

"Yeah. I've even made a couple of my shorts on it. Today, of course, only digital."

Emily carefully replaced the camera where she had found it, then turned and pointed to a poster that occupied the wall above the TV. It was a French-language reproduction of *La Maman et la Putain*, Jean Eustache's masterpiece of a tortured love triangle where, it turns out, after nearly four hours of agonizing dialogue between one man and two women, nobody emerges emotionally unscathed. "That's a brilliant film," Emily acknowledged.

"You've seen it?" asked Joel, his mouth opening in feigned surprise.

"I thought you knew I did a stint at Berkeley Film Archive. They have a print up there. Pretty beat up. Needs to be restored."

"I know! I've been trying to get them to let me do a digital restoration here, but you know Helena. The title alone probably offends her La Jolla-ite sensibilities."

Emily chuckled. "Yeah, I don't think that would be her cup of tea."

Joel's expression grew thoughtful. "It was one of Nadia's favorite films. She turned me on to it, in fact." He opened the paper bag with the seafood tacos and set them on plates he had thoughtfully brought from the kitchen. He plunked down an already uncorked half-liter bottle of Societe beer and a glass next to Emily's and beckoned her to sit on the couch.

Emily eased onto the couch, picked up the bottle and examined the label. "'The Savage'," she read. "I like that."

"They make all different kinds. I'll take you out to their brewery someday if you'd like."

Emily nodded at Joel's offer, but didn't reply one way or the other. She poured a glass, took a sip, then looked at Joel with eyes blinking suspicion. "How did you know I liked Societe beers?"

"I didn't."

"I bought some when I first got here—deliciously hoppy," Emily critiqued.

"Goes great with the tacos." Joel offered her some hot sauce in miniature plastic containers. She took one from him, poured it over her fist-sized taco, and bit into it.

"Mm, that's good." With a paper napkin she wiped hot sauce from the corner of her mouth.

"Within one mile, I have the best seafood tacos and the best coffee." Joel produced a self-deprecating smile, as if even he couldn't convince himself that he had found heaven in San Diego. "What more could a guy want?"

Emily blushed a smile at his sarcastic humor, reached an arm over her shoulder, and scratched her back. Joel noticed.

"Would you like to take a rinse-off? Salt water itching you?"

"No," said Emily. "That's cool. I'm fine."

With a plastic lighter Joel lit a joint he picked up from one of the abalone shells, sucked in smoke, and offered it to Emily. She shook her head no but smiled.

"You don't mind?"

She shook her head again.

"Would you like some more beer? You should try The Highwayman."

Emily smiled, held up her still half-full glass and said, "No, I'm fine."

Joel took another hit on the joint, held the smoke in his lungs, then slowly exhaled it through his nostrils, dragon-like.

"Where's your bathroom?" asked Emily.

Joel pointed toward a hallway.

Emily rose from the couch and crossed the living room. She passed more movie posters hung on the walls in the hallway. In the small bathroom, she relieved herself, then studied her face in the mirror. She turned on the faucets and splashed cold water on her face, dried herself with a hand towel, then leaned close to the mirror for one last look. She rehearsed excuses to leave because she wasn't feeling comfortable, but she sucked in her breath and returned to the living room.

"Ready to watch my short?" Joel asked.

Emily sat back down on the couch. "Yeah. I thought that's why you invited me over."

"Okay. Just making sure." Joel reached for the remote. "It was shot in sixteen millimeter and the sound isn't all that professional, so don't be too critical."

"Oh, don't be ridiculous. I'm not a film critic. I'm not some film snob. I save that for literature."

"Okay." Joel pushed a button on the remote, and the large-screen HDTV came imagistically to life. He had already cued up the DVD with his film. With a second remote aimed at a sensor, he lowered the lights. Emily shifted to the armrest on her side of the couch and slouched at an angle, her legs thrown out on the table as a kind of cautionary barricade.

"Comfortable?" Joel asked.

"Let's watch it," Emily said.

Joel pressed Play and settled back on the couch, respectfully a cushion apart. He took another hit on the joint, then set it back in the ashtray to extinguish itself.

The black-and-white images were grainy. Daylight scenes boiled like sand in a windstorm. A woman was introduced walking under neon lights at night. She had jet-black hair and piercing black eyes and a body wrung from lust. Cast as a lady of the night, she rendezvoused with men at hotel rooms for anonymous trysts, but during the day she scribbled furiously in notebooks and painted surrealist images on big canvases in what must have been bold and vivid colors. The short experimental film cut back and forth between these two realities of her fictional life in a rapid montage-like fashion. Without sync sound, were it not for a voice-over and the classical music on the soundtrack it would have resembled a silent film. The narration was the languid, mellifluous voice of, presumably, the actress. She spoke eloquently and lyrically about what she longed for in life, about her depression, the wars waged in her head that were growing less reconcilable with every passing day, about how she hoped her black depression, if confronted, would bring her to a deeper understanding of it, and hopefully deliverance from its torment. Her voice-over bordered on the religious—words like *suffering* and *redemption* were used frequently—and the philosophical. In another life she might have been a failed academic. In her present life she had been reduced, fictionally, to prostitution. Was it a metaphor for something else? Emily wondered as the film unspooled. Or a dream? It wasn't clear. Joel's eye for composition was daringly artistic, she admired quietly to herself. Though perhaps there was a little too much of an infatuation with the actress's beautiful features: face, breasts, bottom. She seemed to be in a state of undress a lot, but she performed her frequent disrobings in a kind of unapologetic and unhesitating naturalness, not bashful being in front of the camera. In fact, she expressed a kind of uninhibitedness that even embarrassed Emily at moments.

At one point the film held on a close-up of the lone protagonist as she applied makeup in an oval mirror in imitation of a famous photograph by Ed van der Elsken that depicted a woman kissing her twin image in a similar composition. Wrenched from the strangeness of the movie, Emily reared back slightly, recognizing the mirror from Joel's bathroom. *Was this his girlfriend?* she wondered, feeling her brow knit. As the camera slowly zoomed in, another fulguration of recognition went off in Emily's imagination. Holy shit! she exclaimed half out loud to herself. She unconsciously threw a hand to her mouth. Her heart was beating in a panic, and the blood ran hot in her veins. She was seized by such crisscrossing thoughts and presumptions and emotions that she had no choice but to turn to Joel and ask.

"Is that Nadia Fontaine?" Emily practically gasped out the query, at first in shock, then with a creeping sense of disconcertion.

"Yeah," answered Joel casually, his eyes locked on the TV in what Emily sensed was an elegiac sadness. He seemed as enrapt with Nadia as Emily was but, having known her, dragged by an undertow of emotions dissimilar to her own. She searched his face for a moment, then slowly rotated her eyes back to the screen. Nadia's character started sinking deeper into depression. It was in the voice-over narration, which had become a kind of confessional suicide note to the world. A lament about a man she had once loved, but it had ended. She wanted to escape her life of prostitution, but she needed the money. Then, in an eerie, almost phantasmagorical montage of shots and rapidly edited sequences, she drove to a moonlit beach and, like Virginia Woolf a half century before her, slowly waded into the ocean's teeth of incoming whitewater, incandescent with every breaking wave, until she had disappeared into its watery darkness. In an homage to the *Nouvelle Vague* of '60s French films, the last credit was punctuated with *Fin* and a forte in the classical music chosen for the score.

Joel paused the DVD on *Fin* and let it burn white through the black title card. An uneasy silence fell over the small living room. Emily slowly sipped her beer, haunted by the film. Not because it was any profound work of cinema, but because her predecessor seemed to have stripped bare a tranche of her soul and immortalized it on the screen, for the few eyes who watched it at various film festivals where Joel had submitted it and won acceptance.

Questions swirled in Emily's mind. Each came with a qualification and a fear of the consequences if she broached them. She looked at Joel, who was still staring at the TV, and studied his melancholy expression for any ulterior motive in choosing to show her the film, given that they barely knew each other. Despite the politics in Special Collections, the omnipresent feeling was that everyone wanted to bury the memory of Nadia Fontaine and treat her passing as though she had never existed.

"Were you a couple?" Emily ventured.

"No, friends," Joel answered enigmatically.

"She had no problem undressing for you," Emily said, stiffening a little, realizing now, after seeing the movie, that their relationship had forever been altered.

Joel shrugged. "Nadia was a free spirit, a truly liberated woman. She didn't play by the rules. She flouted them. She felt constrained being an archivist." Joel turned to Emily. "No, we weren't lovers, if that's what you were implying."

Emily searched his dark eyes for elaboration. They blinked impassively, blank, swimming in the sorrow of his grief. He seemed to be lost deep in thought, tunneling back to a time when Nadia was alive.

"Plus, she was an artist." He wrenched himself from his hypnotic spell. "You know she published a book of short stories?"

"Right. You mentioned she was a writer."

"One of 'em won a Pushcart," Joel said in a defensive tone.

"Really?" said Emily. "I should check them out."

"They were on the shelves at Memorial until one day they went missing."

Emily furrowed her brow in question.

"Somebody took them out of circulation," Joel elucidated, a tone of disgust harshening his voice.

Emily's jaw dropped to her chest. "What? Why?"

Joel shook his head in response, as if words were unnecessary. He rose and angled over to the wall. He slid out a book from his crude bookshelf, turned, and held it out to Emily.

She took it from him and read softly out loud. "*Knife in the Heart.* Short Stories by Nadia Fontaine." The cover was designed around a famous photograph by the tragic photo-surrealist Francesca Woodman, who committed suicide at the age of twenty-two. "Francesca Woodman?" Emily muttered. Joel nodded and resumed his spot on the couch. Emily flipped the book over. The back cover featured a full black-and-white photo of Nadia. Framed by shoulder-length dark hair, her depthless black eyes tunneled into the camera's lens from the youthful face of a woman Emily's age. Staring at her, Emily's transfixion moved her to ask, "How old was she when this was published?"

"Thirty," shrugged Joel.

"Her only book?"

"Her only published one." Joel picked up the half-smoked joint but set it back down. "She had an agent and everything, but . . . it's a tough world." Joel titled his head to one side in a gesture that summed up the futility of artistic aspirations, of which he himself had tried his hand and knew all too intimately.

Emily held up Nadia's book. "For me?"

Joel opened both hands in invitation. "As you can tell from the worn dust jacket, I've read it one too many times." Joel's eyes strayed off, blinking back tears. "The last, as if she were speaking to me from the grave."

Emily laid the book down, reverently not taking her eyes off it for a moment. When she looked up at the screen, *Fin* still burned its ghostly white letters against the black background. "Your movie—when was it made?"

"Last year," Joel said, collecting himself.

"Whose idea was it?"

Joel turned to her as though it were a rhetorical question. "You mean, Who wrote the screenplay?"

Emily nodded.

"Nadia did."

"It was entirely her idea?" Emily asked, slightly stunned.

Joel nodded slowly, then pointed at *Knife in the Heart*. "It's based on one of the stories in there. You'll recognize it. She didn't want it in the credits." He picked up the joint, lit it, took a hit, then set it down in the abalone shell, where it smoldered, scorching another black sphere in the shell's iridescence.

"She was married?" asked Emily hesitantly.

Joel ran his tongue over his front teeth, and his upper lip bulged where it had traveled in thought.

"Were you in love with her?" Emily risked.

Joel's face disorganized into an awkward and embarrassed laugh. He threw out an arm at the TV and opened his hand as if his gesture were spilling the words of an answer that was obvious to him. "She's beautiful. Smart. Deep. Creative. For a guy like me, a dream come true. Alas." He lowered his eyes to his chest and cast them down at the coffee table. A sorrow like a swiftly approaching storm seemed to sweep the once sanguine sky of his face. He brooded for a moment accompanied by an almost imperceptible nodding. "I guess I was in love with her, yeah," he confided. "It's not healthy to always be wanting someone you can't ever have."

"You made a movie with her so you could always have her close to you in some way?"

Joel's eyes found Emily's in the still dark living room, and in them he found a grieving truth. He tilted his head to one side. "It's tough for a guy in this anti-intellectual wasteland of a city called San Diego to meet a woman like Nadia and to realize that the bar is now impossibly out of reach." Almost absently, he rested one of his large, masculine hands on Emily's knee.

Without embarrassment or outrage, Emily simply grabbed his hand by the wrist and lifted it off her knee. "You're a nice guy, Joel. We've had a wonderful day. But I'm not going to be the one to have to say goodbye. That's a compliment, by the way." She sprang to her feet—not with anger, but deliberately, conclusively—in her mind, so as not to rupture the nascent friendship. To let Joel know she was never going to be his next Nadia, she added, "I'm not the one for you, Joel." She threw him a crooked smile to cushion the rejection.

"Understood. Sorry." He turned to her and smiled. "Don't go to Human Resources."

"Oh, please." Emily relaxed. "I had an awesome time. Thanks for showing me your film. It was pretty . . . interesting. I'm sorry about Nadia. I can see she meant the world to you."

A palpable solemnity fell over Joel. He loomed bigger, more ponderous in the dark than he had only hours ago at Black's Beach. Still only in his thirties, he seemed a hulk of a lonely man in his one-bedroom Pacific Beach apartment. He breathed in deeply and rose cumbrously to his feet. Emily gathered up her belongings. They stood a few feet apart. Emily stepped forward, and they came together in a conciliatory hug.

"I had a great day," said Joel, hugging her tightly.

"I did too," said Emily. "And thank you for showing me your favorite haunts."

"Anytime."

They dropped arms and disengaged.

"How do I get out of PB?" Emily asked.

Joel pointed through walls and walls of apartment complexes and rivers of freeways, painting the air with an index finger as though it were a map.

Emily left Joel's apartment and hurried out to her car. Following Google Maps, she drove east to Cass Street, turned right, and cruised down to Grand Avenue. Two- and three-story apartment complexes, all with marine-themed names it seemed, bore the cheerless alienation of all the beach hamlets that dotted the coast of Southern California. Gas stations and convenience stores were the only establishments still lit up and open for business.

Emily drove the empty thoroughfare of Grand Avenue in the direction of the freeway, every traffic light green. Shuttered stores in strip malls, their parking lots grimly deserted and bathed in sulfurous light, streamed bleakly past.

The freeway north back to Del Mar reminded Emily of a vast subway train empty of passengers. She closed her eyes when she remembered Joel's hand warm on her knee. It was innocuous, she decided. He took a shot. That's cool. He liked her. He thought she was attractive. At thirty-five maybe he was a little old for her, she decided. Her thoughts traveled once again to Nadia. The letter was still replaying in her head. She had practically memorized it. Nadia had had an affair with Raymond West. Of that much she was positive. Then something awful had happened. Reflecting on the film, Emily wondered if Nadia bordered on the manic-depressive, the story, choppy and hard to follow, was that unrelentingly bleak.

Onyx was waiting for her when she opened the sliding glass door to her apartment, a jumble of thoughts still swirling in her mind. "Sorry I was gone so long, little guy. Did you miss me, huh? I missed you." She squatted to pet him. He arched his head back and meowed. Suddenly she no longer felt all alone in the world.

CHAPTER 8

Nadia's File

8/13/18

I dreamed I was on a path cut through a field of golden grass. The skies were threatening. Someone shadowy was after me, shouting at me. They were imploring me to come back, that I was making a mistake. The person had no name, no face, was more of an ominous presence than anything else. I recall an epic peregrination of some phantasmagorical nature that lay ahead, but I didn't know where. Then the dream changed, and I was under water, held down by a large wave.

Woke to the alarm clock and crying Onyx.

Nadia's letter, her film, haunts me.

Regents was beginning to show signs of life. Fall quarter started in a month and orientation sessions and other pre-enrollment activities were underway. The firefighters still could not get control of the blazes and the skies billowed with columns of smoke. As Emily, glancing anxiously at her watch, hurried to work from the parking garage, mammoth Memorial Library stood sentinel on the slate-gray plaza against the orange-and-red-colored sky, quietly observing the natural world burning behind it, impervious to its destruction.

When Emily climbed the steps to the eighth floor for the Town Hall meeting, she found the westward-facing section had been cleared of desks and shelving. Approximately 150 fold-up chairs had been arranged in neat rows in front of a movable podium with a microphone mounted at its head. The harsh overhead lights had been banked for the ad hoc event assembly, and the room was illuminated only by the yellow sunlight flooding in through the tinted windows. Emily sat in the back on the aisle periphery, not wanting to be hemmed in by gum-chewers or coworkers who reeked of perfume. The attendees were a democratic, nonhierarchical mix of library staff and other employees, from Security to Facilities to archivists like Emily. Everyone who worked in the library, in any capacity, had been invited to the event.

The elevator doors clanged open with a jarring, cacophonous bang, and Emily turned abruptly. University Librarian David Verlander stepped off, shoulder to shoulder with Helena Blackwell, a spring in their steps. A seat in the first row had been saved for Helena and she blundered her way toward it, using shoulders and the backs of chairs for handholds, her one bad hip staggering her progress, as if fearing she might topple over. She greeted coworkers and other staff with her lopsided smile and air of bonhomie she was practiced at summoning on cue, but it was clear that her presence inspired fear in all who greeted her in return.

Verlander took the podium, set an iPad down on the desk and powered it on. Behind him, a luminescent projector screen had been unrolled from its ceiling housing and blocked out one pane of windows. Verlander lowered his glasses and smiled out at the crowd. He brought a fist to his mouth and cleared his throat. Emily found Joel in the crowd, smiled and tossed him a little wave, as if to allay his fears that he had overstepped his bounds on Saturday. Joel returned the wave with a discreet shaka shake that drew a smile from Emily. They were developing their own coded language of hand signals and the like, the common denominator being the unspoken Nadia, or so Emily wanted to believe.

"Good afternoon," began Verlander in a hoarse voice coarsened by age and pipe tobacco. "The reason I called this Town Hall meeting is that I want to share some exciting news with everyone here who works at Memorial Library before it goes out next week in an official press conference."

Verlander paused to let his opening remarks sink in. "A couple months ago, our esteemed Head of Special Collections, Helena Blackwell—whom I'm sure you all know—paid a visit to a very special person." He paused again for dramatic effect and gazed benevolently down on an unabashedly beaming Helena. He tilted his iPad so he could gain a better view of its rainbow of options. With a pudgy forefinger, he tapped tags on an app he had preloaded. Behind him, the projector screen filled with a washed-out image of a blown-up still photo. It depicted Helena Blackwell and Elizabeth West exchanging what looked like a bank check in a photograph apparently staged for publicity purposes. Seated in the back, Emily was too far away to read what was on the slip of paper. In the blown-up photo Helena and Elizabeth were both smiling broadly, as if egged on by the photographer.

Verlander's voice climbed an octave. "Some of you may recognize that very special person as one Mrs. Elizabeth West. She, of course, is the wife of decorated writer Raymond West. They have been married for an astonishing twenty-five years." Scattered sardonic laughter punctuated his speech. Verlander raised the palm of his hand. "Mrs. West, as many of you know, is one of the most significant donors to Regents. Scion to a media empire, she has generously given large percentages of her inheritance for many charitable causes." Verlander lowered his glasses to the brow of his nose and smiled at his audience. The eighth floor's AC hummed with the hidden engine of the library's power. "And now we learn that"—Verlander drew an index finger to his shut lips—"Professor West has seven-to-one odds to win the Nobel." Gasps shivered through the crowd, and a few clapped in a spontaneous demonstration of collegial pride. Verlander silenced the scattering of applause with a raised hand. "I'm sure Professor West wouldn't want us to jinx it." He widened his eyes admonishingly. He gripped the podium with both hands and his voice grew serious. "As most all of you know, Raymond West's papers have been donated to our Special Collections. It's an understatement to characterize what a privileged acquisition this is, what it means to this library." He gazed down at Helena again. "And we—everyone here in the library—have Helena to thank for that. We have long coveted the papers of someone of West's esteem in the literary world. It's been a process. Stanford, Princeton, Yale, Harry Ransom . . . they've all come courting, but"—he raised his voice dramatically—"he chose Regents, his beloved alma mater, and Helena worked years to make this dream a reality." Verlander swept an outstretched arm over the podium and extended it to Helena in the first row. "Stand up, Helena. Take a much-deserved bow."

Helena brought a hand to her mouth as she stood. In the crowd she looked smaller to Emily, a buoy bobbing in a vast ocean. Applause greeted her upraised arm and seemingly humble wave to the audience. Thirty-five years of service to the library had brought her to the eighth floor and this moment of triumph. Her face colored red, blushing with the recognition of her accomplishment. She had summited her own personal Mount Everest, the dream only now to be made manifest in the rest of David Verlander's announcement. She sat back down with the same pained effort it took to rise.

Verlander politely waited until Helena was settled back into her chair and the applause abated. He leaned his elbows on the podium, cradled his face with his hands for a moment and smiled broadly at the audience. "Oh, but it gets better," he rhapsodized in a jubilant voice. "As most of you know, Mrs. West gave a generous donation of ten million dollars to inaugurate the library renovation, beginning with"—he motioned with his arm to indicate the vast area of the floor which they occupied—"the eighth floor. Fundraising wasn't easy. Ten million went a long way to begin the redesign on the first and second floors. But our dream was always to transform this top floor, the glorious eighth floor, into, let's call it, a luxury reading lounge during the day, but a multipurpose floor we can strike and reconfigure for a spectacular event space at night. That was the dream of our head of Special Collections, the dream that she spent years—yes, years—courting Mrs. West to fund. So, when I say two months ago was a special day . . ." Verlander twisted his head and glanced over his shoulder. He tapped his iPad again, and the image on the screen changed to an extreme close-up of the check. In the upper left-hand corner was printed "Elizabeth West Foundation." Next to "Payable to" was typewritten "Regents University Memorial Library." The amount was $25 million.

When the staggering size of the donation had registered in the crowd, there were gasps, muffled shrieks, and sporadic, almost hysterical, applause. As if he were minister in a church announcing a miracle where a wheelchair-bound man had risen to his feet to a chorus of hallelujahs, Verlander raised his voice and boomed, "Yes, ladies and gentlemen, that's twenty-five million dollars!"

Half the assembled spontaneously sprang to their feet, clapping. Emily noticed that some stood with hands clasped at their faces, tears welling in their eyes. It was an emotional moment for many who had been employed in the library for years to witness this kind of financial support pour in to ensure their futures. For a moment, as the applause grew more deafening, Emily imagined that the collective emotional reaction was going to raise the eighth floor from the seventh and float above it, held aloft solely by the power of its majestic promise. The world—especially the literary and library worlds—would soon know about this famed collection and this wondrous eighth-floor crown. Like a giant magnet, it would draw scholars and the general public from all over the world. It would be a marketing tool par excellence for an ever-expanding Regents University. With the $25 million gift and the ambitious eighth-floor remodel, the donation of Raymond West's papers soared far higher than the typical archival acquisition. Should he win the Nobel—My God! you could almost hear the crowd exult in a collective gasp—the procurement of his papers would be enviously deemed a coup beyond coups. In Helena's proud, swelling chest, all those teas at Elizabeth West's, the myriad hours of banal socializing, all the favors she had no doubt granted, all the years massaging this fragile connection, were now dovetailing into a truly momentous confluence. Nothing could separate her from the grandiosity of this achievement. Her likeness would be painted by an artist and hung on the wall leading into Special Collections. A video would be commissioned and displayed on one of the flat-panel screens, immortalizing her accomplishment in a celebratory timeline. And if West won the Nobel, Helena could weep thirty-five years of catharsis and exultant joy. It would truly be a life's work encapsulated, and ensconced forever, in this one comet trail of glory.

Emily could feel from the audience's rapturous appreciation, from the near-unctuousness of Verlander's words, the gravitas of the moment. Especially what it meant for Helena. But as a project archivist, an outsider, unaffiliated with the university, she felt distant from the emotion that was palpable in the room.

Verlander prattled on in the exultant spirit of the moment, his voice nearly inaudible to Emily in the excited clamor that ran through everybody. He detailed the three phases of the remodel and how the eighth floor would soon become the veritable crown of a library, whose capstone would be the Raymond West Papers. In exchange for the donation, the library would be rechristened, he announced with raised octaval fanfare, The Elizabeth West Library, its ascendant glory now always associated with its benefactor's name.

Bored and tuning out, Emily found her head bent to the left, her eyes darting down the corridor to the shelf where she had found the letter in the book, speared now in the gut by its mesmeric power. Oblivious of the assembly and Verlander's announcement of the exciting new developments, she was startled out of her reverie when the woman sitting next to her tapped her on the shoulder. Emily looked back. A colleague with raised eyebrows was pointing to the podium.

"A welcome to Emily Snow," Verlander was saying in a booming voice. "Our new project archivist for the Raymond West Papers." Verlander's arm was raised at a forty-five-degree angle in the direction of Emily, urging her to stand.

Emily, unsettled, reluctantly stood. She combed the hair out of her face and manufactured a smile to erase the apprehension that had gripped her thoughts moments before. Emily shrank diffidently and blushed at all the heads turning to look at her, to gain a glimpse of the privileged archivist who was now vouchsafed the West Papers. Pride and anxiety were locked in combat as she resumed her seat.

The meeting adjourned finally on a celebratory chorus of applause, shrill whistles, and a collective spirit where everyone floating high on the eighth floor was part of some unsurpassable exaltation the library—indeed, the university—might not see again for another thirty-five years. Young or old, man or woman, facilities worker, archivist, librarian, its momentousness was a collective triumph.

The hubbub in the crowd as everyone rose from their chairs buzzed with crosscurrents of electricity. Nobody was jaded to its occasion. Verlander gave all of them, Helena, and his presentation, his own private round of applause. On the eighth floor, they were, as Verlander buttoned his stunning announcement, "literally and figuratively on the greatest high the library had ever experienced."

Joel caught up with Emily, who was moving away from the throngs who gathered at the elevators. It wasn't just her misophonia and the maddening *bing bing* of the elevator's floor signal that she was deliberately avoiding. She also worried about being sardined in the car's tight space, pressed to the back, squeezed shoulder to shoulder with her new coworkers, panicking that the elevator would stop at every floor and she might lose her mind and try to escape. They all knew her now because of Verlander's diplomatic introduction, from which the introvert inside her recoiled.

This entire narrative raced through her mind when Joel asked, "Where're you going, Emily?"

"I'm going to take the stairs," said Emily. "Claustrophobia issues."

"Gotcha. Can I join you?"

"Follow me," she joked, since it was obvious that Joel knew every floor of the library more intimately than her.

Joel opened the heavy door that led to the stairs and held it open for Emily as she passed in front of him. Their voices reverberated in the cavernous, cylindrical shaft of concrete and steel as they conversed.

"A couple weeks before you came," Joel started, "a homeless guy climbed up here and threw himself off."

"That's awful." Emily shook her head at the image. "Why'd you tell me that?"

"Sorry. Didn't mean to upset you."

"Fuck, that's horrible," Emily shuddered.

They spiraled downward in tandem on the steel-treaded stairs, Emily trying her best not to glance over the railing into the void of conical space that led to the concrete floor below, closing her eyes and wincing at the appalling image Joel had planted in her head.

"That's something you never want to see," said Joel. Emily continued to descend, her head focused on each step, each left turn, and nothing else. "Helena's big moment," chirped Joel from behind her.

"Yeah, it's an accomplishment," said Emily. She whistled under her breath. "Twenty-five million. Wow. That's a *huge* gift. For any institution."

"The eighth floor is going to be something," Joel exclaimed.

"Sad to see all the books go," said Emily.

"Analog is history, Emily."

"What happens when there's a global energy crisis and all the server farms are shut down?" Emily heard Joel's footsteps stop. She brought herself to a halt at a midpoint in the floor's landings and threw him a backward glance.

"I hadn't thought about that," Joel said.

"When it's all digital," Emily elaborated in a serious tone of voice, "if we lose that, and we have no power to bring it back to life, we will have wiped all historical records of art and history and humanity from the face of the earth."

"What are you, an archivist eschatologist?"

"I know what *eschatologist* means," said Emily, as the shadow of a smile appeared on her face.

"I have no doubt," said Joel.

"I'm worried about the fate of the planet," said Emily. "And the preservation of our individual legacies." She threw him another backward look, and qualified with a raised index finger, "When there is merit."

"Ah. When there is merit. The sixty-four-thousand-dollar subjective question."

Emily started back down the vortical stairwell again, listing to the wall and away from the railing. The flights turned and turned in downward spiraling circles until they had reached the door that opened to the main floor.

"Are you nervous about being West's archivist after all of that?" Joel pointed his arm overhead up the eight floors to the top of the library.

"No," said Emily. "Should I be?"

Joel smiled slyly. It was clear that he was enamored of her, but he was one of those men who knew where the boundaries were drawn, and he feared personal rejection more than recrimination in transgressing them.

"But it would be a lot easier if I had Nadia's personal file," Emily blurted out. She stopped and confronted him. Joel looked over the top of her head at nothing. "Surely, Nadia kept one. All archivists do. You know that." Emily locked her eyes on Joel's with a face of fierce determination. "Jean said she didn't find one when they cleared out her cubicle. Bullshit. It would help immensely if I had that."

"Maybe she took it home with her," Joel suggested.

"Maybe she didn't have time. Maybe she gave it to somebody she was close to when she learned she was being terminated." Emily's eyes pierced Joel's for any semblance, any insinuation, of dissemblance. He blinked her gaze away, then looked down at his feet, which he shuffled in place. "Or did someone take that out of circulation too?" Emily persisted. She waited for the longest moment before unlatching the door that opened out to the main floor of the library and the noise of the staff disgorging from the three elevators.

"Talk to you later, Emily." Joel walked off, his mind focused on something unspoken.

Emily watched him disappear back into Special Collections. She swiveled her head all around, disoriented, confused about the politics. In resignation to the obfuscation, she sighed to herself, then followed Joel back to her cubicle.

Feeling guilty that she had turned down her previous invitations, Emily agreed to lunch with Chloe at Tasmania. A creature of habit, she ordered the vegetarian chili. Chloe had also invited Deborah from the information desk and Julie, another colleague in the department. They were keenly interested in the West Papers, especially after Verlander's euphoric morning announcement. The girls also teasingly tried to pry into Emily's love life, and Emily parried them and said she wasn't in the market for one, that she preferred being single, that men were a waste of time. Chloe suggested that her boyfriend's business partner and she would hit it off.

"Oh, why?" Emily wondered.

"He's cute. He likes literature."

"What does he do?"

"My boyfriend and Clint make artisanal distillates," she proudly informed her.

"Clint? I can't date a *Clint*." Her remark elicited congenial laughter from the girls.

"You'd like him," Chloe countered. "Drinks and dinner? They make an awesome absinthe."

Emily actually was fond of absinthe. After college she had spent a summer touring Europe. She was introduced to absinthe in Prague in a week drunk in longing: a Czech painter had minorly broken her heart, and shots of absinthe chased with lager had helped her forget. "I'll think about it," Emily promised. With a paper napkin she wiped the chili from the corners of her mouth and rose abruptly. "Back to West. I just remembered something, and I don't want to lose it."

When Emily returned from lunch, she found a manila folder with about a half inch's worth of hand-scrawled pages on lined, pale blue legal paper inside. A yellow Post-it on the manila folder read, "You didn't get it from me."

Emily tore off the Post-it note and shoved it in her fleece vest pocket. On the manila folder cover, written with a black Sharpie, it read WPF. "West Personal File," Emily murmured to herself. A smile broke wide on her face. Joel! Her pulse quickened with excitement and anticipation. But suddenly, something bothered her, a metronomic *tick tick tick* that was driving her crazy. She frantically searched the two-desk cubicle, her head swinging like a lighthouse beacon. Above the adjoining station she spotted an analog clock mounted on the wall. Its hands were ticking off the seconds like a dripping faucet that had gone unattended. She set Nadia's file on her desk, crossed the room in a lunge, snatched the clock from the wall, turned it over in her hands, and grappled with the device in an effort to disable it. Not finding an off switch she popped open the battery cover and flicked out the batteries with one finger. Spring-loaded, they shot across the room. "Ow, shit," Emily cursed, bringing her middle finger to her mouth. She looked at it. The cuticle was torn, and blood was seeping from it. She returned it to her mouth to stanch the bleeding.

Emily plopped back down in her office chair and shut her eyes, but nothing was relaxed in her. A silence hung over the cubicle. The lights hummed overhead. Any unwanted noise now would almost for certain shatter Emily's fragilely regained cocoon. When she opened her eyes, she noticed a swath of red on the manila folder. Ironically, it had slashed across the WPF, making it look like a logo for a new company. The red of her blood against the black of Nadia's block-written letters, she imagined romantically, married her somehow to her, Nadia's, fate.

Chloe popped her head in, and chirped, "Thanks for lunch."

Emily smiled, her bloodied hand flattened on the personal file.

Chloe's eyes narrowed. "What's with the clock?"

"I have a hypersensitivity to sounds," Emily laconically explained. "I disassembled it."

"Well, okay. I hate that ticking noise, too." She smiled, waved and slipped away.

Emily longed one day for an office that was all her own, one where she could close the door and immure herself inside with her neuroses. *I am not a misanthrope; I just prefer the company of no one.* With renewed fervor, she redirected her gaze to the bloodstained folder with WPF written on its cover. She gripped it in both hands. Technically, she wasn't allowed to remove it from university property—assuming Joel had *found* it on university property. But if she left it in one of her drawers, it might be discovered by the wrong person. If she did remove it, and Jean or Helena found out what she had taken home, she realized with a sudden shiver of dread, she could be fired on the spot, word might spread from the wrong people . . .

Emily moved the mouse and her computer screen blossomed to life. She clicked on the instant messaging app, waited a second for it to materialize, and found the string that had begun with Joel. She started to type "Thanks," but stopped with her fingers poised over the keyboard. She played air piano with her fingers, as if rehearsing a message she was ambivalent about writing. If she did remove Nadia's file, and she had messaged Joel, would he be incriminated? Could he, too, lose his job? Should she go to Jean and say she had found her "predecessor's" personal file and risk the consequences of that confession? And what if Jean confiscated it? Its potential mother lode of riches would remain forever interred.

She glanced at the time on her computer. It was nearing 5:00 p.m. now. She made a cursory assay of the piles of document items she had started to assemble from the new addition, but she had already decided the fate of the folder. Pretending there *were* security cameras monitoring her activities, she covertly slipped the folder into her tote bag while pretending to recover something she had dropped on the floor.

"Emily," Helena said, as Emily passed by her office at the same moment she emerged from hers. "Exciting announcement this morning."

"Yes." Emily instinctively drew her canvas tote closer to her and glued it to her hip. "Congratulations. It must be thrilling for you," she managed. It wasn't Emily's wont to serve up compliments. She had never mastered that sometimes-valuable resource: being phony. But here she was, manufacturing speciousness the best she could, to distract the director of Special Collections.

"Everything okay?" Helena asked. Her face was flushed red, and Emily could swear she detected wine on her breath.

"Yeah, fine," said Emily.

"I'll walk you out," said Helena, bulling ahead.

"Aren't you going to lock your door?" Emily said.

Helena laughed and shook her head. "I dare anyone to steal from me."

Emily threw a furtive look into Helena's office. The floor was still a jumble of documents of all size, shape, and color. Had it always been like this? For thirty-five years? Its disorganization disconcerted her to the core of her being. She could never work for this woman full-time, she realized in that moment.

She caught up with Helena as she careered toward the library's main entrance.

"How's West coming along?" inquired Helena, speaking to the library with a roving head and not to Emily.

"With the new addition, there's a lot there to process," Emily said. Helena didn't say anything, but her frown and accompanying nod suggested an air of concern. "I've got a good feel for what I have to do," Emily added.

"Good," barked Helena, as they climbed the stairs to the plaza. The sky flowered into view, ominous in its fiery mien. Wordlessly, they crossed the desolate plaza.

Helena came to a halt when she reached her Lexus in one of the privileged "A" spots, wheeled around and faced Emily. Behind her, the hexagonal Memorial Library framed her like a nimbus whose fortresslike halo she had earned. "The eighth floor's going to be fabulous," Helena exulted. "Oh, the Town & Gowns we'll be able to hold up there!" Her pride was etched in her expression and the way she admired the magnificent edifice her eyes were dreaming up at. She looked like a timeless statuary in its foreground, gazing reverentially up at the structure that had been her home half of her life. She threw Emily a backward glance and displayed that implacable face, stolid as her library, weathered as the cliffs, ageless as some rare, endangered reptile. "It's been a journey," she muttered more to herself than to Emily. She grabbed a smile from the palette of smiles that she used and flashed one. "See you tomorrow, dear. Let's get West wrapped up soon, okay?"

Emily stood still for a moment as Helena shoehorned herself into her Lexus and motored quietly away. She gazed up at the sky. It was blackened with soot, a ceiling of ashes in a riverine of orange-red lava. An elderly Asian woman marched past Emily wearing a surgical mask, looking like the lone survivor in an apocalypse, the enormity of which seemed to not affect Memorial Library, standing impervious to whatever had brought about the end of mankind. It did not escape Emily that Nadia's file—a veritable treasure map to all that an archivist worked on—potentially held secrets that were interred in its catacombs. Urged on by the thrill of her transgression, her legs broke into a resolute walk. The library could possibly withstand a cataclysmic event—fires, heavy rains, revolution—but maybe its Achilles' heel resided in a seed sown fatally from within.

The commuter traffic was gridlocked on the freeway. From an airplane it must have resembled a colorful band of metal writhing like a mythological snake, awakened from its dystopian slumber. Emily flowed with the slow-moving traffic on the I-5 until she reached the Del Mar Heights turnoff and veered off from the automotive anaconda. Hungry, she swung the wheel right at the light and drove east. She pulled into Jimbo's, her new favorite grocery store, and loaded up on some necessities, still in a daze from the walk with Helena, Nadia's personal file on Raymond West bouncing on her hip, an item stolen from Special Collections, something she had never done before. In the dairy cases, when a passing employee asked her if she was finding everything okay, she reared back and replied curtly, "Yes, I'm fine," and crabbed over to the next case to get away from the unwanted presence. Emily couldn't bear anybody else crowding the precious real estate in her head.

She lugged her grocery bags out to her Mini, locked them inside, then walked into Urban Plates, stood in line, and ordered the salmon dinner. Armed with a receipt printed with her order number, she retreated to a table in the far corner of the restaurant. While she waited for her number to be called, she slipped Nadia's file from her tote, laid it down in front of her, and leafed through the documents, turning the pages slowly, inspecting them like the manuscripts processor she was trained to be. The block-lettered handwriting was small, but meticulous. Easy to read but mystifying at first glance to decode. Every archivist employed a different system, and since personal files were generated for the archivist's eyes only, often there was a sloppiness to them, an indecipherability, useless to anyone else. But then, most archivists didn't generate a personal file with the prospect that they were going to be handing it over to a successor. Which possibly explained why nobody thought it important that she have it. Usually a *new* personal file was generated by the project archivist or the collection was hurried to completion without the aid of one. But as a project archivist, as someone who took over unfinished projects, that's not how Emily worked.

"Number seven," a young man's voice barked over the intercom. "Your order is ready. Number seven."

Emily closed the folder. She slid out from the bench with Nadia's personal file tucked under her arm, paranoid that someone could swipe it. Who? Why? It wasn't a laptop. But Emily felt protective of it, for reasons she would not be able to express to anyone without them fearing she was unhinged.

Emily claimed her order, added plastic utensils to her tray, and returned to her table. She set the file to her left, opened it and ate absently, barely paying attention to her food, her eyes focused on the pages in the file. The writing was in lettered and numerical abbreviations, and Emily could easily decode most of it. Titles of Raymond's West work were the first letters of the title, for instance. "Corrs. bet. GGM & RW" clearly referenced the epistolary exchange between West and Nobel laureate Gabriel Garcia Márquez. The coded entries were wedded to numbers that would be found on the document boxes in West's archive. To perform a truly thorough job, Emily calculated that she would have to double-check these entries against the finding aid, as well as make sure the coded items were in their respective boxes.

But that was not what she was looking for in Nadia's file and she fucking knew it. Given the letter she had found in the Vindas novel of erotica, Emily was scouring for something out of the archivist's routine indexing. She came to it at the end of the torn blue legal pages. The last document in the folder was a printout of a screenshot taken of her desktop. Two salient things jumped out at Emily, and her heart broke into a run as she zeroed in on the screenshot. "Drive C: Dark Storage." Or, as it was more colloquially and lyrically known in the archival world, "the dark archives," a digital cosmology containing anything and everything that for reasons of privacy should be undiscoverable by the road map of the public finding aid. But findable if, armed with the navigational tool of an archivist's personal file, the DNA could be decoded to produce a chunk of the historical record. What made Emily's blood run hot was why Nadia had had access to the dark archives and she, Emily, didn't! *What the fuck is out there in the West Papers that I don't know about?* she spoke out loud to the document that trembled in her fingers, her voice muffled by the terrible music on the stereo system. But not muffled enough for the elderly couple at the table wedged next to her, who both bent their heads in her direction with furrowed brows and expressions of disapprobation.

The other detail that drew Emily's focus was the date of the screenshot, which appeared in tiny letters in the top ribbon of the toolbar. A relatively recent date, she was certain—and it was easily verifiable—that it was mere weeks before Nadia had died. Would she still have been an employee at the library if she had been taken off the project?

Then something alarming materialized, the way a camera lens swiftly focuses from a near object to a far object, dramatically changing the whole tableau. Chloe and a man a head taller than her could be seen standing together in line through the customers who crowded the low-illuminated room. If Emily's heart had broken into a run, now it was in a full gallop, untethered and uncertain of the twists and bends that lay ahead. She quickly secreted away Nadia's personal file in her tote and rummaged frantically for West's *Lessons in Reality*, brought it to her face and feigned absorption in it.

But Chloe's eyes were the searching, watchful kind too, and she caught sight of Emily dining all alone. A smile exploded like an ocean swell on a rock in the dark and she waved with an extroverted flourish of her arm. With no other option, Emily smiled and held up her hand in collegial recognition. When they had finished their orders, Chloe grasped the tall man by the elbow and, as if jerking a leash, directed the two of them to Emily's table.

"Hi, Emily."

"Chloe."

Beaming, Chloe proudly turned to the man shuffling in place next to her and wearing a sheepish smile, "This is my boyfriend, Jesse." Jesse was a hirsute man, sporting a thick black beard and scraggly shoulder-length hair, but handsome in a blithe flannel-shirt/mountain-man, fuck-all vibe. He extended his large hand, and Emily politely took it. It was incongruously limp and damp for a big, strong man like Jesse.

"Jesse's the one I told you about with the distillery," Chloe said.

"Artisanal distillery," Jesse corrected, with no sense of irony.

"*Artisanal distillery*," Chloe mocked. "Absinthes, flavored vodkas . . ."

"I'd like to try the absinthe sometime," said Emily. "Feel what it's like to be Baudelaire." Her social awkwardness caused her to laugh, as if she didn't mean the sarcasm insultingly.

Jesse visibly blushed, a sucker for pretty girls who name-dropped literary illuminati. "You know your authors and spirits."

Emily blushed a smile. Chloe played ping-pong between the two of their eyes.

"How's West?" Chloe said, pointing at the book in Emily's grasp.

"It's getting there."

"Nervous about the Gala?"

Emily beetled her brow. "Pardon?"

"Well, there's a temporary target date of late October for the eighth-floor unveiling."

"I'm not too stressed," said Emily with one shake of the head.

Chloe smiled at Emily. "Well, we'd love to have you come out with us some night, wouldn't we, Jesse? Meet his partner, Clint."

Emily contemplated lying and confiding she had a boyfriend in another city, but she had vowed recently not to make excuses for arrangements she didn't want to have orchestrated. "I'm still settling in, Chloe."

"Clint's a cool guy," affirmed Jesse. "He knows his literature way better than me."

His literature? Emily almost said something snidely in reply. Did Jesse know she was working on the collection of a writer who was an odds-on favorite to win the Nobel Prize for Literature? That she already had claimed a front row seat to literary genius? That her standards were exactingly high, her dreams of a relationship far beyond an artisanal distiller in San Diego? Not wanting to come off as an elitist, Emily found herself nodding, as if she were giving the invitation consideration, but really internally monologuing and wanting them to vanish and leave her in peace. How do you get a guy to go away without offending him? Especially when his girlfriend is a coworker? Especially when your mind is orbiting something foreign to what their minds are fixated on: Chloe fantasizing a double date; Jesse hoping to set up his best friend; Emily about to descend into . . . the dark archives?

"Sounds like fun. I'll let you know when some time frees up," Emily finally said, invoking a variation on a smile that she hoped wasn't transparently disingenuous.

"Oh, there's our number," Chloe said, as the designated orders announcer bent forward and spoke into a microphone a second time. "See you at work." She cupped a hand around her mouth again, an annoying affectation of hers. "You and Clint would so hit it off." And then they were swallowed up by the crowd, vacuumed away by the noise and gentle tumult of the popular eatery. Emily had once told an older woman friend that she believed it was easier for a man to be alone than a woman. The friend agreed, but with the qualification "When you're young." And those words haunted Emily. For some anomalous reason, in that moment she thought of Elizabeth West, who also owned a front row seat to literary genius. *Owned* with a capital *O*, chuckled Emily, still gleeful that she was in possession of Nadia's personal file.

Emily finished her meal, then slipped out into the unwelcoming night. The Santa Anas had picked up, as they were wont to do at night, and she blinked her eyes to keep them from drying out. The fronds of palms clattered high up on the crowns of their trunks, the gusts of wind dislodging the dead brown ones, which crashed to the asphalt with lethal power. Emily looked all around her. The San Diego night was empty, that existential way only a San Diego night can be.

She walked through pools of lamplight that mottled the desolate parking lot, feeling alone but not lonely, alienated but not unhappy, small but unafraid. Felicitously anonymous, she decided, the private recess she preferred vanishing into.

When she got home, she changed into pajamas and crawled into bed with Onyx purring next to her. "Did you have a good day? Huh?" Emily whispered, stroking Onyx's lustrous fur. Nadia's personal file on the West Papers was splayed open on her lap, the pages spilling out as she drifted into sleep and a Hadean world of disturbing dreams.

CHAPTER 9

The Dark Archives

8/14/18

In my dreams, I wandered lost and frightened in a postapocalyptic world all alone. I came to Memorial Library. It stood, in the aftermath of the catastrophe that had decimated every living creature on the planet, an impassive, unblinking witness to the end of earth. I tried to get in, but the doors were locked. I had left Nadia's personal file on my desk and I was afraid that Jean had been trapped down in there and was going to find it. But why was I worried if the world had indeed ended?

I started reading my predecessor's only collection of short stories, Knife in the Heart. *Troubled characters. Erotic scenes. Frank dialogue (whew!). Powerful. Deeply personal. They're so realistic, I wonder if she lived it to write it, or if she had this vivid of an imagination, this desperate yearning that all her characters have to break free. I particularly liked, "Her Body Cried out for Sex."*

For reasons that were perhaps unconscious, Emily applied some concealer, penciled her lashes, and brushed them with mascara, accentuating them with a flourish of red lipstick. She had found a staff photo of Nadia, the only one she could find. Nadia had deliberately tried to make herself look pretty for the photographer. *Must have been happier times*, Emily thought to herself.

Jean materialized in the door. She tapped her watch. Emily locked eyes with her, debating whether to make another excuse, to apologize, or deploy another tactic.

"Does the university have laptops connected to the servers?" Emily inquired.

"I have two."

"Given the urgency of this project," Emily said, "I'd like to have one to take home so I can work weekends."

"I'll talk to Helena," replied Jean.

A current of tension streamed between them. Jean pointed at the disassembled clock lying face down on the table next to a pile of West's manuscripts. "What's with the clock?"

"I have misophonia," said Emily. Jean furrowed her brow. "An aversion to certain sounds."

"Never heard of it." She glanced at the disassembled clock again, frowning. "Is it something we should be concerned about?"

"No," said Emily, chopping her off. "It doesn't interfere with my work."

Jean seemed uncomfortable with the topic. She swept the cubicle with her large searchlight eyes. "Looks like you're . . . making a lot of progress here." She took a threatening step over to one of the stacks and lifted one of the folders.

"I'd prefer you not rearrange the documents." Emily stopped her by half standing from her chair.

"Where's your student assistant?"

"I don't need him," Emily answered with a hint of defiance. "I excused him."

Jean threw Emily a backward glance and set the folder back down. "We use a visual organizing app in the department where every project has a board, under which are lists, which we check off . . ." She made a move toward Emily's computer, as if prepared to give her a tutorial.

"I'm not interested, Jean," said Emily. "I'm here for one project, then I'm gone. I can't be bothered to learn a whole new piece of software, nor do I like to be micromanaged. It's counterproductive and a waste of my time."

Jean stiffened. Emily had drawn the boundary lines and dared Jean to oppose them. Instead, Jean stretched her lips across her face in a forced smile. "I'll check on the take-out laptop and let you know. Carry on." She turned to go.

"Oh, Jean?" Emily reined her back. Jean made a half turn and planted her chin on her shoulder. "I can hear every word of every conversation you have on the phone in this open-plan environment." Emily swept an arm around in a half circle. "If it's something private, I'd suggest you take the call somewhere else. I have the frequency range of a beagle."

"Good to know." Jean knifed away and was gone, except for the rapid thumping of her heels on the threadbare carpet.

Emily pouched out a cheek with her tongue and shook her head. She realized Jean was trying to control the West project. And now that the big donation to the library was no longer a secret, Emily better understood the hierarchical politics. She wanted to demarcate boundaries so that nobody interfered with her work.

Emily left her office and walked down the corridor. She passed by Chloe's cubicle, tossed a little wave without breaking stride, not wanting to give the confabulating Chloe a chance to engage her in office politics or dating orchestration.

At the end of the corridor she stopped at Joel's office and knocked on the frame of the entrance. Joel was in headphones, watching a YouTube video of surfing on his computer. He jumped when Emily knocked louder, ripped his headphones off, and spun around in his chair. "Emily. You scared me."

"Sorry." Without asking, she rolled out a guest chair and plopped down. She pointed at his monitor. A professional surfer had disappeared inside the gigantic barrel of a peeling thirty-foot wall of water somewhere in the South Pacific.

Joel grabbed his mouse and paused the video. "Just taking a break."

"Hey, I'm not your supervisor. Chill."

"I am chill. What's up?"

From her vest pocket, Emily produced the screenshot printout she came across in Nadia's file, unfolded it and showed it to Joel. Behind him was a framed film poster for Fellini's *8½*. "Brilliant film," she said, nodding at the poster.

Joel threw a look over his shoulder. "A dinosaur. Could never make that film today. Thank God there's a 4K conversion. But who knows. In ten years, the formats might all be radically changed you won't be able to see it. All of film history will be wiped out."

"It'll all be surfing videos on YouTube," Emily teased.

"Ha-ha . . ." He held up the sheet of paper. "So, it's a screenshot of your desktop." He opened his arms questioningly.

Emily shook her head back and forth, back and forth, for repeated emphasis. "I found it in Nadia's personal file."

"Oh, Jesus," he said, burying his face in both hands.

Emily bent forward at the waist so that their conversation would be sotto voce. "Why don't I have access to the C drive and dark storage?" Emily, no wallflower when it came to her archival duties, stabbed a finger at the page that was now levitating on the edge of Joel's desk like the most delicate of feathers.

"I don't know," Joel replied tersely. Emily drilled her eyes into his, forcing him to come up with something better. "Have you talked to Jean?" he asked.

She shook her head in contempt of the question. "No. And I wouldn't. And you fucking know why."

"Why?" Joel challenged.

"Because she'll want to know why I want access, and I'm not going to give you away by showing her Nadia's file." She poked her index finger at the document to underscore her point.

"I appreciate that," Joel said.

"What's out there, Joel?" she asked with a bemused look, not mentioning the cryptic letter found in *Le Rêve d'un Flagellant*. "I'm already coming across some items in the finding aid that don't jibe with items in the document boxes."

"Oh, yeah?"

"Yeah." Her unblinking eyes didn't leave him.

A silence fell over their newly drawn, tacitly demarcated little world, Nadia's personal file being the instrument that had forged it. Joel shut his eyes and pulled on his nose with thumb and forefinger.

"Can you get me into the dark archives?" Emily asked.

Joel's expression indicated that a swirl of scenarios more complicated than a Fellini film were convoluting in his mind. He smiled while shaking his head. "I shouldn't have given you Nadia's file on West."

"But you did. And you know I'm an archivist. And you know what archivists are like. If we care about, and are thorough with, our job"—she leaned in until their faces almost touched—"we notice everything," she finished inscrutably. "Joel? There's a reason you gave me her file."

Joel raised his heavy head to hers. With splayed fingers, he combed his saltwater bleached locks out of his face. In a barely audible voice, he said, "I know Richard, our IT guy. He's going to want some kind of authorization."

"I'm not going to go to Jean." Emily tapped her finger on the screenshot. "But I would like access to the dark archives."

A laugh erupted from Joel. "Dark Archives. I haven't heard that one in a while. You know who always used that term?"

"Nadia," replied Emily, with a sly smile.

"How'd you know?"

"Because she was a poet." Joel's face went slack. "You miss her?"

Joel nodded slowly up and down, lost in memory. A dark river seemed to stream across his sun-fissured face like a flash flood on a cracked creek bed, restoring it to life. When it had passed, he smiled bleakly. "Her death tore me up," he said, blinking back tears.

Emily rested a hand on his shoulder and squeezed it gently. She got up, reached over and retrieved the printout. They said goodbye to each other without professing promises, but there glinted an unspoken understanding in the way their eyes never broke contact before Emily finally turned to go.

Emily took her lunch and walked outside. At Joel's suggestion she strolled down the Alexis Smith Snake Path, an eight-foot-wide outdoor pathway sculpture that depicted, in a mosaic of tiles, the back of a giant anaconda. Subtly contoured, and gently humped, it weaved its sinuous way toward the College of Engineering and Humanities. Halfway down the mammoth snake, shaded by the dense pillars of eucalyptus trees, a little arbor furnished with a cement bench rounded into view. Emily found it unoccupied and sat down. The burning sun slanted through the tall trees in mote-filled spears of yellow-orange light. From her Japanese lunch box,

Emily produced a plain yogurt and two carrot sticks. Next to her was a monumental granite stele in the crude shape of a book with a quote from Milton's *Paradise Lost* etched into it: "Then wilt thou not be loath to leave this Paradise, but shalt possess a Paradise within thee, happier far." Emily knew for certain she had not found that paradise within her yet, but she knew, because her mentor Professor Erickson at Harry Ransom had frequently reminded her, that she had youth on her side. She wondered, in the quiet of the literary-themed nook, if Nadia had found that paradise within her before she met her fate in the icy waters of Black's.

When Emily returned to her cubicle, she found a note from Nicola saying he would drop in on her tomorrow and see if she needed his assistance. Such a polite, well-mannered kid, she thought to herself. She sat down and swiveled to face her computer, moved the mouse in a tight little circle until her screen bloomed to life. She typed in her password and the next screen brought her to her desktop. A smile as wide as a serpent's mouth split open her face with an irrepressible joy. She clicked on her Outlook Messenger and IM'd Joel: "You're awesome." She waited. His delayed emoji reply was the face of Lucifer baring his teeth in a wicked smile.

Emily threw a backward glance to the entrance of her cubicle to make sure no one was dawdling there, then turned back to her screen. And there it was: "Drive C: Dark Storage." Everything in Special Collections & Archives that had been digitized was stored on that server. Everything that was not in the finding aids of all the Special Collections & Archives donors resided there, items that had been digitized and not made available for the public, either because of restrictions placed on them by the donors and their heirs or because they had not yet been processed. Or . . . just because.

Pandora's Box. In reality, it was a jar, an earthenware vessel, that when opened could wreak havoc on anyone's world. The metaphor was not lost on Emily when she clicked on Drive C: Dark Storage. The screen scrolled with directories, each identified by a code. Under each directory were seemingly endless ladders of subdirectories. In some instances, pages and pages. Emily was swimming now in Special Collections' prodigious galaxy of archives.

She navigated to yet another abstruse directory listing, under which was vertically rowed an immense amplitude of yellow folder icons and their accompanying descriptions. Like computer code, they scrolled forever. And forever. Until she hit gold: "_West_Collection." She froze the screen. A thrill ran hot through her blood and seized her with a kind of apprehensive naughtiness. The dark archives, _West_Collection! Her cursor hovered over it like a quivering dowsing rod bending downward into truth. It was a reckless moment. Emily stood perched on the precipice of descending into an impermissible world. She closed her eyes. Impropriety and curiosity, unauthorized access in an unholy marriage with fascination, waged a furious battle of ethics inside her. *Fuck it*, she thought, *What's the worst that could happen*?

The screen refreshed again. Soon she was buried up to her eyeballs in the West Collection folder. Buried within this folder there materialized a multitude of subfolders, like new galaxies suddenly discovered in minutes with the mere switching on of a new, powerful radio telescope that probed deeper into the universe than ever before. Her heart pounding, Emily scrolled through them slowly, studying every one of the folder names. Inching forward, as if the dark archives was booby-trapped with invisible security sensors, she stopped at one of the folders that drew her immediate attention: "_The_Archivist_Drafts." She clicked on it. The folder spilled a ladder of unfurling files: "The Archivist – 1st Draft." "The Archivist – Notes." "The Archivist – 2nd (abandoned)."

Pulse racing, Emily darted her cursor across the screen to the back arrow that returned her to the West Collection folder, her initial foray into the dark archives aborted, and exhaled audibly through flared nostrils. She cocked her ear for coworkers. Jean could be heard clacking away on a keyboard through one of the cubicle dividers. Reassured she wasn't going to be barged in on, Emily resumed her spelunking in the dark archives, scrolling more carefully. Heart still racing, she halted at a folder named "RW_Corrs." With a hesitant, apprehensive, feather-light touch, Emily clicked on it. The screen re-effloresced with several dozen folders: "Nick_Peterson_Corrs," "Elizabeth_Corrs," "Lit_Dept_Corrs," et al., and . . . a folder that read generically "Misc_Corrs."

Emily's brain was speeding. She paused, drummed her finger against the mouse in indecision, debating, measuring her next move, beat by beat, against the weight of its parlous consequences. She could always reverse her steps. Joel would know if someone had a record of who came and went in the dark archives, but she was pretty sure she was alone in this archival netherworld, that no one was electronically eavesdropping. Emily had never transgressed like this before in her young career. She was journeying into uncharted territory, but she wasn't going to be denied. She wanted to know what that letter meant! Vaguely, the ramifications loomed. But hadn't Joel nudged her? Nadia's personal file? Access to dark storage . . . ? She seesawed dangerously between the twin poles of professional duty and reckless abandonment. *Dark Pursuits*, the title of one of Nadia's short stories, came back to her suddenly as her hand hesitated over the mouse.

Sucking in her breath and holding her lungs expanded, Emily, eyes squeezed shut, clicked. When she opened her eyes, another folder file burned yellow on the screen: "_Your_Archivist_TBC." *The fuck?* Emily ran a hand up her face and raked her hair and held it tightly. With her free hand still cupping the mouse, she opened that folder and tripped over yet another folder file, this one named "_Dark_Love." Huh? She hovered her cursor over it, and it fluttered like an electronic hummingbird. Emily let the air exhale from her lungs and clicked again. Slapping her in the face like a glass of cold water was "NF/RW_Corrs." Nadia Fontaine, Raymond West—could these really be emails between the two of them? She clicked again. Deep down in the lowest geologic strata of the dark archives, her monitor mosaicked to life. Files icon-denoted as PDF after PDF after JPG after WAV after MOV after PDF scrolled down the screen, each thumbnail file name with its own unique creation date followed by the opening words of the email's subject heading.

Like a caver who had found a glimmering vein of gold but didn't have the proper equipment to extract it, Emily scurried back to the surface, meticulously marking her path in her personal file so that she could retrace her steps—not that she was exactly Alice in Wonderland anymore—and then switched off her computer and spoke out loud: "Holy shit." To the universe outside her little microcosm, nothing had happened. But to Emily, a powerful earthquake centered in her being had shaken her like a rag doll, and when it was finished scrambling her brain, the world was born anew. No one but an archivist working on a collection like West's, could truly comprehend the magnitude of her discovery. And she hadn't even begun her descent!

Floating on a mixture of dread and dazed uncertainty about her next move, Emily signed out on the staff whiteboard, announcing she was on a break, then ambled over to the Barnes Center. She felt like a snack, but her stomach was knotted in apprehension. Her mouth felt like tissue paper, so she bought a canned iced tea that tasted like industrial waste, but at least it stemmed some of the lightheadedness she was feeling from dehydration.

Seeking fresh air and a change of venue, she walked outside and sailed through the automatic sliding glass doors into the bookstore. It was more than a bookstore. They sold Regents University sweatshirts, T-shirts, and sweatpants. They also retailed electronics: computers, tablets, cells, and . . . flash drives.

Emily rang up a 128-gigabyte flash drive at the register, her imagination still unspooling everything she had slammed headfirst into in the dark archives. She barely heard the pink-haired girl with the eyebrow piercings remind her to type in her PIN so she could complete the transaction.

Back in her cubicle, Emily put the dark archives out of her mind as best she could and worked on another pile of folders that Nicola had neatly arranged for her perusal, but her hypersensitive ears were tuned to the voices on phone calls, the fritzing sound of computers being shut down, the rise and fall of footsteps of coworkers heading home.

Jean stopped at Emily's door and peeked in from the threshold. "Sorry I was a little testy earlier." Emily shook her head as if no apology were necessary, still nonplussed by her discovery. "We're all under a lot of pressure with the eighth-floor renovation, the library rededication."

"I understand, Jean," Emily chopped her off. Had she taken an anti-anxiety pill? Emily wondered. Her mood seemed profoundly improved.

"Are you wrapping up?" She jerked a thumb over her shoulder. "I'm in the Jameson structure if you want to walk out with me."

Emily couldn't fathom accompanying her supervisor to where her Mini was parked. What would they talk about? *Le Rêve d'un Flagellant*? Nadia's short stories? "I'm going to stay late, get through some of these." She gestured to the stacks of West documents that now occupied an entire desk.

"I asked about the laptop," interjected Jean. "It's okay. Just got to get it approved and checked out with IT."

Emily freaked for a second, blinked back her anxiety. Would Richard in IT tell Jean that he had given her personal station access to the dark archives? A fistful of antianxiety meds wouldn't placate Jean's anger if she found *that* out. "You know, on second thought, I don't think I need it. I was just stressing, but I have this under control." Emily nodded with an expression of confidence.

"Okay. See you tomorrow then." Jean turned away. Her heels clicked down the corridor and were swallowed by the monotone humming of the overhead lights.

Emily sat unmoving in her chair, her microphone-sensitive ears tuned to the frequencies of Special Collections. She knew what she was about to do was forbidden. She knew she had bitten into the proverbial apple, and any more bites would excavate a deeper realm of guilt. The covert requests to Joel, the removal of university documents from the library, and now, what she was plotting, the saving of documents to a personal flash drive to surreptitiously spirit home. She had taken the required course in ethics when she was getting her master's in library science, and this same issue had surfaced again and again. The line was blurred. But there was no question pursuing this chain of clues and the personal documents that it yielded without going to Jean or Helena was an unambiguous taboo, an unequivocal breach of ethics. But what was this correspondence? And who performed the ingest into the dark archives? Would Nadia know how to do that? Emily's mind fountained two streams: one conservative . . . and one dark.

Emily tapped the flash drive against her lips. Her outstretched hand found the on-off switch to her computer and her finger pressed lightly against it. She pushed harder and heard a click. Her monitor opened to the home screen. Certain that Jean, and everyone else in the department, was gone, Emily popped open the USB connector on the flash drive and ported it into her computer. She opened a pull-down menu and copied the entire "_West_Collection" folder, then dragged her cursor over the icon of the flash drive that appeared on her screen. She opened a menu over it. Her eyes closed almost involuntarily. She tried to weigh the repercussions but kept drawing an unnerving blank. Her principal fear was whether her movements on her computer were being monitored by Security, but that seemed unlikely. It was possible a digital forensics expert could come in after the fact and trace her actions back to her if there was reason to suspect a hacker, but what reason would there be?

She opened her eyes and clicked "Paste Item." A progress bar showing the number of files to be copied bloomed in the center of the monitor. Panicking that there were so many files to be copied, in a defensive move, Emily gripped the edge of the desk, pushed back her chair and straightened to her feet. She was ready to block anyone from coming into her cubicle while the data migration of files was underway. Between the entrance and her monitor was a shaky footbridge over a dark abyss into which she was about to tumble of her own volition. She wanted to go there. She had to know. The progress bar was crawling like an earthworm on hot asphalt. *Come on*, she urged out loud to the monitor, as if it were another person in the room under her employ.

Approaching footsteps sounded down the hall, rising in volume. Instinctively, Emily backed toward the entrance, all the while her eyes locked on the monitor and the glacially advancing progress bar. She wasn't erasing the files, or redacting them, or diverting data . . . she was *copying* them, she rationalized to herself.

The footsteps clomped past. She guessed it was a man, probably one of the Facilities guys. It wasn't Joel because he had left early to catch the evening glass at Black's. The footsteps receded down the main passageway, turned a corner and vanished. With a hand to her breast, Emily could feel her heart throbbing. *How can a heart beat so fast?* Adrenalized by the moment, she found herself talking out loud to the monitor. "Come *on*!"

The progress bar ended its journey and a message popped on informing Emily "File Transfer Complete." With swift actions, Emily ejected the flash drive, shoved it back into her bag, shut down her computer, then stood for a moment, tensed like an animal surrounded by predators, debating her next move. It was so freezing cold in Special Collections her exhalations were almost visible, ghostly breaths in the dark. When had she switched the lights off? She couldn't remember. It was as if she were emerging from a trance where time had frozen and now was starting up again and reality was once again surreally omnipresent. In that moment of returning to consciousness, she internally warred with herself if she was losing her grip on that precious real estate of reality she clung to.

Needing to get out of the library, Emily clutched her wallet, claimed her tote from the lockers at the entrance to Special Collections, and bid goodbye to the university archivist staffing the reference desk without breaking stride.

The Santa Ana winds, still howling, bent the creaking eucalypti like giant petrified men, night still a violet blue through their peeling trunks. Taking an opposite route, Emily made her way to the Widmer structure on the east end of campus. Now that she knew Jean parked in Jameson, she wanted to avoid running into her. She stopped midstride, startled by a cacophony of avian croaking. From another dimension, a flock of ravens winged in from the ocean, their blackness zigzagging against the midnight-blue sky, and settled in their perch on one of the many eaves of the eighth floor. She didn't know if it was her imagination, but one of the ravens appeared to have dipped and banked in her direction to take a look at her. Joel, without a trace of sarcasm, had informed her that the library's ravens knew the regular personnel, recognized them individually, were discomfited by the appearance of anyone new, cawed joyfully when they distinguished a familiar face in the crowd of pedestrians moving in the ant farm of the university below. She thought he was fucking with her. No, Joel was serious. Possibly, he even believed one of the ravens was the spiritual reincarnation of Nadia—a totem bird, as it were—and now Nadia was watching sentinel over the library where she had toiled thousands of hours. He did like to get high. The raven who peeled off from the flock swooped low for a closer look and screeched at Emily in apparent acknowledgment of a supernatural bond before soaring upward on furiously beating wings and disappearing into the eaves at the last region of light.

Emily drove home, her heart still palpitating. If the flash drive with all those personal email files could be measured in plutonium, her purse would have glowed on the passenger seat. She still worried over whether IT would be able to mirror her activities on her office computer. Joel would know if she asked, but she didn't want to risk compromising him any more than she already had, and she definitely didn't want to divulge what she had found, what she had done in stealthily copying the files off the server, fearful of his chastisement, anxious about losing his friendship and, now, conspiratorial support. And IT would probably have to have a legitimate reason before they backtracked on their servers and squandered the man-hours on an investigation into her activities. Would they even have the technology to go back and mirror her monitor, the erratic movements of the cursor, the copying and pasting of files from the West Collection? No way, she concluded, as she climbed out of her car in the semidarkness of the carport adjacent to her complex.

Fumbling with the key in the frustratingly tiny slot to the door of her unit, she heard a noise that sent shivers through her. Directly above her, the palm tree whose fronds had been scratching the roof when the wind blew, were flexing all their gnarly brown dead fingers, unsettling her with their strident, repetitive scraping. If she had pruning shears, she would lean a ladder against the trunk and climb to the palm's crown and dismember all the fronds that had now taken possession of her as new triggers of misophonia.

Once inside, she managed to muffle the noise by shutting the sliding glass door and quickly switching on the white noise machine she had ordered online. From the middle of the living room, Onyx raised his head, bared his fangs, and meowed, and his sounds comforted her. He flipped onto his side and rolled over on his back in anticipation of his nightly neck massage. Emily ignored him for the moment, crossed the living room into the kitchen, grabbed a Societe—the Thief—from the refrigerator, popped the cork, and filled a glass nearly full, admiring the head of foam. She took a long drink to quiet her nerves, forearming the foam that clung to her upper lip. Stepping back into the living room, she squatted down and stroked Onyx and talked to him in soothing whispers. She threw a backward glance to his food and water bowls. They didn't need attention. The scraping of the dead fronds on her roof was distant now, but because it was fainter, it annoyingly worse. She knew what was really rattling her and stood up.

Emily carried her laptop into the back bedroom to escape the grating noise. A needy Onyx followed her, broad-jumped onto the bed and fashioned himself into a ball next to her. She opened her laptop and typed in her new password: Onyx11. No one would ever figure out that one, she chuckled to herself. She stared fixedly for a moment at her screensaver. It featured a photo of Memorial Library she had snapped with her cell at twilight with the wildfires frozen like red, serrated teeth over the mortuary mountains behind. It was dramatic. Symbolic. A harbinger? She inserted the flash drive into the USB port and waited for its icon to materialize on her screen. She quickly renamed it "NF—RW."

For a long moment, Emily just stared at the icon, thumb and forefinger caressing her lips in contemplation, but soul-searching analyticity unearthed only more uncertainty. Tired of the suspense, she double-tapped the icon. The directory tree appeared just as it had on her desktop monitor at work. She directed all her attention to the screen, sipped her beer, breathed deeply in and out, in and out, trepidation seizing her. Onyx, oblivious of Emily's anxiety, looked at the world with unblinking, expressionless green eyes. She scrolled down to the deepest folder in the tree: "NF/RW_Corrs." Her heart thumped audibly in her chest. By the abbreviation "Corrs" she knew it meant correspondence and she knew who it was between. She moved the cursor over it and lightly double-tapped her touchpad again. Her screen exploded into a full page harboring a single pale blue folder icon named "2017." Still apprehensive about what she was doing, she tapped it open. Embedded in its flowering subterranean world she found individual blue folders for the months. They began in early September 2017 and progressed sequentially. Emily opened the September folder. Ordered chronologically, every day of the month, beginning from September 11, were laddered files. She double-tapped on the individual dates. A quick inspection revealed over a hundred PDF, JPEG, and MOV thumbnails blossoming into red and blue on the screen. Emily sucked in her breath, as her hand unconsciously stroked Onyx for comfort. She reached blindly for the glass on the nightstand and brought it to her lips. She sipped the cold, hoppy beer, starting—no, needing!—to get a buzz from it.

Before she opened the individual PDFs, she went forward in time to the various months in the "e-pistolary"—a neologism that Emily had herself coined for epistolary exchanges in email—correspondence. From September to October to November, the number of files multiplied almost exponentially. On one Saturday in late November alone she counted a dozen emails.

And then they abruptly stopped. Questions abounded. Her mind was dizzy with thoughts shooting in all directions. Her heartbeat quickened.

Emily was about to get out of the November folder and return to where the correspondence had begun when she noticed a file, named simply "MS." Her fingers hesitated over the touchpad. Her curiosity won out over her anxiety, and she double-tapped. The file that blossomed on the screen was a manuscript, written in first person, double-spaced and properly indented, as if its author had intended to submit it for publication one day. It was titled *My Story* (thus the "MS" file name), and Emily scrolled hurriedly through it. She scrolled and scrolled until she reached the end. It was a nearly three-hundred-page document. Judging by the explanatory opening paragraph and the highly personal nature in which it was written—the few places she stopped to scan a passage confirmed that—Emily, with fear constricting her throat, realized this was Nadia's memoir, the key, presumably, to everything that had happened, a narrative summation of the events that had come before. And it had to have been written in a veritable torrent of writing because, going by the date of the file's creation, it had to have been composed in the weeks just before she died.

Should she read *it* first or go back to the beginning of the email correspondence? Emily raised her head and let her eyes come to rest on the blank bedroom wall. Should she read it at all? It wasn't just the unethical nature of the urge, she anguished over the fact that she was prying into someone's personal life. But that someone was dead. And she had taken a lot of care to hide all these items in the dark archives. And, too, there was something plaintive, almost surreptitiously painful, about the title *My Story*. As if it were a cry in the dark, from the dark, across the crevasse of time, from the other world. After all she had gone through to reach this point, it was inconceivable to Emily that she wasn't going to cross the threshold into her predecessor's terrible truth. She already had.

Deciding that it would be less personally invasive to begin her exploration with the emails, rather than launch into what disquietingly promised to be a bombshell of a document, Emily backtracked to the September folders and let her cursor rest over the earliest dated one. She shut her eyes in contemplation. Onyx purred contentedly, oblivious of the portents forming in the room. Emily had heard one too many stories at the few Society of American Archivists conventions she had attended to instinctually know her world now teetered precariously over the uncharted abyss.

She cycled back in her mind over the past two weeks since she began working as the project archivist at Regents. The job was not a complicated one. It involved processing, describing, arranging and organizing items in the Raymond West Papers and making sure that they found their way into the properly labeled archival document boxes and that those selfsame items were cataloged and indexed for a finding aid for future scholars and researchers. If he won the Nobel, they would be converging on Memorial Library in droves, so she wanted to archive the shit out of it and hone that finding aid to perfection.

Of course, there would be other levels of double-checking by her supervisory archivist, Jean, who would go over the finding aid with a perspicacious eye. There would be time to correct misspellings, time to rearrange things if they weren't filed or indexed to her specifications. When it was done, Emily, hopefully armed with an adulatory recommendation, would move on to the next job, wherever the winds of fate blew her. She already had feelers out to Boston Public and the Congressional Library, and she knew she could always return to Harry Ransom whenever she wanted. Professor Erickson had left an open door, an unclaimed office. He liked Emily, praised her to the rafters in the recommendation for the project archivist job at Regents. She was assiduous, possessed the imagination to grasp the bigger picture, she made smart choices in economizing her time. She took her collections home with her . . . Emily stopped herself. Was this what she was doing? If she confided to Erickson that she had downloaded the e-pistolary exchange, it would seize him with terror. The consummately ethical archivist in him would rebuke her for certain, expostulate with her to stop immediately! Yes, but what would *he* do under the circumstances? Would he recklessly set off on this unapproved, unsupervised, career-jeopardizing journey? Would he want to know where the email exchange came from? Why it was there? Who put it there? Should it be listed in the finding aid? Maybe it was an innocent, albeit retina-damagingly extensive, correspondence between donor and university employee. But Emily knew those relationships were more than frowned upon; they were tacitly forbidden, professionally taboo. And yet, she knew they flourished because they were written about in articles in journals and websites devoted to the archival profession. Because in the archival world, behind all the document and record boxes, behind all the finding aids, were human beings, swept up in irrational human emotions. With some collections it was hard for archivists *not* to fall in love. With the collection. Not, God forbid, the donor. But at twenty-seven years of age, and with only a handful of years in the profession, Emily had never reached this crossroads before. Erickson never prepared her for this kind of explosive discovery, and she was scared. This was delving into the personal lives of real people, one very much living, and one very much dead.

Staring fixedly at her laptop, Emily sucked in her breath and held it deep in her lungs, tasting smoke and ash, a wave cresting and frozen before breaking. She knew she was wading into treacherous, hip-deep, fast-moving waters. Assuming her actions weren't being tracked by IT, she could always backpedal and walk away at any time, she rationalized. The fictionally suicidal archivist, who had spellbound Emily in Joel's short film, dragged her fascination into deeper and more dangerous waters. The tortured letter from the torn soul of her predecessor to, presumably, Raymond West—concealed in a book of erotica, no less!—suggested the stones that made up the footpath from initial meeting to denouement didn't cross a manicured lawn but a rickety footbridge over an abyss. If nothing else, as Emily warred in her own tortured dialectic of rationalizations for illegally—yes, illegally!—opening this correspondence and beginning its narrative, she would at least learn why the emails were hidden in the antechambers of the dark archives. Or would she? Maybe there resided a deeper truth than the salacious one Emily was anticipating. The even darker and more personal chambers that the antechambers unlocked? Doors behind doors, in room after room, beckoning with a vortical, emotional force Emily wouldn't be able to resist.

All alone with these personal archival items, Emily decided, against her prudent judgment, to trespass into the forbidden frontier. Once she started, she knew in her heart there would be no turning back. You don't drop a riveting novel after the first chapter, you don't walk out of movie a third of the way in because you're afraid of the trajectory of the director's journey.

With trepidatious heart, Emily opened the first email, realizing it had exacted a passionate, obsessive effort from someone to convert all of them into PDFs. An experienced archivist like Nadia would know how to do that. But she would also have to have a reason, a driving motivation. And then to bury them in layers of subdirectories in the dark archives so that nobody could easily find them, unless they were looking, unless they were following a treasure map . . . unless they were Emily Snow.

From: Nadia Fontaine <Nfontaine@RegentsU.edu>
To: Raymond West <Rwest_Lit@RegentsU.edu>
Subject: Faculty Club
Date: 03 September 2017

Dear Professor West,

It was a pleasure to meet you at the Faculty Club dinner. Archivists usually don't get to meet the artist whose papers they're working on. Usually they're dead, or maintain a rarefied life somewhere far away, never deigning to see what their archivist does. But that doesn't mean that our souls don't intersect through their work. We comb through the collection carefully. Sometimes we take a special interest, especially if the donor's archive comprises works we admire. And then we're vouchsafed a private view. So, when I met you briefly at the Faculty Club, it was as if I already knew you. Could you read it in my eyes? Feel it in my trembling hand as I shook yours? Because for me, I felt an electric current course through me like no other. As a writer myself—if one published book qualifies me to call myself a writer—I have such admiration for what you do, what you have accomplished. To read of your early struggles in your nakedly personal journals, well, it's inspiring. To be pulled into that undercurrent of your youthful, failed, stabs at finding your voice, it gives all of us aspiring writers hope. I do hope we might get to meet again one day, where the prying eyes of your adoring fans aren't tugging at your coat sleeves, pulling you this way and that.

Your archivist, Nadia

Emily lowered her laptop screen. She closed her eyes and tried to dream back nearly a year ago. Then she opened her eyes, lifted her screen, and decided to go to the *My Story* file in an effort to lend the email context, switching back and forth between the two as warranted. In Nadia Fontaine's mellifluous, sultry voice—the identical one from the voice-over in Joel's film—she could hear the words, was wrenched back in time to last September . . .

Nine Months Earlier

NADIA'S STORY

December 2017. I'm all alone. The first storm of winter has arrived, and I can hear the rain beating against the window in this hotel where I'm holed up. I feel like my life is over. While it's still fresh and raw in my memory, I want to record what happened. This is my story:

Last September:

The night was electric, and I was in high spirits. At a round, white-cloth table at Regents Faculty Club, I sat with Nathan, my husband, accompanied by a couple we often socialized with. I wore a low-cut black dress concealing a lacy bra that left exposed cleavage, nothing too risqué for a night out on the town, but for the Regents University Faculty Club dinner celebrating the acquisition of the Raymond West Papers I probably stood out as more than dressed up. The morning of the event I had my hair professionally styled, something I rarely treated myself to. A colleague said my side-parted look reminded him of recognizable screen beauties of the forties. At forty-one, I still possessed the power to stop a professor dead in his tracks, cause him to crane his neck over his wife's shoulders and follow my swinging, voluptuous gait retreating from his leering line of view. Twice a week I swim the half a mile from La Jolla Cove to Scripps Pier, even in the frigid winter waters. That, and my love of surfing, accounts for my sinewy shoulders, the ones that rippled out of my sleeveless dress and elicited in men fantasies of lust. My husband is a mild-mannered man with a round, bespectacled face, a PhD in engineering who had successfully ventured into the private sector, forsaking a career in academia. Mine is a world filled with art and intense devotion to work, but I am a deeply private person. Our married life teeters between the monotony of compatibility and the unremarkable, rarely devolving into the acrimonious.

Raymond West stood six foot two—I knew his exact height because in his archive there existed documents with every personal detail about him. He was casually attired in a white button-up shirt broken at the collar, a black linen coat, faded jeans, and vintage Clarks boots. I suppose if one were to compare him to celebrities, he resembled an amalgamation of Peter O'Toole and the legendary playwright Sam Shepard. His boots lifted him up another two inches, and when he was introduced by Helena Blackwell at the Faculty Club, he seemed to rise up from the VIP front table, treelike, Southern California–tanned, a wry smile creasing his face and masking a diffidence I knew all too well from poring over his journals. He looked uncomfortable as he ambled his way to the pair of steps that led to the low-rise stage.

Our table was in the center middle, the front tables reserved for the major donors and more esteemed guests who had flown in from as far away as New York to attend. The capacious room was full, over three hundred people at fifty tables, comprised of mostly the rich La Jolla elite, faculty, and alumni of Regents. The table that Raymond stood from was front and center, lit by spotlights as if floating in its own ethereal world. Wait staff threaded their way in and around the tables, refreshing guests with more wine and champagne, and changing the courses.

I paid particular notice to Elizabeth West, a regal woman with a voluminous head of blonde waves, clapping politely as her husband was introduced. Her garments were dark rich colors, tastefully bespoke. An impossibly large diamond winked from the ring finger of her left hand. When Raymond's wife rotated her head to survey the crowd, I thought of a lighthouse beacon searching dark, stormy waters for ships in danger, or shipwrecked stragglers impinging on her inviolable shore. Next to her sat a beaming Helena, who climbed down from the stage to resume her seat. It was her night as much as Raymond's, given the decades she had devoted to massaging this relationship with Elizabeth West. The night was about more than a mere announcement; it was a coronation of a personal triumph.

The Dean of Humanities, Professor John Richards, a gnomish man with a wisp of white hair, stood from his chair and shook Raymond's hand. Raymond had to bend at the waist to reach his outstretched hand and meet his crinkling smile. He folded himself into an upholstered armchair that he seemed to squirm in, then casually crossed one faded trousered leg over the other to get comfortable, his whole being restless and reluctant in the limelight. Dean Richards was wearing a tweed coat, slacks, light blue shirt and black tie. In contrast, Raymond looked the part of the literary rebel, a man who would leave the event when it was over and mount a horse waiting for him at the entrance. His tanned face lent him a rugged outdoors aspect, and the slightly tinted shades—he joked in interviews, like Jack Nicholson, he was sensitive to the lights—haloed him in a movie star's allure. He had graced the cover of many magazines, even national publications, especially after capturing the Pulitzer for *Lessons in Reality*. He was dubbed the "Voice of SoCal," and his lanky physique and shoulder-length brown locks made him look more youthful than his fifty-one years

Raymond West, microphone in hand, assumed command of the stage. Responding to Dean Richards's first question, he self-deprecatingly chronicled his modest beginnings—all of which I knew in intimate detail, of course—growing up in a middle-class San Diego subdivision, parents marking time with commonplace lives peddling real estate in the burgeoning Southern California environs. Raymond said he always valued words, but it wasn't until the age of fourteen when he read Rimbaud's *A Season in Hell* that he experienced his own epiphanic illumination. He abruptly quit surfing and stopped going to the beach, withdrew from his stoner high school friends, became a recluse, a nose buried in books night and day, an old army satchel stuffed with them wherever he went. Ostracized by his friends, and feeling alienated and all alone in the world, he traveled to Europe and hitchhiked peripatetically right after he graduated from high school. Europe broadened him, he said, and he flirted with scholarly ambitions. But the words started raining down on him like a visitation. In Europe he was writing in his head as he roamed unfamiliar, cobblestone streets, internally monologuing poems, short stories, then novels, which he transcribed furiously, always in the first person, in various youth hostels. And he read copiously. Back in San Diego, in his senior year at Regents, his first novel, he told the stunned audience, poured through him in a frenzy of writing—a thirty-day cataract of creativity that he poetically characterized as "the Drowning"—and after winning the PEN/Faulkner for best first novel, his destiny was preordained. His would be a life of words. The rest of his story was one of a meteoric rise with few stumbles, an ascent that took him vertically to ethereal literary heights, which he downplayed with his aw-shucks humility. "The blank page knows no god," he said about the difficulty he had faced with every work. To laughter he said, "The revisions kill me because I put every word, every sentence, on trial."

Dean Richards took us through a thumbnail of Raymond's writing life, then the man whose papers I had been working on for six intense months turned to the audience to field questions. With his tinted eyewear, he could have been looking anywhere in the crowd, but I truly believed he was directing his words to me—as if he had divined something! as if a fulguration of synchronicity had wedded our minds in that moment forever—when he said in a drawling articulacy, "I'm not sure where the ideas come from. I usually start with an emotion, or an emotional beat. My characters are born from emotion. But they originate in real life—sometimes to the dismay of those who recognize themselves in my books." Scattered laughter greeted what all his fans knew: he drew personally from relationships and he didn't spare anyone, he didn't bowdlerize himself, he abhorred self-censorship. "They're all roman à clefs," he finished, throwing out his arms as if, in the velocity of his creative force he was only a mere medium through which these ideas sluiced. "I extract from the personal, then I fictionalize from there according to my needs." Raymond lowered his handsome head, gazed down, and smiled. "My lovely wife Elizabeth was the first to read my debut novel." He paused for dramatic effect. "She advised me, in no uncertain terms—to burn it." Laughter exploded deafeningly in the room. Elizabeth blushed an embarrassed smile, lowered her gaze to her lap and shook her head. "You were wrong on that one, dear." He pointed a joking accusatory finger at her. She raised her proud head and nodded in agreement. More laughter echoed. "But it was personal," he admitted, as if to excuse his wife's harsh reaction to his first novel that brought him fame, if not fortune. "And it must have been hard for her to read," he said conciliatorily. "However, you can never write with the shackles of what other people are going to think. It was a valuable lesson. And I thank my wife for pushing me to the edge of despair, because I loved her, and I valued her opinion, but I knew I had to persevere or else forever rue the day I abandoned *The Decision*." He paused. I imagined our heads floated above the crowd and met somewhere the air was thinner. "Her editorial was insightful, however. Once she came around." The ensuing laughter brought me back down to reality. I'm ashamed to admit, I was enjoying his ridiculing of his wife.

Listening to him speak, I was captivated by his every word, as if I could visualize his hand clutching a pen and scrawling feverishly in one of his Moleskines. That night I melted into a world that was only me and Raymond West. It wasn't sexual, it wasn't even emotional; it was aesthetical. My husband and the couple seated with us had been unwittingly abandoned to an alternate universe—this was not their world; it was mine, and goddamn it, I was going to claim it. When I ventured to look at them—the few times I did out of politeness—it was as if they were secondary characters in a movie where the sound was muted. Their laughter was all lopsided faces, their chatter indistinct murmurings. Unbeknownst to them, I had fashioned in my reality, one wholly separate from theirs and the rest of the attendees, a secret tunnel to Raymond West. When he talked about his youth growing up in San Diego, I could fill in the blanks better than anyone in the room because I had read every word of his early journals of the *poète maudit* in the making, the Sturm und Drang of those callow years coming alive to me in a melding of spirit (words) and flesh (the man). I knew the names of all his lovers, or most of them, the ones he had received heartbroken letters from. In one of the first record cartons I unboxed, I had found a list of all of them, complete with dates and time spent together, what they were like as lovers, often in cringe-worthy graphic detail. The list stopped with Elizabeth. The list—but not the affairs. I knew things she didn't know unless she had personally curated his collection, and that I doubted. There were moments during the lively Q&A when I desperately wanted to insert myself into the conversation and remind him of a time and get his elaboration on a personal detail, but I knew it would be boundary-crossing, especially with Helena seated like a traffic cop between us. I desired him to go deeper, to color in the adumbration that Dean Richards, lacking the intimate knowledge I possessed, was skating over. I wished *I* could have been the host. The questions I could have asked him, the answers I might have elicited. The depths I could have taken him to. I found myself leaning forward out of my chair when Dean Richards asked Raymond about his process.

"I let the book build in me, until it becomes like a great pressure." He cupped his hands and held them tightly together near his chin. "I start to see the characters and hear their voices. From there, a narrative starts to take shape. Then"—he raised a single index finger—"I have to have an ending. I will not write without an ending. I do not want to—cannot!—set off on a journey and strand myself in an emotional desert. I need to know where I'm going. I believe in story, I'm resolutely of the belief that I have to have resolution. Once that process has all formed up here"—he touched an index finger to his temple—"and in here"—he placed a hand on his heart—"there's now a blueprint, inchoate as it is. Then I buy these large, black Moleskine notebooks and go into what I literally and figuratively refer to as the Drowning. I write—in longhand—all morning, take a short lunch, write all afternoon, have dinner, then write until ten thirty or eleven. This now all happens at a little oasis I have in Del Mar where I can be lulled by the waves. I sleep there when I'm in the Drowning. Elizabeth loves it because she gets a reprieve from my snoring for a month!" Laughter reverberated in the room. When the laughter died, Raymond concluded, "Thirty days for *The Decision*, my first novel. It all comes out of me like a fire hose turned all the way open. I lived and breathed that book in those thirty days like the most explosive, most exhilarating love affair a person could ever experience. It ends with exhaustion, depletion, a feeling of being emptied out in a way that's hard to describe. A part of you has died in the birthing. It's a part of you that you will never get back again. But you have the book as a record. And now, to know that record is here at Regents, here for however many years before the pages yellow and disintegrate into carbon, is the reward, the reminder that you created something that is not ephemeral. At least you hope not."

His words left me breathless, my face flushed, my . . . I am the designated caretaker of those words. I have read the Moleskines of *The Decision* in West's distinctive cursive and have voyaged with him vicariously to those fictional lands. I, and few others, have taken that journey with him. In that reading, and other readings of his work—which caused the processing of his papers to go on far longer than it should have taken—I have delved into his soul in a way that no one else has, and in that moment, as he spoke, I felt a kinship to him that was inviolably ours and ours alone. An invisible wire streamed a powerful electric current across the room, connecting him to me, and at any moment I thought it was going to overload and burst into flames, and everyone would see that I had fallen in love.

I was lifted out of my chair and cast adrift on a cloud and all I could see was the man whose papers I was lovingly processing and arranging and organizing and cataloging and foldering, and the nimbus that enhaloed him. It wasn't his fame; it was his words. It wasn't that I was physically attracted to him—and I was—it was that he emanated a humility and a tenderness, qualities that most of his fans wouldn't associate with his work. He used the word *truth* frequently. And *soul.* And *intimate being.* Before this night, his work had taken me where I had never been taken before. His presence only validated both my professional, and personal, exploration of his work. My heart beat furiously. From that point forward, I was no longer married to my husband.

I barely heard Dean Richards ask Raymond, "One final question: What are you working on now?"

Raymond grew suddenly introspective. With his gaze on the feet, he nodded to himself as if trying to promote the seed of an answer. He seemed uncharacteristically at a loss for words. Part of me wanted to rush across the room and hug him because I knew where he was. I knew he had found himself adrift in a proverbial Sargasso Sea, eddying in circles. I knew he was lost, and I wanted to save him.

"We haven't seen a book from you in five years, I believe," Dean Richards remarked, oblivious of the fact that—to me!—this rankled deep down in the twisted suffering of his soul. I was probably the only one in the room privy to his aborted attempts because it was I who printed them out from digital files and foldered them and assigned them descriptions. It was I who had charted his soul and no one else. "What are you working on now?" Dean Richards persisted.

Raymond pursed his lips. He raised his head. His eyes, covered by the lenses of his tinted glasses, searched the crowd. He wrestled in his silence for an answer. I remember he smiled wryly, self-deprecatingly. "The floodplains are dry," he managed. "Those voices and stories and words that once came to me in a veritable inundation seemed to have diminished to a trickle. There are brief flashes, little coruscations, and I let myself go there, but it doesn't build like it once used to . . ." He trailed off in a tone of solemn fatalism, self-effacingly honest to the last breath, and what I loved him for. "When is the artist used up? I don't know. These thoughts oppress me, haunt me. Am I now just a turnstile of recycled ideas?" He shrugged. "Barren? I don't know. Inspiration is a mercurial thing."

In an effort to conclude on an upbeat note, Dean Richards added, "Well, maybe your next book will be about artistic rejuvenation."

"Yes, maybe." Raymond affected a smile, hearing the audience silenced and the mood in the crowd growing a little too sepulchral for a man who had only minutes ago been charmingly risible. "Yes, for sure, I need to fall in love with an idea all over again. I'm not finished."

I need to fall in love with an idea all over again. My head exploded. *I will be the seed to your rain.*

A smattering of applause and, breaking my connection with Raymond, the fulsome laughter of Helena exploded, like that unwanted party guest who breaks up intimate conversations just when they're heating up and amorous fantasies are forming. Helena's disingenuous expressions and garish laughter reminded me that she was the reason I had almost not been here to see the man whose work I had immersed my soul in for over half of year. Presiding over the reference desk, stationed next to Helena's cluttered office, I had eavesdropped on a conversation about a Faculty Club dinner featuring Raymond West and the announcement of his collection, the collection I was actively processing! I was infuriated. Did Helena fear that I would steal the limelight if I came? Maybe that's why tonight I wore my most revealing dress, applied more makeup than I had in months. In defiance of Helena. Humiliatingly, I was forced to go online to learn the details of the event. I couldn't believe I hadn't been invited! Me. His archivist. At first I thought I would go by myself but then decided, so as not to arouse suspicions—as if already knowing that I was going to get what I wanted!—that I would make a night of it and invite my husband and Julian and Marina. Not to arouse suspicions that I had already begun to form a fantasy that I would seduce him.

Though Raymond West's novels displayed flashes of humor, they were celebrated more for their literary sublimity, self-insertion of the first person, and their courageous mining of autobiographical content. They teemed and roiled with longing, heartbreak, and despair, as if Raymond were forever seeking something that he yearned for but hadn't found. The vicissitudes of his life had been quarried for every last nugget of refinable ore and it was as if he was insinuating that it was time to close the mine. Even after his marriage to scion Elizabeth in his late twenties, his novels seemed to grow bleaker. It was as if he were spurning the good fortune that Elizabeth had brought him, the good fortune that every aspiring writer dreamed of: having the freedom to wake and write every day without fretting over the quotidian struggle of earning a living. It wasn't until the Pulitzer that his works brought him money along with international recognition. But it was as if he always wanted to disavow the notion, bruited about in literary academia, that he was a writer of privilege, the insinuation being that he might not have climbed to such Olympian literary heights were it not for the support of his wife. In his journals, I had read entry after entry where he bemoaned being thought of as a bird trapped in a gilded cage. This perception picked at him like a scavenger bird, perhaps so much that when Dean Richards asked him what he was currently working on, he shrugged, let his chin sag to his chest, and opened up in his inimitably personal way. "I might be all dried up, John," he replied in his caramel drawl. "Literary recognition has maybe brought me to a desertification of the soul." *Desertification. Soul.*

"Maybe you raised the bar too high," Dean Richards remarked, when

Raymond complained that he had summited pinnacles he had never expected.

"I can't kneel anymore and pick the low-hanging fruit," Raymond said in brutal candor. "If the work doesn't hoist me to a place I've never been, if it doesn't kick open doors to new frontiers, new vistas, horizons unexplored, then I'm just penning obituaries of my past, aren't I?" he ended pensively, self-defeatedly I thought, with sinking, empathetic heart. "So now they're offering me screenwriting work!" he said in a rising tone. The audience, relieved, roared with laughter. "They're paying me handsomely to disembowel my own work."

At this point I was three glasses of wine to uninhibited, felt my face flush hot. Tears had moistened my eyes, and I brushed them away with the back of my hand. My husband touched me lightly on the shoulder in sympathy as if he understood. No, he couldn't understand that my heart was flushing out—and now raining jubilant water—on the desertification of *my* soul.

Dean Richards thanked Raymond West for coming, acknowledged the audience for making it another successful sell-out Faculty Club dinner—"Even Rushdie didn't sell out," he joked—and thanked Raymond for donating his papers to Regents, underscoring for emphasis, "And we hope it will be a collection that continues to grow and that you will be adding many more works to it."

The audience applauded enthusiastically for a local celebrity. More than half rose from their chairs with clapping hands raised aloft. Elizabeth remained seated, applauding politely, her hands looking diminutive framed by the blown tumbleweed of hair that crowned her slim figure.

I leaned across the table and informed my party that I was going to go say hi. "I've never met him," I lied, because I had met him once before, if glancingly. "This is the first time I've actually seen him in person, can you believe it?" I hoped my enthusiasm would come across as nothing more than an excited archivist with the rare opportunity to meet a donor.

"You've never met?" asked an incredulous Marina. "But you're his archivist, aren't you?"

I nodded, pushed back my chair, clambered nervously to my feet, and, heart leapfrogging lily pads floating on a lake of deepening desire, threaded my way through the guests to the front of the room where faculty and alumnae were already converging on Raymond, many clutching first editions in their hands, eager for West's autograph. In the bustling crowd I furtively rooted out a compact and quickly looked at my face in the tiny mirror. I combed back my shoulder-length raven-black hair with splayed fingers, moistened a finger with the tip of my tongue and corrected a smudge of deep crimson lipstick, bold against my skin. I widened my eyes and fixed my gaze on them, studying their blazing brown intensity, as if I was looking for that woman I longed to be. When I looked back up, I felt luminous, I dared him to not single me out as someone who had a special connection to him.

The semicircular crowd thronged three deep at the knee-high stage that Raymond had stepped down from to mingle with his fans and colleagues. Centered among them, he was sequoia-like, incongruously larger than the media images of him, in contrast to many other celebrities, who appeared smaller and less incandescent in real life than was fictionally displayed on the big screen. Raymond didn't need up-angles or diffused lighting to emanate a magnetism that was both infectious and palpably real.

As the crowd surged forward, I pushed with it, elbows flared, as if it were a wave I had paddled into and was now warning other surfers with my body language and glowering expression not to snake me.

Raymond spotted me, the mystery woman in black, the one who had pierced the center of the crowd, an osprey, wings folded, plummeting out of the sky, talons of hope deployed, hope that he wouldn't be disappointed, that he wouldn't treat me like the others, disingenuously polite smiles and obligatory thank-yous, a warm or clever remark scribbled on their books, moving mechanically in a succession to receive all his well-wishers before he was whisked off by a woman of wealth to a seaside house where the booming surf drowned out the spotlight he openly detested. No. He saw me, and he froze!

When I reached the front of the receiving line, I offered Raymond an outstretched hand, a head tilted to one side, hair cascading over bare shoulders, and a crooked smile that I feared radiated to him the pounding of my heart. I looked him straight in the face with an unblinking gaze, defying him to break eye contact. Up close, finally, I could see through the translucent neutral tint of his sunglasses to the sea-blue of his eyes, which glinted like mica when he blinked me into focus.

"Hi," I greeted him breathlessly, "I'm Nadia Fontaine, the archivist on your collection."

I'll never forget this as long as I live. Raymond raised a hand and lowered his glasses dramatically from the bridge of his nose. He studied me for the longest moment, in the tumult of that buzzing crowd, with lambent eyes, visibly taken off guard, a curare-tipped dart having struck his chest and paralyzed him momentarily. "My archivist?" His words dripped on me like the blood from the flesh where my talons had landed and clawed his heart.

"Yes. Nadia Fontaine," I repeated nervously. My heart was beating clamorously, the excitement sped my pulse. Blood rose to my face and colored it, I imagined, a crimson to compete with my lips. I blurted out words in a veritable torrent, aware my time with him in this setting was preciously short, fearful I might utter something I had been speaking in my head. "I've read everything you've written," I sputtered, in a fluster of pent-up elation. "Letters. Journals. Everything."

Raymond's eyes leveled on mine and locked. The crowd ceased to exist when he said, "Then you know me better than I do," as if my words were a revelation that left him speechless. I had hoped for better; I had hoped for more. I knew a wealth about him. Not only from reading his work; I knew his most intimate thoughts. I could recognize his handwriting at a cursory glance, pick it out from a dozen samples in an instant, unmistakably. Tell him exactly where he had a mole on his chest from photographs of him: Raymond in his swimming trunks, Raymond at work, Raymond accepting a prestigious literary award. I was an archivist who had swum deep into Raymond's world. Studied him like a doctoral student. Worshiped him as a writer with the zeal of a believer. To walk up and shake his hand, to feel its warmth and perspiry flesh.

I was oblivious of the clamor around me when he leaned forward and whispered into my ear, "You're my eavesdropping angel, aren't you?"

His warm breath clung to my ear. I could feel my face color hot at his words. Expecting nothing, I had never heard anything as beautiful in all my life. Something aroused in me, like a cat waking to the pangs of a hunger that was more than a cry for mere sustenance. I could feel the crowd importuning behind me, shoving to get in front, calling me to a reality that was the quicksand of my unfulfilled Sisyphean life toiling in virtual obscurity. I stood stock still, refusing to cede ground.

"Your eyes," he said, in a voice as if we were the only two in the Faculty Club. "They're slightly different shades. Or am I imagining things?"

I shook my head. "One is slightly off brown. No one ever notices," I stammered.

"Beautifully unusual," he said. "I must give that trait to a character someday."

"Thank you," I blushed, then recovered. "You should come down to Special Collections and have a look at your archive," I managed as casually as I could, letting go his hand—but not wanting to!—and passing him a staff business card, which he discreetly palmed and slipped into his coat pocket. "I have a few questions for you, actually."

"Okay. I promise," he drawled, molasses in his voice, desire twinkling in his pale blue eyes that ever so subtly tried to drink me in with the seconds remaining before suspicions would be aroused. We exchanged knowing smiles that seemed suspended in time—or was it my imagination?

An arm with a book was thrust rudely over my shoulder. With a smile on my face, I could feel myself growing lost in his transfixing, burning stare, the one now lost and drifting back out to sea. My talons had sunk and momentarily stunned their prey. Our eyes locked like powerful magnets one last fleeting second, but long enough for me to know: he couldn't resist me.

The crowd of admirers pressing toward him was now inexorably jettisoning me away, like a scene in one of those movies they don't make anymore. I was sucked back into the vortex, my eyes concentrating on his as he lifted his sunglasses back to the bridge of his nose—his unshielded eyes only for me! Only I know your depths, I spoke silently. *Only! I! Know! Your! Soul!* I fiercely ventriloquized through my still unblinking eyes. Until finally, the crowd separated me from Raymond, my husband's gentle hand touched my shoulder, his familiar voice spoke, and I was reeled back to a reality that I had already left.

The next morning, I found this in my inbox:

From: Raymond West <Rwest_Lit@RegentsU.edu>
To: Nadia Fontaine <Nfontaine@RegentsU.edu>
Subject: Re: Your Visit to Special Collections
Date: 04 September 2017

Dear Ms. Fontaine,

It was a pleasure to meet you. I'm thrilled you came to the event. I'm sorry if I didn't say anything too profound. Sorry, too, if I was remiss in knowing that a single, and singular, archivist had been assigned to my papers. I suppose I assumed all my writings would just be stored away in some catacomb of the library, the boxes scrawled with Sharpies, waiting one day for some ambitious PhD candidate to unearth them and write a pointless book on me and how I sanctified the flesh over the intellect, or some such rubbish that we in academia are prone to squander our time on. But, no, my work has been archived by an individual... and one as lovely as you!

So, yes, I accept your invitation to come down and see what you've done with my scribblings. Let me know what's a good time for you.

Raymond

I was overcome with joy that he had taken my invitation seriously, written back and with such alacrity. I replied and asked him to meet me at 6:00 p.m., near the time I got off. I hoped that Helena would be gone, knowing that West's appearance in Special Collections would cause a stir, incite tongues to wag. Perhaps, I fantasized, I could talk Raymond into a drink at Manny's. Perhaps we would stay in Special Collections until it shut down, and it would just be the two of us in the thrumming silence, discussing literature and art, topics I was dying to engage in, so desperate had I become in my search for an intellectual equal.

I devoted a little extra time to my attire that morning, tight black jeans and a midnight-blue, V-necked silk blouse rolled to the elbows, that I always received compliments on. My husband left early, giving me a routine peck on the cheek. When I heard the door close and his car start up and drive off, I felt liberated to run riot with my fantasy. When Nathan was around, I felt stifled. His ears seemed to be tuned to my comings and goings, and he had an annoying habit of asking me to chronicle my day, when the truth, if expressed, would have spoiled his. We tried couples' counseling, but it hadn't bridged the chasm of two lives that had long ago bifurcated. He made an effort to be less intrusive, but some habits between couples were difficult to unwind. We quickly retreated into the familiar because that's where we felt most comfortable. I felt hollowed out by my marriage. I had broken free several times, once experimented with a six-month clandestine affair, but it was not one I was proud of, and I shook off its distasteful memory as I fed my cat Clarice and left the house, sailing on the exhilaration I was going to get to spend time alone with Raymond.

Jean and Helena were skirmishing loudly when I made my way into Special Collections. Catching snippets of conversation, I gleaned they were embroiled in a contentious argument over something to do with one of Jean's new software organizational tools and Helena's Luddite disdain for the introduction of any new system promising to disrupt the old one. I tuned them out as I settled into my office, a smile creasing my face as I looked up at my bulletin board and saw Raymond's picture pinned to it. I had to hear about the Helena/Jean fracas from an intrusive Chloe, who always came by to say good morning, but Chloe's gossip was deflected away by her suspicion of loyalties in the department and whom to trust. I debated telling Chloe that West was coming in for a visit, float by her what Helena or Jean would think of such an unceremoniously, last-minute planned appointment. Would Helena think I was going behind her back if she discovered we had already emailed each other without cc'ing her? She may have been reluctant to accept the changing times, instead adhering to old protocols like a barnacle to its treasured hull.

Concluding there was no choice, I knocked lightly on the frame to Helena's open door. My eyes swept the floor and the visitors' chairs. They were littered with piles of papers and folder files spilling documents in the disorganization that was Helena's signature rebuke to the organization that typically characterized the profession. She wasn't an archivist by profession, I sneered to myself, she was an administrator, the self-appointed head of a department, and a discipline, that had outrun her intellectual grasp of it. But her power at Memorial was daunting, and her office bore witness to the fact she lived and breathed Special Collections & Archives, with the emphasis on *lived.*

"Can I have a word with you, Helena?" I asked.

Helena raised her eyes from the clutter that obscured her desk. "Come in, Nadia," she said affably, because she liked me, because she knew I had one foot in her world where we both still believed in the value of archiving with the meticulous eye of a philologist, and the human touch of someone trained in the ways that still valued the instinctual in an archivist. Helena half stood, then sat back down, realizing she would have to thread her way through books and hillocks of folders to reach me for a proper greeting.

I wordlessly cleared folders from a chair, neatly set them on the floor, and sat down. I worked up a smile. "It was good to see Professor West the other night," I began.

"Yes. I was glad you could make it," Helena said, ignoring the salient fact that she had deliberately, I suspected, not informed about the dinner. Was she jealous of my youth? my looks? the scuttlebutt that I was tapped to assume her position as director of Special Collections when retirement or a catastrophic event crowbarred her from the only world she had ever known?

"Yes. I'm glad I found out about it," I said, my sarcasm undetected, still rankled by her passive-aggressive attempt to keep me from meeting Raymond West in the flesh. "I shouldn't have to go online to find out that the donor whose papers I'm processing is speaking here at the university," I said, to awaken her to my hurt.

"It slipped my mind. I didn't think you'd be interested. Besides, I thought you didn't like university functions."

"Helena. I'm the archivist on this project. Have been for six months. And I'm a SAA fellow now," I reminded her.

"I know! Congratulations on becoming a fellow." She had a shifty, practiced way of sidestepping the uncomfortable.

"Anyway. Water under the bridge. The reason I came in was to alert you to the fact that West said he might stop by for a visit."

"When?" Helena inquired, leaning forward, mildly alarmed.

I knew damn well when, but instead I shrugged. "Just said he might drop by sometime. I know you like to know about these things."

"How did *you* find out?"

"I introduced myself to him last night as his archivist," I said defiantly. "He casually mentioned he would be interested in seeing the work I've done." I swallowed hard and cast my eyes to the windowed wall. "He emailed me directly," I confessed.

When I looked back, Helena was staring at me with frozen green eyes. My announcement had unsettled her. "Well, I wish he would tell me these things."

"I'm sure he's very busy. And he probably assumed I would tell you." I stood. "And I just did."

"Thank you," Helena bristled.

"I think he's curious what we do down here. Plus, I have a few questions for him."

"What?" Helena barked.

"Just some clarification on a few items in the collection."

I turned and left Helena to chew over this piece of information as I returned to my cubicle down the hall, a tingling of excitement mounting inside me. I sat down and brought up a video of Raymond's Faculty Club dinner that had already been posted on the staff website and watched it for a few minutes before deciding that I didn't want to be caught in the act of reveling in my burgeoning infatuation.

The hours crawled by in anticipation of Raymond's visit. I buried myself in his collection, paying overzealous attention to an early handwritten manuscript I had already read, an abandoned book chronicling his university years' romantic exploits. Deliciously titillating. Engrossing afternoon reading after a morning of answering departmental emails.

Sometime after lunch, Jean poked her micromanaging head into my cubicle. "I hear West might be coming in for a visit."

"Word gets around," I needled her. "Yeah. He mentioned something to that effect," I added nonchalantly, without looking up immediately from a draft of his book of erotica. I set the Moleskine on my lap and raised my head to Jean. I wasn't fond of her, and she knew it. Nobody was. She was devoid of the soul of a pure archivist and instead had the gnat-like qualities of a hovering micromanager. As the Supervisory Archivist she was senior to me, but as an employee of the university for a longer stretch, I knew things that could quickly put Jean in her place, and Jean didn't test *those* waters. Technically, we were both archivists, but we came from different spheres, graduated with different undergraduate degrees, and improbably intersected at the junction of the same profession. Worse, she harbored ambitions to succeed Helena and sized me up as an obstruction to her goal.

"I like your blouse," Jean complimented. "Miyake?"

"I don't know, Jean. I don't look at labels."

"I don't see you get dressed up that often."

I studied her for a moment, ferreting for the subtextual in her expressionless face. Was she being snarky? "I have an early dinner date," I lied. I forced a smile to let her know that was all the information she was going to get.

Jean pointed at my corkboard. With her index finger she sketched in the air the way it once was, the way she remembered it. "You took some pictures down."

"Did I?" I threw an obligatory backward glance. "I don't remember."

"You used to have pictures of your wedding up there."

I glowered at her, eyes burning through hers, silently seething, letting her know she shouldn't cross into my personal space. She must have gotten the message because she unfastened her gaze from my board.

"How's West coming?" she asked.

"Right on schedule, Jean," I answered with histrionic buoyancy, annoyed at the oft-repeated question. "Wrapping up. If it wasn't for all the interruptions, I would probably be done."

"Ha-ha."

"Is Helena still here?" I asked.

"No. She's left for the day."

"Another one of her fabulous Town and Gowns?" I said, impersonating Helena's high-pitched voice. Mirthless Jean barely cracked a smile. Even when I tried to lighten the mood it was futile. "I hope she raises more money so we can all get a raise," I joked, in a conscious attempt to slacken the wires of tension that were always drawn taut when we interacted.

"I hope so too." Jean slung the strap of her purse over her shoulder. "I'm going. Got to pick up my kids."

I exhaled with relief at Jean's departure. Her retreating footsteps were like the melody of a song I loved to hear over and over again. A glance at the clock indicated that I was now mostly alone in Special Collections. Occupational fatalist that I am, I obsessively checked my cell for emails, momentarily depressed that Raymond might not honor his appointment with me. I put pen to my personal file and scribbled some notes that had been lurking on the penumbra of my mind before Jean's interruption me. I obsessed for a few moments over Jean's noticing that I had taken down my wedding photo. Happier times best left to the dustbin of memories was my reasoning. And, guiltily, I wanted my life to be tabula rasa when Raymond came calling.

It was freezing in Special Collections. I shivered and pulled my black cashmere cardigan over my designer blouse. Jean had noticed what I was wearing. Yeah, it was fucking Miyake, so what? Was she fashioning an incriminating narrative too?

I was so intent on what I was reading that I reared back like a startled horse, threw a hand to my breast, and exhaled air when I saw Raymond West standing in the open entrance to my cubicle, Deborah smiling beside him, the top of her head barely reaching his shoulders. "I have a guest for you," Deborah said in hushed tones.

I blushed and caught my breath. "You scared me."

"Didn't mean to," Raymond said in his sonorous baritone where each word was enunciated as if chiseled from marble. A warm smile crinkled the corners of his eyes. He was wearing a long-sleeve black T-shirt that clung to his flat stomach and fell to his trademark faded blue jeans. Beige Clarks boots lent the impression he'd prefer adventuring in some remote corner of the earth time had forgotten instead of parking himself behind a desk and baring his soul over another Pulitzer Prize winner.

"I'll leave the two of you," Deborah said softly, her eyes widened conspiratorially at me behind his shoulder as she backed away.

An indescribable excitation trembled in me as I rose, reached for the back of a visitor's chair, and rolled it in front of him. "Sit down," I said. "I'm glad you came."

Raymond eased himself into the chair. "I would always keep a promise to my archivist," he said, winking one eye. Pausing for dramatic impact, he added, "Now that I know who she is."

Our narrowed eyes coupled with mutually interpretative looks, burning into each other, flashing with flirtation while suppressing smiles, gleaming viscid with palpable desire. Last night's sparks were not an aberration, I thought, relieved. I could still feel his warm breath in my ear when he said, "You're my eavesdropping angel, aren't you?" The immediate, tectonic, attraction foundered all the professional barriers I had come to erect after nearly a dozen years in Special Collections. We had just met and we were already out of the harbor, sails billowing, I wildly fantasized, and could glimpse the white-capped oceans beckoning to us. "I wasn't assigned your papers," I broke the silence. "I requested it," I finished definitively, never once losing eye contact with him.

He held my gaze. "I'm glad you did. But I believe, if I have my story straight, my wife asked for you."

The mention of his wife momentarily bled the mystery from my fantasy, and I worked up a smile in response. Was he trying to dampen the mood, or was he just summoning up the reality that we would inevitably have to face?

"But of course, I didn't tell her I was coming to meet you," he added, tugging me playfully back down into the romantic fantasy and eliciting an embarrassed smile.

"Oh? Why not?" I asked in my most sultry of voices.

Raymond made a gesture with his hand as if stating the obvious. "A woman as preternaturally beautiful as you? Delving deep into my writings?" He leaned forward and lowered his voice. "Inhabiting my soul?" His eyes leveled on me until I had to pry mine away for fear of spontaneous combustion.

I fleetingly debated telling him Helena already knew he had planned to come, but I didn't want to douse the flames of my excitement with the extinguisher of *my* reality. When I looked back at him, he was still leaning forward and staring fixedly at me. "I'm married too," I found myself confiding.

"Well, then, good," he said. "We have nothing to worry about."

We shared a mordant laugh that erupted spontaneously and seemed to break the ice.

"Marriage is a tough gig," he said.

I lifted my eyes to his. Like mourning doves, who mate for life, we seemed to know something that no one else knew by locking eyes. His life's work and my profession had auspiciously collided, I wanted to believe in my heart, in a kind of strange but humanly bound synchronicity. Where it intersected was instantaneously profound, heightened not by its serendipity but by whom we both were at that moment in space and time. I could feel him drawing toward me and he wasn't even moving. I could feel him hypnotized by my longing, and I hadn't even voiced it. If I closed my eyes, I could feel my hands pressed against his chest and my lips pressing against his full mouth, his hands clutching my ass and hoisting me up in the air and toward him like a dream I had dreamed in another life.

He glanced at the pile of Moleskines that he clearly recognized on my auxiliary desk. "How deep have you gone into my work?" he asked.

"As deep and dark as one could go," I said, enunciating each word. I let my eyes linger on his as my words throbbed in the silence that ensued.

Raymond smiled sheepishly. "I imagine that others in your profession wouldn't have taken such a . . . personal interest."

I bit my lip and slowly shook my head from side to side, an invitation not to stop.

"All those journals?" he asked.

I nodded up and down a couple times for emphasis, smiling knowingly. "You were a bad, bad boy, Raymond." I lifted the Moleskine next to my keyboard and shook it at him. "*An Ocean of True Feeling*?"

Raymond smiled self-consciously at the embarrassingly trite title and closed his eyes as if traveling back in time. "One of those youthful indiscretions." When he opened them, he came face to face with me, this woman who had chronicled his life's work, and he tried to reconstruct the journey I had taken, the islands where I had harbored, the turbulent storms I must have weathered. "I had no conception of how deep an archivist dived into a collection," he admitted.

"I took a special interest in this one," I said unhesitatingly. "Was getting fucking sick of the Language Poets."

He laughed and then looked at me warmly. Was it my imagination or were tears blurring his eyes? "I meant what I said the other night." He waited until my eyes had adjusted to his. "You really are my eavesdropping angel."

My heart disintegrated at his words. They were like a christening, acknowledging my role in the work I had done on his papers, his life work, and conferring on me a gratitude an archivist rarely experiences. It made me feel appreciated, wanted, needed, by a man who presumably didn't need anyone, his talent the solid foundation on which his whole life rested and successfully revolved.

I stirred impatiently in my chair. "Would you like to see your sarcophagi? What your *eavesdropping angel* has done with your life's work?"

Raymond smiled wearily. He wanted to go with me, he would follow me anywhere, but maybe just then he didn't want to be presented with the corporeal image of his life's work ensconced in archival boxes, his soul reduced to the heavy solidity of paper, sectioned by folders, cataloged by abstruse codes, chronologically and categorically dismantled so the world could now find him at any given place in his artistic trajectory. I sensed that he wanted to go with me, just not where I was offering to take him. But he hadn't yet surrendered to the paradise where I really wanted to take the both of us.

We rose together from our chairs out of a lacuna of nascent desire and profanely forming dreams. Raymond stepped aside, outstretched his hand, and let me turn and slip past him. I shifted unavoidably toward him on the way out, and my sweater brushed his T-shirt, and I smelled the faint odor of a scent I had never encountered, and I suddenly wanted to burrow into him, the closeness was that intense. In the corridor I threw him a backward glance, but I had to angle my head to the ceiling to meet his eyes boring downward into mine. "This way," I instructed, leading the way.

In two strides he caught up with me, before slowing his pace and matching mine half-stride for stride. His head towered over me. A glance brought back his face from the countless photos of him I had cataloged in the collection—but it was alive with moving expressions now.

"What was it like to win the Pulitzer?" I found myself asking, as we approached the locked door to the stacks.

"It was surreal," he said. "I didn't believe it when they called."

I dropped my eyes. "I was at Columbia when you gave your speech."

"You were?" he said, surprised.

I nodded. "I was doing my PhD in comparative lit."

"Didn't want to teach?"

I shook my head. "Loathe departmental politics."

Raymond laughed sardonically and shook his head. "Boy, do I know."

"I wanted to meet you, but I was too intimidated to initiate anything, not knowing . . ." I trailed off and looked up at him, seeking reassurance. His eyes were riveted on mine. My pulse accelerated.

I keyed in a number, then pressed down on a lever and pushed open the door. "Welcome to the final resting place of the Raymond West Papers."

"I feel dead already," he said.

I laughed and escorted him into the stacks, the restricted-access section of Special Collections & Archives. I deliberately slowed my pace, conspiring in my galloping heart to draw out the moment. The light grew more tenebrous, and shadows fell on us as we glided between the metal shelving lined with pebbled, gray document boxes meticulously and uniformly labeled. We walked single file along the narrow corridor. I could feel his presence brushing my back like a ghost.

"The lights are kept low for preservation reasons," I said.

"I'm glad. It'll make me look as young as the guy in the picture you have pinned to your bulletin board."

My wine-colored lips parted to an embarrassed smile. "I always have a picture of whose collection I'm processing," I said unconvincingly.

"Oh. And I mistakenly thought I was special."

"Yours might stay up after I'm finished. I'm going to miss you," I said plaintively. "We don't get collections like yours often. Plus, the fact that you're still alive." Without breaking my stride, I tossed him a backward glance. "Most of the collections I'm assigned are people who are dead, you know."

"I didn't. I'm just learning about the archival world." I could see him looking with a keen curiosity all around at the rows upon rows of boxes arrayed on the shelves. "A fascinating world."

"And this is only the analog part of the collection," I explained, as we continued to descend into deepening zones of literary greatness. "And then there's the dark archives."

"The dark archives?" he asked, intrigued.

I came to a stop, dwarfed by shelving laden with document boxes stacked floor to ceiling, and gazed up at Raymond with batting eyes, dreaming he would kiss me. "That's where everything goes that we haven't decided what to do with, or items that might compromise the donor, or . . ."

"Or?"

"Items that someone decided to preserve, for the sake of your collection, that might otherwise be destroyed."

"For instance?"

"*An Ocean of True Feeling.*"

Raymond's face disorganized into laughter. "Please. Don't remind me. I'm mortified enough."

"But you wrote terribly convincingly about transgressive . . . love," I teased.

"I was smart enough not to submit it. Obviously not smart enough to destroy it."

"I'm glad you didn't." I came to a halt in the middle of an aisle flanked by two ceiling-high rows of shelves. "Here we are." I extended an arm. "The Raymond West Papers. Seventy-seven linear feet."

Raymond took a slow, deep breath and followed the imaginary line I indicated with narrowed eyes, tinted glasses dangling from one hand, suddenly choked with emotion at the soldier-like display of all the boxes that constituted his papers. He raised a hand to his mouth and blinked rapidly. His eyes closed as if he was gathering up the years into a single moment of impossible reflection. Then, as if a deeper well of emotion had surged up and flooded him, he drew both hands over his face and hid his eyes. He was seized by a shudder. I sensed that the view of his life's work, like cinderblocks in a building that took years to erect, had toppled on him all at once and buried him alive in the catacomb of memory. "I didn't know," he said in a voice trembling with palpable emotion, devoid now of any trace of irony or self-deprecation. A silence fell as profound as any that one might experience in a cathedral. In the depths of the stacks, entombed under eight floors of concrete and steel and soundproof fenestration, nothing could be heard except the low, monotone hum of the ventilation system. With deep understanding, almost empathy, I could feel the upwelling of feeling emanating from his being, luminously alive with the sorrow of an artist no doubt forced to reflect on a life lived solely in the imagination. Devastation and glory must have been locked in combat in the cavern of his being.

Raymond opened his hands but kept his face hooded. Tears of sentiment had filmed his eyes and he was blinking back the feared cascade of emotion, I thought, that might topple him to his knees. Three decades of a prodigiously creative life presented in a single view, all at once, the weight must have been oceanic, crushing his soul in ways I couldn't fathom. "One day, when I was fifteen," he began haltingly, "I wrote a poem. I got it published in my high school paper." He laughed with a short exhalation spat out his nose. "It was a dumb poem called *Mr. Pencilhead.* It satirized the principal, but apparently not cleverly enough because he called me into his office to explain why I had metaphorized him as an insensitive administrator with autocratic tendencies." With tears wetting his lashes, he shook his head and laughed. "That's when I experienced my first epiphany of the power of words."

"I'm going to search for that poem, because I didn't find it," I said, genuinely displeased that I had failed, after exhaustively archiving his collection, in some infinitesimal way.

"You do that," he turned to me, "my eavesdropping angel." He winked. "I would love to see that."

"If it can be found, I'll find it," I reassured him, making a mental note.

Raymond seemed cast adrift in memory. He raised his eyes again to the three room-length shelves of boxes and stood motionless, positively transfixed. "That's all I ever did, write. From the beginning. And now it's embalmed."

"Not embalmed," I corrected. "Preserved for others to discover as if it were as alive as when you wrote them. Isn't that the power of art? Its timelessness?"

"Lovingly preserved," he murmured in a faint voice. Raymond turned to me and said with sentimental feeling still hobbling his words, "It's a real honor, Ms. Fontaine . . ."

"Nadia," I chopped him off, enunciating every vowel of my name to imprint it on his memory. "I feel like we've known each other forever."

"Yes. Nadia. Sorry to be so formal. We intersected at the junction of art, didn't we?"

I nodded slowly with widened eyes. "Yes. At the junction of art."

He returned his gaze to the rows of boxes. "It's humbling. The work you've done . . . How long did you say all this took?"

"Six months. And I've got another two, at least, to go," I answered. "Unless you've got a new addition you're holding out on."

Raymond shook his head sadly. "Nothing the last two years. Dry as a desert. Not even so much as a Fata Morgana on the horizon."

I risked a hand to his shoulder and touched him lightly with my fingertips, as if bearing his defeatism. Through the scratchy cotton of his shirt, I felt what I imagined was his physical strength. I let my fingers crawl down his biceps barely an inch, as if telegraphing a message through the conduit that our intersection over his work had given us unique access to each other. "You'll get back into it again," I said softly. "That's what you do. The sea turtle returns to the shore where it was hatched ten years later to lay its eggs. That's what they do. It's in their DNA."

"I hope it's not ten years." He laughed sardonically. "Then I'll know I'm finished." He looked at me down the slope of his shoulder where my fingers rested like a drowsing tarantula, ready to be awakened at the slightest tremor in the feeling air.

I raised my face and sailed into his over the ladder of my fingers until my vehement eyes found his and coupled like train cars on a track, inaugurating a new line, embarking on a new journey.

"It means the universe to me," he spoke softly, as if he wanted me not to hear so that I would lean my face in—the face whose lips I imagined he wanted to kiss—summoning me closer with his mumbling incantation.

"And it means a lot to *me*," I said in the same lowered tone as his, "that you came here to see, and acknowledge, what I've done."

He inscribed an arc with his finger. "If you've read everything I've written as you say"—he turned to me—"You know me better than my wife," he stated frankly.

I wished he hadn't mentioned his wife again, because it briefly broke the spell I had spent all day creating just to be here with him now, alone, in the stacks, everyone gone. This was my moment, not his wife's.

He looked longingly at me as if threatening to kiss me. My fingers dug lightly into his shoulders, as if pressing spurs into the underbelly of a horse to prod it into action, and my head tilted up just a little as if imploring *please! now!* He glanced away, locked in combat with the lost opportunity and the fear of greater consequences.

Disappointed, I withdrew my hand like an ebbing tide, feeling bereft that the charged moment had spent itself on a phantasmal shore. "There are security cameras everywhere in here." I darted my eyes to one in the corner of the ceiling. His eyes traveled with mine on an aborted journey to damnation.

"Are they watching us now?" he asked with mild anxiety.

My body was crying out for sex. I shrugged. "I doubt it." His eyes, now wide and bright in the dusky light, returned to mine as naturally as the tide surging back in. "There's nothing suspicious." I raised my eyes to his questioningly. "Is there?"

Another silence fell between us. It swarmed with unquantifiable crosscurrents of emotion. It wasn't fair, I thought.

Until he whispered nonchalantly, "We'll have to find a place where we're not being watched," as if he could qualify his words if he waded in too soon. His eyes suddenly swam deep into mine and lapped their mystery. I knew he knew he was tiptoeing into dangerous waters. And I didn't want to betray his murmured overture with reality, or—God forbid!—dissuade him from going deeper. That's what I longed to tell him then and there with racing heart and desire welling up inside me, but it was all delicious feints and parries, and I restrained myself from leaping headlong into the fire and initiating the first move.

I recovered hope in his lingering over his archive and not appearing eager to leave. He wants to be with me, I thought, he just doesn't know how to broach it. He looked off and scanned the shelves with a mingling of nostalgia and a searching memory, as if he could remember every hour bent over every one of those dozens of Moleskines. He shook his head again in astonishment and exhaled a short laugh through his nose. "I can't believe I wrote that much. It doesn't seem like work when you're swept up in it."

"Why do you think you've been dormant the last couple of years?" I ventured.

Without turning to me, he shrugged his wide shoulders and let them slump. "Maybe the critics were right: after the Pulitzer, I lost the velocity of my voice, lost the nerve to go where I need to go to produce my best." He narrowed his eyes. "My last, *A Time of Uncertainty*, wasn't the real me. Too . . . overtly commercial. The one that will probably be adapted into the hit movie. It lacked the raw emotional urgency and honesty of my legacy work." He cast his eyes to the floor. "Somewhere between needing to write and the superficiality of fame, I lost my connection to something vital."

Not prone to platitudes, I offered, "Do you know about the emperor penguins and their catastrophic molt?"

He turned to me with beetled brow and piqued curiosity. "No."

"In the Antarctic, emperor penguins shed all their feathers at once. They frantically, maniacally, pluck them out with their beaks until they are ridiculously bald, goose-pimpled birds. Fattened up on weeks of gorging, they wait until their plumage grows back, otherwise they'd perish in the frigid waters. It's known as a catastrophic molt. For a brief time they are utterly naked to the cold. They huddle together in large groups and shiver uncontrollably, and some of them don't survive the drastic process. And then, miraculously, the ones who manage to survive, their plumage grows back in all at once in a veritable rush of self-transformation. And when they're newly fledged, they return to fishing in the cold waters, now properly outfitted for the task of finding food."

"A form of self-rebirth?"

I bit my upper lip and then nodded metronomically for emphasis. Our eyes stayed locked on each other's. Something had stirred in him, a ghost seemed to emerge out of him.

"What makes them do it differently from other birds?" he asked.

"In their barbarously cold world, they don't have time to wait for the individual feathers to grow back in one by one, so they perform the molting all at once, brave the freezing cold, and then march forth, yes, reborn anew as they once were."

Raymond gazed down at me with piercing eyes. A smile slowly materialized on his face in the subtlest expression of recognition of something ineffably metaphorical. To me, his archivist, the keeper of his flame, his head bore the weight of literary nobility. Now shipwrecked on the shoals of a desolate shore like hulking driftwood, he feared, I worried for him. A mad beachcomber in search of a large shell that would roar in his ear a new tale from an uncharted continent, one that had gone unexplored. From his journals, I knew he thirsted for originality, a frontier where he could endure a catastrophic molt and be reborn too. I hoped the blatant metaphor would unmoor him, cast him back to some recognizably fecund creative cauldron where the fires roared as they had in his youth.

"Catastrophic molt," Raymond said, as if it were incanting in his head.

I kept nodding with ever widening eyes, hoping against hope he would take me in his arms and kiss me and seal my brilliance.

"Hmm," he said, his eyes drifting away to a swirl of new thoughts.

"Shall we go?" I asked quietly, hoisting both of us back to reality.

Together, we walked back to my cubicle like grave robbers who had chickened out at the penultimate moment. Something had changed in him during the tour of the stacks and the visual presentation of his archive. Something had been awakened. Without manipulation, and purely by instinct, I knew I had opened a new door in his imagination and given him a glimpse of another shore, unwittingly inspired something I hoped was already taking chrysalis form.

When we returned to my office, I shut my computer down and switched off the table lamp, then, in the subdued light, where shadows cast us both in a more youthful aspect, presented him with a copy of a book. He peered at the cover, which depicted an abstract, photo-realist image of a woman standing at an ocean's edge at night, a surfboard planted in the wet stand, whitewater eddying above her ankles, staring off at the horizon, where gold had spilled through the clouds and the sun had dropped off the face of the ocean and, it appeared, set off fires on the far side of the planet.

"*Knife in the Heart*," he said out loud. "Short stories by Nadia Fontaine."

Trembling inside, I didn't say anything. He rotated the book in his hand and read on the spine, "Bloomsbury. Impressive." Without looking at me, he added, "I love the title. It's better than any of mine." Now he looked at me. "From Kafka's *Letters to Milena*?"

"You read it?" I asked.

"Are you kidding? It's my favorite Kafka of all. I've devoured it five times. The artist stripped bare. Without the artifice of modernism he too often hid behind." He smiled for the first time since surfacing from the emotional tumult of seeing his archive. "Like your emperor penguin and his catastrophic molt."

I returned his smile. He opened the book, leafed through the opening pages, adjusted his glasses and intoned, "*She had feelings so deep they were ineffable. Sometimes she wished she could surgically remove them they tortured her so. The forbidden is always the most sublime. She longed for disobedience, a subversion of all norms, a surrender to the senses.*" He lowered his glasses. "I didn't know you were a published author, Na-di-a. The things Helena doesn't tell me." I smirked disdain. "For me?" he asked, holding up my book.

"If you haven't given up reading literature too," I teased.

He smiled wryly. Glancing down at the book, his eyes caught something. "You already inscribed it to me."

"Yes," I said, blushing.

"*To Raymond. Your Archivist. Nadia.*" He closed the book and held the back of it up next to my face. A black-and-white author's photo filled the entire rectangle. He glanced between the two of us in a comical dance. "You're even more ravishingly beautiful today," he declared.

I could see my eyes fluttering rapidly because he was going in and out of focus. "I'm going to hold you to your promise."

"What promise?" he asked, avoiding my eyes.

"Meeting where we're not being watched." I blushed a smile. "It will come after the catastrophic molt," I suggested.

We laughed nervously in unison. I slung my purse over my shoulder and started out. Raymond held out an arm and gently blocked my passage. "I should probably go out alone."

"All right," I said, understanding. Understanding that this is how it would be. *If* it was meant to be.

Raymond held up my book. "I look forward to learning . . . what thoughts were so deep that they were ineffable."

"Good. I hope you do." I extended my hand. He took it in his much larger one, and I could feel a sentiment pour through his veins.

"Thank you for showing me my archive," he said, the spell broken. "It was eye-opening."

"Any time," I said. He started off. "I'm sad you're leaving," I called out.

He stopped and gave me a backward smile of hope, then walked off.

I knew he could take me somewhere I had never been before, pinwheeling away to that dark abyss of an imagination. Did he know I could take him somewhere he had never been before too? That's what vexed and saddened me when his lanky frame drained from the room and abandoned me all alone with his retreating footsteps. To face the commuter traffic east back to Black Mountain Ranch and the place I once called home.

EMILY

Emily stopped eating pizza once she left college, but now she was gorging on some local takeout that rated 4.7 stars on Yelp, between sips of cold Societe, the craft beer she was loyal to now. Onyx was the unwitting beneficiary of unconscious petting and whisker caressing, as Emily opened more PDFs chronicling Nadia's and Raymond's nascent romance and lowered her bathysphere in the dark archives and the seafloor they possessed all to themselves.

From: Nadia Fontaine <Nfontaine@RegentsU.edu>
To: Raymond West <Rwest_Lit@RegentsU.edu>
Subject: Your Visit to Special Collections
Date: 07 September 2017

Dear Raymond,

What a pleasure it was to take you on a tour of Special Collections. The emotion you displayed was as moving to me as it must have been for you. I know you were being self-deprecating when you said that the critics were right that you are washed up. That's ludicrous, and you know it. Maybe you're gestating something and not even aware of it. A famous writer once advised: "Start at p. 1 and write like a bat out of hell." Oh, wait, that was you who said that.

I do hope you're not too critical of my modest collection of short stories. I hope we can meet and talk about them. It would be a shame if your visit was the last time I saw you. Something stirred in both of us, and I know you know we both felt it.

Nadia

From: Raymond West <Rwest_Lit@RegentsU.edu>
To: Nadia Fontaine <Nfontaine@RegentsU.edu>
Subject: Re: Your Visit to Special Collections
Date: 08 September 2017

My Dear Nadia,

Yes, it was moving for me to see my work memorialized in all those boxes. That's a lot of being alone. And I don't want to be alone so much anymore. That's what I was thinking when I grew misty-eyed and maudlin. Forgive me.

But there was something else. I almost wished I hadn't come down to Special Collections. And there you were, more lovely than at the Faculty Club, in your work environment, devoted to my writings. Six months, you say? Yes, you're right. Something stirred in me. Something stirred in me for the first time in ages.

I haven't been able to stop thinking about the "catastrophic molt" of those emperor penguins. Maybe I'm reading too much into it, but was there a clairvoyance in your regaling me with this? Because something quiescent in me shuddered. A seed was sown somewhere in the intracranial theater of my imagination. (I'll tell you more if it starts to come out of the earth and is anything. But, if it does, it's owed entirely to you.)

Raymond

PS: I started your collection of short stories. They're visionary. You write in the same nakedly personal vein that I was once celebrated for. I particularly enjoyed the one titled "Burning." And this line, I highlighted: "She knew her damnation was lasciviousness." Borrowed? We should explore over a coffee, no?

From: Nadia Fontaine <Nfontaine@RegentsU.edu>
To: Raymond West <Rwest_Lit@RegentsU.edu>
Subject: Catastrophic Molt
Date: 08 September 2017

Dear Raymond,

I know it's been difficult for you the last couple years. The symposiums in Europe and abroad—yes, I stalk your journeys online. It must be hard to get into a writing rhythm. It must be frustrating to have an idea seize you, grab you by the throat, and then be tossed this way and that and not be able to give it your full attention.

On another note: I have questions for you about your papers. It could be an appropriate excuse for donor and archivist to get together, to meet again . . . Let me know when you have time.

Nadia

PS: thank you for the kind words on *Knife in the Heart*. It didn't sell well, but I'm proud I got it published. One was even made into a short film I might show you one day, though I'm a little shy. You see, I star in the film . . . and, yes, my damnation is lasciviousness."

From: Raymond West <Rwest_Lit@RegentsU.edu>
To: Nadia Fontaine <Nfontaine@RegentsU.edu>
Subject: Re: Catastrophic Molt
Date: 10 September 2017

Nadia,

Forgive me for not getting back to you sooner. I meant what I said about your writing. I feel like you vouchsafed me a glimpse into your soul. I feel like I know you intimately through your work—as it should be. I know how it feels to mine the personal. Rejection can be that much more painful.

I shouldn't say this, maybe it's inappropriate, but I feel like we're inexorably drawing closer and closer to each other, so I'll risk it: you've ignited something in me, and I don't know what it is yet. Reading your wondrous work, I have this fantasy of writing something with you. Maybe what I need is a collaboration to break through this Arctic ice of stasis, fecklessness, otiosity (is that a word?). My question—and we can explore this when we next meet—is: are what we're writing here in this email that seed that I told you that had formed unwittingly in my imagination? And does that seed need watering? And if it's going to be a love story—because a love story it must be—then is it necessary to fall in love and risk opprobrium on a scale undetermined—unimaginable!—given our discrete positions here at Regents?

Just a thought. Your Raymond.

PS: I continue to read *Knife in the Heart* with a fervency not experienced since, I don't know, I fell in love with the stories of Lispector. You're a sensually possessed archivist, Nadia . . . if the curtain between fiction and reality is as diaphanous as I suspect it is. And I experienced my first pangs of jealousy reading that BDSM story of you and that almost anonymous man and the afternoon of wanton fellatio. My imagination ran into your vivid descriptions and didn't want to believe it was true. Because, in that moment, reading you, falling in love with your writing, I wanted you all to myself, and didn't want to know that any other man had had you like that. I experienced such intense jealousy, you don't know. Isn't that silly? I tried to bury it, but my unconscious hurled it back in my face in disturbing dreams where a siren called to me in a voice much like yours and I wandered a desolate world in wounded hurt.

Of course, I want to see that film of yours!

From: Nadia Fontaine <Nfontaine@RegentsU.edu>
To: Raymond West <Rwest_Lit@RegentsU.edu>
Subject: Collaboration/Liberation
Date: 10 September 2017

Raymond,

It means the world to me that you're reading my modest little collection of stories. Especially coming from you. Although the title story did win a Pushcart, and there is a second collection (unpublished), it's dispiriting when your book sells fewer than five thousand copies, and you wonder if you're only writing for yourself. So, your words mean the world to me.

Yes, like you, I write from a personal place. Remember, I've been reading you since the beginning of your career. Your work hasn't just crossed my path since we were gifted your papers. Can you imagine my excitement when Helena said that your papers were coming here? And to think anyone else would touch your work, can you imagine my jealousy had that had happened? I would have quit. I would have sunk into a suicidal depression. You were mine from the beginning. But I had to approach

Helena and Jean with a dissimulated ardency lest they think I had a too personal stake in it. At one point I threatened to resign if I wasn't given them. It helped that I had just made fellow from the Society of American Archivists, they were scared to lose me. And then I got you.

Yes, I write from a personal place, a deep dark well, and wail, of despair and desire. Don't be jealous. We all have a past. Yes, I've explored. And I'm not going to stop exploring! It's what feeds our art. But isn't what we want is to explore with somebody who is not ephemeral, explore with somebody whom we can go deep with, shackle ourselves to with pure, unadulterated happiness?

I'm intrigued by your idea of a collaboration. Who wouldn't be flattered? And there's no question that living a work before it's written is what makes it three-dimensional, raw, personal, and can connect with people who realize that it has, to borrow your phrase, "the ring of verisimilitude."

I fantasize writing a whole book of short stories devoted to a future where we explore everything you've ever wanted to explore . . .

Your archivist . . .

From: Raymond West <Rwest_Lit@RegentsU.edu>
To: Nadia Fontaine <Nfontaine@RegentsU.edu>
Subject: Re: Collaboration/Liberation
Date: 10 September 2017

Nadia,

I am terribly jealous! Wracked with jealousy. The sexual frankness of your work has me locked in combat with salacious salivation and morbid despair over imagining that I'm the aggrieved husband who discovered the video on the cell of your character Natalie (ha-ha) masturbating to a man urging her on. My God! Did that happen? Or is that just a product of your perfervid erotic imagination run amok? It must be a personal story for it to have had such a profound impact on me. I can see it clearly now the beautiful way you write it, and I'm raw with anguish. I'm an albatross whose lifelong mate has perished in the waves on the windswept cliffs of the Galapagos and is croaking now in despair. And I haven't even had a chance to make good on that promise—forgive me!—whispered in the stacks.

If collaborating is a liberation—for me, not you, at the very least—and if being together engenders that collaboration, then I suppose it's the risk we take, isn't it? And if it launches me out of this eddying whirlpool of creative stasis where I've been in vain for months, then the risk supplants its opposite, doesn't it? Death here on the beach with the surf ceaselessly breaking, in a passionless marriage with a woman who loves me, but who has colonized my unconscious to the point where I no longer feel free to write what I want to write. She doesn't know this. I can't tell her this. Therapists are worthless because they will never understand artists. And, so, I write to you, my friend (for now), my archivist (always), because I know you understand, I long for a soul that mirrors my own! Isn't that the definition of pure joy and contentment?

The quarter hasn't begun yet. The Santa Anas remind me always of Raymond Chandler, who lived a mile south of me, and has always inspired me. So, with that in mind, I went back in the short journey of time to the beginning of this correspondence, and I started to ideate an epistolary novel that would have to, alas, be explored to find out how it ends. And my title? *The Archivist.* Do you like it? I was thinking of *Eavesdropping Angel*, but it feels taken from something too personal between us, and there are some personal things that I want to keep personal.

I'm still jealous!

Your Raymond

NADIA'S STORY (CONT'D)

I was smiling at the email on my monitor when a voice startled me. "What are you reading?" I spun around in my office chair and faced Joel.

"Joel? Don't you ever knock?" I said, with wide indignant eyes, one arm bent behind me and a splayed hand instinctively covering the screen.

"Hey, Nadia, I just wanted to stop by and say our film got accepted at the Naples International Film Festival."

"That's great, Joel," I stammered, trying my best to whipsaw from rereading the charged exchange of personal emails between Raymond and me to the quotidian reality of my obligations at Special Collections.

"Maybe one day we'll expand it into a feature," he fantasized wistfully.

I smiled wordlessly, my mind already writing the reply email to Raymond. "I'm an archivist, Joel, not an actress."

Joel nodded at me, a little wounded. "Gotcha. So, I was wondering if you wanted to hit a little evening glass at Black's?" He pointed a thumb in the general direction of the ocean.

"I'm buried deep in West," I replied laconically, wanting him to leave.

"How is that progressing?"

"The correspondence is prodigious." My tone was sharp and discomfiting.

I waited until Joel had gone, then eased back into my chair, dropped my fingers to the keyboard, and glued my face to the monitor and the fantasy that was preoccupying me, that had ignited my blood aflame, and wrote the following email:

From: Nadia Fontaine <Nfontaine@RegentsU.edu>
To: Raymond West <Rwest_Lit@RegentsU.edu>
Subject: When Shall We Meet?
Date: 11 September 2017

My Dear Raymond,

Of course, we would have to live it in order to write it. And I *love* the title. I don't think anyone has ever written about what someone like me does, from the inside. How we come to be assigned a collection, and then how we, if it's, like you, a donor whose work we admire, invest our souls in it, become enveloped by it. It does become personal. You come to life in our imagination. And what if it did, as I'm assuming you're insinuating, cross the line, transgress into the forbidden, and not the sin of salacity, but the blue ether of pure love, born both of the passion of the flesh and the desire of the mind and its need to create?

Oh, the forests that we could explore! The seas that we could sail! The creatures that we could discover and taxonomically name! . . .

I'm ready. Nadia.

I hit Send without hesitation, thinking it should be "Sin." I shut down my computer, rose from my desk, gathered my belongings, and walked out of Special Collections. I had a status update on "West"—it felt weird to depersonalize him as West now—with Helena and Jean in the afternoon and I wanted to get a bite to eat to fortify myself for the meeting that would unwittingly try to do everything to founder my fantasy under the bright lights of my professional duties.

The air was baking hot and dry. It stung my eyes and dehydrated my skin as I made my way to the food courts at the Barnes Center. Even though I wore dark sunglasses, I shielded my eyes from the mirrored windows flanking the pathway that reflected light back at me like lasers. I escaped the fierce heat and blinding white light and found the cool, air-conditioned oasis of Tasmania. Fall quarter was a week from getting underway, and it no longer possessed the blissful peace and quiet of summer when I could escape here and write and be alone. I ordered fish tacos and a beer, hoping Helena or Jean wouldn't be eating at Tasmania too and casting reproving looks at me for drinking alcohol in the middle of the day. I inserted my earbuds and thumbed through songs on my ancient iPod. Scrolled my way to OMD's "So in Love." It wasn't loud enough to block out the house music, so I jacked up the volume to an ear-deafening amplitude.

I was engrossed in the song to the point where I found myself singing out loud in a state of pure exultation, gyrating on the stool in a dance of controlled ecstasy, oblivious of the world. Patrons were staring, some of them smiling. They could feel my joy at the prospect of breaking free from everything like corralled wild horses set loose upon an untrammeled plain. "I was so impressed by you, I was running blind," I could hear myself singing in full-throated defiance. I reached for my beer and slammed it back as if I were on holiday or had just aced a dissertation defense. I smiled abashedly when the server brought my tacos and commented, "Nice voice."

"Thank you," I replied sheepishly, popping out one earbud to hear him.

"Did you get a raise?" he joked.

I returned his smile. "I wish." Everyone can see my elation, I thought to myself. Swiveling around on the stool, I searched the café, but I didn't recognize anyone, and exhaled with relief. My reputation was not that of someone who belted out '80s New Wave tunes in public places. I was thought of as a mystery woman, an archivist who came and went as surreptitiously as I could, the enigmatic one who wrote stories that got published, the one who was frequently reminded of her beauty but who guarded her private life and kept it away from Regents. Until now. Maybe it had started with Joel's film. Possibly I wanted to reveal a side of myself that nobody knew, not repress it anymore, shock people who didn't know me. Who knows if anyone read *Knife in the Heart*, but if they had—like Raymond—it would have given them a shudder. Who would have thought the girl who grew up an only child with an unfeeling mother and an absent father, matriculated with a BA in English at University of Chicago, got her doctorate at Columbia, hopscotched to an internship at the National Archives, and found herself in California at Regents would be the one to write such daring and shocking stories and successfully get them published by a legitimate press? My background, my résumé, suggested a woman destined to be entombed in libraries the rest of her life. They didn't know me. They never would know me.

My life has taken such an odd path, I thought. Now, I really want to go somewhere different, I really want to take risks.

I glanced at my cell. No email. Raymond would write back when he was ready to set a date, I decided. I need to be careful, I cautioned myself. I can't risk throwing myself into this without some circumspection. But the thought of a writing collaboration with Raymond West, at his behest, catapulted me out of Special Collections and bore me on wings to someplace thrilling, and that emotion I just could not suppress. Not since my collection of short stories had been published had I felt such happiness surge in my heart. I had reached my own desertification of the soul and I, too, needed something to kick me in the ass. This collaboration—if it happened—would be everything I ever wanted in life. It would hoist me out of this cultural desert where I had found myself: San Diego. I couldn't conceive of dying here. This is not where I want to end.

EMILY

Emily looked up from her laptop screen. In the file folders of their e-pistolary exchange sat a file uniquely unto itself, the revealing *My Story* memoir Nadia had written, chronicling her and Raymond's relationship. It explained in greater, more chronologically narrative, detail Nadia's personal feelings separate from the emails, filling in the interstices, charting its trajectory, like any archivist–cum–accomplished writer might. After all, she was a published writer. *My God,* Emily shook her head to herself at the point where she had paused, *they haven't even kissed!* She noticed that the time was 11:38 p.m. and realized she should get some sleep, but this narrative was driving her now. Exploring forward, she established there were weeks, months of emails, a story that had just unfolded and one that now possessed her. Having been in Special Collections for two weeks, her imagination, borne by her predecessor's words, was now set afire. With pounding heart, she double-tapped another folder and a whole new weft of emails blossomed on her laptop screen, each scorched by a date, each promising another rung on their ladder to perdition. When she had consumed a week's worth of the fervent exchange, she opened Nadia's *My Story* file, in a continuing effort to put it all into context.

NADIA'S STORY (CONT'D)

I arrived for the meeting late, the OMD song still playing in the music hall of my head. Helena, shrouded in a beige skirt, blouse and woolen sweater dripping with costume jewelry, threw me a professional smile that was a barely disguised scowl. Jean smiled perfunctorily too, as if the only joy *she found* in life was balancing her checkbook.

Helena interlaced her fingers, telescoped her head forward and got right to the point. "Where are we at with West?"

No confabulation, no "Do you believe these Santa Anas?" or "That's a cute blouse you're wearing, Nadia." No, right to the point.

A madness almost took possession of me and I could feel myself tensed dangerously on the edge of blurting, "We're in love and we're going to write a novel together!" That would have set the room ablaze! Instead, I, the professional archivist who always maintained—in the eyes of the department—a sangfroid, an unruffled cool, a walled-off privacy, combed back my hair with my hand and smiled. "It's a big project, Helena. Even though the collection is boxed and meticulously arranged to the item level, the finding aid requires a lot of tedious cross-referencing. And I know you want me to get it right for Elizabeth," I replied through clenched teeth.

"We appreciate that, and we know this is a big project," interjected Jean tersely. "We're wondering if you're getting too deep into the details," she finished, clearly ventriloquizing Helena's darkest suspicions.

I snapped my head to Jean's. "What do you mean?"

Jean deferred to Helena, who said with barely disguised incredulity in her venomous tone, "Six months, and you're projecting another three? Don't you think it's getting a little obsessive?" She thrust out her jaw and invited my excuses so she could pounce on them.

I bristled with contempt at their vitiation of my work methodology and fumed wordlessly for a moment. In a calm voice, I said, "I made the decision to print out and folder some of the digital files for future researchers. A lot of the revisions were done on a computer and never printed out."

"What?" asked Helena, glancing at Jean. Jean shrugged, signaling that she hadn't been aware of this. "Revisions?"

"Typescripts of later drafts that contain minute changes. I want everything, all these computer-generated items, printed out," I seethed. "I don't have faith these old digital formats are going to be accessible, and I don't want to lose a single word of a single draft of a single manuscript of Raymond West." My words echoed in the conference room. I was resolute in my conviction, but deep in the recesses of my soul I knew I was stalling for time.

"Disk images have already been made of the digital items for ingest into dark storage, I thought," Jean countered.

"Disk images of hard drives and diskettes in their old formats," I retorted. "I don't want future digital archivists complaining they can't access some of the collection because it was backed up as raw data that is now in obsolete formats and totally inaccessible without a huge pain in the ass. Time should be allocated for some of these files to be printed out," I demanded. "And I want to go through them thoroughly and find out which ones." I could feel veins throbbing at my temples.

Helena and Jean collectively sucked in their breath, frantically searching for a counterargument that wasn't forthcoming. I knew this was news to them, but it was time to unload it. I didn't want to let West go. Not now. Not ever.

"Our timeline has been revised so many times," Jean protested, as if she and Helena had rehearsed this inquisition and were ganging up on me—and it wouldn't be the first time.

Helena traded looks with Jean and asked, as if I were an invisible presence, "Maybe we should consider team-processing West."

Before Jean could respond I stood half out of my chair and exploded, "If you order this team-processed, I'm going to quit. And then you're going to be totally fucked!"

Helena's eyes widened with consternation. My outburst pressed her back into her chair.

I sat back down, the room still echoing with my words.

"There's no need for that kind of language, Nadia," Helena reproved.

"It's an important gift. I want to do it justice," I said in a lower octave, still seething.

"We have a big announcement coming up," Helena said with a smile that showered the room with promise.

"What is it?" I asked ominously, worried that any new news about Raymond might topple my fantasy of a collaboration.

"This is a high-priority collection, Nadia, as you well know, which is why we assigned it to you. It has time constraints imposed by new information," Helena said evasively.

"What time constraints?" I asked, my voice rising.

"It involves a sizable donation by Elizabeth West."

My heart slipped like a sun over the horizon, purpling the sky. Elizabeth, I almost spoke out loud. I shook my head in quiet, selfish, disgust.

"That's fine that you want to make hard copies of some of the digital items, but we simply urge you to step up your processing, that's all," Helena said firmly.

"We only discussed team-processing to give you a break," Jean added to placate my wrath. Without me they were fucked, and they knew it, and they knew I knew it.

I leveled my eyes at Helena, but her stony stare gave away nothing. I hated her. I hated everything she stood for. Money, timelines, linear feet, donor fundraisers, Board of Trustees bullshit . . . She only cared about the collections insofar as she could boast their acquisitions, not how they were processed and cared for. She was probably capable of deaccessioning a collection and tossing the archive out into the alley if she thought it reflected badly on the university's, and, most importantly, her reputation, her legacy. And with no qualms about the destruction of the cultural record. I wanted to shout, *You're the reason archivists like me leave the profession!*

"Do you have a timeline for completion?" Jean inquired, the ensuing silence too discomfiting for her fragile psyche.

I took a slow, deep inhale to compose myself. "Assuming there are no new additions, assuming you don't order it team-processed and force me to train a project archivist and bring her up to speed, which would be a massive waste of my time and counterproductive, I think I can have it wrapped up in less than three months," I spoke to Helena, averting Jean's steely gaze.

"What about two?" pressured Jean.

"Maybe," I said. "But I would be rushing the finding aid. And West deserves an extensive, carefully written biography, one that only I can write at this point," I boasted, risking their growing concern I was getting too close to the collection.

Helena, with no change of expression, studied her fingernails, debating her response. We had locked horns before, but never over someone as prominent, or as politically complicated, as Raymond West. She spoke to her painted cuticles instead of me. "I know you're a fan of his writing, Nadia. We all are." Bullshit, I thought. "As an aspiring writer, I'm sure the collection holds a special fascination for you."

Aspiring writer? I almost screamed in defiance of her insult, but I contained my outrage. "It does," I admitted in a soft, but firm, voice. I paused, admonishing myself not to let my emotions run away from me for fear it might jeopardize everything Raymond and I were clandestinely dreaming. "I'm thinking of writing an article for *American Archivist* on . . . the journey I've taken in processing this incredible collection."

"I'm sure it would be a terrific article, Nadia, but we would prefer it if you didn't," Helena expostulated with quiet authority. "It's an extremely . . . delicate negotiation with Elizabeth," she said. "When we make the official announcement, you will understand." Helena raised her head to me and met my eyes. She held the look long enough to semaphore to me that this wasn't open for discussion, that the news was hermetically sealed. Jean waited, expression grim with the realization that she was not, seniority-wise, authorized to elaborate. Besides, it was not her meeting to chair. Helena possessed all the power. The vortex sucked all the energy to her person. Her decisions—what collections to acquire, how to present the collections—forged the future, for better or ill, of Memorial Library's Special Collections & Archives. Mad mariner and pathological hoarder that she was, she charted and steered its destiny. And if she sensed that the ship she had equipped and outfitted was off course, she was going to do anything in her power to get it back on course. And as the director, short of the egregious, she answered to no one. We, including Jean, were steerage, and she never let us forget it.

"I'll try to step up my workload on West," I acquiesced. My conciliatory words brought a barely perceptible smile of relief to Jean's tense face. Helena didn't seem completely appeased.

"Other than making hard copies of the digital items, what's taking so long?" Helena wondered. "It's not like you."

I brought a fist to my mouth and cleared my throat. In a deliberately lofty tone, I said, "I have come to the incontrovertible belief the future reputation of Special Collections rests on how meticulously I process this once-in-a-lifetime gift."

"Understood," said Helena. "But things have changed now. There's a heightened sense of the materials in the collection. Anything that might offend Elizabeth, we'll have to reevaluate them in terms of the restrictions."

"For example?" I asked, mildly alarmed.

"West has lived a, shall we say . . . colorful life."

"You want me to bowdlerize his papers?"

"No. No, we're not saying that," Helena affirmed unconvincingly, glancing away at her watch. Turning to me as if I were as inanimate as a strand of seaweed, she said, "It's now as much Elizabeth's collection as it is her husband's."

Her words infuriated me. "I've made notes in my personal file on anything that might offend certain sensibilities . . . of the *donor's spouse.* Now that I'm apprised there are extenuating circumstances. Maybe at a future date we can go over them. At your convenience, of course."

Relief flooded the room. Jean audibly exhaled. "Well. Good." She closed her supervisor's folder in anticipation of the close of the meeting.

Helena smiled, baring yellowed teeth stained from the exotic teas she drank. "I appreciate that, Nadia. Once again, congratulations on your becoming a SAA fellow," she complimented, having extracted what she wanted. "I'm sure that will go a long way to being recommended for one of the endowed positions."

An endowed position? I tilted my head up and turned it to Helena inquiringly.

"It's one of the conditions of the donation we're negotiating," Helena said, reaching for her handbag and planting one hand on the table for support.

I was suddenly seized with confliction. My reckless heart was now locked in combat with the dream of something I always wanted: the equivalent of tenure in my profession. The proverbial carrot had been dangled, and the proposition came freighted with the admonition to conduct myself like a professional and be a team player. It would secure my future. Other archivists would have wept with joy at the news.

The meeting adjourned as the three of us clambered to our feet in unison. Helena crashed out of the room with all the impoliteness she was notorious for. Jean, businesslike, if occupationally frosty, remained.

"I'd like a written update when you get a chance," Jean said.

"Don't address me like I work for you, Jean. I'm the one who got you hired. Helena was on the fence about you." Jean looked at me with that implacable stare of hers. "I'll have something for you tomorrow, but don't hassle me about it."

"Thank you," stammered Jean, still quivering.

I returned to my cubicle, dispirited by the tone of the meeting, condemned to my anger. *Aspiring writer? Fucking bitch.* I stapled my arms across my chest and fretted that any news about the West Papers could claw at the delicate web we had begun to fashion, the inviolable collaboration of a work that was growing now in the most complex of formations. It was not rooted in the thing itself. A fickle cloud could close off its photosynthetic-warming sun. Helena probably wouldn't dare risk taking me off the project for fear of throwing her precious timelines into chaos, but she had that right. Apprised of the gift, I assumed Elizabeth West almost for certain had that authority. If the library was going to be rechristened in her name—and that was the rumor!—in exchange for a generous donation, if she was going to take possession of its spirit with her inherited fortune and her husband's coveted bequest, Helena would acquiesce to her wishes.

As I sat paralyzed in a state of gloom, surrounded by piles of Raymond's manuscripts, I wondered if I shouldn't back off, hunker down, and stop postponing the completion of the collection. My heart could weather a flirtation nipped in the bud if I focused on the potential consequences and didn't surrender to that first annihilating kiss. But Raymond was matching me email for email, ratcheting things up, and I was already spinning vertiginously upward in the dust devil of our mutual desire. With me as a promising catalyst, he was—if his emails could be believed and were not just a subterfuge for undressing me as a conquest—how dare I be so cynical?—emerging from his creative dormancy with a fervor that only I could nurture. And only someone nosy and overcompromised like Helena could thwart it, especially if she had cause. And with Elizabeth West's imminent gift to the library, Helena certainly had motive to pull me from the project and punish me by giving the endowed chair to someone less deserving. It was curious to me that they hadn't asked about Raymond's visit. Were they already warning me to stay away but afraid to voice it without having any proof that something was brewing? I always wanted to live my life irreproachably independent of all constraints, but now I was debating my own resolve to be recklessly free. Before it was too late. Before the endowed chair handcuffed me to San Diego and a future deathbed of tearful remorse.

I moved the mouse on my desk, and my computer monitor frizzled to life. I click-click-clicked straight to my email. Nothing from Raymond. It had only been two days, but it felt like an eternity. His absence worried me, made me heartsick. Was the bloom off the rose? I was already glimpsing dark waters if he never wrote to me again. What was wrong with me?

The clock on the wall ticktocked as if the second hand were traveling backward. I had brought it in to daily remind me that digital was an uncertain future, could be the cataclysm that some archivists, like me, believed might destroy the historical record forever. I had written eruditely, eloquently—I was told—about it. But ironically, it was digital, the internet, that was now forging the relationship that I desperately, selfishly, wanted to fan into a conflagration, damn the consequences. I laid my long fingers—the ones that had caressingly clawed his arm—on the keyboard, felt the reassuring pimples of the "F" and "J" keys, and knew it was now impossible to stop myself from somersaulting into the void. I didn't give a shit about the endowed position; I wanted him inside me, physically, artistically, spiritually . . .

From: Nadia Fontaine <Nfontaine@RegentsU.edu>
To: Raymond West <Rwest_Lit@RegentsU.edu>
Subject: Where are you?
Date: 12 September 2017

My Raymond,

I haven't heard anything from you all day. I would hate it if you concluded this exchange of ours should be aborted for whatever reasons. I learned today that your "wife"—the one who has colonized your unconscious and recommended you burn your legacy work—is about to gift the library with an undisclosed sum. I don't want you to think I'm the Countess Aurelia of *The Madwoman of Chaillot*. I understand we have to be careful. But what an exultation it brought me to hear you come alive for the first time in years and be excited about writing again, even if it is only the germ of an idea, even if it involves working with someone who could compromise you reputationally. Do you know how badly I want to see you and hear it in your own voice and live it in the cocoon we've constructed in these emails? You know you can count on my discretion, don't you?

They're pressuring me now to speed along the processing of your papers. I can't tell you how much I dread finishing. My dream, of course, is that I will never be finished. There are, however, some questions I would love to ask you. They would save me a lot of research time. If that's all that's left, if those are the tattered ribbons dangling now in the void of this nascent fantasy whose light was extinguished before ever being born.

Sorry for being dramatic,
Nadia

After hitting Send, I pushed back from my desk, swiveled in my chair, stood and walked down the hall to Joel's office. Joel, in headphones, didn't notice me come in. I swung out an extra desk chair and plopped down in it, folded my arms against my chest and forced him to look at me. When he finally noticed me in his peripheral vision, he started, tore off his headphones and turned to face me. "Nadia. Jesus."

"Can you rip me a DVD of our film?" I asked.

"Uh. Sure."

"Have you heard the news?" I asked, leaning forward into Joel's face.

"Santa Anas are still blowing, and it's corduroy to the horizon with perfect offshore winds?" he said.

"Probably that, too." I smiled, relieved now that I had written that email and sent it.

He glanced at his watch. "You should come out, Nadia. It's going to be epic."

Epic? He had no idea. "I'm working late."

"What's the news?" he asked apprehensively.

"I guess West's wife is giving a huge gift to the library," I said.

"Oh, yeah?" Joel said. "Changes afoot?"

"I heard a rumor they're going to endow a couple positions," I told him, as if it were priceless gossip.

Joel thrust two thumbs in the air. "Yes. New boards for the quiver."

I couldn't suppress a smile, but then my chin slumped to my chest. "I'm under a lot of pressure to get West done. They threatened to team-process me."

"What?" said Joel, mouth agape in empathic horror.

I nodded, narrowing my eyes. "I'm in love with this collection, Joel," I confided. "I'm not ready to let it go."

"I know." He was resigned to the fact that the processing of Raymond's papers had kidnapped a big part of me away from the time we spent together, the films we conceived of making, the long talks on film and literature. Our surfing sessions had to be put on hold, our lunch breaks in the bower were less frequent.

"I told them I was producing hard copies of everything digital in the collection."

Joel's eyes bulged. "I bet that made Helena happy."

I shook my head with exaggerated ominousness. "Since you've been doing the raw ingests to the dark archives, I wonder if you could help me start printing out some of the files." I fished in my pocket for a sheet of folded-up paper, opened it and handed it to him. He looked down at it. "I'd prefer if you didn't show this to anyone. They're tightening the noose. I don't want them micromanaging us."

"Okay. Anything for you, Nadia."

"I don't mean to dump all this work on you," I said.

"No problem, hot stuff."

"I'm going to Human Resources for that." I brandished a teasing index finger at him as I rose from the swivel chair.

"Who's the DVD for?"

"I just want a copy for my personal records." I said unconvincingly.

"You're naked on it," he said.

"I know, Joel." I smiled. From the cloud that scudded across his face he intuited why I was smiling.

I returned to my cubicle, eased into my chair and stared in contemplation at all the folders stacked high on the table, mentally calculating the work that still lay ahead. I glanced at one of the container lists and then flung it aside. A sigh surged and ebbed in my chest at the prospect of the work that remained and the arbitrary deadline I had committed to. Two months would be barbarous. I would have to devote weekends. Important to get to it though. West was mine and mine alone. And no, I wouldn't quit. I spun around in my chair and moused my screen to life. The clouds parted and my heart leaped to infinity when I saw his email:

From: Raymond West <Rwest_Lit@RegentsU.edu>
To: Nadia Fontaine <Nfontaine@RegentsU.edu>
Subject: Re: Where are you?
Date: 13 September 2017

Can you come by my office in Arts & Humanities around 4:00 tomorrow?

—RW

From: Nadia Fontaine <Nfontaine@RegentsU.edu>
To: Raymond West <Rwest_Lit@RegentsU.edu>
Subject: Re: Re: Where are you?
Date: 13 September 2017

I'll try. Kidding. Of course!

EMILY

Emily, in an eerie déjà vu of her dead predecessor, strode into the library late for her West status update meeting. She proudly, but invisibly, wore the numen of Nadia's presence. It was as if Nadia brought her into the room by some otherworldly transit to face the selfsame cold, inquisitional stares of Helena and Jean.

"Good morning, everyone." Emily slung her purse over the back of the chair. Could they read the guilt on her face? Had someone in IT been mirroring her actions on her work computer and this was the real reason for the meeting, not a status update? Jean chewed gum with an annoying snapping and popping sound.

"How are you, Emily? Settling in?" Helena offered cheerfully, spearheading the meeting.

"Yes," Emily said. "Thank you. Del Mar's beautiful. And every time I come to the library, I'm in awe of the architectural design. Sometimes I see arrogance. And sometimes I see eternity." She smiled. She had an idiosyncratic habit of setting boundaries by holding people at arm's length with a burst of non-sequitur lyrical description that often took them by surprise, momentarily stunning them into speechlessness. "The treasures it must hold."

Emily noticed Jean's eyes widening, her brows bowing. "Well, then," she began, "Can you give us a progress report on West?"

Emily rummaged in her purse and produced a square of paper and unfolded it to the full letter size of a page. She set it on the table and smoothed it out with both hands and began to read from it. She itemized the work that she had processed since the new addition, the items that had been inputted into the finding aid, recommendations on what to do with certain digital materials whose final archival domain was yet to be determined. She looked up from the comfort of her notes. "And there are some items missing from the document boxes that are cataloged in the finding aid."

A silence dropped with the weight of her declaration. Jean and Helena exchanged looks of wordless consternation.

"What items?" asked Jean in a quavering voice.

"I'm not sure. They're denoted by carefully coded abbreviations on the folder and item level," Emily said.

"Where?" asked Helena, examining her nails.

"In my predecessor's personal file."

Helena's face turned to stone. Jean tensed for an explosion.

"Where did you find her file?" Helena inquired, eyes blazing, head telescoping in Emily's direction.

"In one of the document boxes," Emily lied. "She must have kept it hidden there for security reasons." She shrugged.

Jean stiffened. She glanced at Helena for a reaction, but all she got was granite.

Helena's eyes shifted to Jean's. She pouched out a cheek with her tongue, rose noisily from her chair and muttered, "I have to make some calls. Carry on."

Jean waited until Helena had stormed out, before she got up and closed the door to the conference room. The soundproofed quiet of the room now magnified the popping of the gum she was nervously chewing. Emily inured herself to it as she best she could.

Jean shuffled some pages on the desk in front of her. "I'm glad your predecessor's file has been helpful to you," she began in a clipped, specious tone. Emily waited for the elaboration, arms folded across her chest. "You understand that she left under very sensitive, *very acrimonious*, circumstances." The words of Nadia's and Raymond's early emails now burned on the lenses of Emily's glasses like movie subtitles. A flare went off in her head. Given West's literary prominence those emails should be a part of his collection. Is that what Nadia was thinking when she jettisoned them out to the immense dark archives? She only caught snippets of her supervising archivist's lecture—"broad strokes;" "eighth-floor remodel;" "the rechristening of Memorial Library"—when she finally brought herself to look at gum-chewing Jean after she realized she had come to a halt in her demeaning of Emily and was waiting for a response with unblinking black eyes.

"I understand the exigencies of the changed circumstances," Emily said.

"You need to work within our parameters."

Emily suppressed an urge to snarkily correct Jean on her misuse of the mathematical term *parameter*. "I am working within our *boundaries*."

Jean, frustrated, for reasons Emily couldn't ascertain, pushed her chair back from the table and stood. From an up-angle she appeared older than her late thirties. For a brief moment Emily felt sorry that she was nailed to the cross between a domineering, Argus-eyed Helena and archivists like Nadia and Emily who devoted themselves to their work with a respect for the collection, a passion to preserve the cultural record, a pride in the finished process. No matter how much effort Jean employed to wrench herself free, she would always feel the nails tearing into her flesh. Resurrection would only come at retirement. And even then, Emily thought witheringly, the memories wouldn't amass into anything worth remembering.

"There's nothing in that personal file I should be concerned about, is there?" Jean pried, as she stood at an angle in the doorway.

Emily returned Jean's questioning eyes with a blank expression. "I'll let you know if I think there is."

NADIA'S STORY (CONT'D)

I slipped out of work early, unnoticed, moving swiftly. With seniority, with the prestige of being elected a fellow by the Society of American Archivists, I didn't have to account for my comings and goings the way others might have felt obligated to.

Adrenalized by my "appointment" with Raymond, I crossed the main lobby in a few coltish strides and disappeared into the bathroom. Out of the chill of Special Collections, I hurriedly shed my sweater. Underneath, I wore a cleavage-revealing black scoop dress. From my tote bag I rooted out a pair of ankle-high black boots and replaced my sneakers. Leaning into the mirror, I refreshed my face with some foundation and a touch of concealer, and I painted my full lips a dark and striking garnet.

The door banged opened, startling me. A figure loomed in the mirror like a harbinger of shattered fantasies. Helena's unmistakable perfume assaulted me with its floral fetor. She drew up next to me at the adjoining sink and turned on the water. *Did she just come in to wash her hands?* I wondered.

"That's a pretty dress, Nadia," Helena said to my image in the mirror. "I don't remember you wearing it earlier."

"I have an audition," I blatantly lied, enjoying it.

"Oh, that's right. You sometimes act in amateur theater."

I silently seethed at the pejorative *amateur theater. Aspiring writer; amateur actress.* What pissed me off even more was I knew it was deliberate. It was so like Helena though, this territorial belittling of everyone, that it wasn't worth it for me to take offense, even if I did feel like slapping her in the face and announcing I was quitting to write a novel with a famous writer. My retribution would be in my love affair—if it happened—and the subterranean fault line it would open up beneath her.

I finished up, collected my purse, and turned to go. "Sorry about my little contretemps earlier," I said. "I'm fully aware of what's at stake."

"Good luck, Nadia. I hope you get the part."

Escaping the bathroom, I exhaled a sigh of relief and crossed the main lobby in lengthening strides and emerged outside. It was still baking hot. A traveling sun burned butterscotch through the towering eucalypti. A flock of ravens was wheeling high overhead in lazy circles, croaking warnings to me before settling in the branches to rule sentinel over the sprawling university campus.

As I made my way from the library, I glanced down at the gigantic tongue of the anaconda that balefully announced the start of the descent of the Alexis Smith Snake Path, the irony not lost on me that I was metaphorically entering some gaping maw of mythological peril. The colossal snake sculpture seemed in arrested peristalsis, its fanged mouth devouring me, pulling me inexorably down to Walden College and the Arts & Humanities Building where Professor Raymond West was waiting. Against the twilight sky, Bruce Nauman's subversively colorful, pulsing neon *Vices and Virtues* art installation festooned the top of one of the engineering buildings in a frieze of ever-changing word contradictions. Pairs of vices and virtues were superimposed in blue, yellow, pink, and white, composed of a mile of neon tubing in flashing composited arrangements: FAITH/LUST, HOPE/ENVY, CHARITY/SLOTH, PRUDENCE/PRIDE, JUSTICE/AVARICE, TEMPERANCE/GLUTTONY, and FORTITUDE/ANGER. The horizontally moving paradoxical word combinations wrapped around the eaves of the building, traveling swiftly like an electronic stock market ticker tape. Virtues moved clockwise and vices counterclockwise at a faster rate so that every conceivable combination of opposites could be displayed.

"Prudence" was not uppermost in my mind as I made my way down the back of the enormous reptile. "Desire" for connection for anything other than the life I was emotionally suffocating in was pulling me magnetically, and "Hope" teemed in my heart like a river overflowing its banks, the true siren that was calling to me through the swaying and creaking trees. Don't let me get that old and not have lived life, I cried out in my head. In my fatalistic mindset, and now keenly aware of the gigantic stakes that bore the future of the library and all that Elizabeth West's gift promised, I feared Raymond was backpedaling. Email can be unnervingly misleading, I reasoned. It heightens fantasy, but too often fails to deliver fulfillment. I shook out my hair in an effort to dislodge the memories of the handful of affairs I wasn't proud I had conducted that had originated in email correspondence and then burst aflame like prairie fires. A business card was passed, smiles were exchanged, a furious back-and-forth exploded like antinomian currents driven by loneliness and lust, exaggerated by mutual fantasies of something new and forbidden, expectation doused by disappointment. One recent encounter had crossed into the prurient and then leaped a black river into the world of light BDSM. The barrens of my marriage had driven me to such a state of desolation that it propelled me into wanting to be with some anonymous man, bound and blindfolded, my bottom spanked crimson and ravished savagely just so I could feel something, anything. I cut it off abruptly to the man's unhappiness, not because I felt afraid or guilty, but because I felt nothing—even though he felt everything, he importuned in unreturned emails, bombarding me with compliments and a deluge of requests for assignations he described in luridly salacious detail. The only aspect of it that excited me was the email leading up to the profane encounter, material I would later cannibalize for my Pushcart winner, much, it appeared, to Raymond's dismay. Did he judge me for it because I had dared to mine the personal? How hypocritical if that were true? I shrugged off the sordid memory, glad I had been able to at least alchemize it into *art*. In the end, I felt exploited by the experience. It didn't make me feel alive as I had fantasized. It deadened me to sex and numbed me to love. What made me feel alive, however ephemerally, was the hope in the furious email exchange that led up to the encounter that it *would* make me feel alive.

It didn't. I longed for something deeper.

These few trysting past encounters that had suffused me with equal measure of thrill and shame played on my mind as I entered the ground floor of the Arts & Humanities building. I waited for the elevator. When the doors clanged open an older, goateed man boarded with me and shuffled his way to the rear of the compartment, perhaps to gain a fuller, more unobstructed view of me, my revealing black dress, my muscular thighs, my kissable neck. I could feel his goatish eyes preying on me, the ghost of his hands pawing me. I threw him a backward glance, and he smiled at me with the moist gleam of lechery. I looked quickly away. He disembarked at the third floor, but not before drinking me in one last time as the doors scissored him off from view.

At the fourth and top floor, the elevator doors swung open to the administrative assistant Eileen, who gyrated in her office chair like a two-tentacle octopus managing her cluttered desk. I approached her with an ever-widening smile. We had met before, probably at a university event, but I blanked on her name. She was in her forties and had the weary, road-mapped face of an overworked drone for demanding academics. Professors disgorged from their offices, dropping items off for her: packages to be shipped via campus mail; requests to put in calls to various individuals to arrange appointments; questions she was supposed to know the answers to, but promised she would find out. When she recovered a moment of sanity from the chaos of her duties, she looked up into my anxiously waiting face.

"Hi, Eileen," I furtively read from the name plate on the desk. "I have an appointment with Professor West. Nadia Fontaine."

Eileen cast me a sidelong look. "Hi, Nadia. That's a pretty dress."

"Thank you. I have an event this evening."

She raised her head. "Ah." People were hard to decipher at the university. Was it a compliment or was there a dissimulated meaning that women like me shouldn't be wearing something blatantly provocative for a visit with a man as prominent as Raymond West?

Eileen picked up the phone, punched three buttons with a painted nail, waited, and spoke into the mouthpiece. "A Nadia Fontaine here to see you, Professor." She waited. "Okay. I'll send her down." She smiled back up at me. "Do you know where you're going?"

"Yeah, thanks." I peeled away to the west-facing corridor, feeling Eileen's suspicious little thumbtack eyes tracking my exit. I tried not to sashay down the corridor in a burst of euphoria, hurrying to his office, even if that's how I felt. Proverbial tongues would proverbially wag. Rumors could flare up and had the combustible power to rupture reputations and ostracize faculty and staff without warning, isolating them, islanding them, destroying their lives and reputations. Rumors of forbidden romances were particularly insidious in academic settings where envy, and adultery, were pandemic, and imaginations were annealed in the cauldron of timeless literature.

I walked with a professional gait and a serious mien as if I had come seeking answers to pressing archival questions. Professors I knew casually passed me in the hall and their eyes darted fugitively in my direction, wondering perhaps, from their expressions as they passed, if they knew me. I felt twin pangs of nervousness mingling with affirmation as I knew I was probably the most dressed-up woman to visit the fourth floor that day.

At office number 411, before I could knock, the door swung inward, and I found myself staring into the face of a woman ten years my junior. Straight brown hair tumbled to her shoulders, and the oversized glasses and nervous tremor in her voice made me surmise she was a Lit graduate student. She had a file folder bracketed to her chest and was looking into the office on backward retreating steps. Raymond's face appeared, filling the room with presence and—dare I admit?—celebrity. "Okay, Professor, I'll revise my thesis proposal and have it to you next week. Thank you." Raymond smiled at the woman, then his eyes shifted over her shoulder and met mine. The graduate student turned and ran straight into six feet of woman. If she had harbored any fantasies about Professor West, she had met her competition, and by her disappointed expression, a thunderstorm had erupted over that prairie fire.

"Okay, Michelle," Raymond said, his eyes locked on mine.

Michelle smiled up at me perfunctorily. "Excuse me."

I stepped aside, and the grad student slipped past me. I followed her leave-taking for a moment and then turned back to Raymond. He was wearing faded jeans, Clarks desert boots, and an off-white muslin button-down shirt, sleeves rolled to the elbows, tanned arms visible, as if he had emerged from an exhaustive session of writing.

"Hi, Nadia" Raymond eventually greeted me. "I waited all day for you." He opened the door wider to his office and motioned me in. I stepped into his inner sanctum. With beating heart, I could hear the door close with a powerful solidity, a finality, like the door to a tomb, closing on a future that I hoped would be ideated and charted in detail for all eternity. I would sail with him anywhere, damn the consequences.

When the door thundered closed, I realized that we were suddenly all alone in his office, ensconced away from the world. I approached him and offered my hand. He took it in his and held it meaningfully for the longest time before saying, "I missed you. That time in Special Collections still haunts me."

"Oh," I said, lingering on the *oh*. "Why *haunts*?"

"Because I can't expunge it from my mind," he said in a serious tone. "Seeing my work arrayed like that. Meeting you . . . my archivist . . . I'm still there in my imagination."

Our eyes swam in the dusky light until they met. Flecks of mica glinted in his, agitated and excited by my presence, I sensed, wanted to believe.

He opened an arm to a two-cushion couch and beckoned me to sit. I eased into the smooth black leather and drank in his office with inquisitive eyes. Bookcases crowded every available wall, rising from the tiled floor to the paneled ceiling. Unopened padded envelopes containing more books were stacked against one of the bookcases. Raymond occupied a chair with a high, flexible back so he could throw his Clarks boots up on the desk if he felt inclined. On the west-facing wall, a half-shuttered, amber-tinted, rectangular window divided the cement in two. Silhouettes of paragliders at the nearby Gliderport—a popular cliffside recreational spot for experienced aeronauts who leaped off the sheer face of a precipice, only their chutes keeping them from a plummet to their doom on Black's Beach—passed by it like blips on a radar monitor.

I raised a finger to the bookcase behind him. "All of D. H. Lawrence," I commented, my voice quavery.

Raymond threw a backward glance at the row of Lawrence stationed behind him. "The plays I regret reading."

I laughed knowingly. "Unstageable."

He pointed to the ceiling. "I would turn the lights on, but the overhead lights in here were designed by a sadist who apparently wanted to punish middle-aged people like me."

I slipped him a smile and glanced down at my hands, warring with each other like scorpions in my lap. I stilled them and raised my head. With his left hand Raymond pushed the laptop on his desk to the side so he was afforded an unobstructed view of me. I could feel his eyes dreaming me to life. "I missed you, too," I finally confessed.

"Did you?" he asked.

He could see coals burning emphatically in my flashing eyes. "Email can be both exhilarating and frustrating," I said.

"You are one beautiful woman," he said matter-of-factly.

I could feel my face color and looked away with a blushing smile. From the corner of my blue eye, I could see him staring at me with what looked like an awestruck gaze. He bent forward and picked up the copy of *Knife in the Heart* that was resting prominently on his desk, and which I had noticed when I first came in.

"I love these stories in a way that's hard to express without you thinking I'm coming on to you."

"God forbid."

He chuckled, raised my book to his heart. "There's a soul-baring personal truth in your writing."

"The truth animates me," I said. "I'm drawn to extreme states of feeling." And then I transfixed him with a stare.

"I can tell," he said without unlocking his eyes from mine.

"I like being overwhelmed. I thirst for intensity," I added with a strong, deliberately husky voice for good measure.

A laughter rattled him. "You're no saint."

"It's fiction." I smiled in a lopsided way that indicated I was lying.

Raymond smirked doubtfully. "The detail is too exacting, the verisimilitude too piercingly real. What did your husband say when he read them?"

I shrugged. *Husband, wife, could he just lay off those words for once?* "He thought they were an expiation. Of the imagination."

"Naturally." Laughter shook Raymond again until it wrung tears from his eyes. When his laughter quieted, he nodded at the window. "Your time is nigh, Nadia, and if damnation is my fate, is that worse than a life of jaded torpor?" he poeticized to some invisible force. I wasn't sure what he was referring to. He shook his head in apparent disgust. "Fundraisers. Charity balls. I'm a pet chimp on a retractable leash reined in by money and measured daily by the calipers of fame. Crucified on a cross of my own conflicted carpentry. No wonder I'm dried up."

I gazed sympathetically upon the man I admired as he stared vacantly out the window, charting in vain, it seemed, the lost continent of his current writing life. Looking at him and hearing his words, I had an image of a beautiful caged bird, once a fierce raptor, imprisoned now in the administrative bureaucracy of academia and in a marriage that had poisoned his creative well and stilled his once fiery drive to bleak quiescence. His outstretched arm could reach the window, I thought, but the paragliders, seemingly insouciantly independent in their courting of death, were as distant as the wing-suited base jumpers standing high on a cliff overlooking a fjord in Norway on the opposite side of the planet.

"One day your work will be in an archive like mine," he mused to the world that sneered back at him.

"Are you shamelessly flirting, Professor?"

He relaxed his chin to his chest and smiled. "No." He raised his eyes to mine for emphasis. "Why don't you quit your job and give it a go full time?"

I shrugged and looked away. "It takes a lot of courage, doesn't it?" I finally managed. He didn't take his eyes off me. "Besides," I looked up, "if I had I wouldn't have met you."

Raymond's face creased into a smile. He bent his head to the window again and, hawklike, journeyed away for a moment. I worried suddenly whether he had been wrestling with second thoughts. Had the fervency of the email fantasy already disintegrated into the rubble of reality? Had the fourth floor of the Arts & Humanities building and his coveted corner office reeled him back to his senses? Had he forgotten his passionate words to me? Was this the moment he caressed and rotated the snow globe of my fantasy in his hands, shook it vigorously, and presented it back to me, when the fluttery flakes had settled, that *this* now was the stark reality? Was I no longer his beautiful archivist? This was not the man I had surrendered to in fantasy. Even though he opened by saying he had missed me, the dream seemed to be evanescing under the cold weight of his responsibilities, the institution we were both entombed in, that embodied, contained, and was the repository of, everything he would be risking. The paragliders, even if they lost the updraft, even if their chutes collapsed, still carried emergency parachutes. Desire this irresistibly powerful, given our mutual obstacles, provided no safety net between us and the void. The landing would be harder, grimmer, uncertain, that was for sure. But if it wasn't, I raced through these thoughts in my mind, it wouldn't plunge us to the depths we both needed to dive if we were going to write this book. I wanted badly to tell him this. Going back to those anonymous online encounters was depressing to contemplate, and I had to suspect that Raymond had wearied of the young women the university campus paraded before him, every year a new flotilla, every year him growing a year older but the girls remaining immutably youthful. It had to be depressing. Surely, like me, he longed for something deeper, more powerful, a bond that would produce something more lasting. I marshaled these thoughts to my expression when I looked up at him, hoping he would read me, waiting on the verdict.

And then my heart swelled with excitement when he murmured, "So, tell me, Nadia, about this mysterious, erotically named, dark archives." He winked, as if igniting the kindling in anticipation of the fire to burn.

My face colored and tears almost sprang to my eyes. Raymond threaded his fingers together and produced a little dome that he rested his chin on and waited. "What do you want to know?" I asked, enunciating each word as if were some form of flirtation game that literary-minded lovers engaged in before they threw off the intellectual pretenses and reverted to animals.

He grew serious, his tone almost interrogative. "What's out there? What's potentially out there? What—fictionally—could be jettisoned out there?"

"Is it beginning?" I wanted to know, a thrill suffusing me like a startled nest of spiders originating from my heart.

Raymond nodded slowly and definitively as if he had already given the proposition careful thought. "I'm not going to die in peace without going through this door that you've opened, Nadia. I'm glimpsing it now." He leaned on his elbows, held his head in his hands and bent toward me with eyes blazing so intense I thought I was going to faint. "I have a creative obligation now. You stomped open that door in Special Collections the other afternoon, wittingly or unwittingly. I would be miserable the rest of my life if I didn't venture a step through it." He leaned a few inches closer. "With you." He grabbed my modest collection of short stories and shook it with near thundered conviction. "I have no doubt that you can do this."

"Oh, I can do this. Just try me." I met his fierce gaze of conviction with one of my own. "It must be risky, in your position, to embark on a project in total secrecy?"

"It must be risky, in your position as an archivist working on my papers, to set sail with me as your co-mariner. We're both daft. But if we don't risk it, we will always wonder, won't we?"

"I wasn't sure," I heard my voice stammer.

He tapped an index finger on the cover of *Knife in the Heart*, which he still held in the air between us. "I want to go where you've gone."

"I would have thought you'd gone there and then some," I parried obliquely.

He shook his head. "Not with the likes of a woman like you."

I tried valiantly to suppress a smile but lost. "Jealousy is a swiftly moving stream. And its current devilishly runs both ways."

"That's *one* of the themes I want to explore. Among others."

"And what are the others?" I parried.

"Truth. Because truth is the last residue of all beings. And I want to descend into its burning, white-hot core one last time." He tapped my book again to underscore his declaration. "Like you." He paused dramatically. "With you."

I was momentarily paralyzed by his words and took a deep breath. I exhaled slowly out my nose toward the window and the diorama that metaphorized my freedom. "The dark archives is a vast network of servers," I started. "When an archive comes in, like yours, sometimes it's not completely curated. It all falls to me. Some items slip through the cracks—wittingly or unwittingly. And I stumble across things. Like the letters from Livia Galotti." Raymond shut his eyes in remembered embarrassment. "Besotted with you she was. Beautiful girl. Immortalized in your *Lessons in Reality*. What a lucky girl. Wrote you every day." Raymond nodded with his eyes still closed. I changed back to a more serious tone. "And I'm thinking, as your archivist"—I lowered my voice to a whiskey-throated whisper—"that maybe certain donors, or their heirs or their estate, wouldn't like this to be available for all the world to read. Because, you see, Professor"—I deliberately uttered *professor* like it was something wicked—"your work, because of its prominence in the literary firmament, is going to be made available to the public." Raymond opened his eyes questioningly and waited on my words, spellbound by my—to him, eroticized—intellect. "So, I'm thinking, these lovelorn letters—my God, she wrote to you every day, in longhand, poor thing!—are valuable precisely because they formed the basis for one of the characters in your legacy novel." Raymond leveled his eyes on mine, and I could see that he was already beginning the ideational process, the catastrophic molt. "But I'm guessing I'm going to meet some resistance if I choose to make these available. *Choose* being the operant word. But there's another alternative."

"The dark archives?" he asked, knowing the answer.

I nodded. "You're entering my world," I said in the sexiest voice I could muster.

"Because you believed they were of research value," he said.

I nodded vigorously now, enjoying the creative dialectic that had begun with this celebrated writer who valued me, I desperately wanted to believe, as an equal. "Yes. But more important, I thought, as any archivist, they should be preserved as part of the collection of Raymond West. Without which, in my perfectionistic way of going about things, your archive wouldn't be complete. And I would have to live with that omission the rest of my life in a grievous way that only archivists can relate to. We don't like to lose anything, be it to the ravages of time, the ineptitude of data managers, or the actions of bad actors, like certain higher-ups we fucking despise."

"The dark archives," Raymond incanted, blinking.

"You wouldn't believe what's out there that nobody knows about," I continued, growing excited, free-associating rapidly now. "Only two percent of what the Smithsonian has in its collections is available to the public. Did you know that?" Raymond shook his head. "The rest resides in these huge repositories, because they can't decide what to do with it, or it goes out to the dark archives, where it lives in a kind of island universe, findable one day if someone is diligent enough and has the motivation to want to travel there."

"An *island universe*," he said, smiling.

"Superannuated. But I prefer it to galaxy, don't you?"

He arched his eyebrows in assent. "And that's where you and I will live, in *The Archivist*," Raymond concluded inscrutably.

I swallowed hard, and my throat throbbed with nervous anticipation. In the hundreds of books that occupied his walls, my eyes alit on a title. As if following the mesmeric pull of a dowsing rod, I straightened from the couch, daring to cross his office without permission, and went directly to the book with an obscure but instinctual objective. I slipped it out, opened it, pretended to leaf through the pages, but now that I was that much physically closer to him, I was expecting something more. "*Le Rêve d'un Flagellant*," I murmured. I rotated to him slowly, fire smoldering in my eyes.

He seemed to be studying something in his mind and didn't answer, but his unblinking eyes were yearning.

I feigned immersion in the book. A second later, I heard a chair creak, releasing the weight it was holding, and it excited me; the delicate hairs stood up on my forearms, a sable softness. A patch of warmth grew closer to me, like the breath of an existence. I felt it the way an animal feels the approach of another animal, but in a nonthreatening, comforting way. I didn't hear him stand, he had unfolded his legs effortlessly, quietly, as if he had transmogrified into something spectral inhabiting me. I deliberately didn't turn to him for fear that whatever it was he was about to do, I would contaminate the mood. I held on to Vindas's book for support as my heart leaped about in my chest and those once-again agitated spiders disgorged from their wounded nest and swarmed in every direction, skittering across my nerve endings. Never in my life had I felt as alive as when his fingers lightly touched my perfumed nape. His hand traveled up my neck and combed my hair off one ear with fingers that gripped my head with an ardency that sent a shiver knifing through me.

"I've never seen such a beautiful neck in all my life," he ventriloquized through the ghost that brushed my back. To me, his voice was a susurration, like an angel wind rustling leaves in a quiet forest. I, of course, wanted him to think I was beautiful beyond anything he was ever going to find in his lifetime, but what I wanted most, what I had yearned for desperately all my life, was for him to imagine me creating something with him, where the rowing was equally shared, the plotting coordinated together. Creating as one.

"I don't want to be your muse," I whispered back, looking down at the cold, waxed tiles that shone back at me with a darker truth I hoped never to experience. "Or your amanuensis."

"No," he assured me. "It will be a true literary pas de deux." And then he bent penitentially—because we both knew in that instant that if we were to write this book, it would have to be everything or nothing—and touched his lips to my neck. Another shiver seized me, and all the spiders swarmed afresh in my being, and my blood was in tumult, coursing hotly. I spun and rushed to meet his mouth. His came to mine with a force that was unmistakably one of deferred longing—*All the goddamn emails*, he must have been thinking—as we kissed with a powerful, and equal, force of mutual desire. It was as if we were now bolted together by a pact voiced by the mutual stirrings of our hearts. I could feel his strong hands spread open like the wings of a bird on my back pulling me toward him. Mine were pressed to his shirt and my thumbs were tickled by the fine tufts of hair that sprawled out from where his shirt was unbuttoned at the collar. I felt an urgency in me to unbutton two more, reach my hands in, and feel his warm chest, feel his heart through his flesh to convince myself he was real. With his lips still planted firmly on mine, I grew disoriented. The floor momentarily gave beneath me, and I was floating. He broke the spell by withdrawing, but his eyes bore into mine with the unmistakable intensity and incandescence of a man who was as desperate to feel alive again as I was.

"I can only write if I am free and free from censure. I don't want to live any other way. I can't. I won't," he finished defiantly, as if he were speaking to other, more oppressive, forces impinging on his life. Still stunned by the kiss and the pact we had sealed, I found myself nodding at his profession of newfound purpose, and I trusted him. Not for a moment did I believe that it wasn't paramount in his intentions. He had too much at stake to fabricate a collaboration if all he wanted was to hike up my dress and ravish me against a cavalcade of toppling books. If all he wanted was an affair with his archivist, then as compromising and clandestine and risky and messy as it would have been, I would have given him that too. It could have followed the soul-destroying trajectory that those relationships usually do, and I wouldn't have cared. This was a deeper avowal of intent, born from the work I had done on his papers, from the short stories I had published and that he had frankly admired. Here was a man, a successful man in the arts, who could have me for my body but who desired me even more for my imagination, for my talent, for my creative powers, what some referred to as my "blinding intellect." I blinked back tears. The validation that our coming together was more than physical, was something divinely, privately cathartic. Together, we would produce something as intangible as air, as ungraspable as a dream, as timeless as a memory.

His lips found mine again, he kissed me forcefully, and to me, in that vertiginous moment, it was as if he was affirming our collaboration with a hot wax seal.

"Keep writing me email," he exhorted breathlessly, as if sand was running out of the hourglass. I nodded, my black lashes flashing back tears in my eyes. "And I'll write back. And it will start to take shape of its volition." My hooked fingers, desperate for more physicality, lightly clawed his chest through his shirt. "And I'll make arrangements for us to be together." He paused, and his eyes tunneled into mine. "We can't just imagine this." He paused for blatant dramatic effect. "We have to live it with all the intensity required to write it."

"I know." We were conspiring to be adulterers, but I was yearning to be swept up in this tumult of promise, fuck the consequences. *I want to live. And this is how I want to live!*

And our mouths closed again with each other's and this time it was sexual, my hand traveling where it shouldn't have, his tracing my nipples beneath the fabric of my dress, burying his head in my cleavage. I gripped him more firmly. Looked into his eyes and gave him silent permission to be taken.

One hand had pulled up my dress to my buttocks when a timid knock sounded at the door. Raymond's hands moved swiftly, and instinctively, from the flesh of my ass to the front of my shoulders and gently shoved me away. All the fire and romance of our incipient collaboration had drained from him as his eyes darted to the door.

Sensing his alarm, I reluctantly withdrew. Then I grew scared. "It's not . . . ?"

"No. God, no. She wouldn't come here."

I hastily put myself back together, drew in my lips because my lipstick had no doubt smeared my mouth with his fierce kisses. Raymond combed his hair with his hand, looking agitated, the consternation in his expression unassuaged.

"You were here asking some questions about my archive," he whispered to me.

"Okay," I whispered back.

"Okay." Worried suddenly that he had spoiled the moment, he fixed me with one last tunneling gaze, raked a hand through my thick hair, held my head by the scalp and shook it ever briefly, lovingly—that look a contract!—then turned to the door with a fraught look.

It was a male colleague, wanting Raymond's opinion on the preparations for an upcoming lecture event.

Raymond opened the door wider. "This is one of the archivists working on my papers," Raymond introduced me, without divulging my name.

The older professor glanced between the two of us without overt suspicion, smiled benignly. I returned the smile, then turned to Raymond as I stepped past the colleague, "Thank you for your time, Professor. It was extremely . . . enlightening."

"We'll talk soon." He shot me a furtive wink.

Dizzy, I walked crookedly out of Arts & Humanities, swerved around

Eileen's panoptic station, and sailed down the stairs because I didn't want to wait for the abysmally slow elevator, not with all the energy that had built up in me. I levitated across the campus to the Widmer structure, fantasizing about informing Helena that I had nailed the audition and been offered the part but, in reality, irrationally eager to inform her that I had unblocked Raymond West and that a new work was in the offing. That would raise the roof on the eighth floor! I rhapsodized deliriously in a head that was a kaleidoscope of pure, weightless bliss.

I floated across the campus, bounded up three floors in the Widmer parking structure, and climbed into my car. In the relative privacy of the parking structure, I quickly changed into my wet suit. I squealed tires turning around the spiral that led out of Widmer and roared to where the surfers parked for Black's. I would surf until the sun had set, and since it was a waxing full moon, I might keep surfing into the encroaching darkness, when the waves exploded in white phosphorescence out of nowhere. I had all this pent-up energy to discharge, and the exhilaration of surfing until exhaustion wearied all my limbs was the anodyne I needed.

EMILY

Emily let her head loll to the pillow, threw her arm back like someone feeling faint and fell into a state of lassitude. Her laptop had slid off her thighs, the last email from Nadia dimmed on the screen as the battery-saving features had kicked in somewhere when Emily had lost herself in Nadia's recounting of her and Raymond's first kiss. Shame of her voyeurism quickly surrendered to the quicksand of a love affair, Nadia's nakedly intimate memoir, presumably written for the replenishment of her sanity, providing Emily the connective tissue between the emails, and a damning personal account in its own right. Following a strange and fortuitous trail, Emily had tunneled her way into the beginnings of a remarkable exchange, mined personal gold, but she wondered if she should stop. She needed to talk to someone, but there was no one—not even Joel—with whom she could confide what she had read. A married archivist and a married donor, concurrent with an archive that was actively being processed, falling in love and kissing wildly—in a campus building, no less!—was beyond inappropriate; it knifed dangerously close to the heart of the stated ethics of the profession itself.

Emily glanced at her cell: 1:11 a.m. As per her superstition, she waited patiently until it turned 1:12, then she closed her eyes. A swell had arrived from a hurricane off Baja California, as Joel had predicted, and she could hear the waves cracking like liquid whips on the backs of shallow waters in the quiet of the night. Sets were composed of four or five waves, thundering one after another in short intervals, and then the ocean went silent like a large animal pausing, tensing in the dark. The occasional rise and fall of a car speeding past seemed to jump-start her thoughts all over again. "I can only write if I am free and free from censure," Emily whispered out loud to the walls. "I don't want to live any other way. I can't." With only the existence of their words, Emily tried to travel back in time and imagine what Nadia felt when Raymond told her that, holding her in his arms, staring into her tear-filmed eyes. She tried to teleport herself into Nadia's shoes at that precise moment, but the scene wasn't materializing, wasn't coming alive. And three months later, she was dead. Surfing at night, according to the articles. Another powerful set of waves approached the shore, exploding one after another in a concatenation of blasts. Hard to imagine being out there all alone at night. It was too much for Emily's tired mind. She was too exhausted to try to fathom the unfathomable.

CHAPTER 10

The Archivist

8/20/18

I've been remiss in writing here. The reading of the e-pistolary exchange between Nadia Fontaine and Raymond West has consumed me. I'm in possession of materials I shouldn't be in possession of. Without permission, I removed them from university property—there, I admitted it. What I have on my computer, if it were ever discovered, could get me ostracized for life from ever getting another job as an archivist in a university setting. It's a small society, Professor Erickson always warned me. Disrepute is worn like a tattered garment.

My predecessor, Nadia Fontaine, risked this, too, when she fell in love with a donor and started communicating with him, sneaking around the Director of Special Collections and her Supervising Archivist with these impermissible exchanges. Complete breach of all protocol, at the very least. Why would she risk it? Love? The book they were conceiving of writing together? Surely she knew the consequences. Was she that unhappy in her job? Or had her definition of happiness changed? Had the collection itself transformed her in some way I'm at a loss to comprehend? I should stop, but I can't.

I continue to labor away on West's papers, but there's another river of truth, a corollary to the one that I'm preparing to be presented to the public. A subterranean river, on whose banks the water is rising.

Emily took a late lunch. Following Nadia's path to the Arts & Humanities Building on Walden College, she sauntered down the back of the Alexis Smith Snake Path. Its scales were replicated by oversized hexagonal tiles, in grays, whites, and pastels smoothed by years of foot traffic. Its skin was slightly rounded to give pedestrians the subtle sense that they were tightrope walking on the back of a giant, slumbering serpent that could awaken at any moment and pitch them into the trees and bushes that lined the winding path. But Nadia *really had* walked on the back of that serpent. Nadia really had tickled the tail of the dragon, Emily thought as she looked down at her tennis shoes, flashing suddenly on a description of an early experiment in nuclear fission where a physicist had slowly moved two blocks of subcritical masses together to find its criticality and, in what must have been a tense moment, brought them too close.

A reckless skateboarder whooshed past, carving a turn around Emily, rattling her nerves, rudely disrupting her ruminative moment. His approach was sudden and discordant, and she reached her hands to cover her ears, but it was too late. Crouched low, he screeched away from her on clacking wheels.

"Hey!" she shouted. "Not cool, asshole!" She kept her hands clasped over her ears until she was sure the skateboarder's grinding, squealing cacophonous wheels had receded into the distance.

Halfway down the snake path, Emily settled on the concrete bench in the bower with the quote by Milton about leaving Paradise now more meaningful than ever. She wondered how many times Nadia had sat here, lunching all alone, recovering from another broadside delivered by an often splenetic Helena, or fulminating in her head over a new manifesto posted by Jean bolstered by spreadsheets and impossible-to-meet goals of linear feet needing processing, and dreading the drive back to the generic bedroom community of Black Mountain Ranch and a husband who loved her for all the wrong reasons, debating delaying that drive with an evening glass paddle with Joel or by herself, romanticizing the West Papers that she was processing . . .and then swept up in fantasizing the way their affair would unfold—like flowers fated to wilt and die, or trees that grew tall and whose bark was flesh and pearled with perspiration.

"Mind if I join you?" A familiar voice startled Emily.

She looked up and found the tanned face of Joel and his bleached blond surfer locks tumbling down his shoulders over yet another T-shirt announcing his affection for an obscure writer or avant-garde filmmaker, this one Luis Buñuel. "Sure," she said, relieved that it was Joel.

Joel eased onto the bench next to her, careful not to brush her with his thigh. "I'm glad the fires have stopped. But not the Santa Anas. I am digging those offshore winds."

Emily smiled at her interlaced fingers in her lap, relieved to be hoisted out of her introspection by inane chitchat with someone she felt comfortable with. She wanted to metaphorize that the fires might have been finally contained in the foothills of San Diego, but new fires had flared in her life and were conflagrating within her soul, ravaging treacherously in unpredictable directions, and that she was powerless to stop them. Instead, she absently peeled the tangerine that she had laid out on a napkin. Joel popped the top on a canned cold brew coffee, threw back his head, and quenched his thirst.

"How can you drink that shit?" Emily asked, her annoyance arising more from the sound of the pop-top snapping and the drink releasing its carbonated pressure than any concern for Joel's health.

Joel held up the can. "Hey, Bird Rock cold brew. It's awesome." In an outstretched arm he offered her a taste. She took it from him and sipped.

"Hmm. Not bad." Emily handed it back to him.

A silence, born of unspoken questions, descended. A gust of wind rustled the dry leaves high in the branches of the groaning eucalyptus trees, trunks creaking as they bent. The sudden croaking of ravens overhead made them both raise their heads and train their gazes straight up.

"They're loud," Emily said.

"They know we're here," Joel speculated, head still bent skyward.

"Yeah, you told me. You really believe that?"

"Yeah. I've seen evidence of it."

"What evidence?" Emily asked.

The family of ravens alit on discrete branches, settled and quieted, becoming invisible. "When your predecessor—when Nadia, sorry—died, the ravens were in a state of discombobulation and agitation for like a week or longer."

Emily swiveled her head to Joel's. "How did that manifest itself?"

"They would see me, but they would fly round and round, wheeling in circles, as if something was aberrant in their world, croaking like crazy, as if in mourning, as if they knew, sensed, intuited, whatever . . . that she was gone." He mimicked the best he could their anguished cries. "I'm telling you, it was a collective, heartfelt cry, as if they knew her physical being was no more and her spirit had risen to somewhere they were calling out to in collective sorrow."

Emily looked at Joel with bright, flashing eyes. "That's kind of beautiful, Joel."

"I'm no Neruda, but I've written my fair share of poetry." Joel shrugged. He let his head sag.

"And you believe it's because the ravens were missing her? Divining her absence?"

Joel nodded. He took another sip of his cold brew. "I don't want you to think I'm another weirdo wearing a tin foil hat. But yeah, I do." He turned to her. "They know the regular staff here. Trust me." He pointed at both eyes with straightened index fingers. "They can spot us like gophers. And I've even seen them swoop down to get a closer look if there's a new hire like you."

Emily lifted her eyes to the tops of the trees. "You think that's why they just now swooped down?"

"They never come here when I'm alone," he said. "They know me. But they're just getting introduced to you. They're watching us. Absolutely."

"You're creeping me out," she said.

"Birds are smart, Emily. They see this whole scrambled pattern of Earth from their unique vantage point unlike any other creature. They only lack the language to convey their knowledge to us. What man has done to them is one of the worst genocides." He shook his head in pained disgust.

Emily separated a section of her tangerine and raised it to her lips. When she bit down on it, the burst of tart citric acid puckered her mouth.

Joel dropped his chin on his shoulder. His melancholy eyes made him look forlorn. "Haven't seen you around much. You've been distant."

Emily could feel his eyes resting on the side of her face. Explanations weren't forming, and words lacking conviction were not her forte. In answer, she raised another section of tangerine and made it disappear into her mouth.

"I hope I didn't offend you that night at my place," Joel apologized sheepishly.

Emily shook her head. "I'm not looking for a relationship, Joel," she said honestly. "And I'm not into a casual thing." She turned to him. "But if I were, you'd be at the top of my list."

"I'll consider that a Pyrrhic Victory."

"You haven't lost anything, what's Pyrrhic about it?"

"Definition noted," Joel smiled.

They looked away from each other. A minute crawled by, but it felt like ten. Joel raised his head to the sky and asked, "What have you come across?" He said it with a distinct bite to his query, as if this were the real reason he had tracked her to the bower and pretended to come upon her by happenstance.

Emily turned to him and their eyes met beneath the watchful ravens who, perhaps startled by Joel's blunt question, without a signal to one another, took flight, wings beating, croaking agitatedly, flying their way to some unsettled matter in their own impregnable universe.

"Do you ever think about suicide?" Emily murmured into her lap, not sure where the unspooling non sequitur thread was taking her.

"Sometimes," he confided. "Why do you ask?"

Emily absently separated another supreme of tangerine, feeling the connective tissue of the fruit as if it could experience human pain as it was pulled apart. "I mean, have you ever been close? Have you ever been at its precipice?" She looked up at him.

He concentrated abstractedly on his canned cold brew. "Once I felt that way."

"What was it?" Emily asked.

"I guess it was a feeling of hopelessness, that life, or whatever I was going through, wasn't going to get better."

"What wasn't going to get better?"

"I was hopelessly in love with this woman. I thought she had feelings for me. I hadn't heard from her in a few days. Or maybe even like a week. I did something stupid." Joel paused and a guilty look darkened his expression. "I started to follow her." He shook his head in apparent disgust at himself. Then he threw out his arms in a gesture of self-deprecation, wanting to come clean, but half-afraid. "I know, you think I'm a creep."

"No," Emily assured him.

Joel's eyes narrowed. "She lived in one of those California-style beach cottages, so the windows were very accessible. I stole up to her bedroom window one night and there she was in bed with another guy." Joel kept shaking his head at the memory. "It wasn't only that she was with another guy. It was the way they were with each other." He stopped like he wasn't going to keep narrating this awful moment in his life.

"What do you mean?" Emily asked.

"They were doing things I couldn't imagine her doing." He chopped himself off, afraid to say any more.

"You felt doubly betrayed?" Emily asked, puzzled.

"Yeah! And I was fucking blown away!" Joel threw his arms up in the air.

"What were they doing that had you blown away?"

"I don't want to talk about it." Joel's tone insinuated he regretted what he had already confided. "It was all my fault. I shouldn't have followed her," he muttered. "But love is a fucking crazy trip. Cruel and paradoxical."

"Yeah. But what you saw was powerful enough that it made you contemplate taking your life," Emily said, reeling him back to the start of the conversation.

Joel nodded and then fashioned an expression suggesting it was in the past and the past had performed its job of smoothing the sharp, serrated edges.

"What do you think it was?"

"Well, for one thing, I knew she didn't love me. For another, I wondered how many others there had been. Most of all, I couldn't get the image out of my head. It plagued me for months. Drove me to suicidal despair." He turned to her with the cold brew raised to his mouth. "Does that answer your question?"

"Didn't mean to dredge up something unpleasant," Emily apologized.

"I lied to you about something." Emily waited for him to correct himself. "It wasn't her house. She met the man at his house."

"You followed her in your car?" Emily asked.

Joel shook his head. "No. I had her email. I followed the whole affair in email."

"Why didn't you call her out?"

"We weren't lovers," he confided, annoyed she had dredged an even more painful truth out of him. He stood abruptly, discomfited. Emily was hurt that she had upset him. But her curiosity couldn't be restrained.

"How did you have her email?"

Joel gazed up at the sky and the ravens that had winged their way to another location, their absence not buying him the solace he was seeking.

"Was she a colleague here?" Emily probed.

A lump worked rhythmically down Joel's guilty throat.

"It wasn't Nadia, was it?" she asked.

Joel staunched his answer with another drink of his cold, bitter coffee, but there didn't seem to be anything left in it because she could hear him sucking at its opening, a noise that grated on her. "You asked me about suicide, Emily. We may live in a sexist world, but women have a lot of power over men. They hold the keys to love through the gauntlet of jealousy." He waited a moment to see if the ravens would return, but help was not forthcoming. He started off, stopped, threw Emily a backward glance. "You never answered me."

"What?"

"What are you finding out there?"

"Exactly what you wanted me to find, Joel!" she practically shrieked at him.

Joel lowered his head and leveled his eyes at hers, Emily's blazing back at his for elucidation. They coupled in the bower's eucalyptus-perfumed air. An unspoken understanding streamed between them. Joel had given her the access to the dark archives without getting permission; Emily had ventured in. A single raven cawed. One had returned by herself. She perched on a tree, waiting restlessly for her lifelong mate.

Joel, with nothing to say, walked up the snake path back to the library, his chin hung on his chest. Emily watched him until he disappeared from view, then she withdrew her laptop from her tote, opened it, and went straight to the dark archives:

From: Raymond West <Rwest_Lit@RegentsU.edu>
To: Nadia Fontaine <Nfontaine@RegentsU.edu>
Subject: Subject to Subjective Subjects
Date: 18 September 2017

Dearest Nadia,

I booked us a room at Estancia, perilously situated across from the university because I know you said you were a dangerous woman who, in one of your short stories, "lived for treacherous waters." This Friday. I keep ruminating over what you told me about the dark archives. I've been in a febrile state ever since, scribbling notes and ideas like crazy. To quote Hemingway, "The pressure is building." It's eerily reminiscent of that halcyon time when I was gearing up to write *Lessons in Reality.* The. Same. Exact. Feeling. It's alternately exultant, it's thrilling, it's terrifying, all the things a writer should feel getting ready to set sail. I meant what I said when I told you this was now a creative imperative. And it's to you I owe that feverish impulse to write again. To you I owe that wanton feeling of liberation.

Now, I need for you to blow that door open and set these horses free!

Your Raymond

PS: Wait for my final instructions on Friday in case plans change—God forbid!

From: Nadia Fontaine <Nfontaine@RegentsU.edu>
To: Raymond West <Rwest_Lit@RegentsU.edu>
Subject: Re: Subject to Subjective Subjects
Date: 18 September 2017

My Raymond,

I want you to know, first off, how much your words mean to me. Though I doubt my paucity of works will ever be in an archive one day, it was nonetheless validating to hear you think so. And especially coming from you.

Yes, I want to blow the doors open, too.

My ass awaits your spanking hand!

From: Nadia Fontaine <Nfontaine@RegentsU.edu>
To: Raymond West <Rwest_Lit@RegentsU.edu>
Subject: Re: Re: Subject to Subjective Subjects
Date: 21 September 2017

My Raymond,

It's Thursday and I haven't heard from you about Friday. I sent you a letter through campus mail, but possibly you didn't get it. Maybe you're angry at me for sending you a letter—I swear it was discreet and anonymous. But after our meeting, our pact to begin this creative journey together, that heavenly kiss that still lingers in the heartstrings of my being, I wonder if you're not having doubts.

Please don't leave me hanging like this.

Nadia

NADIA'S STORY (CONT'D)

I signed out of Special Collections two times that morning, which was unusual behavior for me. On my second exit, Helena craned her neck across her desk and watched me stride by the always annoyingly open door to her office. I glimpsed her out of the corner of my eye, and her brewing suspicion, beetled brow and all, concerned me as I gushed out of the cold, air-conditioned library and emerged out into the punishing, blinding sunlight, fumbling in my bag for my dark sunglasses. I saw myself, the mysterious figure I cut, all in black, reflected in the paneled mirrors that flanked the entrance to the library like the individual frames of a film, blown up to real life and distorted like in a fun house attraction in some amusement park of academe.

I crossed the campus on winding walkways to Walden College in the direction of the Arts & Humanities Building, believing with a sly smile that I was the dark woman of mystery. I had no intention of going inside and confronting him. I had decided I wasn't going to be one of those clichéd women who, when ghosted, stalked their men until they gaslighted her. It was he, after all, who had supposedly made the arrangements for us to meet in the hotel. It was he who had said I had kindled a fire under him like no other. It was he who had sealed the promise with a kiss so powerful it still lingers at the forefront of my memory. I can close my eyes and feel it to this moment, as if it were flesh. His gift to me was this collaboration, no matter how fraught it was with danger. Wasn't that danger the seed of the core idea? I rationalized to myself as I sat perched on the precipice of an affair, my legs swinging over the void, my whole being ready to leap. My gift to him was in my purse. As his archivist, I knew, of course, that his first drafts were always written in longhand in the large, black Moleskine notebooks. Inside, on the title page, I had written,

The Archivist
(An Epistolary Exchange)
By Raymond West & Nadia Fontaine
Vol. I

It had thrilled me almost to a sexual excitation to fill out that title page. It evoked memories of the time when I printed out and bound my final proofed manuscript of short stories and sent it off in the mail, like writers once did before computers and email attachments. It was such an indescribable sense of accomplishment. And to be embarking on something new, it felt like I was turning a corner in my wretchedly lonely life, my stale and passionless marriage, my too often thankless job. I didn't need, or want, Tuscany or San Sebastian, Paris or London. I didn't need or want a string of dispiriting affairs and the dramas of spurned lovers that consequentially ensued. I needed this book! I needed him. He had wanted me, and I had wanted him ever since I began processing his papers, ever since I learned he not only lived close to where I worked, he was faculty. Why else would he say the things he did? Why else would he touch me longingly and kiss me deeply in his most private chamber? His heart was burrowed into mine too, wasn't it?

In the swirl of these unresolved self-recriminations, I found myself on a cold cement bench at Walden plaza, shifting uncomfortably, one leg crossed over the other, elbows dug into my thighs. From my purse I rummaged a rumpled pack of unfiltered Gitanes. I carried them with me, even though I had quit smoking, to remind me that I had quit smoking. Like a scorned Frenchwoman in a Rohmer film, I jerked up the pack and fished one out and planted it between my lips with trembling fingers. From months of being jostled in my purse the cigarette was a jagged line, the kind a bum might fish out of a pocket with gleaming eyes. Anyone who saw me lighting it—with shaking fingers?—would probably conclude I *was* mad or an addict going through withdrawals, but I was determined to light it anyway. It tasted acrid, the tobacco stale, the smoke hot and dry. I spat flecks of tobacco that clung to my lipstick in disdain of my wrecked beauty. Yes, I had reapplied lipstick on the walk to Arts & Humanities in that unconscious way that women do when they are in a hurry to meet their lovers. *But he wasn't my lover yet!* I crucified myself with self-abnegation. But what if he did come? What if he did see me? I wanted to look my best. My desperation was devouring me from inside. The cigarette sped my pulse and made me more overwrought. I quivered in fear that I had lost him, that he had come to his senses.

I raised my eyes to the entrance to Arts & Humanities. Hidden behind my dark Ray-Bans and far enough away I doubted anyone would recognize me, forlorn and shifting on that hard cement bench that dug into my ass, the minutes crawling interminably. Professors and graduate students and staff disgorged from that cold, gray cement fortress and spoked out in all directions like harried ants from a concrete hole in the first floor of the tomblike structure. I lifted my head to the fourth floor, where a single narrow window marked Raymond's corner office. I couldn't see in, but he could see out. If he was in there. If he was standing at the window, looking out, searching for me. And what would he think if he saw his archivist, pretzeled on a concrete bench with a bent Gitanes smoldering in her red-lipsticked mouth? Would he give up on me, if he already hadn't? I had no way of knowing. He hadn't responded to my last two emails, and I wasn't going to humiliate myself by bombarding him with any more. I couldn't call him; I didn't have his number. Though I fantasized doing so, it would be professional suicide if I stormed into the Arts & Humanities Building like Isabel Adjani stalking the desolate streets of some Newfoundland village in Truffaut's *The Story of Adele H.* It would be professional suicide—me, now a fellow of the Society of American Archivists!—if I accosted him in any way that appeared predatory or aggressive, hurt or spurned—or worse, moldering in tears. I told myself I had to wait like the jungle leopard, concealed behind the tall reeds, crouched, picking my moment, if that moment even came. And what if it didn't come? I wondered with a nausea spreading in my stomach, which the stale Gitanes was only exacerbating.

A half an hour was all I could afford to be AWOL. Raymond West never emerged from the building. My aggrieved conclusion was that he wasn't on campus and that the thrill of Friday across the street at Estancia Hotel had now perished on the most terrible Tuesday of my life.

With dejected resignation. I glanced at my watch. Suddenly, petulantly, I didn't feel like returning to work. I hurriedly composed an email to Jean on my iPhone, fabricating a doctor's appointment, then assured everyone, especially an anxious Helena, to whom my email would also be forwarded, that West's papers were on schedule and that, yes, I had given it some thought, but, no, I didn't need for it to be team-processed. Angry that the suggestion was once again putrid in the air I stormed to my car and broke the speed in driving to Scripps Pier.

In the empty parking lot, I changed into my one-piece swimming suit with the agility of a contortionist, then I walked down a flight of wooden steps to the water, broke into a run, and pierced the ocean, confronting the incoming waves with lunging body and heart crushed with a hellish emptiness. In a waterproof fanny pack I carried my wallet, phone, and car keys. Soon I was swimming past the breakers and out into the open ocean, free as a dolphin. Heading south to La Jolla Cove, I paced myself with long, languorous but powerful strokes. Now and then I glanced at the horizon and saw it bleeding orange, but my arms kept climbing over my head, one splash after another, never breaking stride.

An hour later, winded, lungs burning, I waded ashore at La Jolla Cove in ankle-small surf. Dripping wet, I mounted a flight of concrete stairs and climbed to street level, the open-ocean swim an obliterating balm to the desolation of rejection. I rinsed off in an outdoor shower, then unzipped my waterproof fanny pack and fished out my cell. No email. Exhausted, but still euphoric from the swim, I ordered a Lyft to take me back to my car. The driver, a nervous young man who seemed uncomfortable with a woman in a bathing suit, was incredulous when I informed him I had swum from Scripps Pier to La Jolla Cove. And that I did it often, summer and winter.

I ate dinner alone at Roberto's, a Mexican joint occupying a garishly colorful, ramshackle building overlooking Los Peñasquitos Lagoon, a protected wetland where migratory birds wintered and the Pacific overflowed when the surf rolled in from deep waters, and battered the shores with giant waves. As I ate my taquitos, I texted my husband that I was going to see a play at the university and would be running late. My double life was cleaving me in two and I longed to be one, either with myself or someone like Raymond. I was growing tired of the lies, as blithely as my husband seemed to allow them to pass through the sieve of his oblivion, or no longer caring.

As the sun fell heavily over the horizon, streaking the sky with scarves of orange and mauve, the water bled a deep crimson. Improbably, it all went dark, as if I had blacked out for a spell, and the lights of the cars on the street below were suddenly pinpoints of blinding white. I waited for the commuter traffic to abate. To the east, the I-5 was still a slow-moving river of lights. Across the Coast Highway the ocean now was an impenetrable black. I closed my eyes and imagined myself walking toward it. How would I drown myself if I was such a good swimmer? I laughed mordantly. If I go in with those velcroed ankle weights that runners sometimes wear, maybe that would hold me down, I contemplated. Despair had seized me in its viselike grip. Days ago he had cleaved to me so fiercely, kissed me so passionately . . . I needed a pill—or something—to hoist me out of the quicksand of depression that had claimed me.

Feeling lonelier and more bereft than I had ever been in recent memory, I untangled myself from the restaurant picnic bench, now moist with dew, and headed off in the direction of my car. San Diego lured you with its sun and surf, but it dismantled you with its alienation, it robbed your soul of sustenance, the kind I was looking for.

Aimlessly, I drove along Carmel Valley Road to the 54 freeway, a motorway as cold as ice water in my veins. I had spent a third of my life on the 54 freeway, commuting to Regents, and what did I have to show for it? One book of short stories and becoming a fellow in the archival profession. Big fucking deal! Since moving to San Diego, I had spent thousands of hours bleeding my soul empty on this network of freeways that linked all the bedroom communities, acned here and there with sad shopping centers, sad people coming and going, lugging their sad purchases. Late at night, driving the freeways, the shuttered, neon-lit shopping malls looked as lonely as Hopper paintings. I closed my eyes to block out their horrible symmetry, but when I reopened them, it was more of the same.

Stop being self-pitying I exhorted myself. The fantasy is over. It was never going to work; the obstacles were too insurmountable. The freeways swept me along on a subterranean current of thoughts about what I might do, where I might go, how I could change my life with a snap of my fingers. I didn't have to stop; I could have kept going. It was the California dream: from a car in your garage, loop onto any nearby freeway, and except for stops to get gas, you could be anywhere in America without a single red traffic light. Some of my few friends and colleagues equated this with freedom; I viewed the car as a symbol of prison. For me, freedom was through the senses, though the flesh, through the crying birth of creation, not in a car where rubber rolled endlessly on asphalt and concrete until retirement spat you out in a condo on a golf course in a desert clime where death inexorably, grimly awaited.

Mortally tired from driving around the city in circles obsessing about Raymond and why he hadn't emailed me back, I gathered my last ounces of energy and navigated the now empty freeways back to my home in Black Mountain Ranch. The neighborhood streets were mausoleum quiet. The dead slept in their two-story tombs identified by five-digit numbers on prosaically named streets chosen by a public official who possessed zero imagination. A skunk, blinded by my headlights, darted into a row of hedges, the only extant living creature in this depersonalized subdivision I likened to an abandoned outdoor mall. Who chooses to live here? I asked myself.

My loneliness and suffering capsized me when I entered my home. My husband was listed on the couch. Snoring noisily, he unconsciously scratched his head. A remote was slipping from his other hand. The large-screen TV was tuned to a sci-fi movie where superheroes were locked in combat with malevolent-looking robots marauding the earth. Feeling sorry for him, I gently removed the remote from his hand, slowly powered down the volume on the TV so as not to wake him. I stood back and drank in the sad tableau: the empty beer bottles, the half-eaten bag of Kettle chips, the bowl of pistachios, the dystopian war waging on the TV. My hand gripped my mouth to stifle the sobs, and I veered on unsteady legs to go down the hall for fear my husband would wake and hear me weeping, the one sound that could rouse him out of unconsciousness.

I lay in the guest bedroom where I had slept for the past year since my husband had learned of an affair. We tried couples therapy, but it was hopeless, it was worse. It only amplified our differences, didn't bridge them. For economic reasons, we cohabitated, but it's not what either of us wanted. We were both imprisoned in a purgatorial stalemate where life trundled on, heedless of fulfillment. I needed something definitive to end it—a new archivist position somewhere perhaps—but I didn't want to move out, not here in depressing San Diego, and live all alone in some generic apartment, the divorcée. I almost preferred the hypocritical mask of marriage.

I shut my eyes hoping I could refresh the screen of my insomnious mind. Out of habit, I opened my laptop and logged into my work account. No email. I started to reply to a string that now seemed like a boat adrift in the middle of the ocean, rudderless, pitched by crosscurrents.

From: Nadia Fontaine <Nfontaine@RegentsU.edu>
To: Raymond West <Rwest_Lit@RegentsU.edu>
Subject: Re: Re: Re: Subject to Subjective Subjects
Date: 22 September 2017

Raymond,

Trite as it sounds, I guess it wasn't meant to be.

Your Eavesdropping Angel in absentia,
Nadia

My finger hovered, trembling, over the Send button. Should I pour out my heart more explicitly? Fuck that. I'd rather swim as far out to sea as I could until my limbs gave out and I sank beneath the swells. I tapped Send and fell back on the pillows in a heap and gazed up at the wooden paddles of the ceiling fan that wheeled in drowsy circles, circulating the hot, stale air to little avail. I would have turned on the AC, but my husband and I had decided it was too costly and so we kept if off at night and only ran it when it was stifling. That was one of the few things we could agree on. I raised my head and dragged my laptop back where my fingers could reach the keys. I opened a journal file, a new one begun when I first met Raymond. They were notes to myself in the event I decided to write a memoir of our relationship one day. The words came pouring out of me, a palliative to my bottomless despair. As I was typing furiously away, I saw a notification alert slide in from the top right of my computer. My eyes widened, and a current of electricity shot down to my toes.

From: Raymond West <Rwest_Lit@RegentsU.edu>
To: Nadia Fontaine <Nfontaine@RegentsU.edu>
Subject: Re: Re: Re: Re: Subject to Subjective Subjects
Date: 24 September 2017

Dear Nadia,

I've been spirited away by obligations. Austin, Philadelphia—don't ask—apologies galore for having to reschedule. Please understand. Wait for me. Give me another day. Please. Tomorrow.

Your Raymond

Relief washing over me, I slowly folded close the lid of my laptop, tears of joy mixed with cascading laughter, hand clutched over my mouth to stifle my exultant sobs. It seemed like weeks, but it had only been a few days. I had worked myself up into a frenzy of dire pessimism over the disappointment of our coming together—the kiss, the exploratory hand—so that the resulting reassurance was like a whiplashing force, and all my confidence flooded back into me, all that impetuous, and depressive, resolve to end it in dark waters voided with one short email, and now I was going to show him what a deep and transgressive love truly was. I was going to lead him to the book he was meant to write!

EMILY

Emily closed her laptop and shut her eyes. Her contacts burned and they needed solution. The sound of the surf ghosted in through the open bedroom window. Nadia's journal had colored in a picture of a complicated, deeply unhappy woman. Had Raymond been privy to her tortured memoir he would never have been so cavalier in the dilatoriness of his email replies. He must not have realized how much she hurt, how much she believed in his words, how much she ached for him. It wasn't the flirtation and the stolen kiss. It was the six months she had labored on his archive where she had fallen bottomlessly in love.

Emily could intellectually grasp Nadia's obsession with West, the man and his work, but she would never be able to inhabit it the way Nadia had. She meditated on Nadia and the events in her life that led to her infatuation with Raymond, and the perilous consequences she was courting. At some point Emily realized she, herself, had crossed the Rubicon and was now rooting for their romance to take hold, rooting for that book to be written, a story whose ending was foretold, but whose trajectory wasn't filled in. Rooting for it, as if it were fiction and the consequences weren't real. And was he the lover who had stolen her from Joel?

Emily climbed off the bed, went into the bathroom, and removed her contacts. She debated a shower but decided against it. And she knew why. She wanted to dive back into their correspondence, Nadia's memoir; she was hungry for more.

NADIA'S STORY (CONT.)

Joy of joys. I was buoyed with hope when I got his email. I feared that he had spotted me when I was spying on him outside the Arts & Humanities Building, deemed me mad and too big a risk. I don't know why he ghosted me. It was the shortest of emails, as if he had typed it hurriedly in between pressing obligations. Austin? Philadelphia? Right. The lecture tour? No. I had googled and came up empty. Had he accompanied his wife on one of her many whirlwind philanthropic soirées? Was he lying? Did he have another "eavesdropping angel" in Austin?

I was slumped in my chair in Special Collections, sleep-deprived, but strangely hopeful. I had been short with my student assistant—I had ceased to trust anyone in the department—then apologized and excused her to do something else with the rest of her day, assuring her she wasn't doing anything wrong. It was hard for me to be alone with the mammoth West Collection, especially now that I was presumably climbing into it, however anonymously. The ocean we had just begun to descend into seemed filled with so much promise. Forests of seaweed. Rare marine life. Depths that would only be discoverably ours.

I obsessively checked my email. It had been three days since the apologetic one, and I wanted to believe the urgency in his words was the selfsame passion that had swelled up in him in his office, caught in slow-motion attempting to crest. I'm an impulsive woman, a woman of urgency. When I get an idea, I write it down; I don't wait; I don't wait for anything. I wasn't born equipped to abide the waiting. It drives me to madness. Especially when it revolves around the molecules of love.

My office phone rang, and I shot out an arm to answer it. It was Deborah at the information desk. "Nadia, there's a delivery here for you."

"What is it?" I asked.

"Why don't you come out and see?" she trilled.

I pushed away from my desk, straightened to my feet, careered out of my cubicle and across the main lobby to the information desk. When Deborah saw me approach, she lifted a vase of red roses and presented them to me.

"Secret admirer?" she asked.

I smirked. "My husband forgot our anniversary," I joked, forcing a smile, knowing that that was not who had sent them.

Jean slipped by me in the corridor as I carried the bouquet back to my cubicle. "Nice," she remarked, without breaking her stride.

I set the flowers down next to my computer, settled back into my chair, and meditated on them for the longest moment before opening the small envelope that accompanied them. I plucked it from the thorns. Inside was a small vanilla-colored card. It read,

> *Meet me at Estancia tomorrow at 4:00. I'll email you the room number. It's been a hellacious week. Forgive my absence. I just didn't know if I could. Now I know I have to. I can't bear the thought of being without you.*
>
> *R.*

I folded the card and secreted it in my purse. No one could read this. The dozen roses now exploded conspicuously into two dozen and were a borderline liability. The hands of the clock had transformed into wings. I dived into the unprocessed manuscripts of West next to the stack Joel had printed out and piled on my auxiliary desk. I came across a book of poetry he had self-published when he was only nineteen and grandiloquently daydreamed he was the next Neruda. They were imitative but showed promise. They reminded me of a time when he was young, a time before Elizabeth entered his life and promised him the security he needed to incubate his talent. I fantasized taking him back to tabula rasa, the earth he knew before the formation of marital compromise.

Then, remembering something, in a state of unadulterated happiness, I went on a mad, obsessive search for *Mr. Pencilhead*, the satiric poem he had written in high school that had sown the seed for his writing career.

On my evening swim from Scripps Pier to La Jolla Cove I mentally went through my wardrobe and debated what to wear for the rendezvous. By the time I dragged myself up on the beach, panting for breath, I decided on the burgundy skirt, the black stockings, and the matching black blouse. I wanted to look pretty for him, but not too risqué, an outfit that would say business attire if anyone from the university happened across Torrey Pines Road—God forbid—and encountered me in the lobby of Estancia.

Having emailed in sick, I slept in, pursued by dreams that for once were not themed around fractured narratives of desolation. By the time I climbed out of bed my husband had left for work. I took a long, unhurried shower and sponged myself clean. With my legs braced against the tile I painstakingly shaved them, drawing long languorous strokes, until they were marble smooth. I left the rest of me unshaven—I had read all his work and knew his predilections as intimately as anyone, which is why I also massaged in a drop of lavender oil, a scent that wantonly excited him.

When Raymond won the Pulitzer for *Lessons in Reality*, he stated in a *Paris Review* interview that his goal in life was always to be "going against traffic." It was both a clever use of metaphor and a literal summation of someone who grew up in Southern California with the ubiquity of cars. If you were going against traffic, it meant you weren't yoked to a nine-to-five job, it meant you were one of the fortunate few, in Raymond's case a real working writer. I found myself on Friday deliriously going against traffic, driving into the university when everyone was leaving. The thrill of the reversal didn't escape me. All those people heading home after another mentally draining day and here I was, in the throes of a fantasy about to be a reality bursting out of my chest. Nothing now could stop that imprudent voracity of my heart for adulterous love—the most exhilarating, the most dangerous, the most transcendent.

Estancia Hotel was a boutique spa resort hotel across from the university.

Hidden from Torrey Pines Road by an embattlement of palms and dense verdant shrubbery, it was an oasis in La Jolla where everyone from visiting professors to distinguished lecturers to celebrity guests, and others, bivouacked when in town for business in the area.

A valet leaped off his stool and greeted me when I pulled into the circular drive in my cream-colored Ford Falcon Futura with red, tuck-and-roll bucket seats—a car I bought on a whim when I knew my marriage had turned Sisyphean and needed a physical force that would make me feel free. "Just here for drinks," I cavalierly tossed at the bronzed young man who held open my door for me. He handed me a ticket with a practiced smile. Halfway to the entrance of the hotel I threw a brief backward glance. The two parking attendants were staring, mumbling to each other, possibly wondering if I were some Hollywood celebrity they didn't recognize but thought they should: the dark sunglasses, the jaunty red cashmere scarf. As soon as they saw me looking at them, they broke for the cars waiting to be parked, chagrined that they had been caught staring. I smiled to myself. I guess I still had it.

Having stayed at Estancia before—*good grief, not Associate Professor X, I shuddered, banish him from my mind!*—I passed straight through the lobby and out onto a sun-splashed garden patio, the warm air and fragrant flowers permeating the inner courtyard with a piquant anticipation of something new and utterly revivifying. Intermittent gusts of seasonal Santa Anas shook the fronds of the tall date palms and flexed their rough-skinned trunks in groaning protest, as if they, too, ached for the new, to be uprooted and blown oceanward, cast on currents to a new shore. I felt in my purse for the fishnet stockings and the spare underwear I brought in a small accessory bag, panicking for a moment thinking I had left them at home. I organized and arranged everything to be perfect, the way I would approach a collection.

In the open-air café, I swiveled onto a stool at the empty bar and faced a wall of variegated distillates. I needed a drink to steady my exuberance. My heart was beating fast now, and not because I had strode through the lobby and steered into the bar with the gait of someone who was late for an appointment. My long legs were propelled by the prospect of passion. It had been months since I had felt about a man in this way—in any way!— but it was surging back again, atavistic, primordial; I could feel it, like the harbinger of a new world born from a mass extinction, oozing and pullulating from the bubbling pit of a great rebirth. I wanted singularity, a life ushered in as a singular new creation, not one wrung from habit and a fate destined as a conciliation with old age and the remorse of what could have been.

A young woman bartender with a black skirt and white blouse approached, finally having emerged out of the back when she realized she had a customer. "What can I get you?" she asked.

"Drunkenness calls to me," I quipped with a wide-mouthed smile, stripping away the scarf and bunching it into my purse.

"I hear you," she replied in tacit solidarity.

"What wines do you have by the glass?" I asked.

"What're you in the mood for?"

I propped my elbows onto the bar and seized the wine list with eager hands and pretended to focus on it with a self-indulgent gaze, but everything in me was elsewhere. My eyes darted briefly to my dark red nails that I had painted that morning, and they brought a wry smile to my face. Lifting my arms, I felt my underarms already humid. The Santa Anas and Raymond's roses had opened my pores and made me already a spigot of desire. Everywhere. I wanted something cold and bracing, something that would quiet my nerves but not make me sleepy—I wanted to be ready for him. "I'll have a glass of this Chilean Sauvignon Blanc. I need to get out of California," I added enigmatically, closing the wine list.

The bartender promptly set a wineglass on the bar in front of me. She lifted a bottle from a bed of ice under the bar, uncorked it and poured generously. "You're my first customer."

"I drink early and lustily when it's a Friday," I said brazenly.

She tilted her head to one side. "Sounds like a plan."

I didn't feel like striking up a conversation. Who knows, maybe she was a grad student at Regents and bartending was supplementing her student loans. I had to be careful.

The bartender drifted off to a table where a gaggle of women had gathered and were chattering like an aviary of mynahs. I glanced at my cell. It was still early. The wine was astringent and floral, and it teleported me to a vineyard with a view of the ocean somewhere in Valle de Casablanca. If

I closed my eyes, I was there. I sipped greedily. On an empty stomach the alcohol launched into my bloodstream and hit my brain like spring streams coming to a confluence at a headwaters and surging skyward. With every sip I felt myself growing bolder, sexier, more sensual. My blood was molten lava, and it seemed to reawaken collapsed arteries and veins my body hadn't needed to keep my heart beating, hadn't summoned in years.

When the bartender held up the bottle in lieu of asking if I wanted a refill, in a rising tone lifted by tipsiness, I said, "Sure, why not!"

Sensing my need to obliterate something, the bartender filled my wine-glass dangerously near to the rim.

I was on fire now, my emotions gathering and billowing like storm clouds in a tropical sky and closing off the burning sun! I would race to him with all the ardor of a woman who had waited too long for this moment. The wine unchained every last one of my inhibitions and set me free. My mind and body were locked in a dangerous conspiracy. I was fully committed to this afternoon of lust. Instead of dragging me down or making me slur my words the wine emboldened me. When the email banner notification lit up my screen and I saw the room number pop up, I slammed back the rest of my glass, tossed down too many bills on the bar, snapped my purse shut, pirouetted off the stool, and tore off. The bartender seemed to intuit where I was headed, and I caught the scintilla of knowledge in her sly, curled smile.

In the lobby bathroom, I quickly pulled on the fishnet stockings and changed my underwear, the sexy pair that had no other purpose but to showcase my swimmer's ass. I reapplied my lipstick, the deep carmine that matched his gift of roses.

As I passed the desk clerks in Reception, I deliberately avoided their sweeping eyes, but I could feel them trained on me as I headed down the corridor to my final destination, the place where my life would change forever.

Tipsy on two generous glasses of wine, I walked along the long, carpeted, tunnellike passageway, giraffe-like on my four-inch, black high heels that I never wore, swaying back and forth, balanced on the fast pace of my forward momentum and the reckless pursuit of a dream, a woman on a gallant mission to save a writer from the "desertification of his soul." How incredible, I thought, that you could walk down an empty hall, past one door after another, open the one assigned to you and enter a carnival of desire. I paused at a customized antique mirror hung on the hallway wall and appraised myself one last time. I pursed my lips and pushed them back out so my lipstick glistened. Was the fake mole I drew in with my eyeliner pencil overkill? I leaned forward and stared into my widened eyes. He had noticed the subtle different shades of brown. Now, even closer, would he see the gold fleck suspended in my left iris? I stared into the mirror and found another woman. *I am ferociously beautiful!* I slurred into my disorganized face. I am fucking hot! I leaned back from the mirror, teetering in place, and unfastened one more button, splayed open my blouse. Why not? I was almost there. It was now or never for me; it really and truly was. When I still ran moist at the sight of his smile. Didn't he compliment my writing by saying I had a "fluency in the language of love"?

I pried myself away from the mirror, confident in my final steps, and slowed to a stop at 211. I could feel my heart leaping out of my chest. No one in my sphere of colleagues and acquaintances knew I was here. I had told no one. It made me feel spectral, wraithlike . . . haunted . . . hungering to live . . . Like someone free-falling into an abyss, heedless of the ground. Somersaulting into the void. Hoping to find the touch of flesh and the entanglement of limbs and the oblivion of mouths and not the barren desolation of a banal extramarital tryst.

I arrived at the door to Raymond's room with nothing but my body weaponized for love, my mind heady for any proposition. If there were a new kind of love to be charted and explored on this godforsaken planet it would originate here, I exhorted myself with reckless abandon. I will make it come true. I raised my fist to the door, threateningly. *Warning: I am about to begin making you mine.* I rapped with my knuckles. My heart kept trying to broad jump out of my chest, it was beating so furiously.

Raymond West answered. He was taller than I remembered, but my high heels brought me level to his face with only the slightest upward tilt. He smiled down at me without a trace of anxiety, his turquoise linen shirt unbuttoned two buttons at the collar, his face clean-shaven, his blue eyes impish with the same expectation that had me frozen in place. My eyes burned into his like twin lasers, and he fixed his gaze on mine with wordless intensity. My blood was boiling in my veins. We shared a moment of shocking recognition of what was about to happen, and then my arm shot out and my hand clutched his Adam's apple and throttled his throat. I pushed him back into the room and slammed the door closed with the backward kick of a hormone-fueled filly. I clasped my mouth to his, and he eagerly reciprocated with a famished mouth of his own. Words from a famous writer and from a woman who spent her life with words were obviated by our too-long-deferred desire. Our kissing was an atavism of pent-up animal longing, hungry, avaricious, desperate for a love that dived subterranean deep, zones below the normal.

Without ever taking my mouth from his, my hand still gripping his throat, I shoved him back onto the king bed and his lanky frame crumpled without resistance, smiling like a man who craved excitement by a woman taking charge. I was savage now with my desire as I devoured his mouth, covered him on the mattress like a large cat its prey, my fangs at his neck. I almost wanted to exclaim, *This is what death will be like if you're so lucky.* Wordlessly, we grappled, frantic to be rid of the world, both afraid that if either uttered even a single word, the spell would be snapped in two. We wanted this inviolable world of ours to explode with the exaltation of life, the joy of being, the transcendence of raw, animalistic fucking. This was the preternatural portal to the other side we were both looking for, and though we were both writers we didn't need to voice it.

I fumbled for his belt and pulled it undone. I loved the feel—and smell!—of its heavy leather and the brass buckle as it clanged like the clapper of a church bell tolling our clandestine assignation. At six foot two, I expected I would not be disappointed when I plunged a hand into his underwear and grabbed hold of his cock. He throbbed in my fist with a wild turgescence, bolting out like a bouquet of pure male desire. In my mouth it was a fat white asparagus reaching for the sun. I maintained my hand on his throat with a halfback's stiff arm while I lubricated him with my saliva. From time to time I steered my eyes in his direction, drawn by his muffled moans, at his reddened face and closed eyes and recognized he had surrendered wholly to me. His sighs were not remonstrations, but urgings for me not to stop. He had transited—unhesitatingly, unashamedly, with no holding back, no reservations—to my sexual wantonness. I attacked him with a ferocity I could tell he hadn't felt in ages, I wanted to engrave on his memory forever. I was primed for this carnal moment! This voluptuous body of mine was honed from years of long-distance ocean swimming, and I used it to ravish him unrepentantly, indefatigably. I wasn't going to stop until the skies bled violet, or he cried, *Enough*.

I raised myself up and kneeled bestride him. His hands hiked up my skirt the erotic way I had fantasized. They pulled down my panties and his fingers spread out and clutched my muscular ass. The same fingers that had written millions of words, those millions of words I had spent months processing and organizing and carefully foldering and arranging into boxes. And now the flesh of my ass was the keyboard, and his elegantly long fingers gripped me and explored me as if wanting to use every letter and symbol to reciprocate my desire. I let go of his throat, and he gasped for air. His eyes bloomed open, and I could tell I had transformed him, converted him to my religion, equal parts passion, a slapping of hurt, and a feather of tenderness. His arms reached up to caress my face, comb my cascading black hair with his strong spidery fingers, and I could tell from the look in his eyes that he, too, was hopelessly, deliriously in love.

I knew I was ready when he guided himself against me and my opening began to claim him with a seizing enveloping, as if a woman's sex were an anemone times one thousand. Throttling the base of his cock, I slowly and carefully fitted him inside. My eyes widened as if all the air had vanished from the room, and I was on the verge of the most intoxicating pleasure of suffocation I had ever known. I wanted to exult in his reaction the deeper he rose up inside me, so I stood tall above him, my torso vertical, hands pressed against his chest. Pleasure like heroin roared through my veins, burst the capillaries in the whites of his eyes, tensed every muscle in his body. I examined him dying beneath me as he acquiesced in the struggle and surrendered himself completely over to me. To be filled up this amply felt like putting down the roots of a sequoia. Rocking on his horizontal body, I raised my arms and raked my hair with my hands in the act, and simultaneously in a moment of triumph. His fingers climbed up the vertical cliff of my back and fumbled with my bra clasp. My breasts tumbled into space, and he caught them with his sandpapery fingers and celebrated their liberation with gentle touches. I, too, felt gravityless and stroked into him like a cresting wave and carved the face of his body up and down as he prolonged his climax, on his back, a prisoner to my strength and the ardor that made me feel more powerful than ever. I rose high on the wave and glided atop its feathering lip, levitating over the ocean. And then I let go, the whitewater enveloping me, not knowing whether I was facing up or down, left or right, a blissful vertigo of the senses as I collapsed, breasts heaving, to his side.

When I emerged from my trance, I saw that he was smiling over at me, all the tension drained from his body, a happiness suffusing him. He had disappeared under the water as well and had surfaced, I wanted to believe, reborn. My mouth found his, tenderly this time. His face was smooth, and I realized from the smell that he had shaved for me before I had arrived. A gust of wind rustled the palms, and they rattled like maracas, a calling to dance wildly on an empty equatorial beach. It was only then that I noticed the room service tray with the bottle of wine in the ice bucket and the plates of hors d'oeuvres he had thoughtfully ordered. But I didn't want to leave the feast of his body, not just yet, and I held on to him like a foundered mast. He stroked my hair as my head rested sated on his shoulder and my lips nibbled his ear. We still hadn't spoken. My soreness was a satiated ache I had longed for seemingly forever. I hoped he felt the same. I reeled him back to reality with fluttering eyes and the widest of smiles. He reached down to stroke my fur with the tips of his fingers. As if he were writing on my moist pubic hair, I could tell he adored me.

And then he whispered, "Well, at least now we have the first chapter."

My laughter was muffled with my lips pressed to the side of his face. "That's all you have to say, Mr. Writer?"

"You know you're incredible," he said admiringly. "Beautiful and smart." He lolled his head in my direction. "And in every other way."

Our lovemaking humanized the city for me, cratered the night freeways and transformed the shopping malls into quaint peasant villages. I drew nearer to him, and he pulled me close to him in a reassuring deliquescing of bedraggled bodies. And then, before making love again, we talked intensely about *The Archivist* and the work that would hoist us both out of our trapped existences, each in a different manifestation of plumbing the truth.

"What are you feeling?" I asked, when I rolled over onto the mattress, naked now in his presence, winded from another devouring and exploring of each other, this time an affirmation of the first but with deeper knowledge of each other and a tenderness supplanting the collision of comets that was our inaugural coming together.

"Like I'm home," he whispered in that deep baritone without a trace of irony or facetiousness, nodding, staring up at the ceiling fan. "Like I'm home." He turned to me. "I'm sorry I went radio silent for so many days. Truly sorry."

"Shh." I brushed the hair off his forehead. "It's not going to be easy; I know."

We each had a glass of wine, snacked on the hors d'oeuvres, talked breathlessly about the book we were going to write, then, with heavy heart, I gathered up my belongings and put myself back together as best I could. On the outside. Inside, I was forever changed: ravaged now, windswept, clinging to dreams, fearful that it would all evanesce like affairs often do.

He kissed me passionately at the door. Whispered promises into my ear. Raked my hair with his fingers. Gazed admiringly into my eyes with an intensity that I believed meant to convey something, to reassure me that it wasn't just an ephemeral fantasy finally consummated, but a true love scorching a desiccated plain, leaving a scar in its wake.

He playfully shoved me out the door. I retraced my zigzag path down the hotel's saffron-colored corridor, a smile broadening my mouth, tears of joy streaking my face, happier than I had ever felt in my life. And in that upwelling of happiness, more anxious than ever before.

A torrent of emails rained:

To: Nadia Fontaine <Nfontaine@RegentsU.edu>

Our love is made of incandescent matter.

To: Raymond West <Rwest_Lit@RegentsU.edu>

If I lost you, my soul would cleave in two.

To: Nadia Fontaine <Nfontaine@RegentsU.edu>

I've witnessed fires in my soul that I didn't think were capable of burning; your love is what fuels them.

To: Raymond West <Rwest_Lit@RegentsU.edu>

I'm prepared to go to Hell for this love.

To: Nadia Fontaine <Nfontaine@RegentsU.edu>

The beauty of your flesh; the thunder of your eyes; the rainfall of your orgasms.

To: Raymond West <Rwest_Lit@RegentsU.edu>

The exaltation of our dark pursuits . . . in hotel rooms . . . in cars . . . wherever/whenever you want me . . .

To: Nadia Fontaine <Nfontaine@RegentsU.edu>

To our "dark pursuits" never abating, lasting forever . . .

EMILY

Emily, the blood drained from her face, rose from the bed, startling Onyx to a standing position, staggered to the bathroom, collapsed to her knees, jackknifed over the toilet bowl, and vomited. Pizza, beer—it all came back up in a sour stench of nausea elicited by the emails and Nadia's shockingly frank description of their lovemaking. The ardent back-and-forth in which Nadia and Raymond professed their passion for each other in postmortems was startling to read. It wasn't as if Emily was taken aback by the candor of their words per se, but more by how personal they were, how personal her predecessor had become to her, and in finishing up the West Papers, how much she, too, was now invested in him.

With one hand clutching her stomach, Emily shambled back into the bedroom on unsteady, quivering legs. She was all alone with this. She couldn't rule out that Joel knew what she had found; she couldn't be sure; he had been close to her. If he did, had he read what she had read? If he were in love with Nadia once, he probably wouldn't want to read what she had read: "Being inside you was like heaven on earth if Satan had commandeered all my dreams." "Dark pleasures, transgressive fantasies. When you touched me there where I have never been touched before . . ." In email they maintained a velocity of an electric current of prose whose sheer salacity bordered on the pornographic, vulgar if it weren't for the fact that Nadia was hopelessly in love and Raymond smitten beyond redemption. And the profuse professions of love: "I've yearned for someone like you all my life." "I love the look in your eyes when you climax." "I want the more, not the less. And if I have to suffer the more, then I will embrace it with a fatalist's leap. You, Nadia, are what I've wanted all my life. God help me." "Words that you speak bundled under the sheets but not meant for other's eyes."

Emily knew what she had waded into, but she didn't realize the depthless bottoms she would sink and churn in, like the wave she had wiped out on, until she started reading. And as their love affair got underway, in its turbulent and clandestine madness, it wasn't only the perfervid velocity of their words, it was also the pictures that Emily was privy to! The software program Nadia had used to preserve their emails had also captured each and every attachment. Nadia loved to tease Raymond with a photo here and there. As a photographer, she had an artist's talent for composition. She took one from the point of view of her eyes looking down the length of her, her panties titillatingly hooked around her ankles, her crotch a blot of sable in the photographic journey to her panties. Emily had *never* been that free with the few lovers she had enjoyed in her life. Partly because she never fully trusted any of them enough to let herself go that wantonly, that brazenly, to this kind of exchange. In Nadia's case, she probably didn't feel any fear that Raymond would show or forward the pornographic photos, because he sent a few himself. But the exchange was still risky. The emails were another story. In the wrong hands, they would have been all that was necessary to poleaxe their conflagrative romance. But the times apart, the desperately short trysts, must have galvanized them to exchange this rainstorm of emails, emboldened Nadia to torture him with photos of her body, to keep the desire aflame. And it was this same love they were presumably conspiring writing about in their collaborative project *The Archivist.*

Emily didn't know what had made her throw up. Was it that she felt like a voyeur, ghostlike in a private world between two people—one now tragically dead—and that entering their inviolable dominion of scorching adultery was as transgressively, and ethically, wrong as the relationship Nadia and Raymond had voyaged out to sea on? Sans compass, sans provisions, guided only by their impassioned hearts set aflame in Special Collections when he gazed at sheer immensity of his career and fell in love with the woman who archived it? It wasn't the sexual excitement of the emails and their lyrical descents into the dark and the deep and the taboo—after all, he was a Pulitzer winner and Nadia was a published writer in her own right—it was Emily's fascination with the epistolary book Raymond West had started to write inspired by their email exchange. They competed with each in email to better inflame their project.

And Emily could identify with Nadia, if only in her own nascent way. Her loneliness. Forty-one and "on the declivity" and feeling she had little to show for the first half of her life. She longed for something grand. Emily did too, but perhaps she felt like she had more time, its urgency not as pressing and omnipresent as Nadia's. Also, and almost as alarmingly, Nadia's depressive psychology ran like a dark river beneath it all. The amplitude of her mood swings, abysses in which she was prone to free-fall, the obsession with contemplations of suicide when all seemed bleak and hopeless.

And then there presumably existed the literary chronicle of their love, already titled and whispered as *The Archivist.* What had happened to that? It didn't just disappear.

Emily opened her Gmail and wrote a tactfully unburdening email to Professor Mark Erickson, the Head Librarian at Harry Ransom, the person who had given her her first chance and encouraged her, and whom she had grown close to over the few years she interned there. To Professor Erickson,

Emily was that rare breed of new archivist who cared profoundly about the work she was processing, who still read books and screened films and grew engrossed in both, damn the linear feet. He liked to tease her that she was a Luddite, and she liked to believe that she was proud of the fact that, as a so-called millennial, she rebelled against much of what her generation embodied. She was either a futurist who believed in a future where a return to aesthetics was imminent, or she was a young person with a baby boomer's soul who longed for the day when sinking into a good book was not an anomaly, not a superannuated activity.

After writing to Erickson, she glanced at the plethora of emails in the Nadia/Raymond correspondence. She had only begun, she realized, with twin forces of alarm and fascination pulling at her soul like the riggings of a billowing sail. The PDFs scrolled for pages. The cataract of emails. The memoir of her love affair Nadia had written for her own personal archive, obviously not for publication. The erotic thumbnails. In each other they had unleashed a veritable torrent of creativity that flowed in alternating currents, between them, and the work that Raymond had begun to write.

CHAPTER 11

The Danger of the Anima

8/28/18

Classes will begin in a few weeks. The university will be swept up in swarms of students. I dread their coming.

That's not what I wanted to write. I'm almost afraid to write what I need to confess. I've started the email correspondence between Nadia and Raymond West. Going back and forth between them and the memoir Nadia had written just before her death. Conflicted about whether I should keep reading. I know I can stop any time. But if I stop, I will never know. Will never know what led up to her drowning.

If Christ on the cross represents the torment of a conflicted soul, then I am his female equivalent. I know that sounds lofty and self-serving, pretentious and hyperbolic, but that's how I feel: Nailed to the cross. Damned if I do; damned if I don't.

"I'm invisible today / A little spider yo-yoing / On a silver gossamer hangman's noose." Nadia wrote about this in an essay she published in American Archivist. *Note to self: must reread her essay.*

Joel, in jeans and his *The Endless Summer* T-shirt, found Emily in her office, dwarfed by record cartons and tottering hillocks of documents she had unearthed. She was attired in a black fleece vest over a white long-sleeve shirt and black corduroys. Joel stood among the literary civilization in miniature for a moment in quiet awe until she finally looked up at him from the office chair where she was hunched over her files. "Are they threatening to fire you?" he asked.

Emily was taken aback. Had her secret life with the emails somehow been exposed? She swallowed hard. "Why would you say that?"

Joel painted the air with his index finger with a reproving flourish. "Looks like somebody's getting seriously behind."

Emily lifted her chin defiantly and held it up to him. "Oh, yeah?"

"Be careful, Emily. Fascination can turn to obsession."

Emily started to sputter an explanation but ran out of gas when she realized her voice lacked conviction.

Joel held up both hands in surrender and rescued her from a lie. "I don't want to know."

Emily lowered her chin and grew contemplative. A page from her personal file stared back up at her as if she didn't have her glasses on, blurred out of focus.

"Feel like surfing?" Joel asked. He raised a flattened hand above his belt buckle. "It's only chest high. Water's warm," he said temptingly, waving her to the imaginary beach that awaited just outside her cubicle.

Thinking of Nadia and that day she took off and raced to Estancia to meet her lover, Emily slapped her file down on the table. "Okay. Let's do it."

Joel raised a fist. "Are you in the Widmer structure?"

"Yeah."

"I'll meet you there at five fifteen," he said.

Emily skipped lunch and made headway on the new accession organizing items in the records cartons, poring over the container lists, wanting badly to stop and read early drafts of manuscripts or linger over photographic memorabilia. But she couldn't lose this job. Joel might have been joking, but he might not. He had an allusive way of speaking, a shifting personality that was at times hard to pin down. He had given her Nadia's personal file that had led to the dark archives, and Joel was the one who had arranged for her to have access, so . . . But she wondered about his ulterior motives.

After work, Joel met Emily in the Widmer structure, and they shifted her belongings into his Element. They drove to the private road that led down to Black's. He was waxing on about the new six-foot-one quad-fin he recently had a friend shape and glass and was eager to give it a test ride. Emily's mind was still at work, and Joel could sense it. His eyes darted to her now and then between navigating the curving roads out of the university's labyrinth of cement structures. In the shared silence, their unspoken thoughts crackled with electricity.

Emily suddenly turned to him and blurted out, "You're aware they were having an affair?"

Joel sucked in his breath, tightened his grip on the steering wheel, whitening his knuckles, and peered forward with a grim, implacable countenance. "Why do you want to go there, Emily?"

"Because I'm deep into it, Joel."

Joel exhaled through flared nostrils. "I figured."

"You knew she swam three times a week from Scripps Pier to La Jolla Cove." Joel didn't respond. "That's almost a mile, Joel. And she did it year-round."

"What's your point?"

"The official ruling on her death was accidental drowning." Emily gazed out the passenger window. "A woman who swam three miles a week in open ocean, summer and winter, drowned?" She whipped her head back to Joel and glared at him with burning eyes for an answer. "Are you fucking buying that?"

Joel, feeling ambushed, closed his eyes behind his sunglasses, drawing deep, slow breaths through his nose and exhaling them with worry.

In the affluent La Jolla Farms neighborhood, Joel found a space between two cars and parallel parked. With the subject of Nadia's death still lingering in the brackish air, they changed into their wet suits in silence. Joel handed Emily her board and locked up his car. They threaded their way around the swinging metal barrier and started down the single-lane asphalt road toward Black's. The sun floated heavy in the ash-bronze sky. The ocean hemorrhaged crimson all the way to the horizon where it burst into ragged flames at the edge. A squadron of pelicans striped the water in a traveling black ellipsis.

"A tax attorney I hired to work out a settlement with the IRS back in my drinking and drugging days," Joel said out of nowhere, "once said to me when I started to mention some monies that I had, let's say, come across in an ill-gotten way, 'Don't tell me anything I don't need to know, Joel.'" He turned to Emily. "No, I don't think she drowned. I never did. I told you." He was agitated now. Because of where Emily had gone. Because he had pushed her there. "Yes, I knew they were having an affair. Okay? Does that answer your question?"

Emily nodded. She pulled up to a stop and leaned her board against the curb. Joel looked over his shoulder, silhouetted now against the crimson, immortalized unhappily like the surfer he would forever be.

"What's going on?" he asked petulantly.

Emily looked at Joel and then rushed toward him, encircled him with her arms, thrust her head against the neoprene of his chest, and held him tightly. "Don't get the wrong idea."

"Furthest thing from my mind."

"I just need to know you're there for me," she cried out in a spasm of emotion.

"Of course, Emily. We're in this together." He patted her back. "If you've found correspondence—and I know you have—be very, very careful whom you talk to."

"I promise." Emily squeezed him hard one last time to affirm their pact, held him at arm's length and made him look at her. Tears had welled in her eyes.

"Let's go shred some waves."

"All right!" Emily said.

Emily retrieved her board, and they traipsed off for the evening glass at secluded Black's Beach. It was a fun hour in waist-high waves that languidly crested and crashed like rose-colored oil in a lava lamp until darkness fell over them like a velvet curtain.

Emily had begun taking her lunches off campus. She found solace in the nearby Gliderport, where a grass palisades sloped to the vertical drop-off of the cliff. Paragliders staggered in place, braving the prevailing onshore winds and manipulated their webs of lines in an effort to billow their chutes and raise them off the ground. Once that was accomplished, harnessing the wind with their equipment, they duck-walked to the edge of the cliff, their chutes flapping and fluttering, and, in a leap of temerity, were soaring aloft, carving turns in their colorful gear.

One afternoon, Emily ate an egg salad sandwich and sipped an iced coffee and watched the paragliders glide effortlessly, like the native pelicans, never venturing out too far for fear of losing the updraft when the wind slammed into the sheer face of the cliffs. The soaring, silhouetted geometries of men in flight captivated her. She shook her head, realizing she could never leap off a cliff like that with her faith placed solely in the wobbly hands of a parachute and harness to hold her beneath by a network of nylon cords. No way.

"Would you like to try?" a male voice asked her.

Emily started. She corkscrewed from her sitting position, tented her forehead with a flattened hand, and found herself within inches of the sunburnt face of a young man in a T-shirt and board shorts. She forced a bemused smile.

"I'm an instructor here. We do tandem."

"No, thanks," replied Emily. "I'm scared of heights. But I like watching them. It must be exhilarating."

The young man in the mirrored shades gazed off to where the cliff's edge met the dark blue expanse of the ocean and above that the blue-yellow sky. "Yeah, it's a rush." He turned to her and handed her a business card. "If you want to conquer your fear, my name's Rick."

Emily took the card from him, glanced at it, then set it down on the picnic table where she was sitting all alone. "Okay," she said tersely, expressionlessly, not wanting to encourage any more conversation.

Rick took the hint and sauntered away with a nirvanic smile. Emily wondered why she was occupationally standoffish, guarded and stiff. She decided it was because she didn't want to get comfortable with San Diego, didn't want to begin imagining this was a place where she might settle down. She extricated herself from the picnic bench, threw her lunch bag into a vandalized trashcan, then strolled back to her blue Mini across the vast dirt parking lot that bordered Torrey Pines Municipal Golf Course. On a putting green that abutted a chain-link fence three middle-aged white guys in colorful outfits waited patiently while their fourth bent over his ball, gripping a putter, taking his time. What a stupid game, Emily thought. They could be soaring along the cliffs. One of them caught a glimpse of her, fashioned a V with his index and middle fingers, thrust them in his mouth and whistled at her. Emily jerked her head away, climbed into her car and started it up. She had come to the Gliderport, the snoop in her realized, because the second time Nadia and Raymond met, it was here. They had agreed to rendezvous in separate cars at the far end of the vast lot, where it met a canyon. Their kissing—"God, how luscious your mouth was, how much I missed you," he had gushed—was seismic. He: "You're an electric current." She: "I needed to feel you inside me, I would do anything." In the salacious, flirtatious emails leading up to the tryst, she wrote, "I want to suck your cock," which made Emily blush and grow nauseated again. She started up the car and drove slowly over the washboard-rutted dirt lot to the end where the two had met over a lunch hour nine months ago. She imagined Nadia leaping out of her car and disappearing into Raymond's Range Rover—after the sexually exhilarating afternoon at Estancia they were both desperate to be in each other's arms again. He would have backed his seat as far back as it would go from the steering wheel, she hurriedly and wickedly unbuckling his belt because time was short and the sounds of belts and zippers turned her on, and she unzipped him and disappeared from view, shrouded by tinted windows. No one would have seen his perspiring face, hands gripping the steering wheel, head thrown back in ecstasy. To passersby, there were only hawks wheeling over them in the windblown sky as she made him imagine a blood moon in the blue. Emily read Nadia's lyrical aftermath with a hand clasped to her mouth. But it was Raymond's email thanking her for the Moleskine, which captured Emily's attention—the archivist in Emily wondered where that Moleskine was. *Fuck the graphic descriptions of their lovemaking—I want* The Archivist.

As Emily drove on, a sadness enveloped the emptiness reflected in her rearview mirror: the sandy brown dirt landscape bordered by the shrubbery of the canyon, the sky streaked coral and red. Was it the combustion of the fiery romance—chronicled in the torrid emails and Nadia's memoir, dredged to the surface by her binge reading—that made their affair come vividly alive in her imagination? Or was she more haunted by its incontrovertibly tragic end? It did end; that she knew. And there was no finished book; that she presumed. It wasn't anywhere in the West records. Emily found herself shaking her head in puzzlement. A nondescript sorrow suffused her as the Mini found smooth asphalt, Torrey Pines Road, and the short drive back to the university. It was as if she had relived it all herself, their voices were so intensely vibrant in their emails.

Vowing not to read any more of the voluminous exchange until she consulted with Mark Erickson at Harry Ransom for some much-needed professional advice, Emily buried herself in her work on West's archive. But how could she plug the dike when she lived with West all day long, as if he were a living thing? *How do you professionally detach yourself?* Emily wondered. He wasn't an abstraction. She had seen him in the flesh. Albeit, she remembered, broken down, hunched over, hobbling on a cane, pensive, distant, not at all the man in the emails to his raven-haired lover.

As the day wore to an end, Jean appeared at Emily's cubicle, as if she had waited for the precise moment when she knew time would be short and conversation truncated. Without preamble, she blurted out, "We have a big status update tomorrow."

Emily, tired, inwardly troubled, nodded. "Okay."

"Elizabeth West is going to be in attendance," she added ominously.

"Should I get dressed up?" Emily attempted a joke. Jean was immune to jokes. In the three weeks she had been the project archivist for the West Collection, Emily couldn't honestly recall a moment when Jean had laughed.

"Can you pull some items that might go in the projected display?" Jean wondered, not really asking, working her wad of gum so she could blow a bubble, which she did and then popped it, as if underscoring her request by flouting Emily's misophonia.

"I'll bring some things, yes," Emily said, gritting her teeth.

"How's it coming along, if you don't mind my asking?" Jean said, her gum hopping from side to side in her mouth, almost as if weaponizing it to galvanize Emily into action.

"I feel like I'm right where I need to be," Emily replied ambiguously, crossing her arms against her chest defiantly as if erecting an invisible, but palpable, barrier between the two of them. She wanted to hold off on hostilities until pushed to the brink.

"That's what we like to hear." Jean pivoted on her heels when she heard her office phone ring and stole away down the corridor.

Emily stayed late, busying herself pulling items from document boxes she thought would be appropriate to include in the exhibit Helena was masterminding. The stacks were quiet. It was just Emily and the West Papers. She closed her eyes and imagined Nadia and Raymond here together, alone in this windowless room, his work lovingly archived in boxes and Nadia overjoyed witnessing his emotional appreciation of the work she had done. What writer wouldn't fall in love with his archivist at that moment of recognition? What archivist wouldn't have been bursting with love for him before she even met him? Raymond was the only one Nadia had ever led into the stacks to view their archive. Her heart pumped blood into a river that suddenly diverted and jumped the levees that held all propriety and ethics at bay. An avulsion of ethics in the archival world of epic proportions, reverberating potentially with monumental consequences. Emily wondered if she, herself, could have resisted. The emails, especially Nadia's, which were long and pulsed with the stylish phraseology of any renowned epistolist, painted such a vivid picture, it was as if they were scenes in a movie unspooling in her head. She could hear their voices. Raymond had called Nadia's "mellifluous"—Emily strained to hear it! His Nadia likened to a "red wine river." And Emily could feel them in the spectral past close to each other and how electrifying that must have been, how Nadia had "wished it would have gone on to eternity," and how he had "never met a woman with such incendiary beauty." Emily heard a scraping of footsteps and, for a sidereal moment, she thought the wraithlike figures of Nadia and Raymond had materialized to life, and she was eavesdropping on the sowing of the seed of their monumental love.

"Hi, Ms. Snow," greeted David Verlander. "Not surprised to find you down here."

Reminded of Jorge's exhortation about the guy who was stalking staff in

Special Collections still at large, Emily threw a hand to her chest in relief, bent forward, and gasped. "You scared me, David."

He backed away a step. "I'm sorry. It sounded like you were talking out loud to yourself."

"Yeah, uh . . . I do that sometimes." Emily knitted her brow. "Don't all archivists?"

"We can get a little nutty," Verlander chuckled.

Emily managed to wriggle out of the shroud of fantasy that had momentarily enveloped her in its erotic allure.

"Must be a product of this device-driven world we live in where too many interactions, alas, are just with ourselves," Verlander philosophized.

Emily looked up into Verlander's amiable face framed by owlish eyewear enlarging his twinkling, limpid eyes. He turned his head and drank in all the document boxes in the West archive, as if paying respect. The room hummed a low monotone roar. Wordlessly, Verlander paced along the row of boxes, slid one out, angled it downward, and dropped it into his arms. He squatted down, set it on the floor, unsealed its lid, and removed an accordion folder, meticulously labeled. From the folder he extracted a black Moleskine with the care of a rare book collector handling an ornate, filigreed volume of the Book of Kells. He bent his head over his shoulder and threw Emily a backward glance.

"Have you seen this, Emily?"

"I haven't been through all the boxes, no," she answered.

Verlander rose as if he were holding something precious and priceless and was standing precariously on a floor iced over by a recent storm. "Come have a look."

Out of fear, or because she had just been imagining Nadia's and Raymond's visit of a year ago, she glanced up at the security camera, reassured that one was pointed down at her. She stepped toward Verlander and stopped an arm's length away. She could smell the piquant scent of pipe tobacco clinging to his wool coat. He opened the Moleskine and presented it to her like some relic of literary lore. "A first draft of *Lessons in Reality*," Verlander said in hushed tones.

Emily, adrenalized by the mention of the title, telescoped her head forward and zeroed in on it. Capital print handwriting filled the page in an, at times, indecipherable scrawl, as if written by someone whose narrative had outrun his physical ability to keep pace. Words and whole paragraphs were often crossed out. Marginalia in the tiniest of print poured down the sides of pages as if West had obsessively gone over these first drafts before transcribing the text to a computer. To Emily, it looked more akin to a lost mariner's demented log than the beginnings of a Pulitzer Prize–winning novel.

Verlander seemed far more excited by the manuscript than by the beautiful young archivist standing next to him in the dusky light. "He wrote this in a fevered dream of thirty-four days. I mean, look at this." His voice rose an octave in enthusiasm, imagining West's hand racing across the page in a state of hypnosis. "You can see the creative tumult of this man's mind on the page," he intoned, tracing his index finger over the page he had opened the Moleskine to, as if trying to decode its cryptic birth by touching its tortured scrawl. He turned the pages slowly, with an air of mystery, as if each held a single breath of life of life that was now extinguished. "It's like you're looking into the unadulterated soul of pure creation."

From Verlander's words Emily could feel his awestruck reverence, and she knew instantly what Nadia had fallen in love with. No wonder Nadia had written floridly about the author's fingers clutching her naked ass. Her ass was that Moleskine, and her skin was the parchment where his next soul-deepening love would be imprinted. Nadia wanted her soul to transmigrate through her skin to his fingers and that feeling to be transferred to the page, immortalized in a book, with a dust jacket, set in legible Sans Serif or Garamond or Bodoni, it didn't matter, she would preserve it and here it would be, something final and immutable because she knew that love died with lovers, but books outlived their hearts that ceased to beat.

"Wow," exclaimed Emily, then shrank abashed at the inanity of her expression. "Thirty-four days?"

Verlander nodded, still entranced by the pages he turned with solemnity and an archivist's care. "Writing a novel is an emotional journey, and here we have the pulsing heart of that record. It feels alive to me looking at it. This is why I fell in love with this profession." He turned to her. "This is what Mark at Harry Ransom said about you." Emily raised her eyebrows questioningly. "That you loved the origins. That you got excited by going back and seeing the beginnings."

"Yes," admitted Emily, with a lump in her throat.

"But you don't ever want to write?" Emily shook her head definitively. "I would have thought differently."

"I don't believe I have anything important to say," Emily said self-deprecatingly.

"Everyone does. They just don't have this." He held up the West Moleskine for evidence of creative genius, an imagination touched by the unearthly. He squatted back down and carefully replaced the notebook in its folder. He ran his index finger over all the other folders in the box as if he were in a seminal archive in Europe and this might be his last opportunity to view a particular rare collection. "This came like a prairie fire," he murmured. He fitted the lid back on and lifted the box up from the floor. "Bewilders me why he's no longer what he once was." He leveled his eyes at Emily.

She shrugged, not knowing what he meant.

"The sagging shoulders, the sadness, the absence of humor. West can be wickedly funny. Get a few tequilas in him, and he can command the room like Rushdie." Verlander's eyes gleamed mischievously. "And his mind ranges over . . . many disciplines."

"I wouldn't know," Emily said.

Verlander carefully slid the box back in the empty slot on the shelf and, like a seasoned archivist, arranged it so it was smoothly aligned with the others in the row, his wrinkled, liver-spotted hand patting it for good luck. "Makes you wonder if the creative impulse isn't destroyed by success rather than emboldened by it." He turned to Emily. "Or money. Maybe the geniuses need the wolves howling at their door." He chuckled sardonically. "Are you coming out?"

Emily shook her head. "I've got some work to do here."

"Okay. It's going to be quite a celebration on the eighth floor. Or, as Helena is fond of saying, *fabulous*."

Emily chortled at Verlander's mild derision of the director.

"Carry on." Verlander turned and walked off.

Emily waited until he walked out of view. The black Moleskines, she thought to herself. A flare went off in her head. *The Archivist.* He didn't need the wolves at his door—she mocked Verlander's words because she knew the truth: he needed love to ignite those capital print letters scorching the page. Where were the *Archivist* Moleskines? How much had they written? How deep had they gone? Could she go to Verlander if she found them? Surely he would understand their cultural value.

It was nearing nightfall when Emily drove back to Del Mar. The tributaries of the Los Peñasquitos Lagoon were colored candy orange, sinuous in between the dark olive hue of the reeds flattened by an onshore wind. In the distance, the freeway flowed red and white in arcing crosscurrents, one person to a car mostly, Emily concluded, each ensconced in their own world of podcasts or music or text messaging, commuting back and forth, back and forth, until time inexorably ground them into old age and disintegrated them to carbon. Nadia didn't want to end up that person. The house, the pension, it was all part of a sorrow that she would never be able to come to terms with. That was why she ventured out in the dead of night to swim to La Jolla Cove. That was why she had no compunctions about falling in love with *the* most famous donor in Memorial's Special Collections and risking professional opprobrium and personal ostracism, her career in tatters. Nadia would have gleefully accepted the offer of a tandem ride with that paraglider instructor, Emily thought defensively. Hell, she would have probably had her own rig and leaped into the abyss without an instructor. She already had. "I have a passion for the void," Emily had read in one of her short stories and she believed Nadia was speaking autobiographically. Emily realized in that moment she was jealous of Nadia, that she knew she could never be like her.

Back at her apartment, Emily showered, fed Onyx, then opened the cork on a Societe half-liter and poured a glass. An alarm jangled on her cell, a reminder that she had an appointment to talk with Professor Erickson, and she silenced it. She combed and blow-dried her hair and threw on a comfortable, but elegant, blue-and-gray checked flannel shirt because she didn't want her image on the other end of their Skype call to mirror dishevelment. Archivists picked up on little details like that. And she had important things to talk to Erickson about.

Emily settled comfortably on her couch. In the middle of the living room,

Onyx stretched out his forepaws, arched his back and yawned, oblivious of wars, the depredations of climate change and forbidden romantic affairs between archivists and donors. Then he padded over to her like a dreamy miniature panther, launched himself into the air on powerful legs and landed softly next to her thigh. Emily stroked his thick lustrous fur and massaged his bony spine. A feeling ran across her and she wondered if Raymond didn't feel the same thing when he raked his fingers through Nadia's hair. She shook free the image and opened up the Skype app on her computer. Her screen status indicated Erickson was online, so she tapped his contact and heard an ancient rotary phone ring. After a few moments, his face filled the screen. He was a white-haired man with crinkly eyes underscored by bags, physiognomic evidence of the hours he spent poring over manuscripts and other archival items that exacted its toll on his eyesight. The bifocal glasses with the gleaming gold rims only accentuated his age and years of toil in the vocation he had devoted his life to. Emily assumed he was gay, or a lifelong bachelor, because he had never been married, never been seen with a woman, or otherwise talked about such things with any interest. Possibly he was asexual, an archival troglodyte for life.

"Hi, Emily," Erickson croaked.

"Hi, Professor."

"How are you?"

"Okay," Emily said. "You?"

"They're trying to push me out here, think there's a cottage outside London with my name on it, but I'm not ready to go yet. We just got a new accession of Arthur Miller. And, of course, still a lot to be done with Márquez. They're going to have to drag me out of here kicking and screaming." He glanced off. "I would be lost without Harry Ransom."

Emily nodded and smiled, wanting to empathize with Erickson, but her mind was on other topics. She absent-mindedly ventured a sip of beer.

"How's West coming along?" he asked, turning back to face Emily.

"I get asked that every day," she said, shaking her head in mock exasperation.

"I bet you do. I read the news about the remodel of the eighth floor over there at Memorial. I've visited. Stupendous views. I can imagine they're anxious to have you wrap up."

"Don't remind me."

"Stunning library on the outside, by the way," Erickson remarked. "I'm jealous."

"Yeah, it is," replied Emily. "I marvel at it every day when I go in." She chuckled. "Sometimes I think it's ugly, sometimes I think it's beautiful. The jury's out for me."

Erickson laughed in agreement. "It's a beast of Brutalist architecture, that's for sure. Probably outlive all of us." He played with one end of his trademark handlebar mustache, an affectation dissimulating contemplation. "What's on your mind, Emily?" he asked finally.

"Remember the SAA conference we both went to a couple years back in Portland?" she asked.

"Terrific beer there. And wine," he recalled fondly.

"Yeah." Emily held up her glass. "Anyway, do you remember that lecture on archivist-slash-donor ethics?"

"With Ms. Danielson, yes. Eloquent speaker; beautiful lady."

"Question: You're working on an archive; you come across compromising items—happens almost every time, right?"

"We're dealing with human beings." Erickson shrugged. "Most of the time, anyway."

Emily smiled and took a deep breath. "Let's say, hypothetically, that you believe the items are of cultural value. Part of the truth of the archive Ms. Danielson talked about. And that future researchers would definitely want to have access to these items. But you know if you go to your supervisor, or the director of Special Collections . . ."

"Helena Blackwell?" Erickson interjected.

Emily tilted her head to one side. "She's the director here, yes."

"I know," he said, "I met her when I was out there. Not really an archivist like us, is she?"

"No. More of a social facilitator is what I glean," said Emily. "She doesn't know her DAMs from her acid-free folders, but she's good at raising money."

Erickson raised an index finger. "Not to be discounted."

"No. Anyway, as I was saying, you know, because of the nature of the compromising items, they're going to want you to destroy them. Or, at best, put serious restrictions on them. Hell, I read Caroline Kennedy has some restrictions on items in her mother's archive that go into the twenty-second century." Emily paused and sipped her beer. "These potentially compromising items I'm talking about are digital files, by the way."

"Okay," said Erickson, waiting.

"In the dark archives."

"The dark archives. My favorite place to roam these days," Erickson mused archly.

Emily fortified herself with another sip of beer. "But there's an ethical issue—aside from the nature of the items themselves." Emily paused. "The hypothetical archivist who discovered the items didn't get access to the dark archives through proper channels."

"I see." He resumed toying with his mustache, but a dark ray had crossed his face.

"She was led there by a series of, shall we say, bread crumbs. And not heedlessly thrown either. I would say deliberately, leaving a road map as it were."

Erickson narrowed his eyes in contemplation. "Compromising items?"

"Yes," replied Emily.

"Of a prurient nature?" he asked, tilting his head suggestively.

"It's deeper and much more . . . interpersonally complicated than that."

"It always is." He looked up into the camera. "Why can't you—I mean, your hypothetical archivist—just leave them where they are in the dark archives?"

"That's what I'm wrestling with. But what if I think, as the sole project archivist of this collection, that they belong in the archive, but no one else does?"

"You're the hypothetical archivist."

"Yes," admitted Emily.

"The archive is West's?"

"Yes."

"What does the estate say?" he asked.

"The estate is Elizabeth West. The one you read about donating twenty-five million for the eighth-floor renovation." She paused. "Raymond West's wife."

"I see. A little wayward, was he?"

"It's a little deeper than that, Professor," Emily said candidly. "I'm going to go out on a limb and say she would be stunned if these items were brought to her attention." Emily polished off the rest of her beer. "I'm positive she doesn't know they're out there."

"How do you know that?"

"Because they didn't do, or authorize, the digital ingest of the items."

Erickson recoiled in alarm. "Who did?"

Emily fell silent. The warning bell of an approaching Amtrak clanged on the bluff below, rising and falling. "I don't know," Emily answered feebly, trailing off.

"West's archivist?" he asked, incredulous.

Emily shrugged as if she didn't know the answer. She was now regretting the call. She needed advice, not an inquisition of her methods.

"Were they having an affair?" Erickson asked, assembling and disassembling the puzzle Emily had presented to him.

Emily looked down and blinked her eyes, not answering.

"Did you get to these items without permission" Erickson asked point-blank.

Emily looked off, bunching her lips with thumb and index finger until they were vertical. The train clanged out of earshot. "I've got to go, Professor. My phone is ringing, and I've got to take this."

"Emily! Did you come upon these items *illegally*?" he thundered in an accusatory tone.

His words jolted Emily. She felt her stomach knotting and her voice went into hiding as she succumbed to the invasive echo of her thoughts.

"Don't jeopardize your—"

"I'm losing you, Professor," she cut him off. She quickly moused over the red End Call button and tapped the touchpad. The screen refreshed to her home screen: a picture of a weathered wooden bench at the top of the bluff overlooking the ocean in her temporary home, Del Mar. Seized with anxiety, she sat up on the couch, her breathing rapid, her heart pounding against its will. Onyx meowed, as if he sensed an emotional shift but couldn't apprehend its repercussions.

Erickson tried calling back, his face blooming ominously back on the screen, but Emily slammed her laptop closed, her heart beating hard.

She sprang to her feet, grabbed a sweater, threw open the sliding glass door, patted her sweatpants pockets for her keys, locked the latch on the door, bolted down the concrete stairs, past the garbage bins, and sprinted out into the alley on wings of fear. She slipped by an apartment with its curtains open. Inside a party was in full swing. The music blared. Voices poured out in a collective cacophonous din. Everyone seemed to be in high spirits, enjoying alcohol, weed, and conversation. She felt wretchedly alone suddenly, skulking in the dark, the wind brushing her face, her arms stapled across her chest. Erickson knew Helena. Had met her! "He wouldn't call her, would he?" Emily worried, then realized she had said this out loud when a woman walking her dog on a leash turned to look at her, thinking perhaps she was being addressed by Emily. Emily waved and moved on.

She made a left and walked down Sixth Street, but when she arrived at her favorite bench, she found a young couple occupying it, silhouetted against the moonlit blue ocean and starless sky. He had his arm around her, and her head rested on his shoulder. Both of them held cells that lit up their faces ghoulishly. They're here alone in the night and they're both looking at their phones? Madness!

Emily scrabbled down the first section of the cliff. She stopped in the middle of the railroad tracks, squatted and put her hand on one of the rails. She could swear it still felt warm from the sparking wheels of the train that had just rumbled passed. Raising her head eastward, she got an eyeful of a full moon over the gabled roofs of the seaside homes. Behind the veil of the ash-strewn sky it resembled a giant cataract-afflicted eye. Emily could almost feel its gravitational pull drawing the tide toward the cliffs. The waves battered them now in relentless thunderclaps. The ocean sounded, and felt, metaphysical in the dark, a mysterious, implacable force reaching out and pulling her inexorably toward it.

Feeling her way in the moonlight for the footholds that surfers had sculpted into the sandstone, she clambered down the zigzag pathway to the rocks below. She wanted the distant roar of the surf to drown out her conversation with Erickson, which she was replaying in her head with mounting anxiety, and pretend she had never initiated it. Feeling all alone in the world, she felt crucified by her solitude as she crouched on the wet rocks at the bottom of the cliff and let the whitewater subside at her feet, spitting spray into her face. All at once, as if she knew a sound was coming that she was going to loathe with all her being, she threw her hands to her ears and screamed. She screamed until she had emptied her mind and was panting for breath. She screamed intentionally loud enough that if someone had happened by, they would have almost for certain called 911. She screamed until the wave-ruptured ocean was but a distant roar. She screamed until she believed she was the only human alive on a planet that had met its final extinction, the one that would incinerate it to carbon. That's how desolate and alone she felt in the world now, watched by a jaundiced Cyclops eye of a moon looming ever more immense in the night sky.

Her breathing stabilized. The ocean's numinous powers of sound and smell and an infinite darkness showered her with relief. The ocean's unceasing pumping of waves shoreward weirdly tranquilized her. Then and there Emily realized she could always count on it to claim her if she got in too deep and all the exits to safety were boarded up. A quick glance all around reassured her that she was alone, so she wriggled out of her pants and peed. Feeling better, she straightened from her animal crouch, turned, and clambered back up the cliff, the soles of her tennis shoes slipping, fingers gripping and clawing until they were roughened and raw.

When she reached the crest, she was suddenly blinded by lights. The paced clanging of another approaching train's klaxon rose quickly in volume. It hurtled past, not more than a dozen feet from her, the rail cars shaking, a brutal terrestrial force. She flung an arm to her face to shield her eyes from the dust it kicked up at her. Through the blur of windows, the passengers sat sanguine in the brightly lit compartments like lonely people do in all-night diners. Except these diner cars were speeding past at seventy miles per hour, oblivious of Emily. And why should they care? The steel wheels clack-clack-clacked in retreat until they were nothing but a tapping in the night, then an invisible nothing, and finally a silence. The ground had stopped rumbling. As Emily crossed the tracks it hit her: with one leap she could experience liberation.

CHAPTER 12

Lives in the Stacks

8/30/18

Broken sleep. Ellipses of sleeping and waking. Dreamt of a deep, committed love, but it was only an abstraction. Woke. Whole body sweating. I opened the windows, but the damn dead palm frond kept scratching the eave like a giant, maniacal finger itching a scab. Went back to sleep. Dreamt of Nadia and Raymond in their lovemaking. Graphic. Woke again, the dream still playing like a film on my computer.

Skype with Professor Erickson unnerved me. I thought he would be understanding, but he started to turn on me. I realized I didn't want to tell him about the correspondence I had unearthed. What if he advised me to let it go to Helena or Jean or just leave it be? It's mine now, I thought. I found it! Nadia led me to it. Wouldn't I be betraying her?

Against my better judgment, I continue to read "the correspondence." Some of the pictures they exchanged are hard to look at; or impossible to look away from. The words are poetic though. I wish I could write like her. I wish I could find an "ineffable" love like she found because I've never found it, I've never been in love. I think I know why people risk it all, what she means when she talks about there being "no limits." And I can see how this excited West too. How freeing it must have been for him to have met my predecessor.

But what haunts me most is that I'm writing about her in the past tense.

Emily drove to work on a bright blue morning. The Amtrak Surfliner that had barreled past her the night before approached lazily, from the south this time, cutting diagonally through the Los Peñasquitos Lagoon, a lumbering silver snake that slithered on a trestle under the Coast Highway, glimmeringly innocuous now in the sunlight. Emily wondered again if she had the courage to end it all if life got too stressful. She wondered, too, if Nadia's obsession with suicide had dredged up fantasies of her own.

Holed up in her cubicle, Emily and Nicola busied themselves with the collating of items that had come in the new West boxes, feeling the pressure of the anticipated deadlines and archiving in a more concentrated fashion to hurry the project to completion. To her professional dismay, Emily continued to find inconsistencies between the finding aid, Nadia's meticulous personal file, and what was in the document boxes.

At one point, Nicola returned from the stacks and—exasperated, as if he were about to be reprimanded for doing a poor job—apologized in a defeated tone, "Couldn't find it."

Instead of scolding him—not in Emily's arsenal—she nodded contemplatively, then excused him to go and get some lunch. She needed to be alone.

"Am I doing something wrong?" he asked.

"No, Nicola. You're doing a fantastic job." She found herself smiling. "We'll get through this."

As Nicola slipped out, Jean appeared, as if their beings had swapped places. She rapped her knuckles on one of the record boxes that formed part of the wall that blocked out the corridor. Emily turned to her and waited. "Am I disturbing you?" Jean asked.

"No, Jean. What's up?"

"How are you coming with the display items?"

"It's the least of my concerns right now," Emily said, irritated.

"Not Helena's. Mrs. West is going to be in the meeting, I think I told you."

"I'm well aware." With paddling feet Emily crabbed in her chair across the room to the desk opposite her workstation and tapped on a box. "I've got them pulled right here."

"Do you want to go through them with me?" Jean asked.

"I feel confident I've selected items that will make for an impressive display." Emily crabbed back to her desk, not hiding her annoyance. "I'm sure there'll be input."

"Okay," said Jean. "Three o'clock. Don't be late." She toggled her index finger at Emily's computer. "You got a message."

"Thanks, Jean." Emily didn't break eye contact with her until she had left. When she was gone, Emily swung her chair around and bent toward her monitor. It was an IM from Joel.

It read, "IT says they can't monitor in real time. They have the technology but not the funding or the authority."

Relieved, Emily cursored over the reply pop-up window and typed, "Thanks, Joel."

"Are you ready for the big meeting?"

"Will you be there?" Emily typed.

"Of course. Have to."

"Question?"

"Fuck."

"What's RA stand for?"

"Why do you want to know?"

"Because." Emily waited. Joel's reply was not immediately forthcoming.

"Where did you find the initials?" Joel typed.

"You know where." Emily typed back.

"Emily!" Next to his reply the trembling emoji of a red-faced devil punctuated his exclamation.

Emily smiled, then typed, "What's RA? Please tell me."

"Regents Annex. Analog overflow and items waiting for deaccessioning," Joel reluctantly explained.

"Thank you."

"Surfing?"

"Can't."

"Cool. See you with Helena the Horrible in a few."

Emily closed out her messenger app, drummed her pen against her pursed lips. She closed her eyes and listened. The analog clock had been silenced. Voices of staff from the other cubicles had mercifully vacated to grab lunch. There were no footsteps. As if her cubicle were booby-trapped,

Emily stood up, careful not to cause the chair to squeak, crossed the room to the light switch, and clicked it off. The room fell into a dusky quiet. The record boxes and stacks of stuff she had pulled from them formed shadows that looked like an architect's rendering of some ancient city in silhouette. Eight floors of concrete and steel and windowing pressed down on her from above. Emily craned her head back and looked up and could almost feel its massive tonnage weighing down on her through the diffuser panels directly above. If she meditated any more on its collapsing and burying her in its rubble pile, it might fuel the beginnings of an anxiety attack.

As she crept back to her computer and moused her way into the dark archives, scrolled down to "West," she could feel her pulse quicken realizing suddenly that if she played this as recklessly and irresponsibly as Nadia and Raymond had conducted their love affair, the permanence of Memorial Library could be compromised, the way a hairline crack in a dam could one day, without warning, bring down a cavalcade of water and the inundation of a civilization drowned forever in a watery fate. She thought of Elizabeth West and her sea-level home and her fear her house could one day be a component of that fate, and her consequent plans to relocate to higher ground.

I'm going to find out what happened, Emily voiced to herself in the soft light of the cubicle. *I opened a barred window to an archive, and I'm going to find the truth.*

Ignoring Professor Erickson's remonstrations, she grabbed her mouse with renewed resolve, pierced the membrane of the forbidden and dived into the correspondence where she had left off. *I will not be deterred. I will not play by your rules. I'm redefining the rules*, Emily could hear herself speaking out loud now with a firm determination, a fierce conviction that felt inspired, marionetted, by Nadia and the treasure map she had left to a future archivist who dared to disinter the truth.

From: Nadia Fontaine <Nfontaine@RegentsU.edu>
To: Raymond West <Rwest_Lit@RegentsU.edu>
Subject: What I Want!
Date: 09 October 2017

My Raymond,

I can't live with limits. I don't travel where there are borders. I want to journey where the foliage is dense, succulent with life, pollen oozing, primates howling, colorful birds shrieking. I want streams rushing in spring, not placid in fall. I want to feel alive. I want every fiber in my body vibrating like finely tuned piano wires plucked by your desire; I don't ever want them to slacken. I want the flesh of a man to deliquesce with mine. You. I want the numinous. I want the night. I want to be the owl hooting invisibly in the eucalypti, as you pass under, then swoop down and claim you, prey to my predation, heart to my hunger.

It won't ever stop until you have depleted me, looted every fantasy in my profane imagination. I defy you to deplete me! I am no stranger to insatiety. I am no stranger to the taboo. When I drive to you, I am already fervent with expectation, bursting with desire, avaricious for your scent.

When? Where? Soon? Please!

Your Nadia

PS: Have you started?

"Knock knock," an effervescent woman's voice announced.

Emily wheeled around in her office chair, an outstretched arm behind her with the hand splayed against the screen. "Chloe!"

"I'm not looking." Chloe brought a hand to her eyes and fashioned a pretend blindfold. Emily seized the moment to close out the screen. Nadia and Raymond's galaxy was sucked back into the seemingly boundless vortex of the dark archives as if an astronomer had turned off his telescope; Nadia's voice, summoned from the past, now muted once again.

With her computer shut down, the wires of tension in Emily slackened. She scolded herself for bringing the highly sensitive items back into her office life. The threat of being found out was even that much riskier, she realized. "So, what's up?" Emily finally said to a waiting Chloe.

"I know you've got a big meeting with all the muckety-mucks, so I thought you might need to blow off some steam later." As if in reply, Emily adjusted the glasses on the bridge of her nose and blinked in response to Chloe. "Jesse and his partner Clint and I are going to have dinner at this cool place in Encinitas. They're celebrating a new client they just scored. Should be fun. No pressure."

Feigning exasperation, Emily swept her arm across all the boxes and folders stacked high in her cubicle. "I've got a lot of work here, and Helena's breathing down my neck."

"I know, that's why I thought it would be good to get out, explore San Diego a little." This always happened to Emily: the extrovert in her coworkers trying to coax the introvert in her out into the world. It's one of the reasons she made it a point to remain aloof. Girlfriends were always trying to set her up, as if all she burned for, deep down, was a man to entertain her, maybe romance her, maybe corral her into a relationship doomed to end in an awkward flurry of texts where she felt compelled to explain their blatant incompatibility. Did she look like the wallflower they treated her as? The Nadia/Raymond email correspondence flickered across Emily's heightened state of consciousness, and she reasoned that if she opened herself up a little, perhaps she might tamp down any suspicions in an office setting where gossip flourished like equatorial undergrowth. Make friends, Professor Erickson had advised her, you never know whom you might need to confide in.

"What time?" Emily found herself asking, as if her voice were disembodied, ventriloquized through an Emily who wasn't her.

Chloe brightened, lit up with a smile of triumph. "Like seven thirty? I'll IM you the details. You live in Del Mar, right?"

Paranoia gripped Emily. How did Chloe know that? Joel? Had *she* said something? Had she been talking out loud again? Was there a staff list of addresses and phone numbers she wasn't aware of? Emily wanted her bubble of privacy to remain impermeable. "Yeah. How did you know I lived in Del Mar?"

"Well, you were eating at Urban Plates," she said. "I just sort of figured you were in the general vicinity."

Emily's fickle anxiety quieted. "Okay, text me the details, but don't hate me if I have to bail."

"Totally cool. See you in the meeting." Chloe left an empty hallway in her blustery exit. Emily swung around to face her computer and switched it back on. When it came to life there was already a text from Chloe. It read, "Solace & the Moonlight Lounge. 25 East E St., Encinitas. 7:30. See you there!" In the place of her name was one of those idiotic smiling yellow emojis that Emily worried would negatively define her generation for ages to come.

Restless, Emily left her cubicle, crossed the main floor and was about to turn to go into the bathroom when she changed her mind and decided to take the stairs to the eighth floor, not only to get some exercise but also because the bathrooms on the eighth were private. The immense concrete stairwell echoed with every footstep.

She started up from the second, main, floor. Raising her head, she saw the circumvolution of the stairs around the cylindrical center, guarded only by a waist-high railing. She never counted the number of steps she ascended because she wanted to be surprised when they ran out. Sometimes, like today, the ascent seemed to go on forever. Her thighs burned the last two flights, so she trusted she must be nearing the top. Her mind was a confusion of cross-currents: the disturbing Erickson call that she had abruptly truncated; the status update meeting with Helena and Elizabeth West; the date with Chloe and her boyfriend's business partner; and the salacious correspondence she couldn't stop reading. This last on her list of troubling items was the one she feared the most, the one that made her not want to look down the stairwell as she approached the top, for fear that she would be consumed by her own vertigo and cartwheel over the railing as if pulled by a powerful magnet . . .

On the eighth floor, Emily locked herself into the small all-gender bathroom. It was dark and claustrophobic inside, but she felt comforted being cocooned in there. "Solace & the Moonlight Lounge," she mouthed out loud to herself. *So fucking SoCal.* She shook her head. It wasn't like her to go on a double date . . . and how was she going to look Mrs. Elizabeth West in the eye with all that she now knew about her husband! And what did *they* know?

The oppressively tiny bathroom imploded in on her. Seized by anxiety, she heard herself beginning to hyperventilate. She pulled up her panties, smoothed down her skirt, rummaged in her purse for her lipstick and thrust her face in the mirror, hands planted on the sink. She started to apply some lipstick and then had second thoughts. With a sheet of toilet paper, she wiped the mascara from her eyes. Didn't want to look anything like Nadia, she thought. She opened her mouth and exhaled, fogging the mirror and blurring her face. Suddenly an inscrutable image materialized. Her hot breath had educed the tracings of a past greasy finger that had drawn a heart with a jagged line running diagonally across like a sheared aorta. "The fuck!" Emily hissed, horrified. She wiped the fog and the omen of the heart shot through with an arrow from the mirror and studied her countenance one last time. Inconspicuous, plain, without suspicion or ulterior motive, she thought, nodding once to herself and a quick readjustment of her eyewear. I'm ready, she declared to her doppelgänger.

Bolting out of the bathroom, she emerged into the blinding sunlight of the eighth floor. The study carrels and book shelving had all been carted off, leaving the linoleum gray and bare, and the resultant empty geometry of concrete and glass mosque-like and cavernous. As Verlander had detailed in the Town Hall meeting, it would be carpeted with a luxury weave. Plush reading chairs would replace the outdated, evacuated furniture and face a spectacular view that would make it hard to study. But why study when there are no more books? On two ladders, electricians were dismantling the harsh overhead lighting—chandeliers would plunge gloriously from the ceilings in their stead. If Emily closed her eyes, she could imagine this eighth-floor space, wrapped rectangularly around the elevator shaft and stairwell, as if it were the university's version of New York's iconic Rainbow Room, without the slow rotational gimmick. Helena's Town & Gown fundraisers would be privileged invites for La Jolla's snobbish high society. To think it had once been a sacrosanct floor of learning was now almost unbelievable in the midst of this ongoing transformation to the bookless, digital future. The library would finally be crowned as Helena had always dreamed it. At its epicenter she would stand tall like the mast of a sleek sailing vessel, her vision polished to perfection. She didn't need the house on Windemere with the waves breaking just out of arm's reach. Her legacy would be this metamorphosis of a public institution into her image of the future, a multipurpose structure that paid tribute to a vertically steep hierarchy of wealth and privilege. She would be the envy of everyone at the university who knew what she had accomplished in getting Elizabeth West's checkbook to open and steering the argosy of Helena's master plan into the harbor. If you were Helena, Emily thought, it must be breathtaking to see it all evolving and now materializing before your eyes.

Perched at the top of the stairwell en route to her meeting, Emily finally forced herself to look down, as if hoping to conquer her acrophobia with one gaping eyeful of the view of the void. Eight floors to the concrete below. She reared back from the railing in terror, the back of her hand pressed to her forehead, a little feverish, a little faint, the ethereality of the height discomposing her. The stairs were wide enough that she could descend by cleaving to the walls if she felt an imagined centripetal force was pulling her into the shaft's cylindrical free fall. She redirected her gaze to the wide metal stairs that reverberated loudly with her every step. She started down, listing to the wall, afraid of that colossal empty cylinder and its tragic pull, briefly pausing at each floor's landing to collect herself.

At 3:00 p.m. everyone in Special Collections who had anything to do with the West Papers convened in the seminar room. Emily was second to arrive after Jean, who was busy fussing with the finishing touches on a movable whiteboard that detailed a timeline for the West Papers. At the top of the whiteboard, in case there was any doubt, "The West Papers" was written in black block letters and double-underlined in red for emphasis. Jean did love her colored dry-erase markers. It validated her job title. Annoying, Emily thought as she took a chair and plopped her folder with the items she had pulled for the display down on the table. Chloe, with her mismatched bohemian garments, trundled in next. She bent down to Emily and asked if she got her text. Emily smiled and nodded, almost glad now to have a female friend, even if she had to meet her boyfriend's business partner as the quid pro quo for having one. Joel, wearing a blue work shirt and black jeans, sauntered in and sat a chair away from Emily. "Hi, everyone," was all he offered, before directing his gaze to the whiteboard. He swung his face to Emily's, pointed a derisive finger at Jean's back and shook his head briefly. Emily replied with a downturn smile, as if to say, *Do you believe this?*

The mood in the room turned serious when Verlander bustled in with Helena. Verlander, in blazer and dress shirt, greeted everyone amiably, in his typical bonhomie, but Helena, expressionless, midi skirt and a ballooning blouse, looked overwrought, camouflaging her anxiety with an all-business scowl. As she collapsed into her chair at the head of the table with a menacing thud, Emily noticed she had dyed her hair a light pearl gray and then, as if throwing caution to the wind, had it streaked with jet black for dramatic effect. Chloe visibly sucked in her breath at the spectacle. It made Emily think of a skunk's pelt, if the white striping were gleaming silver. It was cropped short, styled in waves like a frozen yogurt, and she was sporting new eyewear. It was as if the eighth-floor renovation had been completed, and she were already dressing, and styling herself, more fashionably for its apotheosis.

"You're looking . . . nice, Helena," Joel offered, though Emily knew he was cackling like a hyena inside.

"Hi, Helena," Emily greeted her.

Helena forced a smile that disappeared from her face as quickly as it had come.

Everyone assembled around the canoe-shaped table. A woman's voice could be heard outside the door, and a figure could be seen through the window panel, a phone tilted close to her mouth. Words were not discernible, but Helena glanced frequently in the direction of the woman, as if indicating to everyone else in the room that chitchat had ceased to be appropriate.

Elizabeth West entered the room, concluding her call and slipping her cell into her purse. The badinage among colleagues came to an abrupt halt and expressions turned serious. She was sophisticatedly dressed in black silk slacks and a flowing white blouse that unfurled over her womanly hips. The black pearl necklace around her neck made Emily think of Nadia's hand on Elizabeth's husband's throat at Estancia, rousing an imaginary spider who then tiptoed down the nerve endings of her spine. The unspoken was truly ineffable. Emily thought, *If my mind were a snow globe and you could see inside . . .* The guilt momentarily paralyzed her.

Verlander chivalrously pulled out a chair for Elizabeth, greeted her deferentially, then resumed sitting next to her. She set her stiff leather handbag on the table where it stood sentinel over the meeting. Through closed lips she smiled at everyone in the room, swiveling her head left then right, a lighthouse beacon illuminating a dark ocean, its creatures and wayward crafts with a searchlight that she, and only she, could switch off. She practically owned the library. For all intents and purposes, she owned everybody in the room. Her sangfroid was quietly alarming.

"Hello, everyone. Sorry I'm late." She directed her imperious presence to Helena. "Helena."

Helena laughed nervously and tried to control a loose-mouthed smile. "I know it's been a few weeks, but you remember Raymond's archivist on the project, Emily Snow." She pointed a crooked finger in Emily's direction.

Elizabeth swung her head to Emily seated midtable. "Of course." Her expression bore a spooky impassiveness that made Emily wonder if she hadn't recently undergone facial reconstructive surgery. Wrinkles didn't form naturally when she smiled. Her beauty was incontestable, and Emily could clearly see vestiges of the woman Raymond had fallen in love with, but it gleamed like Roman statuary under the mercilessly unsparing overhead fluorescents. "How are you finding my husband's papers?" she asked sincerely.

Emily nervously adjusted her glasses on her nose. She noticed that Helena was making a gesture with an upturned hand for her to sit up straight. She quickly corrected her posture, cleared her throat with a fist thrown to her mouth, and finally replied, "Such a prodigious archive for someone still relatively young. It goes forever."

"Yes. He was born with it. God knows where he got it growing up here in San Diego. A cultural abyss," she put in dismissively of the city they had all chosen to live in. Her flashing acerbity surprised everyone. And that trenchancy, too, Raymond had no doubt fallen in love with. And no doubt quailed in the face of when it was turned on him for whatever reason.

"Something we're going to change," Helena said, smiling optimistically.

"It's an honor to be working on his papers," Emily enthused in a rare moment of ebullience. And in that moment she almost decided she couldn't go on reading the correspondence that had taken her on such a dark and compromised detour. She just couldn't. The iniquity of it all! This woman couldn't bear it, even if Emily were so recklessly stupid as to bring it to the university's attention. Couldn't bear it; didn't deserve it.

"Do you want to begin, Jean?" Helena said.

Jean, at last with a purpose, smiled and rose from her chair. She took two steps to where the double-sided whiteboard was positioned. For dramatic effect—since it was her only apparent moment in the limelight—she flipped it over and displayed the timeline of the West Collection she had been strategizing. Everyone's heads bent to the front of the room for her presentation while Jean flanked the whiteboard brandishing a dry-erase marker. Its squealing on the board every time she touched it grated on Emily's nerves. Each arrow that she drew was like a spike hammered into Emily's head. When she completed the arrows with the vees of the arrowheads, the slashing of the two lines almost made Emily want to scream.

"This is when Emily began." *Squeak squeak.* "We had a project assessment date for August fifteenth." *Squeak.* "Determined that with the new addition, Emily would need a week to get up to speed on where we were on the general level." With dry-erase marker poised next to her cheek, Jean turned to Emily with raised eyebrows, silently asking if there were any qualifications to what she was outlining. Emily let her continue with a wordless nod. Jean turned back to the comfort of the whiteboard's narrative. Left to improvisation she would have had a panic attack. "And then as we got into a feel for the folder and item level of the collection, David was kind enough to make the big announcement—which surprised us all"—Jean attempted a parenthetical of light humor that drew a chuckle from everyone—"and we decided to move up the timeline."

Jean took one step back from the reversible whiteboard and slowly flipped it over. At the top it read "West Collection—Phase II." Underneath was a series of dates. With a nod, Jean turned the presentation over to Helena.

"September twenty-fourth, before the quarter starts, we would like to be close to having the first exhibit in the foyer to Special Collections," Helena said with quiet authority. She addressed Emily. "I understand you've brought some samples of items that will go in the display cases."

Everyone swung their heads to Emily, who tapped the manila folder in front of her with a flattened hand to reassure them.

"Good." Helena readdressed the room. "Beginning the first of October, we would like to go out with the press release about the acquisition of the West Papers." Helena leaned back in her chair and smiled. Polite applause greeted her announcement.

Emily, looking around, realized it was important to join in to celebrate this. Not having been a fixture at the library like Verlander or Helena, she could have only vaguely grasped its importance, but not felt it emotionally like they did, given all the years they had sacrificed establishing the prominence of this institution. When Emily ventured a glance at Helena, she was dabbing tears from her eyes with the knuckle of an index finger. Years in the planning, the eighth-floor renovation must have been a cathartic triumph for her. Memorial Library was shedding a skin and was about to be reborn anew. It was the dawn of a proverbial new day. Even though Emily was replaceable, as she looked at the timeline and endured the high-pitched squeaking of Jean's manic, obsessive, unnecessary double-underlining of dates, she realized just how integral she was to this timeline now unchangeable in red, blue and black on the whiteboard. To lose her now would capsize this boat midvoyage; they would have to begin all over, bring someone new up to speed. Emily suddenly felt like one of those early astronauts who awoke to the realization that he, indeed, was going to be strapped into the cockpit of the rocket and launched into outer space. If he had doubts, it was too late.

"How-*eh*-ver," Helena said, dividing the syllables in *her* dramatic fashion. "On October fifth, the Nobel Prize for Literature is announced. And though I know no one here wants to jinx it, we have to be ready for the media, in the event . . ." she trailed off with widened eyes of excitement. In large block letters Jean wrote "October 5th." She finished it with two exclamation points, and then triple-underlined it. The *squeak-squeak-squeak*ing of the bold, exclamatory strokes involuntarily forced Emily to rush her hands to her ears. "But our focus needs to be on the Gala."

Emily let her hands drop to her side and returned her attention back to the whiteboard where Jean had double-underlined "November 11th—The Eighth Floor Gala."

Joel raised a hand to eye level.

"Yes, Joel," said Helena.

"What happens if he wins the Nobel?"

"We're in uncharted territory," chuckled Verlander in his raspy pipe tobacco voice.

"It'll be a fabulous problem to have," enthused Helena.

"We would have to go to Stockholm," Elizabeth interjected dryly.

"While we all sat here in Stockholm Syndrome," Joel quipped. The collective relief of laughter brought a rare moment of collegiality to the room.

When the laughter died down, Helena directed her gaze at Emily. "Emily, do you want to fill us in where you're at in the timeline? Show us what you've pulled for the display? Pose any questions? We know it's been a hit-the-ground-running project for you . . ." Helena extended an outstretched arm. "The floor is yours."

Jean remained standing at the whiteboard. Everyone waited. Emily chose to remain seated.

"First of all," she began, "thank you for the opportunity. So far"—she turned to Elizabeth—"your husband's papers have been a joy to work on." Elizabeth smiled, and not a wrinkle creased her beautiful face. Emily opened her manila folder. "I'm a big believer in origins. Where everything started." Like a card dealer she pushed some photos of Raymond in his early twenties to the middle of the table for all to view. "I found these."

Everyone let Elizabeth have the first look. Drawing one toward her, she smiled fondly at a black-and-white photo which captured Raymond, no more than twenty-five, bent over a writing slope stationed on a desk, pen poised in hand, a cigarette dangling from his mouth, a plume of smoke curling wispily past his intense hawklike eyes. She set it down, a smile aglow on her face.

"He's smoking in this one," Helena worried, her PC antenna tuned to the zeitgeist of the current moment.

Elizabeth shook her head. "That's the way he was back then," she reminisced wistfully. "I like it. Brilliant choice, Emily."

Helena had trouble disguising the fact that Emily took a chance on something that she would have feared offending a major donor by pulling for the first exhibit. "Yes, I like the chronology," she admitted. "No need for us to disguise anything."

Emily fanned out some more photos and they were carefully passed around. Everyone handled them delicately by their edges with flared palms and set them down gently like antiquarians might do with rare letters. The manuscript pages Emily had pulled from the boxes in the stacks that had already been processed and cataloged were treated with the same careful regard for their long-term preservation.

Over one photo of a young Raymond and Elizabeth, both smiling radiantly, Elizabeth, staring fixedly at it, remarked, "Such a lovely time in New York with his play. New York is fun when you have a hit play." She lay the picture down on the table, her eyes not leaving it, with an expression that traveled dreamily back in time.

"His only play?" Emily inquired.

Elizabeth found a frown, and this time her forehead broke into fine lines. "He despised the director. Called him the Idi Amin of theater." Everyone laughed. "He didn't like collaboration."

Emily thought this was an odd comment but refrained from asking why. She circulated some more items for the team to inspect for their archival relevance. Elizabeth zeroed in on one, picked it up, and held it at arm's length, her eyes narrowed, her mouth tightening. Her ominous silence drew everyone's attention. Helena's jaw went slack. Everyone could see that it was a yellowed newspaper clipping. Slowly, deliberately, dramatically, with thumbs and index fingers holding it like a spider's pinchers, she tore it in two. Verlander slowly reared back in his chair with interlaced hands over his chest, stunned. Helena's eyes enlarged with an animal's consternation. The shock traveled like an electrical current through everyone else in the room. Elizabeth West had just destroyed an item of university property. Had anyone else in the room taken the liberty to tear or otherwise deface an artifact from the West Collection, they would, depending on their standing in the hierarchy, either be fired on the spot or rebuked in a prelude to an inevitable firing. Even Helena, queen of Special Collections & Archives, would almost certainly be called into Human Resources to explain her actions. Any misgivings they had over Elizabeth's destroying of university property were suppressed in favor of the opacity necessary to assuage the feelings of such a donor. She controlled the collection with an iron fist. And the West Papers overshadowed every other collection in the library by a long shot. And lest anyone thought otherwise, Elizabeth defied them to challenge her preeminence in the library's hegemony with her steely gaze.

"I don't like this one," Elizabeth announced, setting the now two items of the *New York Times* Arts Section article on the table as if they were toilet tissues blotted with excrement. The headline read, "Raymond West Wins 2005 Pulitzer for Fiction." The grainy black-and-white photo that accompanied the article pictured Raymond surrounded by a semicircle of smiling fans. "Remove it from the collection," Elizabeth fulminated. "Now."

Emily, taken aback, withdrew the two pieces of yellow-faded newspaper, already remedying in her mind a plan to restore it. "I'm sorry. I didn't . . ." she started haltingly.

"I just don't like it," Elizabeth spluttered in an attempt to collect herself. She waved a bejeweled hand in the air as if chasing away a pestering swarm of flies.

Everyone exchanged looks of disconcertion with one another, at a loss as to how to palliate the suddenly changed mood that had begun on such a high note. It was as if the room had suddenly darkened and grown fraught and everyone was left to wonder why.

"I'm sorry," Elizabeth said. "I haven't been sleeping well."

"It's okay, Elizabeth." Helena patted her solicitously on the wrist. "We, of course, all want you to be happy."

Emily secreted the torn newspaper clipping into her folder and closed it so that whatever was offensive about it was cut off from Elizabeth's view. "Is there something specific about the photo, so I don't . . ."

"I don't want to talk about it," Elizabeth said sharply. "Just take it out. Get rid of it."

Helena attempted to restore a professional order back to the meeting. "Why don't you tell us where you are with the timeline, Emily?"

"Well, as you know," Emily began, the contretemps of the newspaper clipping fleeting like a dark ray across her mind, "we had a new addition to the collection. I've had a chance to go through it on the general level, check it against the container lists, and I think we're in pretty good shape. I'm still identifying some items that I'm not finding in the records or document boxes, but I'm sure now that I have Nadia's personal file, it's going to go even faster."

The room fell quiet. Everyone seemed to stiffen. The overhead lights buzzed. In the shared silence, the name *Nadia* hung in the air like a cloud of poison.

"I don't recall giving that to you." Helena held a clenched smile that fissured her face and turned her mouth into a rictus of startled alarm.

"She discovered it in one of the records boxes," Jean explained to exculpate herself.

Joel heaved a sigh of relief that anyone in the room who noticed interpreted as a yawn.

Elizabeth, still seated, wore a faraway expression as if an ear was bent toward an imminent emergency.

"Anything else, Emily?" Helena asked, maintaining her composure, "Before we adjourn here."

"Is it possible I could talk to Professor West? I have a few questions—"

"He's too busy," Elizabeth snapped, visibly disturbed, her earlier aplomb crumbling in front of all of them.

The room fell silent. Elizabeth's words still vibrated in the air. She looked visibly jolted by Emily's apparent impertinence. Everyone waited.

"He doesn't want to be bothered with all this"—Elizabeth flung a hand in the air on a disjointed wrist—"this administrative shit. He doesn't like to remember. He never reads his books once they're published. Never," she punctuated the air with a raised index finger. "New beginnings," he always said. "He was appalled when he heard Philip Roth, upon retirement, had taken it upon himself to read all twenty-nine of his novels. What an act of narcissism, Ray said. He would never go back."

"Not even to something he left unfinished?" Emily ventured meekly.

Elizabeth rotated her large head toward Emily and let it loom over her. "Never." She smiled. "What would you like to ask me, Dear?" *Dear* had the inflection of an adult addressing a small child.

Emily screwed up her courage. She knew she was wading into overhead waters but the ethical archivist in her couldn't halt her blurting out, "In the . . . file . . . there's mention of a project, ironically titled *The Archivist.* I can't find it anywhere in the document boxes, even though it's clearly indexed in the finding aid. Can you shed any light on what this title refers to?"

Elizabeth's stony silence reverberated through the room like a low-frequency current that only certain species of living creatures could detect. The tectonic jolt in Elizabeth was subtle, but everyone's antennae were suddenly tuned to a different frequency, and the fugitive glances that darted from one to another were a frantic attempt to read her complex psychology. It was not uncommon in the archival world to have a misplaced item. Unless, of course, it was a manuscript that had tickled the dragon's tail.

"It was abandoned," Elizabeth quaked. Then, in an effort to regain her usually unflappable composure she qualified, "An immature effort that my husband dismissed as youthful folly, I believe is how he characterized it to me," she finished with a forced smile, her thunderous words bringing the room to a hush.

"Thank you," Emily said. "I'll stop looking for it."

"I hope you do." Elizabeth glanced at her glittering jeweled watch. She hooked her thumbs under the table and pushed back her chair suddenly, stood, reached for her purse—Emily could have sworn it was still trembling at the force of Elizabeth's words—and said curtly, "Carry on." As she strode out, she stopped next to Helena, stooped over and put her mouth next to her ear and hissed so that everyone in the room could hear, "Get control of your employees!" She scurried out the door as if cast out into a storm, leaving the power vacuum for Helena to fill. The tension in the seminar room hung over it like a cloud, throbbing invisibly. Faces wore expressions of befuddlement.

"Well," began a conciliatory Helena. "I think despite the little faux pas of Emily's that we're all on the same page here, moving forward. I think we all understand that Elizabeth is under a lot of pressure with the Eighth Floor Gala approaching, the move to the new house . . ." She cut herself short and turned to Emily and telescoped her head toward her like a preying, coiled, threatening snake. "I thought I told you to run anything you had concerns about with the West Collection by me."

"I didn't know," Emily said in an apologetic tone.

"Well, now you do," she chastised. "Now you realize how delicate this project is." She sat back and fingered the fake pearls that festooned her neck, not real ones like Elizabeth wore. "If Elizabeth wanted to pull her gift, this rededication, everything, *everything* would collapse," she finished in a veritable tizzy that surprised everyone.

"That's a little hyperbolic, Helena," Verlander interjected, rising to Emily's defense. "Given that the deed of gift has already been signed and the money is in the process of being transferred." Without looking at her, he threw out a hand to the chagrined Emily. "I think Emily was just asking an innocent question. How could she know it would touch a nerve?" He was the only one in the room higher up than Helena and able to adopt an opposing position.

"She could stop the transfer of funds any time, David," Helena barked back.

"I don't think this is a topic of conversation for the agenda of this particular meeting or for the ears of our staff, who are working their butts off to make your dream a reality," Verlander rejoined, pushing his chair back sullenly, rising, grabbing a worn leather briefcase, sweeping a smile across the room before exiting.

Joel and Chloe took Verlander's leave-taking as their cue to excuse themselves. Emily gathered all the archival items back in her folder, preparing to leave when Helena stopped her.

"Emily. Could I have a word with you?" Helena requested.

"Sure," replied Emily, closing her folder and resting her hands on it.

Helena raised her eyes to Jean, who intuited the hint and stole out the door without a word, closing it behind her.

Helena waited until Jean's footsteps retreated out of earshot. She interlaced her fingers and brought them to her mouth as if shaping the beginning of a disquisition in them and holding it at bay. Then she rocked them prayerfully in front of her. "I realize you're being professional. That's why we hired you." She forced a smile. "Elizabeth is an emotional, high-strung woman. You realize?"

Emily ran her tongue over her front teeth, bulging out her upper lip, and then nodded.

"You're not, I hope, digging into digital items that are out of scope?"

Reflexively, Emily shook her head, but the veil of her opacity had been pierced.

"There's a *lot* in the West Collection." Helena's tone was tremblingly hostile.

"Seventy-seven linear feet and counting," Emily said, just to hear her voice, for fear that the inviolable bubble she had created around herself was an ectoplasm of developing madness.

Helena fixed Emily with an icy stare. "To replace you at this late juncture, with all that's happening, you realize would seriously set us back, if not downright"—she threw an arm like waving a dead snake in the direction of Jean's timeline—"dramatically throw everything into turmoil. We can't have you go tunneling into every nook and cranny because you want to do a thorough job. There'll be time for that after the Gala."

Chastened, Emily muttered, "Okay."

"*Anything* you have a question about, you don't go to Chloe, you don't go to Jean or Joel—or even David." Emily looked up into Helena's cracked makeup and bagged eyes. "You come to me." She stabbed a finger at her chest.

Emily nodded. "I'm just trying to do my job, Helena," she replied matter-of-factly, in an effort to defuse the situation, understanding full well that she had deliberately tempted fate.

"It's not always about preserving every item in a collection," Helena said. She raised an index finger and pointed through seven ceilings to the eighth floor. "Sometimes there are higher things, more important. And I don't mean God."

Back in her cubicle, Emily sat in contemplation with her legs thrown up on the desk, crossed at the ankles. Eyes fixed in contemplation, she tried to process what had happened in the meeting. Mind-blowingly unprofessional perhaps to bring up *The Archivist*, but she didn't know that Elizabeth or any of them knew about the affair. If they did, they would have kept it buried. But *The Archivist* was a real book, a tangible thing, something, Emily stubbornly believed, that should be in the archive, even if restrictions were imposed. The person who would know where it was, of course, would be Raymond West. But, given what had just gone down in the meeting, *that* conversation was not going to be brokered.

Emily let her feet drop down from the desk. She replied to a text from Joel asking whether she wanted to go surfing. She typed a reply that she would take a rain check. He replied, "Don't ever let them know I gave you Nadia's personal file. I have student loans."

"Okay, Joel," she wrote back, not appreciating being admonished, as if Joel thought she were idiotic and cruel enough to give him up. A text from Chloe came concerning the double date with her boyfriend and Clint. Emily still couldn't believe she was going out with a guy named *Clint.* She wrote back that Saturday was still fine.

Emily opened the folder that she had brought into the meeting and slid out the two pieces of the *New York Times* newspaper clipping. Like only two pieces of a jigsaw puzzle, she fitted them back together. With a groping hand, she opened a drawer and fumbled around until she found a photographer's loupe. She lowered it over the torn clipping, bent her head down and pressed her eye to the cup. At eight times magnification, the black-and-white photo looked like a promotional still for an old movie from the '60s. The grain was the size of small pebbles. In the center of the photograph stood a handsome, joyously smiling Raymond. His shoulder-length hair tumbled to the collar of a white button-up shirt. Taller than everyone else in the photo, he dominated the center of the image. Emily moved the loupe over the other faces grouped around him she couldn't see in detail with the naked eye, until they bloomed into focus. She stopped on one. Directly behind Raymond to his right, a hand placed on his shoulder, was a young brunette woman, tall, striking, head cocked to one side and smiling coquettishly. She looked familiar. Emily raised her head. She switched on her computer and went spelunking into the dark archives, descending quickly down the ladder of directories until she found the one she was looking for: "N/R Corrs." She remembered a picture that was in the file, a topless Nadia, wearing only black bikini bottoms, arms flung behind her head, fingers intertwined, smiling that crookedly sultry smile of hers. Was it her? Emily minimized that screen, and then found her Google search window. She typed in "nadia fontaine death." The internet quickly spewed forth the handful of articles on her drowning. In all of them, the same stock university website photo had been given to the press, the standard one that was taken of all the employees. Looking back and forth between the photo on her monitor and the one in the loupe, Emily was positive the woman was Nadia.

Emily leaned back in her chair and sucked in her breath. Had Elizabeth recognized Nadia in the photo? Had Nadia been stalking Raymond long before the library acquired his papers? She could only imagine her predecessor's thrill when his work *was* acquired, and at knowing almost for certain that she would be assigned to it. She must have been over the moon. She probably interpreted it as destiny. Emily breathed in slowly through her nose, and her chest swelled.

As per archival protocol, Emily photocopied the torn clipping onto acid-free paper, fully intending to replace it in the document box where she had found it. Then she rooted around in her top drawer and found a dispenser of Scotch Tape, which she always kept handy, even if archivists were forbidden to use it to repair anything. She carefully laid the two pieces of the torn clipping face down. She measured a length of tape, broke it off at the serrated cutter, and caught it before it curled and taped itself into a Möbius strip. As she laid it on the two pieces of the clipping, the static electricity caused the newspaper to levitate, as if animated, freaking Emily out. She pressed down on the tape, trimmed the overlap with scissors, and turned the clipping over. It wasn't a perfect tape job. A jagged diagonal line fissured across Nadia's and Raymond's hearts, victimizing and stigmatizing them for their infidelity. It made her briefly reflect on the utter illogicality of their love. *Love goes where it will; the arrow can only follow* . . . She recited the words to herself in a murmur. Had she read them quoted in one of their emails, evoking her own dim memory of the famous line? Was it déjà vu? She carefully folded it and placed it in her pocket, a keepsake for her own personal file.

Footsteps sounded. Through her bookcase where the West record cartons had amassed, Emily could make out the willowy figure of Jean walking briskly past. She didn't stop to say goodbye, but that was her custom. Chloe waved as she went by. Joel leaned in on his way out, had to perform a semicircle to get Emily's attention because she was wearing headphones, tossed her the shaka shake. Emily smiled a laugh, and then he was gone. Emily removed her headphones and went out to the reference desk. Samantha, a cataloger whom Emily didn't cross paths with much, was staffing the desk.

"Going to the bathroom." Emily pointed across the lobby as she marched past. And as she did, she glanced at the door to Helena's office. The light was switched off and the door was closed. She would have asked Samantha if Helena had left for the day, but her paranoia was mounting. She crossed the lobby and disappeared into the bathroom. All alone, hands braced on the counter, she looked at her face in the mirror as if she hadn't looked at herself in weeks. She breathed in and out deeply several times, then, as if deciding something, washed her hands and returned to her cubicle.

Except for Samantha, Special Collections had fallen silent. Emily basked in the serenity. She sat down at her desk and mouse-clicked her way quickly into the dark archives. Looking for more coded references to *The Archivist*, she didn't find anything. Frustrated, she clicked her way into the correspondence between Nadia and Raymond and picked up where she had left off.

From: Nadia Fontaine <Nfontaine@RegentsU.edu>
To: Raymond West <Rwest_Lit@RegentsU.edu>
Subject: Truth is the final residue of all beings . . .
Date: 10 October 2017

My Raymond,

I was born into a race that split off from its tribe and embarked on a different journey, one that went from light to darkness. We traveled tumultuous seas on balsa rafts. We inhabited islands and procreated a species that knew only passion, knew only the blood scalding in our veins. We evolved into a race that fed on voluptuousness . . . this is who I am. This is the I who met you, was thrown at you, the woman you needed to ignite that dormant desire . . .

Yes, I will meet you, of course I will meet you, whatever you say, my love . . .

NADIA'S STORY (CONT'D)

The heat was ferocious that morning. With the Santa Anas blustering out of the mountains, I put the convertible top down on my Ford Falcon and squealed my tires out of the lot to turning heads and startled pedestrians, my blue scarf trailing like a torn pennant over the back seat. Day had surrendered to twilight, and the sun had long since departed to other warm latitudes of the world.

Out of the university city, I veered right onto Torrey Pines Scenic Drive, a two-lane road that led to the Gliderport. Raymond told me he only had half an hour to spare, but he desperately wanted to see me. The Gliderport parking lot would be patrolled by Regents PD looking for students drinking and drugging, so we agreed it was too risky to meet there like last time. We decided on an ill-lit street, across from an industrial park. Swiveling my head left and right, I spotted Raymond's black Range Rover with the charcoal-tinted windows. I pulled ahead of it, located a space, and recklessly parallel parked in two twisting moves, my car jutting out at an angle, but I didn't care, I was floating on a cloud. I knew his scent now and I could already smell the odor of the soap he used mingled with the underarm deodorant and I longed to drink it in. His breath would be coffee-scented. The top two buttons of his shirt would be undone, and the sparse chest hair would feel the electricity of the first grasp of my hand and swell on goose-pimpled flesh. He may or may not have run an electric razor over his fine stubble—I didn't care. His mouth would come to mine as eager as an animal, as impetuous and passionate as the lover he had become and the woman he was besotted with.

I hurriedly reapplied lipstick in my rearview mirror and leaped out of the car, not bothering to put the top up. The only streetlights were on the opposite side of the street and they cast it in random pools of melancholy yellow. The waves breaking at Black's Beach could be heard over the Gliderport cliff like an urgent voice. A swell must have come in, but I wasn't interested in surfing tonight. With no sidewalk on the passenger sides of the parked cars, I tightrope-walked the curb between the cars and shrubbery with mincing steps, a gazelle giddy with happiness. Was it the warm, dry air or the furious exchange of last-minute emails cementing the details of this hastily arranged clandestine tryst that had made my whole body damp with sweat? My underarms were sticky. My face was flushed. The insides of my thighs were dewed with desire, the short, tight skirt I had changed into in the parking lot squeezing them together. In the short amount of time we had, I wanted him to have willing access. That's why I had unsnapped my bra, wriggled out of it like a contortionist, and flung it cavalierly over my shoulder and into the back of my car. I wanted him to have my breasts without him having to pace his desire. This was not a languorous afternoon that bled into evening with two or three sessions of lovemaking, showers, and drawn-out, ardent goodbyes, promises as lovers disconsolately parted. This was "I'm coming for you at your behest, and you'd better be ready."

I opened the Range Rover passenger-side door and found Raymond lounged in the bucket seat, the back inclined halfway into the rear, easy ingress for his lover. I kissed him hard on the mouth and wouldn't let go, didn't want to hear his voice, didn't want to snap the moment like dry twigs in wet towels with conversation. Smothering him with my ardency, I could feel his desire swell beneath me. His whole body ached for me—I could feel it like the electrical storms I knew from my youth. Dark, swollen rain clouds would scud in low and fast, and the electricity would jerk the sky, and it was important to get down, even in the beating rain that quickly followed, and not be near anything that the lightning could target. Once I witnessed a tree split in half with an ear-splitting crack, and that's exactly how I felt when his confident hands found my bikiniless ass, raised up my skirt and guided me up on to him, my fingers flailing at his belt and pants and underwear until I found what I had fantasized all day while I was holed up in that soulless cubicle. And then, like a flock of birds scared into flight all at once, we were one in the car, a whirling dervish of two bodies that hungered for the depthless ocean of pure desire. I had him now and I knew he couldn't give me up without experiencing a deep sorrow. He waited for me to come, and then the low-flying thunderclouds in the humid air burst inside me and unleashed a torrent of rain, and then it was as if the sky's tumult had quieted and passed. He closed his eyes and groaned deep from his thorax, and I collapsed on his chest, gasping for breath, as his limbs trembled, then sagged still. He laughed a little and shook his head.

"What?" I whispered.

"You're too much," was all he could manage, sighing the consummation of his pleasure over and over until he finally quieted.

I kissed his ear and raked a hand through his silky hair. I wouldn't wash that hand until the next morning because I wanted to sleep with it cupped against my mouth and nose as my husband snored away in the master bedroom across the hall that had been barren for months.

Raymond reached a hand out over my shoulder. His eyes opened into my larger, firelit ones. They were inches from his and they stayed on him, boring into him with a fierce intensity, a jungle cat who had subdued her prey and now licked her bloodstained lips in serene satisfaction. He could tell from my eyes this was going to be a hard love to ever abdicate. We were in deep now, adults screwing like teenagers in cars parked dangerously close to the university. He held up a black Moleskine to the sides of our faces. As I felt him retreating from me with the diminishment of my desire, he replenished it with something better. "Volume Three," he announced proudly. His free hand clutched my ass and squeezed it goodbye with one last pulse of desire. "It's coming fast now, my love."

"I'm thrilled." Without taking my unblinking eyes off him, I took the Moleskine he offered. "I can't tell you how elated I am."

"We're immortalizing this." He clutched my hand to his heart, a man, I believed in all the untapped hollows of *my* heart, was now apocalyptically in love with me.

I held him tight. I couldn't bear our uncoupling. Not just yet. Don't look at your watch. Please. Stay with me a while longer. Let's run on the beach. Devastate me with your kisses.

And then our cars parted . . .

EMILY

Emily found herself stuck in rush-hour traffic on the Coast Highway, wedged between two long lines of slow-moving cars. Three lanes merged into two, choked to one where the road shallowed out at the ocean, before the climb back up the hill to Del Mar. Emily cursed herself for leaving late, knowing damn well that the traffic would be a gridlocked bitch. She had wanted to visit that side street off the Gliderport where Nadia and Raymond met and fucked and traded literature in the making—he writing, she transcribing—their love and emails, the loam where the seed had been sown. It was a lonely stretch of asphalt at night. The streetlights weren't amber as Nadia romanticized in her *My Story* memoir. They were an icy blue/white. She had no doubt that the windows of West's Range Rover had fogged them from view and provided them the perfect cover from the eyes of stray pedestrians.

Emily banged her fist on the steering wheel, as if that would promote movement in the traffic, but the cars just idled. White lights flowed down the hill on the other side, but all she saw was a sinuous river of red, a vein of coagulated automotive blood. She motored down her window and hyperventilated ocean air in heaving gulps. The ocean, once calming, now rose up like water in an aquarium where she was held fast to the bottom with weights. As if she had momentarily blacked out, a space in front of her opened up and she let go the clutch too fast and her Mini stalled. A horn blared behind her. The frustrated asshole just stood on it with the palm of his hand, his fat head, Emily noticed in horror in her rearview mirror, tilted grotesquely to the side in puerile, mocking rebuke. She pressed the ignition button and held it in until her car roared back to life. She slammed the gear shift into first, and it shrieked metal as she didn't have the clutch depressed all the way. She lurched forward again and then had to slam the brakes because the serpentine line of cars had come to yet another dead stop. Her heart was racing uncontrollably now. She glanced out at the ocean, seeking an anodyne to her overwrought state. The changing twilit sea met her gaze in a kind of phantasmagoria of disturbing colors: violet, swirling reds, descending midnight blues heralding nightfall. The clouds were churning in the sky like an enormous celestial fire. Her mind started to spin out of control. Elizabeth West's fury and the tremors of anxiety that had gripped the department; the ardent emails and her inability to stop reading them; her fear that she was going insane. Her heart revved up its cadence. She clutched it with her right hand and could feel it throbbing behind her breastplate like two hands gripping the bars of a prison cell screaming to be set free. The now palpable reality of her rapidly palpitating heart made it beat faster, runaway anxiety, not the traffic jam, the jet fuel that pulsed it. She plunged her hand into her purse on the passenger seat and fumbled frantically for her cell. Soon she was panting through flared nostrils like an exhausted horse.

She found her cell and raised it to her face. She tapped the icon for Google Maps, thumbed in "ER" and tapped "Directions." The green route directed her to make a U-turn at the next light. But the cars were at a standstill, the light wasn't even in view! In that cell ellipsis, she had lost her place in the segment of the automotive serpent now preventing her from getting home and to the medications she knew would quell the panic attack she now truly believed was bringing on imminent cardiac arrest.

The horn of the monster behind her blared shrilly again, an aural assault. Emily twisted her torso and gave the irate harasser the middle finger. He retaliated, honking back loudly in juvenile spurts, ratcheting up Emily's now full-blown panic attack. She whipped her wheel to the left, let go the clutch, slammed her foot down on the accelerator, and jumped the median divider. Her wheels crashed into the curbing hard, the Mini lurched upward, slamming Emily's head against the roof. The angry motorist behind her glowered in disbelief, then shouted through his open window, "You fucking crazy bitch!"

Emily executed the most insanely illegal U-turn in her life. Didn't give a fuck she was knocking the front end out of alignment. Didn't give a fuck that it was a $500 citation first offense. She power-shifted into second and then third, tearing up the hill in the direction Google Maps pointed her. Fourth gear, and she was dangerously swerving her Mini through thick but fast-moving traffic, doing her best impersonation of her Formula One idol, Senna. Didn't care if she crashed. Didn't give a shit if she heard sirens, police dispatched to pull her over and arrest her. There would be wailing sirens aplenty if she let go of the wheel and let the panic attack take her to its inevitable collision. Her needle pegged at ninety miles per hour, vibrated there like a hovering hummingbird as she flew against traffic. Her heart was pounding out of her chest. When she glanced down, she could see it! Like an organ in a transplant surgeon's hand.

Past Torrey Pines Golf course, she hung a fishtailing left on Genesee Avenue, sped across the I-5 on a gray scar of asphalt and wheeled into Scripps Memorial Hospital La Jolla, a sprawling, two-story complex. Her rear wheels fishtailing, dodging startled pedestrians, nearly sideswiping slow-moving cars, she followed the red-painted Emergency signs with blurred, peering eyes. She braked to a halt in the drop-off area under harsh fluorescent lights and parked in the red, ignoring the signaling protestations of a security cop advancing on her across the parkway, a hand reaching instinctively for the weapon on his gun belt.

A stricken Emily leaped out of her car and staggered into the ER on stilt-stiff limbs, buckled to her knees in Reception, tears of anguish and full-blown panic flooding her eyes and screamed shrilly, “I’m having a heart attack! I’m having a heart attack!”

Reception was galvanized into action. Emily rose out of her tortured, corporeal, fetal-contorted being and watched it all with ghostly detachment. A gurney was wheeled in. A male and a female nurse helped her onto it with strong arms and grave countenances. Patients and next of kin in the waiting room were gawking, some with hands thrown to their mouths, half up and off their Plexiglass chairs to gain a better view of the drama unfolding with a stranger who had gone mad.

Emily was wheeled down a fast-moving corridor, babbling incoherently, her hand pressed to her heart. She tried her best to answer questions. “Drugs?” “No, God no.” “Allergies?” “Yeah, to douchebags honking their horns!” The female nurse bugged her eyes out at this. “You’re going to be okay; you’re going to be okay.” At which point Emily sprang up bent at the waist like a woman possessed by an evil spirit and screamed, “I’m dying! I’m dying!”

They wheeled her into the ER. Emily was involuntarily heaving her head back and forth like a sick animal in the throes of death. Tears streamed down her anguished face. Fear had locked hold of her. Her nerves were in a tightly wound coil now, and she was seized by its implacability. The ER doctor, a young man with short spiky hair and eyes the size of a bullfrog’s calmly looked down at Emily and barked at the nurse, “Let’s do an EKG, Valerie.”

As the nurse unbuttoned Emily’s blouse and attached monitoring devices to her chest, the doctor patted her forehead and asked the same routine questions the nurses had asked and Emily finally shouted, “I’m not a drug addict. I’m an archivist!” The nurse and doctor met each other’s eyes with puzzled, consternated looks that suggested to a barely cognizant Emily she was either crazy or in the throes of a tumultuous nervous breakdown, outcome uncertain, an institution on the other side of a narcotizing injection. Unnerving Emily even more was all the screaming and anguished cries from the other ER patients, some ambulanced in from horrific car accidents, others who *were* having heart attacks, one clutching his bleeding stomach from an apparent knifing. All the world’s human misery was sucked into this vortical maw where she now lay helpless to her untethered fears of mortality.

The nurse bent over Emily and stroked her forehead as the doctor studied a monitor with narrowed eyes. "You're going to be okay," the nurse incanted in a soothing voice.

The ER doctor shook his head and scowled, turned to the nurse and hissed under his breath. "She's not having a heart attack. She's having a bad panic attack. Give the fucking Jane Doe two milligrams of Valium and get her the hell out of my ER." He stalked off in apparent disgust.

Emily heard his harsh assessment through her panic-stricken caterwauling, and the mortification at crying wolf strangely started to settle her, especially now that she was reassured she wasn't dying. A few minutes later the nurse returned—when had she left?—and gently slapped the crook of her right arm, hoping to distend a vein. When her finger touched a throbbing candidate, she expertly wriggled in a needle. Emily remembered glimpsing the plunger depressing, and a few seconds later calming into a hypnagogic state. Her labored breathing stabilized. Her tears abated. Then the shame of it all struck her like a brackish wave and she tasted acrid water and felt like a fucking fool for all the commotion she had engendered at the expense of so many.

Emily's eyes were focused on the white-paneled ceiling in the brightly lit ER. The last time she had experienced a crucifying panic attack was when her mother had been felled by a stroke and she had felt all alone in the world, her foundations foundered, the world spinning out of control. But it was nothing like this one. Now, with her mother in an assisted living facility, she felt even more alone in the world. Her phone back in her hand, the nurse urging her to call someone to come retrieve her, she realized that she didn't have anyone she could call. She didn't know Joel's number. They had only texted and emailed through work. She should have given him her number when he asked her for it that first day they surfed and hung out, but her privacy paranoia had won out. If she hunted and pecked online, she could probably locate it, but she didn't have the energy or the wherewithal and she let her hand with the cell collapse to her side. Did she even want Joel to know? She brought a hand to her eyes because they now welled with tears at the realization of just how alone and terrified of the world she was.

Clambering to a sitting position on the edge of the gurney, she ran a hand through her matted hair. She had sweated profusely during the ordeal and her clothes were soaked through. She had journeyed heroically back from a mythological world of demons and ogres who, in the moment, appeared all too real and frightening.

Seeing her calmed and sitting up, the nurse returned through the hurly-burly of the ER and gently removed the monitoring devices taped to her chest while Emily, sedated to near-somnambulance, fumbled with the buttons on her blouse. "How'd you get here?" the nurse asked.

Emily lowered her gaze to her feet and said in a drugged voice, "I drove."

"I'd wait a while before driving," the nurse advised. "Do you see a therapist?"

Emily, lost in thought and foundered by humiliation, shook her head.

"It was a bad panic attack," the nurse said, massaging Emily's shoulder comfortingly. "And I've witnessed some humdingers." Emily smiled a weary laugh. "Besides, you're way too young to be having a heart attack."

Emily nodded in agreement. The nurse helped her off the gurney and ushered her back to Reception on tentative steps. In a passive state, she was required to sign some forms before they would release her.

Outside, Emily stood, a hand tenting her forehead from the blinding fluorescent lights, and scanned the parking lot for signs of her car. It certainly wasn't where she had illegally parked it and jumped out an hour ago, an hour that seemed like four. She felt enervated, debilitated, emotionally drained, and desperately needed familiarity with something, anything, even a car.

The security cop approached her with a stern expression. "Are you the lady with the blue Mini Cooper?"

"Yes," Emily said.

"We could have towed it, but you left the keys in it, so we parked it."

"Thank you," replied Emily in the Valium-induced voice of an automaton.

"Here, I'll take you to it." He handed her her car keys.

He headed off with a heavy, booted gait. Emily's legs moved, but she didn't know by what means of locomotion anymore, they were wobbly in the aftermath of the grand mal panic attack.

"Are you okay?" the middle-aged security guard asked as he slowed his pace, noticing Emily with a hand clutched over her mouth and terrified eyes. "You were pretty out there"—he chose his description carefully, Emily could tell—"when you pulled up."

"Yeah. It was a bad panic attack," Emily confided tonelessly. "I'm not a crazy person."

They reached her blue Mini. The security guard squatted down and noticed the bottom fender was dislodged. It looked like a giant, twisted arm, sprung from its mooring. He squatted and wrenched it back into place the best he could. "You might want to get that looked at," he suggested.

Emily nodded listlessly, the memory of jumping the median to get to the safety of the ER now rushing back at her in embarrassing waves. "Thank you." He opened the door and, with a hand grasping her elbow, steered her inside, shoehorning her in behind the wheel. He closed the door gently and let her go back to the civilized world, a worried look on his face, as if freeing a wounded bird not ready for release into the wild.

Coast Highway back to Del Mar was an unbroken ribbon of black, nearly devoid of cars. The sloping road featured loneliness and an overwhelming feeling of mortification. The commuters were back in their homes in the sprawl of bedroom communities that dotted all of North County San Diego. Still under the tranquilizing effects of the Valium, Emily shifted her Mini in slow-motion. When she hit a pothole, she heard scraping and made a mental note to get the front fender looked at.

Fumbling with her key in the lock, she could hear Onyx meowing in distressed tones, as if he had been supernaturally witness to Emily's frantic U-turn, the out-of-control dash to the hospital, and the frightening episode in the ER and knew something was wrong with the woman whom he counted on for food and water.

"I know, I know," Emily comforted Onyx, stroking his head. "Just a little panic attack. It's okay now. I hope." Onyx trailed her into the kitchen, clinging to her ankles. She opened a can of cat food with listless fingers and Onyx's meows rose impatiently at the piquant fish odors that permeated the air. He bent his head into the bowl before Emily could even finish forking it all out. She filled his water bowl, then walked slowly, haltingly, into the bedroom and collapsed on the bed, immobilized by the velocity with which the panic attack had conflagrated through her—a frightening first. Her last bad panic attack had only incited rebuke from an insensitive Louis, who accused her of overwork, too much sugar in her diet, and a host of other lame etiologies. Not only was he *not* a comfort, he was an impediment to conquering her panic anxiety. He blamed her. As if she had control over these sudden and wild episodes where she transmuted into something strangely spectral and otherworldly. The trigger could be anything, but usually it was claustrophobia. The claustrophobia, however, was always perched on the dormant volcano of something deeper, something more perniciously malignant.

Nadia and Raymond. The sweeping ethics of it all. The pressure of the Eighth Floor Gala. Elizabeth's scowling rebuke of her picking that newspaper photo that showed Nadia clinging to Raymond. It was a confluence of stressors she couldn't have anticipated conspiring to intersect at a headwaters in her overworked brain and caused the imaginings that spiraled out of control and made her think she was suffering a heart attack. She could resign, but what reason would she give? This was the crucial moment, a rite of passage in her young professional life, the treacherous Strait of Magellan navigated in a ship captained by one. Turn back now and forever rue your cowardice? Forge ahead and face the consequences? Turn back and never know? Plow forward and discover what you might never want to know? Would she stand up to this moment of truth and mature into the woman from the girl, or would she forever be self-branded a simpering fool? Crossing the archivist's Rubicon, a declaration that the truth, as Raymond had emphasized in email after email, was the final residue of all beings. What she preserved imparted a rush of emotion that connected her with the enduring and the profound.

Emily fell asleep with all these crisscrossing thoughts converging in her exhausted mind.

PART II

THE FIRES INSIDE

CHAPTER 13

The Cruciform of Desire

9/7/18

More broken sleep. First bad panic attack since the one in San Francisco. Drove myself to the ER. Don't know how I made it. Fear of death like I've never known. Thought I was having a heart attack. Okay now.

No one to call. No one to text. Even if I could have texted Joel, I was afraid of what he would think. All alone in the world.

The deeper I go into the correspondence the more I want to know. The more I know the more isolated I become. It's the isolation that triggers the panic attacks. So terrifying to be in that state. I want so badly for someone to envelop me in his arms.

If I let it go, if I do my job, if I keep my nose out of what I have found, beginning with that letter in the string-tie envelope, I can walk away from this job, this library, this city, with my name and reputation intact.

I don't know if I have the will to go on.

Summoning all her strength, Emily drove to CVS to get the Xanax prescription filled that the doctor had scribbled in quiet contempt at the ER. While she stood in line, she checked her messages. There were the usual business emails from the university now that she was in the system. Announcements, other junk she could clear out of her inbox. Then, disturbingly, she noticed one from Professor Erickson. The subject heading was "Are You Okay?!" She closed it out, not wanting to read it until she had pulverized half a milligram of Xanax, let it dissolve sublingually, and waited for it to calm her. Her attempt to reach out to him for advice didn't yield the empathy she was searching for, instead only fomented suspicion. Emily was also acutely aware of how small the archives community was. Erickson had already admitted he knew Helena Blackwell—possibly even on a personal basis. In fact, that's probably how she got the job. He knew about the West Papers, and the $25 million gift, because it had gone out in a press release—with her name, Emily Snow, in the news articles, credited as the project archivist. Nadia Fontaine was never mentioned. She had seemingly been expunged from the official Memorial Library Special Collections & Archives register of staff and faculty, just like her *Knife in the Heart* had been removed from the library's shelves. The past had been erased, whitewashed. Except the past was now bubbling back to the surface, its star-crossed lovers as alive to Emily as any characters in a novel.

Emily left the brightly lit CVS with its grim, shambling cast of dramatis personae, vial of pills securely in her purse, and drove the stretch of Coast Highway that connected her to Regents. Wet-suited surfers pimpled the blue Pacific that refracted the sun like a million mirrors shifting and rocking on its trembling waters. A squadron of eleven pelicans—Emily counted—glided low across the faces of the cresting waves, their wings extended and barely moving, their beaks and deep gullets bent downward for the feast of minnows that awaited them in the translucent waters.

At the bottom of the hill, she lowered her window, slowed, and scrutinized the divider she had jumped the night before in the straitjacket of her panicked condition. She didn't notice any damage, or otherwise identifying marks, thank God! The protective shrouding of her car's undercarriage, dislodged in the manic U-turn over the median, scraped when she went over a pothole, and there appeared to be a shuddering in the wheel when she climbed past fifty miles per hour, leading her to speculate she had knocked the alignment out. A visit to the car dealer would take care of that, and she probably needed an oil change anyway. She inhaled/exhaled a sigh of relief thinking that if a cop had spotted her, she would have had a nervous breakdown on a main artery from the university to the bedroom communities north, and God knows who might have seen her, taken a picture, posted it on social media . . . Emily took slow, deep breaths to calm the infestation of paranoiac thoughts that were mounting once again.

On legs propelled by anxiety, Emily detoured into the bathroom before heading into the bowels of Special Collections and the coworkers she was dreading bumping into. She felt different now after the panic attack and the visit to the ER, as if she couldn't hide its ignominy, as if she wore it and others could see it on her like a garment of shame. One of the announcements in her inbox had been regarding a sexual assault committed near the Gliderport. A week ago the university reported a suicide: a young man had leaped from a bridge into four lanes of oncoming freeway traffic. Any occurrence of an emergency nature within a two- or three-mile radius of the campus was broadcast to faculty and staff to place them on alert. For a second, Emily catastrophized her self-admission to the ER would be recorded and duly sent out in a mass email: "Project Archivist Emily Snow was admitted to Scripps Memorial Hospital ER suffering apparent cardiac arrest. Doctors examined her and determined it was an anxiety attack brought on by . . ." Emily shook her head. If she weren't so sleep-deprived, she might have gotten a sardonic chuckle out of it, except that, in her still-fragile post-panic-attack state of mind, she worried it could be real.

Emily studied herself in the mirror. She stretched back the skin from the corners of her eyes. Were there premature wrinkles? Was her upper lip trembling or was she imagining that, too? She attempted to stop it with a stiff index finger pressing her lip to her teeth. She thought about Nadia and all the times *she* had fled into this same bathroom, sometimes to change into something sexy, times she had no doubt covered her face with her hands and wept at the misery of her life. From the explicit images in Joel's movie, Emily had glimpsed a much different woman than herself. Nadia was five foot ten at least, maybe five eleven, compared to Emily's slight five five. Her hair was a waterfall of cascading black; Emily's was short, chestnut in color. Emily glanced down at her small breasts. She wasn't flat-chested, but she didn't spill out of her bra like the buxom Nadia. She imagined Nadia strolling through the library carving a swath through the air, sleek as a yacht bent at an angle in white-capped blue waters. By contrast, Emily knifed through the air, more unnoticed, not everted to the world like the more striking, full-figured Nadia. Nadia was the kind of woman who mesmerized men the way a giant magnet agitates iron particles and draws them into its vortex, cratering their inhibitions. And Raymond was the magnet to her magnet, two forces of enriched uranium drawing together to create a veritable critical mass.

The door to the bathroom burst open, startling Emily. Jean slipped in, wearing all black, as if in mourning or attired for a micromanaging assault on staff with updated Excel spreadsheets and deadlines. Her stork-like figure pulled up next to Emily at the dual sink. One could detect no joy, no emotion, in her perpetually baleful countenance.

Emily, in a hurried effort to paint the ghostly pallor out of her face with some foundation and a swipe of lipstick, jammed her makeup accessories back into her little pouch and pushed it into her purse.

"Hi, Emily."

"Hi, Jean."

"Everything all right?" Jean asked.

"I had a doctor's appointment," Emily said. "My annual."

"I didn't see it on the board," Jean said.

"Sorry. I didn't notice until it was on my To Do calendar when I woke up." Emily made to leave. "Back to West," she said in specious cheer as she went out the bathroom door.

Emily strode across the main floor into Special Collections, not wanting to give Jean an opportunity to catch up with her. She glanced in at Helena's office across from the reference desk where Samantha was buried in her phone, thumbing texts on social media. She looked up and said hi.

"Did Helena come in?" Emily asked.

"Not yet," Samantha, torpidly chained to her post, replied.

"Thanks." Emily was relieved that Helena had not made it to work yet.

In her cubicle, Emily fished her hand into her purse, groped around a little until she found the vial of Xanax. It comforted her knowing it was there. She didn't like resorting to medication, unless she felt an attack coming on, and she didn't want to get dependent on them, but the safety valve was reassuring when the stress plunged her back in the pressure cooker again.

She switched on her computer. As she waited for it to boot up, she swung in her desk chair and examined the boxes on the table. Nicola had moved the previously processed ones into the closed stacks where the West Collection rested. Emily flicked a pen against her lips. She couldn't free her mind of *The Archivist*. How far along had they gotten in the writing of it? Had it been abandoned? Where were the Moleskines they wrote the first draft in, now that Emily knew Nadia and Raymond were trading the iconic notebooks as Raymond wrote in a feverish pace?

A notification popped up on her screen, and she tore herself away from the thoughts nobody wanted her to be obsessing over.

Joel texted, "How goes it?"

Emily typed back, "Fine." She started to type in a question but froze her fingers as they were poised over the keyboard.

Joel: "Up for a paddle?" Tacked at the end was an emoji of a surfer on a blue-and-white wave.

Emily: "Maybe a late lunch at the Gliderport?"

Joel: "Cool."

Emily blushed to herself. Joel genuinely was becoming a friend. The link to Nadia and her death—and the affair—was palpable, though she had only been on the job for a month and circumspection and occupational distrust still walled her off.

Remembering something parked in her mind since picking up her prescription at CVS, Emily opened a window on her computer that listed a directory of university services. She scrolled down and stopped when she saw University Staff Counseling Services, followed by a phone number with an extension. Emily reached for the handset on her office landline, crabbed quietly to the side of her desk farthest from Jean's adjoining cubicle, then cupped a hand to the mouthpiece like a baseball pitcher speaking to his catcher, when she heard it ringing on the other end.

A cheerful woman's voice answered, "Regents University Staff Counseling Services. Jennifer speaking. How can I help you?"

"I'd like to make an appointment," Emily spoke in lowered tones, not identifying herself, hoping to remain anonymous.

"Are you staff here at the university?"

"Yes, I am."

"What's the nature of your request?"

I'm a project archivist, and I've just discovered a treasure trove of salacious emails between my dead predecessor and a famous novelist who is also about to be named chair of the Lit Department and maybe win the Nobel Prize for Literature and whose wife is a fucking multimillionaire who is transforming the library into a luxury event center and endowing positions left and right, and I just had a massive panic attack, lady!!!

"It's, um, work-related," Emily whispered.

"Okay. What's your name?"

"Emily Snow," she said, as if it were one word.

"Could you speak up please and enunciate, I couldn't make out your name."

Emily went blank. She regretted her rash impulse to seek professional help. She didn't like talking about herself. And now she could see it all spilling out of her in a confessional torrent and the mortification that would follow as she dredged up all the personal details of her life.

"Hello?" the receptionist spoke louder into the silence.

"Em . . . you know what? Never mind."

Emily replaced the handset into its holder and drew both hands to her face. Employing her feet as flippers, Emily walked her chair back to her computer. She clicked around until she found a map of the enormous, sprawling campus, cross-checked a directory, noticed with some relief that the University Staff Counseling Services' offices were across Torrey Pines Road. If she decided to seek free counseling, at least it would be less likely that she'd be spotted.

Emily occupied herself with the piles of manuscripts she had neatly organized and made ready for perusal. Some were typescripts riddled with marginalia, and she was tempted to stop and read them, but she had a job to do. She moved back and forth between them and the finding aid for the West Collection, building a day's work. Now and then she couldn't help but stop and examine a manuscript page of a now famous work with childlike enchantment. Raymond's marginalia on some of the printouts were fascinating. In poring over the finding aid, it appeared the reason Verlander had singled out the Moleskines for *Lessons in Reality* was because it was the last book Raymond had written his first draft in longhand. Until—Emily thought, leaning back in her chair—*The Archivist.* The weight of the affair and the book fell on her suddenly like a toppling eucalyptus. She tried not to let herself be pulled down into the rabbit hole of that potentially labyrinthian search—document boxes, finding aid . . . dark archives.

At 2:30 Emily drove over to the Gliderport to meet Joel for lunch. She found him at one of the picnic benches holding a pair of sandwiches nested in reusable plastic baskets, the blustery wind threatening to launch them into the air. A red-and-white wind sock snapped horizontally on a tall pole like a gyrating cloth snake.

"Hey," he greeted her. He was wearing a gray T-shirt with the black silhouette of John Cleese's "The Ministry of Silly Walks" stamped on its chest.

"Hi." Emily slid in next to him so that they were both afforded views of the colorful paragliders leaping into the void. "Cool T-shirt," she said, pointing.

"Yeah, the Pythons were awesome."

"They were," Emily agreed. "Do you ever watch old *Pete and Dud* shows on YouTube?"

"Yeah. Love 'em," Joel said. He pointed at her sandwich basket. "I ordered you the turkey like you asked. No sprouts." Emily chuckled. "Didn't know what you liked to drink, so I got you a sparkling water. Is that okay? I can get you something else."

"That's fine. Thank you." Emily unscrewed the cap on the mineral water, and it hissed. She took a sip. When she looked at Joel, she discovered to her surprise a twelve-ounce bag of Bird Rock Coffee Roasters coffee beans standing on the planked bench between them. "Joel!"

"I live practically right next door. I'm happy to do it."

Emily reached for her purse. "How much do I owe you?"

Joel shook his head. "Get me back next time we go to Oscar's."

Emily clutched the bag of beans in front of her face. "Panamanian Geisha. Natural process." She faced him and experienced a pleasant sensation that she had cultivated one true friend from the barrens of San Diego and the fraught political hierarchy of Memorial Library's Special Collections & Archives. "I've never had a coffee from Panama."

"They told me it was awesome."

"Thank you." Emily set the bag down, took a bite out of her sandwich, then looked up. The wildfires had finally abated, and the sky had been restored to a milky blue. A paraglider launched himself off the cliff. He shifted his harness basket to horizontal, caught an updraft and soared north, held aloft by favonian winds. Emily extended an arm in his direction. "Could you ever do something like that?"

Joel turned to her with a mock look of bewilderment. "Emily. I used to be an instructor."

"What?"

"Yeah."

"Really?" Emily asked.

"Yeah. Really. Banged up my knee in a crash and gave it up. Expensive sport."

"'I was lunching here the other day and a guy offered to take me on a free tandem ride. No way, I said."

"A free tandem ride?" Joel repeated her words sarcastically.

"Yeah. That's what he said."

"It wasn't free."

"No? He was going to sell me a package of lessons?"

"No! He was going to ask you out on a date. While you were soaring over the cliffs, when you couldn't possibly say you'd take a rain check." Emily shook her head in mild disbelief. "Are you kidding? You're totally hot. And before you get the wrong idea and go to HR, I get it—you're a rolling stone, you don't like entanglements. Coworkers are a no-no. That's cool." Joel gestured out to the four or five paragliders now painting the blue with their colorfully patterned chutes. "But if you ever want to go up, no strings attached, let me know. I still got all my tandem gear."

"Really? You'd take me up tandem?"

"Absolutely. When you're up there, you're not thinking about anything else. And the view is heart-stopping. Once you're aloft, you won't be afraid anymore. You won't be afraid of anything. You'll feel free as a pelican."

Emily bit her upper lip. She conjured an image of Joel behind her, his strong surfer arms enveloping her, propelling her to the edge, the chute ballooned with wind and bouncing them up and down in preparation for launch, her no doubt screaming with eyes squeezed shut, then the ground beneath them giving way to an abyss of air a thousand feet above the blue of the Pacific.

"Okay," Emily said. "Maybe when this project's done, we'll celebrate."

Brought down to reality, Joel nodded thoughtfully. A silence fell between them and the wind off the ocean filled the gap with white noise. Direction pennants flapped against their pole mounts like cloth whips. Circling seagulls cawed a warning to the next paraglider in the queue stutter-stepping haltingly to the edge of the cliff as if he might be the one-tenth of one percent who didn't catch the updraft and spiraled to his death.

"So, you want me to get you into the Annex?" Joel asked the wind, staring darkly forward, the confabulation over, the true reason for the lunch date.

"Yeah. If you don't mind." Emily was relieved that he had brought up the subject and that she didn't have to press.

"What are you looking for, if I might ask?"

"Evidence of a deep and troubling love," Emily said.

"Oh, good Lord."

Emily stared at Joel. The side of his face was whiskered from not having shaven. Tawny like the hair on his forearms, they glinted like mica in the sun. Her eyes stayed on him, but he wouldn't turn to meet hers.

"Let me think about it," he said with a resigned exhalation.

"I want to get in there," demanded Emily. "And you know I can't go through the normal channels."

"All right," said Joel in an exasperated tone.

Remembering the panic attack and the visit to the ER, Emily held up her phone. "I still don't have your number." Emily looked at him meaningfully. "In case I need to text you when you're not at work."

Joel dived a hand into his back pocket and fished out his phone. "What's your number?"

Emily recited her number as Joel inputted it into his phone. He tapped Send and waved his phone at her. "There you go."

"Thanks," Emily said and then smiled. "Didn't realize you were an emoji guy."

Joel smiled a laugh, set his phone down, and bit into his sandwich.

Emily wasn't fond about handing her number out to anyone, but after the ER visit she decided it was a good idea to have a local contact she could trust. She gazed across to the immense dirt parking lot where Nadia often met Raymond. It would hurt Joel to know what she, Emily, knew, and she was sensitive to that no longer impalpable quiet Joel slipped into every time the West Collection and the affair reared its head.

Half an hour later and more mindless talk of surfboards and trading enthusiasm for old British sketch comedy, Joel crawled out from under Emily's Mini. He clambered to a standing position and clapped dirt off his hands.

"What'd you do?" he asked in mock alarm.

"I accidentally drove over one of those cement limiter thingies up at Jimbo's," Emily lied.

"Well, it's all cool for now. Next time you take it in, get 'em to bolt it down better."

"Okay, thanks, Joel." She came toward him and reached her arms around his wide waterman's torso and laid her head on his chest for a brief second. Her fingers didn't even meet at his spine, he was that muscularly thickset. She stepped back.

"Coming back to work?" he asked.

"Where else?" She held up her bag of prized Bird Rock coffee. "Thanks for the Panamanian."

When he was gone, she started up her car. The first bump on the washboard dirt road she came to didn't produce a scraping sound. Men *were* good for something, she chuckled to herself.

She drove past the University Staff Counseling Services building. It was a four-story cement structure with narrow windows. Emily had seen a therapist before for her misophonia, but it didn't cure it and the tête-à-têtes always strayed into uncomfortable emotional regions she didn't like venturing into. But a pressure was building inside her. Half of her wanted to park, get out, march in, unload everything she was holding all alone in her being, but the other half of her was conflicted. She worried confessing archival transgressions to a stranger—even a professional—risked revealing, to herself, that her obsession with the affair bordered on foolishness. She drove on, comforted that she had Joel.

The rest of the afternoon was swallowed up by work. She buried herself in the finding aid and tried to block out the private lives of her predecessor and this literary luminary. But it was hard. It was the occupational hazard of an archivist. To Emily, it was never an issue of data and records, processing and arranging; these were human lives, and they burrowed into you like corn weevils. She had always been able to distance herself from a collection, but this one was obviously, and strikingly, different.

After work, the drive back home to Del Mar was easier, the traffic lighter than the day before when it had bottlenecked and ignited her uncontrollable panic attack. She had weathered it. She knew she wasn't having a heart attack. There is power in self-knowledge, she consoled herself.

Back at her apartment, Emily, per the routine they had established, fed a hungry Onyx, who was contentedly back on schedule now, his meows perceptibly less anxious. She finished off a half-eaten Urban Plates takeout because she was too tired to climb back in her car and perform the monotonous San Diego freeway dance in order to get something to eat. One day, she mused, I'll have a place where I've put down roots, a full refrigerator, and the time to cook.

Emily tried to sort out her life as she walked down the stairs out of her complex in the direction of the pounding surf, drawn by its peaceful cadence. The thought of carrying through seeing a therapist ping-ponged around in her head again. Could she trust them? Would she say too much? It wouldn't be a private shrink; it would be a university employee. They'd know about the Raymond West Collection and the huge gift by his wife. No, it was simply too big a risk to take.

Emily came to a stop at the end of Sixth Street. The sun had set a half an hour ago, but there were still pastel vestiges of its fading light. The scent of marijuana wafted from a young couple sharing a joint and spluttering with moronic laughter on the splintered, planked observation bench Emily felt to be her own possession. After a while, they got up to leave and drifted off like apparitions down the crest of the bluff's dirt pathway.

Emily took their place, the bench still warm from their presence. A twinge of remorse that she didn't currently have someone in her life came and fled like the sweeping headlights of a swerving car. Look at Nadia and Raymond, she thought. What drove them into this dangerous love affair was the despair and emptiness of their longstanding relationships, the uncertainty of it all versus the limitations a relationship imposed. If she had a man in her life, would she have been able to keep quiet about this opening of the Pandora's Box? Would he have supported her in this ostensibly unethical decision, despite the complicated qualifications to the contrary? Or dragged her into ambivalence and doubt and reined her in like a horse rearing back and pawing the ground, aching to be uncorralled? Emily started to realize that Nadia and Raymond had forged a special union that hoisted them both out of the morass of their lives. He thought he was dried up, a literary accessory on a wealthy woman's arm. And for Nadia, the brilliant woman who inspired him, to be the one whom he had chosen to collaborate with on his first book in five years—and his only ever collaboration—what a privilege! Emily watched the last of the fading light with rejoicing eyes. Together, Nadia and Raymond had conspired, against the parlous obstacles, to elevate each other, to raise each other, to new heights—indeed, the very obstacles to the consummation of their love had become their intimately fecund ground. He saw in Nadia not the affair but the mind of an artist in her own right who drove the nail of an idea—one that quickly possessed him and seized him with a sudden jolt of creativity—straight into his own tortured heart.

Tears welled in Emily's eyes, and she was flashing them back now with rapidly blinking lashes. She stood abruptly from the bench, her hand now clasped over her mouth, her bulging, newly panicked eyes beseeching the sea, which featured only a moonless blackness. She closed her eyes. The ocean spoke to her in a rhythmic murmur, but it provided no answers. What happened to end all this literary and romantic exultance?

Repudiated by the ocean, where Nadia had met her fate, Emily retraced her steps and walked the quarter mile through the quiet seaside neighborhood back to her apartment. The acrid stink of ash was gone from the air. The blazes had finally been contained and all that was left were charred hillsides. The damage was massive, the rebuilding would take years. But for Emily, while the fires may have been extinguished outside, they had flared up anew inside and were raging out of control across another kind of landscape. A raccoon darted across the street, stopped, frozen in place, and gazed at Emily with gleaming yellow eyes. She couldn't help but be reminded of Helena's new hairdo. She shook the image free from her mind and hastened on.

Ensconced in her apartment, she uncapped an ale and took it and her laptop into the back bedroom where another world was about to engulf her. She flipped open the lid on her laptop and the screen brightened to an image of a beach in Costa Rica. Onyx leaped up onto the bed and padded over to her, licking his whiskers. He curled up next to her warm thigh like he always did. Emily distractedly reached out a hand and stroked his fur. "If only you were Carl Jung," she whispered to him, "I could go on this journey and not risk my sanity." Onyx yawned in reply.

Emily moved her cursor over the folder "Dark Archives" and let it hover there. "Fuck this," she spoke out loud. "I'm going to find out what happened." And she double-tapped her touchpad to continue the journey where she had left off.

CHAPTER 14

Love Goes Where It Will . . .

From: Nadia Fontaine <Nfontaine@RegentsU.edu>
To: Raymond West <Rwest_Lit@RegentsU.edu>
Subject: Vol. 5: Our love . . .
Date: 15 October 2017

My Raymond,

The truth of our love is inviolable. Nothing can desecrate it. It runs underground like an uncharted river, alive and pulsing, like a new vein throbbing with the earth's blood. Seeing you is pure transcendence, and it exults me to hear you say the same, to read into your words the exact feelings I'm feeling.

I was all alone and miserable when I met you. God is a monster sometimes! His cruelty can be unforgiving. I live for passion. I live for epiphany. Our love has hoisted me to a realm where I've never been before. I don't know the rules up here. Are there any, in this celestial madness we now inhabit?

I think secretly that all archivists want to fall in love with the one whose papers they care so lovingly for. But of course, not just any creator, scientist, whomever. It's a lunatic love because it's almost always unrequited: they're no longer living; they're physically revolting; many reasons. And yet, we can still fall in love. Even if it's only with the work. But then a collection like yours comes in.

Archivists live in quiet worlds, cold worlds. They come and go apparitionally, anonymously. Few others know what they even do. But archivists have feelings, of course. I would venture to say their feelings are more intense, precisely because they're built up in the pressure cookers of the collections. I read your words, I see pictures of you, I know you're alive, and that makes me come alive! . . . Can any archival ethicist explain this? Am I supposed to not fall in love? Am I supposed to repudiate any hope that this love will one day have its apotheosis?

And will that apotheosis only be *The Archivist*? You are five beautiful volumes of Moleskines in now, and to see our words in this cataract of emails melding as one is to see my perspiry body coiled around you like a snake, squeezing every last . . . word out of you. You're writing again, Raymond! And when you told me that you told your editor at Scribner's about the book, can you imagine my thrill? My love. Tears of elation are blurring my eyes even now. I can't read what I'm typing. I'm laughing through my tears, I'm so impossibly happy for the first time in my life.

And then there are the obstacles. The book that you say will be your "death knell" if you let it go to publication. That we will only be remembered for this "infamy" wounds me to my core. It's art. It's an alchemization of what we have. It's always what you said you thought the truth in literature was: the annealing of the intimate and the personal in the cauldron of love and forging an immutable work of art.

I need to see you. I need to be with your naked body, hot in my arms, for hours. I can't bear the abbreviated meetings, euphoric as they are. I think about having to leave before I even arrive. I'm just getting the smell of you and then I'm orphaned . . . to a dirt parking lot . . . a hotel bed and a lazily circling fan and your footsteps retreating . . . and the despair comes flooding in all over again.

I have Volume 5 of our *The Archivist* transcribed. I type through my tears, obsessed with when I'm going to hear from you next, obsessed with when I'm going to be in your arms next time for an hour—two?—one day?—forever?

Nadia

From: Raymond West <Rwest_Lit@RegentsU.edu>
To: Nadia Fontaine <Nfontaine@RegentsU.edu>
Subject: Isla Negra
Date: 15 October 2017

My Eavesdropping Angel,

There is no artifice in your words. They are stripped bare, and the soul, translucent and naked, trembles. What writer wouldn't be enamored of meeting in the flesh his distaff mirror and epiphanically reaching the terrifyingly beautiful recognition that without her he is nothing? Yes, terrifying *and* beautiful, because without both, neither would exist.

I write everything at my little cottage in Del Mar, nicknamed Isla Negra after Neruda's seafront home in Chile. No one comes here. My wife is even forbidden. It's an inviolably private and haunted place. Haunted by the ghosts of my past works. Sometimes I close my eyes there and listen to the ocean pleading for me to write.

I want you to come there. Our book is everything now. I'm envisioning 12 volumes—a magical number, symbolizing supreme wholeness—and then it will be done. And then our love will be known to the world. If this work has to court "infamy," then so be it. I fear more for you than for myself. If you're not afraid, neither am I.

Will you meet me at Isla Negra and lead me into the dark hold of your voluptuous wiles? The deeper we descend to the seafloor the more *The Archivist*—this golden child of ours—will resurface and achieve its just resurrection. You have taught me that there is another membrane to pierce. And no doubt, one after that. The doors keep opening to new doors in an infinite succession, and I'm writing now in a veritable trance. How could you think for a minute that I could ever stop loving you?

Your Raymond forever and anon

From: Nadia Fontaine <Nfontaine@RegentsU.edu>
To: Raymond West <Rwest_Lit@RegentsU.edu>
Subject: Re: Isla Negra
Date: 15 October 2017

My Raymond,

My heart flutters wildly with joy at your words. I read and reread them, and I consume every one of them as if they were rationed morsels on a long ocean crossing to what island we might elect to maroon ourselves on, exiled outcasts that we surely will become when *The Archivist* sees the light of publication—O, joy of infamy!

Of course I will meet you at your Isla Negra. I know all about your hideaway, except where it is, the whereabouts you've guarded so zealously. I've read about it in your journals. In interviews I've heard you lyricize about it as your sanctuary in the storms, the place where you would retreat—the loves you have weathered there!—the loneliness, the creative battles, your dark night of the soul with the bottle when your editor Nick Peterson at Scribner's wasn't "feeling it" with *A Time of Uncertainty.* I know it all, my love. You're a diarist par excellence and I, your apparitional snow leopard, have devoured every word.

You supply the red wine; and I will bring darkness . . . I want desperately to go beyond the limits of my life.

Your Nadia

From: Raymond West <Rwest_Lit@RegentsU.edu>
To: Nadia Fontaine <Nfontaine@RegentsU.edu>
Subject: Re: Re: Isla Negra
Date: 15 October 2017

Nadia, my dark love,

How could I not love someone who knows everything about me? How could I ever forsake you? I would hurt worse than you if you left me. Especially if you left me for another man. You have filled me up with a hope that this second half, my life on the declivity, won't be a pathetic ceremonial succession of personal appearances, an embalming of my creative soul. You have breathed life into me, and I wake now each day with this book aflame in my head as if my imagination were the pounding heart of a runaway horse.

Isla Negra. 115 Little Orphan Alley (corny, I know). Bet. 7th and 8th. Where the road dead-ends at the train tracks and the ocean beyond. Fri. 8:00. When darkness falls. Don't come down the alley and park in the driveway. Too dangerous. She's gone to New York for some fundraiser or whatnot, but fame has caused the unfortunate crumbling of Isla Negra's once-exclusive privacy.

Your Raymond

PS: Bring the latest photocopies!

PPS: It would be better if you came straight up from the ocean and walked right onto my back porch. In a white dress like the angel you are. Now that would be a sight to behold.

NADIA'S STORY (CONT'D)

After work on Friday, I took a long swim in Regents Natatorium. I loved the way the turquoise light of the pool shimmered and shifted and how the sky faded to deepening shades of lavender whenever I looked up. I swam half a mile, all alone in the Olympic-size pool, wanting to exhaust all the restlessness out of my body. In the quiet of the locker room, in a collapsible tote, I withdrew a pair of outfits that I hadn't decided between.

Earlier in the day I lied to my husband and said I was attending a play with a coworker. He wished me a good time and said he would be "out with the boys." I didn't like to lie, but I knew it was going to be like this until Raymond and I could finish *The Archivist*. Paradoxically, all I wrote about in my short stories and in my articles on ethics in the archival world for various trade journals was the preservation of the truth and the consequences of lying. Did I rationalize that to get to the emotional truth I had to abase myself through the gauntlet of a lie? Was there any rationalization that couldn't be invoked if you were swept up in the most transformative love of your life?

I drove down Coast Highway in the direction of Isla Negra, haloed happily in a nimbus of self-absolution. The sky was painted by Van Gogh if he had chosen San Diego over Arles, and the sky could move in his painting like a forever cinema. A purplish-yellow light from the setting sun leaked at the horizon as if pinched there by the thumb and forefinger of a miserly god, reminding me that day was beginning for other creatures on the other side of the planet. But for me, night not day was calling me to an awakening, an awakening of my senses, a dream of a kind of illuminated and transcendent union gathered out of the sky by giant hands in both flesh and spirit. I wrote all the time in my head when I was alone like this, remorsefully aware of what was slipping through my fingers in the cruel, inexorable advance of time. I sensed this must be how it feels to be a true, uncompromising, artist. The words flood in from an invisible place in a veritable cataract and all one can do is hope to be ready, craft at hand, to etch them into eternity. Raymond and I were doing that, I truly believed, as I glanced nervously over at the empty passenger seat where lay the latest printouts of his Moleskine explosions.

I coasted down into the sleepy neighborhoods of Del Mar that fronted the cliff. An older couple walked by in the dark on the sidewalk, holding hands. I imagined he was a retired professor and she had been his mistress and they had made it through the baptismal fire of ostracism and academe's unforgiving recriminations of frowned-upon fraternizations and found peace on the other side, beyond the cinders of the ruin their love had engendered for all involved, all those whom they had hurt.

As instructed, I parked my car on Stratford Court. Little Orphan Alley was a mere block of houses that ended in a cul-de-sac at the bluff. My heart was beating exultantly knowing that I would have, at last, an entire evening alone with Raymond. A rogue Santa Ana gust rustled a palm above me and shook its marimba of moon-silhouetted fronds. The warm wind heightened my senses, enlivened my stride. The walk to Raymond's seemed scripted from unconscious memory.

The sound of the pounding surf poured up through the echo chamber of the alley and grew more thunderous as I neared the dead end. I could feel the waves detonating in my heart, as if it were the sea and the waves were the blood that coursed through it! A crooked grin rent my face in two as I strolled down the alley toward Raymond's literary Shangri-la, accompanied by the roaring of the ocean, drawn by his passion for me; he, touched by my burrowing into his soul in a way no one had before. To me, the dimly lit alley was a parade route for one, and I was the one being coronated in secrecy.

When I reached the end of the block, I stopped to drink in Raymond's famously secretive Isla Negra. It was a simple, wood-framed California-style bungalow, faded, weathered blue-gray, untouched by renovation, edged by a waist-high picket fence, deteriorating naturally, pristine in its ramshackle abandon, its contempt of modernity. The tin eaves were rusting, the landscaping was a riot of untrimmed hedges and weed-fissured walkways, and fan palms clustered together ruled over the house like some arboreal open jaw, guarding its entrance. Warm orange light leaked through the blinds in the windows, reminding passersby, if they had any suspicion of who lived there, that the midnight oil was burning in a cocoon of creativity. Compared to the other homes in the wealthy neighborhood, it looked lived in, even a little dilapidated, standoffish, a repudiation of anything that didn't have to do with the writer's imagination. It warned visitors, *Stay away! You're not welcome! Herein resides a man who lives only for what he's capable of imagining. Who doesn't give a shit about appearances. Who doesn't have to.*

The front door was hidden away down a narrow driveway where I noticed Raymond's black Range Rover parked. I felt nervous. I was glad I had exerted myself in that swim, exhausted my body and quieted it of all anxiety. Suddenly I heard a noise. It was the clanging bell of an approaching train. Lights swept the train tracks directly below the bluff. The clanging grew louder. The bluff palpably rumbled. As the Amtrak hurtled past, it obliterated in an incandescent flash everything in my mind. The ensuing silence that fell seemed to leave nothing in its wake but a new beginning, as if the train had wiped the slate clean, and here at Isla Negra, with Raymond, it was all tabula rasa, the way it was meant to be. I slipped into the dark of the narrow driveway . . . and back into the perdition of our love affair.

With my heart in my throat, I knocked lightly on the door. Raymond met me with a wordless smile of recognition—not of who I was, but of what we now had forged in the subterranean hold of our shared secret. It was a smile of our dark union, our sacred pact, his moldering writer's den where the Moleskines filled with the fervency of his prose, poured from a cauldron heated by the words I was showering him with in an unstoppable flood of emails, galvanized by this work I was sure was going to transform my life forever.

He raised a hand and brought it admiringly to my hair, his pianist's fingers splayed, his eyes on mine. He raked his fingers until they disappeared into my sable darkness, and my eyes closed because I wanted to dream myself into this other world. When his fingers found the back of my scalp, he pulled me toward him, but it took no effort at all because I came willingly unmoored in his grip. Our ravenous mouths met in hunger and need, loneliness and suffering, death and rebirth. We wanted the more, we had agreed to court the more, damn the consequences. I knew he was intoxicated by the magnanimity of my kisses and that made me unsteady with desire, my hand flung recklessly from the rudder, wanting to be adrift on a dark, uncharted sea.

With his mouth close to mine and his eyes blinding me, he said, "I missed you."

"I missed you," I echoed, with pounding heart.

He kissed me again reassuringly, his mouth held fast to mine until we were both gulping for air. I could feel my breasts swell and press against his chest. Another strong gust of the Santa Anas blew down through the alley rustling the palms like a warning signal, and he pulled me inside and closed the door, immuring the both of us in his hideaway. I wanted to believe with all my heart that this was something final, that this was the beginning of a new life for the both of us. That I, too, would one day write here and reinvent myself, live another life.

I walked inside and swept my eyes around the main room, whose details came eerily to life from journals I had read in Raymond's archive. It seemed to fill the whole house, as if all the walls had been knocked down to create this one unobstructed, undivided space. The remaining walls were occupied with bookcases with shelves stuffed full, heavy with Raymond's intellect and range of aesthetic interests. Lamps burned under orange shades on side tables, lending the room an eternal sunset refulgence. The west-facing wall was a sliding glass door that faced out to the ocean. A simple planked desk rested in the foreground, like a wheelhouse of a small boat awaiting its captain. On it was planted a chipped and worn wooden writing slope, angled at about thirty degrees. My heart leaped when I saw one of the black Moleskines I had given him held open with a coffee cup, a pen glittering to one side, the image seared into my memory forever.

"So, this is the legendary Isla Negra," I said more as a remark than a question, nodding to myself as I reveled in the thrill of finally being in his inner sanctum. I could live here someday, I dreamed. We will listen to the metronomic sighing of the ocean, ideate future collaborations, and grow old like that couple I saw taking their nightly constitutional like a pair of ambulatory penguins. The rest of my life unspooled before me in a kaleidoscope of years that ended in fulfillment. I vowed I wasn't going to be the bitter woman of my mother's generation who, when they hung the morphine, regretted she hadn't lived.

Raymond's mouth curved into a wry smile. "Legendary? No. Just a humble beach cottage and a guy who got lucky." He came up behind me and wrapped his arms around me. "You're the one who's legendary," he whispered in my ear. "The one who is about to be legendary."

I smiled, broke free from his embrace, and crossed the room and went directly to his writing slope, drawn to objects, drawn to the tactile. Running my hands along its burnished contours, I felt the hardwood earth where all of Raymond's works, until recently, were sown. The muffled ocean touched my ears with a breathing infinity. I lifted the heavy pottery coffee cup from the opened Moleskine. His capital block lettering was almost supernaturally familiar to me—for six months it had been in my face in Special Collections; nights when I stayed late to read every word of those first drafts for the sheer pleasure of his racing cacography. It was as if the floating world of the dream had crashed-landed into the planet of reality and the two were now forged in this creation of ours. I couldn't help but throw him a backward glance and feel the seam of a smile widen the corners of his mouth knowing he had intuited my feelings. To be here finally where his brain had disgorged all his memorable works, it was as if I had finally entered by the vessel of whatever he saw in me the turbulent and intimate sea of his soul.

"Almost to Volume Eight." I feared for a fluttery moment that I might have violated the unspoken rules of his creative process.

"You keep feeding me the most extraordinary, inspiring material," he replied, unaffected. "The emails, the journals . . . it's a cornucopia of riches, Nadia."

I blushed with pride and my blood ran hot. "Does it feel strange to have me here?"

"Not at all. Without you, Nadia, I'm nothing now. It's a true collaboration. And that's the God's truth. You've given me the road map out of my despair. My mind is on fire. Every day ends in exhilaration. If something happened to you, I would stop writing, it would all come to a screeching halt. I would be demoralized, unable to go on. Not just with writing, but with life." He threw his arms to the ceiling. "Thank God I took a sabbatical for fall quarter."

I returned my gaze back to the Moleskine and flipped to the first page. In his handwriting it read "The Archivist—Vol. VI—A Novel by Raymond West & Nadia Fontaine."

"It's really going to be a book." I batted back tears at the sight of my name written in his own hand.

"I'm afraid so," he said with self-deprecating resignation. "I'm in the Drowning now."

"The Drowning. Yes." I turned to face him standing in the center of the room. "That *bathysphere* you sink to all day and into the night, six days a week, until you're done."

"You know me too well, Nadia," he said. "I *can't* let you go."

My eyes devoured the Moleskine for fear it wasn't real. I leafed through the pages and pages of his feverish capital print lettering until I landed where he left off for the day. It was a thrill to find myself in the middle of his process, teetering at the precipice of what was to come next, our minds at the region of a creative twilight. Was I looking at an item in his collection one day, one that would be pored over by scholars for decades to come? And here it was, hatched from its literary shell, fledging, gangly, tottering, becoming, soon to be soaring! The catastrophic molt in pimpled efflorescence. From behind me I heard his slippered footfalls drawing near to me. I dared not move. A hand fell on my shoulder like an angel's scepter, bestowing upon me with its warm touch his unspoken love. He massaged my shoulders. I could feel his moist, wine-scented breath on me. His arms enveloped me again and squeezed me tightly the way I had always longed to be held.

"I have something for you," Raymond said. I looked down. He opened one hand and presented me with a small box that he had concealed inside his fist and now opened dramatically like a flower in time-lapse photography.

I lifted the box out of his hand with delicate fingers, untied the ribbon, my back still turned to him. I wriggled off the lid. Inside gleamed a gold pendant, the figure eight of a fang-baring snake devouring its tail. I touched it as if were a live butterfly, its iridescent wings beating furiously to be free.

"The ouroboros," I said, lifting it out by its delicate matching gold chain. "The Egyptian symbol of rebirth."

"And recreation of life. And perpetuity," he whispered, taking the necklace from me, slipping the fragile chain around my neck, and clasping it on the nape, kissing me there as if to seal it with a wax melted from his lips.

"Thank you," I said. I offered my face to him. We came together in a languorous kiss. We had time to luxuriate now, time to explore; we didn't have to rush. In one sense it was a fairytale. It was so wrong, and yet so deliciously perfect.

"In celebration of our mutual rebirth," he said.

I cast my fluttering lashes down at the buttons on his shirt, smothering my smile of contentment in his chest.

"Me writing again for the first time in years, and your coming so otherworldly to me, to inspire me to new heights by taking me to new"—he raised his eyebrows—"unfathomable depths. You're the first woman I've ever met in my life whom I feel I can really talk to, open up to, without fear of judgment or opprobrium, or criticism of my work." He held my shoulders in firm hands and made me look at him. "Do you know how freeing it is to be with you?"

"And me you." My hand reached up and touched his chest to see if his heart contradicted his words. It fluttered against my open palm, throbbed with a life force I wanted to believe I, and I alone, had resuscitated from the dead.

"Come." He took me by the hand and guided me across the plainly furnished room.

We came to a narrow door. He turned a brass handle, verdigris by oxidation. Still holding my hand, he stepped inside a dark space. He yanked a chain from the ceiling and a yellow bulb bathed us suddenly in a golden light. A narrow staircase sank down into an even deeper darkness. *Le Rêve d'un Flagellant* flashed in my mind, but his mood was too winsome, the moment too sudden for *that.*

"This house was built in the fifties," he started, escorting me by the hand down the staircase. "They installed a fallout shelter." His voice was echoing now in the concrete tomb. I still thought for a moment I might find a room outfitted with accoutrements for sexual exploration, but when he pulled the chain on another overhead bulb, the tiny room blossomed into a wine cellar. Disappointment that he wasn't going to ravish me in some new way might have been visible in my puzzled look.

"You've got a lot of bottles," I said in astonishment, my eyes scrutinizing the wooden racks and the capsules jutting out from their assigned slots, all of them neatly labeled. "Who organized all of this?" I asked, running a finger over the labels, a twinge of jealousy that he had brought in some beautiful, female oenological archivist and that this moment at Isla Negra between us was not as special as I wanted to believe.

"I did. When I'm writing, I embrace chaos, but down here, I prefer order. Pick a bottle," he suggested, opening a hand. "Any bottle."

My eyes swam for a moment in the racks of bottles that gridded the walls in a Dionysian dream. I felt like red. Red was warmth. Red was blood. Red was passion. Animal. Primordial. I desired to go deep into the earth, not into the ethereality of the clouds. Red would take us down into the igneous rock, to his Murphy bed, which I had noticed tucked against the wall when I had first come in.

I slid out a Syrah from Chile and presented it to him. "Let's journey to Chile in honor of Neruda, shall we? I've never had a Chilean Syrah."

He smiled and then took the bottle from my outstretched hand. He pulled the overhead chain, and the wine cellar was again possessed of darkness. To me, every moment with him was magical. Every touch was profound.

Upstairs he uncorked the Viña Casa Marín Syrah but plugged the cork back and laid the bottle on its side in a picnic basket. "It's such a warm night, the water's still improbably in the seventies—let's go down to the beach, shall we?"

"I didn't bring a bathing suit," I said.

"You don't need one," he replied lasciviously.

It was a waxing full moon night. Together we stepped off Raymond's planked patio and crossed the train tracks that ran along the top of the bluff. The night was ours, and ours alone, except for invisible nocturnal creatures only audibly present in the scrub that huddled close to the ground.

"I see now why the train is featured in so much of your work," I remarked, as he helped guide me across the rails. "And the Santa Ana winds. And the pelicans." I turned to him, my hair whipping all around my face. "And the ocean!"

"It's what I see and hear every day when I'm here writing," he answered.

"Be careful now." He reached for my hand and I took his in mine. His grip was strong. It didn't feel like he was ever going to let me go.

Raymond led me down a zigzag path that was hewn into the bluff by industrious surfers who didn't want to trek all the way from Torrey Pines Beach to surf the reef below. The Santa Ana wind had calmed and was warm on our faces. When we reached the sand, Raymond spread out a blanket and set down the picnic basket. It was medium tide and the chest-high waves crashed bioluminescently in the dark, in a rare marine phenomenon brought about by an algae bloom. Every unannounced eruption created a new white-and-turquoise-toothed smile from the face of the ocean. The lowering moon, in a bending of optics laws, smeared out its reflection and replaced it with a rectilinear spear of narrowing light that launched all the way to the horizon like some spiritual road to infinity.

Raymond filled two stemless wineglasses with the Chilean Syrah and handed one to me. I couldn't help looking at him. It was as if it were a dream and I was trying desperately to hold onto the fleeting moments. I fingered the ouroboros at my throat, running the tip of my index finger over the figure eight of the snake. With every caress I felt closer to him than ever, as if we were braided together like this. I had so many things I wanted to ask him, but half of my questions—why are you still married?—would no doubt contaminate the mood. If it were a dream, it was a purgatorial dream. Our relationship, if it ever happened, if it was ever made official, would be a wailing, complicated birth. We both knew that. We both were reluctant to talk about it. We both wanted badly to live in the bliss of the present.

"I wanted you to see the bioluminescence," he said, pointing to another set of waves rolling toward us in a surreality of incandescent blues, as if lit by underwater floodlights.

"I know. The plankton are alive tonight!" I exclaimed, my heart racing.

He hooked an arm around me. "God, I love you," he said in a voice deep with conviction. "God, I love you."

I nodded. No one had ever loved me like this. I had never felt this fulfilled in my life. "What's . . . going to happen?" I finally ventured in a quavering voice competing with the waves that thundered in the dark, close to where we lay. I instinctively knew, like the addict's ebb of his dopamine surge, the moment was temporally fraught. I needed reassurance.

Raymond sucked in his breath and took a sip of wine. "We really got ourselves into something, didn't we?" He swiveled his head across his broad shoulders and peered down at me. "It's going to work out," he assured me, sensing that the vertiginous height of the moment had exacted its opposite: the fatalism sewn in the fabric of its descent.

"'When two people fall in love, there is already sown the seed of tragedy,'" I quoted him from one of his books.

Needing it, Raymond drank more wine and smiled a laugh. "Is that what you fear?"

"It's too perfect of a moment." I met his eyes, mirroring moonlight back at me. "But I wouldn't trade it for that fear and risk not having this." I opened an arm to the ocean.

Raymond craned his gaze away to the ocean and the booming surf, and held it there, borne by a thought, or an image of where he would pick up the writing the following day. I looked at him. I glimpsed a mariner who had voyaged there in all his work, and I wondered in that moment whether I would someday be the one he waved goodbye to, or if I would be the port he always sailed back to. He hooked an arm around my shoulders and drew me close to him.

"You made me realize how imperative it was I change my life if I wanted to go on living as an artist," he said. "Look, I'm fully aware of what we face. But the deeper I get into the book—our book"—he hugged me closer to him until we were crushed together—"the more I see how much of a lie I'm living and how necessary it is to live the truth." He nodded resolutely to the panorama of the ocean, to the thoughts orbiting in his head, that rectilinear moonlit road that led his mind to some other shore where he wanted to journey. "The truth of this love, immortalized, if one can be so arrogant, in *The Archivist*."

I hung on his words and let the ocean's eternal roaring fill the void that was now our uncharted, mutual silence. "When I started on your collection, you realize we had already met . . ."

"That's right. At Columbia. The Pulitzer."

"You don't remember me at all. You were surrounded by all these women." I stabbed him in the ribs with a teasing forefinger, and he flinched in chagrin. "That's why I didn't introduce myself."

"I wish you had." He raised his eyebrows mischievously. "What might have been," he spoke to the ocean in a forlorn voice.

"There's a picture of you with me in it—and all those other female admirers—somewhere in your archive."

"Maybe remove it," he murmured, his words muted by the crashing waves.

Slightly offended, because I didn't want to be expunged from his life like that, I studied him with a searching look, but his eyes were fixed on that rectilinear shaft of light with the narrowed eyes of a brooding captain, one arm wrapped around the mast, me. "I don't want to be one of them," I said softly. "I don't want to be left stranded on the sands of despair." I clawed the ground and brought up a handful of sand. Then, dramatically, I let it go through splayed fingers. "My heart couldn't stand it."

"It won't happen," he said, eyes daring disbelief. A wave exploded in the dark and then lit up incandescently with the agitated plankton, as if to punctuate his solemn promise with an exclamation point.

I sipped my wine, leaned into him and hugged him tight to me. He drew me closer to him until my hair cascaded over his shoulder. He kissed me hard, fierce, eyes blazing, then he looked once more in my eyes.

"Okay?" he said, squeezing me.

"Okay," I said.

"I'm almost at the halfway point," he said, shifting the mood with his hopeful words.

"You're not going to abandon it?" I asked, half kidding.

He looked at me as if I were unhinged. "I would never abandon it. The book has set its hook in me." He pointed an index finger to his temple. "It's churning inside me right now. I wake and live and breathe *The Archivist.* How could you say that, Nadia?" He grabbed my chin with his free hand and forced me to look at him. "It has taken total possession of me." He let go of my chin.

"I believe you." I raised my eyes from his shoulder where they were buried in dreams and fixed them on his. "But you have before."

"Not when it's pulsing like this I haven't," he said resolutely.

"That makes me happy. As both your cowriter *and* your archivist."

"When I really get into the Drowning," he said, narrowing his eyes at the ocean with a fierce determination set in his expression, "I always go to this place in Baja to finish." He turned to me with boyish excitement. "Then celebrate. Can you get a whole week off?"

"Yeah. Of course. And if they say no, I'll fucking quit!" I needed to follow the trail of this excitement wherever it led, even if it doomed me to destitution.

He lowered his arm and found the hem of my T-shirt. He lifted it up. I turned to him and raised both arms. He wriggled it off me. My breasts faced him and all he could do was stare and shake his head.

"God, you're fucking beautiful." Then, in an uncharacteristic moment of youthful effusion, he announced, "Let's go swimming."

We clambered to our feet. Laughing, shrieking uncontrollably like teenagers, we stripped naked. Raymond reached for my hand and I took his. Together we ran tangle-footed headlong into the oncoming surf. The shock of the water's late summer bracing seventy-two degrees was quickly supplanted by its refreshing emollience. The sweat was washed from our skin. Together, we swam out to head-high and bodysurfed like spinner dolphins, both equally comfortable in the ocean and unafraid of the dark waters and what creatures lurked there, swimming euphorically in the bioluminescence.

Refreshed, we thrashed to the shore, exhausted, limbs entangled, kissing clumsily with wet faces. We fell bedraggled to the blanket and made love, me on top, riding him, as he preferred. I could have sworn a train roared overhead when I came, but maybe I'm only retrospectively poeticizing the moment, as the writer in me is wont to do. We lay, limbs entwined, spent from exhausted, pent-up desire, and the tension wrought from fear of the absolute forbidden that imprisoned our world. Wicked laughter punctuated our apprehensions. I've never felt freer. Raymond spoke of the writing of our book with such intense verbosity, he drowned out the waves. And then lust consumed us again.

We toweled off and drank more wine, gathered up our spontaneous picnic belongings, and climbed back up the sandstone cliff with its primitive steps. On the planked porch, under the palm thatch awning, we finished the deep and haunting Chilean red, wondering out loud if it haunted Neruda back in his day. And then it began. The kissing now was deeper and led us ineluctably back into the house where our clothes flew off again, and we tasted the crystallized salt on our profanely naked bodies.

At one point, I excused myself and disappeared into the bathroom. I returned wearing only a black T-shirt and matching panties. My breasts swung loosely under the T-shirt, which I'd had personalized with Gothic stenciling reading "Your Nadia Archivist."

Raymond sat up, his eyes widened with excitement, "My naughty archivist, indeed."

I interlaced my fingers and brought them behind my head and posed, one hip cocked to the side.

Raymond reached for his cell and started recording. I danced for him like my character in Joel's film, the archivist wrung from lust. I sashayed toward him and knelt onto the bed. I wriggled seductively out of the T-shirt, one thread at a time, and my breasts tumbled out and I fell onto him. The gold ouroboros scintillated at my throat, but it was the dangling jewelry I had clipped to my nipples that I could see excited Raymond. I tossed the black T-shirt across the room. I was coming for him in a way that no other woman had ever come for him. The jewelry tinkled like salacious wind chimes ignited to life by the Santa Anas moaning through the open windows. I let him finger them adoringly and then lowered my head to his erection. I heard him sigh and imagined his head was thrown back and his eyes had closed to take me in in all my sensorial splendor. Once I lifted my face up, black hair stringy wet, eyes ghoulishly inflamed, the anima manifest in reality of every man's dream, staring straight into the lens of the camera, a savage beauty, confident and unashamed of my ardor. My lips glistened with him and with both of us and desire had never been more radiant. The video ended when I rose up on my knees and closed in on him where he wanted to be obliterated so badly and where nothing was left for his eyes to see except the physical poetry of my unbridled lust.

From: Nadia Fontaine <Nfontaine@RegentsU.edu>
To: Raymond West <Rwest_Lit@RegentsU.edu>
Subject: Post-Isla Negra
Date: 22 October 2017

My Raymond,

And the waves lapping at our feet . . . but my happiest moment of all was seeing the latest volume of the Moleskine copious with words . . . racing to the finish!

EMILY

Emily slowly closed the lid on her laptop. A tortuosity of thoughts gripped her mind in the vice of a headache of exacerbating ambivalence locked in combat with a weft of psychological terror she had never experienced before. The video was mind-blowing enough. Her predecessor, naked—with a donor, no less—captured on video and launched like a corked bottle into the dark archives. Holy fuck, Emily thought, as she slithered off the bed and walked into the kitchen. She knew what she wanted in the refrigerator, but her mind was paralyzed by her latest dip into Nadia's dark well of recounted—and recorded!—salacity, as she held the door open, her thoughts trying to thread into some semblance of coherency. *My God! What was she thinking?* Emily shook her head.

As if the neurons had delayed their journey to her hand by the length of her internal wrangling, she finally reached for the last bottle of Societe ale, uncorked it, filled a glass half full, then crossed the small living room to the picture window and gazed out at the night. Holy shit, she mouthed to herself, staring down at her cell to the colorful image of Google Maps. Raymond's Isla Negra was located mere blocks down the hill and around the corner from her apartment in Del Mar. She shivered at the thought at how close to her it actually was.

Following this trail of mystery, impelled by her own unwanted, but motivated, place now in its chronology, Emily stepped into her sandals and threw open the sliding glass door as if she, too, had a lover to clandestinely run to. The same dead frond scratched the eave above her head as she locked the door, but she didn't even hear it this time. In her hand was her cell with its flashlight app and the address of Isla Negra—info that fans of West's books would die to have. She was officially stalking him now, she thought, and she didn't care.

Did she see the same elderly couple taking their nightly constitutional when she walked in the same direction Nadia had a year ago? The husked silhouettes of two adults, whispering anxieties for palliative purposes, stole by her on the other side of the depopulated street, moving in and out of pools of dim streetlights. Maybe Emily was too inside the taboo Nadia/Raymond correspondence to know the difference between reality and a year ago. She glanced back over her shoulder to reassure herself she wasn't hallucinating the couple from Nadia's account, but they had vanished. Must have turned down one of the alleys that led to the bluff, Emily decided.

Emily sauntered on with mounting ambivalence until she came to Little Orphan Alley. The night hummed with insects. Her heart raced as her eyes blinked at the modest street sign in disbelief, as if she were imagining it somehow. But the literary way Nadia had vividly described the rendezvous in her memoir was exactly how Emily relived it now, and it imparted an eerie sense of déjà vu. The ocean, no longer blocked by the homes, audibly boomed with the white noise of crashing surf. The hoot owl that slipped overhead like a phantom jet alit in the thick of a tree, calling to its mate in a sorrowing *tu-whu tu-whu, tu-whu tu-whu.*

Emily started down Little Orphan Alley with hesitant, halting steps, gnawing on the cuticle of an index finger. She didn't know why she was creeping along so slowly. Did she fear Raymond West appearing? The moonless night gave her more cover, but would he even recognize her? Had going back nearly a year in time merged the past with the present because their words were so powerfully passionate and alive as if their affair had all happened mere weeks ago? Lights blazed in some of the houses, but she hadn't heard, let alone seen, a single car pass since she left her apartment. She could feel the wind brush her back, but it wasn't the buffeting Santa Ana that Nadia had described—was she fabricating this rendezvous? Emily almost couldn't believe that emails in the dark archives had taken her here. Past and present had surreally merged.

One step at a time, Emily crept up toward 115 Little Orphan Alley. She came to a stop before the driveway and peered over a row of hedges. No cars. A solemn silence seemed to have fallen over the house. Through shuttered windows, the hideaway that was moments ago so aglow and lifelike in her mind with laughter and love, soul-searching kisses and heart-pounding sex, was plunged in ghostly darkness. Emily ventured to the end of the alley, still moving slowly, step by step, tensed to turn away and run at the slightest apprehension. She came to a halt at a concrete culvert a few feet deep running north and south. She crossed it, but slipped and skinned her knee on the rough, hard surface.

"Ow, fuck," she cursed, rubbing her knee where the concrete had shredded a hole in her pants. She clambered to a standing position and skulked to a spot with a view of the patio. The dead palm fronds fashioned into an awning were exactly as Nadia had painted them with her superior command of words. Behind the sliding glass door, a curtain was drawn closed. Emily shimmied back across the culvert, this time without incident, and bushwhacked her way through a row of hedges until she found herself standing on the plank decking. A gust of wind rustled the dead frond awning, and the marimba-like noise startled her for a moment, and she whipped her head up with a glance that strained her neck. She took her hand away from her heart as if pulling out an arrow embedded there. She took two more steps to the sliding glass door and pressed her face against the pane. Through a fissure in the curtain, she was afforded a fragmented view inside, like looking through a keyhole with one eye. Nothing but darkness. She pressed an ear against the glass, but it seemed to only reflect the sound of the inexorable surf. Frustrated, she pulled up her flashlight app, set the intensity bar to low, laid her cell against the windowed door, and held it at chest height. An otherworldly glow illuminated the inside of Isla Negra, the hidden inner sanctum of Raymond West. Peering inside, Emily recognized it exactly as Nadia described. The desk was still parked in the foreground, an archeological relic now without its author. And on it, his writing slope, worn by forearms, pen to the paper in a primordial connection to his once fathomless well of epically emotional personal journeys. The Murphy bed where they had made love was a forlorn tangle of bedcovers, appearing as if it hadn't been slept in for months. The only object missing, described in Nadia's memoir, was the Moleskine splayed open on the writing slope held open with the weight of a coffee cup. Isla Negra a year later had a sepulchral feel, abandoned by its lovers, as if it were now a museum with the barest vestiges of their love remaining visible.

Emily caught herself holding her breath in a bursting chest pervaded by a yawning sadness. If he one day was fortunate to capture the Nobel, acolytes and fans and press would swarm this ramshackle oasis. If she could find it, so could they. Or could they? Emily inhaled and exhaled in anxious breaths and felt the heavy ocean air stream in and out of her like a dense fog. Something trembled in her. She heard a noise, and she realized her legs were shaking involuntarily; the planks beneath her soles were creaking with their movement.

She needed to move to stop her legs from trembling, so, convinced that no one was inside, she pulled up one of the chairs and sat at the table where Nadia and Raymond had polished off the bottle of Viña Casa Marín.

The thoughts swirling in Emily's head had only grown more webbed and Byzantine. She realized in that moment that she wasn't just an archivist—she had become a private investigator, unstoppably and inexorably following clues stumbled on in the dark archives. She was, to quote the title of one of her favorite diarists, a spy in the house of love. She was positive no one knew what she knew. And—she was convinced of it!—it was implausible that Nadia had drowned accidentally! This relationship was too fraught with hurdles, the lines of tension too gridded and taut, for that too-convenient forensic ruling on her death. Now she wanted more. She wasn't going to be deterred.

Emily rose from the deck chair, the roar of the ocean over the dark side of the cliff thundering in her ears, and started away. She stopped on the street and cast a final look at Raymond's Isla Negra. Something she hadn't noticed when she approached was a For Sale sign, discreetly nailed flush to the clapboard façade. Coastal Premiere Properties. In an inset was the garish picture of a blonde Realtor dressed in a red coat as if she were headed off for a fox hunt, smiling idiotically with a maw of white teeth. For no reason other than posterity, Emily took a picture of it. When her phone's camera flash went off, she noticed that the driveway was windblown with debris, and that West's once legendarily secret writing hideaway—whereabouts undisclosed, and carefully guarded, to everyone but a few—was in a state of dilapidation. The salt air of the ocean was oxidizing its aluminum rain gutters. Through fissures in the pavement the earth beneath was sprouting up with the hardiest of weeds, drought-resistant species that could survive the apocalypse. The earth-shattering love that had been conducted there, the book that had been conceived out of that love, but apparently abandoned unfinished, was now part of a ghostly memory possessing the creaking ruin of an old seafront bungalow moldering in neglect, shuttered to the world. The historian in Emily wondered if Isla Negra would go off the market if Raymond won the Nobel. Wouldn't it be enshrined as an historic landmark? Wouldn't it be immortalized like Hemingway's Finca Vigía in Havana? Wouldn't Elizabeth West be desperate to preserve it? The outside would be professionally landscaped and the house restored to its *Lessons in Reality* former glory, wouldn't it? *The Archivist* would not be part of its history, but its literary ghost would haunt this house for all eternity.

The only time Emily had seen Raymond West he appeared gaunt, was limping, employing a cane to walk. The West in the emails to Nadia was unabashedly buoyant and exuberant and hopeful about the future. The West she briefly encountered in the La Jolla home cast the sad silhouette of a broken man, a saturnine cloud of solemnity, or resignation, hovering over his hitching gait. Writing screenplays? He didn't need the money, Emily reasoned. She knew he loved movies, even if he didn't admire the tepid, bowdlerized screen adaptation of *Lessons in Reality*. They "missed the heart and soul and strip-mined it for plot," he mordantly confessed to an interviewer at the time. He couldn't be infatuated with a place as venal and shallow as Hollywood, could he? Surely, his heart was in literature, but somewhere over the course of a year his heart had blackened, the fires had been extinguished again, not even embers glowed in his milky blue eyes. He needed the life force Nadia had inflamed his imagination with. Emily alighted on a phrase in one of the emails he had written to her: "Without you, I'm nothing." It could have been the hyperbolic effusion of a man in love, but Emily wanted to believe it was something more; he had excitedly written about it to his editor at Scribner's, for Christ's sake! He truly believed this new, deeply personal, work, *The Archivist*, had opened his eyes to a new form of intimate autobiographical writing, a transcendent comingling of fecund imaginations. A *pas de deux*, as he had written Nadia, a conjoining of twin sensibilities racing headlong toward a confluence of two mighty rivers pouring from mountain heights at such severe angles. Hyperbole or not, he wanted—he needed!—to believe it, Emily presumed, in order to write it. Nadia desperately *wanted* him to believe it too. He had let himself go, unshackled, fully into the Drowning, where he descended in a symbolic bathysphere to the seafloor, cut off from the world, existentially alone with only his imagination as sustenance. And Nadia. Nadia there with him in this sacred immurement of pure alchemical transmutation of base matter into gold.

And then the literary experiment had ended. For reasons unbeknownst to Emily, the bathysphere surfaced and floated adrift, rudderless, its captaincy vanished overboard, on never-ending seas. What had happened? All Emily had gleaned from scouring the public records was that a midnight surf session led to a leash twisted around Nadia's neck, strangling her long enough to lose consciousness and not have the wherewithal to make it back to the surface before her lungs filled with water and stopped breathing. A beautiful woman in a wet suit, slapped by spent waves at the shore's edge all night long, discovered by a lone surfer in the salmon hue of daybreak. A drowning? A woman who had once competed in triathlons, according to her staff biography? In her labyrinthian way of thinking, Emily felt lost in a maze of misdirections and contradictions that didn't add up.

Having overstayed her sleuthing, feeling guiltily voyeuristic bringing this affair back to life in a way no archivist probably would dare, Emily reluctantly walked away from the bungalow, its shuttered emptiness summoning a sadness, the relentless surf now a lamentation. Having spent a month now on West's papers, she felt an animallike kinship to the house, surprised at the propinquity of its location. It was an overwhelming experience to see it, ironic that it was strangely close to her apartment, but not unusual given that Del Mar was a small hamlet and home to many university faculty and staff. His prodigious library existed still intact, the spines of the books staring back at her with their many titles of fiction and poetry. And his legendary writing slope! *My God*, Emily thought, *that burnished walnut artifact alone should be in Special Collections.* Why did Raymond leave it if he wasn't writing here anymore? Did he plan to return one night, grief-stricken from the death of Nadia, and pick up the revisions on *The Archivist* where he had left off, absolve, once and for all, the entanglements of this tragic love?

As she strolled back to her apartment through the quiet neighborhood,

Emily was firmly resolved to find out what had happened. And something *had* happened. Turning back was no longer an option. She'd rather die than not know. She, too, wanted the more, not the less, she decided then and there in the gloom of Isla Negra. Besides, she rationalized, it was now a matter of Raymond's papers, and Emily couldn't live with an ellipsis—a gaping hole!—in his collection.

The white-haired couple passed her on her way back, headed in the opposite direction. She wanted it to be Raymond and Nadia, younger, walking arm in arm back to Isla Negra, their faces aglow with lifelike laughter, their eyes only for each other, a happy ending for a couple who had risked it all for love in all its sublimity.

It was late when she got back. She was having trouble shaking off Nadia's account of her and Raymond's first clandestine meeting at Isla Negra. If she closed her eyes, she could picture them coiled around each other like the ouroboros of the pendant. She smiled enviously at the image of the two of them splashing into the warm waters, laughing and naked, as the bioluminescence lit up the waves and the moon hovered celestially above. Emily felt deeply the warmth Nadia must have felt as Raymond held her tightly in his arms after they exhausted their bodies in wicked exploration. She could feel Nadia's despondency, piercing her, when she had no choice but to leave to get home at a decent hour so she wouldn't be interrogated by her husband. And she felt the pure rush of joy Nadia must have experienced when Raymond pressed that key to Isla Negra into her hand and invited her to come unbidden anytime. When she closed her fist around the key, it sealed a pact that this was far deeper and more immutable than anything she had felt before. When she doubted his love in her gush of emails, he reminded her he had already told Nick Peterson, his editor at Scribner's, about *The Archivist*. For a book is a fragile thing. It's nothing but the spores of plants blown by a wind until it's captured on paper. And once it's on paper it still must be a book. Nadia had yet to hold that book in her hand, and until she did, she would always doubt its existence, and in doubting its existence, she would perforce always question the constancy of his love.

"Nick Peterson, Nick Peterson," Emily repeated out loud in her apartment. She had remembered seeing "Nick_Peterson_Corrs" in the dark archives but hadn't yet had time to venture in and read through it. Tunneled in on what she wanted to do next, she didn't see the walls, she barely heard the welcoming *meows* of Onyx. She rushed straight into her bedroom, crept onto the bed, and opened her laptop. In the dark archives, like the sleuthing spider she had become, she found the brief email exchange between Raymond and his trusted, steadfast editor at Scribner's, the only one Raymond ever worked with.

The first email was an effusive one from Raymond. After apologizing for not writing in many months, he began by confessing the affair with Nadia. But he took pains to explain in an unedited torrent of superlatives that something had awakened in him. He had begun, in collaboration with the woman, a new work, one that he was writing in an Ishiguro-like thirty-day frenzy, driven by an inner fire that was consuming him whole. "Conflagrating my brain and heart to ashes." To Emily's eyes it was an extraordinary profession of both his love for Nadia and his rekindled desire to find a way to put that love down on paper. It didn't comport with the slow-moving, cane-supported man she had briefly met in the seaside house in La Jolla. It was another man all together. His editor's astonished reply was predictably mixed with excitement and worry, privy as he was to Raymond's personal life. But the editor in him, encouraged by his star writer's apparent return to form, eagerly awaited its birth. Raymond wrote back with the confidence of a writer in the thrilling crucible of creation: "You will see."

Emily slowly pulled down the screen of her laptop, inhaling in tandem with its closing. Nadia had been Bcc'd on the emails! He had wanted her to see that their love was not something that existed anonymously in the cocoon of an affair, wrapped up forever in the shroud of clandestinity, or worse, a fraud, and he manipulating her for sex. He wanted her to know that he was tiptoeing with their love—and the book that would both celebrate and immortalize it—into the public. He had wanted her to know that he was prepared to risk it all for her. And that one day, inevitably, they would be together.

CHAPTER 15

The World Outside

9/14/18

I dreamt as vividly as I had ever dreamt before. The dreams were like the fragments of long, multilayered novels that had no beginning, middle, or end. I know Jung said the unconscious tried to sort out the irrationalities and bewilderments of consciousness using the symbolic language of dreams to communicate to the dreamer, but I didn't wake with any sense that the disorder of my life had suddenly righted itself and found order. The world seems more chaotic now than ever.

Surfers bobbed in the waters at Torrey Pines State Beach, catching a few waves before work. The morning skies the fires had previously bled red were once again a shimmering light gold to the east and an opalescent blue to the west. The water was azure, touched by invisible offshore winds that held the waves up long enough for the surfers to carve up and down them out of reach of the crumbling white water.

The fall trimester had not begun yet, but orientation was underway, and the university was fast becoming an ad hoc city. Inhabitants who had once abandoned it were now returning, spoking in and swarming its walkways, bringing color and movement to the concrete, quickly creating wide crisscrossing streams and filling the library's desks and carrels like wine overflowing the rim of a vast goblet.

Emily slipped into her cubicle at Special Collections. Helena's office door was closed. Samantha at the reference desk waved and chirped hi at a tense-faced Emily, who smiled without breaking stride. Nicola had been let go to prepare for the fall quarter, and Emily was glad to have the West Papers once again all to herself. She also remembered Jean would be working at the Annex, so the department this morning was blissfully quiet. The tautened lines of tension that had developed over the West Collection would slacken, if only for a day, if only until the next status update when the push to be ready for the Eighth Floor Gala would once again rear its head, bringing with it a new set of pressures.

Emily ignored the Excel spreadsheet Jean had set over her keyboard so she wouldn't miss it. She flung it aside, turned on her computer, and scrolled through her email. As she trashed email after email, Joel messaged her:

"What's up? How R U?"

Emily typed back, "Want to have lunch together?

"Your place or mine?"

"Ha-ha. In the bower. 1:00?" Emily suggested.

"Can I get you anything?" Joel asked.

"I'm fine."

"How's West?"

Emily tapped her fingers lightly on the keyboard as if pretending to type, afraid to press the keys, then closed with, "See you at 1:00."

Emily leaned back in her flexible-back chair until her eyes could see the ceiling without having to bend her neck. She flicked her favorite pen against her lips, trying to sort out her thoughts. From another cubicle she could hear the rise and fall of a voice talking on the phone, but the words were indistinguishable and didn't bother Emily. It was when she could hear what they were saying, and they wouldn't stop, and they kept saying the same fucking thing over and over again, that she became irritated, then silently enraged.

Emily lowered her eyes and caught something glinting back at her. On one of the two desks crowded with boxes and West items she noticed a small pile of folders. Emily rose out of her chair as if an apparition out of a horror movie. With an outstretched hand she approached the items, tensed to strike. Before she touched them, she spotted a handwritten note. It read, "Found these in the doc. box where you said to look for the Barnes Corrs.—Nicola." Folded into a small triangle like a flag was a black T-shirt. The object glinting on top of it was the gold ouroboros! Next to it was a single brass key. Emily fingered the ouroboros in her hand, the necklace Raymond had clasped around Nadia's neck, and the night at Isla Negra surged up in her like a rogue wave. Closing her fist around it to conceal it from view, she darted a glance at the entrance to her cubicle. She cocked an ear and listened. The humming of the AC roared in her ears, but she couldn't discern anything else. Even the voice on the phone had concluded its complaint. Emily pocketed the ouroboros in her fleece vest and then picked up the black T-shirt and let it unfurl before her. On the front was stenciled in silver Gothic letters *Your Nadia Archivist.* Galvanized by fear, Emily's hands flew to her face, and she clutched the shirt against her nose and mouth, inhaling deeply its scent. Unmistakably lavender, the same lavender scent Raymond had rhapsodized about. And, God, if she couldn't detect behind the firewall of lavender, the scent of their commingled sweat. She breathed in deeply, like a master sommelier might the aromas of a fabled Burgundy, trying to identify every single piquant phenolic still clinging indelibly to the cotton. She could picture Nadia, stark naked except for this T-shirt, approaching him confidently, ruling the imperium of their lovemaking as she hurled herself into the void with complete and utter abandon. Raymond, too, wanted to let go, loved to let go to her, because he trusted her, because he loved her deeply, because he wanted desperately to see where she would take him. Where she could take him. And here it was, all their unconventional and unmentionable lovemaking lived in this black T-shirt, still redolent of their orgasmic furies. Oblivious of the complex of cubicles in Special Collections, Emily breathed it in and out, in and out. Transfixed by its sexual odors, she didn't hear her visitor:

"Knock knock." Then, louder, "Knock! Knock!"

Emily withdrew the T-shirt from her face in a panic. From the lavender-scented blackness of the garment, her world was rudely replaced with the round, smiling visage of Chloe. "Chloe!"

"What are you doing, Emily?" She reached out a hand. "Let me see."

Emily tensed, instinctively pulled the T-shirt away from Chloe's hand, imagining trying to explain *Your Nadia Archivist*, what fabrications she would have to concoct, and knowing how transparently inept she was at lying.

"What? Why can't I see? What did you find?" Chloe's eyes darted furtively around Emily's cubicle. The pendant and key could be explained, Emily quickly reasoned, but not the T-shirt—oh, no, God no, not the T-shirt. Nicola didn't know whom Nadia was, but her coworker did. Chloe cocked her head to one side and set a hand on her hip "Come on, Emily, what's up? Find something in the West Collection?"

"No!" Emily almost screamed but caught herself. "No." She looked down. "It's an old gym shirt. I was just . . ."

"Smelling to see if it needed to be washed?"

"Yeah, something like that," Emily said in blatant voice of sarcasm.

Chloe nodded with a smirk as if Emily's words lacked conviction. "The way you had it smushed to your face was kind of weird, Emily."

"Is there like no privacy in here?" Emily retorted, looking around, as if addressing the whole nonexistent ensemble of the department. Gossip was political capital, and the Nadia/Raymond affair was an archivist's kryptonite.

"Hey, I'm not trying to pry. So, are we still cool for tonight?"

"With Jesse and Clint, right?" Emily asked.

"Yeah." She cocked her head to one side. "I can't keep rescheduling."

"Okay, sure," Emily said to get her off her back.

Chloe brightened. "Great."

"If anything changes, I'll text you," Emily said.

Chloe frowned. "Ciao."

When Chloe had gone, Emily crumpled Nicola's innocent note into her fist and tossed it into the wastebasket. She was suddenly seized with paranoia, rummaged around in the wastebasket, retrieved the ball of paper, and shoved it into her back pocket. The brass key went into her right front pocket. The T-shirt was unnerving her, though. Thank God, Nicola was a naïf! She bundled up Nadia's stenciled black T-shirt and jammed it into her purse. Its existence in the Raymond West Collection had no explanation, and even less of an explanation why she would have pulled it and had it brought to her cubicle for . . . processing? As memorabilia?

With Chloe out of her cubicle and the contretemps of the T-shirt smoothed over, Emily sought refuge and structure in the finding aid. She found the Nick Peterson correspondence listed, which almost shocked her. Jotting down the identifying codes on a piece of paper, she took them with her and walked in the direction of the stacks. She slid her passkey through the reader, the buzzer sounded, and she pushed open the heavy door. It slammed shut behind her with a boom, and she panicked for a moment that she had locked herself in.

It felt even colder in the stacks, and she crisscrossed her arms against her breasts and moved in that defensive posture she had been chided about before. She wandered through the shelving, through the pillars of slanting light, into the shadows of the stacks where the catacomb-like silence was a soothing balm to her misophonia, exacerbated now with all the stress. She knew in all these rows of flannel-gray document boxes there were geologic layers of mystery. It would take millions of archivists in thousands of libraries, and all the whirring servers where the dark archives lived, to disinter them all. And if the human heart could speak truly nakedly, we would know, Emily firmly believed, the real truth of humankind. Inchoately forming in her still-evolving understanding of an archivist's role, this was precisely the reason why she had gravitated to the profession, then fell hard for it. Like a first crush, an epiphany at a crossroads, and never wanting to let go, cleaving to it like a foundered mast. Tears pooled in her eyes thinking that her predecessor had needed to let it go and reinvent herself in some way that would only be an apparitional vestige of who she, deep down, was. Before she died. Or was her death because she couldn't let it go? Suicide? Emily was struggling with the tragedy, but the archivist in her believed its answer lay in the records.

Emily ran her forefinger along the labels on the boxes like a bored kid dragging a tree branch along the spikes of a wrought iron fence. She stopped when she came to the box she was searching for. It rested on the top shelf. She leaped up and got a hold of it, tilted it toward her until gravity dropped it into her hands. She set it on a cart, the way a corpse might be displayed on shining, antiseptic steel. Death is unspectacular, cold and final, Emily morbidly thought, as she shimmied the lid off the box.

Inside, she looked and she looked, but she couldn't find a folder with the correspondence between Raymond West and his editor at Scribner's, Nick Peterson. And yet, it was in the finding aid, and it had been digitized and put in a folder in the dark archives. If it had been scrubbed from the boxes, why not the dark archives too? It was starting to feel like one of those Russian nesting dolls; every time Emily pulled one out, she confronted others concealed inside, begging to be freed.

Joel was already seated in the bower when Emily arrived, lunch box in hand, a head of worries and deepening confusion sequestered inside her. Joel chivalrously, if histrionically to draw a laugh, wiped the concrete bench where she was preparing to sit. Memorial Library loomed above and behind them, its windows in sun-reflective mode, shooting off blinding bolts of light. It was so immense, it eclipsed half the sky through the eucalyptus branches, an indomitable presence, as if they could never be umbilically detached from it no matter how far they gravitated from it.

"There you go, Ma-dame," Joel said.

Emily smiled a laugh. She opened her Japanese lunch box and removed an already peeled hardboiled egg wrapped in a napkin. In one of the compartments a few sticks of carrots rested. She snacked on them as Joel started to maul a Styrofoam container of fish tacos, beans, and rice.

"Is that all you're eating?" Joel asked.

"I'm not that hungry," Emily replied, her eyes on the dirt where ants skittered through dead, fallen eucalyptus leaves.

"You seem depressed . . . ?" Joel said solicitously.

Emily shrugged. "I don't want to get you in trouble, Joel."

"Please." Joel held up both hands in surrender. He turned to her. "What do you need?" he inquired with an exasperated exhale.

Emily swiveled her head and met his eyes. "I want to get into the Annex."

"I know. You told me." Joel sucked in his breath, then let it go with a sigh. "My buddy's working security there tomorrow."

"I only need fifteen minutes," Emily said.

"I know you're going to think this is me being paranoid, but there are cameras all over that place. There's no reason on the planet for you to be in there without authorization . . ."

"You want me to wear a disguise?" Emily half joked.

"I'm not saying go all out with a wig or shit, but if they wanted to go back and look at the videos they could. And we both would be busted."

"All right."

A silence fell. It was shattered by the grinding noise of skateboard wheels that rose quickly in a hideous clacketing as a young Asian girl wearing a black antiviral face mask weaved her way dangerously over the tiled scales of the back of the enormous anaconda as if she were surfing it. Emily instinctively brought both hands to her ears and held them tightly as the student streaked by. She had come to loathe that noise with a passion. It ruined the serenity of the bower.

"What the fuck!" Joel hollered, hands cupped around his mouth.

"I fucking hate when they do that," Emily cried, dropping her hands from her sensitive ears.

"I'm with you," Joel agreed.

"Completely unnerves me every time. They shouldn't be allowed to desecrate this beautiful outdoor sculpture."

Joel rested a hand on the bench next to her thigh, careful not to touch her. "You seem tense."

"I'm filled with a lot, Joel."

"Suggestion?" She refused to meet his dark probing eyes. "Lay off the dark archives. Lay off the affair. It's in the past. Water under the bridge."

She swung her face to his. "I can't, Joel. Shit happened. That West archive"—she flung an arm over her head in the general direction of the mirrored library—"is a mess. And I'm not going to put my fucking name on it."

"Jeez, Emily. Relax. Chill."

"I can't chill, Joel. Someone's dead. And I'm positive she didn't drown." Still seething, Emily resumed eating her egg. "I should just *fucking* resign." Emily exhaled a blast of air through her nostrils.

"No," said Joel, taking her seriously. "Don't do that."

A silence fell. Emily looked off. "You know the fender on my car that you tried to fix?" Joel nodded. "I jumped the divider on Torrey Pines down by the beach." She shot Joel a look. "I had a panic attack. I drove myself to the ER at Scripps. I thought I was having a heart attack."

Joel blinked and looked down at his lap, his face gravely serious all of a sudden.

"I didn't want this, Joel. I was excited to come here and finish up the papers of a writer I deeply admire. And then I find all this . . . stuff." She exhaled sharply through her nose. Her voice rose an octave. "And it keeps unraveling. And I don't know where it goes. But I can't stop." She nodded to herself as if to gather her emotions. "It's why I've been so wound up these last few weeks, so tense. I almost made an appointment at Faculty & Staff Assistance, but I don't feel like I can trust them. Is that paranoid?" She looked at Joel.

Joel adjusted his sunglasses on the bridge of his nose. She imagined his eyes enlarged behind them. "I feel guilty that I've been your Deep Throat."

"No, don't," Emily said, setting a reassuring hand on his thigh. "You're the only one I can trust." Joel seemed ambivalent to speak. Emily dropped her hand to the bench. "This collection is like a beating heart, one party alive, one dead, so palpable, so real, so intense, so intensely personal. These are human beings, Joel. The chronicle of their love is over in there"—Emily threw a hand over her shoulder and pointed at the library—"in that cold repository, but as alive to me as it was to them." She cast her eyes down. "Isn't this what we signed up for? And what do we do when faced with it?" She shook her head. "Everything is so . . . ephemeral these days, so shallow and trite and meaningless. This was real. This was deep. No, I can't let it go."

A gust of wind rustled the dry leaves of the giant trees, dislodging a cluster of dead ones and sending them fluttering to the ground. The family of ravens weren't in the trees today. Maybe they had found a new home. Emily wondered as she dreamed her eyes upward through the highest branches and the sunlight that yellowed them in faded gold.

Joel rose from the concrete bench with heavy limbs that took a few seconds to get straightened. He arched his back and stretched his sore surfer muscles. "I got to get back. We just got in the new Lasergraphics ScanStation, and today's the first day of training."

"Really? You're getting into film to digital conversion?"

"Yeah. I'm hoping to get promoted to digital film preservationist."

"A new position here?"

"Yep. I'm hoping. Film's my first love."

"That's awesome, Joel."

"Yeah, then apply to UCLA TV and Film Archive, move to LA and sell my screenplays and make it in Hollywood." His head bobbed on his shoulders.

"I'll come with you," Emily said gaily.

Joel peered down at her, eyes covered by his dark sunglasses. "Don't worry, Emily. I'll get you into the Annex."

"I appreciate that," Emily said.

"Like I mentioned, I've been here almost a decade. I've got student debt. I spend too much money on surfboards. I don't want to have to move."

Emily brought her eyes from the sky back to his. "I understand."

"What's in the Annex, if I might ask?" he inquired, his tone modulated as if he feared the answer.

"It's better if you don't know," Emily said in a neutral undertone.

Joel nodded resignedly. "Okay." He turned his head and squinted through the trees toward the library. "Did you know they did a recent study on the earthquake preparedness of Memorial Library?"

"No. I've only been here a little over a month."

"Well, they did." Joel kept his gaze cast to the library and spoke to it. "Now, you'd think, looking at that concrete monstrosity, that nothing could budge it, that even in a 9.0 damage would be minimal." Emily waited. "So, they completed the study and came to the conclusion that they have no idea what would happen if an earthquake the magnitude of a nine, say, struck. No clue!" He threw up his arms in disbelief. "Would windows shatter and explode and tear through the bodies of students? Would the concrete fissure and the whole thing list and go down like the Twin Towers?"

"Pretty morbid, Joel. You're freaking me out."

"Well, we're down there on the bottom floor." He turned back to Emily. "You're only here for a few more months. I'm probably here for life. I don't want to be buried under all that concrete with Helena and Jean."

Emily laughed. "What're you saying, Joel?"

"There are earthquakes, Emily, and then there are earthquakes. Ones that cause the ground to tremble violently and topple civilizations. And ones that cause the collective psyche to tremble and implode from inside," he added enigmatically.

Their eyes met in a fusion of nascent conspiracy. Emily knew what he was metaphorizing, but she didn't want to scare him off her quest to find out everything she could before her time ran out. His eyes strayed away from her.

"I'm with you, Emily, all the way. Just keep me out of it. I want that film curator position." He brooded for a moment. "And I agree wholeheartedly, no fucking way Nadia drowned accidentally." Joel turned and walked up the rounded back of the anaconda. His tacit support of Emily's sleuthing was reassuring to her. For one wistful moment she wished he weren't a coworker. That was one of her hard-and-fast rules: no coworkers. She had witnessed too many breakups and awkward aftermaths, in one instance leading to a friend having to find another job and relocate to another city. Maybe Joel sensed this too. Or maybe Joel thought because she was only there for a limited time, on this one project, they could have a romantic interlude. But that wasn't Emily, not what Emily wanted. If she wanted to have an affair, she either wanted it to be a forgettable and fun youthful oblivion or something as intense and deep as what Nadia and Raymond were once desperately entangled in. Maybe Joel was lonely. Southern California, with its vast network of interconnecting freeways, the hours imprisoned in your car, the cheerless apartment complexes, and the total absence of a village-like culture, robbed your soul of meaning, reduced your life to one of isolation. One true friend could be a whole extended family.

Emily was deep in thought as she trudged uphill back to the library. Helena still wasn't in her office, and Jean—thank God!—was signed out for the day. Emily still had to worry about Chloe on her stealthy rubber-soled shoes sneaking up on her, but her cubicle was quiet. Ever since Joel's little lecture on the library's earthquake preparedness study, Emily felt the oppressive tonnage of all that concrete towering eight floors above her. Her worst fear would be the library imploding during an earthquake, entombing many in helpless silence, rescuers unable to reach them for days. She made a mental note to bring in an earthquake preparedness kit.

Emily switched on her computer and navigated to Google. In all lowercase lettering she typed "nadia fontaine drowning black's beach." She had performed this search before, but only out of professional curiosity. Now it took on a more profound aspect. Her pulse sped. Her intensity level was heightened. Several web pages of articles and clips of local newscasts bloomed on her screen. All were dated December 12. "Nadia Fontaine, Regents archivist, was found dead in the early morning hours at secluded Black's Beach . . ." "The County Coroner determined cause of death to be drowning . . ." "Surfing at night, archivist Nadia Fontaine apparently was strangled by her own surfboard leash, then drowned . . ." The newscast clips were from the early morning, when her body was discovered. In one, local news reporter Dave Atkinson—microphone gripped in one hand, head bent into the camera—was interviewing a Detective John Taggart with the San Diego Police Department. Taggart—Emily made a written note in her personal file—was saying that "the drowning is under investigation, but at this time we have no reason to believe that foul play was involved." The few obituaries Emily could find spoke highly, if too briefly, of Nadia Fontaine. Her university faculty picture showed that same serious, smoldering, decadent beauty of hers that Emily had seen in Joel's film, in photos sent to Raymond . . .

Emily froze the news segment with Detective Taggart. He was a world-weary Black man, looking out of place standing in a suit and tie on the beach. Behind him, lying on the sand, Nadia Fontaine's body was draped with a sheet. Gloved forensics personnel were still completing their investigatory work, taking photos, sifting for clues. Emily found herself stroking the armrests and staring down at her office chair, realizing that the woman under that sheet had only eight months ago probably been sitting in the same chair, surreptitiously typing emails to Raymond West, aflame with desire. A wave of nausea stirred up in Emily's stomach. She remembered the part in *My Story* that brought back to life the happy moments Nadia spent with Raymond West at his secret hideaway, the now derelict bungalow which at one time glowed with the fires of creativity inside. If it wasn't an accidental drowning, as Joel indignantly dismissed, was it suicide? Did the university want to cover that up? Because surely suicide had the potential, if investigated, to lead to the affair, to Raymond West, to his wife Elizabeth . . .

Emily grabbed her purse and fled her cubicle. With a hand clutching her collarbone, she rushed across the main floor, gulping air. No, no, no, she wasn't going to have a panic attack. She rooted in her sweater vest pocket for the vial of Xanax, unscrewed the cap, fingered one out, and pulverized it under her tongue. It would take at least twenty minutes to quell the escalating anxiety, but at least relief was just over the horizon. The nausea in her stomach, however, wasn't panic. It was a whole other palpable level of dread and sickness now manifesting in her body.

Emily eschewed the elevators and the *bing bing* at every floor, which she knew was going to drive her batshit, and entered the stairwell. Her heels pounded on the hollow metal steps and echoed up the enormous cylindrical concrete shaft. She deliberately kept her gaze on her feet as she trudged up, one hand now holding her stomach, her throat constricted, refusing to glance left to the increasingly longer fall to the bottom floor. If she looked down, she knew she would be overcome with vertigo and she knew she would throw up, and if someone found her and called Security and they came, everyone in the fucking library would know. For all she knew, a campaign might already be underway to replace her. As Helena had threatened, Elizabeth had that authority, given it was her money funding a project archivist to finish up the processing of her husband's papers. Emily had to make it to that top floor! She had to make it to that private, one-person, all-gender bathroom, lock herself in, and sort out this mounting anxiety.

It seemed like every step led to another step and it was forever before she summited the final platform and located the heavy door with a big number 8 painted on it in bright red. Her thighs burned. Lightheadedness accelerated her heart rate. The image of the dead Nadia under that sheet was burned into her memory now like a flesh-sizzling cattle brand.

Finally, she burst out onto the eighth floor into an explosion of sunlight. Her nervous system was staging a rebellion. She rounded the central pillar to the bathrooms on the other side. Thank God the first one she tried was vacant. She locked herself in the small gloomy room and plopped down on the toilet without undoing her pants. A thunderstorm of tears exploded in her eyes. She gulped air in frantic inhalations, her head rocking violently up and down. She clutched her mouth with her hand and desperately attempted to suppress her hysterical weeping. Tears puddled in her eyes like a hemorrhage beyond the reach of placation or cautery and spilled down the sides of her face like two miniature waterfalls. She was suddenly aware of cawing sounds issuing from her mouth through the diffusion of her fingers as if an angry crow were tearing at her entrails. Emily sat huddled like that in a contorted, overwrought state, trying to contain her emotional outburst. She was wracked in sobs, and her whole body was convulsing like some mortally wounded animal in the process of dying and petrified of the beyond. And then, as if she had crested this awful outburst, just as quickly as the nausea and tears had sprung upon her, they passed. The pill's effects had launched into her bloodstream, and she could feel her breathing normalizing. The nausea receded like an ebbing tide, leaving her feeling raw and exposed.

Drained, she climbed slowly to her feet, one hand gripping the handicapped wall mount for support. She bent toward the mirror and inspected her tearstained face. Her eyes were splotched red, and her mascara had smeared. She gaped horrified at her distraught doppelgänger, not recognizing herself for the first time in her twenty-seven years. She dabbed at her face with toilet tissue and, fearing another paroxysm of emotion, attempted heroically to regroup, not wanting to return to the cubicles in an overt display of emotional dishabille. She chuckled at something someone had once told her, quoting Elizabeth Taylor, "Pour yourself a drink, put on some lipstick, and pull yourself together."

Badly shaken, she applied some lipstick, turned the latch to unlock the bathroom, and stepped out into the punishing bright light of the eighth floor with the slow, halting steps of someone whom tragedy had taken hold of, shell-shocked, weighted down with torment and emptied of tears. Not ready to return to her cubicle, she rummaged in her purse for her sunglasses and drifted across the wide empty space previously occupied by dense rows of book shelving and study carrels. She plopped down into one of the remaining upholstered chairs at the window and gazed west as if in a trance. A dense fog was streaming in off the ocean, advancing on the cliffs and pouring through the dense forest of eucalyptus trees like a ghost tsunami, wreathing the university in mystery. The still-exposed buildings jutted upward like a floating city, a modern-day lost Atlantis in the process of sinking into the lethe of history.

Feeling disquieted, Emily rose shakily from the chair. As if crossing the enormity of a battlefield in ashen-faced incredulity as the sole survivor, she made her way back around to the stairwell, carrying the radioactive weight of the Nadia/Raymond affair and its unknown consequences in the fragile repository of her psyche. The antianxiety med had ameliorated the panic, but queasiness still plagued her stomach like an etched memory of mortification that wouldn't go away.

Emily felt wobbly on her legs as she stepped into the stairwell. Descending back to Special Collections, she couldn't help but look down the eight-floor cone of emptiness. Only a two-bar railing, easily scaled, prevented someone from putting themselves out of their misery. That homeless man Joel told her about had done precisely that the week before she started her job. It must have looked inviting to him, Emily mordantly mused, as she cleaved to the shaft's wall and began the downward spiral of stairs, pausing at some of the landings to collect herself, as if in a giant centrifuge and being spun in her fear by a powerful gravitational force.

She crossed the main floor on unsteady legs, jostled now by students, in orientation mode for the fall quarter, moving in a constant stream perpendicular to her. She smiled a hi to Samantha at the reference desk, whose nose was buried in a bestseller Emily would never deign to read. Back in her cubicle she shut down her computer and turned off the lights. She had to get out of the library. Its eight floors were suffocating her. With no Helena or Jean in the department, no one would know she'd left early, so her spirit lifted. She felt something hard in her vest pocket and she thrust a hand inside. It was the ouroboros necklace Raymond had clasped around Nadia's neck. She tried it on. Fingered the figure eight of the snake devouring its tail. Coming full circle. Rebirth. She needed to be reborn, delivered from this narrative that had taken her into the depths of her being like no other challenge she had encountered in her short life.

Emily drove home, vowing to herself to give the correspondence in the dark archives a rest for the night. Seeing Nadia in the naughty videos only exacerbated her dismay. She wouldn't email Chloe and cancel. She would go out. It was Friday night. She would have fun, or at least pretend to have fun. Hell, maybe Clint would be cute. He didn't work at the library. According to Chloe's boyfriend he was a literary snob. Well, we'll see about that, Emily thought, as she pulled into her parking space and climbed out of her car.

The Xanax knocked her out and Emily fell into a broken sleep of disquieting dreams abruptly interrupted by the sound of her alarm. Daylight was still bleeding through the curtains, but the sky was painted orange as the sun sat perched on the horizon when she sauntered out into the living room, rubbing her eyes with the palms of her hands. She fed a hungry Onyx his favorite can of tuna, then showered. Emily was decisive when it came to her attire. She selected a black, button-down sweater and allowed one extra open button, teasingly exposing the cleft between her breasts. If someone taller than her looked down, he would be able to make out the color of her bra. She matched it with her black cigarette felt jeans and ankle-high boots to boost her up to five foot seven from five five. She said to hell with any makeup—she would save that for the Annex disguise!—and instead ran two thick lush lines of lipstick over her protruding lips. In the end she broke down and applied a little mascara in order to keep the guy's focus in the event she sensed even the semblance of a connection.

Emily stood back from the mirror appraisingly, imagining she looked chic. Arty spiked pixie cut, a ripple of muscles bulging inconspicuously in the tight sweater. Glasses or no glasses? Contacts? In the end she opted for glasses. It was a defensive choice, a bit of a deliberate paradoxical contrast to the sensual cleavage. Finally, she cavalierly looped Nadia's ouroboros around her neck and clasped it closed. The snake consuming its tail hung around her neck like a talismanic charm. His eyes would travel there for sure, she thought. And he would ask. And, like a tattoo conversation starter, she could regale him with her knowledge of Jung and that would either alienate him or challenge him to determine if he was a true intellectual or another pathetic poseur.

Dressed as pretty as she had been in months, Emily drove with her car windows open up the coast in the direction of Encinitas. She put on her mixtape of '80s classics—OMD, the Cure—and found herself singing out loud to music that was composed and danced to before she was born.

The Coast Highway snaked along the ocean through the seaside hamlets of Solana Beach, Cardiff, then into Encinitas. The water in the two lagoons she passed were winding ribbons of gold between dark swatches of reeds.

The ocean was dotted with the silhouettes of wet-suited surfers on placid waters of darkening blue. San Diego North County seemed to be in a perpetual cycle of surfing and work, work and surfing.

Coasting into Encinitas, announced by a banner hung over the road, on hopeful wings, Emily was afforded her last view of the ocean as she passed by Swami's Point, named after a Buddhist retreat that occupied its cliffs. Encinitas had once been a haven for surfers bunked four to an apartment, but progress, the lure of living in Southern California, the relentless sprawl of Los Angeles, and the ability to work remotely and not have to be tethered to a city as ugly and gridlocked with traffic as LA, had gentrified it. There were still surfers, but they were now coders with six-figure salaries. The Coast Highway split local businesses on both sides into indulgences to attract the new millennial wealth: hair salons, trendy restaurants, day spas, antique stores . . . It was all generic, Emily sneered, utterly unimaginative. Where were the movie theaters and the bookstores, or the playhouses? She was ready for an argument with her date. Date? Was that what it was? A thrill suffused Emily suddenly and she started singing out loud to the music, directing her voice out the car window at the top of her lungs. Maybe she would give herself away for one night, what the hell? As Nadia had written, "I want to live intensely; I want to feel alive."

Solace & the Moonlight Lounge was situated next to the train tracks in the heart of Encinitas. Night had fallen by the time Emily arrived. The restaurant/bar was on two levels. As she approached the entrance her sensitive aural canals were assaulted by a cacophony of voices and music pouring down from the upper level.

A hostess, a few years younger than Emily, greeted her with a white-toothed smile, carefully crafted by a week's job orientation. "Party of one?"

"No, I'm just meeting some friends."

"Cute necklace," she complimented.

"Thank you."

Emily mounted the wooden stairs and climbed them with clunking steps. The décor was all planks and timber, as if Midwest barn met Pacific Ocean in a marine-themed bric-a-brac production design. Emily was greeted at the top of the stairs by yet another hostess. She had to raise her voice over the noise in order to be heard in the crowded room. "Just looking for some friends," Emily half shouted through cupped hands.

"Enjoy." The second young host smiled occupationally.

Emily stepped around the host's stand and scanned the beautiful zinc bar that flanked the east-facing side of the upstairs. The loud, bass-driven music came up into her legs through the floor and, with a few guys throwing her appraising looks, gave her an evanescent thrill of femininity. She didn't see Chloe right away. The capacious room with the high-beamed ceiling was ringed with tables. The west-facing wall opened to the night in a romance of more candlelit tables. Planted stolidly in the center of the raftered room was a long, thick, communal table designed out of more wavy, resined timber. Through the dark, Emily caught a woman's arm flung out and motioning like a traffic cop. Chloe.

Emily weaved her way through the crowd to the elbow of the table where Chloe, flashing a big smile because she knew Clint would be happy with Jesse's offering, and how Emily—usually seen in white button-up shirts and gray fleece vests—had turned herself out into the kind of attractive, if intellectual and serious, woman who men couldn't pry their eyes from.

"Over here," Chloe shouted over the din of the popular eatery.

Emily jostled her way across a row of patrons in their twenties and thirties until she reached the elbow of the baronially long table. Clint, a tall, rangy man in his early thirties with shoulder-length dark hair and sideburns like stirrups hanging on his face, stood up with an almost embarrassed smile at his good fortune and gallantly pulled out a stool for Emily.

"This is Clint, Jesse's business partner," Chloe enthused, thrilled to see Clint's crooked grin of excitement.

Emily thrust out her hand. "Hey."

Clint took it, almost as if it were an injured bird he was caressing, shook it with one hand, but closed a second over it reverentially as if to assure her when he said, "It's a pleasure, I've heard so much about you."

"Yeah, like what?" Emily asked over the hubbub, hoping she didn't sound obnoxious, but feeling feisty.

Chloe, a few drinks into eventual intoxication, interfered. "Clint works with Jesse at the distillery."

"Oh, right," Emily pretended to remember.

"Hi, Emily," Jesse said, leaning forward and throwing her a friendly wave from a propped elbow.

Emily swirled down onto the stool Clint had politely pulled out. She wriggled it closer to the table. She didn't feel like going through the motions of conversation. Deliberately histrionically, she pounded her fist on the timbered table and declared, "I need a drink!"

"All right." Clint clapped his hands in front of his pleasantly rubicund face, as if the day at the distillery wasn't all work lifting kegs or whatever they did that Emily didn't give a shit about.

Chloe, the flaunting extrovert, waved to one of the servers, who bustled over with an urgency born of duty. He had marcelled blond locks, dyed by too much exposure to salt water, and a face bronzed by a boyhood squandered in too much sun.

"What can I get you?" he leaned down and asked Emily.

"Why don't you try one of our absinthes?" suggested Clint.

"Yeah, and we'll get another round of oysters," Chloe filled in. "Do you like oysters?" Chloe asked Emily.

"Yeah, sure, why not," Emily said, liberated by the wall of noise that didn't trigger her misophonia, and animated by the company she hadn't enjoyed, other than Joel's, since she first moved to San Diego. And after she got warmed up on a few drinks, if Clint didn't say anything too aesthetically stupid, she might even be able to overlook those Paul Bunyan sideburns and envision a fun date, ending who knows where.

"Fucking bring on the absinthes!" Emily hollered, looking daringly alive.

"All right, my kind of girl," Clint gleamed.

Emily studied her drinks menu with an exaggerated furrowed brow, then slapped it on the communal table. "And a stout to back it up."

Clint raised his beer. "TGIF."

Chloe was wild-eyed with excitement. She was one of those fun girls on the weekend, and she had that look to Emily like she had scored a coup in getting the aloof and occupationally distant Emily to break out of her shell. As Chloe turned to her right to elbow Jesse, as if to say it was going auspiciously, Clint swung his big head to Emily with his sweet, sad face and retro barbering.

"Chloe tells me you're an ar*chi*vist."

"*Ar*-kuh-vist," Emily hastened to correct.

"Huh?"

"*Ar*-kuh-vist, not ar-*kive*-ist. Accent on the first syllable."

"*Ar*-kuh-vist. Okay," parroted an amiably chastened Clint.

"Everybody gets the pronunciation wrong, don't they, Chloe?" Emily shouted across to her.

Chloe raised her mug of beer. "Nobody understands what we do. So, I long ago stopped explaining." This elicited chuckles from Jesse and Clint, but not Emily. Why disparage the profession? The banality of the conversation was already boring her.

Just in time to rescue her mood, their drinks arrived. Dark beers in frosted refrigerated mugs and shot glasses of an apple-green liqueur materialized on the table. A second server materialized bearing trays of shucked oysters packed in crushed ice.

Emily, nervous, unaccustomed to socializing, energy bottled up in stress and the secret world of West and Nadia and the Moleskines of *The Archivist*, reached for one of the shot glasses of absinthe, held it up to the bar lights, turned it around in her hand and studied it with narrowed, interpretive eyes.

"It's real wormwood we import from Czechoslovakia," Jesse explained.

Emily put the shot glass to her lips, tossed her head back and performatively drained it in one gulp. She chased it with an oyster. A quaff from the mug of beer left a moustache of foam on her upper lip that she less than daintily forearmed off.

"Whoa, there, Ms. *Ar*chivist," reproved Clint, rearing back a little. "That's one hundred proof. That'll get you shithoused in a hurry."

"Good." Emily slammed the shot glass onto the timber. "I've had a stressful week. I need some action."

Clint and Jesse exchanged bulging frog eyes.

"Emily's working on the Raymond West Papers," Chloe explained. "She's under a big deadline."

"Raymond West," began Clint in a drawl, twisting his long sideburns in thought, "he's a famous writer, isn't he?"

"Hell, yeah, he's famous," hollered Emily, the absinthe already launched into her bloodstream and racing to her head. "Short-listed for the fucking Nobel. He wins that," she continued, reaching recklessly for another shot glass of absinthe and draining it, "your library here in San Diego is going to be a magnet for scholars from all over the world." She flung out an arm in a grand flourish to indicate the imaginary world she was defining. The two shots were warming her up. She could feel the ground slipping beneath her and she liked the feeling. Everything that had been bundled up inside her seemed pushed away, shoved into the corner, replaced by a pleasantness where dreams felicitously swirled and romance was simple. This was a new space where she could be herself again.

"Clint," Emily said, grinning loosely at him, "what do you do over there at the dis-till-ery?" She was already slurring a little.

"Well, Jesse and I distill high-end booze. All-natural ingredients. Not that commercial junk."

"Sounds like a noble ambition," Emily enthused. "The world needs organic distillates."

"Are you making fun?" he asked, rearing back and squinting at her.

"No, I'm serious." She reached for her third shot of absinthe. "This stuff's fucking awesome." She tossed it back with uncharacteristic abandon.

Clint turned to Chloe and Jesse and raised his eyebrows in excitement, or concern, it was hard to tell. "This chick's cool," he said to them turned away from Emily.

The server returned, smiling nirvanically, as if he slept the night at the Self-Realization Fellowship Temple overlooking Swami's. "Can I bring anyone some more appetizers?"

Chloe spoke up. "We're going to have two of the seafood platters."

"And more absinthe!" said Emily.

"Okay, coming right up," replied the server.

"Slow down there, Emily." Clint touched her forearm with comforting fingers.

"Don't tell me to slow down. I want to feel alive. I can drink all of you under the table."

"Okay," Clint said, grinning warily at the sexy, increasingly inebriated Emily, now pressed up against his shoulder in the crowded room.

Emily reached up a hand, grabbed the sideburn nearest her and tugged at it. "And if I have trouble walking, I'll just hang on to your sideburns and steady myself."

"Be my guest."

Emily released his sideburn. She realized she hadn't touched a man intimately in months. The feel of his facial hair remotely excited her. Pent-up energy she had repressed, energy that had vented like a pressure cooker exploding when she suffered her panic attack, was now gathering turbulently inside her. She was feeling herself growing aggressive. A sudden fantasy to attack Clint amorously with sloppy kisses fulgurated across her mind, but she managed to restrain herself.

The seafood platters arrived, high on open palms in a bit of fanfare, a colorful plentitude of raw and cooked seafood: shrimp, mussels, oysters, lobster. A pitcher of dark stout sloshed in front of the four of them. Shots of absinthe were replenished with alacrity. Talk ranged from surfing to the production of distillates. Emily could feel her face flushing, her words bolting ahead of her thoughts like a runaway horse. She was feeling exultant. In her tight jeans and low-cut sweater, her body had started to perspire a little. Something was flowering. Voices rose and fell in volume in the noise of Friday night revelers. Drunkenness was a matter of degrees. Maybe Emily wanted to get drunk to lose self-awareness. When she wasn't talking, she was belted by erotic flashes of Nadia and Raymond fucking passionately in all the places she'd quarried from their emails. When she was talking, she found herself free-soloing to the rim of belligerence. She threw back shots with increased intemperance. Instead of making her embarrassingly sloppy, the absinthes seemed to energize her—fire her up! Another woman rose out of her tiny frame: a fun woman, an assertive devil-may-care woman, a woman who could kiss a man in public and not give a damn, maybe flash her breasts and shock the hell out of everyone. She was feeling dangerous, unleashed, pawing the dirt in advance of bolting headlong into the void. The unconscious was displaying its contents, animating them, volcanically spewing them to the surface, and over the rim, and into the world!

"Pour me another absinthe," Emily demanded, slamming her empty shot glass down on the table. At the request of Jesse and Clint, the bartender, a friend, had brought over their company's antique bottle to show Emily. And from its thick, wavy blown glass, they poured Emily another lethal green shot.

Emily held up the bottle and inspected it with bleary eyes, moving the bottle in and out to find a point of true focus. "This is a cool bottle."

Clint blushed. "Thanks."

Emily set it down and reached for her fifth shot glass of absinthe. Or was it her seventh! "And this quaff is awesome." In one motion, she threw back her head and the shot glass. She followed it with another mouthful of stout, slurped an oyster unrepentantly, shook her head with exaggeration, then reached for another oyster.

"Chloe tells me you're a big reader of books?" Clint tried to make conversation and normalize the bacchanal.

"Yeah. I am."

"What're you reading these days?"

"These days I'm reading"—Emily paused because she realized a truthful answer was about to be the biggest mistake of her life—"Uh . . .uh, I'm seriously deep into the West Papers and don't have time for recreational reading, but I dip in and out of *Le Rêve d'un Flagellant*. Do you know it? Maurice de Vindas."

Clint shook his head. Her French accent distanced him a little. Emily could see that he was one of those San Diego guys who kind of liked smart women but hopefully not too smart.

"You read French?" he inquired.

"*Oui!*" Emily squealed.

"What's it about?" he asked.

From the far side, Jesse and rosy-faced Chloe leaned in, eager to hear Emily's sophistic explication.

"Well," Emily started. "It's erotica. BDSM."

"BDSM, what's that?" Clint asked.

"Bondage, domination, sadism, and masochism."

"Oh, you mean like de Sade?"

"*Absolutment!*"

"Are you into that?" Clint asked, more out of curiosity than judgment.

Emily shrugged. "I'm fascinated by people who live at the edge. I love people who live intensely. Isn't that what life is?" She raised a stiff index finger to the ceiling to gather everyone's attention. Their heads leaned in so they could hear. "'Would you rather love the more and suffer the more, or love the less and suffer the less? That is, I think, finally, the only real question.'" They blinked wordlessly at her in thoughtful stupefaction. "Julian Barnes."

"Who's he?" Clint asked.

"British novelist. Man Booker winner." Emily took another eye-popping quaff and slammed her mug of stout on the table with a loud blow, then grinned in their faces.

"Okay. Got to think about that." Chloe and Jesse nodded in thoughtful concurrence.

Realizing she might be alienating him, Emily tried to reel Clint back in by raising his proud bottle of absinthe. "Like your absinthe here." She poured a little more into her shot glass. Everyone marveled at her tolerance. She leaned in close to his face and slurred, "It's in-tense."

"And clearly you love the more," Clint joked at Emily's expense. Laughter exploded from Chloe and Jesse.

"That's right," Emily agreed, chin raised defiantly upward, reaching for her refilled shot glass.

"And you will suffer the more if you keep drinking at that pace," Jesse tossed in. More amiable laughter exploded. As if she were a distilled beverage critic, Emily concentrated on her shot glass with narrowed eyes and turtled for a moment, absorbing solitary offense at not being taken seriously. She rehearsed a rain of sardonic insults and then smiled them away.

After an awkward ellipsis, Emily faced Clint and peered at him through slightly fogged glasses. Her engines were revving up, and he was looking more handsome in that lumberjack flannel and that muscle-bulging hard body of his. "What are you reading these days . . . *Clint*?"

"Well," he began, "I'm reading Tom Robbins's *Even Cowgirls Get the Blues*. Do you know it?"

"Hippie rubbish!" declaimed Emily. "Couldn't get through it. Drivel!"

Clint withdrew his head, not accustomed to having his taste in books blatantly, and trenchantly, skewered. There were thresholds for Emily. In literature. In film. In her mind she saw no future in a guy reading Tom Robbins, but she could probably sleep with him if she were horny enough. Such designs were forming madly in her whirligig of a brain, as the absinthe coursed in her blood, and a kind of rage against her loneliness waged war inside her.

"Didn't mean to insult you," Emily backpedaled. She noticed her hand patting Clint on his hairy, manly forearm, as if her hand were disembodied and someone else other than her had initiated the conciliatory gesture. Then, even more shocking to her, she found her hand climbing up his arm and, forming a claw, gripping his biceps. "You've got nice arms." Emily looked up into Clint's face with a sloppy expression. "I apologize for being too harshly opinionated."

"That's okay." Clint risked a hand grazing her hand touching his biceps.

Chloe intuited that this was the moment to disengage and let the matchmaking proceed apace. She stood up from her stool, Jesse mimicking her action. "We're going to take off," Chloe announced over the pounding music.

Emily noticed Jesse circling the air with a forefinger to Clint, indicating something about the bill. Clint nodded confidently, as if, *no worries, thanks for the intro.*

"Okay, guys," Clint said.

"Have fun, you two." Chloe waved. "See you at work Monday, Emily." She hooked her arm in Jesse's, and they disappeared into the now three-deep crowd thronged at the bar clamoring for drinks.

Clint tilted his head down at Emily. "You know, you're kind of an obnoxious snob, but you're paradoxically sexy, too."

"I've lived my whole life in academia. My mom was a professor. You have to hold your own where I come from," Emily explained in an apologetic tone. She looked up at him seductively. "Do you like to explore, Clint?"

He gazed down at her. "You mean BDSM?"

Emily widened her eyes and flashed a risqué smile.

"I'm an open-minded guy." Clint winked.

Their mouths were close. His breath smelled of absinthe and impeccably clean raw fish. She thought of Nadia and Raymond skinny-dipping at night, and she reached around behind Clint's head and pulled his mouth toward hers, met his lips and plunged a tongue into his mouth. She released him like a tuna on a taut line, and his head snapped back in astonishment, bewilderment, and excitement. He smiled at her.

Emily reached for her shot glass and held it up. "To Baudelaire. Who went down with absinthe!" She drained it, closed her eyes tight, and shook her head.

"I think you mean Coleridge," Clint corrected.

"No, Baudelaire! Coleridge was into opium."

"I think you're wrong there, Ms. Smarty Pants," Clint countered playfully.

"I'm never wrong," Emily replied aggressively. "Archivists are the best researchers in the world." She rummaged around frantically in her purse, produced her cell, googled with the efficiency of all archivists, found Baudelaire on Wikipedia, zoomed the text so that bleary-eyed Clint could read it, and shoved the screen into his face. "Baudelaire. Absinthe. Coleridge. Opium."

"Okay." Clint held up both hands in mock surrender.

Emily remembered pouring more absinthe, spilling it over the rim of her shot glass. Then came the ellipses in her memory, the blackout lacunae. Clint paid the bill and helped her shambling, limp figure out of Solace & the Moonlight Lounge. Raucous laughter and more obstinate argumentation burst from Emily as they clomped down the stairs to street level. She walked on spraddled legs out onto Coast Highway, Clint holding her by the elbow to keep her from falling. They stopped and kissed one more time. This time she could feel his whole body pressing against her, and it felt big and exciting. The night air reawakened her, reawakened the dormant woman in her. She remembered the streetlamps, the yellow pools of light, and the total absence of cars. And urging Clint, "Let's go into the Daley Double Saloon. I heard it's cool. Heard they got bands. I want to dance."

"No, I got to get you home," Clint was saying solicitously.

"You're no fun."

"Where's your car?" Clint asked.

"Over there." Emily threw out an arm like a dead snake, whirled around and almost toppled over in the middle of the street.

"No, no, no, you're not driving," Clint said, bending down to help her up.

"You're not driving," Emily said. "I got my own car. Zoom zoom."

"Yes, I am driving. I was pacing myself. Cops up here will ruin your night."

Emily slurred, "Alll rigghhhtt, Clinty."

Clint, with an arm now slung around Emily's torso, walked her to his retro 1968 Ford truck. He opened the passenger door and hoisted her up and in with strong arms. Emily rolled down the window and rested her head on her forearm and looked ahead at the empty road like a dog sticking its head out the window and panting for fresh air.

Clint shifted through the gears of his truck old school as they drove down a desolate Coast Highway.

"This is a cool truck." Emily banged the outside of the door with an open hand. She swung her body loosely and wildly to him. "This your buddy?"

Clint slapped his hand on the dashboard. "Yep, this is my buddy."

"Bet you got a dog at home too?"

"Yep. How'd you know?"

Emily leaned over and grabbed his arm with both of her smaller ones and hugged him. She tugged playfully at his sideburns, yanked them a tad too hard, then bit his shoulder.

"Hey," protested Clint. "Tell me where you live, Ms. *Ar*-kuh-vist."

Emily threw out a loose-limbed arm toward the windshield but miscalculated the distance and her hand struck the glass. "Ow. Just keep going down here. I'm right on the Coast Highway."

"Okay. Let me know when we get there." Clint reached over and grabbed her hand. "Hurt?"

"No," said Emily coyly. "Not if you kiss it." She offered her hand. Clint, growing confused, kissed it.

"Better?" he asked.

"Getting there."

Clint kissed her hand again, and Emily pierced his lips with two fingers and felt the wet warmth of his mouth. "This is what it must feel like to have a cock in a woman, huh?" Emily slurred, her face disorganized from all the absinthe.

"I don't know what you're feeling." Clint gently removed her fingers from his mouth.

She slipped her mouth to his ear. "It feels like *this*." Emily thrust her tongue into his ear and mauled it as if she were an animal eating it ravenously. Then, mercurially, her moods flashing fickle and unpredictable, she pulled away and threw her head out the window again. Clint thought she was preparing to vomit. Instead, Emily extended an arm into the night and erected a middle finger, "Fuck you, San Diego!"

"Hey, Emily. Chill."

Emily muttered "Sorry," and went quiet. Just as the alcohol had uninhibited her and rocketed her up to a plane of false exaltation, it now lowered her down into a state of disheartenment. She was riding shotgun in the truck of a nice guy who was a friend of the boyfriend of a coworker. Her car was abandoned because she was too drunk to drive, and she would have to Uber back in the morning to retrieve it. The roadside establishments, most of them closed, flew by in a blur of Southern California emptiness. Surf shops, taco shacks, realty offices, New Age claptrap, a slide show of cultural bankruptcy. The only thing that had given her life meaning since taking this project archivist assignment was her total immersion in the West Papers. And stumbling headlong into the passionately romantic correspondence in the dark archives. A trapdoor had sprung, and the new earth had drawn her, captivated beyond anything in her life heretofore, down into the darkness, without a flashlight, without a road map. New territory. The outside world, the world outside her imagination, was the one foreign to her. Solace & the Moonlight Lounge with coworker Chloe, and now this Clint guy giving her a ride home.

"Pull in here," she heard herself saying with a wildly motioning arm.

Clint pulled into the apartment complex's parking lot and let his truck idle.

"Number eleven." Emily gestured to her empty parking space.

Clint coasted into it and shut off the engine. He got out of the car, circled around, and opened the door for Emily. She fell into his arms like an injured baby deer. Lonely suddenly, she rose to meet his mouth. The kiss adrenalized her, and scalding blood surged to her head. She didn't want to feel depressed and lonely. She didn't want to go to bed all alone with her cat. I'm twenty-seven years old, damn it! she caviled in her head. I want to live a life of passion like my predecessor.

"Who's Nadia?" Emily thought she remembered Clint asking as he half carried her along the walkway to her unit.

"Forget it," she remembered waving him off.

Clint had to wrest the keys from her stubborn fingers to open the sliding glass door because Emily's drunken, fumbling attempts were unsuccessful. They bustled inside, as if cast in from a storm.

"You want a beer?" Emily asked, finding a second wind.

"Sure," said Clint, looking around. "Nice place."

"Yeah." Emily went into the kitchen, clanked two beers noisily out of the refrigerator, thrust one out to Clint, now standing in the kitchen, looking dreamily down into her eyes. She didn't wait. She lifted up on her tiptoes and kissed him lustily.

"We need some fucking music!" She circled around him, found her computer, opened a music app and somehow managed to begin playing songs from the '80s out of a speaker. Onyx darted out from under the kitchen table, scampered into the second bedroom, and hid.

Emily, holding her bottle of beer in one hand, started dancing. Clint observed with questioning eyes. "Come on. Dance with me, Clint."

"I don't dance." He raised his beer to his lips.

"Oh, come on." Clint shook his head. He pointed to a whiteboard with Emily's writing on it. "What's this?" he asked.

Reality smashed Emily in the face. If she wasn't drunk, she would have remembered a week ago buying a dual-sided whiteboard and some dry-erase markers from a nearby Best Buy and, in an effort to make sense of her labyrinthian journey through the emails of Nadia and Raymond, fashioned an adumbration of a timeline. At the top she wrote "Nadia" and "Raymond" and underlined their names. There were dates, details about their clandestine assignations, intersecting lines, other interspersing dramatis personae and crisscrossing lines. The Faculty Club meeting, the dates of the first emails, arrows drawn, a veritable blueprint of their affair. Emily suddenly woke to the possibility that Clint could tell Jesse; and Jesse, Chloe—her privacy violated. She flipped the whiteboard over. The other side was blank.

"What were all those dates? And who's Nadia?"

"It's work-related," Emily explained loudly.

"And I saw the words 'torrid affair.'"

"None of your business, Clint." Emily pressed her back to the whiteboard.

"Come on, let me see," he protested, taking a step toward her.

"No!" She threw out her arms like the wings of a caged raptor, as if that would obscure the whiteboard from view.

"Are you like writing a novel or something?" he asked, looking at her out of the corners of both eyes as if pretending she was this reclusive, mysterious genius.

"Yeah, I'm writing a novel, okay? It's titled *The Archivist*. They're all my characters. And a writer should never talk about what she's writing until she's ready to show it!"

"Okay. Cool. Sorry," said Clint, raising both hands, fingers splayed.

Emily came forward and threw her body at him again, hoping he would forget about the whiteboard, because if anyone knew . . . ! He kissed her back. Okay, Emily thought, he's more into the kissing. She collapsed to her knees and started rubbing her hands over his bulging groin. "Oh, you're fucking hard, aren't you?"

Clint placed a hand on her head, not to encourage her, but to pull her up, more confused and apprehensive than turned on. "Emily . . ."

"Come on, you want your cock sucked; you know it." She reached out her hands to unbuckle his belt. Clint let her, but also semi-tried to discourage her. Either the powerful absinthe or the loneliness or the turbulent hormones that exposed all her nerve endings and left her damp with desire and open for exploration reignited her aggressiveness, and she was able, against his tame expostulations, to get his belt undone and his jeans unzipped. She reached around him and grabbed the waistband of his pants and yanked them down. With one hand she slapped his flanks. Her hands then flew back to his underwear and she snaked a hand down into his crotch and pulled them down. She got hold of his cock in the fist of her tiny hand, and it sprang into her mouth.

"Emily," Clint sighed, with pleasure, but clearly conflicted.

"Come on, you want your cock sucked," she said, staring at it, the first one she had seen and felt in months. She desperately wanted it inside her to trigger that rainstorm, that storm inside carrying her away, raining out all the stress and tension of the past weeks.

"I want to be fucked," she announced, drunkenly determined.

"Emily."

"No, come on, Clint, let me suck it. Please." He relaxed and let her suck his cock.

Suddenly, as if inspired by a dark impulse implanted by Nadia, she whipped the belt out of his loops and ordered, "Get into the bedroom."

"What?" said Clint. She showed him the coiled belt. *BDSM time?* he wondered mischievously.

She kneed him in the thigh. "Get into the bedroom. Come on." She brandished his belt and again nudged him with her knee in the direction of the bedroom.

Clint—twin emotions of thrill and fear warring inside him—complied, and they hurtled down a short hall and into the bedroom. Emily pushed him onto the bed, and he toppled willingly, wide-eyed with bemused anticipation.

"Turn over!" she commanded with belt brandished.

"Wha—"

"Turn over!"

Clint, looking confused, rolled over until his ass was facing her. With a ferociousness she had never possessed before, she turned to his exposed ass. She gripped the belt by the buckle, took a wide stance, and whacked him with all thirty-six inches of it.

"Ow!" exclaimed Clint, throwing her a backward look of genuine terror.

She whipped him again with all the repressed frustration in her being and raised a red welt on his backside like a swollen river of coagulated blood. Channeling Nadia from her most perfervid emails to Raymond, she yelled over the Psychedelic Furs, "I want to live intensely. I want to fuck intensely. I want to open doors that have never been opened before!" *Thwack.* "Get your fucking ass out there." *Thwack.*

"Ow!" Clint didn't know what to do. He reached around and rubbed his swollen buttocks.

"I'm going to climb you; I'm going to ride you; I'm going to fuck you like you've never been fucked in your life," sputtered a wild-eyed Emily, "and you're never going to leave me!" *Thwack.*

This time Clint leaped up from the bed. "You're fucking wack, Emily."

He stood on the other side of the bed, pulling up his underwear and pants and hurriedly buttoning the fly. He circled around the bed. He was now indifferent to the prospect of getting laid, resolute about escape, assuming charge. "Give me my belt."

Something imploded in Emily. With an outstretched hand she compliantly handed him back his belt, and he snatched it from her as if she might use it on him again. Emily collapsed to the edge of the bed. Both hands went to her eyes and she started crying in hot shame. "Just go, please," she said in a plaintive voice, not angrily or wounded that she had been rejected, but more in abject humiliation than anything else. From behind fist-blind eyes she heard the scuffle of footfalls. The sliding glass door opened and then closed shut. A lock latched. When her apartment had fallen silent, Emily rose slowly to her feet, walked somnambulantly into the living room, and killed the music. An orchestra of frogs croaked from the man-made pond on the terrace of the apartment below hers. She returned to the bedroom and crawled under the covers as if into a sleeping bag, the sheets and comforter all twisted around her.

Emily woke in the dead of night. She glanced at her phone. It read 3:11 a.m. Fuck, she thought. She raised a hand to her forehead. It was damp with perspiration. Her hair was matted and clung to the sides of her face like jam. She discovered to her dismay she was still in her clothes from the night before and her whole body was sweaty. Sticky and bedraggled, she gripped her head in the vise of her hand and pressed hard. The pressure headache from all the absinthe felt like someone pounding a sledgehammer against a pier piling underwater. Her mouth was parched, and she thirsted for water.

Hurting everywhere, Emily crept out of bed and slipped across the tiled floor into the kitchen. In the refrigerator she grabbed a flavored green tea drink and drank until she felt sufficiently hydrated. Her head was throbbing murderously. Onyx was curled up on the couch in the living room, still processing the previous night's unplanned events in his limited sentience. He looked up at Emily with an expression of empathetic consternation. He sensed something was out of order.

Emily paused at the whiteboard that she had begun a week before, inspired by Jean's timeline whiteboard and wanting a countervailing representation of the West Collection to keep her sane. She slowly flipped it over. Clint's naive glimpse of her obsession returned to consciousness with blinding, mortifying, fury. The blueprint and timeline of the affair was meticulously detailed, and she didn't think that Clint could have made much out of it. Unlikely he would mention "Nadia," and even if he did, would Chloe be able to connect the dots? She wasn't that intuitively bright or observant to put two and two together. Emily picked up a dry-erase marker and popped off the cap. Next to the date and the words "Nadia Drowning" she wrote, unbidden, from the depths of nothing she could put her finger on, "Could it have been murder???" She double-underlined it for emphasis, stepped back from the whiteboard, and absorbed it in its entirety, all alone with her suspicion, wondering if she had gone mad.

Emily, head belonging to someone else, undressed, threw on her pajamas, and climbed back into bed. She lay supine with her head propped up on two pillows, an arm flung over her sodden forehead, hoping the weight of it would quell the headache if the two Advil didn't take effect. She cycled through the rhythms of remembering, the way drunks must do after a Homeric bender. She remembered Clint, of course. The parade of absinthe shots. She raised all her fingers on one hand and stopped when she got halfway through the other counting the number of shots she had consumed, then closed her eyes and let her head loll back and forth in self-deprecation and lonely remorse. She touched her crotch. Thank God nothing had happened, she consoled herself.

Almost out of earshot, she heard the dead frond on her porch scratching the eave like fingernails on a chalkboard, but her misophonia was the least of her maladies. What had possessed her? Was she envious of Nadia? The famous man she had fallen in love with? That mature, all-encompassing, all-consuming love, not some guy with a jacked body and a nice smile, but someone who could take her deep like West had plundered Nadia and she him, heart, body, soul, art? If she hadn't eavesdropped on their correspondence, she would never have known the fathomless depths to which two people could plumb. Trapdoors were lying in wait beneath Emily, but she had managed to keep them latched until the alcohol sprang one and hurtled her into a sinful encounter with her darker self. Jung had taught her that if you keep repressing one side of yourself—and he meant the erotic, the dark arts—it would only, in a sudden uprush, return to plague you in other manifestations. That energy has to go somewhere. It had transformed Emily into a feral cat, and all it took was a night out on the town and a nice guy like Clint to get in the way, and now she was terribly hungover and there seemed no escape from her indignity.

She opened her eyes and thought she should email Chloe and apologize, make light of the date gone haywire, but she reasoned that Clint had probably already texted both her and Jesse and told them Emily was a freak. That she had weaponized his own belt and went after him like a dominatrix. However it got narrated, it would be mortifying. Had the oftentimes salacious Nadia/Raymond emails produced a wellspring of unconscious desires? But for Emily to uncontrollably launch them on an unsuspecting guy she had just met—the friend of a coworker, no less . . . ? Emily shut her eyes in more self-recrimination and self-loathing, the punishing hangover exacerbating the dull throbbing in her head. But what angered her about the night more than anything was letting another person into the sanctuary of her apartment and him seeing the whiteboard. She felt unmasked, but of her own stupidity. It wasn't like her. She prided herself on being fastidious, careful, guarded; this wasn't like her. She never forgot anything. She never lost her keys. Never an assignment she didn't finish on schedule with the highest praise for her work. Everything was in order. Nothing resembling chaos could be detected in her life. And she always maintained an impervious wall of privacy, even with Joel. She cringed at it having been scaled and her being spied on, forever violated.

Saturday passed sluggishly. Emily, nursing a humdinger of a hangover, managed to do her laundry, but spent the rest of the day staring benumbed at websites, unable to concentrate on the unceasing tsunami of articles that presented themselves. She avoided the dark archives as if they were a malignant force that had ineluctably transformed her into someone who she wasn't. There were no postmortem emails from Chloe, but that didn't mean anything. Clearly, the double date had not gone according to plan. No need to recount its pathetic downward arc into shame.

Weary of torturing herself over the date, Emily emailed Joel and asked if he wanted to go surfing on Sunday. He readily agreed. She needed to get out and be with people. She needed the memory-obliterating adrenaline rush of pounding surf, exhilarating wipeouts, one's entire body spent from the physical exertion, where the mind ceases to exist.

They rendezvoused at La Jolla Farms Drive, and together they trekked down the twisting private road to Black's. Joel inquired about her weekend, but Emily shrugged off the question. "Pretty quiet." The closer they got to the beach the more vividly Emily saw the news clippings of Nadia and realized all over again that it was this same beach where her body was discovered. The sandstone cliffs, the La Jolla skyline that outlined the drowning scene, were identical to what she had seen in the news clips. The more she had read in the e-pistolary exchange, the closer she had grown to Nadia and Raymond's deep and forbidden love, and the more she yearned to get back on the trail to find out what happened.

On the beach, waxing their boards, Emily asked Joel out of the blue, "On that night Nadia drowned, was it overhead? You would know."

Joel looked up at her from his board. "No. It was two-to-three. Hardly a swell."

"Was it a full moon?"

Joel looked at her as if a cloud had drifted in front of the sun. "I don't know. Could easily find out."

"She wouldn't surf on a moonless night, would she?" Emily asked.

"That would be insane," Joel said. "No surfer goes out on a moonless night."

Emily furrowed her brow. "If you don't think she drowned, what do you think happened?"

Joel's head slumped. The waxing of his board grew slower and more deliberate, as if he didn't have his heart in Emily's private, single-minded investigatory journey anymore. Then he stopped altogether and sighed. "I think, when the affair ended, she . . ." He looked out at the mottled surface of the ocean. "She couldn't handle it anymore." He started to wax his board again with renewed vigor.

"But how?" Emily persisted, looking at Joel as he struggled for an elaboration, depression over the tragic memory darkening his face. "She was found here, right?"

"She was depressed when Helena fired her, no doubt because Helena suspected the affair. Or worse, was informed of it by someone. She went out, drunk or on antianxiety pills, and slipped anonymously under the waves. Virginia Woolf did it—put stones in her pockets and walked into the River Ouse. It's not hard. And the university did everything to cover it up."

"Helena fired her?" Emily asked rhetorically.

"Yeah."

"For what cause?"

Joel turned to Emily. "Uh. Fucking a donor."

Emily looked off. She knew this, of course, but she bristled at Joel's use of the word *fucking* and sensed that his jealousy over Nadia and Raymond's affair still disturbed him.

"And especially if the donor's wife is going to give a gift of twenty million fucking dollars to the library . . ." Joel angrily shoved the bar of wax into his wet suit pocket.

"Then why was her death ruled an accidental drowning?" Emily asked.

"I don't know, Emily. Probably because they were afraid it would instigate a more thorough investigation and turn up the affair and all the tawdry details. It's one thing Mrs. West could for sure bury in private. No doubt she's done that before with a womanizer like West. But to have it publicly in her face—with Helena's own handpicked archivist—one can only imagine the pain, the repercussions." Joel stood up abruptly, clapped sand off his hands, then bent to pick up his board. "She was his archivist, Emily. She was not some starstruck Lit undergrad. That would have threatened Mrs. West, wounded her on a more primordial level. And suicide would have boomeranged back to her. That's my theory. She's a tough lady. But nobody's that tough. Even I was jealous when I found out. Okay?"

"And how would they cover it up as an accident?" Emily asked naively.

Joel smirked at her. "She's the richest woman in San Diego. Her money can buy a face-saving narrative. And don't think your literary crush Raymond West is so lily white either," Joel said, his tone modulated now with a trace of nastiness. "Nadia committed suicide because she probably couldn't handle how a love affair that blew up in her face irrevocably destroyed her career," he added, in a voice now thick with hurt and fury, "They all conspired to want her dead!" He started off, then stopped and turned to her. "Say you're Nadia. You come to the realization that after the West Papers the only job you're going to get as an archivist is records management for, uh, I don't know, San Diego Gas & Electric. I'd be fucking depressed, too," he fulminated. "To be barred from Special Collections, from her life's work, work that Nadia loved when . . ." he trailed off.

"She got a collection like West's?" Emily finished for him.

Joel turned and walked off, leaving forlorn footprints in the sand. He stopped at the water's edge and threw Emily a backward look. "Are you coming?"

"In a minute." She was immobilized by his interpretation of what may or may not have been the cause of Nadia's death.

He regarded her for a moment with warning eyes. "I hope you don't find their book. But I'm not going to stand in your way. I like you too much."

Squinting into the sun, Emily stared back at Joel, pondering his words.

Joel wheeled away from her, set his board in the ankle-deep water, walked it out until it was waist-high, then climbed onto it and began paddling out into the lineup.

A squadron of thirteen pelicans—Emily counted each one—glided over the water, as effortlessly as the paragliders. In unison, it seemed, they all flapped their massive wings once, banked in formation into an almost imperceptible turn, and created a palpable tremor in the air as they flew past. Their massive beaks hung lugubriously, prehistorically, low on their heads. Their eyes surveilled the water for prey. One broke from the thirteen, folded its wings, and splashed headfirst into the water. A few seconds later, with a furious beating of its wings, the majestic pelican was airborne again, a squirming minnow writhing in its beak, soon to be swallowed whole in its massive gullet. Tritely, Emily reflected, *Life is short.*

As Emily paddled out into the lineup to catch up with Joel, her imagination traveled to Nadia and that night she paddled out, all alone, into the dark ocean, this very ocean Emily was paddling in. Emily had checked an online almanac and it had been a moonless night, but she didn't want to tell Joel for fear he would chasten her again for her obsession with Nadia's death. But he was right. Surfers don't surf on moonless nights, she thought as she pushed down on the nose of her board and let a wave tumble over her. She came up shaking the water from her hair, feeling revivified finally from the Friday disaster date. Surfers can't make out the waves forming in the dark. Maybe Nadia did take a fatal fistful of pills and, in total despair over whatever had happened with Raymond, went to her favorite surfing spot, stroked out into the impenetrable blackness, and let all her hopes, pinned to *The Archivist*, sink into the dark waters. If the book had been abandoned, if things had ended with Raymond . . . She had to locate those Moleskines. And she knew where they were.

CHAPTER 16

The Annex

9/17/18

Humiliating weekend. Got shit-faced and all rowdy with this guy I barely knew, with a sexual fury I have never known before. Something unleashed in me from God knows where. All I wanted was a casual, one-night screw but it grew into something darker. Note to self: stop after two drinks. Jesus. Images from Friday night still haunt me. Something just came volcanically out of me. I was so pent-up, I guess I wanted release from everything, but it seems I'm in the thick of it now. I tried to obliterate it from my mind by preparing for the next status update meeting (ugh!), and surfing with Joel.

More dreams of chaos and disorder. I feel all alone here. Other than a reluctant and conflicted Joel, I don't have any allies. I went in the dead of night to the secret West hideaway where he has written all his works. Serendipitously, it was within walking distance of my apartment. I think of Nadia there less than a year ago, impossibly, consummately, happy, the two of them writing their book together, the waves crashing in the distance, the warning bell of the Amtrak train like a signal to begin a journey of exploration together. I hear all of that, too, calling to me, but it's different. I don't have what Nadia has . . . or had. I don't have her courage. Maybe I'm just fated to live my life vicariously through others like her.

If I let this go, I'll forever regret it, but it might buy me some relief from all this stress I'm experiencing. If I keep going, I'm afraid of what I'm going to find. More than anything, I want to find The Archivist *Moleskines, if they haven't—God forbid!—been destroyed.*

Emily inched slowly through the early-morning commuter traffic converging on Regents University from the four corners of San Diego. Today was the first day of classes and parking was going to be a competition. She'd set her alarm early to make sure she found a space.

An abstemious drinker, if one didn't count her Oberlin College days, Emily was still feeling the effects of all the absinthe Friday night when she walked into the library and parked herself in her cubicle and collapsed into her desk chair. Everything felt dulled, as if the room had been numbed by her hangover. Colors were less striking, sounds muter. Her movements were slower, her thought processes not firing as they normally did. The cloud of her responsibilities on the West Collection weighed more heavily on her now than ever. Everything had a lifelessness to it.

Still in a hangover fog from the absinthe blowout, she switched on her computer and leaned back in her chair. She swiveled around and picked up a folder that contained the Nick Peterson correspondence and flipped distractedly through it. It was all the correspondence except the extraordinarily confessional email she had read from Raymond to Nick in the dark archives. Those email printouts would be of high target value for any researcher. But she could never tell Jean or Helena where she got them from. Or could she? Was it time to open up about where she had been?

Chloe stopped by Emily's cubicle, turned her head over her shoulder without redirecting her body and exclaimed, "Whoa." She widened her eyes as if to underscore that she knew enough about what had happened on Friday. Emily wasn't in the mood to engage Chloe in conversation about it, so she smiled back blankly, defensively, then lowered her gaze, until Chloe started up again and finished the traverse down the corridor to her cubicle. It wasn't exactly the type of gossip she would share with Jean or Helena. What was she going to tell them? Emily Snow had gotten drunk out of her skull and gone nuts on her boyfriend's business partner and sexually assaulted him? Emily shook off the embarrassing memory, but it was still disturbing to her that she had let her guard down.

Emily busied herself in the morning with the collection, her hand firmly on the tiller, staying true to her course now, moving from items she was foldering to the West finding aid on her computer. She was living a double life and she knew it was the reason she was stressed, the reason that her dreams had turned treasonously against her, the reason she got herself drunk and transformed into a wholly different person. Was this other person residing inside her? She needed to align these two worlds, but she felt psychologically split. Emily found herself staring at her desk phone wondering if she should go through with booking an appointment with the university counselor. She shook herself free of the temptation, afraid to dredge up something so raw and complicated, a quandary she feared therapy would make her back away from. And she didn't want that.

Emily lingered over lunch in the bower, oblivious of the world. Random people walked by, but it was as if she were invisible. She was anonymous to the world, alone, conflicted. For some strange reason she was reminded of Saint John of the Cross's poem *Dark Night of the Soul.* Lining her own narrow, snakelike path were ethics on one side and the terror of the truth on the other. But it was where ethics and truth had intersected that had Emily feeling emotionally gutted. She had come to the realization in the ever-changing world of the archives profession there were no true guiding principles, no real ideological pillars to lean on. These were human beings, and the human soul knew only mercuriality, mutability. There existed no one truth; no one, absolute way.

She pulled up a quote from her journal app and read it again for the hundredth time:

> Thus, then, the more pure and simple the divine light when it beats on the soul, the more does it darken it, empty it, and annihilate it . . . It remains for me now to explain that this blessed night, though it darkens the mind, does so only to give it light in every thing; and though it humbles it and makes it miserable, does so only to raise it up and set it free; and though it impoverishes it

> and empties it of all its natural self and liking, it does so only to enable it to reach forward divinely to the possession and fruition of all things, both of heaven and earth, in perfect liberty of spirit.

Emily looked up from her phone and raised her eyes to the sky. An unseen raven cawed in a forlorn preternatural punctuation, more of an acknowledgement than a warning. This was exactly the fork in the road that Emily had come to. As she straightened from the bench, she thought, *It was darkness and then light; or light and a plunge back into darkness.* She smirked to herself.

Emily arrived late to the scheduled status meeting in the seminar room. A sudden hush fell when she entered, voices still reverberating, as if they had been talking about her. Eyes darted away from her. She felt a tacit distancing, as if, in her paranoia, she knew she wasn't one of them. Verlander was the first one to break into a smile. He pulled out a chair for her next to his.

"Hi, Emily."

"Sorry I'm late." With a downcast gaze, she eased into the chair Verlander had offered.

"Hello, Emily. Glad you could make it." Helena smiled. Both superior authority and a shrugging off of Emily's apology could be seen in the cruelly forced smile.

Jean didn't say anything. Her occupational resting bitch face was on full display—who knew what apocalypse lay behind it? The four of them were spread around the oblong seminar room table like too few mariners crewing a colossal yacht.

Not one to waste time with confabulations, Helena leaned forward and asked in a tone sharp as a falling icicle, "So, where are we, Emily, on West?"

On cue, Jean stood and moved three steps to the sanctuary of her whiteboard.

Emily met Helena's withering gaze. "I'm close to finished."

"Excellent," said Verlander, adopting the role of peacemaker, as Jean filled in something on the whiteboard with her dry-erase marker. The squeaking of it sent a militia of spiders up and down Emily's spine, but she restrained herself from saying anything, shut her eyes for a moment at the fantasy of fleeing the room.

"And we've, hopefully, pulled some new things for the exhibit that won't be objectionable to Elizabeth?" questioned Helena with a doubting smile. It hit Emily with the twin forces of elation and anxiety. They needed her! They were dependent on her. Where would they be in Jean's timeline if she resigned now? Or was fired? All their plans would be thrown into irremediable chaos. She looked around the room with a confidence born of this revelation. She was all Helena had to pull off this eighth-floor extravaganza. Without Emily, she would be a public humiliation.

"I think so," said a calmed, and more assertive, Emily. She opened the folder she brought and passed around some pictures and copies of manuscripts in the direction of Helena and Verlander. From a tote she produced one of the Moleskines of *Lessons in Reality* and slid it over to Helena, rising out of her chair to reach her. They both adjusted the glasses on the bridges of their noses and studied the items with redoubled curiosity, given the last, disastrous, meeting.

"These are nice," appraised Helena. She fingered the Moleskine with a cryptic smile, leafed briefly through it. "And this . . . personalizes it even more."

"I would say," echoed Verlander with a laugh. "They are truly one-of-a-kind artifacts."

"And so," began Jean, not wanting to be irrelevant, "when do you anticipate actual completion, Emily?"

"Well, it depends how thorough a job you want me to do," Emily said, fissuring the foundation with her simple words.

Helena reared back in her chair and stiffened in response. Her mouth puckered into a pained expression, as if she had bit down into an unpeeled lemon. "Can you elaborate?"

From her folder Emily produced three copies of a document and slid one to each of them. "It's a printout of an email exchange a year ago between West and his editor, Nick Peterson, at Scribner's."

"We can see that," snapped Helena, setting the document back down.

"Notice the date," insisted Emily.

"Less than a year ago." Verlander spread his arms in an inquiring shrug. Jean looked down from her whiteboard, dry-erase marker poised to write something that hadn't been fully decided upon yet.

"What's your point?" Helena asked Emily.

"There are more."

"How do you know?" Helena added.

"Because they're noted in my file."

An ominous silence took possession of the room. Emily glanced from face to face, wishing she hadn't twisted the knife of truth into them so deeply. But it was too late to reverse course. The proverbial cat was out of the bag. Her soul was about to be annihilated.

"Where are they?" Helena demanded with bilious eyes, terrorized by the truth.

Emily went stoic with seeming indifference, her sangfroid impressive in the face of Helena's wrath. Verlander met Helena's steely gaze, when it swung searchingly to him, and shrugged. A look of dismay suddenly capsized Helena's cold composure. That indignant expression somehow caromed over to Jean, who now sensed a thunderstorm forming on the horizon.

"This has nothing to do with you," Helena fumed at Emily when no one dared produce an answer. "Stay out of it."

"These are original documents," Emily protested. "You want me to ignore items that are part of the West Collection? You don't think this is of enough historical value to be retained?" Emily looked at all of them incredulously. "Especially if he wins the Nobel?"

The hierarchy of power tautened in crisscrossing wires in a room that had suddenly grown smaller.

"Where's the rest of the correspondence?" Emily said blithely, invoking ethical propriety as an archivist, if nothing else. She crisscrossed her arms against her chest, waited.

"Maybe there's a reason it was culled out," Helena argued.

"What reason?" demanded Emily. Helena didn't have a ready answer. Nobody did. "Because according to my file, he was talking about a new work, the one I mentioned in the last meeting."

"The Wests didn't want it in the collection," Helena snapped, her eyes malignant.

Emily sat back in her chair, genuinely flummoxed. "One of the richest correspondences in the collection, and they don't want it in his archive?"

"That's right."

"He didn't want it, or she didn't want it"?

Helena glowered at Emily. "Both," she barked.

"With all due respect, I find that hard to believe, Ms. Blackwell. Especially given the truly personal nature of the other letters."

"You've read them?" asked Verlander.

"Of course," said Emily. "I'm a manuscripts processor. I don't just organize and arrange. I often read. To know what they are."

"Why are you wasting valuable time reading correspondence that's already been processed?" cut in an irascible Helena, finding footing in Verlander's query.

"I'm working on this collection day and night. Am I behind? I don't think so. But I have questions. Between the finding aid, what's been cataloged and foldered in the document boxes, and my West file, this collection where I took it up is a disorganized mess!"

"Why are you taking all this time with the cross-referencing?" Helena asked. "It's delaying the completion of this project."

"Because I'm a professional," Emily asserted, jaw thrust forward. "And this is how I was trained."

"Stay out of it, Emily," Helena bellowed, pushing herself up from her chair with the support of both gnarled hands. She bent threateningly across the desk. "Do what we hired you to do."

"Are you asking me to ignore items from his collection that are in the finding aid but not where they're supposed to be if someone inquired?" Emily countered in disbelief. "That's unprofessional."

"Don't tell me what's unprofessional!" Helena snatched the Moleskine of *Lessons in Reality* and launched it across the room in a paroxysm of rage. Emily ducked and simultaneously threw up both arms to shield her face. The book slammed into Jean's whiteboard and windmilled it around. Jean bent down and retrieved the Moleskine from the floor. It looked like a bird that had been hit by a shotgun at close range and had sustained some damage, its spine broken, pages torn and dangling out. The shock of everybody in the room was palpable.

Helena crooked a bejeweled finger at Emily. "Finish up. And stop asking questions. Remember, your position is being fully funded by Elizabeth. *Anything* that might be offensive to her is going to get redacted, regardless of what her esteemed husband might think!"

Emily realized anything she said would bump up against the wall of Helena's hostility, so she just silently seethed.

Helena stormed out of the seminar room like an immense bird on broken wings. Her voice seemed to still carry in the poisoned air like a canyon echo after she left.

Jean handed the Moleskine back to Emily. "I think you need to repair this."

"This is a one-of-a-kind item, a first draft of a Pulitzer Prize–winning novel. Where I come from, do this"—Emily looked at the Moleskine with disgust and shook her head—"and you would be gone."

"You're not the director of Special Collections," Jean reminded her.

"I don't destroy university property." Emily reverently closed the book, still shaking her head. "Fucking unreal." She looked up. "Why doesn't she just fire me?" Emily asked in exasperation.

"She can't," said Verlander soberly. "To get somebody else up to speed, with the"—he looked straight up at the ceiling—"Eighth Floor Gala approaching would not be possible." He lowered his head and leveled his kindly eyes at Emily. "We didn't know about this unpublished, or abandoned, manuscript of Raymond's. But it seems to have Elizabeth upset. And whatever upsets Elizabeth is going to rankle Helena." He narrowed his eyes at Emily. "She spent three decades cultivating that relationship. Give her some credit. We owe this entire renovation project to her. There are always compromises, Emily."

"You don't think it wouldn't be of enormous value?"

"Of course I do, Emily. But this is a complicated situation. Sometimes preserving the cultural record has to take second base to the"—he pointed his index finger to the ceiling—"bigger cause."

Verlander's mollifying words infuriated Emily and her jaw tensed in response. Even though she had forayed into the dark archives, ignoring items and destroying rare manuscripts was truly unprofessional behavior. Of course, she knew what the underlying issue was, and there's no question she was trying to push it out into the light. At the risk of what Verlander was explaining to her. She didn't care anymore. She wanted it all to come out!

Seeking clarity but finding the waters more muddied than ever, Emily gathered the copies of Nick's emails and ordered them neatly back in her folder. She closed it, put it and the priceless Moleskine in her tote, pushed back her chair, and rose from the table. "I want to see the deed of gift."

Verlander and Jean exchanged portentous looks. Emily left them with a new thundercloud looming on the horizon as she left the room.

Special Collections cleared out promptly at 5:00 p.m. Jean strode right past Emily's cubicle without saying goodbye, but Emily was used to her unfriendly exits. Helena had locked her hoarder's pigsty of an office after the meeting and disappeared somewhere, probably the Faculty Club to douse her indignation with some cold Chardonnay. She was the director and could do whatever she wanted. From a tote, Emily pulled out a black hoodie and stretched her arms into it. Then she took out a black antiviral mask that was popular among many Asian students on campus and slipped it over her face. She walked down to Joel's digital archivist station. He gasped when he saw her in the ninja disguise.

"Emily. Jesus. You scared me half to death."

Emily lowered her mask. "Are you ready to take me to the Annex?"

"I heard there were fireworks in the status update meeting." Joel fixed her with a look of concern, not making a move.

"There are items missing from the West Papers, and I'm going to find them," said Emily in a crystalline clear voice not lacking in conviction. Emily produced the mangled Moleskine and showed it to Joel. "One of the volumes of *Lessons in Reality*. Hurled at me by you know who."

"Helena?" Joel asked, astonished.

Emily nodded up and down in ominous affirmation.

"A handwritten original?" Joel said, stunned, his mouth frozen open.

Emily tilted her head to one side, widened her eyes in exclamation, as if to say, *Do you believe that?*

Their gazes locked in mutually disturbed recognition. Shaking his head in disgust, Joel switched off his computer, grabbed a small backpack, and turned to Emily. "You look cute in the hoodie. Not sure about the antiviral mask, but it's an imaginative touch. Let's go."

They drove out of the university in a dense fog that painted the university in a gray watercolor outline. In the shared silence their hearts beat with apprehension at the espionage that lay ahead.

"Ever surf in a fog like this?" Emily asked.

Joel nodded. "It's spooky." He swung the wheel to the left and bent around a corner. "What are you looking for exactly?"

"As I told you before," Emily turned to him, "it's better if you don't know."

"Allow me to rephrase—the items you're looking for, what are you going to do if you find them?"

"That I don't know." She glanced at Joel. "It's moot if I don't find them."

Joel nodded without pressing further. She sensed she had his respect. "If Security shows up," he instructed, "don't volunteer anything, let me handle it. I have access to this place; you don't."

"Okay," she said.

"This fog's incredible," he said, a non sequitur to get his mind off his imminent aiding and abetting of a departmental violation that could lead to his dismissal.

Visibility was less than the width of a soccer pitch as Joel steered onto Torrey Pines Road and headed south on the sinuous downhill road that sloped into La Jolla. On most days they would be able to see La Jolla Shores and the turquoise waters of the cove, but even Scripps Pier, just over the hill, was obliterated from view by the dense fog. Silently, Joel turned into a single-lane driveway. They coasted past a wooden sign with painted lettering that read Scripps Institution of Oceanography. They rode through a cluster of wood-framed buildings set in the hillside overlooking the ocean. Joel parked his Element and switched off his engine.

"Come on, let's get this over with," Joel said.

Emily pulled the hood of her sweatshirt up and tied it at the neck, then brought the antiviral mask back to her face and said in a muffled voice, "Is this okay?"

Joel shook his head. "Yeah, it's fine. You look like a cat burglar."

They climbed out of the car together. Emily followed Joel through the horizontally traveling fog to a large, box-shaped building. They stopped at a door. Joel swiped a plastic card through a reader. A moment later the red LED turned a flashing green, and he pulled the door open.

They found themselves inside a large warehouse, stretching two stories high to the exposed ceiling. Shelving for the sundry items of archival stuff ran in crowded, overstuffed, seemingly disorganized rows across the cold concrete floors. The individual shelves were heaped with cardboard boxes, piles of folders, even plastic trash bags overrun with debris. Its cluttered messiness was in stark contrast to the pristine orderliness of document boxes in the stacks.

"Welcome to analog overflow." Joel held out his arm in a grandiloquent gesture of greeting. He turned to Emily. "I'd turn the lights on, but I don't think it's wise."

"I came prepared," Emily reassured him. She held up a small, black pocket flashlight pinched between thumb and forefinger.

Joel nodded and then pointed to the cavernous space. "Everything on the far wall is for shredding. The rest is spillover. I'll leave you to your call numbers."

"Okay," said Emily.

"I'm trying to be cool, but I'm fucking nervous."

"I appreciate it."

Joel made a gesture with his thumb. "Text me when you hit paydirt."

"All right."

"You've got fifteen minutes, Emily. I'll be outside, trying to hatch some appropriate lies."

"Thanks, Joel."

Joel went back out the door they had entered. It clanged shut behind him, ensconcing Emily all alone in the Annex. A scattering of lights that were left on all the time flickered high up in the ceiling, but they didn't afford much visibility. Emily switched on her flashlight and checked the item code she was looking for: "2017.RW.NBM.V1-V12." She walked along the first row, spraying the flashlight over labels on the shelving, raising up and crouching down. To her initial frustration she realized that nothing in the Annex was organized alphabetically or numerically. It was a total hodgepodge. Probably somewhere in the department's bowels, someone had a map rendering items discoverable, but moving through the crepuscular light, Emily was flying blind. And, worse, on the clock.

Five minutes into her search, she texted Joel after having no luck: "Still looking. Could it have been shredded already?!"

"Possibly. Unlikely if only in last year."

His text lent her renewed hope, and she slithered quickly through the rows, hunching and rising, her flashlight swinging back and forth between shelving flanking her on both sides. "Fuck," she muttered to herself. "Fuck!" A text came up from Joel: "5 more mins." She ignored it. She wasn't going to leave until he came in and forcibly dragged her out.

Her frustration was suddenly broken when she stopped at a code that began "2017RW." She shined her pocket flash on it, recognized it as an all-purpose code for the West Collection. She pulled down the box closest to her, hurriedly tore open the top. Inside, as she frantically rummaged, she discovered old newspaper clippings and duplicate items that an archivist would not find of use in processing a collection and would deaccession to reduce bulk. She hauled the box back up on the shelf. Needing to get to the one on top of it, she looked around wildly. Spotting a knee-high stepladder, she noisily dragged it over, propped it against the shelving, and mounted its two steps. With the flashlight gripped in her teeth she noticed that the box above had the code she was looking for. Excitedly, she wrestled it out of its space and let it plummet to the concrete, where its crash echoed throughout the facility. Worried, she cocked her ear and listened. When she didn't hear anything—no footsteps, no voices—Emily leaped off the ladder, ripped open the top of the box, but only came upon copies of various editions, English and foreign language, of West's novels. More typical overflow.

"Fuck!" Emily could hear her heart pounding. She wasn't anxious, she was exasperated; she wasn't afraid, she was pissed; she wasn't going to surrender to failure—she had seen the code, she knew it was somewhere! The Moleskines had to be here. Nadia wouldn't have sent her successor to the Annex on a wild goose chase, would she? Or had they already been destroyed by bad actors scrubbing the collection to the uncorrupted literary posterity that Elizabeth demanded of her "poodle on a leash" writer husband?

With effort, Emily lifted the box back up and shimmied it into place. She noticed that it wouldn't go all the way back. She pushed, but it stopped short and still hung suspiciously over the ledge. It looked out of order now. She noticed some space next to it and she arm-wrestled it to the side, the flashlight still held between her gritting teeth. As the box turned, the flashlight sprayed the gap between the adjoining boxes. Emily's heart froze. A less than foot-high stack of manila string-tie envelopes, secured with elastic bands, lay concealed behind the box. Emily reached an arm to the back and was able to get a finger-grip on the heavy-duty elastic bands and yank the item toward her. The string-tie envelope had "TA-V1" handwritten in block capital letters. Emily sucked in her breath, descended the stepladder with the parcel. She pulled off the elastic bands and fanned out the string-tie envelopes on the empty lower shelf. Volume I, Volume III . . . Volume XII. They were all there. She didn't dare open them. She knew what they were. She could feel them with her trembling fingers in the envelopes! Rejoicing, tears sprang to her eyes, and she wiped them with the back of her hoodie sweatshirt. Her joy, her relief, veered sharply to terror when she heard a man's unfamiliar voice:

"Excuse me," he said, politely but firmly.

Emily corkscrewed to a standing position and met a column of bright light. Behind it, she could make out a uniformed, middle-aged Asian man standing a few feet from her, blinding her with a more powerful flashlight. She threw a hand to her eyes to block the light. "Could you turn that off, please?" she asked, feigning a tone that verified she had a right to be in the building.

The security cop let the flashlight drop to his side, where it shined a small pool of white on the linoleum floor. "Are you authorized to be in here?"

Emily lowered her antiviral mask. "I work in Special Collections."

"What's your name?" The guard jerked a notepad from his front pocket and clicked the plunger on a pen into readiness.

"Emily."

"Emily who?"

Emily hesitated. "Snow."

The guard pulled out a rectangle of paper and unfolded it. He sprayed the flashlight over it. "I don't see your name on here."

"I'm new. I work with Joel Beery."

He furrowed his brow. Footsteps came fast down the aisle and, to Emily's relief, Joel bloomed into view, his eyes bloodshot from reefer.

"Lee, my man, how's it hangin'?" He held out his hand with the thumb extended.

Lee took his hand, and they exchanged the peace shake. "Joel." He jerked a thumb at Emily. "You know this woman?"

"Not the way I would like to." Joel slipped Emily a wink to show that he would do or say whatever was necessary. Lee chuckled in tacit understanding.

Joel waved him over with a knowing nod after he noticed Emily had scored what looked like a prized possession secured under her left arm. Joel and Lee drew a few feet away out of earshot from Emily.

Emily could make out Joel whispering to Lee something in a pacifying tone. "Not authorized . . . Needed to find something . . . Last minute . . . Totally cool . . ." Emily seized the opportunity to conceal the string-tie envelopes in the tote slung over her shoulder. In the dim light she could make out Joel watching her over Lee's shoulder with widened eyes warning her to keep quiet. She saw him pass Lee what looked like a joint in a plastic tube, running it by his nose as if to emphasize its potency before giving it to him. Joel clapped him on the shoulder. Negotiations concluded, they turned back to Emily, shuffling in place.

"So, Emily," Joel began in an affected voice, "did you find the items that were earmarked for the shredder?"

"Uh, yes, I did, Joel. Thank you."

"Great! Another tragedy averted in Special Collections, courtesy of our new diligent project archivist here." He turned to Lee, clapped him on the shoulder again. "All right, my man, we're out of here."

The three of them trooped out of the Annex together, Lee waving goodbye to Joel and Emily at the door. He locked himself back inside, his expression shifting to sullen at the prospect of another brutal night shift.

Joel remained in an incomprehensible silence until he steered his car out of the constellation of buildings and back out onto Torrey Pines Road.

It was night now and the fog flooded in off the ocean in denser currents, reducing visibility to mere feet.

"Fuck, man." Joel exhaled a sigh. Emily didn't say anything. Joel turned to her. "Did you find what you were looking for?" Emily nodded. "Thank God I knew Lee. I didn't realize they had full-time, twenty-four-hour security now." He brooded, head bent over the steering wheel, squinting.

"When do you think that started?" Emily asked.

"I don't know. I mean, I knew they had someone who checked in, but I didn't realize it was a full-time position. Weird." Joel shook his head confusedly. "Wonder if they're tightening security around West with all the stuff that's coming up," he muttered.

"Is there a lot of West overflow there?" Emily asked.

"Probably. It was a huge collection when it came in."

"Do you think they've doubled down on security because of it?"

Joel wordlessly shook his head.

"Sorry I told him my name."

"It is what it is," he said resignedly.

"What'd you tell him?" Emily asked.

"You were working on West—he didn't even know who he was—and that you needed to check for some things that might have gotten misplaced." Joel shook his head exaggeratedly as if attempting to shake free a narrative that had a bad ending.

"Do you think your friend Lee would say anything?"

"I doubt it." Joel stared forward, peering over the steering wheel through the fog. "Unless he was grilled specifically. Remember, that whole interaction is probably on tape somewhere, but no one's going to do shit unless there's a reason to do shit." Joel whipped his head to her accusatorily.

Emily averted her eyes from his glowering stare. They rode in silence through the thickening fog back to Regents and the Jameson Parking. Emily's car was the only one visible on the depopulated fifth level, all alone in a sea of concrete. Joel braked to a stop and let his car idle. With his hands gripping the top of his steering wheel he let his eyes fall heavily on Emily.

"I'm glad I could help you," he said. "I didn't mean to be uptight."

"I appreciate it."

"Helena was asking about you the other day."

"Asking you?" Emily said.

"Yeah, me. Who she never talks to."

"What'd she want to know?"

"She was sniffing around about the dark archives," Joel replied, looking away.

"What'd you tell her?"

"Something nebulous, I don't remember."

"Is she afraid of what's out there?" Emily asked.

Joel shrugged noncommittally. "I didn't even know she knew there *was* a dark archives or what it even is," Joel attempted to joke. "I doubt she's going to bring in a digital forensics guy to scour it, if that's what you're worried about." Joel turned to Emily. "She can fire me, you realize? I'm sticking my neck out for you."

"What else did she want to know?" Emily pressed.

"She wanted to know if you were getting too possessive of the West Collection."

"What'd you tell her?" Emily asked, increasingly agitated.

A dark ray passed over Joel's face. "That you were intense. Like Nadia. That you took these collections personally because you're a professional and a lover of literature and want to get them done right . . ." Emily waited, sensing that Joel had more to confide. "Something I never told you," Joel started in a more somber tone. "Shortly before Nadia died, she showed up unannounced at my apartment late one night and banged on the door. She was crying. She was totally distraught." Joel swung his melancholy eyes to Emily. "I knew about the affair because of that time I followed her. But it was the first time we had talked about it. Of course, there's a lot she didn't tell me, a lot more that I don't know. And don't want to know." He banged the palms of both hands on his steering wheel to vent his frustration. "I have a lot to lose. I don't have rich parents. I didn't make it as a screenwriter. Still owe fifty grand in loans," he rattled off in a state of high anxiety. "Special Collections has been good to me."

"I'll be careful, I promise," Emily said. A thought flared in her head suddenly. "When was it that she came to you crying?"

"Emily!"

"Rough idea."

"Just before she was fired. Okay?"

Emily fixed her eyes on Joel, who wouldn't meet her gaze. "Do you honestly think she committed suicide, Joel?"

Joel shut his eyes and exhaled through his nose. "The affair had ended. She was fired. Excommunicated from the library. Exiled to wherever the hell she lived with her husband. A disgraced pariah. She wasn't going to get a recommendation from Helena, or even Verlander. Her next job was going to be in, I don't know, some corporate repository. Nadia? If you knew her." Joel shook his head. "She was an artist. Her life was ruined. Over." He turned to Emily. "She took a hell of a risk with that affair. She couldn't have fallen for a worse person."

Emily's jaw tensed in Nadia's defense. "She wanted to live. She didn't want to die a nobody." She grew misty-eyed.

"Whatever," Joel said, still visibly shaken.

Emily held up her tote with both hands and shook it. "And I've got the proof."

Joel raised a hand to shield his face. "I don't want to know. I'm glad you found what you were looking for, whatever it was. Please be careful. This is serious shit, Emily." Joel closed his eyes, let his forehead sink to the steering wheel, and sighed.

Emily played with her lips with thumb and index finger, as if debating whether to divulge anything more. "I did some research on something," she said hesitantly.

"What now?" Joel asked wearily.

"Did you know that drowning as a method of suicide in women is less than one percent?"

Joel swung his head slowly to Emily and leveled his eyes at her.

"And even in that one percent it's mostly women over sixty," Emily added, wild-eyed with conviction.

Dark thoughts clouded Joel's visage and seemed to momentarily disassemble him. "What're you saying?"

"I think she had a lot to live for." Emily opened the door. She gripped her tote with the thickness of the string-tie envelopes glowing radioactively within. "Thanks, Joel."

Joel reached over and enveloped her in a brief, but fiercely caring hug. He whispered into her ear, "Forget about it, Emily, it's Memorial Library," paraphrasing the famous movie line. He withdrew, smiling crookedly.

"I can't, Joel. I'm past the point of no return. I would regret it the rest of my life."

He nodded in dejected resignation. "You and Nadia are so different and yet so alike. I miss her. And I'll miss you when your job is over."

"I'm sorry I dragged you into this," Emily said, laying a hand on his forearm.

"I'll wait until you get in your car."

"Okay. Thanks, Joel."

Emily stepped out of the passenger-side door.

Joel's Element idled as Emily climbed into her Mini and started the motor. Satisfied she was okay, Joel drove off. The squealing of his tires as Emily rounded the spiral-shaped structure seemed to sharply etch the audio landscape, a monotone of recirculating air.

When Emily came down to the stop sign out of the parking structure, she braked to a halt and put her gear stick in neutral. She telescoped her head over the steering wheel and tilted her head up through the windshield. Memorial Library's mezzanine was wreathed in fog. You couldn't make out the massive concrete pedestal that held the whole structure aloft. The dense ground fog had the effect of lifting the upper floors high up into the night, their lights illuminating them like a brilliant, enormous diamond, fixed in the sky as if floating ethereally on a cloud. Emily could make out construction workers in the brightly lit eighth floor where they were working overtime now, racing against the calendar to get it ready for the Gala. They resembled citizens of an alien society going about making their spaceship an inhabitable place on an inhospitable planet. It would be a new city when it was completed. It would capture worldwide attention and transform the university into a magnet drawing students and faculty from all over the globe, a renovated Memorial Library its glorious epicenter. Emily wondered if Helena, who made it all happen, had also stood in the ground fog one night, staring up at this extraordinary architectural masterpiece of a library and dreamed the dream that was soon to be realized. There had to have been many bumps along the road, and every one was represented by a wrinkle line in Helena's deeply fissured countenance, strained from the vicissitudes that had brought her to the precipice of the crowning moment the workers on the eighth floor were readying now.

Emily glanced down at the tote bag lying rumpled on her passenger seat. *Holy shit*, she mouthed. *Holy shit.* Could words do what no 9.0 earthquake could and bring it all toppling down?

Emily drove in second gear all the way back to Del Mar in eerie, deep fog, her heart contracted like a small fist closed tight over a secret, deeply conflicted. Who was she? The effrontery? The internal pummeling of accusations assailed her. If she assigned faces to them, she would be in a fun house of repeating images reflected on warped mirrors. Red emergency lights pulsed in the gray, sirens shrilly rose and fell, and Emily slowed. An accident involving two cars was blocking one of the lanes. A man held a hand to one ear as blood spouted from it. He emerged wraithlike out of the fog in staggering disorientation, groping the air in vain for handholds that didn't exist. A woman was kneeling on the asphalt, her face covered by her hands in anguish, screaming inconsolably. An SDPD SUV was parked by their askew cars, its emergency lights strobing surreally red and yellow. In the distance, Emily could hear the rise and fall of sirens, EMTs, local fire trucks, converging on the horrible scene.

Emily passed by the accident site with parted lips of shock and then climbed the hill into Del Mar.

The accident still gruesomely fresh in her imagination, Emily emptied the contents of her tote onto the kitchen table. A slumberous Onyx, looking as half-conscious as the accident victim clutching his bloodied ear, wandered in on disjointed paws, yawned, ambled over to his bowl, found food, and didn't complain.

Emily undid the elastic bands on the bundle. Excitement comingled with fear and apprehension raised her blood pressure. She fanned out the manila envelopes on the table. In the upper middle of each envelope was a hand-typed label. The first one read "TA #1—RW/NF." The others were all progressively labeled the same. As if handling hazardous materials, Emily lifted the first one. She felt its contents through the envelope, and she closed her eyes in relieved satisfaction. It unequivocally formed a notebook. Her heart accelerated. Her blood burned wild. Slowly, as if defusing a bomb, she undid the string tie, turning it in a figure eight, the way it was fastened. She flipped open the flap, reached in and took out number 1. It was a black Moleskine, the 7½" × 9¾" oversized one that Raymond had handwritten the first drafts of all his works in. On the cover, in silver Sharpie, in beautiful handwritten calligraphy, was written "The Archivist." Under that, "(An Epistolary Exchange)," and under that, "By Raymond West & Nadia Fontaine." Below that was "Vol. I." The handwriting was unmistakably Nadia's. From the tiny string-tie envelope and the catalog card and the tortured love letter to Raymond she had found weeks ago, Emily would recognize Nadia's mellifluous cursive anywhere. A thrill suffused her as she pictured Nadia handing her cowriter/lover these Moleskines, one by one, presumably, already titled. Emily clasped a hand to her mouth. Tears spilled from her eyes. She could almost hear Nadia saying to Raymond, "Here, my love. Go deep. Write whatever flows from your heart. I don't care how scandalous. Write it so the world will know." And he would write and pass them back to her, presumably for transcription, the preservation, and the secrecy that he trusted Nadia would maintain.

Slowly, methodically, Emily breathlessly opened the other eleven envelopes and removed their identical black Moleskines. Unconsciously, she gathered the string-tied envelopes into a single pile and set them aside. Now she had a rainbow of black and silver no one even knew existed, not even its principal author, Raymond West. She reached for the first one and caressed its cover with both hands, as if the mere touching of it would launch her back in time to its creation. She stroked it like she petted Onyx, fondled its contours, almost afraid to open it. Would it only be blank pages? She opened the first one. It wasn't blank pages. Inside the black cloth covers a wide-eyed Emily, with hammering heart, found lightly ruled pages overflowing with the distinctively recognizable capital block letters of Raymond West that she remembered from the *Lessons in Reality* Moleskine Verlander had shown her. Emily's mind was seized with an odd conflation of panic and exhilaration, as if torn apart by opposing forces. As she turned each page, venerating the Moleskine as if it were a rare, almost sacred text, she realized the words had poured forth in a veritable torrent, spilling over the ruled lines with the gushing of water from a burst dam. The only pauses were for dates. And there weren't many. Volume I had been written, it appeared to Emily's practiced eye, in three days in a trancelike state of total artistic possession.

Another siren screeching in the night flew by Emily's apartment complex, escalating in *whoop-whoop-whoops*, heading in the direction of the accident that Emily had circled around. She threw her hands to her ears, this time not because of her misophonia, but because she didn't want to be reminded of the hobbling man with the bloodied ear and whether he had died on that fog-slickened pavement. When the siren passed, she returned her attention to the Moleskines. Her eyes traveled over the twelve volumes, a time bomb of professional suicide for Nadia, personal suicide for both of them—if it corresponded to what Emily imagined was in those volumes: the very alchemization of what she had read in the daily back-and-forth fervor of their emails, the quintessence of their affair in all its fictional profanation. She knew he was deep into the Drowning. She knew he was relying heavily on Nadia's emails—they were her words too. Imagining it in print must have terrified them. The guarded, private side of Emily shuddered at the thought.

Emily took a long, hot shower in hopes that when she emerged, she would view her mission in a changed light, but intertwined in all of it, and refusing to go away, was Nadia's death. She knotted a towel around her head and changed into pajamas. From the refrigerator she fished out an ale from a fresh six-pack and uncapped it, moving in a veritable daze. She had made up her mind. She knew what she was going to do. From the box of archival supplies that she always traveled with, Emily produced a pair of white cotton inspection gloves and fitted them onto her small hands. She picked up the Volume I Moleskine of *The Archivist* and carried it with her into the bedroom with the care of an antiquarian bookseller. Looking at the cover, unable to pry her eyes from it, she slipped into bed, switched on the bedside light, and opened the Moleskine to the first page. Her heart thumped in her chest; it had never stopped its intense hammering since she'd found them in the Annex. Emily, all alone, was about to begin Raymond West's last unpublished work of prose. And she already guessed it was a love letter to Nadia, of a lyrical beauty. To think of Nadia tossed back and forth at the shore's edge, her once-beautiful face cyanotic with the mask of the death, and to think of these black volumes hiding in a storage facility, one day destined for the shredder by an unthinking archivist tasked for clearing out space, produced shivers in Emily.

Emily slowly opened Volume I. The spine cracked like something waking to life. She began reading. The pages flew by in a blur, turned seemingly by themselves. The words devastated her. Raymond had taken his obsession with alchemizing the personal into fiction and given it new life in this epistolary novel. It was raw, diaristic writing, a vein of molten gold running through the darkness, composed with such self-effacing honesty, written almost as though its author(s) prefigured its fate as posthumous and not meant for the light of publication while they were alive. They wrote, and bared their souls, with reckless abandon, holding absolutely nothing back, leaving little to the imagination. The sex was graphic, the emotions heightened to a fevered pitch. Their affair was laid out in all its transgressive splendor, and all its self-incriminating honesty. A roman à clef of bombshell proportions. Its publication would have shocked anyone who knew Raymond West. Nadia would be the literary Helga to Raymond's Wyeth, and the achievement would be fodder for the literary tabloids, excoriated and lauded, condemned and celebrated, its future in the fate of the beauty of its prose.

Emily woke in the middle of the night. Waves exploded and echoed in the mausoleum silence of her complex. Were she at Isla Negra, they would roar three times as loudly. Her hand roamed to the side of the bed where there hadn't been a partner in nearly a year. Eyes closed, she caressed the covers of the Moleskines on the bed covers as if they were a litter of kittens slumbering away. She cycled through the rhythms of remembering. Volume XII had reached its cathartic, redemptive end. It was the last volume, as Raymond had predicted to Nadia in the middle of the writing. Raymond had penned a note when he finished it: "My Love, it is completed, and our fate is sealed." Raymond's words, ventriloquized through literature, haunted her.

CHAPTER 17

The Reckoning

9/24/18

I found the black Moleskines referenced in the correspondence. I read the whole book in one electrifying sitting, enrapt. I'm positive I've never read anything like it. But before that . . .

There are questions. Nadia had sequestered them in the Annex, that much is certain. I discovered them behind a box I was led to by cryptic notes in her personal file. I'm assuming the typescripts are with West, unless he destroyed them. I know Nadia transcribed the handwritten first drafts and gave him the copies for annotation.

The book, titled The Archivist*—the writing is beautiful, both Raymond's and Nadia's. It's as if they were feeding off each other. As if they were both haunted by the twin recognition that their love was both highly flammable and potentially damaging to others. Much of it goes over my head. Much of it I don't understand or can't relate to. Why, how, two people could so be so self-effacing, why they felt the need to go where they did. At times it feels like they're deliberately destroying their personal lives and rebuilding new ones all over again in a hard-to-fathom act of rebirth, or something Jungian—I don't know. Maybe one day I'll have the literary chops to fully grasp what they were reaching for when they decided to launch into this collaboration.*

The sex is at times cringe-worthily explicit! But by book's end, it's a hieratic celebration of their love.

I felt like I was in the thrall of an unfinished literary masterpiece, to which there is no comparison, because of its extremely personal nature.

I am still in a state of shock.

I don't know what to do. Part of me thinks I should retrace my steps back to the Annex, put them back where I found them, dismantle the dark archives from my computer and go back to being an anonymous project archivist. Finish the job and get the hell out of here.

And part of me knows that I will always know, and the professional in me knows that this work, destined for the collection, has to be addressed one way or the other.

I'm all alone with highly sensitive materials.

I stopped to cry many times during my reading, knowing that Nadia, my beautiful predecessor, is dead and gone. Knowing that Isla Negra, where this was written, is now abandoned and up for sale.

The question that haunts me: What if I gave them back to Raymond?

Emily drove to work in an early-morning fog that seemed to mirror her sleep-deprived mind. *The Archivist* had consumed her like a fire fueled psychically from inside. She seemed to be missing the necessary brain cells to process all the ramifications and potential consequences were the Moleskines ever to come to light, but she shuddered at the thought. The red brake lights in the fog shone like the eyes of animals in the night. They blinked on and off, as the commuter traffic trudged up Coast Highway in the direction of the university.

Emily wondered why Nadia—if it had been Nadia—had put "Restricted until 2020" on the string-tie envelopes. The eighth-floor renovation would be completed in 2019, so perhaps she was thinking that would be a safe-enough date. *Assuming* anyone found them. She had found them. She, Emily, was the archivist Nadia had hoped would find them, Emily firmly wanted to believe. But what a responsibility to drop on an unsuspecting archivist. And what if it had been someone who didn't know what they were? Would they have automatically assumed that "RW" referred to Raymond West? And if they *had* found them, would they have taken the time to read them? Would they even have the aesthetic wherewithal to comprehend what they were in possession of?

The library was aswarm with students when Emily came inside. A majority of them were bent forward, their eyes glued to mobile phones, texting adroitly while walking, and then had an annoying tendency to carom off one another like bumper cars. They pinged off Emily like inhabitants of a new civilization that was forging a future, Emily believed, with machines, not love; STEM, not art; disjointed, not deep, immersive, reading.

Emily was taken aback to find Helena in her cubicle when she arrived in Special Collections, flinging open drawers in an animallike fury.

"Helena?"

Helena stood up, startled, flustered. "Uh, I was just looking for a . . . Sharpie. You wouldn't happen to have an extra, would you?"

Emily narrowed her eyes at Helena. She took two steps, opened the top drawer, grabbed a black Sharpie and handed it to her. "Here."

"Thank you. I'll bring it right back." Helena stopped at the entrance. "You're aware, Emily, that the Gala has been moved up."

"Yes. I read my emails," Emily retorted.

"Good. Carry on." Helena bustled out. Emily kept her gaze on the empty entrance until the sound of retreating footsteps was replaced by the more commonplace sounds of Special Collections: the copier whirring, muffled voices. She sat down at her desk and turned on her computer. Panicking that she had forgotten something, she threw open all her drawers. In one of the file folders, she noticed that Nadia's personal file on the West Papers showed pages that had been partly lifted out. She grabbed it, spun around in her chair, and faced the cubicle entrance defensively. The pages, full of codes, were the ones that had to do with Regents Annex. Had Emily been careless in leaving them drifting out of the folder? Had she put them back too hurriedly? All the pages in the personal file were numbered progressively and Emily, with some semblance of relief, took note that none were missing.

She raised her head and eyed the empty entrance suspiciously. Was Helena spying on her? Had the unauthorized Annex visit been reported?

For the rest of the afternoon Emily, still shaken by Helena's appearance, holed up in her cubicle and went through the motions of continuing the processing of the collection, but her mind was circuiting some far penumbra of the West Papers.

After a solid morning of archiving, sleep-deprived and still wracked with paranoia, Emily shut down her computer and walked the length of the corridor to Joel, worried she hadn't heard from him. He had his headphones on and was watching a surfing competition streamed in from Australia.

"Joel?"

He didn't answer right away. Emily swanned forward and waved her arms histrionically. Joel tore off his headphones and gawked at her, jittery every time he saw her now, perhaps fearful of another compromising request.

"What?" he asked.

"What's the scuttlebutt?"

Joel regarded her like she was a little deranged. "What do you mean?"

"Helena was in my cubicle going through my drawers." Emily imitated a frantic Helena with wildly waving arms.

"The fuck?"

Emily planted her hands on her hips and tilted her head to one side with a questioning look.

Joel shifted restlessly in his chair. "I don't know, Emily. I'm just a digital archivist."

"And I'm just a manuscripts processor." She dropped the facetious tone. "Are they gossiping about me or what?"

Joel let his face muddle into a sheepish look. He glanced at the entrance to his cubicle.

Footsteps resounded in the corridor, interrupting their conversation. Helena and Verlander lumbered past, talking animatedly in earnest whispers. Helena shot a glance in Joel's cubicle, smiled without parting her lips, and continued keeping pace with Verlander.

Joel turned back toward Emily, his face bit by worry. In a forced undertone, he queried, "Are you ever going to tell me what you found?"

"I thought you didn't want to know," Emily said.

Joel closed his eyes and heaved a sigh. He waited. They had reached that juncture in their relationship where the tacit only required its spoken response.

"You told me not to tell you anything you didn't need to know," Emily said.

"How heavy is it?" Joel asked.

Emily tilted her head back ninety degrees and gazed up at the ceiling and the eight floors of the library pressing down on her conscience with the weight of consequences impossible to gauge. "They're collapsing, Joel. They're coming down."

"Don't tell me that." Joel swung his chair back to his monitor.

"Do you want to get coffee later at Bird Rock? I need to pick up a bag of beans. We can talk."

Joel found sanity in his monitor, stricken with paranoia suddenly. "Text me," he said tersely.

"Okay," Emily said, feeling a little abandoned, but glad she had kept the revelation of her discovery to herself. To Joel's back she said in parting, "I'm not going to give you up, Joel."

He nodded, but it was clear from the hangdog profile of his expression his confliction had intensified into a wordless dubiety.

Emily took a late lunch in the bower and then crossed the crowded campus to Farber College. The fog had dissipated, and the sky was a panorama of spreading blue through the trees. Oh, the poetry of those treetops, Emily thought, remembering a line from *The Archivist*. Students swarmed like ants on the maze of pathways, hurrying erratically to classes.

Following a campus map, Emily came to DuBois Lecture Hall, a large building with glass doors, and slipped inside. A few students with backpacks, their faces hunched zombified over cells, were clustered in the foyer. Emily accosted a group of them.

"Is this Professor West's creative writing class?"

"Yes," replied one of the young girls, who turned to Emily with an insouciant expression.

Legs fueled by an emotion she couldn't define, Emily went through the doors into the 150-seat, tiered lecture hall. A buzz of voices in the packed auditorium signaled an air of anticipation.

Emily settled inconspicuously into a seat against the wall in the right-of-center section in the extreme rear. She cinched up her hoodie and hunched down in her chair, rooted from her tote a Moleskine she had bought at the campus bookstore, opened it to the first page and wrote in ballpoint, "RW—Autobiographical Fiction."

A few stragglers migrated down the steps and settled into the remaining seats, some having to resort to sitting on the carpeted aisle steps. The class appeared to be comprised predominantly of women—some older, possibly grad students or even university professors, Raymond's privileged appearances were that rare, in addition to the fact that 2017 was a sabbatical year. Emily noticed three young women in the front row, right in front of the lectern, who were seized with giggling. When the right side door, the one for faculty, opened, the auditorium dropped into a sepulchral hush.

Raymond West appeared, tall and rangy, briefly backlit by the sun until the door banged closed behind him. With the support of a cane, he hobbled across the ground-level stage of the auditorium to where the lectern stood, his cowboy boot heels clicking on the laminate, heralding the approach of something momentous. In the hand not gripping his cane he clutched a weathered leather briefcase designed in the retro style of a postal bag. He slapped it onto a thigh-high table, leaned his cane against it, then stepped up to the lectern and smiled at the class. He combed his shoulder-length hair off his lined face with the splayed fingers that Emily had read described by Nadia. What he had lived and experienced, and what they had yet to live and experience—the juxtaposition was chasmic to Emily.

"I didn't realize how many young people today hoped to be writers," Raymond opened. His words were met with scattered, nervous laughter. "But who's going to read what you write if your generation doesn't read anymore?" he added cynically, but Emily could tell from the tone of his voice that it was something plaguing his conscience. The death of the novel, its readers dispersed to other content mediums, never able to get back.

Raymond gripped the lectern with both hands and steadied himself behind it. "Welcome to Creative Writing 198. If you're here to learn about quadratic equations"—he swept an arm behind him to the long blackboard scribbled with inscrutable numbers and formulas—"then you're in the wrong class. You're free to leave." Raymond allowed his eyes to stray over the sea of youth. No one stirred. "You're all here to learn to be writers?" he asked, incredulous, wanting to inject a note of sardonic humor into his presentation. He nodded at the collective murmurings of apparent assent. "Okay. My name is Raymond West. I'd prefer if you called me Raymond and not professor." He paused and his eyes met his hands gripping the lectern. "I profess to know nothing." A relieved chortling filled the auditorium. Raymond nodded to himself, as if promoting the generation of his opening remarks, which, once begun, would carry him extemporaneously through the hour as if on autopilot. He bent his head in the direction of the burnished black walnut cane. "That cane there. There's a story in it. How did I end up with a broken femur?" He lowered his voice. "Thus, the limping, in case you were interested." He seemed to be fumbling for an opening, until he hit his stride. "What led me to a situation where I would break my femur?" He turned back to the eager young faces gazing down enrapt at him and refound his footing in their laughter, their hanging on his every word. A pensive smile like a dark cloud scudded across his face. Emily started to feel an eerily emotional connection to him, as if he were speaking metaphorically and solely to her. "The class I teach is autobiographical fiction. It takes many forms. Memoir. Imaginative fiction . . ." and Raymond was off and running, delivering a colorful, unscripted lecture.

Emily pretended to take notes. After detailing the requirements for the class, Raymond launched into a definitional scope of autobiographical fiction, distinguishing it from other genres of fiction. A pedanticism graced some of his opening remarks, but then he appeared to veer off topic and rambled on free-associatively about mining material from "real life," about how it "could compromise others," and then, most absorbingly to Emily: "There are things so vividly, and powerfully, personal others might think you lived them." He looked up. "And will judge you. Because the fiction is so well written they can't differentiate or disentangle it from the truth." His words were halted by a saturnine pause. His eyes blinked and he seemed to have grown lost in his own labyrinthian maze of thoughts and memories. Then he recovered. "Until you win a Pulitzer." He raised both arms to the height of his ears in mock triumph. "Then all is forgiven!" The collective laughter made him feel human, less professorial, and that mischievous smile returned to his face again.

In that moment Emily caught a glimpse of the emotionally excitable, even voluble, Raymond West whom Nadia had fallen in love with. Not the man before her now, borne by some concealed or confidential tragedy, who had limped in on the support of a cane, appearing to have given up on life, a jaded professor put out to pasture and exiled to stories of fame and broken memories, his passions tamed.

After the laughter died down, one of the women in the front row threw her hand up in the air and waved it frantically to draw his attention.

"Yes?" Raymond said, lowering his glasses, pointing at the besotted undergrad dying to ask him a question, but also, Emily cynically imagined, dying to get him to notice her.

"Professor—I mean Raymond," the girl nervously corrected herself. "When you first came in you pointed to the cane on the desk and started to say that it was the beginning of a story. And that you broke your leg. Could we maybe hear what that story is?"

Raymond's eyes roamed to the cane aslant against the desk, then settled on it as if it were a sleeping animal that could awaken at any moment and assail him with the past. He unconsciously pulled on his nose and grew reflective with slow nods of his head. "There are some stories," he addressed the cane in a baritone that students craned their heads to make out, "that are too painfully personal to share." His words stretched out as if he were speaking in half time.

"Even if they would bring you the 'catharsis' you once talked about in an interview I read?" the persistent student asked.

Raymond nodded, lost in thought, hypnotized by the cane. "Yes. And those are the ones you should dare to write." He had traveled back somewhere looking at the cane. Emily could see he was wrestling on one hand with the past and trying to come to terms with a manifest hypocrisy in the present, even if it all floated ethereally high over the heads of the students, none of whom had experienced suffering on the scale Raymond's expression bore silent witness to.

Finally, he seemed to snap out of his trance and turned to the class. "I started to write that book." He lowered his head to the lectern and paused. "Sometimes you have to know when to abandon books, or stories. Sometimes," he looked up, finally having found footing in a train of thought, "as my editor once told me, 'Reality is more fiction than fiction.'" He brought a hand to his mouth and spread a forefinger and thumb over his lips, a tic of his when he wasn't sure what his next thoughts were, or, Emily wondered, when trying to quash an emotion.

"So, the cane is not a story you're going to write?" the undergrad pestered.

"I don't think I can," Raymond replied enigmatically. "In autobiographical fiction writing, if you don't feel like you have total emotional access to something, if you're not willing to be completely truthful and forthcoming, if you're afraid of hurting others, it's, well"—he looked up—"the peril of being a writer."

A silence fell on the class as if the 150-plus students, entranced by his words, were still straining to apprehend his subtextual meaning.

"One day I might write the cane story." He smiled wistfully. "There will come a moment when I'm ready to write it. But that moment isn't now." He turned his head and glanced up at the clock above the blackboard, then back at the class. He rallied: "My advice is quantity over quality. Especially at your age. Try to write five hundred to a thousand words a day. Try to finish a short story every week. Write even if you don't know what you want to write. Writing begets writing. Ideas beget ideas. And one day you'll have something, and maybe it'll be something that will make others want to take that journey with you." Animated now, he produced a smile. "I'll see you all next Monday, when we'll talk about the autobiographical genesis of Hemingway's *The Sun Also Rises* and . . ." He paused and gazed at the young faces. "Clarice Lispector's *Collected Stories*. A brilliant writer whom many of you might not be familiar with." He pounded his chest with a fist. "She wrote from the heart. Read her."

Emily recognized the name Clarice Lispector, and a spider skittered eerily up her spine.

Raymond removed his glasses and slipped them into his shirt pocket. Students emptied from their chairs and swarmed him. Many of them waved forms in his face for him to sign so they could be admitted into the overflow class. The three girls sitting in the front dawdled, gazing up at his lanky frame and handsome face, hoping to draw his attention. He signed the forms and patiently fielded their eager, overlapping questions.

Emily undid her hood and ambled down the steps from her high perch in the auditorium. Students bounded up the aisle past her in the opposite direction. Emily measured her steps, taking one for every three students who fanned away from the vortex that clustered around Raymond. When he had finally chased away the three adoring undergrads, he turned, now all alone, to reach for his knurled cane wobbling against the desk from all the commotion.

Emily knew she was breaking all protocol of an archivist when she interrupted him and said, "Raymond." He turned and looked at her with squinting, circumspect eyes. "Do you remember me?"

"No," he answered guardedly, "I'm afraid not. Should I?"

Emily thrust out a stiffened hand. "I'm Emily Snow." He looked puzzled. "I'm the project archivist working on your papers."

And at that moment his hand let go of the cane and it rattled against the table's edge. He seemed momentarily shaken. "Ms. Snow. Yes. We met at my house." He took her hand and held it in his without letting go, almost, Emily thought, as if he could sense through the current in her being that she needed his hand in some way that was not of this world. And, maybe, just maybe, he needed hers.

Emily's pulse thrilled. "Yes. Briefly."

"How is it coming . . . my archive?" he stammered.

"Well, that's just the thing." Emily paused and cleared her throat. "I have some questions about it I would like to pose."

"Oh?" He reached for his cane and bag. He slung the bag over his shoulder. "Would you like to walk me to my car and talk about it?"

Emily remained motionless. "No. I can't."

Raymond, mystified, dropped his gaze to hers. Their eyes locked in the cane's ineffable grief. "Why?"

"You're a donor. I'm staff. Technically, we're not supposed to be seen together unless we've made an appointment through proper channels."

"So you chose to come here and accost me?" He shook his head. "I'm missing something, Ms. Snow."

"I have some important personal things I'd like to talk to you about. If I went to the director . . ."

"Ms. Blackwell?" he said.

Emily nodded once. "She would want to know the purpose of my visit."

"I see. And you don't feel you can reveal that to her?" he said somewhat warily.

Emily shook her head back and forth emphatically.

"And why wouldn't they want you to come directly to me?"

"They would consider it inappropriate," Emily explained.

Raymond nodded thoughtfully. "Why would you risk coming to me then?"

A gravid pause elapsed. Raymond glanced at his watch and waited.

"Because I know the story of the cane." Emily said.

Raymond swung his head in her direction like a startled animal to meet her blazingly intense eyes. His face, transfigured by a sudden disinterring of an avalanche of events, colored red, and miniature storm clouds massed in his limpid blue eyes. Unbidden, he blinked back tears with a rapid fluttering of eyelids. The past had smacked him like a wave crashing at night.

"Oh my God," he gasped. He brought a hand to his mouth and looked away, shaking his head, as if the tsunami of the tragedy had brought a second wave into the inundation zone of his sorrow.

NADIA'S STORY (CONT'D)

From the 56 freeway, I headed in the direction of the university, but veered off at Carmel Valley Road and steered in the milky blue morning in the direction of Raymond's Isla Negra. Ostensibly I was on my way to the airport to catch a flight to a Society of American Archivists conference in San Francisco, but instead I was headed to a rendezvous with Raymond and a blissful week with him, alone together at last, across the border in Valle Guadalupe. I hated lying to my husband, but these were changing times in my life, and the truth was going to come out sooner rather than later.

I found a parking spot on Stratford Court, climbed out of my Ford Falcon, grabbed my carry-on bag, and waited for a gray Volvo SUV to pass before I crossed the road. The SUV slowed to a crawl as it went past. I couldn't see through the tinted windows. In my tight black jeans, sleeveless burgundy blouse unbuttoned to my bra, mane of black hair styled that morning into a waterfall of pulchritude over my bare shoulders, bright red lipstick, I would have been a sight to behold this early in the morning. I might have expected a whistle or at least a horn honk, but the car coasted anonymously past, and I skipped across the street and down Little Orphan Alley, paying it no more mind.

Raymond greeted me with an emotionally starved, breath-stealing kiss at the door. It was a lusty kiss, one without reservations, one he didn't look over my shoulder to see if anyone was spying on us, one that promised armadas bearing treasures of exotic surprises. His strong hands gripped my muscular shoulders, his fingers repeatedly raked my hair as if he wanted something of mine to hold on to and never let go. His eyes bore into mine, narrowed with love; it was knee-buckling. He was in an unusually ebullient mood as he pulled away and a smile crinkled his face with fine fissures and his eyes glinted with mica in their miniature Mediterraneans of blue.

"Let's go," he announced in a voice brimming with enthusiasm.

We packed up his Range Rover with our travel belongings and backed out of the driveway. At the top of Little Orphan Alley, I noticed, for some reason—paranoia?—that the Volvo SUV had found a place to park. A man in his midforties, with short-cropped hair, tight black jeans and black T-shirt and mirrored Ray-Bans was leaning against the driver's-side door, a cigarette poking out from his mustachioed lips, a gold lighter in one hand, as if he were waiting for a signal to click it aflame. I noticed that his eyes swept the trajectory of our vehicle as we turned right and traveled south. I stole an inconspicuous glance at the side rearview mirror, but the road remained empty behind us all the way to the freeway. I turned to Raymond. He was smiling contentedly. If we were being watched, and that was my nauseating suspicion, I didn't want to founder the joyous mood with my vague unease.

Raymond pointed to the glove compartment box. I threw him a quizzical sidelong look. "A little present," he said, as if it were of trifling importance.

I pressed a button and popped the glove compartment open. Inside I found a package wrapped in black paper and tied with a silver ribbon. I held it in both hands with a strange, tremulous excitement. I knew what it was by the feel of its outlines, but I wanted to delay opening it because the fatalist in me realized it was the end of something, something momentous and unique, and I worried that once it had ended, Raymond might no longer need me or, worse, desire me. His kisses were powerful testament in contradiction of that fear, but we weren't officially together. He was married; I was married. And he was married to a woman who wasn't going give him up without a fight. These thoughts crowded my sudden feelings of excitement at what I was about to unwrap. My depression worked like this. I needed the high of the climb, but when the summit was near, I seemed to automatically sense the descent and dread its inexorable disillusionment. The addict in me, the woman addicted to finding the love of her life at any lethal cost.

I untied the ribbon with the presentiment of that sorrow slackening my shoulders. Did Raymond's thoughtful expression show understanding of my feelings or did he think this was my way of expressing exultation? Even more slowly than the ribbon, I unwrapped the sheeny black paper, spreading it outward like the foil on a special chocolate. Inside was what I had expected: Volume XII of *The Archivist*. The final volume. Tears sprang to my eyes, and I flashed them to keep from weeping. I squeezed my lids closed and could feel my lashes grow wet as they tried to combat the flood of upwelling emotion. Erased in that moment was a decade of failed and aborted attempts, countless rejections from senior editors at imprints large and small, hopelessness and futility, the conclusion after one published book I was a nobody, a cipher, destined for the dustheap of a handful of libraries where I technically still existed. But with *The Archivist*, they would go back and rediscover *Knife in the Heart*, and they would see, those fuckers, that the fire had never died in me, that I wasn't one of the vanished writers. When I opened my eyes, they were blurred out of focus.

"I finished it last night," Raymond said with a sigh of relief. "Wrote past midnight. Haven't done that since *Lessons in Reality*. I was levitating, my love. Levitating." Celebrating, he pulled me toward him and kissed me wildly, swerved to get back in the lane, and laughed wickedly like a man freed from a prison and launched into a world where hope and redemption ruled supreme. "The catastrophic molt is complete," he said to the wide, empty road ahead. "I did it. God help me." He shook his head once for emphasis. "Correction: God help the both of us."

I drew the back of my hand across my eyes, choking on words backed up in my mind a mile long and consisting of a lifetime of true fulfillment. The concrete freeway and all its steel and rubber were now but a blur of another reality, a river I *wanted* to be carried along on, not the Sisyphean treadmill where hope never glistened. It was as if a turnoff was up ahead, and when we took it, we were the only car allowed on it, and it rose higher and higher and arced like a rainbow over the library that now loomed to our immediate right, and we were way out over the Pacific, tandem paragliders, soaring to an island of eternal happiness where, together, we would dream the literary future. I dared not utter these hyperboles. Like all women I dreamed, but my dream had always seemed an unattainable one. But here, in my tremulous hands—yes, they were shaking!—was concrete consummation of that dream.

I swallowed hard. All I could say was, "Thirty days. A true torrent of creativity. Do you know how truly happy this makes me? To see you like this?"

"When you know what it is," Raymond started philosophically, his sunglasses turning back to the road ahead of us, "when you know what you want, when it's coming from a place and time of pure feeling, it's a dam bursting, and you hope to God you divert, and capture, as much of the water rushing at you as you can." He nodded at the freeway through the windshield. "You can't hold back. You can't censor yourself." He turned to me and rested a hand on my thigh. "You disinterred it, Nadia. You reminded me what once made me who I am lauded for being. And then you gave me the gift of *your* words, which took me—us!—to new heights. It's your book, too. And all the time, in this cocoon, I was writing it to you, for you." He finished in a higher octave, a note of pure elation with all he had accomplished in the thirty days since beginning. I let him ramble. His excited verbosity over our creation heightened the thrill of our escape across the border. Mutual thoughts of lust intensified the closer we got to the Mexican border. I hugged his firm musculature. He clasped my thigh and massaged it, and I could feel his desire through the grip of his strong hand, the one that had held that pen that raced across those twelve volumes of electrifying prose.

"I gave you everything I had," I effused. "And I wanted to give you more. I wasn't sure it would ever be enough. But to see this . . ." I held up the final Moleskine in triumph.

"I know," he said. "I know."

I could feel his gaze on my nodding head, nodding as if it were a perpetual pendulum, stunned and suddenly feeling all alone. "How do you feel?" I asked.

"Exhilarated. Emotionally drained. Emptied out. Like never before." When he realized I hadn't responded, he turned to me. "You seem sad, Nadia. Why? We did it!"

"Because it's over," I said, clasping a hand to my mouth.

"No, Nadia, it's just beginning," he reassured me. And his words bore the deep intonation of truth, as if they had emerged from somewhere deep in his soul, and it was that intonation that I needed, that I clung to like a little girl to her blanket.

I fell into him and cleaved to his shoulder with both hands and wept openly into his blue linen shirt. Raymond remained passively silent. He understood the catharsis of creation and its welling aftermath. He knew that powerful storms left landscapes changed and altered forever in faulted new formations. I only knew, through my sobbing, that, if this book were published, I would be remembered, remembered as . . . *the archivist. His* archivist. Sadness surrendered to happiness and I found myself laughing through my tears. "I can't believe we did it," I gushed. "I'm ready for the fallout." I turned to face him. "Are you, Raymond?"

He patted my knee. "I only know what it is. I can't think about that right now, my love."

We crossed the border into Tijuana. All the logorrheic emails, professions of love and exchanges of erotic fantasies, the phone conversations, the post-lovemaking brainstorming sessions on *The Archivist*, they had all been distilled now into a first draft of a work that one day, when the time was propitious, would be published. We slipped into an unspoken mutual understanding that nothing about what we had done had to be further analyzed.

The final Moleskine had given *The Archivist's* creation a kind of vocal mask. I didn't want to say anything, I didn't want to overintellectualize our creation, our collaboration, for fear it would shatter the inviolable spell its spontaneous inception had constructed. I floated weightless in a bubble of unadulterated ecstasy. I would never admit to Raymond it was more profoundly moving and earth-trembling than any sex we had ever enjoyed. Sex moved the earth in the moment, but the written word eternalized the act of creation.

And how freeing it was to realize that, I thought, when we turned on to Mexico Highway One, the latitudinal aorta of Baja California, that snaked a thousand miles to the Sea of Cortez traversing a wild, desolate desert where cacti twisted a hundred feet into the endlessly blue skies, like the gnarled fingers of some unshakeable god of a forsaken earth. From Tijuana to Ensenada, the smooth two-lane highway curved along a seaside bluff. The blue of the ocean seemed bluer here in Mexico, I imagined. The skies seemed washed of pollution and looked freshly painted in watercolor azure. Waves crashed on black rocks in explosions of blinding white more dramatically than anywhere in San Diego. And we were across the border, in another country, another land almost, no longer lashed to jobs and residences, obligations and routines. Here we could be exultant in our lovemaking and sleep in each other's arms, wake to yearning and longing and chapped lip kisses, not have to be somewhere, no one checking their cells for the time or messages. We had eloped —I liked to believe—in celebration, and we would return in hope, expectation for the glorious future that awaited us. We would run the gauntlet of opprobrium, weather the unimaginable backlash, then triumph, like twin phoenixes rising from the proverbial ashes. I drank in my lover's smiling, contented face, with a lust for insobriety, a lust for his heart. That's all that mattered to me.

As Mexico Highway One opened up to empty, white-sand beaches, the road now felt, both literally and figuratively, ours alone. Midweek, we found an absence of tourists, a desolation of cars, and Raymond drove fast, eager to get to our destination. The Spanish-language billboards made me think we had flown into a new time zone, had circumnavigated a quarter of the globe, that it had been a true turnoff from the freeway into our own inviolable realm. I was delirious with joy and I was sure Raymond could recognize it in my face, the face that had surrendered tears to sun-splashed, wide-mouthed, red-lipped smiles beneath my dark sunglasses, sunglasses Raymond contended made me look like a movie star, causing me to blush. A "decadent beauty," he had described me in *The Archivist*. I may have been that beautiful, and I felt appreciated for it, but it was his adoration of my mind, my imagination, the lifting of my words into a now finished work of art, that radiated the real beauty I felt and hoped wouldn't go unacknowledged.

The dark blue of the Pacific seemed to fall farther and farther beneath us as the road climbed ethereally higher and higher into the cerulean sky and the wispy white clouds that drifted across it, making us feel lighter and lighter, like two arrows launched across a forbidden border and into a lawless territory where the consequences of our love, and the sealing of its pact in *The Archivist*, bore no traces, existed tabula rasa, ready to spring forth from the hard, barren land of our damnable, but necessary, infidelity.

A low, dense, churning white fog had drawn a curtain over the ocean in a section of the highway where we pulled over at one of the many scenic *el mirador*s to stretch our limbs. Raymond stood tall behind me and enveloped me in his arms as the wind shattered the human mast of our lashed bodies on the high seaside overlook. He held me tightly, like he would never let me go. I gathered him into me as if I were a well and he the pure rainwater that gushed from it. In a furious motion, he spun me around and we kissed, my hair whipped by the onshore wind that buffeted us on the precipitous, sun-drenched cliffside.

Mexico Highway One wound down near the ocean where windblown sand dunes rippled like waves pouring out of a desert into an oasis. I rested my head on my arms on the ledge of the door in the open window and let the wind sandblast my face. In that moment I felt sure I had changed the depth of my inner existence forever.

Ten miles before Ensenada, we angled away from the coast and traveled in a northeasterly direction on the single-lane Highway Three. The barren landscape gradually colored into verdant agricultural parcels framed by low rolling treeless hills in the east-facing sky. Remarkably, splendiferous vineyards rose into view, drooping with their October verdancy and pendulous clusters of bursting ripe grapes. Signs indicated we had entered Valle de Guadalupe and its Ruta del Vino. Raymond had not told me where he was spiriting me away to. He had only alluded to Baja and a special place, and I had confessed I had never crossed the border, "not *that* border" I qualified to his understanding smile. We knew each other now; we shared that private shorthand.

The skies were deepening blue and the hills shaded dusky silhouettes when we swung into the driveway at Adobe Guadalupe, a winery resort north of Ensenada. Raymond's Range Rover churned gravel as we braked to a halt in the circular drive of the entrance, centered by a large fountain, whose underwater lights transformed the jets of water into an arcing stream of glittering yellow diamonds. The moonless night gave way to a sky dome of swirling, opalescent galaxies fixed in whorls like giant, motionless shells of fog. The air smelled of scrubland flora, leafy vineyards and the drifting smoke of charred meats and fishes wafting from the kitchen chimneys from an indoor grill burning white-hot with crackling and hissing mesquite.

A smiling, white-toothed valet unloaded our luggage, and another took Raymond's keys and led the two of us into the hacienda-style resort, our ears still ringing from the drive. In the enormous lobby, with its tiled floors and adobe walls and crisscrossing dark-beamed ceilings, we were greeted by Luis, a man in his fifties with black hair frosted at the temples and a face the color of saddle leather. He shook Raymond's hand with obvious genuine pleasure and then turned to me.

"And you are?" he asked.

"Nadia." I caught Raymond raising a forefinger to his lips to Luis.

"*Seguro*," he said. "Come, I'll show you your rooms."

"Rooms?" I teased, as if the spell was starting to fissure and the dream already evaporating.

"I'll explain at dinner," Raymond whispered into my ear, kissing it softly with his reassuring lips.

Trailed by the valet with our luggage wheeled on a clattering cart, Luis led Raymond and me to our assigned rooms through an arched brick portico that faced out onto a vineyard and beyond to the hills now framed by a midnight blue firmament spilt and splattered with stars.

Luis stopped at a door. He turned to me. "Your room."

I glanced over the shorter Luis to Raymond. Raymond slipped me a wink.

Luis held open the door with an outstretched arm and beckoned me inside. He handed me the heavy brass key. Then he set my bag down inside and quietly closed the door.

I felt all alone in the casita. The warm light from the bedside table lamps cast the room in a golden illumination. The décor's motif was dark blue. Curtains were held back by ties and opened out to the stars. I sat back on the bed with my arms spread to the sides of me like a large sleeping bird and dreamed my gaze out the window.

After a while, I picked myself up off the bed, showered the dust and salt air and happiness off my smiling face and recharged body, and changed into the plush courtesy bathrobe, knotting it at the waist with a braided rope. Brushing out my hair, I espied a piece of paper at the buttery band of light where the door met the floor. I bent down to pick it up. It was a small rectangular card. "My door is open. Please hurry."

I rushed to Raymond with a head of wet hair and a milky soft body thirsting for physical, not artistic, validation. He was lying supine on the bed, his head in the cradle of his back-stretched arms, stripped now to only his underwear. I opened my bathrobe and he almost fainted in anticipation of me upon him. I crawled onto the bed like a ravening jaguar, shimmied up over him with writhing hips and locked his skull in the vise of my passionate thighs. Gently at first, and invisibly, he lapped from eternity, knowing it was ephemeral, but immortal in the moment. I clasped my hands behind my bedraggled hair and threw back my head and closed my eyes to the immutable feeling that from that first collision of our hearts at Estancia he had never wavered in his love for me, our book its tangible testimony.

His hands clutched my buttocks and pressed them to him with a fervor I knew was born from a month of intense all day, and nearly all night, writing. Like me, he was in need of lustful oblivion. My cries rose and I made no effort to muffle them, as it felt so fucking freeing to be so far away from Regents. We came in explosive exhalations, liberated from the fears of a prying world. Soon I shuddered and slapped my hand on the pillow and then grabbed his head and speechlessly begged him to stop. I threw a hand to my forehead, tenting a contented smile. My thighs went slack. He heaved me back to his chest with wanton abandon and looked up at me with his own desire unsatisfied. He turned me over, and I willingly submitted to total limbs-outthrust surrender, ceding over the lost continent of my body's voluptuous glory for him to colonize in his quest for the extremes of pleasure. He held back little in his exploitation. I let him ravish me, fling his body at me. Until he was no longer the famished writer, released from his own terrible stresses and obligations and a world that seemed to always be watching him. Raymond completely let go until he had run to the end, where he came to an exhausted halt, winded, drawing lungfuls of a new air, feeling the blood coursing hot in his throbbing heart.

Sweating in the heat of our bodies, we lay coiled together like tarnished angels in the transgression of our escape. Fallen to earth after the pure and exhausted heaven of our collaboration, its cauldron's fires extinguished for now. It had been two weeks since we had made love. To me, it seemed forever. Words would have rendered the aftermath mundane. Would have vitiated the silence, shattered the spirit that flowed like a sacred current through the tips of my fingers to the flesh that shrouded his soul. The screeches of birds carried to our ears through the adobe walls and curtained windows, a language that predated men and communicated a deeper, more ancient, truth, it seemed. Footsteps on the tiled portico walked across our imaginations like masked intruders of another race. Our world knew no other world except this one of unshackled freedom. Even if, in limning the joy of our entwined limbs, the glance of another, more unforgiving, world anxiously beckoned. A glance that would soon grow monstrously into a cruelly judgmental spotlight, one that, sadly, we would have to soon give justification. But for now, in the depths of Baja's Valle Guadalupe, our phones silenced, our alibis ironclad, we breathed an unadulterated evanescence of love.

We held each other in the shower as warm water rained down on us and deliquesced us into one. My hands climbed up the muscles of his back and rested on his shoulders. I pulled him down for a kiss, and he kissed me until water almost drowned us. Were there tears bathing his eyes? Or merely the shower water enclosing us in its waterfall?

"Are you crying?" I touched a forefinger to his eye.

He nodded. "It took a lot out of me. And, of course, she—and everybody else—was dying to know what I was working on. To hold it inside like that . . ." He squeezed his eyes shut and exhaled air from his nose. Reassuringly, he ran a hand through my wet hair. "And to go two weeks without you"—he shook his head with shut eyes—"was hell," he closed in a voice that sounded truly pained. "I missed you so much."

"But I was always there," I said, "hovering over you."

"You were always there, you always will be," he said, in a tone that sounded final to me, as if these were the words he would utter on his deathbed.

He pulled himself away from me in the shower and dressed. Then I could hear him talking in hushed tones on his phone. I brought my hands to my ears and withdrew into myself, the spray of the shower emptying me of reality, drowning out his whispered lies to his wife.

I went back to my casita and got dressed for dinner. Raymond was waiting for me in the outdoor patio dining area. A saffron-colored enclosure rose up to expose star-stippled skies. A fire burned red and spat embers in an open-air pit where a sous chef turned meats and vegetables on a grill with a giant pair of tongs. I stopped and gazed at Raymond from across the patio. He was magnificent, I thought, in an off-white linen shirt, the sleeves rolled to the elbows, the tails flying out over faded jeans. The shirt accentuated his tan, bronzing his lined face and distinguishing his smile in its gleaming whiteness. The flames from the open-pit mesquite grill flickered patterns of light across his life, whose work I had cared for lovingly in the time I spent working on his papers. He looked impossibly handsome to me. A pinprick of insecurity touched me when I noticed he was looking down and tapping on a phone. He put it away when he heard my approach on the gravel path. He rose from the table and pulled out a chair for me. His hand grazed my bare neck. I wore a sleeveless black dress with a V-neckline that revealed my black bra when I leaned forward into his eyes. I caught him staring at the necklace dangling dangerously above my breasts.

"I love that ouroboros." His eyes glinted with delight. "Incredible how certain symbols of mythology run through to today, and we're no different in many ways than our ancestors."

I reached out and placed my hand on his. He poured me a glass of red wine that was standing uncorked on the table.

"Local Tempranillo," he said.

I picked up the bottle and read the label. "Jardín Secreto." I pulled a face. "Secret garden."

"I thought it appropriate." His eyes blinked impishly, then traveled unrepentantly down my plunging neckline and into the well of the woman he now knew intimately. From the delight in his eyes, I could sense his relief that the writing was over, the first draft had been egested, that a tremendous weight had been lifted from him, and from here forward all that would remain would be tinkering and honing until we got it right.

A waiter appeared with a gleaming silver platter heaped high with grilled meats and vegetables and set them down. Rosemary-scented smoke sizzled from it in pungent clouds. The waiter slipped away into the quiet whispering of the other tables that were all a blur to me and Raymond, locked away as we were in our own inviolable world. Nothing but Nature touched us now. If only this suspension of being together could be hung forever, I mused as I sipped red wine and thought how happy I was, how perfect this moment was, how Raymond had carved out a world for the two of us to celebrate, how long ago it was that I sat all alone outside the Arts & Humanities building wondering if we would be here one day.

Slowly, sensually, I buttered a roll from a basket and spoke to the knife, "Tell me you haven't brought your wife here ever?"

"Never." His voice deepened an octave. "Some things are sacred, Nadia."

"Or anyone else?"

Raymond shook his head with his eyes leveled at mine. "Let's not spoil the mood with reality, shall we?"

"Okay," I surrendered. I held the wineglass next to my face and met his eyes. They were squinted seriously, the granitic way a man's eyes can be serious. I waited, with pounding heart.

"Don't worry, Nadia."

"I know we have to wait." I found myself nodding. "I know you can't rush this into publication. I know you can't just . . . ask for a divorce."

Raymond reached a hand across the table and put two fingers to my crimson lips.

"Shh, Nadia." He grabbed my wrist and held it tightly, fearing the madness rearing up in me that he knew ran like a death wish through all my short stories. "When this whole library rededication business is done, it's going to be published. And I know what that means. And I don't care."

I looked up with flashing eyes. "What *library rededication*?"

"She's giving a huge donation to the library. The eighth floor is going to be transformed into a . . . celestial event center, whatever. You can't tell anyone. It's top secret."

I was seized with fear. "Why didn't you tell me this?"

"I just found out. It's been in the works with Helena for a few years now. It doesn't change anything. We just have to get through it."

"You used me?" I said suspiciously.

"No," he protested in a wounded voice. "Why do you say that?" He tightened his grip on my wrist. "No. I love you, Nadia. I love you."

I eyed my wineglass with a hurt look, thinking through the narrative as if ideating another story whose ending was yet to be realized. "They'll know it was me, won't they?"

"If you don't want me to publish the book, I won't. If you don't want your name on it, I won't put it on. But I'm tired of living a lie. You've got to believe that."

I nodded, but the trapdoor had unexpectedly sprung, and my insecurity was in pinwheeling free fall again. I heard the gravity incorporated into his voice and I wanted to believe him. With the admission of the library being rededicated in his wife's name, there were now consequences beyond adultery, ramifications that superseded divorce. I raised my head to him from its downcast stare into the wine I was swirling in my glass. "Of course I'll wait. And, yes, I want it to be published. And, yes, goddamnit, I want my name on it, because half of those words are mine," I underscored with a fierce conviction, feeling my nostrils flare and my self-doubt ebb with my resolute words.

"Okay. I will make it happen." He let go of my wrist, and for a fleeting moment it felt like an abandonment. "I want to protect your professional reputation. I know you're a decorated archivist. I know, Nadia, that what we're doing is unethical, beyond the obvious. That you risk banishment from the profession for life. I know that."

A flicker of worry fluttered in my eyes. "Where do you keep the printouts? You should be careful, Raymond, you know. What you wrote—what *we* wrote—now that I know what I know about the rededication and all, could bring down the whole library."

"They're in the wine cellar at Isla Negra," he said.

"And she never goes there? You swear?"

Raymond shook his head, as if the thought provoked the absolute unthinkable.

I sucked in my breath and exhaled with a sigh of relief. His assurances and the Jardín Secreto tempered my fears.

"And where do you keep the original Moleskines?" he asked.

I shook my head back and forth, back and forth, until my face broadened into a perverse smile. "Nope."

"You're not going to tell me?" he asked, incredulous.

"It's better if you don't know."

"You don't trust me?" he said.

"I want to. But I need them for my own safekeeping."

"You really think I exploited us, you, for this book?" he asked, wincing at the outline of my distrust.

"It would be the most egregious of betrayals," I said, "one whose pain would be irremediable. To let you into my soul like that, and to think it was only colonized for purposes of exploitation . . . I would never get over it, Raymond."

"These feelings don't go away with a book, Nadia. If anything, the book roots them deeper. I would give up the book in a heartbeat if it came down to a choice."

I reached for his hand. We interlaced fingers and stared, searchingly, into the dark tunnels of each other's eyes.

In a move of swift prestidigitation, Raymond produced a small white box with a black ribbon and set it before me with thumb and forefinger holding it as if it were a delicate creature. I looked up at him.

"Open it," he said, nodding at the package.

I extricated my hand from his. Untied the ribbon with smoldering eyes of promise on his. Lifted the lid. Inside, a Royal Blue Burmese sapphire set in a platinum ring winked up at me like the glittering iris of a lynx. I raised it up on trembling fingers, held it to the fire, turned it in the light so its scintillations sparkled the most intensely. Its deep blue color reminded me of the ocean and the depths that it invited.

"When this is all over . . . will you marry me?"

"Of course," I said. "You can't let me go." I marveled at the sapphire, bewitched by the promise it sparkled. "It's beautiful." I slipped it onto my ring finger, modeled it for a moment, removed it, put it back in the box, tenderly fitted the lid back on it, then turned to Raymond. "To answer your question, I will when it's over."

We were interrupted by Luis. Hands folded prayerfully at his dimpled chin, he addressed us. "Will you be riding tomorrow, Mr. West?"

Raymond, blown from the solemnity of his proposal, turned to me. "Have you ridden horses before?"

"Yes. In Virginia, we had horses." I leaned forward. "I rode them fast."

Staring wide-eyed at me, Raymond ventriloquized, "Yes, we will, Luis." He finally tore his eyes away from me, and I could feel he believed I was the love of his life. "After breakfast. Eleven."

"It will be a pleasure," said Luis.

"I want to run them," said Raymond.

"Okay. I will have our best Aztecas ready."

Luis excused himself, then turned and disappeared into the glass-enclosed kitchen that flared orange and red with sauté pans in flames.

"Aztecas?" I asked inquiringly.

"It's a Mexican breed. A cross between an Andalusian, Criollo, and American Quarter horse. They're beautiful." He reached out a hand and ran it through my hair. "With manes like yours."

We feasted on seafood and mesquite-grilled meats, spiritedly debated current literature and film, and finished our celebratory gourmandizing with a quivering Mexican flan.

"How are you feeling about *The Archivist*?" I ventured. "Now that you're finished with the first draft."

"Exultant. Levitating," my Raymond thrilled. "But I won't know until I go back inside and face what we have wrought."

"We. I like hearing you say that," I said.

"Yes. We. They're your words, too, Nadia."

"Are you scared?" I asked.

"I'm always scared." He sipped his wine. "What are *you* feeling?"

"It's hard to have perspective, isn't it? We'll be pilloried for sure."

He laughed a gallows laugh. "The vilification will be launched from all quarters." Raymond's eyes deepened. "I just hope there's praise in equal measure to the excoriation of the soul-baring truth of our story. We put it all out there, Nadia."

"That we did," I acknowledged, thinking back to every transcribed sentence that bore the tortured and frenzied cawing of our love. "Are you ready for it?"

"Are *you* ready for it? It's your coming-out party too. You've been deserving of publication for too long. One could argue you used me as much as I used you."

I smiled faintly, humbly. "I guess we're in this together, aren't we?"

We split a second bottle of wine that left us tipsily weaving back to his room, arm in arm, and crashing onto the bed. We exhausted our bodies plundering our imaginations until we had demolished all the definitions and boundaries of satiety. We indelibly etched the promise of every word professed over dinner with lovemaking that crossed frontiers, the most taboo we had explored. And drenched the sheets sodden, defiled in exaltation and hope of a life like this one day together.

For the first time since our affair started, we woke in each other's arms. Sun slanted through the cracks in the curtains like pillars in the ruins of a building, but not the ruin of our love. With reluctance we came untangled. I threw open the curtains and sunlight gushed with intensity into the casita. Soon we were rejoined in the shower. I shaved his face with slow strokes and adoring eyes. He told me he had never had a woman do that to him before. I reminded him of other things more salacious, and I put a finger to his lips to shush him.

We met Luis at Adobe Guadalupe's stables. Three beautiful

Aztecas—caramel, white, and black—were saddled and waiting. As Raymond had described, the horses boasted beautiful flowing manes, pennants of silk hair that spilled over their powerful necks and shoulders.

"You ride English?" Raymond asked me. He was clad in jeans and a long-sleeve jersey, and I was jaunty in a white shirt and a blue scarf I had picked up in the gift shop.

"That's fine," I assured him.

"Okay," Raymond said to Luis.

Luis and a stable boy paraded the three horses out of the hacienda's arched stables and into a patch of bright sunlight. The snorting horses were spirited, young, smelling the flora and growing excited, aching to gallop across the open landscape. Luis helped me into the saddle, giving me a boost up with his weathered hands. I confidently slid my feet into the stirrups and grabbed the reins with both hands. The Azteca was a sleek, hard-muscled animal, with the flowing curves of ancient statuary. I could sense Raymond was an experienced rider by the way he climbed onto his black mount, ran his fingers through her mane, and murmured into her ear. Luis stepped up onto his beautiful buckskin-and-white mount, and we started off along the vineyards.

It had been a decade or longer since I had ridden, but it felt like yesterday. I stood inches above the saddle and had no difficulty getting into the rhythms of the horse's powerful impulsions. From time to time both Raymond and Luis solicitously looked back at me to make sure I was faring okay.

We walked the magnificent horses along the perimeter of a vineyard, glistening in a covering of dew from an early-morning fog retreating like a ghostly army back to the ocean, regrouping for another incursion in the evening. The sun had climbed over the hills to the east and sparkled on the wet grapevines. A flock of crows banked in the air, then flew low over the vineyards, hunting for rodents with downward-directed beaks and talons hooked for combat.

Luis gave his horse the lightest of kicks with the heels of his boots and his mount broke into a trot. Our horses took the cue and paced their trots accordingly. I found myself rising and falling with the horse's strengthening stride. My hair blew back. I could feel the wind invading my face and cooling it where beads of perspiration had started to form from the hot sun high in the sky overhead.

Luis pulled up to a stop at the edge of a vineyard. The horses gathered together, pawing the dirt, breathing noisily, and chewing their bits. As if to explain why he had brought us to a stop, Luis pointed to the sky. Raymond and I arched our heads, tented our foreheads with stiffened hands. A swarm of black starlings was advancing in a poetic whorl like a vast moving cloud that twisted and contorted in its own lavishly painted geometry. At one point the boiling cloud of starlings momentarily blocked the sun and the terrain around us fell briefly into shadow as though a solar eclipse had plunged the earth into an apocalyptic darkness.

"Beautiful," I exulted.

Luis shook his head and muttered something to Raymond in rapid-fire Spanish. The only words I caught were *pájaros malos.*

Raymond turned to me. "They're starlings. They come in huge flocks in the fall when they know the grapes are ripe. They can decimate a vineyard."

An explosion detonated in the distance, splintering the morning calm. The horses reacted, rearing slightly, then calmed. With a raised hand, Luis explained the noise to Raymond, who translated for me.

"They're bird bangers." Raymond pointed to a cylindrical device mounted on a tripod at the edge of the vineyard. "They use them to scare the birds."

"Why is he concerned?" I asked, adjusting my sunglasses.

"He's being careful. They can spook the horses."

The swirling cloud of starlings, massed like locusts in a Biblical migration, coiled in the sky in massive black circumvolutions and then fled over the mountain in a tortuous retreat. The blue of the sky returned in all its unblemished expanse. Luis broke into a wide-toothed smile, turned his leathery face to Raymond, looking happy. He made a grand flourish with his arm to indicate the birds had been scared away.

Raymond turned to me. "He wants to know if you want the horses to run faster."

"Let's pick it up," I said recklessly, "let's see what they can do."

"*Bien*," Raymond said to Luis.

Luis cinched up the strap on his tasseled sombrero and Raymond and I followed suit. Luis kicked his horse a little harder and it broke into a trot.

From a dead start, our horses erupted into motion. A trail stretched out before us and rose up a hill in the direction of the low-lying mountains watercolored in the distance. Once Luis could see that we were comfortable, he gave his horse an extra kick, and together we accelerated into faster trots. The pounding of the hooves on the dry earth thrilled up through my mount and suffused me with a preternatural excitement. Trailing both Raymond and Luis, I was enthralled by the long, sleek bodies of the Aztecas as they shifted into canters, then gallops. The power of the three horses now charging along the vineyard and kicking up dirt was liberating. My heart was hammering in my bouncing chest. The three horses seemed to be laughing with glee as they teethed their bits and ran out at full speed.

At one moment, I seemed to lose all control, as if I was one with the horse's strength and powerless to stop it. I held onto the reins with both hands and stood high in the stirrups so that my mount wouldn't buck me. I was flying, going as fast as I had ever gone on a non-man-made machine, as fast as I had ever ridden when I was a child.

Raymond threw me a backward glance and the smile he wore was as joyous a smile as I had ever seen crease his face. The smiles in all his publicity photos were either feigned or wry. They were always intense or intimately knowing. But this smile, thrown over the back of his horse's rump, was one of total exhilaration. It was as if he had been unshackled from some ponderous weight that yoked him to a life he wanted to free from. And it was in that moment, his uninhibited smiling back at me, that I understood how writing happened and how writing should be born: headlong, a run on the most powerful horse, headed into the nowhere, heedless of the perils, a full-blown run into pure oblivion. It was in that moment that I understood what I needed to do in my own writing. I needed to unshackle myself. I needed to court recklessness, I needed to create without constraints. The horse was my unconscious and all I had were two hands on the reins. Unbound freedom. Raymond and I were now united in this run to a literary and romantic future whose approaching sky was an amplitude of endless variations, a plenteous plain of infinite potential. My blood was now scalding hot with passion. My face was flushed red with exultation. Galloping effortlessly now on these magnificent beasts, I felt every door in my imagination blown open, each beckoning to a different world, but all contained within the possibilities of my own sentient being. It was the exhilaration of freedom within the corporeal, the way it was when I made love to Raymond, the way it was when he alchemized our words in a fury of thirty days and never let go the reins, never looked back, never for a moment allowed a doubt to slow his pace. Like the Aztecas, they had broken for the horizon and the air was light and nothing could stop them. Tears of unadulterated happiness were wind-whipped from my eyes and luminous on my cheeks. I cried out because my heart could no longer bear the suppression of its joy.

And then, almost as suddenly as I had summited this Himalayan joy, the blue skies grew afflicted. A dark cloud had twisted cyclonically over the shoulders of the mountains and was spiraling downward toward us in circumvolutions of predatory depredation, driven, it seemed, by some occult force. In the blur of our galloping horses, I glimpsed Luis frantically waving an arm. The swarm cloud of starlings advanced on us with alarming speed, closing off the sky and casting a vast dark ray across the vineyards and blackening the sun. Luis was screaming *No! No! No!* but it was too late. A bird banger sounded next to Raymond's horse with a powerful concussive blast. His black Azteca pulled up, reared back, fought the noise for a hysterical moment with hooves furiously paddling the air. Then, panicked, it lowered its massive head and broke jaggedly into the vineyard. Raymond lost control of the reins and, instinctually, he grabbed his mount's mane with both hands, leaned forward on his runaway horse, and tried desperately to hang on.

Luis dismounted, scrambled to the bird banger, and ripped out the electrical cord to prevent it from firing another charge. He whipped his head to me when I drew up next to him, grabbed the horse's bit, and quieted it.

"Stay here," Luis ordered me.

I could feel defiance disorganize my face. "No!"

Luis climbed back on his horse, gave him a kick, and loped into the vineyard. Operating on instinct, I jerked the reins of my horse left, kicked with both heels, and followed Luis at a measured trot. In the far distance, I could make out a funnel of dust pouring out from under the back of Raymond's runaway horse. The sky grew darker as the starling murmuration descended on the grapevines with a feeding avarice.

And then a shrill cry pierced the quiet. The cry mounted into screaming, a human in the throes of anguish. As we approached, we could see at the end of the vineyard where Raymond's horse had balked before a dirt culvert, afraid to leap it. An untethered Raymond had obviously been catapulted over the suddenly motionless horse, the velocity of his hurtling body defying the laws of physics. Pitched high into the air, he had landed hard. When we came upon him, both hands were gripping his thigh. Luis reached him first. He dismounted and scrabbled into the culvert. I was right on his tail. Leaping frantically off my horse, I toppled into the dirt. I picked myself up and, hot tears blurring my eyes, clambered into the culvert. Raymond's earlier smile was supplanted by the most awful look of suffering that I had ever seen on a human being. When I looked down, his hands were clutching the jagged shard of his femur where it had snapped in two and pierced through the flesh and jutted up angrily to the circling swarm of starlings in symbolic condemnation. Blood spurted from the wound as if a major artery had been severed.

Pandemonium seized control of the accident scene. Luis tried to staunch the bleeding with the shirt torn from his torso. My hands were clasped to my face in horror. Raymond's hands held the base of the break of the shattered femur, his face a swollen red of fear and agony. Time stopped. And in that moment I knew something had changed forever.

When Raymond saw me approach, he shouted at Luis, "Get her out of here, Luis! Get her out of here!" His shouted words bore the intonation of the other life he had repressed for us, the one he feared intruding now before he could take control of its narrative. Luis already had his cell to his ear as the blood quickly saturated his shirt and reddened his fingers. Raymond spoke rapidly in Spanish to Luis, and I only caught the word *esposa* several times, but I didn't need an interpreter.

Raymond turned to my crying face, my knees digging into the dirt next to him, one hand on his forehead, as close to the heart of true horror I had ever witnessed. He stared at me with sharply afflicted and martyred eyes. "You've got to get out of here, Nadia. The keys are in the room. Drive back. Park at Isla Negra."

"No!" I shouted protectively, worried that he was going to bleed to death. "I'm not leaving you!"

A wildly unsympathetic Raymond raised his head against the adversity of pain and screamed at me, "You can't be here! Get out of here!"

As if it was happening in the warped time phantasmagoria of a nightmare, I could feel Luis's hands clutching my arms and pulling me away from Raymond. My screaming and crying shattered the afternoon air. My hysterics could not be calmed, but I remember letting Luis mount me back on my horse, slapping the horse's rump, and sending it flying away from my profusely bleeding and screaming love.

I rode away in a dark ambivalence beyond placation. Wailing sirens rose and fell and grew louder. A speeding ambulance passed on a road opposite the vineyard my horse was trotting away from. I wanted to turn back, I wanted to be there for him, but instinctually I knew the trappings of his personal and professional life would descend in force. The media would swarm. If he didn't pull through—God forbid, I thought, clutching a hand to my mouth—the obituaries would be front page. His literary fame and Elizabeth's society prominence would guarantee that.

I left my horse with the clouded face of the stable boy, who only knew from my grief-stricken expression that something terrible had happened out in the vineyards.

I staggered to our rooms and frantically gathered up my belongings. I had the presence of mind to rinse the blood from my hands. In the mirror I noticed that blood had flecked my face and I now bore the freckles of Raymond's agony like a morbid tattoo of imminent death.

Every instinct in my being screamed at me to go back to the culvert where he lay writhing in agony. What if he did bleed to death! I wanted to rush into the lobby and exhort them to call me a driver and speed me back to Raymond, but his beseeching for me to leave had been fiercely definitive, leaving an emptiness where once there had been the fullness of his love. Even if he bled to death, I knew my presence would compromise him and whatever tattered ribbons of the dream were left they, too, would be blown over the cliff and into the abyss of desolation and perennial shame. I would never be able to explain it, I realized, palms pressed against my weeping eyes.

Galvanized by the *thwock thwock thwock* of an approaching helicopter—no doubt the Coast Guard had already been summoned—I rummaged for the rest of my belongings, blinded by tears, careered into Raymond's adjacent room, found his car keys on the dinette table, then snatched the shirt he had worn when he proposed to me and clutched it to my face. I wanted his scent deep in my nostrils if this was going to be the last time I ever saw him. Horrified by my aloneness, I wadded it up and stuffed it into my bag, marched out to the parking area, threw my one piece of luggage into the back of the Range Rover, climbed behind the wheel, and turned over the engine.

A second ambulance sped past me on Mexico Highway Three, its siren blaring its earsplitting tragic wail, its warning lights flashing hypnotically red and blue, as I drove in despair to the coast. The brown scrubland that fronted the highway looked forsaken. I tried to comfort myself. He would be all right, he would survive, help was converging on him from every conceivable direction, but every time I mouthed the words, I saw that jagged, broken femur staring at me from the gash in his thigh, and his lower body saturated in blood. I squeezed my eyes tight, but when I opened them, I had to veer sharply to keep from careening off the shoulderless road.

My anguish and terror and immobilizing despair was bottled tightly in a close-lidded jar when Mexico Highway Three met the main artery of Highway One. I understood *norte* and bent in the direction of the approaching onramp. The ocean loomed to my left, and it instantly evoked the Burmese sapphire. I glanced at it on my finger through the shroud of my tears. I touched it to my cheek, burning hot from the sun and the horror and panic of the surreal last hour. With a frantic hand I found the button to motor down the window and gulped in ocean air as if its brackish acridity would calm me, make me forget I was now all alone in Mexico and would find only oblivion after all I had just lost. A swarm of starlings, the black hand of a malevolent god, punishing us for our taboo love.

Still in a state of shock, time lost its incremental quality and the landscape blurred like film through a sprocketless projector. Somehow—I don't know how—I finally made it to the chaos and confusion of Tijuana's border sprawl, engulfing me now with its stark poverty and dilapidation. The traffic ground to a standstill. My ears buzzed from the roar of the wind through the open windows. The lines of cars crawled, hitching and braking unnervingly. Aggressive vendors thrusting their garish bric-a-brac into my face frightened me, and I motored up my windows. It was their wretched poverty mirroring my despair that so horrified me. US Customs jadedly asked me if I was bringing anything back from Mexico, and I shook my head wordlessly, a whole tragic story unfurling in my head that I could never begin to tell anyone. They asked me what the purpose of my visit was, and I muttered enigmatically, "Valle de Guadalupe." They waved me through.

I was back in the United States, on familiar ground, but its familiarity came rushing at me with obligations, the things I had to do to erase all evidence of our relationship. I tried to think clearly through my despondency and worry, but I couldn't expunge the image of Raymond's shattered femur. It stabbed my consciousness like a dagger, over and over, that jagged end of the break a punctuation mark ending a vivid portent that threatened everything.

Dusk was lowering on the horizon when I pulled into Isla Negra. A dense fog was pouring in over the cliffs like an enormous overflowing cup, or the ghostly adumbration of a powerful tsunami that would one day be real, and erase all history, all archives, from mankind's memory. In a daze, with no one to unburden my grief to—the plight of the mistress, I chuckled sardonically—I wasn't sure where to go. I felt disoriented, lost, as the fog poured inland. If I went straight home, I would have to explain to my husband why the conference ended two days early. The nearest hotel was Indigo, not too expensive and walking distance to Isla Negra so I could keep an eye on the place. I needed to feel close to Raymond in some way. And I needed to be alone, but I didn't want to be holed up in a hotel.

With the key that Raymond had secreted to me I unlocked the door to Isla Negra. Stepping in quietly with watchful eyes, I looked around to see if anything was different. I even sniffed the air! A sheaf of papers was spread on his writing slope, and I went over to look at them. It was the typescript for Volume XI of *The Archivist*, the penultimate volume. His marginalia were spattered all over the document like the insignia of a writer possessed. Volume XII, the final volume, was safely in my luggage. Remembering that Raymond had told me that Elizabeth never came here—wasn't allowed to come here, he insisted—I made the rash, emotionally imprudent, decision to stay the night, fuck the hotel. Scared, hugging myself tightly to prevent myself from shaking, I wanted to be as close to him as I could, damn the consequences.

I retrieved my laptop from my luggage and nestled onto the Murphy bed. Faintly, I could detect the scent of our lovemaking, and it brought a hard smile to my face.

I opened my laptop, went online and typed Raymond's name and "Baja" and "accident" into Google. The stories blossomed on my screen. The local coverage was extensive. The Wests were a power couple, and Raymond's horse-riding accident was headline news. In the first article I learned that he had been medevaced by the US Coast Guard to Scripps Hospital in Encinitas. With a hand covering my mouth and tears blurring my eyes I wept with restrained happiness knowing he was alive and safely back in the US.

My initial fears allayed, I left Isla Negra and walked to a nearby restaurant on Coast Highway to find something to eat, having eaten nothing since breakfast. At a place called Prepkitchen, the hostess's professional smile was incongruous to me at that moment, but I tried to manufacture a smile of my own in return. I sat inside against the wall. Famished, I ordered a hamburger with fries and a glass of Pinot Noir. Two couples in their fifties were sitting at a table two down from me. One of the men kept darting glances at me. Joel once told me I was my most beautiful when I was my most depressed. My uncombed hair made me look wild and ready for anything he had said. I didn't feel sexy. And only one man had my heart, and he was almost certainly in an operating room, drugged on morphine, surgeons working on his shattered femur.

As I torpidly ate my burger and picked indifferently at my fries, I kept checking my phone for messages. Nothing. I replied to one from my husband saying the conference was going well, and I was getting ready to head out with some colleagues to a restaurant.

After a hurried meal, I walked on quiet, empty residential streets back to Isla Negra. Fanned by the onslaught of the Santa Ana winds, a fire had broken out in the mountains and its out-of-control flames were tearing through the dry tinder and coloring the clouds in the sky in yellows and reds.

Feeling paranoid suddenly, I detoured on the walk back and deliberately didn't go down Little Orphan Alley but took the street before, which identically dead-ended at the ocean. I clambered across the culvert and onto the bluff. Seagulls cawed invisibly in the night as if awakened by nightmares or the thrill of heavy surf upwelling prey. I skulked step by step along the bluff until I came to Isla Negra. The patio decking with its palm frond umbrella looked forlorn. I could visualize us together at the table, drinking wine and Raymond reciting a Neruda poem to me that was meant for me and not the lover Neruda penned it for. On the now empty patio I felt our life force mere days ago gust through me like a wind of ashes. I could dream him at the window bent over his writing slope, the words of *The Archivist*, our collaboration, pouring out of him volcanically. I had animated him with life. We had fallen in love, and it was a true love, one forged from the flesh and the mind and not the practicalities of a partnership. Our future was as infinite as the ocean behind me, but as fraught as the fires burning toward the Pacific in the east-facing skies. All alone with my pain, I babbled. Hadn't he affirmed our undying love when he gave me the Burmese blue sapphire? I rubbed its almond-sized jewel as if to remind myself it was real, I wasn't hallucinating this fantastical love. The waves crashed at my back with their inexorable truth. I felt the key to Isla Negra through the fabric of my jeans pocket as if it both unlocked dreams and incriminated me with the adulterous truth. It was real. My torment savaged me in my solitariness and made me fear, not irrationally, that I was spiraling into madness, soon to be the vanished writer I had become before I met him.

The rhythmic clanging of an approaching train sounded in the distance. I spun around to meet its oppressive force. Its Cyclops headlight rotated in a tight circle. The warning bell grew louder. An earsplitting whistle sounded, fissuring the silence. From above the train tracks I could make out the passengers in the upper deck speeding toward downtown San Diego. When it passed with a whoosh and a clattering of steel wheels, I felt the air empty from my lungs, wiping the slate clean. I had decided: I wasn't going home. I was going to stay the night at Isla Negra. With the two days remaining on my alibi, I would type up Volume XII of *The Archivist* and that would occupy my days and help me not to dwell on the tragedy that had cruelly befallen the two of us. I would follow the progress of his recovery online. I wouldn't abandon him for anything. I would request a week off from work, if necessary. Surely, Helena would understand. Cold and unfeeling that she could be, even Helena knew that archivists sometimes got too close to their subjects and weren't immune to feelings of loss and hurt. And with this postaccident strategy I managed to partially calm my anxiety.

Having made my decision, I forded the dry culvert, made a circuit around the house, and locked myself inside Isla Negra. The brackish odor of the ocean reached inside when I opened the door. His writing sanctuary had a claustral feel, which lent me a certain, if fragile, sense of comfort. Remembering where he hid the key to his wine cellar, I opened the narrow door and stepped down into the former fallout shelter, converted into a wine cellar, to pick out a wine. I selected another Chilean red in honor of our last time here together, returned to the kitchen, uncorked the bottle, and poured a glass. It was rich and deep and tasted of the earth, but with perfumed fragrances that issued from somewhere empyreal. That's how Raymond would describe it, I thought to myself, as I carried the wineglass with me to the bed. I climbed out of my clothes and wrapped myself in his voluminous white shirt. I set my wineglass on the nightstand and opened Volume XII. I didn't know how the book ended. It had been following a trajectory that paralleled our own, but now . . . now everything was different. Would there have to be an epilogue?

I spent a night of broken sleep, coiling and uncoiling like the flock of starlings that had brought me such wretched anguish. Anonymously all alone in Raymond's confidentially located Isla Negra, every sound startled me. Once I awoke with a start imagining I heard footsteps on the decking, but when I got up to look out the window, I saw a raccoon staring up at me, swiveling his head from side to side, as if looking for Raymond. In another lacuna of broken sleep, I swore I glimpsed the ghost of Raymond bent over his writing slope, sipping coffee, pen hand moving in a blur, head immobile, eyes blinking with intensity. I half rose, but the image evanesced, and the scratching of his pen was only the dead palm fronds of his patio umbrella animated by a sudden gust of the howling Santa Anas. And then I dreamed the worse: that he was dead. *What would I do? Where would I go?* I thought, as I lay there in the dark. *I'll throw myself in front of the train. I'll—*

I woke with a fright from ragged sleep and disturbing dreams, rubbing my eyes with my palms to wipe them from the harsh light of consciousness. I found eggs in the refrigerator and—on an empty stomach, emotionally weakened by the accident's aftermath—whipped myself up an omelet. On the kitchen counter I found whole coffee beans in a brown bag, ground them in a professional-grade grinder, and brewed a strong cup of coffee. I took it with me steaming into the bathroom. The coffee and a shower revived me a little, but looking back, I was still in a state of shock. Benumbed as I was to the world, I was careful not to venture outside. The excuse that I was house-sitting stood ready on the forefront of my tongue should anyone come knocking. I tried to shake off the horror of the accident lurking always on the penumbra of my mind, but it kept getting dislodged by my terrible fear of the future whose once certain path, professed with a ring, was now shattered like Raymond's femur.

Needing obliteration, I buried myself in transcribing Moleskine Volume XII, typing furiously on my laptop, intermittently flashing back tears at poignantly personal memories from our relationship Raymond had drawn heavily on. They read differently now, as if they were ghostly, in a long-ago past. In-between breaks I checked for email and status updates of Raymond online. The story of the horse-riding accident had spread like a prairie fire and then burned out as it traveled its way over the internet without any real new information forthcoming.

For emotional sustenance I worked at Raymond's desk, the Moleskine on his writing slope, me in his chair next to it, as if next to him. When I was done for the day, I always left the Moleskine closed on his writing slope, giving it a pat, as if for good luck. It's where it was born, so that's where it always needed to be.

By afternoon, my uncertainty and nauseating worry was urging me to get dressed. I locked up Isla Negra and walked out to my car. On a cloudless day, the skies filling with funnels of smoke from the worsening fires, I raced up the freeway to Scripps Memorial Hospital in Encinitas. Wearing dark sunglasses, I walked like a zombie, fear and worry having drained me of all energy, through the sliding glass doors of the main entrance. I hated hospitals. This is where you go to die, I remembered my mother, a nurse, telling me, demanding to die at home.

The main reception desk stood to the side of a large, sun-drenched tiled foyer that led into the bowels of the hospital, wide corridors branching off from it. Nurses wearing drab-green scrubs and doctors in white lab coats clutching clipboards marched urgently about in zigzagging directions, weaving their way between shocked and dismayed family and friends drawn to this temple of horror and death out of both love and obligation, some leaving with their hands clutched to their faces convulsed in sobs, wounded by the darts of suffering.

Disconcerted but undaunted, I approached the reception desk. A busy Black woman with bright red lips looked up into my questioning face, unsmiling, businesslike, ready to parry tragedy with a shopworn platitude or a request she couldn't honor with a reasonable excuse. "Can I help you?"

"I'm here to see Raymond West," I said softly, hoping not to elicit suspicion. "He was admitted yesterday, I believe."

The receptionist's right hand found a mouse, then both hands typed furiously on a keyboard. She paused and turned slowly to me. "Are you family?"

"No, I, uh, am faculty at the university where he teaches," I stammered. "Was in the area. Wanted to see how he was doing."

"Visits are completely restricted."

"I see. Do you know how he's doing?" I asked in a plaintive register.

She placed her fingers back on the keyboard. "You say you're faculty at the university? What's your name?" She turned her head to me and rested a jowly chin on her shoulder.

"I, um, no, it's okay," I said, panic seizing me.

"I could put in a request with the family."

I found myself backing away, my hands rising in mock surrender to my chest. "It's okay, I'll just . . . ask around at the university."

The receptionist furrowed her brow and narrowed her eyes. I noticed security cameras mounted in every ceiling corner. I forced an apologetic smile, pivoted and strode out the front entrance, elbowing my way through another surging ebb of aggrieved humanity.

In my car, I banged both fists on the steering wheel. "No, no, no, you have to let me see him," I spoke out loud to the windshield in angry frustration. I tilted the rearview mirror down and noticed my eyes were bloodshot. Without makeup I looked a fright. I tried grooming my tangled hair with the fingers of both hands, but it kept falling forward onto my face. Disturbed by the real possibility that I could have been recognized, I plunged my hand into my purse and scavenged for my phone. An ambulance came squealing around the corner and careered into the hospital parking lot speeding to the ER, emergency lights strobing, sirens screeching. I instantly flashed back to the ambulance racing past me in Valle Guadalupe and, throwing my hands to my ears, thought for an unsteady moment that I was tilting into madness.

While the memories of the accident and its aftermath were still fresh, I tapped out my longest journal entry ever into my phone. Several hours fled by as I wrote through my anguish, my thumbs unable to keep up with my racing thoughts. I kept glancing in the rearview mirror at the entrance, debating my next move.

Dusk was reddening the skies and marbling them around deepening blues when I finally climbed out of my car. I had to see him, regardless of the risk.

I paused inside the entrance. To my anxious relief I found that a work-shift change had brought a new face to the reception desk: a young man who seemed to be engrossed in one of the two monitors facing him. The hospital interior seemed quieter.

I spotted a wheelchair left abandoned by the wall, hurried over to it, clutched it by the handles, and pushed it down the main corridor and past the reception desk, confident in my disguise. The man at the computer terminal glanced briefly at me, looked back at his monitor, apparently satisfied that I was staff or family.

The wide main corridor ended at a T. Signs fastened to the wall indicated the directions to ICU, Critical Rehab, and a range of individual room numbers. Venturing to the right, medical personnel passed me in the corridor, and though I must have looked odd pushing an empty wheelchair, the doctors and nurses were moving too frenetically from one emergency to the next to register suspicion.

The rooms bore the names of the patients handwritten on three-by-five-inch cards slotted into brackets. I exhorted myself that I would scour the entire hospital until I found him. Unless, a fear seized me, he had been assigned to a room under an alias. Walking and looking left and right simultaneously, as one unfamiliar name after another fled past, I debated my next move. Ask a passing doctor or nurse? Surely they would know the whereabouts of the famous novelist medevacked in from Baja with a fractured leg. No, too risky.

Lost in my swirling thoughts and growing exasperated, I rounded yet another corner, headlong in search of him. Two women were walking toward me from the far end of the corridor. I halted in my tracks. I veered violently away when I suddenly recognized Helena Blackwell with Elizabeth West. Abandoning the wheelchair, I backed around the corner, the clicking of their heels on the linoleum floor growing louder as they approached. The first room that didn't have a nametag I pushed down on the door lever. It gave way to the weight of my shoulder. I quickly shut the door behind me, latched it locked, and leaned my back against it. I threw a hand to my heart. It was beating furiously, pounding like a tiny fist demanding to be released from its cage. I heard women's voices exchanging words through the heavy door. Ten years of Helena's voice distinguished it as clearly as any voice I knew. I knew all its registers, all its octaves. I couldn't discern what she was saying as their echoing footsteps went past, but there was urgency, a gravitas of alarm, in her words. No doubt she was allaying Elizabeth's fears, consoling her, explaining that the project would go forward as planned. I realized it was Helena's ne plus ultra dream, and nothing would thwart it, not a fractured leg, not even a wayward archivist who dared . . .

Staring blankly at the antiseptic room and crisply made bed, I let a full minute pass after the sound of their heels had grown silent before I hazarded going back out into the corridor. Glancing in the direction where Helena and Elizabeth had disappeared, I was relieved the corridor was blessedly empty now. I went in the direction from which they had emerged, as if their presence were a fierce wind I had to battle and which was making forward progress difficult. Halfway down the corridor I found a card in its bracket that read simply "West, R." I pressed an ear to the door until it hurt. At first I thought I heard voices, but then realized it was news chatter from a TV. Nervous to barge in on him unannounced, I inhaled deeply, shut my eyes on the warring questions in my mind, then pushed down on the latch.

At the click of the door opening, Raymond turned a drawn and stricken face to me. He was propped up in a sitting position on a mechanical hospital bed. His left leg was encased in a thick, white cast stretching from his groin to his knee. It had been winched up by a medical hoist and labored airborne on straps. Stitches ran across his upper lip like an ellipsis denoting wounds. His face was frosted with a day and a half's growth of beard. It seemed like weeks since I fled Baja. His eyes darted at me sharply flashing dark apprehension. The perfume of Elizabeth and Helena still lingered in the room like a menacing admonition. I instantly sensed a changed atmosphere between us. It was now tense and cold. He didn't want me here. I was a liability now.

I reached for his nearest hand and gripped it in both of mine. "Raymond."

"Did you see Helena and my wife?" he asked with panicked eyes, ignoring my solicitude.

"Yes. I ducked into an empty room. They didn't see me."

"Nadia." His voice was scornful, and I didn't appreciate its tone. "You shouldn't have come."

"I had to." Tears upwelled from my stomach and found the crevasses of my eyes. "How can you say that?"

Raymond exhaled through flared nostrils all the ominousness of the past thirty-six hours. "You realize if they were to come back . . ."

"I couldn't bear it," I quavered in a grief-stricken voice.

"If they see you in here like this . . ." he trailed off, shaking his head.

"I worried about you so much." It felt like we were talking from opposable spheres of dismay.

Raymond lolled his head toward me and finally met my eyes. "I worried about you getting back."

"Are you in a lot of pain?"

Raymond pointed up at an IV bag. "They've got me on morphine." I nodded. It was so hard to see him like this. "Operated and implanted a steel rod in my femur."

"Oh, God," I said, bringing a hand to my mouth.

Raymond rolled his head away from my tear-filmed eyes, unable to bear to look at me, as if I were the vehicle that had driven him into this unwanted wall of misery. "I'm glad you came," he managed, but he seemed distant, his words lacking in conviction.

I gripped his hand tightly and kissed him lightly on the mouth. His stitches tickled my upper lip, but he kissed me back with his cracked lips that wouldn't open. I withdrew a few inches and steadied my eyes on his, limpid from the morphine.

"I'm glad you made it back okay," he said.

"Yes. I did."

"She wanted to know how the Range Rover got back," Raymond said, his narcotized gaze fixed on some nexus of complicated worry, trying desperately to process all that was orbiting crazily around in his befogged brain.

"What did you tell her?" I asked.

"I don't know. They've got me drugged. Probably that I paid someone to drive it back." Raymond shrugged, shaking his head back and forth as if the repercussions were still settling in. "I don't know if she believed me." I stroked his furrowed forehead. His thoughts seemed to have traveled somewhere dark and foreboding as he tried to sort through the jigsaw of their affair, the accident, and its now consequential aftermath.

"It's going to be all right." I paused. "I'm staying at Isla Neg—"

"No!" he chopped me off, swinging his head to me with pained effort. "You can't stay there, Nadia."

"You told me she never goes there," I pleaded. "I can't go back. I'm supposed to be at a conference in San Francisco."

"Everything's different now." Raymond's drugged tone was in combat with his fear. "How do you think she found out about the Range Rover? If I had someone drive it back, why wasn't it driven back to the house in La Jolla? She doesn't trust me, Nadia."

Desperate, acting on the pure anguish of my feelings, I rummaged in my purse and produced a sheaf of papers in a manila envelope. "I've transcribed Volume Twelve," I said, wanting to palliate his fears, but also realizing by his narrowed eyes that he thought I was delusional, living in an alternate universe. Practicality had flung love and our book out of his soul. I thrust it back at him as if it were the last rope keeping the other from being irretrievably lost downstream.

"I don't want that in here," he said coldly. The typescript of the final volume had suddenly been reduced to an untouchable, radioactive object of danger, imperiling everything. "You've got to get out of there, Nadia."

"Okay," I said, summoning some semblance of sanity, and pulling back the pages.

"And you've got to get all copies of the manuscript out of there," he added crossly, a different Raymond from the one I knew.

"Okay," I said. "Okay!"

Raymond shook his head back and forth like a condemned man. I gripped his hand for reassurance, clung to him, but this time he pulled his hand away and rested it on his chest. An invisible wall grew up from the bed like bulletproof glass. His face went cold and immobile like marble statuary.

"Raymond," I began, wiping tears with my now free hands.

"You've got to get out of here," he cut me off with implacable finality. "And you've got to get rid of those manuscripts."

"Do you mean destroy them?" I asked, incredulous, heart gripped in terror by a brewing storm of fear that had been building in me since he implored me to leave the accident. Was this the last time I was ever going to see him!

Footsteps and voices were suddenly clamorous in the corridor and Raymond tensed. Both of us froze. The fast-moving footsteps and clipped voices passed quickly and retreated down the corridor. Raymond's paranoia abated momentarily. He grabbed my chin and made me look him in the eyes. "We have to cool it for a while. Until this passes." He touched a hand to his massive cast. "All this shit that's going on. The library rededication. Her San Diego mayoral bid . . ."

"Your wife's running for mayor?" I asked, dumbfounded.

Raymond looked at me guiltily, caught in a lie of omission.

"Jesus, Raymond." I sat back, absorbing the shock.

"It's not official. It doesn't change anything with us." His voice was weak and retreating into hiding, to me unconvincing.

I leaned forward. "Do you still love me?" A fusillade of tears caused me to shoot a hand to my mouth.

"Of course, Nadia. But you have to understand . . ."

I bit my upper lip almost to bleeding, braving back the tears. Then nodded resolutely. "I'll take good care of the manuscripts." I couldn't hold back the tears. "I'm your archivist, am I not?" I pleaded.

He seemed unmoved. "Get rid of the manuscripts. Please."

"Okay. I will." Hurt radiated through me as if the blood coursing in my veins was scalded. His eyes had turned cold, castigating, two slivers of ice. His warmth had frozen over. His love was now immured behind a shroud of personal and professional fears. I rose from the hard plastic chair on ground now unstable beneath me.

I left the room sobbing, cast out into a sterile hallway by the violent gust of his angry exhortations, staggering away, eyes blurred with inconsolable grief. Despair fanned out in me like an army of stinging insects flushed from their nest. My heart was that nest. I was tossed now into a darker, more turbulent, world of suffering. I didn't know what was what or who I was, because for two months I had been defined by our love affair and the all-consuming writing of *The Archivist*. The only thing I knew now was that I had urgent business to take care of before Raymond's and my world blew up.

CHAPTER 18

The Black Moleskines

Emily crawled out of bed, rubbing the sleep out of her eyes with the heels of her hands. Onyx was crying for breakfast. Emily fed him and then showered. Her face looked haggard in the mirror. She had spent the night engrossed in Nadia's lengthy, heartbreaking account of the accident. Emily had also read all of the postaccident emails Nadia had written to Raymond, but which he apparently never received, perhaps because he had erased them from his computer for fear his wife would find them. Emily had stopped reading when her eyes grew weary, and sleep claimed her. Her dreams were a jumble, as if the unconscious had taken in too much material and was now creating images and fragments of scenes in a compensatory effort to rearrange and make sense of Emily's psychic world. Nothing patterned out. Emily, a person who prided herself on order, realized that love probably knew no order, that its mercuriality knew no clear explanation. As she drove past the beach on her way to the library, she started to inescapably rise to the belief that love maybe only knew chaos, entropy, that its luminosity and exultation was glorious precisely because its destruction was equally as inevitable, that within its gestation was also, to borrow from a passage in one of Raymond's books, sown the seed of tragedy. She was sorting through it intellectually; Nadia had lived it experientially, and the ocean had taken her. Did love's tumult only find peace in death?

No one in the department seemed to sense the turmoil in Emily's soul when she walked into Special Collections. Helena managed a smile for her and asked if she would like to have lunch. Emily pled off with the excuse of too much work and an appointment over lunch, which she wouldn't specify.

In her cubicle, computer blossoming to life, Joel texted her. He informed her Bird Rock Coffee had opened a new outlet on Carmel Valley Road overlooking Los Peñasquitos Lagoon and they should break it in. Emily smiled at all the seeming normalcy that enveloped her in the library. If she could only let go of what she knew, she could have a normal life without drama, without conflict, drive off into the sunset to the next job. Or toe the line and stay in San Diego. Hadn't there been an insinuation from Helena that Elizabeth might endow a new position at the university and they were looking for a "forward-thinking" archivist with digital expertise?

Emily straddled two worlds: the one she was sitting in and the one she was about to descend into. The present and the past had coiled into one, and a dark red river ran riot between them. The footbridge that forded them had grown more rickety with every Nadia email, with every new revelation, to Raymond and the chronicle that had grown in *My Story*. Especially now with the physical existence of *The Archivist* Moleskines. If she relaxed into the job of the present and let it go like a kite to the windblown sky, no one would ever know. For all she knew, she was the only one who had ever read the book, other than Nadia and Raymond, of course. It appeared as if Raymond had abandoned it after the accident, and Nadia, thinking frantically, had sequestered all the typescripts and their correspondence into the dark archives in hopes one day it would be discovered, be resurrected somehow. She had deliberately put restrictions on the incendiary items. She didn't destroy it as Raymond had recklessly insinuated while he lay helpless in the hospital.

Emily had the black Moleskines in her possession. She had *The Archivist*. She was philosophically and professionally split. Yes, Nadia had transgressed boundaries, following the impetuous trajectory of her heart. A $25 million gift to the library could now be in jeopardy. Raymond had a right to invoke his trepidations to make Nadia see that their love, the book that celebrated that love, was little more than dead leaves pushed along a gutter by a bitingly cold wind in the face of the monumental consequences that now hung in the balance. Nadia, Emily realized, trembled in fear that Raymond was withdrawing, and she was desperately trying to hold on. If their love was going to die on the hill of this awful remorseless fate, then she was going to construct its headstone in all its tarnished honor. And in their love's grave would be buried the truth: *The Archivist*. For truth is the final residue of all beings.

And now their love, like Neruda's body to be reautopsied, had been exhumed. By a nosy twenty-seven-year-old project archivist whose job description was to finish processing a collection and then move on. Emily stood alone on this rickety bridge over this sleeping volcano. She hadn't bargained for the discoveries made in this disinterment. But she hadn't shied away either.

Had it only been the discovery of their affair, had it only been the correspondence, which was incontrovertibly of scholarly value, she might have let it be. But there existed a fully formed first draft of a book, for God's sake. Did Raymond honestly believe Nadia had destroyed it? Had someone tipped Helena off and that's why boxes had gone back to the Wests and returned, scrubbed clean, camouflaged as if a new addition? If the truth meant anything at all, if truth were the defining moment of a person's morality and how their reckoning with death would be adjudicated, wouldn't Emily be cast into a purgatory where she would straddle this split for all eternity?

An alarm rang on Emily's phone. She stared it for a long moment before silencing it.

Emily signed out of the library early and walked determinedly to the parking structure, anxious about what she had arranged to do. In the trunk of her Mini she retrieved a black canvas tote and slung it over her shoulder. When she turned to go to the stairs she stopped momentarily and took in Memorial Library through the open-wall, ventilated views. In reflective mode, the windows mirrored the sprawling campus, surrounding landscape, and blue sky. Its diamond-shaped formidability never ceased to impress her. It stood as a testament to the purpose of the most prominent libraries and museums: man's innate need to be remembered, to leave some manifestation of his legacy, be it progeny or story, scientific discovery, or wild clairvoyance. If these august repositories of remembering were going to preserve the past, shouldn't they, too, be built indestructibly to withstand an uncertain future? Emily believed, in the short time she had been an archivist, that the need to be remembered was greater than the sin of avarice to be wealthy. *Money* will *buy you happiness*, she thought, *in material things, but it will not—it* can *not—buy you immortality.* And in that fulguration of reflection, staring at towering Memorial Library, its reflective-mode mirrors blinding in the hot sun, she selfishly thought: *How will I be remembered?*

And in the black tote bag slung over her shoulder were the sticks of dynamite that could bring it down: the twelve black Moleskines that fictionalized a singular and unique love that was both so wrong, and so right, that it had inspired its own incarnation: a book that would eternalize it. Was its discovery her legacy?

Emily crossed the campus to Walden College in a purposeful stride, threading her way through swarms of students whose futures beckoned and glittered with the promise of a life in a world Emily now darkly envisioned tragically imploding.

Emily climbed the stairs to the fourth floor of the Arts & Humanities Building. Her heart was beating with a physical power like some wild animal caged and looking desperately for any avenue of escape. She paused for a moment, wondering if she shouldn't turn back. A young professor bumped her shoulder and spun her around. He apologized profusely as he backed his way into the open elevator, a briefcase full of books and a lecture organized in his head that had momentarily divorced him from reality.

Emily sucked in her breath and approached the front desk. The Administrative Assistant smiled up at her while her arms worked independently of her mind like a two-tentacled octopus.

"Can I help you?" she asked.

"I have an appointment with Professor West," Emily replied with trembling voice.

"Your name?"

"Emily Snow."

She smiled. "Around the corner. Four eleven." She picked up a phone. "I'll let him know you'll be waiting at the door."

Emily peeled away from the desk and headed down the corridor the administrative assistant had indicated. As she walked on hesitantly, each step a deliberate *click* on the hard laminate, she fell prey to the eerie déjà vu that she had inhabited Nadia's wraithlike presence and she could feel Nadia deep inside her, almost writhing to get out. They were one now, confronting the man who had robbed the two of them of their once glorious love. If Emily closed her eyes, she could hear Nadia's words in her memoir describing the tingly, sensual excitement of coming to Raymond unannounced, him kissing her neck, their sowing the seed of their love through the sheer brazenness of her accosting him at his office. The spirit of Nadia moved Emily's legs down the corridor to her own moment of truth.

When Emily reached 411, she paused, squeezed her eyes shut, inhaled deeply, then rapped on the heavy door. Seconds later she caught the groaning of a chair's springs as it released a weight, footsteps slowly coming toward her. The door opened. The seam of a chary smile drew a line across Raymond West's gaunt face when he saw her. Emily noticed he was wearing the same off-white linen shirt, maybe the one Nadia had described spiriting away from Mexico. Standing in the doorway, just the two of them, she couldn't believe how imposing he was. Up close, the limpidity of his blue eyes was more sorrowing. Wrinkles nested at the corners of his eyes.

"Come on in, Ms. Snow," he said in a phlegmy voice, drawing a fist to his mouth to clear it with a rasping cough. "These Santa Anas dry out my sinuses," he muttered.

Emily stepped into West's office. Just as Nadia had described, books lined every wall floor to ceiling, dominating the office's decor, monuments to Raymond's vast ranging intellect. They spilled out onto the floor in tottering piles. The small couch where Raymond beckoned her to take a seat was pushed against a wall occupied by memorabilia. Emily wasn't surprised no pictures of Nadia hung on the walls, but her absence bore a palpable sadness to Emily, a spirit hovering, untethered to anything except memory. The framed photos were of Raymond with literary and film entertainment celebrities. Emily recognized a few from duplicates in his archive.

As she broke away from the wall and started to sit, she noticed Raymond clutching the corner of his heavy, hardwood desk, as if to steady himself. He audibly groaned when he resumed sitting in his chair. It tilted back toward the bookcase behind him on croaking springs. He set his elbows on the armrests, interlaced his fingers, and rested them on his stomach. Light filtered in through the single rectangular window, tinted amber, mixing with shadow, a small window as if to discourage professors from the distraction of a view.

"I'd turn the lights on," he apologized with a raised forefinger, "but they're punishing. And when you hit fifty, as you will someday," he added in his gravelly voice, "and you see your picture on some website or in some magazine, you'll know the true meaning of vanity."

Emily's lips curled into a laugh. A quiet fell. In the shared silence there trembled a palpable, mutual knowledge.

"Sorry to bother you," Emily began, "I know you're a busy man."

Raymond glanced at the cane leaning against his desk and looked fixedly at it, dropping deep in thought. "So, you know the story of the cane," he croaked with effort, his eyes blinking as if trying to bring it all back into focus. He reached for the cane's hooked grip and raised it in the air. It was a burnished, burled mahogany that tore a jagged, lightning-flash line in the air like the trajectory of his life since it had come, unbidden and unwanted, into his possession. "It was a terrible accident," he voiced to the past, a reservoir of excavated memories starting to percolate painfully to the surface.

"I know," Emily said. "I read about it in some of the news clippings collected in your archive."

He nodded, as if still addressing memory and not Emily. He rested the rubber tip of the cane on the floor and leaned the hooked end against his desk. It rattled before settling. Turning to Emily, he intertwined his fingers again but this time into a dome, brought them to his mouth and exhaled through flared nostrils over them as if attempting to blow the last vestiges of embers into a fire of memories he didn't know how desperately he needed, or wanted, to exorcise.

"How is your leg?" Emily inquired.

"I have a steel rod in there about yea long." He widened his hands about a foot in length and then interlaced them again. "Not sure I'll be on the Faculty volleyball team this year," he chuckled.

A silence fell and created unease in the tiny room again. Emily glanced off. She had come with a storm brewing inside her, but she found herself vacillating. If she unloaded everything she knew, the world would change forever; she just couldn't predict how, and that drove her doubt. After weeks of immersion in his and Nadia's personal life, she felt like she knew him better than anyone alive. Her heart raced. A paraglider soared past the window like a forgotten thought.

"How are my papers coming along?" Raymond asked to break the ice.

"Reasonably well," Emily said.

Raymond caught a note of ambivalence in her voice. He said darkly, "The story of the cane?" Emily blinked in reply. "It was quite a cliffhanger you left me with, Ms. Snow."

"How confidential can I be with you?" she asked, a tremor in her voice.

His expression developed fissures of tension. "You're my archivist. The keeper of my flame. Fire away. I'll let you know when you've crossed into consecrated ground."

Emily foraged in her mind for the right words to begin. "You see, Professor West—"

"Raymond, please," he waved her off.

"Raymond." She sucked in her breath, still intimidated being in his presence. "How much do you know about what archivists do?"

"Some. Having had some experience with your predecessor."

"Nadia Fontaine."

He threw his head away from her and out the sliver of a window. He pouched out his cheek with his tongue. "Yes. Nadia Fontaine." His chin sank to his chest.

"Do you know what the dark archives is?"

"I've heard the term mentioned." He lifted his gaze to the window again. "Elucidate me." He knew what it was, but he was acting coy.

"Basically, they're servers. It's a huge repository for all the digital content that's not immediately available to the public."

"I see." His eyes narrowed and alighted on a midpoint between professional obligation and memory. "Go on."

"Well, in going through your collection, I found something in the dark archives."

"Dark archives," he incanted, nodding. "And what did you find?"

"Something that came to Special Collections unfiltered. Or . . ." Emily paused dramatically, "something that was uploaded by somebody who desperately wanted the truth preserved."

"*Desperately?*" he asked in a faint voice.

"There was risk involved."

"What did you find?" he inquired in a more animated tone, waking now fully to a story limned with potentially darker tragic dimensions. He shifted in his chair and a trapezoid of sunlight fell on his shirt like a shard of glass and shimmered over his heart as if threatening to shear it in two.

Emily's eyes traveled to the window as if sage advice awaited her there. "I'm going to be honest with you." She turned and offered her face to his with blazing candor burning in her eyes. He turned to her and opened his hands like two exclamation points, inviting her disclosure.

"I stumbled across . . . your entire email correspondence with Nadia Fontaine."

Raymond drew a hand to his chin. "And you read it?"

"The emails were very carefully curated and saved as PDF files, employing a fairly sophisticated piece of software . . ."

As if it had finally struck him, Raymond held up a hand for her to stop. With eyes squeezed shut, he kept his hand raised like a traffic cop who couldn't bear any more flow of cars. "Have you read them?" he asked again, this time more fearfully.

An interminable pause followed. The silence hung like the prospect of an apocalypse of unspoken truths on which the world's future hinged. Emily couldn't decide if she felt closer to Nadia or Raymond at that moment, but she could acutely feel the tragedy of her death in his gallows tone and knew she was solely responsible for dredging it all up again.

"There are so many. Some still in draft form and never sent," Emily confided softly. "Plus," she continued, looking down, "she wrote an entire memoir of your relationship in rough draft form." Raymond visibly stiffened. "It's a powerful . . . account."

Raymond shut his eyes, hoping when he opened them the world would be reborn to a changed reality instead of the one Emily presented. "How long is it?" he asked in a quavering voice.

"Long," Emily replied. "Personal. Detailed. In the wrong hands . . ." Emily trailed off, realizing Raymond didn't need explication.

Nodding, Raymond gazed out the window again, his face a lined and weary lapidary silhouette of aggrievement. The ensuing silence left Emily feeling momentarily deserted. She couldn't determine if he was angry with this revelation because it was dredging up a past he had hoped to wall off forever or if he was stunned that Nadia had preserved their correspondence for someone to potentially find.

"She also uploaded all the media attachments," Emily admitted. Raymond's head turned sharply to hers. "Photos. Videos. That's why I risked coming directly to you. They're out there in the dark archives, and I'm not authorized to take them down, and the ones who are, well . . . I'm not sure you want me going to them. Nor do I think you want someone else to find what I discovered."

Raymond studied her face as if it were a cryptic text.

"I'm not your enemy here," Emily reassured him. "Just a girl with a problem." She paused, looking off. "What I did was a breach of professional ethics, a serious breach in the archival community. We're in this together, you and me."

"Why did you delve into it?" he asked.

"Why do you begin a new book?" Emily shot back. He looked at her quizzically. "Can I quote you?" He offered a hand in a gesture of assent. "A book must be the axe for the frozen sea inside us."

He smiled wryly at the floor in recognition of his words. Then shook his head. "I was paraphrasing Kafka. He burned ninety percent of what he wrote. I should have followed his example." He chortled.

"In this digital day, you don't have that luxury," Emily said.

"I was in love with her," Raymond started haltingly with downcast eyes. "Deeply in love. The kind of love that blinds you to everything." He turned to Emily. "I don't know if you've experienced what Nadia and I had."

"I've never really been in love, no," Emily admitted. "Someday."

Raymond nodded imperceptibly.

Emily leaned closer, elongating her neck. "They're beautiful, lyrical emails. And the memoir. Even in first draft form one can recognize the true writer in her."

Raymond drew in his breath and held it for the longest moment before exhaling. He sized up Emily with questioning eyes.

"There's more," Emily started, summoning up her courage, soaring now far from the cliffs where the winds were more unpredictable. From her purse she removed the small catalog card in the string-tie envelope and the folded page of the letter she had found in *Le Rêve d'un Flagellant* and set it on Raymond's desk.

He looked at it warily, motionlessly, as if it were not inanimate. After a pause, he extended an outstretched arm, touched the item with hooked fingers, and drew it toward him in a slow deliberate motion as if he both feared it but couldn't look away.

"It's a letter she wrote to you that she had meant to send through campus mail, but never did. She hid it in a book, as you can see." She watched while he glanced at the card and then slowly unfolded the letter. "It's heartbreaking." Emily drew a hand to her mouth to quash her feelings. The last thing she wanted was for Raymond to think she was personally, emotionally, involved, but she was coming unglued under the weight of the disclosure and she needed this moment to collect herself.

Raymond reached absently for his glasses on the desk, adjusted them on the bridge of his nose, focused on the origami-folded page with Nadia's handwriting overflowing on both sides. He started to read it, but he set it aside after the opening lines, his expression chaotic and troubling. He made a move to rise from his chair as if wanting to escape the thick, fraught air of the room, but winced in pain as he put weight on his leg and sat back, defeated, the husk of a man who once rode galloping horses and loved and wrote with reckless abandon.

"Those were her last words to you . . . before she drowned," Emily finished solemnly.

Raymond squeezed his eyes shut and kept them shut.

"As I think you can plainly understand, I can't go to my supervisor, and I couldn't possibly go to Helena, who is obviously very close with your . . . wife." Emily audibly sucked air into her lungs. "Now, I could have let it all go, pretended I never found the letter, or followed the trail to the correspondence in the dark archives, but then I would have to live with that. And I was afraid of it being out there for *anyone* to discover."

Raymond nodded, sunk deep in thought.

Emily raised her voice an octave and spoke nervously faster for fear he would send her away and never get to hear everything she wanted to say. "She didn't put those emails and photos, and her memoir, up in the dark archives in any vengeful way because you spurned her after the accident." Raymond looked at her furtively. "She put them there to document the truth."

Her words seemed to paralyze him. The only thing that moved were his rapidly blinking eyes.

"The truth you always talked about in interviews, the truth that is the bedrock of your art." Emily's voice dropped to nearly a whisper. "It was the only hope she had, short of betraying you, that she was going to be remembered." She looked at him with fierce conviction, and her eyes never lost contact with his. "I ask you, Raymond . . ." She waited until he looked up at her and met her eyes. "How do you want to be remembered?" Her question thundered in the small office and left the air trembling with hurt and anxiety and uncertainty.

Chained by fear now—fear of his position on campus, fear of his marriage, fear of sinking irretrievably back into the bog of painful memory—he intoned softly to himself, "How do I want to be remembered?" A weary exhalation escaped through his nostrils as he shook his head.

"Yes," Emily said. "How do you want to be remembered? Because for both of us—you for posterity, and me professionally—that is the essential, the only, question. And it helps me to determine what I decide to do next."

Raymond nodded thoughtfully. Then he perked up. "You're my archivist—you found all this; what do you suggest I do?"

Emily broke free from his gaze. The trapezoid of sunlight had shifted to the floor like a modern-day sundial. "I'm not sure. I've never been in this position before. There's no precedent. I'm all alone." She focused her gaze on the trapezoid, wishing it were an entrance to an answer. "There's something else." Emily pried her eyes from the floor and looked up into Raymond's now crucified mien. "I know it was more than a love affair." Raymond shot her a furtive look.

Her eyes fell on his desk and she pointed at the letter from Nadia with a brandished index finger. "In the letter she mentions a book the two of you were working on." Emily paused. She trembled at the cataclysm of her next words. He looked up at her. "*The Archivist.*" She looked up.

Raymond's expression colored dark with shock, as if someone had punched him violently in the chest. "I burned it."

"Well, she didn't," Emily retorted.

The blood drained from Raymond's face. To his developing horror, Emily simultaneously reached for her tote bag and sprang from the couch. She took two steps and upended the twelve volumes of the black Moleskines with the silver Sharpie handwriting onto Raymond's desk. They fell like dominoes into a world not acclimatized for their collapse into reality. *The Archivist Vol. I . . . The Archivist Vol. II . . . The Archivist Vol. III . . .*

Seized with panic, Raymond instinctually drew a hand to his mouth and stared fixedly at the work he thought he had successfully obliterated from his memory, from his life, forever. Now the Moleskines lay there, a broken testimonial, dead for a year, but resuscitated like a corpse buried alive pushing through the casket lid where it had been buried alive and screaming all this time from some deep hole in his soul. He faced its unwanted exhumation with fateful eyes. He shut them tight until he had wrung out the last tears he had wept since Nadia's death. They exuded from the corners of his eyes like drops of dark honey.

"Your catastrophic molt, I believe Nadia termed it."

"You read it?" he cried in a choked voice, a sob rising in his words, through splayed fingers that webbed his mouth closed, his emotions on the verge of collapse.

Emily nodded. "It's the most exquisitely personal work you've ever written. The two of you." Her eyes were blazing. "From her idea. She wasn't only your inspiration. She was your collaborator, your cowriter." Emily planted her hands on the edge of his desk. In a quaking, vehement voice, she said, "Did you think she was going to destroy them?" Tears spilled from her eyes. "She was a professional archivist." She straightened from the desk and wept openly in a catharsis of weeks of pent-up emotion. "She wouldn't destroy what she thought was your greatest work." She slapped a hand on one of the Moleskines. "We preserve things. This is what we live for, don't you know that?"

Raymond drew both hands to the sides of his head and raked his shoulder-length hair with spread fingers.

Emily was still standing in the middle of the room, unyielding, her eyes sodden red. She forearmed tears from her eyes and gathered herself together. She picked up one of the Moleskines. "I've had to live with this, too," Emily murmured, blinking back her tears. She collected herself somehow and found a more cynical voice. "Now that I've found them and returned them, you can destroy them. It's your choice. They're your words. But even if you do, I suspect she'll live on in your conscience for the rest of your life." She looked at him with blazing, demanding eyes. "Ask yourself: Is this the hill you want your legacy to die on?"

Her words and the disclosures, both manifest in the Moleskines and abstracted from Emily's confession about the items Nadia had hidden in the dark archives, had reduced Raymond in stature in some indefinable way. He glanced at her, baffled by the display of the manifest truth in the black Moleskines now facing him, glowing anew from the cold embers of their banishment. Emily recognized in his narrowed, searching eyes how difficult it was for him to see the Moleskines hauled back into consciousness, unannounced, against his will. She wasn't going to let guilt derail her. She had lived with its truth too long.

"What do you want to be remembered for, Raymond?" Emily gently inquired. "This manuscript was written from your soul. From both your souls. If you don't want to go back to it and publish it, at least let me put it in the archive so someday someone else can read it and be as moved by it as I was. This work is not yours alone," she reasoned with him. "It may have been conceived in . . . a compromised, clandestine way, but its aesthetic value, given your literary fame and recognition, is incalculable. Let it go to the world. If you have the courage to. That's my advice to you as your archivist."

Having said her peace, Emily folded up her tote bag into a small square and squashed it into her purse, signaling she had no intention of taking the Moleskines back with her to Special Collections, or her apartment, or anywhere. They were once again his property now.

"In one of the emails," Emily said, "you quoted Kafka to Nadia when she expressed her trepidation about *The Archivist* and what it might mean for both of your futures. Remember what you wrote her?" Raymond, still paralyzed by the sight of the Moleskines he couldn't pry his eyes from, shook his head. "I think we ought to read only the kind of books that wound and stab us. If the book we are reading doesn't wake us up with a blow on the head, what are we reading it for?"

Raymond was nonplussed, preoccupied with a diorama of sorrow whose curtain had been flung open in all its once palpable intensity. He couldn't pry his eyes from the Moleskines; they looked like more than a novel he had written in a furious thirty days; they were the record of an incandescent truth and he knew Emily was right. He wouldn't forget. He reached for the grip of the cane and in a sudden fury of anger, as if wanting to erase the past all over again in one desperate gesture of self-laceration, he swiped it violently at the Moleskines and splattered them all over his desk where they settled in disarray, turned askew, some flared open to their lined pages with his recognizable handwriting. He let go the cane from his hand and it rattled on the tile.

"I'm sorry," Emily said, when the echoing of the cane's rattling had subsided. "I had no choice," she added from her timid frame.

Raymond snapped his head in her direction and regarded her with almost rebuking eyes. He rose cumbrously from his desk chair and hitched his gangly frame toward the window. He wanted to distance himself from the work he was guilty of deserting, but it was as if he could never get far enough away. The dipping sun cast his face in light and shadow.

In the grave silence that took possession of his office, Emily quietly gathered the Moleskines, now strewn on his desk, and, fearing for her own future, arranged them neatly together, and piled them chronologically back in order, reverting to habit. She spoke meekly. "Isn't *The Archivist* representative of what you teach in your class on autobiographical fiction? Risking it all for the truth?" She paused when he fixed her with an arresting backward glance. "I'm sorry. I didn't want this. And then when I fell into it, I couldn't stop. I'm human too, you know."

"You took a tremendous risk in coming here," he muttered to the lowering sun and the silhouetted paragliders, his voice fading in the face of the items Emily had dumped on him.

"Pales in comparison to you and her, and"—Emily pointed at the twelve Moleskines stacked neatly into one pile—"what you conceived together." She looked away. "Besides, if I took them to the director, they would be destroyed. And then they would destroy me because they would want to know how I found them. It wasn't exactly ethical what I did to get them and bring them here." She let her confession hang in the air. "And if I had put them back where I found them, it's unlikely they ever would have been unearthed."

Raymond turned from the window, took one step, and braced a hand on the edge of his desk. He opened the first Moleskine on the stack and flipped desultorily through it, as if resigned to the fact that he would now have to reconfront its existence, either as destroyer or preserver. His face had the look of a conflagration long since extinguished by the rainstorm of tragedy, its aftermath now only a gray landscape dulling his vacant eyes.

Emily watched him gazing at his own handwritten words. What must he be thinking? What had she done? Guilt now divided her where once professional obligation had driven her to this moment of reckoning for both of them. She had come without a filter, wanting only to lift the weight from her chest that had kept her up nights and driven her to an emergency room, and . . . Raymond kept slowly turning the pages, a terrible black dawn rising in him.

"Do you remember what you wrote Nick, your editor?" Emily quietly asked. Raymond shook his head. "You were elated."

"Was I?" he asked in an undertone.

"I believe you wrote, 'I'm writing again with a passion inspired by a woman who transcends the mere corporeal.'"

Raymond blushed a smile. "Did I?" A cloud scudded across his face again and his eyes narrowed, as if he had already, Emily hoped in all her heart, made up his mind to retrace his steps to that time. "I can't believe she saved them," he said, shaking his head in disbelief. He turned another page. "And I can't believe you found them." He then let the Moleskine close as if letting go a handful of dry leaves in a sudden gust of wind. "I can't go back there. Even if I was willing to risk losing everything."

"You once were," Emily countered.

"I'm not the same person who wrote this." He looked away, conflicted.

"I didn't think you were a coward," Emily said.

Raymond jerked his head toward her as if pulled by the bigger, more powerful, magnet of truth. "You're asking me to resurrect a dead woman's memory for the sake of art? Are you out of your fucking mind, Ms. Snow?"

"No. Just doing my job. You asked me my opinion." Raymond dragged a hand across his face. "In my profession we sometimes come across items of a compromising nature. We either open Pandora's Box or don't. I honestly didn't know where it would lead. I'm deeply sorry if what I brought here is a truth you don't want to face."

He slapped his hand in anger on the pillar of notebooks. "A truth I don't want to face? You're imploring me to rake over old bones and relive the most painful period in my life?" he challenged querulously.

Emily quailed in the thunder of his words. Doubt capsized her resolve and she felt shattered by his scorn. She thought she had come on behalf of Nadia, but now she felt that knot of doubt tightening in her stomach again.

"I wish you hadn't gotten into all this," Raymond said testily, hobbling back toward the window. In the distance the sun laid gold leaf over the ocean, and all was tranquil.

"I'm sorry," Emily replied defensively, "but I did. Because *she* wanted somebody to. That's what you need to understand."

"She committed suicide because of me!" he blurted out in self-recrimination. "And you have the audacity to exhort me to relive that?"—he tossed a finger at the Moleskines—"Slingshot back to a happier time and bring it inexorably to its tragic conclusion? Is that what you're urging me to do?"

"She was the love of your life," Emily exploded. "You professed it to her countless times. She lived for your words. She didn't believe in the book because she selfishly thought it was for her. She divined the lyrical brilliance in those pages and glimpsed its monumentality, and she wanted you to believe that it transcended the two of you. She believed it was literature. I think you owe her the validation of that belief." She clapped the Moleskines into a neat pile and in her agitated, overwrought state, aligned them so they were in a perfect quadrilateral mound. She lifted her face to his tall frame, no longer intimidated. "And she inspired these words. And for the first time in years, you were writing again—not some Hollywood screenplay, the real thing. You're an artist, Raymond. You can't dam that river. And you owe it to her."

"I don't owe her anything," he muttered despairingly. "She took her life to spite me."

Emily slapped the palm of her hand on the top volume, troubled by his words. "One day these will be more important than both of you. Your legacies are entwined."

Emily pulled her hand away, plunged it into her sweater pocket, fished out a thumb drive, and set it on top of the pile of Moleskines as carefully as if it were an insect she was setting free. "All your emails and her emails, in individual PDF files, in chronological order. I recommend you read them, especially the unsent drafts and the memoir she wrote of your relationship titled *My Story*—a heartbreaking document—good enough to be published in its own right. In the event you feel the urge to be reinspired to finish what you started." She reached for her purse and slung it over her shoulder and prepared to leave. She knew she would heave into a fit of sobbing as soon as she walked through the door and tried to maintain some semblance of dignity. She gazed at the strained, but still handsome face of Raymond. "You know, Raymond, if I had been given your papers to process . . ." She waited until he looked at her. "I would have fallen in love, too." Their eyes coupled and didn't break contact for an eternally awkward few seconds.

Emily broke away, but before she reached the door, she spun around and faced him again, perhaps for the last time. "You're right. I took a tremendous professional risk coming here and unloading all this on you." She paused until his eyes locked on hers again. "I know what's at stake. I may be young, but I'm not stupid." She flung out an arm in a flourish to include the whole of the university. "The Elizabeth West Library." She went to a lower register. "The reputation of Raymond West." She pointed at the tower of Moleskines. "But the raw beauty of those words." Raymond looked at the Moleskines with downcast eyes. "I'm a fan of your work. And, in my humble opinion, it's your *Letters to Milena*." She blinked back tears clouding her eyes. "Do you have the temerity, the cold awfulness to destroy it?" She studied him, but he was incapable of words. In a conciliatory tone, she said, "There are ways to preserve it, all of it"—she drew a finger across the Moleskines and flash drive—"without anyone getting hurt. And without destroying it."

The tomb-silent office echoed with her words. Emily reached for the door handle. She bowed her head to the floor, then turned it upward to a penitent, and saturninely silent, Raymond West. "And how can you be sure she committed suicide?"

Raymond looked at her, thrown for a moment. "She was too strong of a swimmer to have drowned," he finally admitted. "And besides, everything that happened . . ." He shook his head and trailed off.

"I'm not suggesting she drowned accidentally," Emily cut him off.

Raymond jerked his head to hers, stunned. He could barely form the words; they rattled out like bones. "You think she was murdered?"

CHAPTER 19

Knife in the Heart

10/4/18

I thought a great weight would be lifted when I went to visit Raymond West, but after I left, I felt pinned down by an even greater truth.

Question: Do I now get Joel to wipe everything from the dark archives? Would he? Or would he go down the same path I had if I led him there?

I suppose every archivist is going to come to this fork in the road at some point in her career. Maybe never like this. No. Never like this.

On her lunch break Emily drove to the San Diego Police Department headquarters in Downtown San Diego, determined to get to the bottom of Nadia's death. From her front windshield, blue skies smeared with wispy white clouds collided with cold gray cement. She found metered parking on the street and walked half a block to a six-story, unwelcoming governmental building, its windows latticed with bars. An American flag and a California State flag below it snapped in the freshening afternoon wind at the top of a white pole in need of paint. Emily had consciously dressed conservatively in a knee-length black skirt, white blouse, and heels.

She pushed through a glass door and walked into the capacious facility with its gray tiling and screened windows. The floor was dominated by the desk officer's station, denoted by a plaque engraved in the desk sergeant's name. Above it, behind a wire-mesh window, a uniformed Hispanic woman sat at a computer staring at a monitor, her fingers typing rapidly on a dirty keyboard. Hearing Emily's heels slap the tiling, she swiveled in her chair to face her but didn't smile.

"How can I help you?" she asked through the small hole in the window.

"I have a question, Ms. Melendez," Emily said, reading her name off the plaque.

"Okay," said Sgt. Melendez.

"Sorry, do I call you Officer?"

"No, my name is fine."

"I work at Regents University in La Jolla as a professional archivist. My predecessor in the job was found dead at Black's Beach about nine months ago. I did some online research. The death was ruled an accidental drowning. I'm wondering if there's any chance I could see the death investigation report."

"This was your predecessor you say?"

"Yes. We're both archivists in Special Collections. Well. She *was*. Until the unfortunate accident."

"And why do you want to see the death report?" Melendez asked.

"In the collection that she was unable to finish, I want to include her in the biographical notes. Plus . . . she was a close colleague. A friend." Emily displayed a flash of genuine emotion at the conclusion of her rehearsed lie.

Melendez studied her suspiciously and seemed to reach a decision. She swung ninety-degrees in her swivel chair and placed her hands on her keyboard. "What was the name of the deceased?"

"Nadia Fontaine."

Emily heard the clacking of keys. She glanced around. Detectives dressed in suits and ties moved from the entrance to the elevator in opposable streams, greeting one another collegially. She turned back to Melendez, who was working her mouse and typing additional words. After a minute, Melendez rotated her monitor so Emily could see it.

"Is that her?"

Emily bent forward and pressed her glasses up to the wire mesh-occluded window. Filling the monitor screen was the stock photo of Nadia that Emily had found in the online university profiles. That thick, lustrous black hair, middle-parted and falling like the wings of a raven on a face too beautiful to be marred by a photo with a too-bright flash. "Yes, that's her," Emily said, pursing her lips and nodding.

"What do you want to know?"

"I don't know." Emily opened both hands. "Anything you have."

"Can I see some ID, please?"

Emily rooted her wallet out of her purse, produced a driver's license and her Regents University Staff ID, and slid them into the shallow well underneath the mesh barrier. Melendez fished them out of the well, scrutinized them, looking back and forth between the two IDs and Emily, then swiveled and rose out of her chair in a practiced move with a hand gripping the edge of her desk to balance herself. "Excuse me a moment."

Emily glanced at the time on her cell. She ignored the red badge displaying double-digit email messages.

Melendez returned, carrying a manila folder thick with documents, squeezed back down into her chair, slid the thick folder in the well, and pushed it up toward Emily. "Here you go. I'll keep your ID. Don't leave the building with those documents, or I'll have you arrested." She smiled to show she was half kidding. "I trust you."

"Thank you, Ms. Melendez."

Emily lifted the thick folder with both hands and hauled it over to a window ledge and set it down. She breathed hot air onto her glasses and wiped them clean with her cotton blouse, adjusted them back on her face, and opened the flap of the folder.

Many of the documents in the folder were redacted with a black Sharpie. Leafing carefully through them, Emily came across crime scene photos—some of them lurid and awful; the many pictures of Nadia's cyanotic face and open eyes were the most haunting to Emily. She scanned pages of drawings and sketches and handwritten reports of what witnesses who found the body had testified. Emily also came across write-ups of interrogations with various individuals who knew Nadia, including her husband, Nathan Waters; some of her colleagues at the library, including Joel and Helena and

Jean; and then, Professor Raymond West. They had clearly investigated it as a possible homicide but had evidently ruled that out.

Emily kept neurotically glancing at her phone for the time. Of most interest to her was the final ruling on probable cause of death by the investigating officer. Words like "suicidal" and "depression" appeared frequently. But the words that caught Emily's attention and caused her to suck her breath in were, "Pregnant. 4 months."

Emily inhaled deeply, tilted her head back slightly to absorb the revelation, and held her breath. When she finally let it go, she let it all go. She slapped the folder closed. Thoughts crisscrossed in her head, warring with one another, contradicting timelines, deepening the mystery that now appeared more complicatedly labyrinthine than simply the fallout from a tragic love affair.

It did not go unnoticed to Emily as she walked the folder back to Sgt. Melendez that she had arrived in San Diego nearly two months ago in the employ of a university as a project archivist and now here she was at the San Diego Police Department's downtown headquarters inquiring about her predecessor's death. Was it her sleuthing instinct that led her now to discover a more scandalous truth? Or had obsession clouded her sense of reasoning?

Reluctantly, she set the folder in the well. Reluctantly because she would have killed to take it home with her and study it more thoroughly.

"Thank you," Emily heard herself say, her thoughts distant. She started away, then stopped and made a quarter turn back.

"One more question," Emily said. Melendez looked up and smiled wearily. "The official cause of death was ruled an accidental drowning, and there's language in the various depositions that maybe somehow it was suicide-related. The investigation was closed. What does that mean exactly?"

"Means," said Melendez, "if the detectives thought there was foul play and they had a suspect, in custody or whatever, the DA would be the one to file charges." Emily pinched her lips with thumb and forefinger. "You don't watch your *Law and Order* reruns, huh?"

"I don't have cable," Emily replied. "I don't watch TV. One other question: There's nothing in the report in the way of an autopsy."

"That wouldn't typically be in the report. That would be with the coroner."

"What are the chances I could talk to the coroner?"

Melendez frowned and eyed Emily circumspectly. "That wouldn't be my call. I would have to ask the lead detective."

"Detective John Taggart, I believe?" Emily said.

"You read through that report pretty thoroughly."

Emily nodded. "Is there a chance I could speak with this Detective Taggart?"

"That's not our policy with the public. Unless you were a defense attorney for a suspect in custody, or close family member . . ." Melendez trailed off unpromisingly.

Emily, capitalizing on the desk sergeant's ambivalence, leaned forward and implored in a hushed tone, "What if I told you I had information that goes beyond the scope of what's in the report?"

Melendez's attention was suddenly riveted. The folds in her face seemed to tremble. "Do you?"

"I might," said Emily. "But the information to support my suspicion has restricted access protocols. In other words, I couldn't remove it from university property to convince you to let me speak to Detective Taggart. But it could be subpoenaed. I'm asking you to trust me."

"Do you have a business card?"

Without losing eye contact, and not wanting to break the spell of Melendez's invitation, Emily unsnapped her wallet in her purse. With stubborn fingers she plucked out the business card she had designed online and slid it into the well and halfway up the curved slope to Melendez, as if to underscore her desire to have Detective Taggart call her as soon as possible.

Melendez examined Emily's business card. "What's MLIS stand for?"

"Master of Library and Information Science."

She looked up at Emily. "I'll pass this to Detective Taggart and relay what you told me."

"Thank you." Emily turned to leave. It occurred to her that there would probably be a record of her visit, but she couldn't let that derail her now.

On a soul-dispiriting I-5—the alimentary canal of San Diego as Joel had dubbed it—Emily drove from downtown San Diego back to the university, battling twin emotions of anxiety and elation. Wanting a bucolic view, she circled around Carmel Valley Road and approached Regents from the north. Passing Torrey Pines State Beach, she saw blue through tattered clouds backdropping a windblown ocean.

Back in her cubicle, Emily found a text from Joel about surfing, but she was still too shaken from her visit to the police station, as well as the fraught meeting with Raymond, and she feared Joel prying details of it from her, so she declined.

Emily stayed late in the library. Joel came over at one point and sat down and asked her how she was doing, sensing something was brewing.

"I'm doing fine," Emily said sarcastically, flinging an arm to indicate the document items stacked on the adjacent desk. "As you can see, I've still got plenty to get through."

"Don't let the stress get to you," Joel advised solicitously. He rose from his chair, towered over her, and whispered inscrutably, "It's not worth it, Emily." He wagged a finger at her.

She nodded noncommittally, more in preoccupation with her thoughts than as a response.

"The Nobel's announced in a few weeks," Joel informed her. "There's going to be media here. Ladbrokes has West at one and a half now."

Emily looked up at Joel. Surely Raymond was apprised of the odds. If he won, he would be in front of cameras and microphones with an arrow in his side, blood seeping from a wound. His potentially most important, and enduring, work was now in his hands, and it could die the death of deaths: invisibility. The vanished book. Isn't that what Nadia had called it at one point?

"Sure you don't want to come surfing? Clear your mind?"

Emily shook her head and managed a smile.

Joel flashed her the shaka wave and lumbered off.

The library went quiet. Emily ventured out of her cubicle. She found Samantha at the reference desk, nose buried in her bestseller, the one with the bound woman, eyes closed expectantly for the severe-faced man who was moments from ravishing her.

"Helena gone for the day?" Emily asked without breaking stride.

"Yeah," replied Samantha, looking up and hiding the tawdry cover from Emily's view.

Emily walked down the corridor and entered the administrative assistant's office where the administrative files were kept open in a metal cabinet drawer. With frequent backward glances she rifled through the drawers, flipping past the individual files like an oversized deck of cards. They were filed alphabetically. She came to one manila folder with a handwritten label that read "West, Raymond—Deed of Gift." She lifted out the file. It was an inch thick at least. Emily flew past the publicity announcements, briefly perused the Deed of Gift—which she noticed was in both Raymond's and his wife's name—and then the correspondence. The correspondence included printouts of emails between Helena and various individuals associated with the West Papers. But the majority of them were exchanges between Elizabeth West and Helena Blackwell.

Emily jumped when she heard approaching footsteps in the corridor. She stopped with the manila file folder clutched guiltily in her hands, quickly fabricating an excuse, but the footsteps went by without incident.

When the footsteps had retreated, Emily slipped the correspondence out and made her way briskly down the corridor to the copy machine. Her heart was racing. It wasn't inappropriate or even irregular for her to be checking something in the administrative files on West, but copying correspondence might have raised suspicion. Every page that spat out of the copier into the receiving tray felt like a protracted beat of her heart.

When she was done, Emily returned to the administrative office where she refiled the folder. She retrieved her bag, secreted the copies in her purse, shut everything down, and was the last one out, remembering to arm the alarms.

Emily crossed the eerily deserted campus with the paranoid feeling she was being followed, or watched, without any manifest reason. It was a glimmer of a feeling, a pinprick of an instinct, a deepening, nauseating fear.

Emily drove back to Del Mar. When she reached the bottom of the hill where Torrey Pines State Beach yawned a gap in the cliffs, she dredged up the memory of the panic attack that had driven her to the ER mere weeks ago. It seemed like months, she thought, glancing over at the neon yellow sun touching down on the horizon, silhouetting the surfers bobbing on the gilded waters like stragglers on a planet overcome by towering edifices of water.

A creature of habit when overworked, and overwhelmed, by a project, Emily ordered takeout at Urban Plates and took it back to her apartment.

She fed and stroked a needy Onyx as he wolfed up his tuna, opened her favorite Societe ale—the Henchman, a dark beer with a malty flavor—then plopped herself down on the couch. Out the picture window the sun had set over the horizon. Clouds had caught fire and were swirling in a conflagrative red. A train clacked past on the bluff, its warning horn a lamentation in the encroaching night. Emily wanted to read the correspondence between Elizabeth and Helena, but she was almost afraid to look at it. Its mere existence in her purse was a rolled-up pipe bomb. With no rationalization for having copied those files, it would be automatic grounds for dismissal were she found with them in her possession, and it could ricochet through the archival community and make it hard for her to ever find employment again. She shut her eyes and cycled through the bumpy rhythms of the ramifications. But the one thing that kept surging back to her from the police report was the shocking word "pregnant."

Galvanized by the storm clouds of suspicion gathering in her mind, and heedless now of the consequences, Emily unpacked her laptop, turned it on, waited for it to come to life, then went straight to the email correspondence of Nadia and Raymond, and the accompanying memoir. The growth of a new, cold resolution had taken hold inside her, and she had to know.

From: Nadia Fontaine <Nfontaine@RegentsU.edu>
To: Raymond West <Rwest_Lit@RegentsU.edu>
Subject: The Apocalypse
Date: 29 October 2017

My dearest Raymond,

I left the hospital, depressed, and in an overwrought state, but raced straight to Isla Negra at your behest . . .

NADIA'S STORY (CONT'D)

I swerved out of the hospital parking lot wiping tears from my eyes, tears that seemed to be pouring out of faucets turned all the way open to an inexhaustible well of grief. I drove in a veritable blur. The surf shops and salons were all closed. Here and there were beer pubs spilling out with youth oblivious of emotional tragedy, or so it felt to me as I sped by, Raymond's last words of harsh affection crucifying me with their apparent finality.

Isla Negra was quiet when I pulled into the driveway behind Raymond's Range Rover. My antenna was up, trying to sense anything amiss or out of order since I'd been gone. I heard the ocean, as rhythmic as my heart once beat, and it momentarily soothed me. Seagulls cawed invisibly as they flew overheard to nests burrowed in the cliffside bluff.

I turned the key in the lock, and the door fell open to the quiet of the cavernous main room. Were there two table lamps burning when I had last been there or only one? My memory was playing tricks on me, half-delirious from lack of sleep and the reverberations of shock still heaving through me in seismic waves.

Retracing Raymond's and my steps, I slid the tips of my fingers on top of the door molding that led to the basement wine cellar. I breathed a sigh of relief when I felt the key's cold, cut edges. The wine cellar door opened outward to the room, and I circled around it, remembering how Raymond had gently pushed me into the tight stairwell with a loving hand guiding my swinging hip and made me feel uniquely desired by him. I reached an outstretched hand up into the dark and waved it around until I felt the yank chain and pulled it down. The bulb flickered on, but just as suddenly I heard a pop, and I was frighteningly alone in the dark again. I groped a hand in the murky light and felt for the handrail of the tiny spiral staircase. Its unvarnished wood fell into the grip of my hand, and I started down the short flight of narrow steps, feeling my way as if slipping into Plato's Cave without a flashlight. I was deathly afraid that when I found the chain for the light in the cellar it, too, would fail and cast me again into permanent blackness. I thought I was going mad until my fingers pinched the chain, pulled it down, and the light effused yellow in the small room. I breathed a sigh of relief.

Raymond had only said the typescripts of the Moleskines were in the wine cellar, but he didn't specify where exactly. I quickly deduced they couldn't be behind the bottles lining the racks on the wall. So where? Stacked against the far wall were oaken wine cases of special bottles yet to be itemized and cataloged and slotted into individual wine racks. I knelt next to the boxes and pulled them out one by one and set them on the small tasting island that centered the cellar. I opened every one of them, but found no sign of the typescripts. With my hands gripping the island I leaned back and searched the wine racks from the rot-resistant hardwood floor to the plaster ceiling. The tops of the racks were flush to the ceiling, so they couldn't be hidden there. For a moment I wondered if there wasn't a secret compartment somewhere and I felt along the panels between the racks inspecting for any kind of seam. Was I crazy? Wouldn't he tell me if they were secreted in hidden compartments? How the hell would I find them? This has to be Occam's Razor, I thought. The most logical answer was the most probable. One of the wood wine cases was empty. It had once held two magnums of a legendary Bordeaux, its chateau logo branded smoky black with a hot iron into the blonde wood. Why would he leave the wood wine case here if he had already drunk the bottles?

Defeated, I left the light on and slowly trudged back up to the main room, sans typescripts, depressed, anxious, my mind churning. I flopped supine onto the bed where only a week ago we had cavorted and made love. I closed my eyes, but all I could think about were the typescripts of the Moleskines and Raymond's anguished expression when he exhorted me to find them and "get them out of there." How could he say that? I worshipped those Moleskines. They were my blood, and my heart was their home.

Unable to quiet my mind, I sprang up from the bed and scoured the main room with the frenzy of a thief burgling a house for a particular, priceless item of jewelry. In a panic to find them, I tore the place apart, but came up empty-handed. I fell back onto the bed, rosy and sweating, flung an arm across my forehead in exhausted despair. Text messages pinged at me from my husband, and I wanted to cauterize them. I texted him back and said I was heading to a symposium at the conference, trying to remember when the conference ended and I was expected to return. I received the expected succinct reply: "Okay." I cared about his feelings, but I wasn't going to fucking leave Isla Negra until I found those typescripts! My God, in the wrong hands . . .

I lay on the bed engulfed in a kaleidoscope of thoughts and scenes, images and voices. They rushed at me with a wild, implacable disjointedness like a swarm of flying insects. I kept closing my eyes and transporting myself in memory back to the lovely dinner at Adobe Guadalupe, but it felt like a chimera. I caressed the Burmese blue sapphire ring on my finger now as if to make sure it was real.

And then just at that moment I sat bolt upright in bed in a state of consternation. “Fuck!” I muttered out loud to the room. I looked sharply over at Raymond’s writing slope. It lay barren on the planked desk. I leaped out of bed. Where was it? I had put the Volume XII Moleskine there, the one he had given me on the drive to Adobe Guadalupe. Where was it? I flung a hand to my mouth. Was my memory conspiring against me? Did I hide it in the bookshelves somewhere before I went to the hospital? In a panic, I stood back and let my eyes sweep the titles on the wall lined floor to ceiling with books. Frantically, I ran my hand across every single row, but there were no black Moleskines.

My gaze went back to his writing slope, as if trying to evoke a memory of something that never existed. As clear as yesterday I could picture it there. *The Archivist.* Volume XII. I always left it there as a good luck charm. The words gleaming in silver, in my beautiful cursive. I was positive I’d left it there.

Suddenly I didn’t feel alone in the house anymore. I raced outside and scoured my car for the final Moleskine. Had I hidden it there when I’d returned the Range Rover? My mind was so chaotic from mental fatigue I might have done anything and forgotten it in the trauma of the accident’s aftermath.

Coming up empty, I gave up and returned inside, locking the door behind me. I descended back down into the wine cellar and slid out a bottle of the Viña Casa Marín Syrah, in memory of our night on the beach together. I deliberately left the light on. My eyes wandered the cellar, still obsessed with locating the typescripts. The bottle uncorking reverberated in the tomb-like space. I poured a glass. It was rich, layered, and tasted of the earth of Neruda’s Chile.

I climbed back up the stairs with the bottle in one hand and a wineglass in the other and eased down onto the edge of the bed. Glancing over at the writing slope, I kept shaking my head, as if hoping to dislodge a new memory that would replace the one that still haunted me. I kept hoping it would materialize. I was absolutely positive I had left it there!

The dead palm fronds of the patio umbrella clattered in the wind in a suddenly disruptive commotion, and I tensed. I thought, but couldn't be sure, that I heard footsteps creaking on the patio floorboards. What I heard disappeared as quickly as it had floated through my ears. Once an oasis, Isla Negra was fast becoming an asylum harboring all my fears and now grave anxieties. I couldn't think straight anymore. It had been two nights since I had found more than an hour's sleep before bolting awake in the throes of another nightmare. If I wasn't going mad, I was surely sinking into a realm of irrationality where frayed nerves and tortured feelings were dictating my actions.

I fell back onto the pillows, eyes fixed on a moment in time I ached to return to. I wanted absolution from this despair, transcendence from the desolation that gripped my abdomen with a nausea of severed love I had never experienced before.

Dead tired, I capsized into the void of troubling dreams, heightened by my unconscious, an unconscious trying to disassemble and reassemble all the thrown pieces of my emotional turmoil and make sense of it. I popped awake in the middle of the night, dehydrated from the wine, alone and scared. I noticed with mild alarm that I had drunk the entire bottle of Chilean Syrah. My head pounded. I could feel a vein throbbing at my temple like a juddering insect. I lay back down with my hand gripping my head, the palpitation of the vein undiminished by the force of my fingers pressed against my temples. I was afraid to shut my eyes, afraid of the nightmares that would claim me like a deadly quicksand of the psyche that was impossible to escape.

I ebbed back into darkness and more disquieting dreams. In one, someone was importuning me in a reproachful voice, but as I battled and groped my way to consciousness, the voice did not fade, but grew disconcertingly louder with every step on the ladder I took toward awakening.

"Get up!" a woman's voice ordered.

I blinked open my eyes. Elizabeth West had thrown open the curtains and bright sunlight had gushed into Isla Negra like an audacity of existence, suddenly exposing everything secret and dark to the world in an explosion of light. Her expression seemed to scream, *There! Happy now?* She was wearing a navy-blue pantsuit and a white silk shirt, in sharp contrast to me, who had fallen asleep in my black "Your Nadia Archivist" T-shirt and panties. I sat bolt upright in Elizabeth's husband's bed, facing a nightmare worse than any my unconscious could have conjured from the depths of all the horrors of mythology and fairy tales.

Elizabeth moved away from the window toward the kitchen, casting a sidelong glance at me, words caught in her throat and still unable to face me directly. She circumscribed an invisible fence around me with her presence and I felt powerless to move, hemmed in by her every jarring movement.

"I'll make some coffee," she said almost surreally, in a neutral tone of voice more authoritarian than angry. "Why don't you take a shower and put on something decent." She pointed to the black T-shirt in disgusted disapprobation, further mortifying me. "You know who I am, of course?" she asserted.

I nodded in helpless resignation, at an utter loss for words.

"Good," she rasped. "We'll start there."

I slithered off the bed. In a state of shock, I shuffled my way into the bathroom on uncertain feet. The throbbing of the vein at my temple had passed like a swollen tributary of a wide river having finally found its delta, but my head still consisted of a dull pain. As the shower water rained over me, I tried to anticipate everything I was about to confront, but incomprehension overwhelmed me as I walked back out into the sunlit room, dressed in jeans and the scoop-necked T-shirt I had worn the day before.

Elizabeth heard my approaching footfalls across the room and commanded in the same sharp tone, "Have a seat." She jerked out a chair, more as a direct order than an offering.

Slowly, dispiritedly—realizing it was now all truly over between Raymond and me—I eased down onto a simple wooden kitchen chair. A tea kettle whistled shrilly, unnerving me, and I glanced up. Elizabeth poured water over coffee grounds in a French press and brought it to the table with an air of superciliousness. She set it down so hard on the table it rattled the coffee cups in their saucers. She shifted sideways into a chair and sat erect, face beautifully stoic. Fearing the worst, I held my head in my hands with my elbows propped on the table. I couldn't meet Elizabeth's withering gaze that bore into me like twin blowtorches, lit with the hot blue fire of the indignation of a woman wronged, one who was going to dictate the terms of everything from this point forward.

"So, we finally meet," Elizabeth began softly. She pushed down on the plunger in the French press as if injecting the space that separated us with authority. The coffee rose above the strainer, black as reality, bitter as truth. Elizabeth poured me a cup. "Do you take cream?"

I looked up at her and nodded soberly, waking by degrees to the full ramifications of this horrific reality.

Elizabeth's eyes blazed with barely suppressed loathing. She poured cream from a saucer into my coffee and then repeated the action with hers. I sipped the coffee. Elizabeth sat back, nursing hers. She set her cup down. "You realize the affair with my husband is over." Her voice was without inflection, flattened of emotion.

I pondered my answer. I couldn't, or didn't want to, see that far into the future. A nauseating feeling suffused me. "I think that's for Raymond to decide," I found myself muttering in an unsure voice.

"Not this time," Elizabeth shot back, obliterating my words with the sudden gust of her retort. Her eyes fluttered and she exhaled a sigh. "You're a beautiful woman, Ms. Fontaine. You're not the first. And you won't be the last."

"It's different between us," I said.

"Oh?" she said with thinly disguised contempt.

"Raymond needs me in a way you wouldn't understand," I found myself saying.

"Really?" Her eyes burned into mine, the coffee awakening her to the sharpened weapons she had come armed with.

I looked up at Elizabeth and met her steely gaze with a fierceness all my own. Now that the affair was in the open, I summoned a fighting spirit. If I was going to be expelled from the university, blacklisted from the archival profession, I wasn't going to slink away without a fight. "I'll let Raymond tell me," I said possessively.

Elizabeth scoffed a laugh. "I can break you in two"—she snapped her fingers—"just like that." She held her withering gaze. "Your career, your life . . . The backlash will be unforgiving, will end it all, you realize?"

Eyeing Raymond's wife, I glimpsed in her the strong-willed woman who had been the ballast for his lean years, the rock that stood immutable when he wandered adrift like a lost mariner, but I noticed, too, that here was the woman who had unwittingly robbed him, slowly but surely, of his creative will to go on, the woman who had manipulated his talent and fame for her own reputational aspirations. The man she had fallen in love with was the man she had hoped to remold in her own vision. He would come to heel; he would grow up and write novels that would not stir the air with controversy. At least not the controversy that stabbed her personally in the heart.

"Let's get something straight, Ms. Fontaine," said Elizabeth, "I'm not jealous. I'm not even as angry as you might be imagining. I'm disappointed. Appalled, of course. But I don't feel threatened by you in any way. I'm more sad than anything." She sipped her coffee, her eyes trained on me, patronizing and remote. "I didn't come here to give you a lecture on morality and ethics. Yes, I planned to have you replaced. But I reluctantly agreed to honor Raymond's wishes to at least let you keep your job and not go to Helena with all of this . . ."—she looked around Isla Negra with a sneer of contempt—"salaciousness."

I blinked and waited. That nausea was rising in my stomach now, as if the starlings had somehow swarmed inside me and were forming an inner blackness that coursed through every vein in my body. My heart beat irregularly, thumping against my breast, as Elizabeth lifted a tote bag onto the kitchen table and hauled out a manila folder thick with typewritten pages. I gasped and raced a hand to my mouth. The typescripts that I had torn apart Isla Negra looking for were in Raymond's wife's taloned hands. I felt like I had been struck in the chest by a large fist and was immobilized. In an instant I saw my whole life crumbling away like an ancient civilization in speeded-up time, toppling because of famine, seismic activity, wars . . . It wasn't the end of our affair that crushed me, it was that she could destroy *The Archivist*, wipe it clean from the face of the earth.

Elizabeth, a spider with her victim snared in her web, flipped open the manila folder and thumbed the pages disdainfully, and methodically closed in on her prey. "You were working on a book together, I see," she mocked in a belittling tone, looking down at the pages. My hand was still clasped over my mouth. My nostrils flared over my fingers in silent rage. That was my whole world in this vindictive woman's hands. I hallucinated reaching for it, ripping it from her clutches and strangling my adversary, but I was positive Elizabeth had made a copy. "Do you recognize it?" she snapped.

I didn't answer. A kind of emotional catatonia had seized me.

Elizabeth smiled a mordant laugh as she shook her head at the pages with deep disdain. "I don't even recognize his writing. How you do diminish his talent," she assessed, the former London book editor in her rising to the occasion. She let the folder close and leveled her eyes at me, the wound opened between us not by the affair but by *The Archivist*, a book so personal, spawned by lives so intertwined she couldn't bear its existence. "I bet you fantasized you were collaborating with my husband on his next literary masterpiece." She set her hand on top of the manila folder without taking her eyes from me. "This is vile, rubbish. How you conned him. Sunk him to his literary lowest. My God." She jutted her head a few more inches forward across the table suddenly in a threatening motion. "The vultures on his talent have never been as despicable as you."

I held my eyes fastened on the folder, hypnotized by it, ignoring Elizabeth's words. A tiny flare lit in my adrenalized brain: I had the Moleskines, the originals Raymond had pleaded with me to burn. They were safe. I didn't have Volume XII, but I had the typescript on my laptop.

Elizabeth raised the typescript of all but the last volume with one hand and shook it violently before slapping it back down on the table and letting the pages spill to both sides. "This, of course, will never see the light of day," she proclaimed, stabbing a bejeweled finger at the typescript to underscore her threat. "As I said, Ms. Fontaine, I didn't come here as the scorned woman. This whole sordid affair is beneath my dignity, and I wouldn't even be confronting you like this, sleeping in my husband's bed, unless there was something important I needed to address. Because you see, I don't need to be here in person to tell you this affair is over, I don't need to be the one to inform you you're no longer working on my husband's archive, I don't need to tell you to your pretty face this novel of yours"—she slammed her hand on the manuscript with a thundering blow—"will never, under any circumstances, be published." She inhaled deeply as if trying to compose herself.

I waited for the coup de grâce, sipping my now tepid coffee, my eyes focused on her leonine presence.

Without removing her narrowed, judgmental eyes from me, Elizabeth's hand snaked into the tote bag to produce one more item. It was the Volume XII Moleskine, the one I had left neglectfully on Raymond's writing slope. She held it up to my eyes. She then thumped it down on the typed pages, causing the table to tremble and the coffee cups to rattle in their saucers again. "Where are the other eleven?" she demanded in a quavering voice. "I want the originals of this . . . *smut* the two of you have cooked up."

I pried my eyes from the table and offered them to the righteous anger of hers.

"I want them!" Elizabeth thundered.

"They don't belong to you," I found myself saying softly.

Elizabeth jerked her head upward, as if to an invisible god sitting in judgment above us, and cackled maniacally. "Oh, no?"

"No." I waited until Elizabeth's head had returned to earth. "They belong to history."

Elizabeth snorted in derision, in hysterical incredulity. "Where are they?"

Calmly, I looked up. "You can destroy me with all the character assassination your millions will buy you. You can threaten to withdraw your generous gift to the library. You can publicly humiliate your husband and me with the revelation of our love, if you choose that scorched earth path." I somehow found a reservoir of resolve and defiance. "But you will never get your hands on the originals of *The Archivist*. Never! They're mine. I own them too," I hissed back at her.

She shook Volume XII in my face. "If you hope to salvage your career, you'll see to it that this never sees the light of day." She dropped the Moleskine down on the dining table, rattling the tableware. "You don't own my husband."

"Why don't you ask him what's in his heart?"

"I did. He called you a mistake," she hissed, "an indiscretion he regrets." She brandished a finger at the Moleskine. "The book, an aberration. The *collaboration*," she spat, "a desperate attempt to regain his form, but a failure in every way."

I didn't believe her. If Raymond told her that, he was fishing pathetically for excuses to salvage his marriage. It was hopeless attempting to win Elizabeth over to the truth. A shudder went through me believing the truth might be buried forever. "All I know is he was writing for the first time in years. Positively possessed."

"Drivel." In a mocking tone, "Infatuated with a little whore and her sex games." She looked away. "Literature?" She shook her head in disgust. "Garbage!" In a fluster of emotion, she rose hurriedly from the table and gathered her purse. The humiliation was now an evil spirit possessing all her limbs. Elizabeth had made it to the door in a murderous fury when I stopped her with a voice summoned from the gaping wound of my hurt.

"You can't undo what's done," I called out to her. "History will outlive all of us, and it's my professional obligation to make sure it does."

Elizabeth opened the door and stopped. Sunlight struck her face and revealed her age like fissures in fine china. She craned her head over her shoulder and glowered at me. "I believe he instructed you to burn them," she spat harshly.

"So did Franz Kafka to Max Brod."

She closed her eyes and fumed for a moment in quiet exasperation. In resignation, she said, "Leave your keys here. Return and I'll have you arrested for trespassing." She exhaled in revulsion. "And if you come to your senses on the other notebooks"—she wagged a dismissive finger at Volume XII—"give them to Helena in a sealed container with instructions to give them to me." She fixed me with a scowl sculpted in stone. "And I hope you will. For the love of God. You might still salvage your career." She pushed the door open and took a step forward.

"There's one more thing." I halted her exit.

Elizabeth stopped and vouchsafed me a haughty half-backward turn. The architecture of her face had transmogrified to granite. "What?"

Cold Santa Ana winds gusted over the house and rustled the umbrella of palms. One of the dead fronds snapped and clattered loudly against the patio planks.

"I'm pregnant with Raymond's child."

Elizabeth froze. My admission gored her with a brutality she hadn't bargained for, a brutality all her millions couldn't buy her way out of. "I . . .

I don't believe you," she stammered, as if pretending to be merely inconvenienced by this revelation.

I lifted my cell from the table. "Would you like to read the email from my gynecologist? See the sonogram?"

"Get rid of it!" Elizabeth quaked. And she stepped out into punishing sunlight, slamming the door behind her.

I heard the engine of an expensive foreign car growl to life. Gravel churned in the driveway, and then only dust was visible out the kitchen window. And then not even dust.

I looked down at Volume XII, the triumphant last chapter, its magic now vitiated, contaminated by Elizabeth's dismissal. Did Raymond really utter those awful things to his wife about me and the book?

I straightened wearily, my whole body tender and aching, and crossed the room to the bed. I made it carefully, slowly, as if making it for the last time. In my heart, I wanted to believe the one thing the exposure of our love couldn't destroy, that would outlive me and all the rest of them, was *The Archivist*. In its pages, Raymond's soul and mine had converged to perfection, our hearts had intertwined and our blood had coursed in a two-way flowing stream of pure, unadulterated love. We had chronicled a truth, however immoral in some eyes. My whole being, a life devoted to literature and art, reassured me of that. The pregnancy could be taken care of—I had only recently received the chilling news and I was not going to let it spoil our trip, or, God forbid, his captaincy of the Drowning—but *The Archivist*, even in draft form, was immutable. Elizabeth would never be able to come to terms with that irremediable force. To me, destroying *The Archivist* would be for our other child to die the death of deaths: invisibility.

From the bed, where I sat cross-legged, I gazed at the interior of Isla Negra and wondered if I would ever see it again. I focused on individual objects, as if etching them in memory. The writing slope, where Raymond had poured out his soul so many times, was inscribed on my brain forever. Ironically, shockingly, crazy as it might sound, I felt more violated than Elizabeth. In that moment, it made me want to keep our child and raise her to know the truth and preserve its flame should anyone dare try to douse it.

I straightened to my feet on fatigued limbs. Unconsciously, I fished a brush out of my bag and unsnarled my wet, tangled hair. All alone now, sinking into a chasmic depression, I tried to connect myself to a reality that would offer a solution, but I was adrift like any lone mariner asea without a compass. A storm was gathering on the horizon. Sleep-deprived, nerves frazzled from the events of the past four days, loss of reason perilously encroached.

I left Isla Negra with the typescripts and Volume XII. I left our inviolable world and walked out into the fierce heat of the Santa Ana winds fueling a fire that couldn't be contained.

EMILY

Emily looked up from her laptop. She was stunned to find she was standing in her kitchen and that the time on the stove read 12:11 a.m. Between the tortured email to Raymond and Nadia's own account in her memoir, Emily felt oppressed by the plethora of new, damning information. She gently set her laptop down and closed the screen. She walked, zombified, into the kitchen and opened the refrigerator and stared into it forgetting why she had opened it in the first place, still trying to process the confrontation between Elizabeth and Nadia that had taken place a mere half mile from where she was standing, deciding on whether she should drink a second ale or eat a piece of fruit. She grabbed an ale and closed the refrigerator door. She stood there in the murky light and spoke out loud: "Holy shit. Elizabeth West knew Nadia was pregnant?" With her beer in one hand and a dry-erase marker brandished in her right, she took two steps to her whiteboard and continued to chronicle the narrative's deepening and darkening trajectory.

Exhausted, Emily took her cell to bed with her, opened her journal app and started to tap out an entry in an effort to preserve her feelings at precisely that moment.

CHAPTER 20

The Scales of Justice

10/7/18

Had Nadia really taken her and the unborn child with her to the ocean and ended it all?

In too deep now. Have to know now.

Emily awoke to her cell alarm. She sat upright in bed, rubbing the fading dreams away with fists pressed to her eyes. Plunged into a void of lurid scenes, she realized she had become so obsessed with Nadia's death that their dreams were swirling, clashing together like two storms in an already fractured sky.

On the commute to Regents she checked her work email. One was from Helena requesting her presence at a 9:00 a.m. "check-in" meeting. She replied that she was running late. A second email made her suck in her breath: Detective Taggart from the SDPD. It read,

> I'm happy to meet you this afternoon. I'll be in the La Jolla area.
>
> John

Emily struggled to find parking. Fall quarter was in full swing and the university was a veritable beehive of students and faculty teeming the walkways, zigzagging on bikes and skateboards, texting while walking, oblivious of the world in a way that made Emily nostalgic for a different time and a world not so anonymously alienating.

Memorial Library loomed up at her as she walked out of the Jameson parking structure and marched across the mezzanine, predictably late for the meeting. She always paused and tilted her head up at the mammoth structure, marveling at its architectural splendor. She wondered if Nadia wasn't being hyperbolic, even sentimental, in writing that *The Archivist* would outlast everything, even the seemingly indomitable Memorial Library.

Emily rushed into the library on legs fueled by obligation. She dropped her belongings in Special Collections and headed for the seminar room. As she approached, she could hear voices, she could hear her name spoken repeatedly through otherwise unintelligible utterances.

When she entered, the room fell into an awkward silence. Their expressions were not inviting or amiable. They were guilt-riddled and grim, bearing the thankless, uncomfortable task of incipient reprimand.

Emily took a seat in the chair nearest the door, waiting on the unwelcome verdict as to what she had done wrong. Helena sat at the far end of the large, oblong table. She was dressed for battle in a black sweater and a dun-colored skirt, her neck and hands overdecorated with jewelry. Her expression was a rictus of gloom. On the opposite side sat an erect Jean, her expression cast in the severe mien of the micromanager. Seated across from Emily was a woman in her forties. She was the only one smiling.

Jean opened a hand and outstretched an arm. "Emily, this is Nancy Meyers from HR. She's here to monitor this meeting. Nancy, this is our project archivist on West, Emily Snow."

"Hi, Emily," said Nancy.

"Nice to meet you," Emily replied.

"Shall we get started?" Jean said officiously, less as a question than a statement of fact. She addressed Emily with both hands palms down on the conference table. "The reason we called you in here, Emily, is because we got a call from the administrative assistant in the Literature Department.

Apparently, you paid a visit there the other day." Emily waited. "To see Professor West."

Emily glanced over at Helena.

Helena was contorted in virtual misery like someone rearing back from a malevolently unpleasant image. She shook her head in contemptuous disbelief without meeting Emily's eyes. She seemed huddled in herself sheltering an unspoken, but grievous wrong.

"I had some questions for him," Emily explained in an unsure voice, now with nothing—and everything—to hide.

"What?" shuddered Helena, eyes riveted on Emily now.

"About certain items in restricted access," Emily said.

"What items?" Helena said in an ugly tone.

"Correspondence."

"What correspondence?" she practically screamed.

"A name I didn't recognize," Emily replied meekly.

Consternation etiolated the color from Helena's face. "I want to speak to Emily alone."

Jean looked at Nancy, who shrugged. They vacated the room, taking their coffee with them.

When they were gone, Helena pushed herself up from the table with some effort. "Let's take a walk, shall we?"

Emily followed a silent Helena out of the seminar room. To her dismay, Helena headed in the direction of the elevators. Emily picked up her pace to stay close to her heel. At the elevator, Helena kept her head tilted up at the lighted numbers, as if waiting for a signal to begin the scathing sermon she had, Emily sensed, pre-rehearsed.

The doors flung open with a bang. Students disgorged, half of them bent over phones, thumbs jumping nervously on their displays. Helena politely extended an arm to let Emily board the elevator first. For a fearful moment, Emily almost blurted out that she would prefer to take the stairs, but she knew it would only arouse Helena's suspicions—maybe even give her more ammunition in justifying whatever she was going to do—so she decided to gut it out. A handful of students entered the car, pushing Helena and Emily to the back. Emily knew where they were going—the eighth—and she would have to endure the elevator's dinging signal at every floor with shut eyes and a flinching jerk of her head.

Helena reeked of perfume. Was it the same scent Nadia had remarked on in her description of her visit in the hospital? Emily suffered the elevator clanging to a stop at every single floor before reaching the eighth, the top floor. During the entire ascent, Helena remained close-lipped, her head tilted upward, her eyes fixed on the dinging indicator lights.

They were the only two left on the elevator when it reached the eighth floor. A sign greeted them when they got off the elevator indicating the floor was closed for construction. Sunlight flooded in through the windows and Emily almost donned her sunglasses to shield her sensitive eyes, demurring for fear Helena would think she was not taking this tête-à-tête seriously.

Wordlessly, Helena walked over to the west-facing bank of windows, Emily trailing, and came to a stop. She gazed out over the university with the regal expression of someone who took it for granted that she ruled sentinel over it. As she went through the rhythms of remembering, she nodded to herself. The morning fog was lifting on the campus, thinning to reveal the young life that pulsed in its veins of concrete pathways.

"You have impeccable credentials, Emily," Helena spoke to the university below. "That's why we selected you—out of almost a hundred applicants—to finish this project. This is an important collection, for reasons that have to do both with the collection itself and for other, shall we say, grander ambitions."

"I understand its importance," Emily replied blandly.

Helena bent her head toward Emily. They were the same height, but Helena was bigger in every other way, physically, professionally, in community stature. When Emily met her gaze, a deadly malignancy was burning in Helena's eyes like she had never seen before. "If you found anything in the West Collection you thought might be of a, shall we say, compromising nature, Elizabeth left very specific instructions about those items."

"I've read the instructions in the Deed of Gift," Emily said.

"I'm sure you have." Helena wheeled toward the window and seemed to be absorbing a dark premonition. "You're aware that if, for whatever reason, she rescinded her donation it would mean *death* for Special Collections?" She hissed the word death with a resounding emphasis.

Emily didn't feel that Helena's assertion required any kind of affirmation and she remained silent.

Helena blinked and managed a pained smile. "You know, when I came here thirty-five years ago, it was only David and me in a small office. He was the poetry and literature guy, buying up all kinds of experimental stuff I thought was, well, pretty far out there." She found a laugh in her guarded, walled-off being. "But . . . well, he was right. Much of it has stood the test of time. And he was certainly right about West. I'm not going to take credit for that. It was all David. Huge admirer, supporter of his early work. So I started to socialize with his wife." Helena smiled at the memory, as if Emily were nothing more than a Dictaphone she was recording her words for posterity on. "I realized my strong suit was in fundraising, so I became the Director of Development." She darted a look at Emily, as if remembering she had an interlocuter. "That's how it all started. David and I built Special Collections from the ground up. Do you know how many damn Town & Gown events it took?" Helena emitted a self-deprecating laugh and shook her head. "We've come a long way here at Regents. Opened with two colleges and five thousand students. Now, look at it"—with her bejeweled hand she painted an arc across the window and the campus in the distance—"six, soon to be seven colleges, and nearly forty thousand students." She opened both arms to the eighth floor as if it were a celestial ceiling, built not by construction workers but her vision alone, and proclaimed proudly, "And this library is still the signature building. One of the most iconic in the world." She paused and drank in the magnificent view. Her furrowed expression camouflaged a girlish elation. "I've dreamed of this eighth-floor renovation for years. It's the pinnacle of everything I've worked for. There were a lot of ups and downs, but we're finally almost here. And you, Emily, are now a part of our family too," she finished in a pathetic last-ditch attempt at ingratiation. Helena slowly turned to Emily and waited until Emily met her eyes. "Your predecessor, Nadia"—she enunciated her name if she were a siren of evil—"got too close to this project. Way too close. It happens. It's a liability in our profession. But we can't be imprudent . . . like your predecessor." Helena paused to allow her words to resonate. She waited for a facilities worker with a heavy tool belt slung over his gut to pass. "It's unfortunate that we had to let her go. And . . . it's unfortunate what happened to her. Everyone here in Special Collections was . . . shaken. We, of course, don't want to believe she took her own life," she confided, all but admitting the official cause of death was a fabrication. She gazed off imperially at the sprawling university. "I'm sure you've ascertained that your predecessor and West were conducting an extramarital affair," she said in a matter-of-fact tone.

Emily instinctually stiffened. Her mind was racing now.

"I want to know the real reason why you went to see West," Helena demanded in a cruel voice.

"I had a few questions for him," Emily replied.

"Why didn't you come to me first, as I instructed you on our visit to Elizabeth's?"

Emily didn't respond right away. "I wasn't thinking it was that big of a deal."

"I went to visit Raymond yesterday." She let the import of her words drop on Emily. "I wanted to know why you went to see him." Emily could feel Helena's eyes on her burning hot with mounting recrimination. "And do you know what he told me?"

Emily spoke to the window. "No."

"He told me that you showed him a Moleskine notebook. With a title on it. A title you mentioned in one of our meetings."

Emily processed Raymond's lie as quickly as she could in order to fashion a response.

"*The Archivist*?" Helena's eyes hadn't left the side of Emily's window-gazing face and squinting eyes. "Do you remember giving him this Moleskine notebook, Emily?"

"I couldn't identify it. Return to donor." Out of her peripheral view Emily glimpsed Helena's eyes conflagrating behind her glasses.

"Where are the others?" Helena asked in a rebuking tone.

Emily's heart contracted with fear. "I don't know," lied Emily, relieved that Raymond had covered for her, but disconcerted that he had brought up *The Archivist* at all. She sucked in her breath. "I didn't know there *were* others."

"Did you put them in the archive?"

"Put what in the archive?" Emily feigned naivete.

"*The Archivist* Moleskines!" Helena raged. "The handwritten originals of the abandoned novel," she finished in a lowered voice when a construction worker on a ladder froze with an electric drill in his hand to glance over to see what the matter was.

"I don't know what you're referring to," replied Emily.

"Your predecessor and West were cooking up some book together." Helena searched the sky through the windows as if the admission were too much for even her to hear. "God only knows what it was about. We thought they'd come to their senses and gotten rid of it." She flung her head back at Emily. "But apparently, they've resurfaced. From somewhere. And if you've found them, I want them."

"I gave him back only what I found," Emily bent the truth again. "I was curious what they were." She stammered to a halt. If she told the whole truth, she realized she would be implicating Raymond, and he would be gutted.

"You didn't find all twelve and give them to him, did you?"

Emily made a quarter turn with her head. "Why would West lie to you?"

"You found one?" Helena asked incredulously.

"I didn't know there was more than one. I only knew there was an unidentified, apparently abandoned, work titled *The Archivist*."

"It read Volume Twelve on it!" Helena seethed. She exhaled her exasperation like a giant bellows. "However you've come to that belief, whatever you've found in the archive to substantiate that, I don't much care as long as they don't surface in the finding aid—God forbid!" She tried valiantly to gather her composure, but her mind was a hurricane of roiling emotions. "We've all moved on," she added with a grim, unrelenting finality. She directed her self-righteous eyes at Emily, choosing her words carefully. "We've got a job to do here, Emily. The Wests are counting on us. Elizabeth putting her name on this library is a big moment for her. And for all of us. We can't have anything go wrong. We can't have anything delay this gala again. It would risk the whole future of the library. And with it, this historical university." She drew a half arc across the window with a wrinkled and crooked index finger.

Even though they were standing alone at the university's highest vantage point, Emily felt its weight on her in inverse proportions.

"We can always go back after the Gala and do some of the work you talked about," Helena mollified, a little too transparently. She reached an arm across her chest and clutched Emily's shoulder. It felt like the mouth of a snake, fingers hooked into her by fangs. "I'm concerned you've gotten too close to this collection." Emily stared expressionlessly at the eucalyptus trees poking out of the fog like a forest of giant toothpicks. With her fingers digging deeper into Emily's arm, Helena finished, "You're young, Emily. You've got a bright future. We're counting on you. Don't be foolish like your predecessor." She lowered her voice and hissed, "I can make you very small very quickly. The archives and special collections world is a tiny community. We all know one another. I can ruin you for life," she derided, tightening her grip for emphasis, then letting go, the poison of her admonition injected. Helena massaged Emily's arm where she had gripped it, like a nurse patting a vein.

She turned to go back to the elevator, took one step, stopped, and glowered at Emily. "Don't ever go to West again without my permission."

Emily, immobilized by the director's wrath, remained unresponsive. What she knew could founder the library to a first-floor pile of rubble. A tiny current of power coursed through her knowing that Helena was not completely in control of her own destiny.

Helena started away. "Coming?"

Emily affected a smile. "I'm going to take the stairs."

"Oh, that's right. Your hearing disorder." With her index finger she spun a circle around her ear, a gesture more frequently associated with denoting someone who is crazy.

Emily looked at her wondering how Helena had heard about her misophonia, but that was the least of her concerns. "I'll be ready for the Gala," she heard herself say, as if ventriloquizing the reassurance through the Emily, who had arrived in La Jolla over two months ago.

"Good." Helena burned her eyes into Emily's. "And if you come across those Moleskines, I don't care how or where . . . I want them," she said, her tone rising to a threat. She took half a dozen steps, then stopped, threw her head over her shoulder, and gave Emily a backward look. "Remember, Emily, you're just a *temp*." She held her stare, a look of implacable cruelty, and Emily's blood burned hot. Helena's words were meant to impoverish her contribution as an archivist. She met Helena's contemptuous eyes with fierce eyes of her own. Helena turned away.

Emily listened as Helena's footsteps reverberated on the tile. She heard the *bing bing* of the elevator, its heavy doors banging open and slamming closed, depositing Helena inside and delivering her back down into the bowels of Special Collections.

Emily pivoted away from the window and crossed the empty floor toward the stairwell. With every step she was moving toward a new definition of self. Her feet on the treaded metal stairs echoed in the cylindrical stairwell as she spiraled downward, hugging the wall to assuage her vertigo, back to where it all began, innocently at first, with a string-tie envelope and a card catalog card. She continued the descent, spiraling downward not into her cubicle and the box that Helena had circumscribed around her but into a flurry of emails from a frantic Nadia to an apparitional Raymond, all unanswered.

From: Nadia Fontaine <Nfontaine@RegentsU.edu>
To: Raymond West <Rwest_Lit@RegentsU.edu>
Subject: Post-Apocalypse
Date: 03 November 2017

Raymond,

Where are you? I know you're out of the hospital. We need to talk. Your phone is dead . . .

NADIA'S STORY (CONT'D)

I sat on one of the campus's cement benches, hunched over, puffing anxiously on a cigarette. Seagulls squawked overhead in the thick fog that had streamed in, blanketing Regents in a sepulchral quiet. Classes were done for the day and the campus was mostly deserted. I dropped my cigarette to the pavement and extinguished it with a twist of my foot when I espied a man on crutches limping out of Arts & Humanities, hitching alongside a colleague. The fog watercolored him in a strange ethereality reminiscent of some black-and-white movie of the thirties. The two men shook hands briefly, and then they forked off in different directions. I sprang to my feet.

Raymond, bent forward on his crutches, stopped, helpless, when he saw me advancing toward him. His head revolved anxiously on his shoulders like the beacon of a lighthouse.

"You can't come here anymore," he said when he saw me. *You*? He didn't even deign to use my name.

"I've emailed and emailed!" I cried. "What do you want me to do?"

Raymond planted his crutches in preparation for the next step. As he started off, my next words struck his back like thrown knives.

"I'm pregnant," I blurted out.

He froze, lowered his head gloomily. "Meet me at the Gliderport in an hour," he said without looking at me, then hitched away on his crutches.

I walked alone in the fog and a haze of tears to the Jameson parking structure, somehow, in my anguish, remembered where I had parked my car, drove across Torrey Pines Road to the Gliderport, and parked in a familiar area evocative of more exultant times. Then it was the hot Santa Anas and the blood-red sun and the bounding blown tumbleweeds of our desert-blooming love. Now it was the low-visibility fog clinging to the ground enshrouding me in all its gray despair, shearing me off from reality.

My gaze shifted sharply when I heard the crunching of tires braking on the gravelly dirt. In my side-view mirror Raymond's black Range Rover emerged out of the fog like an automotive leviathan. The air was fraught with tension as I climbed out of my Falcon Futura. My arms crisscrossed my chest, and I shivered against the cold of the fog and the freezing ocean from which it emanated and pulled the black cashmere sweater tight to the knot in my neck. Where once my heart had pounded with skyward-soaring anticipation, now it was tight with fear, a rogue planet in an empty cosmology that mirrored the entirety of my feelings.

I opened the passenger-side door of his Range Rover and hoisted myself up and shut myself inside with stomach-turning dread. Raymond glanced at me and then looked away into the fog barreling over the cliff at us, smothering the world in streaming currents of mist. Immured in the car and the fog, invisible to the world—as we had always been and would always be for eternity, I desolately realized—we sat in a strained silence, both staring at the same enveloping emptiness that was gathering to claim us and our once empyreal love. It wasn't fair, I felt selfishly in my heartache. Cold as statuary, he made no move to touch me or kiss me or comfort me, so I hugged my arms against my stomach to ward off the nausea that flooded me. I didn't know if I could survive this breakup, if that's what it was. The harsh tone of his voice did not ameliorate my heartsickness.

"You can't come there anymore," he said, a different man, an unrecognizable voice, a foreign face, my worst nightmare audibly and visibly manifest.

I swung my head to his averted eyes, feeling all the world like some sick animal. "All you had to do was call. Or email."

"She's watching my every move, Nadia," he tried to placate me. "I'm up for Chair for Christ's sake. And the twenty-five million . . ." He seemed to have forgotten everything, had already unmoored the boat while I still bobbed in the harbor with my desperate hopes that the journey was still ours and that I hadn't been thrown overboard.

"I don't care about your wife's fucking gift," I exploded. "That university is a magnet for money. How dare you reduce it all to money." I raised a hand to my mouth to staunch the tears, hating that it had come to this. His opacity, his detachedness, his rehearsed, unappeasable indifference, pained me to the molten core of my being.

Unable to bear his silence anymore, I bent an anguished face to Raymond, who stared stoically forward, as if afraid to meet the emotionally fraught reality of this past he was inextricably a part of. His dark sunglasses, which persisted on his face, cruelly distanced him even farther. "How's your leg?" I asked, the words stuck in my throat.

"It'll never be the same the doctors say," he rasped, as if he were talking metaphorically about our relationship.

I ventured a hand to his shoulder. "One email. A phone call . . ." I lowered my forehead to his shoulder and pressed it there. I inhaled his scent, and it made me tighten my grip on his shoulder. But in reality, a simple, more fatal truth was being breathed.

"I couldn't risk it," he said in that neutral tone I hated. His hand left the steering wheel and found the top of my head. His appeasing gesture meant so much to me that it prompted a flood of tears. I wept openly and unabashedly against his shoulder as if it were a cracked pillar from the ruins of a long-ago civilization. "You know I still love you, Nadia," he started. "You know I do." He inhaled and exhaled audibly. "But we can't do this anymore. The stakes are too high." He let go his hand from my head and gripped the steering wheel tightly, as if readying to go. "The plan was ruined by that accident. And I refuse to define it as Fate."

"How can you say you still love me but not want to be with me?" I was seized by a fresh choking of tears that almost gagged my words. "How can you say that?"

Raymond seemed to have traveled to a place he had resolved to go on his own solemn drive over to the Gliderport. I could feel it in his withdrawing of affection, the pat on the head all he could vouchsafe me. His emotional rigidity chilled me. I felt that nauseating ache in my stomach all over again, that paralyzing sickness of love that haunts all of us, at one time or another, with unassuageable remorselessness. I hurt everywhere.

"I remember when I drove your car back from Baja and I was so sick with worry about you," I began, still clutching his biceps.

"I know. I thought about you on the helicopter. I can only imagine." He seemed to be softening a little.

"And all I could think about were all the times together and how deep we had gone. And for the first time we were together; we had awakened in each other's arms. And the book was finished and what a joy that was . . ." I raised my wet lashes to his stoic face. "It was supposed to be a celebration, the best weekend of my life." I showed him the Burmese sapphire on my flattened hand. "And to think we would be married." Raymond darted a fugitive glance at the ring. I squeezed my eyes shut, but the tears, with nowhere to go, pressed out anyway and stained his shirt.

"And you went back to him the same as I went back to her," he stated coldly.

"Don't say that, Raymond. You know I was leaving him. For you. For us. It wasn't going to be easy for me either."

"You're pregnant?"

"Don't worry. I'll take care of it."

"You're sure it's mine?"

"Oh, for God's sake, Raymond. You think I could be with anyone else with what we've shared?"

Raymond took a blank check from his shirt pocket and set it on the dashboard. "Whatever it costs."

I batted the check away. "I don't want your money," I spat with defeat in my voice. "It's coming from her anyway," I scoffed.

Neither of us spoke for a long moment, both trying to apprehend the consequences and augur the bleak future. There were no answers, and we both knew it in the shared silence that teetered on the edge of a final parting.

"I'm sorry," Raymond finally said. "Would have been a brilliant child."

I raised my head to his in near incredulity. In defeated resignation all I could muster was, "Yeah."

Sensing my eyes on him, Raymond's right arm reached up higher on the wheel, as if he were preparing to depart, as if he were trying to pry my hooked fingers and crying eyes from his shoulder, but I clung to him for the last vestiges of our desperate truth. I wasn't going to let go until he was gone, until I had no choice but to let go, determined to use every ounce of strength I had left to stitch him back to the fabric of my flesh and be one with him again like we were in Adobe Guadalupe before those fucking birds and . . . I pounded my fist on his muscular shoulder and sobbed, disbelieving our love could not be resurrected somehow.

Raymond reached his hand over and grabbed my fist and held it like an injured bird desperate to fly when an attempt would have ended in death. "There was never going to be a right time given the circumstances of my life right now," he began softly, another man I didn't know, not the man who marveled at his archived work in the stacks, not the man who had let me into his inner sanctum, not the man with whom I had collaborated on a book, not the man . . . "We both knew that. We wanted to forget. In that inviolable bubble that was our love, we wanted to be oblivious of reality. And then reality hurtled at us before we could control its coming, pace out its consequences." He thought he was being consoling, but intellectualizing it made it all the worse to me. I had become an abstraction in his life.

My escalating despair found the ledge of anger with clinging fingertips. "What am I supposed to do? How am I supposed to get over this? Every day I go into work and there are your words, your face, Raymond. It's inside me and outside of me, it's intertwined with my life. What am I supposed to do? Look for another job in another city, export my life there and start anew? After what we've had, what we've explored, how deep we've gone? It's never going to be like this again." I raised my tearstained eyes up from his shoulder into the cragged cliff of the side of his seemingly unfeeling face. I tore off his sunglasses and made him look at me. "For either of us, Raymond. Never. The. Same."

His eyes were fearful pinpoints of blue pivoting on a dark axis that was now his reality, not mine. "You're right. How do you think I feel?"

"I don't even know what you *do* feel!" As if the accident, like the fog, could erase everything from visibility, and when it cleared, everything would return to a certain order. I found myself saying, "You have a career and a powerful and forgiving wife and a whole universe in which you can forget me." I lifted my tortured face to his. "How am I ever going to forget you? I have nothing." I rested a hand on my stomach. "Nothing but this . . ." I trailed off because I knew he would never understand.

He glanced down at my hand on my stomach as if seeing through to the life that beat inside me that was our only connection left. "How am I ever going to forget you? You are forever imprinted on my soul," he said with the barest tremor of feeling that injected me with a desperate, fleeting hope.

I removed his sunglasses and set them on the dashboard and clutched at his shoulder with a surging pessimism, the animal who desired passionately to experience life intensely, that radiant light smothered in me now in the aftermath of a barbarous twist of fate. "You won't."

"In a perfect world we would be together, you know that, Nadia," he said platitudinously, and I despised him for the tone. At least he spoke my name! I could sense his eyes cast down at me clinging to his shoulder. "You know that, right?" I found myself nodding against my will, instinctually hoping surrender, not fighting, would buy me some semblance of a future with him. "I can't do this to Elizabeth. Not after all she's done for me."

I broke away from his shoulder when he wrenched his arm free to look at his watch. I could feel the warmth from his body, but we might as well have been on opposite sides of the Pacific.

"I have a meeting at four." He glanced at me. "I should go."

I nodded to an introspective Raymond and not to his remark.

"Giving you up is the single hardest thing I've ever had to do in my life," he said, not without a quiver of emotion. But there it was: the end. *Giving you up*, I muttered the words in my head, the trapdoor to the void beneath me yawning again, the black depression waiting for me at the bottom of its seafloor where ruthless creatures ravened for one another in the implacable competition for survival, where only death and oblivion triumphed.

"Please tell me I wasn't like all the others."

"Don't be foolish, of course not." Real feeling quavered in his voice, now that he had exacted what he wanted: I wouldn't stalk or haunt him, I would release him from this powerful love and let him suffer it without me in his own distant way. "For God's sake, we were writing a book together," he said, as if its admission finally would be the consolation that would salve my soul.

I looked at him with hopeful eyes. "What's going to happen to *The Archivist*?"

"I don't know." He reached for his sunglasses and walled me off by fitting them once again to his eyes. "I can't do this anymore."

"It's a wondrous work, isn't it?" I fished for time. He didn't say anything. "There's a deep vein of truth that's been lacking in your work for years," I reminded him.

He turned to me with his Ray-Ban-obscured eyes. "Because it was torn from the fabric of truth, how would I write its epilogue?"

"But it's such a beautiful piece of writing," I cried hopelessly.

"I've got to go, Nadia." His voice was final, one I intuited I would never hear again privately between us.

I reluctantly let go of his shoulder for good this time, nodding to myself.

Raymond pulled me toward him and kissed me paternalistically on the top of the head. Even though I couldn't see behind the sunglasses, I could sense by the shift in tone of his voice that tears had formed in his eyes. "I'll miss everything about you. I know I'll never find this again." He let go of my head and my shock of thick hair and shot his hand to the key in the ignition. He turned the engine over and let it idle. "Please. Just go. Let's not make this harder than it is."

"Goodbye," I said, and stepped out of the car.

The Range Rover backed out, turned sharply, spat gravel and drove off in a punctuation of funneling dust, leaving me at the driver's-side door of my Falcon staring off at the vanishing car, all alone. No, that's not what I wanted. I wanted him to turn off the engine and climb out of the door and limp around it and envelop me in his arms and tell me he had changed his mind, he would brave all the repercussions of the affair, like he had promised over candlelight and wine and blue sapphires at Adobe Guadalupe, for the sake of our *The Archivist.* Forged in love.

I stood motionless, gazing with squinted eyes into the now dark void of this fantasy. The fog thickened in horizontal waves, blanketing the golf course and turning the players into eidolons. I couldn't see the family of ravens soaring above me, even if their loud cawing gave me hope that they would find their way back to their nests. Raymond's car had been swallowed up by the fog, and that, too, was gone forever. I parked a hand on my stomach again where the child he had regretted I had promised to give up lay, like our novel, in chrysalis form, wondering if she would ever be born. I was all alone. The wind ruffled my hair, and I turned to the cliffs and faced the incoming fog in defiance of its mercilessness.

Our cars, and our lives, had parted for the last time.

EMILY

Emily drove to Regents with Nadia's account of their parting, the final passages abruptly ending her memoir *My Story* discovered in the dark archives, spreading a deep sorrow in her, throbbing in her heart. Having now met Raymond, she felt a tie to Nadia in an even deeper way than before.

When she emerged from the Jameson parking structure, still staggered by all the revelations, Emily spotted a local network news station van parked at the turnaround, a small dish antenna hydraulically hoisted skyward. As she drew closer to the mezzanine, she came upon a gathering of film crew personnel and curious bystanders. Emily approached warily, circling the periphery. A news crew of three hovered in front of local anchor Dave Atkinson, who was interviewing Raymond West. Dressed in his familiar uniform of faded jeans, cowboy boots, a white poplin shirt, and a black sport coat, West was standing with the iconic hexagonal library framing him dramatically in the background. Emily inched closer to get within earshot. She recognized some of the faces of the faculty and staff who were clustered around. She strained to hear what they were saying, but she was timid and afraid Verlander or Helena, standing watchful nearby like a mother hen, might wave her over to put in a word or two.

Emily sidled up next to Joel, who had come out of his digital archivist cubicle to spectate.

"Hey there, hot stuff," Joel greeted her. "There's your man."

Emily stared straight ahead, eyes focused on Raymond.

"How do you feel about your life's work being archived here?" Dave Atkinson asked Raymond.

Raymond turned his head and contemplated the library towering majestically over him. "It's a tremendous honor. As an alumnus of Regents, it's a coming full circle, a coming home." He turned back to Atkinson. "It's deeply humbling."

"And with your wife's generous gift to the library, there must be a feeling of tremendous pride?" Atkinson said with a practiced smile.

"Yes, Elizabeth has given to educational and arts causes all her life. What it means for this iconic library is almost inexpressible. I'm happy for the city of San Diego, not always recognized for its contribution to the arts."

Atkinson chuckled. "San Diego has its pluses."

"Surfing and Over the Line tournaments," Raymond quipped. "But that's all changing."

Emily's gaze roamed to Helena, who was standing directly behind Atkinson, her presence invisibly micromanaging Raymond's words. She slowly rotated a proud and beaming face to the small crowd, spotted Emily, smiled broadly as if the berating lecture the previous day had not happened, and pointed an excited finger at Raymond being interviewed. Emily forced a smile in reply.

“There are rumors that you’ve been short-listed for the Nobel Prize for Literature,” Atkinson remarked.

“Well, Dave, the Swedish Academy doesn’t short-list for the Nobel. Although I’ve heard the winners have sometimes been leaked, much to their chagrin.”

“Yes, but British betting organizations have you as one of the favorites.”

Raymond shrugged. “I don’t like to think about awards for art. If it happens, it would be a huge moment for everyone here, not only for me. It’s not why I write. I write because I believe in the close examination of the human . . .” Raymond trailed off, his words suddenly caught in his throat. He espied Emily’s face in the small gathering and a tacit guilt running intimately between the two of them tautened his countenance. “The truth of the . . . human condition,” he cobbled his sentence together finally. “We live in a world too omnipresent with lies. Art has an obligation to the truth, I believe. It’s the final residue of all living things.”

“You would accept the award, of course?”

“Of course,” Raymond replied, perking up at the non sequitur, avoiding Emily’s stare. “I’m not going to be a Jean-Paul Sartre. I owe everything to the written word. And to my wife, who has supported me through the years.” He extended an arm and turned to the library as if introducing the TV audience to a new era in the university’s history. “And to this wonderful library which has given so much to me over the decades.”

“You haven’t published anything in almost five years,” Atkinson interrupted, “what might we see from you next?”

“Well, I’m writing a movie now.” He shifted his eyes furtively back to Emily. An electric current coursed between them that no one could feel but the two of them.

Emily whispered to Joel, “I’ve got to get inside.” Emily broke away from the news interview. She couldn’t stomach Raymond being so disingenuous, so specious. A celebrated writer squandering his talent on a screenplay for an industry whose golden age was decades in the past, about to ascend to that eighth floor for a gala when the heart of his true love was entombed in memory in its bottom floors. It appalled her. Her anger pushed her legs to walk faster. She thought about what Nadia and Raymond had said to each other in parting, heartbreakingly rendered by Nadia, that there had been no lies between them; they had gone as transparently and as nakedly deep as two people could go. And then fate had snatched it away from them.

Emily sat in her cubicle in front of her computer poring over the West finding aid when she heard a herd of footsteps. Helena was the first to telescope her head into Emily's cubicle.

"Isn't it fabulous?" Helena enthused, her face a riot of happiness.

"It's exciting," Emily agreed in an indifferent tone.

"Everything okay?"

"Yeah, fine. Right on schedule."

Helena studied Emily with piercing, circumspect eyes. She smiled, momentarily dropped her suspicion. "Okay. Carry on."

Joel appeared after Helena, as if he had been waiting down the corridor for his moment. "Pretty heavy stuff," Joel said.

"Yeah," Emily concurred.

"How are you doing?"

"I'm fine." She swept her cubicle with a thrown arm. "Still a lot of work left if I'm going to be ready."

"Up for an evening glass paddle?"

"Yeah, I might be."

Joel realized Emily was being deliberately laconic in her answers. He dropped brooding eyes on her. "Everything's cool, right?"

"Totally cool, Joel. You have nothing to be concerned about."

Joel smiled relief. "He wins the Nobel that's going to be sick."

"Yeah. Sick," Emily added with thinly veiled sarcasm.

Joel gave her the shaka wave. "Later."

Over lunch, Emily drove to the new Bird Rock Coffee Roasters location on Carmel Valley Road. She walked up a short flight of steps to a planked deck consisting of a variety of seating options overlooking the Los Peñasquitos Lagoon. A protected marsh of waterways and untamed reeds, it was a sanctuary for migratory and local avian wildlife in the Torrey Pines State Natural Reserve.

Detective Taggart, a Black man in his early fifties with short-cropped hair edged silver at the temples, flat jaded eyes that were red with burst capillaries, and a mouth like a bear trap, looked out of place in slacks, sports coat, white button-down shirt, and loose-knotted tie at this hipster North County boutique coffee spot. He was perched heavily on a high stool and sipping a cup of coffee when Emily greeted him.

She thrust out her hand. "Hi, I'm Emily Snow."

Taggart took her hand and shook it briefly. "Pleased to meet you." He dropped his eyes with a puzzled frown corrugating his face. "Hell of a cup of coffee they make here."

"Some of the best in the world," Emily said.

"Goddamn, they had one in there from Panama or someplace and it was twelve bucks a cup." He shook his head in disbelief. "Twelve bucks for a cup of coffee. I'd offer to buy you one, but they don't pay us that well for putting bad guys behind bars." He reached for his wallet. "No, here, I was just kidding."

"It's okay. I'll get my own. Back in a second."

Emily broke away from Taggart and went inside. Wasting no time, she ordered a house blend and a scone. She came back outside and hoisted her small frame up onto one of the high stools across from Taggart and sipped her coffee.

"Thanks for agreeing to meet me," Emily said.

"Beautiful view here," remarked Taggart, gazing off. "Don't get up to Del Mar often. My work usually takes me south and east. And worse," he added more cynically, sipping his coffee. "Damn, that's good coffee." He looked at Emily with rheumy, bloodshot eyes. "So, you came to the station the other day inquiring about a death?"

"Yes," said Emily. "Nadia Fontaine. She was my predecessor at the university." Emily rotated her shoulders and pointed in the direction of Regents University hidden behind the wooded hills of the Torrey Pines Reserve that loomed in the mist above them in the distance. "Just over there." She propped her elbows on the timbered table. "How familiar are you with her case?"

"Pretty familiar," said Taggart. "I know she was some kind of librarian."

"Archivist. Totally different."

"And you're an archivist, too, I presume?"

"Yes. Her successor."

Taggart adjusted his sunglasses. "What did you want to know?"

Emily cleared her throat. "I'm putting together a piece on the author whose collection Nadia was working on, and which I'm working on now. I'm a project archivist . . ." she trailed off when Taggart knitted his brow questioningly. "A hired gun. In for one project, then out. I'm temporary in this time-sensitive situation."

"Ah," said Taggart, raising his head.

"Anyway, I'm finishing up Ms. Fontaine's work and I wanted to ask you a few questions about the police report on her death."

Taggart turned to Emily and knitted his brow. "I understand you have some information that might be of interest to us."

"Possibly."

"Okay, shoot," he said.

Emily sucked in her breath. "Okay. Was Nadia Fontaine autopsied?"

"Of course," replied Taggart.

"I didn't see the autopsy report in the death investigation report," retorted Emily.

"That's because it's kept with the medical examiner."

"But as the lead detective you know what the results of it are?" Emily asked.

"They found water in her lungs," Taggart drawled guardedly. "She drowned."

"What else did they find?"

Taggart brought his coffee to his lips. "I'm taking it slowly because it's a dollar a sip." Emily chuckled. "Why don't *you* tell me what else they found, Ms. Snow?"

Emily met his rheumy eyes through her sunglasses. This was truly the point of no return, she realized. "Did the autopsy reveal that she was . . . pregnant?"

Taggart, taken aback, slowly lowered his coffee, twirled his spoon in it, stirring for a response. "How'd you learn that?"

Emily brought her coffee to her lips and spoke surreptitiously over the rim. "There's a reference to it deep in the death investigation report. Plus, I have some other corroborating . . . I'd prefer not to say," she cut herself short.

Taggart nodded. An onshore wind was kicking up, and the blue waterways of the lagoon were textured in a moiré appearance. An egret took wing, striping a low white dotted line across the green reeds like the most eloquent ellipsis Nature had ever produced. "Beautiful," Taggart marveled. "I should be in Costa Rica now. Alimony on the first wife's killing me." He shook his head.

Emily narrowed her gaze at the egret that had flapped out of view leaving abrasions on the water. "How far did you take the investigation before ruling it was an accidental drowning?"

"Pretty far."

Emily faced Taggart. "And you're absolutely positive it was an accidental drowning?"

Taggart set his coffee cup down with a clatter. He lifted his heavy, weary eyes to Emily. "She had a surfboard leashed to her ankle. There was blunt force trauma to the head, which the ME—medical examiner—determined had been caused by a blow from the surfboard or hitting the reef. It knocked her unconscious. And she drowned."

"I see. No suspicion of suicide? Drugs in her system—?"

Taggart chopped Emily off, shook his head, and spoke in rapid-fire impatience. "Unless you think it's suicidal to be surfing in winter in the dead of night. Which I borderline do. But I'm not a surfer. I'd probably drown in three feet of water with this gut of mine. But in my experience, that's not how people do themselves in. Guns, drugs, poisons, asphyxiation . . . Not surfing."

Emily looked at Taggart. He held his eyes on her. They were both measuring each other's definition of trust, from different levels of experience. Emily sucked in her breath. "Out of curiosity, did you at any time during the investigation think her death might have been a homicide?"

Taggart reared back in apparent incomprehension and took in Emily in a wider aspect. "Whenever we find a dead body, unless there's overwhelming evidence to the contrary, we always first assume foul play."

"Did you talk to Nadia's husband?" Emily asked.

"Nathan Waters. Yes, nice guy. Tragic. I can't imagine. A beautiful wife like that." Taggart shook his head sadly as if crime scene photos of the investigation had been unwittingly evoked.

"Was he the father?" Emily asked.

Taggart narrowed his eyes and offered Emily an expressionless mien. "I shouldn't be telling you this."

Emily waited. She had nothing to lose now.

"No. He wasn't. DNA didn't match. He also confided something else." Taggart's eyes roamed back to the lagoon framing Emily in the background, debating whether to divulge any more of the investigation.

"They weren't having sex," Emily said, plucking the words from his mind, beating him to the punch.

Taggart slowly swung his head until his eyes coupled with Emily's, but this time his orbs were dark with suspicion. "You're a regular little Nancy Drew, aren't you, Ms. Snow?"

"Didn't set out to be, Detective."

His expression shifted. He inhaled deeply and exhaled aloud, suggesting perhaps he was willing to regard her more seriously.

"Did you ever find out who the father was?" Emily persisted.

Taggart pouched out a cheek with his tongue and shook his head. "Her husband said something about in vitro, but he couldn't substantiate it. Don't know if he was covering for her or ego . . ." He shrugged and trailed off.

"What'd you conclude?"

"We assumed it was a one-night stand or . . ."

"Or?" Emily begged him to continue.

"You're not going to quote me in your little profile, are you?"

"Of course not. God, no."

"Your predecessor, the deceased, was, let's just say, sexually adventurous."

"Who told you that?"

Taggart clattered his cup to the saucer again. He was used to doing the interrogating and unaccustomed to being on the receiving end. "She and her husband were having problems. The library was threatening to fire her for performance reasons—inappropriate relations—she was seeing a therapist. She had been prescribed antidepressants, antianxiety meds. Had a well-documented history of depression . . . She might have paddled out that night to risk her life, but I don't think she deliberately killed herself. By all accounts she was half-mad, so that might explain what she was doing out there."

"Did the autopsy reveal anything else besides the water in her lungs, the blunt force trauma, and the pregnancy?"

"Are you sure you're not posing as an archivist?" Taggart teased. "Because you sound like a defense attorney, or his paralegal," he added acidly.

"I can assure you I'm an archivist." Emily dived into her purse and produced her university photo ID and splayed it across the table. Taggart looked at it and nodded. She put it away.

"You claimed you had some information," he said testily.

"There were ligatures on her neck. And you concluded . . . ?" Emily asked, fearing she was losing him.

"Could have been the surfboard leash. Sex games with one of her lovers, I don't know. I'm not into that kinky stuff." He parked his forearms on the table. "Look, when we suspect foul play, we look for motive. The husband has an ironclad alibi—Europe on a business trip, I believe. We don't see motive. We did, however, see motive for suicide."

"Why was it officially ruled an accidental drowning then?"

"That gets into politics. Speculation. Subjective interpretations." Emily kept her eyes intent on him. "Look, I've probably divulged too much. We didn't think there was foul play. The husband was hoping we wouldn't rule it a suicide. Ditto for the university . . ." He rolled his tongue over his upper teeth. "I looked over the case file before I came up here. I guess she was working on some famous writer's papers. And he's married to a very prominent woman here in San Diego. A woman who might be running for mayor. A very influential local personage."

"Did you ever suspect she was having a love affair? And not merely a string of one-night stands?" importuned Emily.

"With whom?" he asked evasively.

Emily sat back and gazed out at the tranquil lagoon with blinking eyes. A flare scratched aflame in her head, and she tried not to smile. It struck her suddenly: she knew more than the police! She searched inwardly, wrestling with her conscience, realizing any revelation to

Taggart could brachiate to the wrong tree. She started to craft a response.

"I'm still waiting for the reason why I drove all the way up here," Taggart groused, shifting impatiently on his stool.

"What if you knew who the father was?" Emily asked. "Would you reopen the case?" Emily could imagine but was almost afraid to look at him to catch his reaction. She turned slowly back to his face. He showed unblinking, poker-playing eyes now.

"We would certainly want to speak to him, yes." He waited. The wait was annoying him. "Don't tell me you also know who the father was?"

"I'm positive I know who the father was, but I'm also reasonably confident that, if it were foul play, he wouldn't be a suspect."

"He would be to us," he deadpanned. "Especially if he were somebody important and had a lot to lose."

"It would go to motive?" Emily suggested.

Taggart nodded slowly up and down, his eyes never leaving Emily's face. "You're not going to tell me, are you?"

"I can't. It would be an ethical breach."

"I could subpoena your testimony."

"I would plead the Fifth."

"On what grounds?"

"I could get into trouble," Emily muttered.

"How?"

Emily didn't feel like enlightening him on the archivist's code of ethics. Which could lead down the wrong path, the dark archives . . . She shook her head. "Let's just say that I'm privy to some information via a way you couldn't be."

"Fair enough," growled Taggart. "So, you asked me to meet you to pick my brain about the police report, but what you really wanted was to tell me you knew more than me. Is that the story?"

"No." Emily was as tired as he of the verbal volleyballing and she leaned into his ruminating face. "I'm saying I don't think it was an accidental drowning."

"And why is that, Ms. Drew?"

"She was at the beginning of her second trimester, correct?" Taggart shrugged as if it was annoying to give her the answer she already knew. "She was," Emily insisted. "She wouldn't kill herself."

"I've seen it more than a dozen times," Taggart disagreed in his world-weary voice.

"No woman would kill herself, with her baby in utero, unless she was some whack job or desperate drug addict, and Nadia was neither. It would be a double suicide."

"What's the difference?"

"You don't understand women, Detective."

"I'm on my third marriage. You might have a point."

"Did they find any drugs or alcohol in her system?"

Taggart shook his head. "Toxicology came up negative."

"A woman, over three months pregnant, walks into the cold waters of the Pacific with a surfboard, stone cold sober because she's, you concluded, afraid to tell her soon-to-be ex-husband that she's carrying the child of another man? She paddles out into waist-high surf hoping that the waves will drown her because she's too craven to put a gun to her head? Is that what you've concluded down there in Homicide at SDPD?"

"Something along those lines," replied a defeated Taggart.

"Do you know how many women kill themselves by drowning?"

"Enlighten me."

"Fewer than one percent. Extremely rare, like you said. I think you should reopen the case, Detective," Emily advised with a dark intensity. "You admit as much that it wasn't a drowning. And that suicide is implausible. Investigate it as a homicide."

"Incentivize me and divulge who the father is. If you do know."

"I can't do that, Detective, "Emily said, casting her eyes down. "If I were deposed, I'd be looking at perjury. And if I didn't perjure myself, I'd be facing career suicide."

"Can I ask you a question?" Emily pursed her lips and looked blankly into space. "Why'd you get into this mess?"

Emily spoke to her cup of coffee that she had drunk to the bottom. "I don't know. I fell into it backward. And I don't think justice was served." She sneaked a fugitive glance at her cell. When she saw the time, she reached for her purse. "I've got to run." She climbed off her stool and thrust out her hand. He glanced at it and then back up at her. "Thank you for your time, Detective. You know where to reach me."

He took her hand and held it in his. "Sorry I couldn't be of more help with this Nadia Fontaine woman. I guess you didn't know her personally."

Emily looked at Taggart. She knew her more personally than anyone in the world, including Raymond, she thought, but she didn't have time, or the desire, to get into the nuances.

"What's your stake in this?" he asked.

"The truth." She locked her eyes on his. "As you said, suicide is more likely the cause of death, but not suicide by drowning. And definitely not an accidental drowning. That's bullshit." She raised her eyebrows and tilted her head to one side.

"You think she was murdered?" Taggart said, incredulous.

His blunt words stunned even her. The line had officially been crossed. Without breaking eye contact, she risked, "I don't think the investigation probed deep enough."

"What is it with this archivist woman?" A sullenness had crept into his voice.

"I feel emotionally linked to her in a way that's hard to explain."

Taggart regarded her circumspectly. "Because you're both archivists who work at the same library?"

"No," Emily retorted. "Because she let me into her life in a way I'm afraid you would never understand. And that's all I can say." She paused because she was afraid of divulging more. "I can help you, if you're willing to have an open mind. I can't if you don't."

Taggart stared at her.

Emily slipped her hand out of his. "One other thing, Detective. The night she supposedly drowned was a moonless night. Surfers don't surf on moonless nights." She raised her voice an angry octave. "They can't see the friggin' waves."

"You're sure it was a moonless night?" Taggart asked coyly.

"I checked. I'm an archivist. We're thorough, if nothing else."

Emily turned and walked down the stairs to her car on the street. As she drove off back to the university, she noticed Taggart gazing out over the balcony, looking out of place among all the young people.

When Emily returned to Special Collections, she passed by the seminar room. Through the paneled windows she glimpsed Helena, Verlander, Jean—and Elizabeth—bending over the table in the middle of a meeting. Their muffled voices were difficult to decipher, but Emily assumed if Elizabeth was in the meeting it had something to do with the West Papers. She also had to assume because she wasn't invited, they were talking about things they didn't wish her to be a party to.

She slipped into her cubicle and switched on her computer. The monitor came to life.

"Knock, knock," said a woman's voice.

Emily swiveled in her chair to find the round, usually smiling face of Chloe disorganized into a frown. "Something heavy must be going on," she observed, gesturing with her head in the direction of the seminar room.

"What do you mean?" Emily pretended ignorance.

"Whenever Elizabeth West shows up, there's something."

"Well, I'm on schedule," Emily said.

Chloe came forward a few steps into Emily's cubicle. She lowered her voice. "Jean asked me if I would be up to team-process on West."

Emily didn't trust anyone anymore, except Joel. She raised her head up to Chloe. "What'd you say?"

"If you needed help—"

"I don't," said Emily, cutting her off.

Chloe nodded. "That's what I thought. Which is why I thought it was weird that she asked me."

"They're trying to take control of this project, wrestle it away from me," Emily said.

"I think they just want to make sure it gets finished on time, Emily."

"No, that's not it!"

"Why do you say that?" Chole asked.

Emily gritted her teeth. "I don't want to talk about it, Chloe."

Down the main passageway a door creaked open, and voices spilled into the department. Chloe fell into silence and her brow furrowed. The voices and shuffling footsteps retreated toward the entrance to Special Collections as the participants of the meeting dispersed.

Chloe turned back to Emily and shrugged. "I think they're all nervous about the Gala." She laughed. "I hope I'm on the guest list."

"I hope I am too," Emily said.

"Of course you'll be."

"What other questions about me have they been asking you, Chloe?"

"Just, you know, how you're getting along, and stuff."

"What do you tell them?"

"Nothing. I despise them. They made Nadia's life miserable at the end." She bent forward at the waist, cupped a hand around her mouth and whispered, "I think they drove her to suicide is what I think.

"Is that the general consensus of the department?" Emily asked, not interested in Chloe's analysis.

"Can you imagine if it *had* been ruled a suicide? They would have gone into everything here."

"*They* who?" asked Emily.

"The police. They didn't want that."

Emily remained stoically silent.

"Sorry to have bothered you," Chloe apologized. She vacated Emily's cubicle.

When she was gone and the honeycomb of cubicles had quieted, Emily tiptoed down the hall to Joel's office. On the entrance she found a sign on standard paper thumbtacked to the frame: "In Digital Film." It was signed by Joel.

One of the catalogers came down the hall. Emily didn't know her, just recognized her. "Do you know where Digital Film Preservation is?"

The young woman stopped, pointed down the corridor. "All the way to the end, down one floor, first room on the left."

Emily followed her directions and found Joel alone in a room with the new Lasergraphics ScanStation, a sophisticated piece of film-to-digital conversion equipment. On the monitor was frozen an image of Nadia from his short film. Joel was adjusting the print of his 16 mm film, his hands hidden in white cotton gloves. Sensing Emily's presence, he tore off his headphones and looked at her guiltily.

Emily sat down in the visitor's chair, swiveled left and right, one leg crossed over the other. She pointed at the screen.

"Yeah, I'm finally getting around to doing a 4K conversion of my film," he said.

"Aren't you afraid if they see her"—Emily pointed at the screen—"they're going to have a cow?"

"Nope," said Joel. "Not worried. Helena doesn't come down here. She doesn't give a shit about the future"—he pointed at the Laser Graphics equipment—"of digital preservation."

Emily was mesmerized by the screen. Staring straight into the camera, Nadia, freeze-framed, looked out at them both, a ghost from the backward lens of death. In the image that Joel had chosen to freeze-frame on, Nadia wore the fey, sultry, deep and tragic brilliance Raymond had fallen tangle-footedly in love with.

"She was beautiful, wasn't she?" said Emily, staring straight at Nadia's image, so palpably alive in her imagination now.

"Yeah," agreed Joel. "And smart."

"You were in love with her, weren't you?" Emily framed it as an assertion, not a question.

Joel rolled his tongue over teeth shamefacedly.

"She was the woman you followed to the other man's house, wasn't she?"

Joel's face hardened to stone. "We were never lovers." He nodded, the truth liberating his guilt in some oblique way. "But, yes, I was jealous of her . . . falling in love with West." He twisted his head around to Emily and looked at her with defiant eyes. "But I wasn't the one who outed them, if that's where you're going."

"I believe you," Emily said.

Joel, upset, turned back to the screen and spoke to Nadia's haunted face. "I was worried for her. I didn't know they were writing a book together. That's pretty fucking heavy."

Emily let a few seconds elapse before she said, "Do you know what the big meeting was about?"

Joel shook his head and shrugged. "Some shit going down with the eighth floor."

"You're friends with Jorge, right?"

Joel stiffened. "We've both been here a decade. He doesn't surf and he doesn't know Fellini like you, but we're cool, yeah." He threw Emily a backward glance. "Why?"

Emily smiled at Joel's sly compliment. Then her expression grew serious. "Do you think he'd have a problem showing us old security video?" She looked up at Joel, whose face was disconcerted.

"He's going to want to know why," Joel said.

"Tell him there are items missing from the collection."

Joel stood from his chair so abruptly it rolled away and banged against the cubicle barrier. He brought his hands to the side of his face and raked them through his curly sun-bleached locks. "Oh, Emily, Jesus." He shook his head back and forth in ominous contemplation. "He's going to want to know why you're going through me and not Helena or Jean."

"Because I don't trust them," she stated flatly.

Joel lowered his head and looked at her aghast. "I can't tell him that."

Emily rose up and her whole being blossomed up in his face in the tight cubicle. "Can you make something up?"

"Have you ever seen *Chinatown*?"

"Of course."

"You know what happens to Jake Gittes?"

"I forget. It's been a while."

"He discovers who did it, and the police tell him to go fuck himself." Joel nodded at her for emphasis. "That's right. You should watch it again. Corrupt power triumphs. The bad guys win."

"Okay, I will. I promise. In the meantime, could you talk to Jorge?"

"Emily . . ." Joel groaned. "I love you like a sister, but Jesus fucking Christ."

"Did you know Nadia was being followed?" Emily asked.

Joel narrowed his eyes at her and didn't answer.

"And I don't mean the one time you did."

Joel dropped his chin to his chest and said, "No, I didn't."

"Well, she was. Some guy in a gray Volvo SUV."

Joel slowly raised his head. "She was being followed?" Joel asked, incredulous. "By whom?"

"I don't know. Private detective?"

"The fuck," said Joel, more confused than ever.

Emily made to go. "Will you talk to Jorge, please?"

"I'll talk to Jorge," Joel consented. "Feel him out. Okay?"

"Thanks, Joel."

The time hadn't changed from daylight saving, so the sky still bore a blue brightness to it as Emily made her way back to her car. She put her phone on her dashboard mount and, sucking in her breath and exhaling, followed Google Maps northeast out of the university to Black Mountain Ranch, the bedroom community where Nadia had lived with her husband, Nathan Waters. The bedroom community consisted of generic two-story, stucco-and-wood homes straight out of some movie satirizing suburban depersonalization.

Emily was directed to the address on Vineyard Drive by an electronic voice with a British accent and parked on the street. With her hands still gripping the steering wheel, she bent her head until her forehead touched the hard rubber, thinking through the what ifs, the repercussions. Impulsively, she pulled up on the door handle, swung her legs out of the car, and marched up to the wide double door of the sandstone-colored house. With the manicured lawn and the winding cement pathway, it seemed incongruous to Emily that someone like Nadia would live here.

Emily pressed the doorbell and waited. She spotted a BMW parked in the driveway, so she assumed somebody was home. She pressed the doorbell again. After a moment a man's voice squawked over an intercom speaker.

"Hello?"

Emily put her mouth to the rectangular bronze grille that constituted the intercom and spoke into it. "Hello."

"Who is it?"

"My name's Emily Snow." She sucked in her breath. "I'm your wife's successor at the university. I'd like to talk to you."

"What about?" replied a voice with asperity.

"I just have a couple questions," Emily said. "Archives related. I didn't have your number, only your address, forgive me for coming unannounced like this."

The intercom went silent. A moment later, the door opened. Nathan Waters was a smallish man with a birdlike face and a sinewy body. He was dressed in tight cycling shorts and a matching body-hugging shirt. Sweat beaded on his brow. He held out his hand. "Hi, I'm Nathan."

"I know." Emily took his hand and shook it briefly.

Nathan opened the door and welcomed her in. "I just got done with a ride. Was about to take a shower. Excuse my appearance. Come on in."

"Thanks." Emily stepped inside to a foyer of rust-colored tile. It broadened to an interconnected open-plan living room and kitchen. Spartanly decorated, the living room featured an olive-green L-shaped sectional wrapped around a glass-topped coffee table facing a large flat-panel TV. A black-and-white mottled cat walked in sleepily to see who it was. Emily squatted to pet the cat.

"That's Clarice," Nathan said.

Emily bent her head up at him, instantly recognizing the name, but decided not to connect it to the framed picture of Clarice Lispector, fearing Nathan growing wary and clamming up on her.

"Would you like something to drink?" he offered.

"No, thanks. I'm fine," Emily replied.

"Have a seat." He motioned to the couch.

Emily stepped over to the sectional and eased down onto the nearest cushion. A gigantic HDTV was tuned to a sports channel telecasting a soccer match, but the sound was mercifully muted.

Nathan returned from the kitchen with a bottle of beer and sat down at the opposite end of the couch from Emily. He picked up a remote, pressed a button, and the TV sizzled to black. His face was lined with sun-weathered wrinkles and his strained expression bore a terminal kind of suffering.

"I'm sorry about your loss," Emily said.

Nathan stared vacantly at the TV. He shook his head in a tight movement as if trying to shake himself free of what he saw. "I just still can't believe it," he said, cataleptic in his bearing.

"I'm working on finishing the collection your wife was working on," Emily began gently.

"I know," he replied with the same brusqueness in his voice, "you said. What about it?"

"You know whose archive it is?"

Nathan's expression darkened. He nodded solemnly. "Raymond West," he intoned morosely. Then, in an escalating, high-pitched sarcastic tone, he added, "The famous writer."

Emily bowed her head and gazed down at her hands, now wrung tightly together. "I'm sorry if I sound too forward, but did you know your wife . . . was having an affair with him?"

Nathan jerked his head in Emily's direction, more shocked that she knew than that he was learning this piece of information for the first time. A current of gray gloom pulsed between them. Emily witnessed Nadia coming back to life in this man's tortured eyes, and she could sense he didn't like what he saw: the death of his beloved, beautiful wife and all the reasons he thought she had died.

"Why do you ask?" He spoke with palpable hurt.

"I'm coming to that," Emily said. "Trust me. What I have to say I hope should be of keen interest to you."

The way Nathan stared absently at the TV he didn't seem to think so. A prime suspect, if *she had* been murdered, no doubt the cops had interrogated him. He reluctantly waited for her to dig the shovel deeper into his memory, but he wasn't producing signals stopping her either. "Yes, I knew she was seeing someone. A husband can tell. When his affections aren't . . . reciprocated." His face grew ashen with irremediable regret.

Guilty that she had touched a still-raw nerve, Emily gazed off to the plate glass windows that led out into the backyard. The lights of a small, almond-shaped pool were glowing turquoise. A pair of mourning doves picked at birdseed that had been thrown for them on the patio. Making up her mind, Emily looked back at Nathan. "Did you know who it was?"

Nathan nodded slowly up and down.

"How much did you know about their affair?" Emily pressed. She was on a mission now and doors kept opening to deeper truths, and it seemed to her there was no end to them.

"Enough," he said.

"Tell me how much?"

Nathan sipped his beer absently. His face was colored red, and he seemed mortally crushed by the affair, loath to return to the still-tender cycles of remembering.

"I suspected there was something more about this one." He looked off. "I guess I'm no match for a Pulitzer Prize winner," he said. He raised his eyes to the ceiling. Something ungraspable corroded his soul. "Yes, there had been one or two others, if that's what you want to know."

"And you found out about them?"

"One. Maybe some I didn't know about, I don't know," he spoke with genuine anguish. "She had a longing in her for something intense, she always told me when we quarreled. Which I apparently couldn't satisfy." His head slumped and he peered sullenly into his bottle of beer.

"You're a forgiving man, you stayed with her—" Emily offered, cutting herself off.

"I loved her. I read somewhere that women grow out of these . . . flings." He threw up his hands in mock exasperation. "A lot of men wouldn't wait for their wives to get it out of their system, but I was willing to." He buried his face in his hands to contain a squall of emotion. "I guess I'm a fool."

"I know this is hurtful, but I have to ask." Emily paused. "How did you find out?"

Nathan tugged at his beer bottle, waxed suspicious. "Why are you asking me all these personal questions?" he asked.

"Because I've found some things that relate to . . . your wife. And if I'm right, they might allay your suspicions that she . . ." Emily's words trapped in her throat, not because she was afraid of hurting Nathan, but because she knew at that moment she was indelibly linked to Nadia's fate.

"That she committed suicide?" he retorted matter-of-factly.

Emily nodded. "How did you find out about the affair?"

Nathan blinked his eyes at the colorfully tessellated Moroccan rug Clarice was curled up asleep on, oblivious of his owner's emotional turmoil. "I tracked her," he confessed guiltily.

"You hired a detective to follow her?" asked a stunned Emily, suddenly doubting the conclusions that were nascently forming in her.

"I didn't need a detective." He turned to her. "I work in tech." Nathan set his beer bottle down with a mild blow on the glass-topped table and sprang to his feet. "Just a second."

Emily heard stockinged footsteps pad down the tile hallway. They returned a moment later. Nathan was cradling a fifteen-inch laptop, already open, already illuminated. He sat down next to her, shoulder to shoulder this time, and turned the screen so she could see it. He opened an app. Emily noted a logo at the top: Brickhouse Security. Nathan cursored over a button labeled Stored Activity. He tapped it. Emily reared back when a photo of Nadia materialized on the screen. Below her photo was a list of dates. Nathan tapped one on. A Google map filled the screen. Red digital pushpins dotted a journey that had been meticulously tracked. It began where Emily and Nathan were sitting and led in the direction of Regents University. There were stops along the way, represented by an ellipsis of red pushpins.

With an index finger tracing the trajectory, Nathan explained, "This was one of her many . . . assignations. I installed this tracking device on her car. It works like a cell. I could plot where she was going, how long she stayed at the various meeting places." He closed his eyes to stifle the emotions. "And this is just one day and part of the night." He quickly got out of that screen, tapped on another date, and presented to Emily a map of a different route Nadia had taken. "And there are more. Enough to make almost any man go insane with rage."

Emily looked away from the screen to Nathan's face. His eyes appeared hypnotized by the map that charted his wife's infidelity. "Did you confront her about this?" Emily pried.

"I would ask her where she was, but I wasn't going to tell her I had a tracking device on her car." He shook his head. "She would have left me."

"Why do it then? If you didn't want to leave her?"

"Jealousy. I don't know." He bit his lip, and his eyes glassed with tears. "I guess I thought she'd play this one out like the other ones," he said lachrymosely, "and return to me, like the others, but this one lasted longer, it seemed different." Weeping drowned out his words. A year of repressed emotions had surfaced like a sewer main backing up with Emily's unexpected, and unwanted, visit.

Emily allowed him a moment to regroup. "Did you ever worry she wasn't going to come back?" she asked as gently as she could voice.

"Yes, of course," he cried. He pulled himself together and tapped the touchpad, producing a different screen. Emily adjusted her glasses and focused her eyes on it. She recognized Little Orphan Alley and the red pushpin that represented Nadia's Ford Falcon Futura. Nathan hovered the cursor over the pushpin. "Her car was parked here for three days. She told me she was at a Society of American Archivists conference in San Francisco. But of course I knew she was lying, so I confronted her." He nodded to himself, as if weighing his words. "She told me she met a colleague here"—he pointed at Isla Negra—"who took her to the airport—for the conference she told me she needed to go on by herself to 'clear her head'—and when I admitted I used a tracking device she exploded at me, and that's when she moved out to a hotel."

Emily didn't feel like toppling him into a deeper quagmire of misery with the truth that she knew from Nadia's memoir, so she remained silent.

"She wanted me to stop following her," Nathan admitted in a voice choked with emotion.

"But you didn't."

He shook his head once. "I lied and told her I disabled the device, but I reinstalled it somewhere no one could find it." He touched his fingers to the touchpad and produced a patchwork of new screens. He pointed an index finger in a stabbing motion. "Here she is at a hospital. *That* location I didn't understand." He moved his index finger to another panel of the screen that showed a different map. "Here she is again back at that house in Del Mar by the ocean. I'm assuming that's where she met him."

"But she still lived here?" Emily asked, confused.

"She came and went. After that phony archivists' conference and the three days she couldn't, or wouldn't, explain her whereabouts, she wasn't the same."

"What do you mean? How so?" Emily wondered.

"Distant. Moody. Uncommunicative. Moving around like a zombie. Wouldn't talk. Wouldn't eat." Opening up as if he had been desperate for months to unload his anguish on someone, to relate his side of the tragedy, he turned to Emily with pleading eyes. "You know how people sometimes come and go like they're sleepwalking? There's a word for that."

"Somnambulant?" Emily guessed.

"Yeah," he said, snapping his fingers. "Somnambulant." His sudden effusion was short-lived. "I think she was just really, clinically, depressed is what I think." He nodded as if his rationalization for their failed marriage and his explanation for her death had become clear to him.

Emily inhaled deeply, because the biggest question of all still hung in the fraught air. With the exhalation she asked, "You knew she was pregnant?"

Nathan shot her an apprehensive look and tried to read her. "How do you know so much?"

"Like I said, I've found some things. Which I don't want to go into right now. But if you help me understand these things, if you trust me, I'll fill you in eventually," Emily promised.

Nathan looked at her with the eyes of a wounded animal for the longest moment. "You know, nobody from the university ever called me or emailed me or anything, to offer their condolences. She was employed there a dozen years. She was made fellow by the Society of American Archivists. We celebrated that together!" A commotion of tears brought a turbid havoc to his eyes. He covered them with the crook of his arm.

Emily gave Nathan another moment to recover, then asked gently, "The child wasn't yours?"

He shook his head and arm as if it were some human apparatus cradling suffering. "No."

"Did she tell you she was getting an abortion?" Emily asked.

Nathan slowly pulled away his arm and looked at her with swollen red eyes. "No. She told me she wanted to keep it."

Shocked by this admission, Emily cast a bewildered expression at him. "Pardon?"

"We tried to have kids, but we couldn't. We agreed to have the baby together, even though I wasn't the father."

"I don't understand," Emily managed, her heart leaping like a frog in a fist.

Nathan grew animated. "We were going to keep the child. She was going to lie to the father she had an abortion. We made plans to move to Portland. She had applied for a job at the Portland State University Library."

Emily was rendered speechless. In an effort to regain her footing, her eyes found the screen where Nadia's car was once parked a year ago, mapped and recorded for all eternity by modern technology. "Do you know where she was the night she died?" Emily asked tonelessly. Dread had crept back into her and uncertainty, in its infinity of repercussions, ruled blackly over her thoughts.

Solemnly, Nathan slowly navigated the cursor around until he produced another animated map with a tap on his touchpad. He leaned back and looked at Emily without saying anything.

Emily leaned slightly forward and narrowed her focus on the screen. "Scripps Pier?" She turned to Nathan with a questioning look.

"She must have walked from there to her favorite surfing beach, Black's," he said, shaking his head in puzzlement.

"When did she first park there?" Emily asked.

Nathan wordlessly hovered the cursor over the pushpin until a pop-up window sprouted above it. In it was the date, time, and GPS coordinates.

"Two thirty p.m.?" Emily inquired of the screen. She turned to Nathan. "Kind of implies that she just went for the evening glass. You know, when the ocean settles . . ."

"I know what the evening glass is. I used to surf with her." He slipped into a sorrowing nostalgia. "A long time ago."

Emily glanced at her phone, noticed it was late, and stood abruptly. It was a bad habit of hers; she had never learned how to gracefully exit awkward interactions. "I should go." She reached out her hand. "Thank you for your time."

Nathan took her hand and then rose as if her hand had provided him a current of power.

"I'll let you know if I find out anything more," Emily said.

"I don't want to know any more about the affair."

Emily spoke to the floor. "I'm sorry to have dredged this up."

Nathan shrugged glumly. "Whatever you can fill in . . ." he broke off, his words hobbled by emotions and fading memories.

Emily waited a moment and then met his eyes. "Do you think she drowned accidentally?"

Nathan nodded somberly. "The waves were supposedly breaking overhead that night, according to the police. But they weren't."

"So, you don't think she killed herself?"

"No way," he said, as if he didn't want to believe it. "She wanted that child." He drew a hand and covered his mouth. "And, fucked up as this might sound, I did too. Even if it wasn't mine," he stammered through a fresh rash of tears.

"Do you have a card?" Emily asked.

From his back pocket he produced a leather billfold and removed a business card from it. "Call or email me anytime?"

"So, you obviously spoke with Detective Taggart of SDPD?"

Nathan nodded. "I think he suspected I killed her because of the affair."

"But you were away on business?"

Nathan kept nodding. "That doesn't mean he didn't suspect me of hiring a hit man or something far-fetched like that. He dropped it, though."

Emily gestured to his laptop screen. "Did he know about any of this?"

"No. God, no. I didn't need to arouse his suspicions any more than they were already."

Emily considered his words for an ambivalent moment and then placed a hand on his shoulder. "I'm sorry, Nathan. What I know of Nadia, she seemed like a remarkable woman."

Nathan nodded solemnly. "She was. Despite everything, we had a good marriage. With the child coming and the move to Portland it might have all been a different story."

Emily blinked wordlessly at his remark.

Night had taken possession of the sky when Emily walked outside into the serenity of the peopleless neighborhood and slid into the smoothness of her Mini. She started her car, still processing the revelations gleaned from Nathan. Her mind was aswirl now.

Emily concentrated with squinted eyes on the three wide lanes of overlit empty freeway, hypnotized by their desolation. She closed her eyes "to block out their horrible symmetry," as Nadia had lyricized in her memoir. The same empty freeways Nadia drove around in circles at night when she couldn't tolerate being home and it was impossible and too dangerous to rendezvous with

Raymond. The freeways connected her to the loci of her dispiriting affairs, syringed out her despair in droplets of warm blood. Emily now had tangible proof of it in Nathan's many maps charting the peregrinations of Nadia's love affair with Raymond and her tortured ending. She began to worry that maybe she shouldn't have returned the Moleskines to Raymond, that perhaps she should have followed Nadia's instructions to keep the imposed restrictions on them. But who would ever find them in the Annex, given the labyrinthine journey Emily had embarked on to get to them? And if they did, if it was someone who didn't know what they were, what would happen to them? Helena wanted them in her possession to protect them from the catastrophic consequences should they come to Elizabeth's attention, but maybe she also thought about how valuable they would be, especially if Raymond were to be awarded the Nobel. Nick Peterson at Scribner's would clamor for them and beseech Raymond to publish his unfinished, most recent, work. There was money to be looted in those scandalous, love-sheared pages. If researchers got wind that there existed an unfinished Raymond West, especially a work this personal, a soul-baring work revealing, unapologetically and uninhibitedly, who he was, they would descend on Memorial Library and the West Papers and turn his archive into a modern-day gold rush.

Starving, Emily swung by the Del Mar Plaza to pick up some groceries at the local natural foods store, but it was closed. *9:05 p.m.? Closed? Shit.* Silhouettes of tall date palms fanned out on the asphalt of the empty parking lot like an omen in some film noir movie as she swung her car out and coasted down a deserted Del Mar Heights Road back to her apartment.

Emily didn't know if she had a sixth sense about things—even though her mother once suspected she did—but when she stepped out of her Mini in the carport, something felt peculiar. The air seemed to tremble. She tentatively opened the door that led from the carport into her complex. The dead palm fronds rested portentously quiet on the eave. Emily heard no sound of thundering waves, as if Nature had shut the spigot off on the swell and turned the Pacific into a lake. The stillness of everything disconcerted her. Suddenly she heard the plaintive meowing of a cat. Emily squinted in the dark. She spotted Onyx, wandering out on the concrete veranda, confused and frightened, head bent skyward, meowing louder and louder now that he heard Emily. He bolted toward her when he saw her. Emily squatted to receive him, but her antennae had sprung. Instinctively, she picked up a quivering Onyx, whispering to him, "What are you doing outside, huh, little guy?" She took one step at a time toward her unit, as if picking a path over broken glass.

When she reached her apartment, she gasped when she saw the sliding glass door to her unit flung wide open. Clutching her mouth, Emily, struck dumb by the sight of the open door, reared back against the wrought iron railing and gaped inside, tensed with consternation. All the lights were on, burning brightly. She cocked an ear and listened but heard nothing. In her purse, without looking, she closed her hand over her phone, held it up and weaponized it with the threat of dialing 911 to report an as yet unseen intruder.

"If there's anyone in here, I'm calling the police!" Emily spoke loudly to her open apartment. No response. She steeled herself and then crossed the threshold into her apartment prudently, a footfall at a time, as if the floor were booby-trapped. The first thing she noticed was that all her belongings on the coffee table had been swept to the sisal carpet as if pitched there by an angry, hurried arm. "Hello?" Emily said in a sharpened voice. "I'm calling the cops, motherfucker." She set Onyx on the couch, but deliberately left the door open in case she had to make a run for it. Hearing nothing, she ventured into the kitchen, still debating whether to call 911, thinking through the ramifications.

Braving the unexplored areas of the small apartment, she cautiously approached the bedroom. She shrieked when she saw in horror all her clothes had been ripped from their hangers and scoured from their still-flung-open drawers and piled into a heap on the bed. The bedcovers had been ripped from the mattress, the pillows hurled to the walls. All the closet doors were swung wide open. An invader's anger had met her apartment in a ransacking fury.

Convinced whoever had trashed her apartment was long gone, Emily returned to the living room, closed the sliding glass door and locked it shut, scared, trembling, filled with dread. The violation of her private space was the panic that assaulted her and had seized hold of her. Hyperventilating now, she plopped on the couch and texted Joel. "I was broken into. Can you come?"

Emily waited. She got no immediate reply. She debated calling 911 again, but she was wary of the kinds of questions they might ask her. Impatient, she dialed Joel.

"Did you get my text?"

"No," he said. "Notifications turned off. What's up?"

"My apartment was broken into."

"What! Are you okay? What's your address? I'll come right away."

Emily said she was fine, a little rattled. She gave him her address and he hung up, assuring her he was already out the door.

Her heart racing, Emily waited impatiently for Joel, stroking a still-confused Onyx. Thank God she had taken her laptop to work. The thumb drive with the Nadia/Raymond emails, the memoir, the photos! She thrust her hand into her purse and sighed with relief when her desperate, groping fingers felt its familiar hard, plastic shape. Tense with anxiety and fear, she battled the helplessness of her aloneness.

Suddenly something dawned on Emily.

She stood slowly from the couch, her eyes riveted on the reversible whiteboard timeline of the Nadia/Raymond affair she had meticulously recreated. She moved stealthily toward it as if approaching an injured, potentially dangerous, animal. The names of the dramatis personae were facing her: Nadia, Raymond, Elizabeth, Helena, Verlander, Joel, Black Moleskines (!) . . . She couldn't remember if that was how she had last left it. She was almost certain the timeline trajectory was the last side of it she had seen. Had pictures been taken of it?

Knuckles rapped on the sliding glass door and she threw a hand to her violently palpitating heart. She hurriedly flipped the whiteboard over so its incriminating timeline was obscured from view. The rapping knuckles sounded louder. Emily crossed the room to the door and opened it to the concerned face of Joel. They came together in a mutually empathetic hug.

"I was broken into," Emily gasped into Joel's ear. "Door was fucking wide open."

They disengaged from their hug and Joel backed away from Emily to survey the damage. His eyes swept the living room. "Anything missing?" Joel, in rumpled black T-shirt and jeans, asked worriedly.

"No, I don't think so." She opened her arm to the disorder every room in her apartment bore the evidence of. "But as you can see, they trashed it."

Emily directed Joel into the bedroom. She stood aside as he absorbed the tableau of the out-turned drawers, the hurled clothes, the violently twisted bedsheets.

"Trashed it pretty good," Joel said in a calming undertone that contrasted with his eyes of genuine alarm. "Obviously, whoever did it was looking for something." He turned to her with inquiring eyes. Emily shrugged. Joel regarded her skeptically with frequent backward glances as they drifted back out into the living room. "What do you think they were they looking for?"

Emily cast her head toward Joel. "I don't know."

Joel looked at her with disbelieving eyes. "I'm just glad you're okay," he muttered. "Do you have a beer or something?"

"Yeah." Emily circled into the kitchen and retrieved an ale from the otherwise barren refrigerator, uncapped it, and brought it out to the living room where Joel was examining the busted lock. She handed him the beer as he turned to her from his crouched position.

"Looks like they popped this open with a crowbar or something. It's not a very secure lock." He glanced up at the top section of the frame. "And the deadbolt can only be locked from inside. Stupid." He opened and closed the sliding glass door, measuring its width. "We need to get a security pole in that sliding door track so there's no way anyone can get in."

Emily nodded. It felt reassuring to have Joel there. Glad she had called him instead of the police, she wanted to hug him again to see if she could bleed the rest of the fear and disquiet out of her, but found herself saying, "What do you mean?"

"Do you have a broom?"

"I think so. Just a minute." Emily went into the bedroom and rummaged around in the clothes closet. She had seen a broom somewhere and then remembered it was in the HVAC closet in the hall between the bedroom and the bathroom.

She brought the broom out to the living room and presented it to Joel. To her trepidation she found him standing motionless next to the whiteboard staring fixedly at it—the side she had turned away from the wall—with an expression of shock.

"What are you doing!" Emily half shrieked, standing the broom at her side.

"What is all this?"

Emily combed a hand through her tangled hair. "It's a timeline of their affair."

Confusion disorganized Joel's face. "What? Why?"

"I'm just trying to assemble it into some semblance of order, to make sense of it all," she replied unconvincingly.

"Make sense of all what?"

"The trajectory that led to her death," Emily replied defensively.

Joel exhaled a deep sigh. He turned back to the whiteboard. Alerted to something, he leveled his eyes at Emily in a look of mounting apprehension. "What's this? Moleskines? The Archivist?"

Emily cast her eyes down at the floor.

"Huh?" Joel implored more accusatorily.

"It was a book they were collaborating on."

"What!" Joel said, his mouth frozen open.

"Nadia and Raymond were collaborating on a book tentatively titled *The Archivist*. It was written in longhand. In Moleskines. Twelve in total."

At a loss for words, Joel finally stammered, "How did you know about this . . . collaboration?"

Emily tilted her head at Joel, as if to say, *Come on, we're archivists*. "It's practically all they wrote about to each other in the correspondence I found in the dark archives."

Joel sucked in his breath. "And you found the . . . the . . . Moleskines of this book in the Annex? Is that what you were looking for?"

Emily raised her head, nodding yes to both questions shamefacedly.

"Did you read it?"

Emily nodded guilty. "It's extremely . . . personal. Graphic. And brilliant. And emotionally powerful."

"Okay, okay! Don't tell me any more." Joel shot one last look at the whiteboard, then charged across the room and plopped down heavily on the couch. His beer bottle thunked on the bamboo coffee table. He brought his hands to his face and cradled it wearily. "And what is my name doing up there?"

"I'm sorry." Emily pulled down the sleeve of her shirt over her hand and smeared *Joel/Annex* into illegibility.

"What if someone from the library saw this and took a picture?"

"Who?" Emily asked. "I don't socialize with any of them."

"Didn't you go out with Chloe on a double date and bring her boyfriend's friend back here?"

Emily's mouth fell agape. "She told you that?"

"That's not important. I don't give a shit." He dropped his hands from his face. "Emily, who do you think broke in and trashed your apartment?"

They were both thinking the same thing. "They were looking for the Moleskines." Emily said matter-of-factly.

"Fuck, Emily." Joel nodded his head up and down, up and down. But something was still bewildering him. "But what were these Moleskines doing in the Annex?"

"The project was abandoned," Emily said without elaborating.

"Why?"

Emily regarded Joel portentously. "I know things you don't want to know."

"Evidently," he said furiously. "Obviously they didn't find them here, did they?"

"No," admitted Emily.

"Where are they then?"

"They're safe," replied Emily.

"They're safe. Uh-huh." Joel puffed out a cheek and shook his head. "You realize if someone found them and turned them in to Helena, we would both be so royally fucked it wouldn't be funny. I wanted to help you, Emily, I really did, but I didn't realize you were taking it this far, this deep." Joel closed his eyes to shut out the world he feared imploding in on him.

"I didn't know where it was going to take me," Emily said in a pleading tone.

"But when you did, you couldn't stop, could you?" Joel's eyes were wide with seething accusation.

"No. I couldn't stop." Emily bent forward at the waist. "And I'm not going to!"

"You're fucking crazy, little girl."

"All I did was plow through the data."

Joel barked a derisive laugh. "All you did was plow through the data." He shook his head dismissively.

"I didn't know I was going to find what I found," Emily protested. "I only wanted to know the truth of Nadia's death. And the more I learned, the murkier and more suspicious it became. It's like one of those matryoshka dolls . . ."

"Matryoshka what?"

"Russian nesting dolls," Emily elucidated. "You pull one out and there's another one inside. Only this got bigger, not smaller, the more I peeled it away."

Shaking his head, Joel reached for his beer bottle, took a long pull, and polished it off, then straightened to his feet and came forward to Emily. "Let me see the broom."

Emily handed him the broom. Joel disappeared into the kitchen with it. "You have nothing to worry about," she reassured him. She heard drawers opening and closing and then a rasping sound. She followed the noise into the kitchen.

Joel had found a serrated knife and was sawing the bristle head off the broom, balancing it on the kitchen counter for support. When he had successfully lopped it off, he wordlessly returned to the living room and tested its length in the sliding glass door track. Emily approached him from behind. He twisted his neck and looked up at her.

"Put it in like this at night." He demonstrated, lodging the sawed-off pole at a forty-five-degree angle and securing it against the door jamb.

"Okay," said Emily. "Thanks."

Joel straightened from his squatting position in a twisting motion, drifted a few steps, and slumped back down on the couch. He picked up his bottle of beer, realized it was empty and set it back down. His eyes strayed over to the whiteboard and zeroed in on it again with renewed consternation. He pointed his forefinger in the whiteboard's direction. "Do you want to talk about that, Emily?"

Emily eased down on the opposite end of the couch. "I'd rather not involve you, Joel."

"My name was on there!" he exclaimed.

Emily shut her eyes, exasperation and shame locked in combat. She could hear the ocean finally. It sounded like high tide because the waves were being pumped into the cliffside with a pounding roar.

"I'm worried about you"—Joel rotated his head to her—"not me."

"I appreciate that." Emily didn't know what else to say.

"Do you think someone is following you? Or us?"

"Yeah. I do." She exhaled, bent forward and gripped her ankles, fighting the nausea she was suddenly feeling.

Joel drew a hand down the length of his sunburnt face. "I know I opened some doors for you. And you know why I did."

Emily nodded between her legs. "Because you didn't believe she drowned either."

"I just didn't know you were going to take it this far. That it had even gone this far."

"I wanted to know what happened," Emily said. "We both know she didn't drown accidentally. I had no idea what I would find. And every time I find something with Nadia, it opens a door to something else."

"What do you think?" Joel asked. "Now that the cat is out of the bag."

Emily gazed at the window. She waited a full five seconds before she declared, "I think she was murdered."

Joel turned to her slowly, as if drawn to her face against his will. "By whom?"

"Whoever had motive to break into my place and try to find what I believe they were looking for."

"The Moleskines of *The Archivist*?" Joel said.

Emily nodded ominously.

"I can think of more than one potential suspect," Joel said trenchantly.

Emily swept the room with her eyes and landed them on Joel's. "Including you?"

"That's not funny," Joel said.

"Sorry. I'm a little overwrought," Emily said, glancing down again, still holding her ankles, averting Joel's reproving eyes. She spoke to the sisal rug: "I came down here as a project archivist, excited to work on the

West Papers. I didn't know this job was going to throw me this dangerous curveball." She started breathing rapidly through her nostrils. "Every day my stomach's been in knots. I've been holding this whole thing inside. I almost went into counseling over it. I could have let it go, but I didn't. You know why? Because of my training. Because of who I am." She looked at Joel in a slanted aspect. "Our job is to get it right. For future historians and researchers. I came to a fork in the road. I turned left. I consciously chose the darker path. And now it's come to me, my home, in the form of some malevolent force. Someone who doesn't want the truth revealed."

Joel remained silent. Emily tried to read his absent expression. Was he angry at her? Was he going to abandon her? Fly into a rage?

"I'm scared," Emily said. She clutched her mouth. Tears leached from the corners of her eyes. "Will you stay?" she asked timidly through splayed fingers.

Joel rolled his head to her beseeching eyes and pleading tone. "Come here." He hooked an arm around her shoulders and drew her up from her crouch toward him. She leaned against his shoulder as he hugged her comfortingly. "Of course I'll stay," he said.

"I love you like silverfish love paper."

"That's kind of sweet," chuckled Joel. "In a nerdy way."

"We're all pretty nerdy," said Emily.

"I guess you don't want to hear my advice," said Joel.

"Let it go?"

"Someone broke into your apartment, Emily. Over some archival items. That's pretty fucking heavy. I've been in the profession a decade, and this is a first."

"I would never betray you, Joel, you know that?"

"No, I believe you." He drew her small body closer. "It's you I'm worried about." He hugged her tighter. Out of the blue he speculated, "What if you're right and somebody killed Nadia over this damn book? For whatever friggin' reason. Are you next?"

Emily withdrew her head from his shoulder, and they looked at each for the longest moment.

Finally, enervated from the night's dismaying events, Emily rose. "I'll get you a blanket."

When she returned from the bedroom with a spare blanket, Joel was lying supine on the couch, his cell in his hand, scrolling through texts and emails. Emily dressed the blanket over him. She squatted down and ran her fingers through his hair. "You're not angry with me?"

Joel shook his head. "Get some sleep."

"You too," she said, kissing him on the cheek.

Emily switched off the lights and went into the bedroom. She felt defiled in absentia. Knowing someone else had been in her apartment made her shudder uncontrollably. Knowing Joel was stationed on her couch by the sliding glass door where the intruder had entered brought her a modicum of peace. As she put her bedroom back together, she labored in her mind to make sense of the break-in. She didn't know how much Joel knew about Nadia and Raymond's relationship, and she was loath to disclose any more than what she had. Unfortunate that he had seen the whiteboard—she couldn't lose his trust; he was her only ally at the library. She climbed out of her clothes, threw on her pajamas, and crawled into bed. After she tucked herself in, Onyx leaped up out of the dark with gleaming green eyes and curled up next to her on the comforter, purring contentedly. His world was ostensibly back in order. His. However, every foreign sound made Emily sit up straight, paralytic with apprehension, even the 10:00 p.m. Southern Pacific freight train that came only once a day to San Diego. It was a long train. A hypnotically long train as it rumbled past, seemingly forever. But tonight it didn't soothe Emily. Its loud clacking wheels seemed like the perfect cover for committing murder.

Emily typed two emails, one to Nathan and one to Raymond. Raymond she needed to talk to. Nathan she wanted to install a tracking device on her Mini and keep tabs on her. She was that paranoid now. Then she tapped her way to the *New York Times* home page. An article headline pulled out of the news read, "Sex Scandal Postpones the Nobel Prize for Literature." Her heart froze for a moment, but then she read on. A scandal had rocked the Swedish Academy and they had decided to postpone the award and announce two winners the following year. Emily wondered how Raymond would react to this news. How everyone in Special Collections would absorb it.

CHAPTER 21
Lessons in Reality

10/11/18

My apartment was broken into last night. Joel came over and settled me down.

I'm convinced Helena is suspicious I've found The Archivist. *All twelve Moleskines. Their discovery would seriously compromise the university. After all, what if I—or someone—put them in a security deposit box and blackmailed them?*

What did Raymond do with them? That's what I'm dying to know.

There was no way I could explain the Moleskines to the police. Not sure about my next move.

Joel was gone by the time Emily climbed out of bed. He left a note for her to meet him at Bird Rock Coffee.

Emily, frazzled from lack of sleep and harassed by nightmares of destitution and desolation, showered, threw on jeans and a black long-sleeve T-shirt, and drove down Coast Highway to meet Joel before heading to work. The sky was a milky blue. The ocean was colored turquoise in the shallows and darker blue where it ran to deeper waters. Surf exploded on the outside reefs in jagged peaks of incandescent white, scarring the blue.

Joel was lounging in one of the cushioned deck chairs at Bird Rock when Emily skipped up the short flight of steps to meet him. He lowered his sunglasses to look at her. She sat down next to him in a chair he had saved. On a small outdoor table between them sat a cup of coffee and a chocolate macaroon waiting for her.

"I didn't know whether you wanted the Panamanian Geisha or the Tres Dragones, so I got you the Tres Dragones." He turned his face up to hers. "With cream, right?"

"Thanks, Joel," Emily said. She raised the coffee to her lips. It tasted of earth and all things tangible that she now craved with her entire being.

Joel turned his gaze to the placidity of the Los Peñasquitos Lagoon. The marsh waters were still, trembling panes of golden glass fallen among the flora. Herons with their sleek bodies could be spotted in the dark reeds, luminously white and reflecting the climbing sun like avian mirrors scattered in the preserve. As if spooked, or suddenly hungry, one of them took flight, wings vigorously flapping against the water and, finally airborne, flew horizontally over one of the inlets, disturbing its pristine surface of gold with scratches of its trailing talons.

"It's gorgeous here," Joel rhapsodized. A night of sleep seemed to have calmed his nerves. He turned to Emily. "How're you doing?"

"Okay," said Emily, venturing another sip of her coffee.

"Sleep okay?"

"Not really," she said. "You?"

"I'm not used to couch surfing, but yeah, surprisingly well."

Emily cracked a smile.

"You should move here, Emily." He tossed out an arm. "Your favorite coffee shop. Awesome surfing breaks." He leaned his chin on his shoulder. "Heard scuttlebutt there was a full-time position for a digital archivist opening."

Emily's eyes tracked the heron until it braked on flaring wings and floated down, swallowed up by the reeds. "I don't think San Diego's for me," she said, the beauty of the view drowned in her dark alarm. Gazing absently at the lagoon, she said, "Was Nadia being followed, do you know?"

Joel could feel Emily's eyes on him like hot question marks. He sighed, rehearsing a preface. "She came to my apartment one night. She was scared.

Didn't want to talk about it." He reset his mouth with his tongue. "She said she thought someone was after her."

"She didn't elaborate?" Emily pried.

"No. Like you, she didn't want to compromise me."

Emily stared at an invisible point in space, deep in thought. "I'm really fucking pissed off." Joel rotated his head to her. "They'll do anything to get their hands on that book and destroy it," she muttered, shaking her head. "They'll do anything to cover up the truth." She could feel her face grow tense with quiet conviction. "Anything," she added inscrutably.

"Who do you think's behind it?" Joel asked. "Assuming that the person who broke in was looking for the Moleskines."

"You don't believe me?" Emily said, startled.

"I don't know what to believe, Emily. It started out as such a beautiful morning here in glorious San Diego."

"How are the waves?" she asked sarcastically.

"Sucky."

"I don't know who's behind it, Joel. Could kind of be any number of people with motivation, couldn't it?"

"Like I said, I can think of a few," he said drolly. "You're not going to tell me where they are, are you?"

Emily shook her head.

"So, you really did read it?" he asked in a strained voice.

"Joel!"

Joel inhaled deeply. He knew the answer. "Even if you gave them to me, I wouldn't want to read it."

"Afraid to find Nadia loved another man, or . . . ?"

Hurt discomposed Joel's face.

"Sorry," said Emily. "You want to know, but you don't want to know, is that it?"

"Something along those lines," Joel mumbled.

Emily gazed off at the peaceful lagoon where pelicans and herons and osprey flourished. She realized she was here provisionally and then gone. The repercussions of her actions might not be as severe as they would for a born-and-raised San Diego surfer-cum-wannabe-filmmaker like Joel. At the moment another brilliant, pristine white heron took flight, as if in a current of synchronicity, Emily said, "Question?"

Joel sipped his coffee and waited.

"How long of a walk is it from the Annex to Black's Beach?"

"Over a mile," Joel answered. "Long trek with a board. Why?"

"Can you figure out any reason why Nadia's car would be parked there on the night she died and they found her body washed up at Black's?"

Joel faced her with a downturned expression. "No. And why would she? She had a key to the private road."

Emily met his sunglasses and not his eyes. "What?"

"She had a key. Drove down to Black's with her many times to surf."

Emily reached into her purse and crawled around inside. She produced a key and presented it to Joel. "Is this the key?"

Joel sat up, shocked. "Where'd you find that?"

Emily returned the key to her purse. She ignored his question. "Did you talk to Jorge?"

"Yeah," Joel said. "Where'd you get the key?"

"Joel. You don't want to know, okay?" Emily threw an arm to the lagoon. "There's all kinds of shit out there if you just go looking."

"You're right. I don't want to know."

"Is Jorge cool?" Emily asked, pressing forward.

"Missing items in the stacks, right?"

"That's right," Emily said. "And there are."

"Deep Throat is on it. I'm going to be on the fucking breadline, or have to go back to paragliding lessons." He sat up in his chair while glancing at his diver's watch. "Ready for the big meeting?" he asked with glaring irony.

"As always," Emily said, toasting Joel with her cup of Tres Dragones.

Joel clomped away on the wooden decking.

The Seminar Room was packed. Aside from Emily and Joel, in attendance were Jean, Verlander, Chloe, Nancy from Human Resources, Helena, and Elizabeth. Opening confabulation centered around the sex scandal that had embroiled the Swedish Academy and postponed the awarding of the Nobel in Literature.

"It buys us another year to be disappointed," sardonically joked an immaculately dressed and coiffed Elizabeth. Not a hair out of place, perfectly manicured nails, clothes never wrinkled, a feline beauty spawned from privilege.

Verlander, ever the cheerleader, clapped his hands together. "Is everybody excited about the upcoming Gala?"

A collective, if nervous, murmur of approbation filled the room.

"So, Emily, how are we coming with the finding aid?" asked Verlander.

"I'm on schedule," said Emily, hoping to defuse a mounting omnipresent anxiety. "A couple of loose ends, but—"

"What loose ends?" interjected Helena, her head cocked to one side, her eyes suspiciously in their corners as if she couldn't meet Emily's head-on.

"In Nadia Fontaine's West file, I realized there are some items in the Annex. I'm wondering if I shouldn't take a look at those."

The room collapsed into a malignant silence. It was as if everybody were waiting for the name *Nadia Fontaine* to stop echoing so that the meeting could continue without its contamination.

Helena broke the silence. "I'm guessing those are items that weren't meant to be returned to the curator."

Her rule over her husband's papers threatened, Elizabeth stiffened, and her expression went blank.

"They're out of scope materials," Jean said before Helena could elaborate, sensing tension. "Duplicates, items meant for the shred aisle."

"Okay, well, if they're boxes my predecessor has already processed and determined were of no value to the collection, then . . . I'm fine," said Emily with an uncharacteristically insouciant smile.

For a moment the room seemed to breathe with collective relief. Helena's eyes, though, still blinked with suspicion. "Have you been to the Annex, Emily?"

"Once," Emily admitted.

Helena shifted her face from Emily to Jean. Jean shook her head in a tight no. Helena turned to Emily, a dark expression clouding her face. "Were you given access?"

"No. Just went down there. It was open. Poked around."

Across from her, Emily could make out Joel, who looked like he was standing in a wind tunnel.

"What'd you find?" Helena asked, pretending casualness, given Elizabeth's presence. "Anything of note that we should be aware of?"

"Just some boxes. Like you said, overflow."

Elizabeth looked up from her phone where she was conducting a texting conversation. "I like what you've found in the collection for the exhibit, Ms. Snow. Nice job."

"Thank you," replied Emily. She looked at this proud, affluent woman. Emily couldn't imagine her crumpled into a ball in a human tortuosity of emotional anguish on the floor of a cliffside mansion where the waves broke on both reefs and hearts. "I hope you'll be happy with the work I've done for your husband's magnificent collection."

Elizabeth smiled into her phone without showing her teeth.

The meeting adjourned in apparent comity. The power lines of tension had, for the moment, abated.

Emily took her lunch of two hardboiled eggs and a carrot to the eighth floor. Ceiling chandeliers were being installed by diligent Facilities employees, working overtime to meet the deadline for the Eighth Floor Gala. Against one wall were arranged the exhibit display cases. Drifting over, an anxious Emily saw her reflection in the glass when she looked down into the black-papered wells where curated memorabilia from Raymond West's papers would reside, possibly for as long as a year. In her imagination, she pictured the Moleskines for *The Archivist* fanned out like a black rainbow filigreed in silver. How beautiful they would look! Perhaps it was never meant to be, Emily thought, staring fixedly into the display case. The politics of propriety would always crush and crucify the irrational forces of love.

Emily wrenched herself away from the array of display cases and took the stairwell back down. The break-in of her apartment still unnerved her. She debated asking Joel if she could stay with him, knowing he would be all too happy to have the company, but she didn't want to cower in the face of whoever was after her. The recklessly fearless but determined Emily wanted to continue to be his quarry to show she wasn't afraid. That *he* should be the one to be afraid because she had Det. Taggart on autodial now. She suspected one thing for certain: somebody wanted those Moleskines, and they assumed she had them. No one in a million years would believe she surrendered them to Raymond.

Emily and Joel traded text messages:

"Have you talked to Jorge?" Emily typed.

"He'll come get you. I'm staying out of it," Joel typed back.

"Understood."

Emily buried herself in the remaining archival items of the West Papers now diminishing in her cubicle and let everyone know she was working overtime by being curt and asocial. Jean stopped in to say hi. Chloe wanted to gossip, but Emily cut her short. Even Helena glanced in on her way to talk to a colleague. Everyone was oblivious of the webwork of mystery that lay beneath the collection and its triumphant eighth-floor apotheosis.

At the end of the workday, Joel dawdled at the opening to Emily's cubicle. She was typing intensely on her keyboard when Joel spoke. "What're you going to tell Jorge?"

Emily jumped and whirled around. "Just that some items are missing and that there was a request to study some video."

Joel grimaced. "I doubt Jorge would go to them, but you realize they would think it was more than peculiar. They would view it as overreach."

Emily's face hardened. "Somebody broke into my rental last night. They didn't steal anything—they were looking for something. And I know what they were looking for." She telescoped forward in her chair, and spoke urgently in a whispery voice, "I want to know who it was, Joel."

Joel bit his upper lip and darted a nervous look down the corridor that he, but not Emily, had a view of. Convinced they were alone, he stepped forward and said to Emily in lowered tones, "Do you truly think somebody *murdered* her?"

Emily's eyes blazed with a luminous blue light. "I don't know, Joel, but

I'm going to find out who fucking broke into my apartment! Because I'm positive it has to do with Nadia."

Joel held up his cell phone. "Text me if you need me."

Slipping on her pair of noise-canceling headphones and cranking up the music on her music app, Emily resumed her work, grew engrossed in it while drowning out the ticking of the clock Jean had gotten Facilities to fix and remount on the wall, as if deliberately to annoy her.

Muffled knocking startled Emily, and she swiveled sharply in her office chair while simultaneously tearing off her headphones. Jorge was standing in the entrance to her cubicle. She forgot how tall and obese he was, with a gut spilling out of a golf shirt. He wore a lopsided smile on his face.

"Are you ready, Ms. Snow?" he asked.

"Yeah," said Emily. She gathered together her purse and loose clothing, shut her computer down, and followed him out.

The library had quieted. There were still rivulets of students flowing in and out, but most of them wore earbuds and were lost, drone-like, in alternate universes of texting and music.

Jorge tried to make small talk. "How are things coming with the West project?"

"Almost done," replied Emily.

"Exciting what's happening, isn't it?" he beamed.

"Yeah," said Emily.

"Eighth floor's really coming along," Jorge said, lifting his eyes up to the eighth floor through the concrete and steel atop them. "They're getting the new lounge chairs delivered this weekend."

Jorge steered Emily down a corridor, walked her a length of a hallway, and pulled to a stop at a gray-painted door. A nondescript black-and-white plaque read simply Security. From a keychain ringed with two dozen keys, Jorge produced the one that fit in the lock. He turned the handle on the door and pushed it open for Emily.

"So, this is the same room where you spy on us," remarked Emily, as she surveyed the tiny, rectangular space she remembered from, what seemed like years ago, the time Jorge had issued her her key card. Two tables were set in an L-shape against the white walls in the gray-carpeted room. Three large-screen monitors and two computer terminals were stationed on them. Each monitor was capable of displaying split screens.

The overhead lights snapped off and Emily jerked her head toward Jorge. Other than a single desk lamp, the only light source illuminating the room came from the monitors.

"Is that okay?" asked Jorge. "It's easier to see the monitors."

"Fine," said Emily, a little tense in his large presence, made even larger by the tininess of the room. At this unsettled point in her employ, she wasn't sure whom to trust. Nervously, she asked, "Did they ever find out who that guy was who was stalking Special Collections staff?"

"Yeah," replied Jorge, collapsing in a heap in his swivel chair, customized with an orthopedic pad for his large backside. "Of course, everybody naturally assumed it was some homeless guy. Turns out it was a PhD candidate in engineering. Believe that?" He chuckled. "Fucking STEM motherfuckers. Pardon my French. Have a seat." Jorge turned the wheeled office chair next to him so it faced Emily. She sat down and swiveled a quarter turn into position.

"I can believe it," Emily said.

Jorge focused his eyes on his main screen. From a high down-angle, it showed a grainy black-and-white image of the two of them in the room. Jorge turned to Emily. "We've got thirty-five cameras in this library, including one in here. Do you mind if I turn it off?"

Emily met Jorge's eyes with a questioning expression.

"Technically, you're not supposed to be in here without authorization." He stabbed a pudgy finger at the screen. "Not that anyone is going to look at this, but . . . Joel suggested I turn it off."

"Go ahead," Emily said, "I trust you."

Jorge clicked his mouse and the screen changed to another high down-angle view of one of the floors. Silhouetted students came and went in zigzagging patterns, their shadows lengthening across the floors.

"Joel said you wanted to look at some recent CCTV from Special Collections?" He turned his friendly, jowly face toward hers. "May I ask why?"

Emily made a steeple of her hands and rested her lips on its apex. "You know I'm the project archivist on the Raymond West Papers, right?"

"Of course. You're under a lot of pressure with the big gala Joel told me."

"Yeah. Unfortunately"—Emily bounced the steeple fashioned from her hands against her mouth—"there are some items in my West file that are missing from the document boxes."

Jorge's eyes narrowed with concern. "There are items missing from university grounds?" he asked, astonished.

"Either that or my predecessor made notes that were bogus. But from what I've heard about Nadia, she was one of the most thorough archivists ever. So I doubt it."

"Didn't know her," Jorge said. "Sad what happened. Beautiful lady."

"Yeah, she was," Emily concurred.

"So, what do you want to see?" Jorge asked.

"I think you told me last time we met the security tapes only go back a month and then you delete them, is that correct?"

"Yes. Although campus police keep them longer."

"But if in reviewing the tapes you saw something . . . unusual . . . you might save that file, just in case, right?"

Jorge drummed his fingers nervously on the desk. "I might. I have. Don't tell anyone."

"Did you save anything in the weeks before Nadia was let go? November/December last year?"

Jorge leveled his eyes suspiciously at Emily. "What are you looking for exactly, Ms. Snow?"

"I'd be massively interested in knowing if anyone went into the closed stacks after hours and scoured the document boxes on the West Collection," Emily blurted out.

Jorge rolled a tongue around the entire perimeter of his gigantic mouth. "Why would you think someone would go in the West boxes?" he probed, buying himself time to consider Emily's line of questioning.

Emily leaned forward slightly and met his eyes and said in an ardent voice, "Because there's a valuable original manuscript in there. Or was." Emily had Jorge galvanized. "I don't want to go into it, but there's also some potentially damaging correspondence. Correspondence certain individuals would definitely *not want* in the collection. But maybe don't have the requisite permissions to remove."

"Sensitive to whom?"

"I would know if I knew who was looking for them. And maybe *stole* what's technically university property." Emily widened her eyes for emphasis. Anything that had to do with theft seemed to engage Jorge's attention with sharper hooks.

"Assuming your predecessor didn't make an error in her file?" he astutely floated.

"She was too professional for that," Emily countered quickly for fear she was losing her grip on Jorge's confidence. "I've never come in on a collection this well organized, except for what was not done. There's something amiss."

The palpable emotion in her voice inspired Jorge's hands to gravitate to his keyboard and mouse. On the main computer screen he opened a file directory. He typed in key words in the slit of a search window. The screen filled with new files. Each file was marked with a code and a date. Jorge clicked one, then stapled his beefy arms against his chest and leaned back in his chair. "The stacks. November twenty-third. Thanksgiving weekend. Last year. Check it out."

Emily bent forward in her chair until the screen filled her whole field of vision. On the monitor, she could make out the shadowed figure of a woman moving through the row of shelves. As she disappeared from view, Jorge moved his mouse and switched to another camera angle that picked up the same woman entering another section of the stacks. From a slightly lower angle, the low-level overhead lights now illuminated the side of her bespectacled face. From a coat pocket she produced a small penlight and switched it on. She turned slightly toward the camera, her penlight spraying the boxes in that direction. Jorge froze the screen. Waited, arms again hugging his chest.

Emily pried her eyes from the freeze-framed image and looked at Jorge, who sat staring at the screen. Her heart leaped in her chest. "Helena?" Jorge nodded. Emily looked back at the monitor. Speaking to it, she asked, "What was she doing down there on a holiday weekend?"

"I don't know. Struck me as odd. That's why I held on to it."

"Did you confront her about it?" Emily asked, her begging eyes on Jorge's half-turned face.

Jorge reared back histrionically. "Helena?" His blubbery face collapsed into a laugh. "Noooo." He collected himself. "Besides, she has twenty-four seven, three sixty-five, to the closed stacks. She can come in on Christmas morning if she wants."

"You didn't talk to her about it at least?" Emily wondered.

"I know," said Jorge. "It's my job. So I brought it up with the Head Librarian."

"Verlander?"

"Yeah, him."

"What'd he say?"

"He didn't even want to see it. Returned an hour later, all officious and shit—pardon my language—and told me to delete it. *Nothing amiss* I think were his words." He trained his eyes back on the screen.

"No explanation?" Emily asked.

Jorge shook his head.

"But you didn't delete it?" Emily said in a conspiratorial tone. "Why?"

Jorge brought an index finger to his lips, shushing her. "I figured if someday, someone came along, like you, and my suspicions had merit . . ." He turned to Emily and scoffed: "Besides, I don't always do what these people tell me to." He laid his meaty hand gently on his mouse, as if a small bird. "Like now."

The security video unfroze, and the now identified Helena Blackwell began her movements again. Emily and Jorge watched her pull down one document box after another, tear off their lids, and rifle through them. She flung open the lids of boxes with increasing exasperation, as if she were annoyed she was even having to perform this manual task in the first place. At one point she slammed a fist in rage at the boxes. Jorge froze on that image.

"This is the West archive?" Emily asked, dumbfounded.

"Yep." Jorge let it play on. Helena rummaged through a few more boxes, indiscriminately pulling out files and putting them back hurriedly, then switched off the penlight and disappeared from view, this time for good. "You can tell she was definitely looking for something. But since she didn't remove any university property from the library and since she does have permission . . ." Jorge trailed off, shrugging. "I'm just head of security. She's the director of Special Collections & Archives."

"But still, you saved it?"

In the voice of a subordinate library employee, he replied, "This is my fifteenth year here, Ms. Snow, and I've never seen a supervisor or an archivist, or *anyone*, go into the closed stacks after hours on her own. Let alone over a Thanksgiving Weekend."

Her heart beating rapidly, Emily blinked back speculations that weren't for Jorge.

Jorge placed his sausage-thick fingers on the keyboard, typed in some key words, rotated the mouse in a tight circle, transited back and forth between the two. "We're just getting warmed up here."

Emily chuckled uneasily, but her blood ran hot.

Jorge moused through his index of files, summoned up another saved security video clip. He swiveled the monitor toward Emily so she had a straight-on view. He leaned back in his chair, interlaced his fingers, and cradled his head in them. Emily realized he was watching her and not the screen, concentrating on her reaction.

The security camera perspectives were looking downward in distorted wide angles. On one, Emily made out the silhouetted figure of a rangy man in his late forties. He was shaven-headed, solidly built, and clad in a black mock turtleneck. He passed through an oblique shaft of shadow and when the minimal light hit him, his face had the polished brown look of rubbed wood. His white teeth flashed in contrast. Jorge paused the video.

"Now this dude I've never ever seen before," he said.

"Who is he?"

"I have no fucking clue—pardon my Spanish."

Jorge laid his right hand on the mouse and performed an optical zoom on the box the turtlenecked man was lugging in his arms. He adjusted the frame so it was focused on the document box label. Emily leaned in closer, blinking to focus. The numbers and letters were pixelated, but legible.

"Do you recognize these call numbers?"

Emily gasped in recognition. "Yes." She looked at Jorge, shaking her head in mystification. "It's from the West Collection. So, who is this guy? Is he in the Facilities Department?"

Jorge shook his head in apparent disgust. "Never seen him before. And I know everyone here. I watch them all day long."

"The closed stacks are a highly restricted area," Emily said, more to herself than to Jorge.

"I know," he said. He shook his head back and forth and wheezed out of wide, flared nostrils.

"Did you go to Helena about this?"

"Nope."

"Why?"

Tired from a long day of watching security cameras, Jorge sighed and leaned forward in his chair with a sag of his heavy shoulders. He pulled the saved files of security cameras back up on the screen, clicked one, then leaned back. He paused dramatically and clicked his mouse to begin playing the video.

Emily put her hands on the desk and practically pressed her face to the screen to gain an up-close look. She observed the man in the previous video go by with the boxes. He stopped when he came to another figure in the stacks. Jorge rapid-clicked his mouse and zoomed in on the two of them. He recentered it, turned up the brightness on the image, and boosted the contrast. He dramatically froze it, raising his hand in a flourish.

"Helena?" Emily asked, more as a question to herself.

"Like I said. She has twenty-four seven, three sixty-five. But not," Jorge added, "the authority to give anyone else permission."

"Why didn't you report this?"

"I've got a wife and two kids. Politics around here can be really heavy. I'm more or less accusing someone of acting improperly. Someone high up the food chain." He looked at Emily with a kind of dejected ineffectuality.

Jorge nervously tapped the leather heel of his shoe on the linoleum. "This was pretty late at night." He peered at a digital clock at the bottom of the image. "One eighteen a.m." He sat back in his chair. "And her accomplice in whatever they were doing doesn't look like any night shift Facilities guy I know. Again, I thought it was highly unusual. The director of Special Collections in the closed stacks at one eighteen a.m. That's a first. So I saved it."

"And you never confronted her about it?"

"The woman screamed at me once. She's sent more people crying to HR than you would care to know."

"Why'd she scream at you?"

"We're all alerted when someone uses a passkey after hours," Jorge explained wearily.

"She was saying she didn't need to be questioned?"

"I guess," Jorge shrugged. His stubborn right hand found the mouse by feel. "It gets even more interesting. Watch."

Jorge refreshed the screen. Helena could be seen standing in the shadows of the closed stacks, looking anxious in the mote-swirling pillars of light. The man in the mock turtleneck entered the frame. They started a conversation, but you couldn't hear what they were saying.

"No audio, huh?" Emily commented, disappointed.

"No, I wish," Jorge said. "Would love to know what they're saying." He leaned forward. "But check this out."

From her purse Helena rooted out a wallet. From the wallet she produced what looked like a bank check. As if it were something important and she were underscoring a point, she held the check up to the unidentified man's face and continued talking, her gums flapping, as if exhorting him about something. The man repeatedly nodded, absorbing Helena's conditions concerning the money. Finally Helena released the check to his hand. Jorge froze the video on the handoff. Using all his video controls, Jorge zoomed in on the check. He had to employ the full capacity of the optical zoom to make the check readable. When he finally zeroed in on the check, the image degradation almost made it illegible.

Emily's glasses were now mere inches from the monitor. "Seymour Catering?" Emily read. She squinted at the address in the upper left of the check, trying hard to make it out, and read, "Regents University Discretionary Fund Special Collections." She threw a deeply perplexed expression to Jorge. "Thirty thousand friggin' dollars?"

"Must be one hell of a caterer. Surf and turf, baby." Jorge centered the handwritten note in the lower left.

"Town & Gown fundraiser," Emily read the words scrawled in the lower left memo line.

"Oh, Helena loves her Town & Gown events," Jorge guffawed.

"You ever attend one?"

"Are you fucking kidding?" Jorge scoffed. "You think I would be invited to the Faculty Club? Maybe to help out in the kitchen."

Emily chortled. "So, this guy's a purported caterer. They're lurking around in the closed stacks on a holiday. Helena's looking for items in the West Collection . . . ?" Emily stared at the grainy image of the check on the screen, shaking her head back and forth like a metronome. She turned to Jorge, her new best friend in all of San Diego, with a look of bewilderment. "Doesn't make sense."

Jorge set his chin on his shoulder and met Emily's bemused eyes. "That's why I saved it. It's fucking bizarre." He let go his hands from the mouse and keyboard. "But, hey, if nothing is reported stolen, I'm cool."

"Can you print me out screenshots?"

Jorge threw her an admonishing look. "I like you, Ms. Snow. But if anyone asks where you got them, say you got them from campus police, okay? Because I could lose my job."

"I won't betray you, Jorge. I swear to God. You've been fantastically helpful."

Emily checked her cell for messages while Jorge printed out screenshots. She was surprised to find a reply from Raymond to her email request to talk to him again. It read tersely: "Why do you want to see me?" Emily typed a reply back: "Because there's something you need to know."

Jorge slipped the printouts into an oversized manila envelope, bent the clasp shut, and handed it to Emily. "Here you go." Before he released it to her, he emphasized, "Be careful. When you're dealing with Ms. Blackwell, you're dealing with a fucking institution."

Emily held up the manila envelope and shook it in her hand as if to underscore the radioactivity of its contents. "Thanks, Jorge."

Emily left the library and walked in the direction of the Jameson parking structure. The university grounds were desolately quiet. Here and there a student flitted past like a nocturnal animal, but other than that Emily was all alone. As she made her way back to her car, the library towered over her in all its otherworldly indomitability, illuminated like a spaceship alit on earth. She could make out the young students bent over their desks, cramming for the midterms. A skateboarder came flying demonically out of the dark like a bad dream and zigzagged by her with a grinding roar of its tiny wheels. He had to veer sharply to avoid Emily.

"Asshole!" Emily shouted at him, but he was oblivious of the world with his earbuds and manic, reckless youth.

When Emily reached the fifth floor of the parking structure, she found it deserted except for her blue Mini . . .and a gray Volvo SUV parked a dozen spaces over. Her heart raced. Sensitive all her life to anything suspicious since an assault when she was a freshman in college that she managed to fend off unharmed, Emily kept her eyes trained on the SUV as she opened her car by feel and slipped inside. She pressed the power button and the engine roared to life. She backed out, turned in the direction of the SUV, her eyes locked on it like human binoculars. As she passed it, its lights flared on like in some suspense movie. Scared now, Emily adjusted her rearview mirror. She heard the squealing of sharply turning tires reverberate in the lot, and it climbed up her spine. Looming in her rearview mirror suddenly, the headlights of the SUV burned two blinding white holes. She raced in circumvolutions to the upper exit, the SUV matching her speed, riding her tail.

At the first stop sign out of the parking structure, Emily's eyes were riveted on her rearview mirror. The glaring headlights prevented her from making out the driver who was tailing her. She shifted into first and headed out of the campus. The headlights of the Volvo stayed close on her bumper. Her heart palpitated with a will all its own. This was an unfamiliar, new kind of panic. The one that sent her racing to the ER was pure hypochondria run amok—this felt perniciously, lethally real.

When the stoplight at Torrey Pines Road turned green, Emily gunned it. She power-shifted into second. Because it was late, the next light at Coast Highway was green, and she fishtailed through the intersection, her back wheel hydroplaning on the fog-slickened streets. She looked up into the rearview mirror and the headlights of the SUV were burning like magnesium, so close to her it felt like she was towing it.

Emily sped past Torrey Pines Golf Course, the night sleepy and half dead, except for her car and the one now pursuing her with apparent malicious intent. Emily placed her cell on the dash mount, tapped Google Maps, typed "Police" and waited. The screen refreshed with a map and digital red pushpins indicating the nearest police stations.

At the bottom of the hill, Emily swung the wheel hard and executed a screeching U-turn at the turn-in to Torrey Pines beach parking. The SUV didn't miss a beat, duplicating her maneuver. She was being chased.

Emily raced back up Coast Highway in the direction she had come, the SUV hard on her tail, a kind of predatory automotive force.

With Formula One–expert turns, Emily flew back onto the campus and followed the map on her cell directly to RPD, the campus police station. Leaving her lights on, she leaped out of her car, leaving the door swung open, and marched toward the entrance. The SUV stopped half a soccer field away and idled, its lights burning like two malignant eyes of a large, otherworldly creature, stopped in its tracks.

Inside the small police station, Emily found an open-plan room with two uniformed officers stationed in front of computers. In a breathless, anxious, heart-stricken voice, Emily cried out, "Someone's following me. He's outside right now." She pointed to the door, worried they might think she was deranged.

Both of the police officers, young men in their thirties, leaped up and followed her lead outside.

Outside, Emily pointed to the now retreating red taillights. "He followed me out of Jameson and halfway to Del Mar, and I made a U-turn and came straight back here," she said breathlessly, fear throttling her blurted words.

By the time the officers had caught up with her movements, the gray SUV was two vanishing pinpoints of red light. Emily spun around and faced them. "He was right on my tail."

The officers watched the SUV drive off with grim expressions, exchanged concerned looks, then, as if reaching a solution to the mini-crisis, one of the officers asked, "Do you want to come in, Miss, and fill out a report?"

Gripped with terror, Emily could hear herself hyperventilating. She worried for a moment it could escalate into a full-scale panic attack, but she was determined not to let it take root in her psyche. If it did, it would boomerang her back to the ER and everything she had worked hard and risked so much personally to uncover would be discredited in a heartbeat.

And she knew how fragile the thread to determining the cause of Nadia's death was that she was clinging to. And she was going to hold on. For Nadia. The officer's question must have gone unanswered for suspiciously too many seconds, because the second one pressed:

"Are you faculty or staff here, Miss . . . ?"

Emily cast her eyes down and nodded without vocally elaborating. Flashing on the unauthorized printouts of the screenshots lying on the passenger seat of her car, she worried suddenly about betraying the confidences of Jorge. She decided she didn't want to identify herself, other than in the vaguest of terms. "Yeah. I'm staff over at the . . . library." Coming to an abrupt resolve, she turned to them, smiled weakly. "I'm tired. I've been working overtime to meet this deadline. I'm sure it was probably some random creep whose idea of charming a woman is to challenge her to a race."

"We'd really like it if you'd come in and fill out a report," the taller of the two advised.

"I'm . . . I'm late for something. I'm sure I overreacted. Do you have a card? In case I'm harassed by the same person again."

They looked at her with downturned expressions of concern. Finally the shorter of the two officers produced a card and held it out to her. Emily took it, glanced at it, shoved it into her jeans pocket, inhaled deeply, and said, "All right, well, thank you, officers."

Emily walked back to her car on trembling legs. She could feel the officers' eyes on her. As she backed out, she watched them turn their backs and disappear inside.

Emily opted for a different route out of the campus, but it wouldn't matter if the guy in the gray Volvo was the same guy who ransacked her apartment, because he could easily have planted a tracking device on her car. She wended her way to the I-5 and headed back in the direction of Del Mar. She debated staying the night in a hotel, but she didn't want to feel all alone in a Hampton Inn—its depressing blue-and-yellow sign looming out of the night at a turnoff—and what about poor Onyx? She thought about calling Joel but realized that by the time she got to Pacific Beach and explained what happened, it would be well after midnight.

Emily didn't pull into her assigned space in the carport and instead settled her Mini in street parking and approached her complex from the west side in murky alley light. She climbed the series of steps to the top floor, invisible antennae extended, ears trained like a dog's for sound. Nothing looked anomalous. Her new key fit in her new lock. Once safely inside, she immediately lodged the broom pole against the sliding glass door and pushed it down into place as Joel had instructed, barricading herself in the apartment.

A sleepy Onyx walked silently in from the back bedroom, black against the white tile, yawning. Emily squatted to pet the little jaguar. She was glad to see him, glad to feel his thick fur through her fanned fingers. He was happy to see her. He raised his head and meowed sanguinity. The waves could be heard lamenting in the distance. The nightly Southern Pacific sounded its foghorn. Emily instinctually knew the trouble was tautening, but as she stood crouched next to Onyx, all was in balance, if harrowingly so, for the moment.

CHAPTER 22

In the Archives Begin Responsibilities

10/21/18

I have descended to the bottom. If you're reading this, Joel, or whomever, know that I feared for my life.

In the seemingly infinite necklace of cars that beaded the coast, Emily didn't spot any sign of the gray Volvo SUV. She had gone back over Nadia's memoir where she had described the exact same car that had been shadowing her. Which means the exact same person, in a fucked-up déjà vu, was now following her.

Emily stopped at Bird Rock Coffee to get her thermos filled. One of the baristas there was familiar with her now, and he was overly friendly. Emily smiled him off, ignored his immature but harmless come-ons, then paused on the planked deck on her way out and inhaled the view of the pristine lagoon. A magnificent osprey took flight with a commotion of blurred wings, rippling the waters, and flew in the direction of the ocean. Its effortless flying made Emily flash on the paragliders. She wanted to feel free like that someday, above the ground, attached to nothing, soaring.

Emily drove to the Gliderport to make her appointment with Raymond. A scattering of cars gleamed in the vast dirt parking area spilling out from the cliffside palisades. An onshore wind was blowing and a dozen or more paragliders were cruising like a squadron of undisciplined pelicans along the cliff, their colorful chutes mottling the blue sky with movable patterns.

Emily cut her engine. She swiveled her head from window to window, over her shoulder and out the back, searching for any sign of the gray Volvo SUV. Paranoia now gripped her imagination in a hellish vise. She was ready to explode. Her breaths came short and fast through flared nostrils.

As Emily waited for Raymond, she examined minutely the last forty-eight hours with a mounting sense of terror. So, Nadia *had* been followed. That proved what Joel had told her that Nadia confessed to him the night she came to his apartment in a state of extremis. As she pieced it all together, Emily shuddered to herself. She was convinced someone had stalked her predecessor. Whether he had killed her or driven her to suicide, Emily couldn't be sure.

Emily was jerked out of her dark ruminations when she heard dirt and gravel churn to her right. A tremor of anxiety was quickly supplanted by relief when she saw Raymond's black Range Rover, the one Nadia had referred to again and again in her anguished account. In the crucible of her fixation, he was her last resort.

Heart pounding nervously, Emily climbed out of her Mini and circled around the back, her eyes darting warily over the terrain around her. Across the canyon ravine that rose up out of a slash in the cliff she could make out the Gliderport café and the picnic tables dotting the perimeter of the grassy palisades where more paragliders prepared to launch.

Emily climbed up into Raymond's Range Rover, leveraging herself on the running board, as if she had risen from the corporeal world to meet his celestial one. Raymond's visage appeared haggard. Vertical lines scored his unshaven face from the corners of his eyes. He was wearing an old, faded black T-shirt, jeans and tennis shoes, as if he hadn't come from the university. He removed his sunglasses, and when he did, Emily noticed his eyes were bloodshot, the skin pouched beneath them as if he hadn't been sleeping well.

"Hi, Raymond," she said, feeling sad for him all of a sudden. "How are you?"

"Since I last saw you?" He blew air through his nostrils and shook his head in a self-deprecating laugh. "You laid some heavy shit on me, Emily."

"I'm sorry."

Raymond noisily filled his lungs through his nose as if taking measure of the almost imponderable situation. "Excuse me." He reached across her and popped open the glove compartment. A flask came out in his hand with a flash of silver. He unscrewed the top, raised the small spout to his lips, and bent his head back. He recoiled at the acrid taste, juddered his head and sighed heavily, quickly screwed the cap back on and replaced it in the glove compartment. With his head bent toward Emily, he turned to her; his eyes quickened to her hand. She could smell his tequila-scented breath as he brought trembling fingers to the ouroboros necklace he had given to Nadia, now glinting in offering from Emily.

"You found the ouroboros," he mumbled, his expression contorted, his whole being teetering on the verge of an emotional collapse.

Emily said with compassion, "I found it with the Moleskines. I thought you might want it as a keepsake."

Raymond played with it in his fingers like the filigree of a membrane that encased a once-beating heart. He lifted it out of her hand. He stared at it, transfixed by the memories it disinterred. In an adroit move he strung it around Emily's neck and clasped it. The ouroboros fell to her jugular where Raymond straightened it with trembling fingers.

"You wear it," he said. Raymond blinked his eyes at the ouroboros as though he were looking directly at Nadia's beautiful face. "Nadia had a passion for the void," he slurred through chapped lips, as if to no one but himself. "She was supersonic in everything she did, in every fiber of her being. She was a true artist." He let go of the figure eight of the snake and rasped with sorrow, "She's tattooed on my soul for life. That I know." He relaxed back against the seat cushion and fixed his gaze on the horizon. The alcohol made him a different person. The façade of the academic in him cracked and the edifices of repression foundered. A gust of wind propelled a funnel of dirt across the parking area. "The silence is oddly comforting," he finally spoke. "It's the words that terrify me." He turned his head to her. "I'm afraid to ask. What did you want to show me?"

From her purse Emily pulled a manila envelope. She bent open the clasp and removed the printouts Jorge had provided her. She handed them to Raymond. “Do you recognize this guy?”

With thumb and forefinger, Raymond tweezed a pair of narrow, rectangular-framed reading glasses from his T-shirt pocket and balanced them low on his nose. He studied the pictures for a minute. “No.” He handed them back to her. She slipped them back into her purse. He folded his reading glasses and dropped them into his T-shirt pocket, then leaned back into the headrest, as if contemplating an unfathomable world that had heartlessly conspired against him. “Never seen him,” he said with closed eyes. “Who is he?”

“Did Nadia ever tell you she was being followed?” Emily asked.

Raymond’s head fell in Emily’s direction like a dead weight. She worried from his expression he couldn’t absorb any more disclosures orbiting Nadia’s death without risking a nervous breakdown. She knew from his papers he had suffered one at age forty that institutionalized him for six months.

“She was,” Emily said. “Trust me. Her husband had a tracking device on her car.” She almost, but didn’t, confess there might be one on her Mini.

A fearful pallor flushed Raymond’s ruddy face. “Oh, Jesus. What next?”

“Her husband wasn’t the one following her. That’s someone else. I don’t know who it is. But her husband geo-tracked all of her movements.”

Raymond threw her a look of wild incomprehension. “You talked to Nadia’s husband?”

“Yes.” Emily’s eyes burned like twin blue gas flames.

“Why?” he cried, the tequila having afforded him a gap of livid clarity between tremulousness and sleep.

“I needed to know what he knew!” she exclaimed.

Raymond shook his head and said in a quavering voice, “Why are you dredging all this shit up? She’s gone.” Tears glassed his eyes. He blinked them back, but they had already wet his lashes a sable black.

“Because somebody’s following me. My apartment was broken into. Ransacked.” They were on different wavelengths, but their fates had intersected in the archives and now they were in his Range Rover at the Gliderport where he and Nadia had once fucked like animals. “I think the same person, hired by whomever, who followed Nadia, is following me.”

“They broke into your apartment?” he asked, taken aback.

"They're looking for *The Archivist* Moleskines, Raymond!" Emily nearly shouted.

Raymond flung his head in her direction like a sick horse. The veins in his neck stood out and vibrated. His face was colored red with fear and glowing with drink. The gravity of the situation punched him in the solar plexus and awakened him to a constellation of new fears.

Emily blinked back her own tears. With extrahuman effort she sprang up into him and her lips found the chapped lips of his mouth and she kissed him ardently, hungrily, not out of romantic passion, but desperate for a palpable connection to this narrative of love that had led her downward into the fires of memory and the unredeemed past. At first stunned, he greedily kissed her back. From the force of his mouth, she felt he needed the same thing she wanted, but he had the ephemeral power of tequila and she possessed only the unmedicated reality of her occupational panic anxiety. They both felt an unexpressed abyss gaping in their souls. They had come together over an archive and the archivist who sunk her soul deep into it, words on paper had stitched them together in some surreal patchwork quilt that made no sense except to the underworld god marionetting it all. They were bound for life, no matter what happened now. And they both grasped it in that cathartic kiss that left both feeling connected to something they needed to be connected to without chancing going mad: Raymond to the grief of the past; Emily to the terror of the present and the dark of her once promising future.

Emily let her mouth drop from his and buried her cheek in his chest, kneading his shirt with her fingernails like an affection-starved cat. She felt his comforting fingers on the back of her head, and in that moment she felt closer to Nadia than ever. Her words had brought Emily to the man, and now she was clinging to him like Nadia had done in that final rendezvous here at the Gliderport. She would never be a writer like Nadia, and she would never attract a man like Raymond West to fall in love with her, but with one sustained, soul-searching kiss, she had pierced his emotional opacity and dragged him down to the flesh and blood, down to the godforsaken human.

Emily felt the weight of Raymond's body shift toward the glove compartment. She gripped his forearm with hooked fingers. "Don't, Raymond. This isn't a time to bury it with alcohol." She raised her eyes to him like Onyx did to her when he was hungry. "I need you here for me now." She tightened her grip on his forearm for emphasis. "Okay?"

He withdrew his arm with a sigh. "You're right."

"I didn't mean to do that."

"We're both clinging to her right now," he said enigmatically, but Emily intuited what he meant.

"Look, I know pretty much everything," Emily stated. Raymond nodded. "I know all about your wife and Nadia at Isla Negra." Raymond kept nodding metronomically, absorbing the one narrative he couldn't control. Emily persisted. "I have to ask you, is there any chance your wife would have hired someone to follow Nadia and try to get those Moleskines back?"

"It's not her style," Raymond answered brusquely.

"Helena Blackwell? Would she give Helena money?" Emily wanted to show Raymond the screenshot of the check Helena had handed to the unidentified man in the closed stacks, but she feared alienating Raymond with the too prodigious amount of information she was in possession of.

"Helena? I don't know," Raymond muttered, staring inexpressively through the windshield, shaking his head, thinking. "As Nadia's employer she would definitely be all over her to make the problem go away, but a PI?"

"Who might then have hired a private investigator? Think."

Raymond turned slowly to Emily, his face drawn with tension. "You need to walk away from this, Emily. It's too potentially damaging. For both of us. She's gone."

"What did you do with the Moleskines?" Emily pressed.

"They're in a bank vault." He paused to let that sink in. "If something happens to me, they go to you. It'll be on your conscience then as my archivist."

His words paralyzed her into silence.

"I gave the bank your email and phone number. If you think they need something more pertinent, email it to me and I'll pass it on."

Emily reared back. "I'm . . . flabbergasted."

Raymond drifted away for a moment from the subject of their conversation and let the alcohol talk. "Did you know that the Gutenberg Bible was created out of the hides of three hundred sheep?"

"I might have read that," Emily said.

"Can you imagine the suffering that went into the first printed word?" he roared, the tequila in him unleashing a moment of rage. He flung his head to Emily's averted gaze. "That's *The Archivist.* But I can't destroy it. Not now that I know it still exists. I can't." He pounded his fist on the dash with a resounding blow and held it there like a flag planted in the sand.

Emily watched the shifting range of emotions that played over his face. His eyes were narrowed like a hawk's on prey, but the quarry was inward and abstract, and a hint of frustration twisted his mouth into a tormented grimace. Emily waited until the animal wailing in him had subsided.

"You knew she was pregnant?" she stated.

He turned his head slowly in Emily's direction, a new alarm glinting in his eyes.

"Like I said," Emily started to explain, "Nadia not only kept your correspondence, she also wrote, as I mentioned in your office, a beautiful—very personal, very detailed—memoir of your relationship, which I came across in the correspondence." Their eyes glanced like obsidian off each other, almost producing sparks. "So just admit it."

"Yeah, I knew. Okay?"

"And your wife knew?"

Raymond looked at her with the dark turbulence of a storm brewing inside him.

"She told her," Emily volunteered.

"Oh, Jesus," Raymond said. He pulled a hand over his face and held it there like the half shell of a mollusk on dark sand. Suddenly, his hand shot out for the glove compartment in a lightning-fast move. Emily made no effort to stop him. He rummaged vehemently for the flask, unscrewed the cap with deft fingers, and took a long, soul-obliterating pull of the tequila. "I told her to take care of it, and she did," he said finally, soothed by the alcohol. He took another bracing swig. Emily let the truth serum exercise its ephemeral magic. Raymond looked despondently into the well of a past he had hoped was capped forever, and now its brackish memories were surging back to him like an inexorably rising tide.

"She told you she aborted your child?" Emily asked.

"It was a tacit understanding," he said grimly.

"What if I told you she didn't go through with it?"

Raymond snapped his head into the crosshairs of Emily's penetrating eyes. Shock drained all the red out of his face and painted it a ghostly white. "What?" She was glad he had his tequila for:

"What if I told you that the autopsy report showed she was still very much pregnant with your child when they found her on the beach?"

The jolt of Emily's disclosure lifted Raymond's eyebrows into an arrested expression. It was now more than the errancy of his heart that imprisoned him in the memory of Nadia. His voice crawled up from deep in his soul. "I didn't know that." He leaned his head back. "My God."

"I talked with the lead homicide investigator," Emily admitted.

Raymond sighed with a snort of air through his nostrils and shook his head in astonishment at Emily's deep well of information on Nadia's death. "I'm afraid to ask." He dropped his head to hers. "Do the police know whose it was?"

"No." Emily's eyes roamed the horizon for a door out, but clouds had closed off the sky. "They only know for certain it wasn't her husband's."

Raymond nodded to himself, girding for the next blow of the sledgehammer from Emily.

She whirled away from the windshield and pronounced with fierce conviction, "Do you really think she committed suicide? Nearly four months pregnant with your child? Having recently been fired? You telling her you had no choice but to abandon the book you were writing with her? And that you never wanted to see her again? What else did she have? Go back to the desert that was her marriage? After you?" She finished in a rising tone with an openmouthed glare of utter disbelief. In her look was everything Raymond West the author had failed to grasp about women in his work, except perhaps, unwittingly, *The Archivist*.

Raymond turned away and muttered more in resignation than in anger, "I sincerely believed her when she wrote me and said she was going through with the abortion. I'm stunned to hear this." He shook his head, dumbfounded. "You're positive?"

"She lied to you because she wanted to protect you," Emily theorized.

"But she wasn't going to give up that child. Not after you abandoned her *and* the book. I wouldn't've!"

Raymond turned to Emily and gazed at her as if the spirit of Nadia had suddenly inhabited this new archivist who had taken over the care of his papers, and the distance between them was now as diaphanous as the sheerest fabric. In the ensuing silence, large surf roared in the distance, the blows of its powerful, unstoppable waves reverberating up through the canyon fissure like the ocean's own heartbeat.

"Her husband was tracking her," Emily started back, in an effort to sort out the labyrinthine timeline.

The realization that their affair had been chronicled caused Raymond's chin to drop in shameful resignation. "You said."

"And aside from all the . . . trysting spots," she continued, "he discovered something else." Raymond braced himself for another bombshell with a fugitive shot of tequila. "She was making regular visits to an OB-GYN." Emily rummaged in her purse and produced a fat, white-colored vial of pills and held them up for Raymond to see. "Her husband also found these." The label read "Prenatal One." "Do you still think she would commit suicide? With your child inside her? Regular doctor appointments? She was going to have that baby, Raymond. And her husband, who knew everything, was going to help her raise it."

"Jesus." He raised a hand and cupped it to his mouth, as if the enormity of everything Emily had told him was unassimilable as empirical truth.

"They couldn't have kids." Emily blinked abashedly into her lap. "He had come to terms with your affair and that it was over." She raised her face up to his. "I know, like me, you're an only child, so the West lineage was going to . . . continue on." Emily looked away. "One day that child—that no doubt beautiful child—would have come into your life—"

"Stop!" Raymond cried. He tilted his head back against the headrest, absorbing the implications. "So, you think she drowned?"

"Not in waist-high surf. Not a woman who regularly trained for triathlons swimming from Scripps Pier to La Jolla Cove."

Raymond cast portentous eyes on Emily. He closed them in quiet anguish, and they disappeared into two nests of wrinkles. When he reopened them, they were twin sapphires glinting underwater. "She was pregnant when she died," he intoned, as if still in disbelief. "Why wouldn't the police tell me?"

"Because Nadia's husband lied and said the child was an IVF baby. Therefore, I'm assuming, they didn't feel they needed to do a DNA test."

Raymond's face sagged in despair. He shook his head back and forth in fathomless disbelief.

"But if he hadn't covered for you—out of his own pride—and they did a DNA test and matched it with you, you would have been a prime suspect." Emily glared at him.

Raymond slowly turned his head to hers. "You think I killed her?"

"No! She was the love of your life. And I found the book to prove it. If I thought you killed her, I wouldn't be here with you. Besides, weren't you giving a talk at Dartmouth that week?"

"You know everything about me, don't you?"

"Just like Nadia. Yeah." She flung her gaze out the passenger window. "Even though your wife and Helena knew about the affair, and probably didn't tell the police, you weren't a suspect, Raymond. And I'm speculating that someone who has twenty-five million to give as a gift and has floated the possibility of running for mayor of a city as large as San Diego has the power to buy a lot of silence, even if you were."

Raymond collapsed onto Emily's shoulder. He wept violently into her blouse. "I don't know how much more I can take. I miss her," he bawled uncontrollably. He looked at her with sodden eyes. "And you, holding all this inside, all alone?" he said, with unexpected sensitivity to everything Emily had been going through. He enveloped her in his arms. She could feel his weeping face trembling on her shoulder, his scraggly beard scratching her neck like fine sandpaper. His sad, tequila-scented breath. This broken man, this once heralded writer, disassembled all over again as he was when Nadia had been found dead. No catastrophic molt and consequent rebirth were forthcoming. In that moment, Emily wondered why she had carried this on her lone shoulders as far as she had. And she knew the reason as she clung to him: she couldn't live with a lie.

"I had to tell someone," Emily said tearfully. "I didn't know whom to turn to. And I thought you should at least know that Nadia was definitely pregnant when she died." She drew air sharply through her nose. She realized at that moment that nothing less than his conscience was on trial.

Raymond hugged her tightly. Then he pulled away from her. A ray of terror crossed his face like a bleak shadow. Holding her by the shoulders, as if afraid she were going to abandon him, he slowly turned to her, as if a new, deeper, horror had finally dawned on him: "Do you really think she was murdered?"

"I don't know for sure. The police don't think so. Maybe she did walk into those dark waters because she was inconsolably depressed." Emily thrust out her jaw. "Maybe my instinct is all wrong. But I think she truly believed you were going to finish the book you were writing together. I think that meant everything to her. And when you abandoned it, told her to destroy it, pushed her away . . ." She trailed off. "I don't know what I would have done if you had told me to go fuck myself. I can't even begin to fathom the depth of her despair."

"What do you want from me?" Raymond asked in a helpless voice.

Emily shook her head. "Nothing. I just wanted to tell you this because I thought you should know, that's all." With a vast rush of feeling for him, she reached up and embraced him, her arms not even reaching around his broad shoulders. Their heads coupled for one last cathartic moment. Emily pressed down on the door lever. It sprang open. She didn't want to leave. She twisted back to him. "If I never see you again, I'm sorry I got pulled into this personal world of yours and hers."

He met her eyes. "You didn't do anything wrong, Emily."

Emily reached into her purse one last time. She took out a single sheet of paper and handed it to Raymond.

"What's this?" he asked.

"*Mr. Pencilhead.* The poem that got you into trouble with your high school principal. The first thing you ever wrote. Nadia found it."

Raymond drew a hand to his mouth as he cursorily examined the Xerox of the original. He closed his eyes and tears leached from them.

"That's how brilliant of an archivist she was."

In a trembling voice, Raymond said, "She told me she would find it."

"She did. And so much more. Goodbye," said Emily to a nonplussed Raymond. She stepped out of the car, dropped three feet to the ground, back in her world. His "Be careful" as she closed the door to his Range Rover trailed her like the faint whisper of a ghost, or the cell door clanging shut on a still imprisoned man.

Emily drove in silence following the coastline. Even though it was still light out, she parked on the street again and approached her apartment, step by step, circumspectly. She had wanted to believe eleven was her new lucky number, but now she wasn't sure it hadn't reverted to its superstitious status of unlucky.

Once inside she locked the sliding glass door and jimmied the broom pole in place. She and Onyx met together in the living room as effortlessly as couples should meet in a contented relationship, thought Emily. Wanting to see each other. Missing each other. Needing each other. In their brief moments she felt that with Raymond, strangely enough, but it was much more complicated.

Emily refreshed Onyx's bowls to quiet his plaintive meowing. A half-eaten Japanese takeout that had gone cold and wilted in the refrigerator served as her dinner. She picked at it unenthusiastically, made it palatable with a bracingly cold Societe IPA. Then, unable to stop her racing mind, Emily went into the bedroom and opened her laptop. Silence enveloped the apartment like a fragile skin.

Obsessing again, Emily googled "seymour's catering la jolla del mar san diego." Nothing. Confused, she tried alternative spellings. Still nothing. The only thing she came across was a Seymour's Catering with a PO box in neighboring Solana Beach. She google-mapped it. It was a PostalAnnex+, one of thousands of the cookie-cutter franchise that offered a variety of mail services.

Emily tensed when the spring-loaded door to the upper-level parking opened and banged shut with a vibration felt in the walls. Not uncommon. A scuffling of footsteps on the walkway stopped after a few seconds. Emily sat up straight. The rap of knuckles sounding at the plate glass window door seized her with terror. The window door was the only way in and the only way out! Unless she crawled out the kitchen window, but that was a fifteen-foot drop to the patio below. Emily tuned her ears to the noise, her heart racing, her breathing irregular, but remained motionless in fear. She heard something slap down on the doormat. Footsteps retreated down the concrete-treaded stairs in the direction of the complex's swimming pool.

Emily rose in slow-motion off the bed and tiptoed into the living room. She craned her head into the living room around the dividing wall. The cream-colored paper shades were drawn shut. Emily stepped to the picture window. She slowly drew back the shade at the edge enough to gain a view of the courtyard. A man silhouetted by the turquoise of the pool fled down the short flight of steps that exited the complex. Headlights rose up on the stucco walls of the apartment complex below Emily's, swept them like a lighthouse beacon, then briefly colored them in red with the taillights of an unseen car, turning away down the alley, tires squealing.

Emily let go of the blinds and stood in solitude breathing in short bursts like a scared animal. She crept over to the sliding glass door. Slowly, she parted the accordion blinds. The outdoor floodlights illuminated an object on the doorstep. Face pressed to the sliding glass door, Emily's eyes roamed the outside. She cocked her sensitive ears. Barely heard the wind chimes from across the way. The balcony verandas were quiet. She dislodged the broom pole and unlocked the door. Quickly, she squatted down and picked up the white manila folder that had been dropped on the square of carpet that served as a doormat. She relocked the door, replaced the security pole, closed the blind, and shuttered herself inside, her heart beating wildly.

On the outside of the white manila folder was a message in black block letters: STOP WHAT YOU'RE DOING! Anxiety clutched Emily in the gut. She bent open the bronze clasp and tipped the envelope upside down. A half dozen eight-by-ten color printouts slid into her hands. Because of the graininess, the critical depth of field, Emily recognized they had been taken with a powerful telephoto lens—had to be, because they were photos of her and Raymond in his Range Rover at the Gliderport . . . kissing! Her hand darted to her throat and tried to stop it from leaping. The last item was not a photo, but a sheet of paper. On it, in the same block lettering: I WANT THE NOTEBOOKS.

Emily imploded with fear. She huddled on the sisal rug in a fetal posture, debating her next move. Every sound—a passing car, the palm frond clattering against the eave, even the waves—engendered a new shudder of fear.

Emily texted Joel: "Can I come over? Important."

A few, excruciatingly long minutes passed, and Joel texted back: "Come on by. I'll be up."

In a flurry of anxious energy, Emily packed her carry-on backpack. She grabbed all the provisions she thought she would need and stuffed it full. With her carry-on over her back, a meowing, disconcerted Onyx under her arm, she fled her apartment.

The freeway unfurled in front of her, that wide undulating river of concrete emptiness with the occasional passing car, its occupants entombed in anonymity. As she drove south past the Genesee Avenue turnoff, she could make out Memorial Library to the west, the megastructure lit up like an enormous cracked diamond mounted on the dark cement shoulders of its massive concrete pronged pedestal. With Emily racing by it, seemingly holding its fate in her small hands, Onyx sitting on his haunches on the passenger seat, looking confused.

Emily bent off at the Garnett Avenue turnoff and navigated surface streets through Pacific Beach to Joel's apartment. Except for a handful of bars and gas stations, everything was closed. Humans had seemingly ceased to exist. Southern California cities desolated themselves out after a certain hour and the streets burned weirdly malevolent, bounded with their Ed Ruscha–like paintings of overlit stores and franchise eateries.

An emotional wreck, Emily collapsed on the couch in Joel's apartment, her hands covering her face. When she looked up Joel had Onyx cradled in his arms, and she was glad to see he apparently had no aversion to cats.

"You remember Onyx?" she said.

"Of course. Love the little guy." He stroked his fur. "Can I get you a beer?"

"Sure," replied an overwrought Emily.

Joel gently set Onyx down and disappeared into the kitchen. Onyx looked around, disoriented, recognized Emily's solicitous voice, and leaped up onto the couch next to her.

Joel brought a bottle of beer in, reached it across his cluttered coffee table to her, then ebbed back into an Adirondack-style chair with a groaning canvas back.

"Thanks," said Emily. She took a sip and then studied the bottle label absently while she sorted through the events of the past couple of days in an effort to summarize them for Joel without compromising him—without further alarming him. She bent her head back and took another swig. The beer foamed in her mouth. She had an image of her head exploding.

"What's up?" Joel said, fully aware of the irony of his casual tone.

"They came again," Emily said.

"Broke into your apartment again!"

"No." Emily shook her head. "Left something on the doorstep."

"What?" Joel asked.

"I can't show you." She raised her head to Joel. In a manic, machine-gun burst of words, she spurted out, "They might come here. They're following me. I'm going to get a hotel."

"You're wound up, Emily. Breathe."

"You would be too."

"I can't help you if you don't tell me what it is," he said sharply, more in an effort to bring her to her senses than a rebuke.

"I don't want to compromise you any more than you already are."

Joel straightened to his feet. "I have to admit, Emily, a part of me thinks the reason you're like this is because . . ."—he turned to face her—"you're losing touch with reality here."

Emily looked up at him, fearing recrimination.

"The whiteboard? The pursuit of everything you found in his archive. Everything. Introverts go mad, Emily. Archivists are introverts."

"You think I'm insane?" she accused, trying to keep her voice lowered. "That I'm making this all up? That I'm delusional?"

"No, I'm not saying that. You know I was with you on this all the way." Joel leaned forward. "Nadia's personal file. The permission to get you into the dark archives. I didn't believe it was a drowning or suicide either a year ago when it went down. It's just . . . this whole thing has spiraled out of control. There are bad actors following you now, Emily."

"I know," said Emily, relieved by the solicitous tone of Joel's voice. "Tell me about it."

"There are moments when I think you've somehow merged with Nadia, you've become her doppelgänger or something in some movie or . . ."

Emily met his words with narrowed eyes of shock and near disbelief. To her, the narrative was clear. To him, it looked like she was marching off the deep end. In trying to rein her back in, she felt like he was asking her to erect a wall around the truth, even if the truth was now under siege behind a crumbling rampart.

Emily set the half-drunk bottle of beer on the lacquered driftwood coffee table with a *plunk* and rose to her feet. She slipped her arms through the harness of her carry-on backpack and turned to Joel. "Can you take care of Onyx?"

"Emily? Where're you going?"

"I'm going to get a hotel."

"No, stay, I don't care. I'm not afraid."

"I'm not delusional!" she nearly screamed, whiplashing back to her distrust of everyone.

"I didn't say that. I care about you. I don't want to see you get hurt. I feel complicit," Joel pleaded.

"Maybe I *am* losing my mind. Maybe I *have* overidentified with Nadia and become too obsessed with the correspondence and *The Archivist* and what happened to her." She adjusted the shoulder straps on her carry-on backpack, ready to exit. "But I'm going to find out the truth, Joel, and no one is going to fucking stop me."

"Emily?" she heard him call as she went out the door, down yet another concrete flight of stairs, across yet another walkway that brushed up against a water-stained stucco wall, broadening out to yet another apocalyptically deserted street with nothing but lit-up signs of two-story apartment complexes all with ridiculously banal names like Paradise Palms. *Paradise Palms*, Emily snorted in contempt.

Emily followed the coast north, hugging the ocean all the way, to the hotel she had booked. Every stoplight was green. Every store was closed. She felt remorseful about leaving Joel's in such a fit of pique, but the stress of the day had built up in her like a massive pressure, for which no release valve could vent.

Emily frequently glanced up at her rearview mirror with the darting, watchful eyes of a bird. It didn't appear anyone was following her. But whoever it was, he had her in his sights now, that she was sure of.

Emily drove through slumbering La Jolla. A waxing, near-full moon produced a shaft of white light that stretched to infinity on the placid dark waters where Nadia once swam, fracturing it into two separate oceans.

Emily checked into Estancia Hotel, the one across from the university, aware of the eerie irony that it was the hotel where Nadia and Raymond had first made love but figuring that if it had been good enough them, it was good enough for her too. Maybe she *was* her doppelgänger after all, and Joel and the rest of them were the sane ones, and she was stark raving mad and just hadn't been tranquilized yet and come to in a narcotized state in a mental institution. Maybe if she could feel the power, the erotic urgency of that love, she would understand why Nadia had risked her life for it. She had felt Raymond's lips on hers, and even if they weren't on hers the way they had no doubt been on Nadia's, she had felt them.

A valet took Emily's car without the same gleam of lechery they had thrown at Nadia, but then Emily, in T-shirt and cords, wasn't in heels and her lips weren't a glistening red, and she wasn't exuding the lust Nadia must have when she roared up in her Ford Falcon Futura in a flamboyant cloud of dust, Emily liked to imagine, to meet her lover, who had checked in earlier, undoubtedly under a pseudonym.

Emily checked in at the front desk and followed a yellow-lit hallway with saffron-splashed walls to a bottom floor room with a sliding glass door that faced out to a courtyard edged by palm trees circumscribing a lawn where shadows of the palms swayed gently against the neon-green grass. And no one. Not even a maintenance worker or a housekeeper.

Emily slumped wearily onto the bed with her laptop and made landfall with the hotel's internet. She logged in to her university account and wrote an email to Jean explaining she was taking the next day off because she wasn't feeling well, but that the West finding aid only needed a few more tweaks with the abstract and it would be finished and ready to go live.

She closed her laptop and threw a forearm over her eyes and lay back on the plush pillows, sapped of strength, physical and moral, dreading being all alone in the world. The convolutions since she first opened that Pandora's box of digital correspondence between Nadia and Raymond had drained her of all her will to fight. She wasn't sure where she was anymore. She wanted to be a pelican soaring along the cliff. Food. Sex. Something primordially simple. Not this booming drumbeat of tortured love and its malignant repercussions.

She tried to find refuge in sleep, hoping it would halt her encroaching sense of disorientation and rudderlessness. Her brain chewed on the marrow of her ontological worth until she dropped into the void of dreams. She dreamed . . .

CHAPTER 23

The Law of the Land

10/22/18

I dreamt of Nadia and Raymond and their lovemaking. I feel haunted by them.

I'm all alone. Called in sick. Joel thinks I should just drop it, but I can't. Not with what I know. I can't prove anything definitively.

I feel vulnerable. Unprotected.

Emily pressed the red button on her Voice Memos app. She knew where it was without looking for it.

A knock at the door momentarily startled her. Through the security eyepiece she saw that it was room service and opened the door. Coffee and a breakfast of scrambled eggs and bacon came rolling into her room on a white-cloth trolley. She signed for it and closed the door behind the young man who brought it. She checked her email. Her heart skipped a beat when she saw one from Detective Taggart agreeing to meet her at Estancia at 2:00 p.m.

In her carry-on she had brought Nadia's personal file, the one she had found at the Annex. There were some grainy photos in it that she didn't think meant anything when she first came upon them. They were photos of the man she believed was the one following her in the gray Volvo SUV. She compared them to the screenshots of the security video that Jorge had given her. It was difficult to compare the faces because of the shadowy light and the indistinct images and find similarities. But she noticed something glinting in the collar of the mock turtleneck. The logo of the clothing brand she noticed a tiny metallic, winged mythological creature and it gleamed unmistakably in all of the photos in an identifying pinpoint of light.

Storm clouds were gathering in the sky when Emily corkscrewed into her Mini and the valet closed the door gently on her. She tipped him five dollars and drove off out of the circular drive, feeling a little bit like she was retracing Nadia's trysting past.

With the low-pressure system overhead, the ocean churned with gray waters and jagged whitecaps. The local surfers had seen the forecast online and stayed home. The birds were hunkered down in the lagoon, waiting for more favorable conditions to prey. To the east the low-lying hills were shrouded in cloud cover, lending them a mythological appearance.

Emily stopped at Bird Rock Coffee to get a real cup of coffee and collect her thoughts. While the barista made her pour-over she checked emails on her cell. Helena had written, expressed congratulations things were wrapping up on West, and forwarded her the announcement on the Eighth Floor Gala. The photo of Raymond West on the news link was not the man she had met the day before. He was smiling that tight-lipped smile of irony. He looked impossibly handsome in the unbuttoned white shirt and black linen coat, hair tumbling youthfully to his shoulders. Nothing at all like the broken man who had staggered out of the accident at Adobe Guadalupe, his life in escalatory turmoil. The accompanying picture of Elizabeth didn't match with him. Helena, arm hooked around Elizabeth's waist, with her silver-and-black, two-toned hairdo, made for an incongruous trifecta of mystery.

Emily got her Ethiopian pour-over in a to-go cup and climbed back in her car. She drove past the lagoon, swung right at the corner where her apartment complex was, didn't notice anything suspicious, then gunned up the steep incline of Del Mar Heights Road.

The PostalAnnex+ that served as the mailing address for Seymor's Catering was in the Del Mar Plaza, sandwiched in a large strip mall of shops—the usual Southern California fare: Rite-Aid, a dry cleaner's, a Thai restaurant . . .

Emily stepped out of her car and strolled inside the PostalAnnex+.

Almost the entire wall to her right was occupied with uniformly sized brass PO boxes. Behind a counter in the center, a woman of Indian descent was engulfed in stacks of packages, absorbed in getting them all sorted and into the proper shipping containers. Emily approached her.

"Excuse me. I have this address for Seymour's Catering," she said, feigning naiveté.

The Indian woman looked up and smiled. She pointed to the bank of post office boxes. "Probably one of them," she indicated.

"Oh, I'm so dumb," Emily said, "I thought I could pop in and sit down with somebody and go over an event I'm supposed to help cater."

The proprietor was not shy about divulging her intuition. "Frankly, Miss, a lot of those people up there don't really exist as who they claim to be. If they show me a business card with a business name, then that's what I write down when I rent them the box. As long as they pay the monthly."

Emily leaned her backside against the counter and gazed up at the post office boxes. "You ever see this Seymour guy come in?" Emily said to the bronze mail slots.

"I see them," replied the proprietor. "They mostly come, get their mail, and go without so much as a hello."

Emily rooted a rectangle of paper from her back jeans pocket, unfolded it, and laid it on the desk next to the proprietor's postal scale. "Do you recognize this man?"

The woman picked up the piece of paper and squinted at it with failing eyesight. She shrugged. "I don't know. Maybe. Can't place him."

Emily leaned forward on her elbows: "Have the police ever been in here asking about him?"

The woman set the picture down and grinned excitedly. "Why? Is he wanted for something?"

"He might be," Emily said enigmatically.

"What are you? Some kind of private investigator?"

"I'm becoming one. This guy owes a client a ton of money."

The woman laughed. "Half of them up there are probably running from something. That wall's for the wanted, and the unwanted," she chuckled. "I just rent them the boxes if they've got a credit card. I don't ask questions."

Emily retrieved the photo, refolded it, and wriggled it into her back pocket. "Thank you."

Emily drove back down Del Mar Heights in the direction of the ocean. As she crested the hill the ocean bloomed up in her windshield, windblown and angry. The sky mushroomed with black and gray clouds. She parked on the street and cautiously approached her apartment complex through the narrow alley. Stopping below the pool, Emily tented her forehead with a flattened hand and looked up two flights of stairs to her apartment. The unit seemed to be repudiating her existence. It was as if she had died inside there and now her ghost was coming back to conduct the postmortem. Now that she had been violated twice there, she didn't know if she could ever return.

With a feeling of dread hovering above her like the foreboding storm clouds over the tumultuous ocean, Emily drove back to the hotel.

With a couple hours to kill before her appointment with Taggart, Emily opened her laptop and googled news and press releases on Regents University's Town & Gown events to promote Memorial Library's Special Collections & Archives. Images of Regents' own magazine with Helena Blackwell, Elizabeth West, other faculty and luminaries of the university—the Chancellor, various deans and chairs comprising a multitude of departments—filled the screen in a quilt of photos. Scrolling forever, Emily finally came to a publicity release about a La Jolla Town & Gown event to celebrate Elizabeth West and the announcement that Raymond West's papers had been donated to the library. Swiping swiftly from one web page to another, Emily froze on the announcement: "Town & Gown Event Postponed." Emily backtracked and double-checked the picture of the check Helena had handed the man presumably named Seymour in the closed stacks. The date on the check was mere weeks before the postponed event.

In an introspective silence, Emily sat alone in a cushioned metal chair at an outdoor table at Estancia's Mustangs & Burros, an indoor/outdoor hacienda-style casual restaurant. Her coffee cup clanked in its porcelain saucer. She glanced through the wide-open windows toward the alfresco bar. Shutting her eyes, she tried to imagine Nadia's excitement, her exultation, as she detoured in to fortify herself with a glass of wine and wait for Raymond's text. That penultimate moment of anticipation, knowing soon you would be swept up into another world, carried off, pinwheeling away in the arms of your lover. Emily had never come close to feeling what Nadia felt in that moment.

Heavy footfalls crunched on the gravel and Emily rose Polaris-like out of her reverie to meet her mind's opposite: Detective Taggart. He was wearing a fitted blue shirt with cuff links, open at the collar. His black hair, flecked with gray, glinted in the sunlight like specks of mica. From his large face and cocked head, he wore what Emily construed as an exasperated smile.

"Hello, Ms. Snow," he barked with a gravelly voice, less cordial than the last time they met.

"Detective." She stood and reached an arm across the table. He took her small, delicate hand in his, held it without shaking as if afraid he would tear her arm from its shoulder socket, let go, then fit himself into the too-small metal chair.

"Nice shirt," Emily complimented.

"Thanks. Wife gave it to me for our anniversary. One of those designer ones," he added, fingering its soft cotton. He craned his heavy head to the sky. "Looks like the first winter storm is coming early," he remarked.

Emily traveled with his gaze. "Yeah," she said. "Looks like it." She dropped her eyes back to him.

His face fell with gravity back to the table. He blinked his heavy-lidded eyes.

Their server materialized, a bubbly cheerful woman about Emily's age.

"Can I get you something?"

"Coffee," Taggart grunted.

"Sugar and cream?"

"The whole thing."

"And you're doing okay, Miss?"

"I'm fine," Emily said. She'd already had too much coffee and was teetering on the precipice of an anxiety attack. As the server left, Emily looked up at Taggart. "Thanks for agreeing to meet with me a second time."

"What have you got for me?" he said, getting right to the point.

Emily scrounged in her purse and produced a manila folder with the printouts from Jorge and Nadia's cell phone pictures she had hidden in the dark archives as evidence. Taggart jerked them out and flipped through them skeptically. He paused and looked up when he was interrupted by the server. From a small tray she set down coffee, cream, and sugar. She turned to Emily:

"Do you want me to put this on your room?"

Emily colored red. "Uh, no, uh, I'll just pay," she stammered.

The server smiled and left.

Taggart looked at Emily with a tilted head. "You're staying in the hotel? May I inquire why?"

Emily leaned across the table to underscore she was serious when she said, "My apartment was broken into. I'm being followed." She stabbed a finger at the pictures. "By that guy."

After a long moment, Taggart withdrew his eyes from Emily and returned to the photos with deepening interest. He paused at one in particular. He turned it so it faced Emily. It was the printout of the check for $30,000 to Seymour's Catering. "Who's Seymour?"

"The event that was for was canceled," Emily said in a hurried, overexcited voice. "The money was for something else."

"What?" barked Taggart.

"Seymour's Catering doesn't exist. It's a PO box," Emily explained in triumph.

"Okay," he drawled circumspectly. He scratched the side of his face as if sowing the seed of a thought.

"This man who was in the library is also the man who was following my predecessor, Nadia." Emily stabbed an erect forefinger at one of Nadia's pictures. "She took those last November."

"Where'd you get this?" he asked skeptically.

"I'm not at liberty to say," Emily replied, realizing her mistake immediately.

"I see," said Taggart. "Not even *on condition of anonymity*?" he asked sardonically, letting her infer his time was being wasted if she didn't offer something additional to substantiate her allegations. Taggart picked up his coffee cup and continued to leaf through the documents with increasingly disbelieving eyes. "If what you say is true, what is he looking for?"

"A book," Emily replied.

"A book," he mocked. "I see. I take it a valuable book."

"In the wrong hands," Emily answered ambiguously. "Yes."

Taggart nodded with deepening doubt.

"I'd like you to run a background check on this guy," Emily said, stabbing her index finger at the photo of the man in the black turtleneck.

"Don't need to," said Taggart into his coffee. "I know him."

"You *know* him?" Emily asked, her small head now halfway across the table.

"Richard Seymour. He's a private investigator. Used to be one of us." He set down his cup of coffee in its saucer. "Went rogue on one too many cases. Had to early retire him."

Emily took out a picture she had taken of the block lettering on the envelope and set it on the table. "That's what he left on my doorstep."

Taggart glanced at it. "I get that. What's in the envelope?" Emily looked off, weighing her answer. "First class tickets to Paris?" he asked, his insolence flaring.

"No," Emily said, angry.

"Something to blackmail you with?" Taggart growled with sarcasm, in hope it would shake loose a real answer from Emily and not all this oblique circumambulation of the truth.

"I need protection, Detective. I'm scared." Their eyes locked. Taggart could tell she was serious, but he was still mistrustful.

"I need to know what's in that envelope before I authorize a detail to watch you here in your beautiful spa hotel," he shot back cynically.

"Nadia Fontaine . . ." she began but trailed off, worried about divulging too much.

"The one who drowned and whose death you're obsessed with?" he finished her sentence for her.

Anger fired her. "She and Raymond West were having a reckless love affair. But it wasn't just, you know . . ."

"Hot sex?" interjected Taggart.

"No. It was a deep love connection nobody knew about."

"Except you?"

"Yes," said Emily. "The correspondence between them that I found is explicit, very detailed . . ."—she brought a hand to her mouth—"And heartbreaking."

"That no one else has ever seen I bet?"

Emily nodded guiltily, then lapsed into silence, incanting to herself to stay calm.

"I get it," said Taggart, "they were in love. A professor and his student."

"A novelist and an archivist, who happened to be archiving his papers," she corrected him caustically.

Taggart shrugged as if it were incidental to him.

Emily didn't like him mocking her. "They were more than in love. They were collaborating on a book together. And it was . . . personal."

"And this is the book that's so valuable?"

Emily was desperate for someone to believe her, someone who had the power to bring about the vindication she sought. "Elizabeth West, Raymond's wealthy wife, is donating twenty-five million to the library, and they're rechristening it in her name. Her husband's archive is the cherry on the top. If she found out about the affair, that donation would be in serious jeopardy of being withdrawn."

"No doubt," Taggart chuckled. "But she did find out."

"She found out some things. But not everything. Things that I've personally discovered."

Taggart's professional curiosity kindled a flicker of interest. He took a sip of coffee. "For instance?"

"When Nadia was fired, she threatened to go public with certain extremely sensitive documents, in hopes of saving her job. And reputation."

"Which was shot. And Elizabeth West, through Ms. Blackwell, hired a private eye to follow her and threaten her?" Taggart finished her speculation for her.

"No." Emily waited until his eyes coupled again with hers. "To murder her."

"Mrs. West?" he scoffed and shook his head.

"Hear me out, Detective." Emily waited until Taggart was steadied. "Helena Blackwell. This library is her legacy. That twenty-five-million-dollar gift was everything she had been working toward her whole life. West's affair with Nadia jeopardized a life's ambition to transform that library." Emily flung an arm in the direction of the library across the street, but which they couldn't see. "That library is everything to her."

"It's still a giant leap to murder, Ms. Snow." He jabbed a finger at the photos. "These photos, I assume, were taken from the security video at the library?"

"Yes," said Emily.

"So, they're the property of university security?"

"Technically," Emily admitted guiltily, realizing how deep she was digging the hole in promoting her version, her suspicion, of the truth.

"How'd you obtain them?"

Emily met Taggart with a cold stare, refusing to answer.

"That's what I figured." Taggart dropped both elbows down on the table, rattling the flatware. "Do you know how prominent a defense attorney Mrs. West and Ms. Blackwell—if what you're alleging has any credibility—can bring in?" He lifted up the raft of photos and slapped them down on the table for emphasis. "Any judge in San Diego would rule this inadmissible and the case would be thrown out and I'd look like a fucking horse's ass. Now, if I had served a search warrant . . ." He looked away and shook his head in manifest disgust.

"Only you and I know," offered Emily meekly.

Taggart jerked his head at her. "And the head of security, who printed these out and gave them to you! Who, for a price, will come in and make us look like liars, extortionists." Emily had stirred up something turbid in Taggart and she could see vestiges of it resurgent. But his whole being resisted it. He spoke through steepled hands: "I'm not about to perjure myself in an internal affairs investigation, Ms. Snow, even if there are some suspicious things in here! Then guess what? I go to where I put people: a federal penitentiary! And after the civil trial all I've got left is a Social Security check!" he finished rebukingly.

Chastised, Emily's eyes strayed to a fountain that gurgled peacefully, as if mocking her frustration. She pursed her lips in apparent defeat. She wanted to go somewhere and be alone and weep uncontrollably for the injustice of it all.

"I can't even show these photos to Seymour because they were illegally obtained. He's a former cop, Ms. Snow. He may be reckless, he may be working in the gray, but he's not stupid."

"He's Helena Blackwell's accomplice. Don't you get it? She needed to get rid of Nadia and he did her dirty work," Emily countered.

Impatient, Taggart scoffed at her. "You've got one wild imagination."

Resignation fell over Emily's face like a shroud of existential defeat. Taggart glanced furtively at his watch, annoyed.

"I should be at the beach with my kids."

Emily nodded, feeling even more desolate than ever. It was a hotel, a cup of coffee, and then blackness.

"I'd still like to see the blackmail items in the envelope, *whoever* left it on your doorstep. If you brought them." Taggart laid his hand open, palm to the sky, and held it there like an invitation to surrender evidence. With a painful feeling of humiliation rising in her, but knowing the truth had to be transparent if she had any hope of him believing her, she risked giving him the stills taken with the telephoto lens. Reluctantly, Emily spread open her purse and produced the envelope. She pushed it across the table to Taggart. She had nothing to lose now. Humiliation had already been supplanted by nobody believing her.

Taggart examined the photos indifferently, slowly shuffling through them, one by one. He wore the expression of a man who had lost all faith in humanity, a man who had once again been duped by another conniving, manipulative woman seeking revenge. He raised the photo of Emily and Raymond kissing, her face slightly obscured. Shaking his head with disgust, he said, "That's you, I presume?"

"Yes . . ." Emily admitted with a sinking feeling.

"And the man is . . . ?" asked Taggart.

"Raymond West."

Taggart nodded as if he already knew the answer to his next question and continued to slowly progress from one character-discrediting photo to the next. When he got back to the first one, he started over again, as if still in a state of incredulity. He held up the one that showed Emily's head out of the frame with Raymond's hand resting on top of her head. Consolingly, to Emily. Amorously pushing her down on his groin, to Taggart. "You know, Ms. Snow, I wish I had not stopped at my master's in criminology and gotten my PhD in literature." He shook his head disgustedly. "In our investigation, you know what I discovered?" Taggart leaned across the table threateningly. "Relations between an archivist and a donor are unethical. Cause for immediate dismissal."

"That's not what happened," Emily snarled, knowing she had nothing to add that would substantiate her claim. "This Seymour's trying to blackmail me for those notebooks."

Taggart didn't want to hear about notebooks, literature, love, or dark archives anymore. He slapped the photos down on the envelope and slid the incriminating items across the table back to Emily. "I appreciate your honesty, Ms. Snow. I have to admit, a part of me thinks you're off your rocker and a part of me thinks maybe you've gotten a little too close to this project and spun all these fanciful scenarios because you've seen too many TV crime dramas. Did it ever occur to you that maybe Mr. West's wife isn't concerned her husband is a serial philanderer?"

"We were comforting each other," Emily desperately tried to explain the compromising photos. "It's been an epically long journey for both of us," she said to the blank wall of a jaded, professionally skeptical cop. "I would hope you could see beyond it."

Taggart exploded. " Beyond it? Beyond *what*? I deal in facts. Admissible evidence. That's how I build a case and present it to the DA. I don't traffic in literary romance and the soap opera narrative of somebody's imagination."

Emily jutted out her jaw and tried hard to avert a breakdown. Taggart slammed back his coffee and pushed himself back from the table and rose noisily from his chair.

"You're a young woman, Ms. Snow. I trust you have a bright career ahead of you." He pointed at the envelope with the photos. "Those get out, I'm guessing that career isn't so bright anymore. But then, I'm not in the archival profession." Taggart planted both hands on the table and leaned balefully into Emily's face. "Nadia Fontaine was burned by a famous writer who wanted dirty sex. Ms. Blackwell or Mrs. West hired Seymour to figure out what was going on. Like you said—and I agree—they both had a lot at stake. Nadia was pregnant, had lost her job, her husband knew and had a cow. That would send a lot of people spiraling into a suicidal depression. And that's what we privately ruled it. But for the sake of the university—one of the city's biggest employers—and, yes, Elizabeth West, we called it an accidental drowning to save egos and protect reputations. Okay?" He brandished a finger at Emily. "And, yeah, less than one percent of women commit suicide by drowning, but this woman was an exception to the rule." He shook his finger reproachfully. "Now they're warning you through my old buddy Seymour not to go mucking around in this. My advice: heed their warning."

Emily smiled at him with bared lips of contempt.

Taggart stabbed the pictures with the knife of his index finger. "I'll pretend I never saw these. For your sake."

"I didn't have sex with him in the car," she cried in frustration.

Taggart picked up one of the close-ups of the two of them kissing passionately, in need of each other, and shook it in her face. "Tell that to a jury," he said in an ugly tone of contempt. He flipped the photo cavalierly back onto the table. "And if you did come across that book and are holding out, I suggest you return it to its rightful owner. Otherwise, I'm going to have you arrested for theft."

Emily glowered at him.

"We know about the ER visit for, what was it? Panic attack? Nervous breakdown?" Emily's mouth fell open. "People are watching you, Ms. Snow. And apparently for good reason. I don't know what your game is here, little lady, but it looks to me like you're just some jealous little whore."

"Don't gaslight me, Detective!" Something snapped in Emily and she jerked her cup of coffee up at him in a violent flinging motion, and it splattered on his wedding anniversary shirt, Rorschaching it brown. He glanced down at it like it wasn't the first time he had been assaulted and flicked his hand at the stain.

"I'm sorry," apologized Emily.

"You'd better hope you don't end up institutionalized. Good day, Ms. Snow." Taggart waddled off, shaking his head in total incomprehension at the world Emily had vomited up at him. Emily wrapped her arms around her chest and withdrew from the world as if shielding some malignant grief.

Distraught, Emily slinked back to her room, battling in vain the inevitable floodgate of tears. She threw herself spread-eagled on the bed and wept violently. When she was all cried out, she flipped over and lay on the bed staring at the ceiling, debating her next move. In resurrecting the past, she had disinterred buried retributions and paved-over crimes, without intending to. They had come to her, unwittingly, whispered, through the treasure map to tragedy Nadia had left. Nadia, who seemed to intuit something mortally consequential was going to befall her. Thus, the bread crumbs to the truth. Emily was the savior Nadia had yearned for when all seemed lost. And now she felt like she had failed her.

At a total loss as to what to do next, cursing herself for having ever traveled out to the dark archives, Emily fled the claustrophobia of the hotel room and hiked to the nearby Gliderport. She bought a bottled sparkling water and parked herself at one of the picnic benches and watched the paragliders filling their chutes with wind, then stutter-stepping to the cliff and leaping off. Every time they leaped into the void they would momentarily disappear from view, then the onshore wind would balloon their chutes and hoist them up into the sky where they banked, like human pelicans, and began soaring along the cliffs.

Day bled into dusk. Emily unfolded herself from the picnic bench as the sun fell to the horizon in a blazing orange orb. As the wind subsided, the paragliders started wheeling in from the darkening sky and landing in an exhausted heap of imploding paragliding gear.

Emily ate alone at Prepkitchen in Del Mar. She didn't feel like making small talk with the waiter and kept her answers short, her eyes focused on her menu when she spoke.

Out of habit, she cruised by her apartment complex, but she didn't feel like she lived there anymore. She was deathly afraid to go inside. Two-and-a-half months had seemed like two years. She missed Onyx, but she decided to stay in the hotel until the Gala, and then leave San Diego for—where? She didn't know. Austin, Texas, and the Harry Ransom Center, if she accepted the project archivist job Professor Erickson had recently floated? If she stopped now, she deliberated, she could get out of this potentially unscathed. There was still the matter of the Moleskines, though, radioactively aglow in a safe deposit box in a bank somewhere in sleepy La Jolla.

On an impulse, Emily wended her way down to Isla Negra. She parked at the top of Little Orphan Alley and climbed out of her car. The air was redolent of the sea. Waves exploded like gunshots in the distance. She walked down the quiet street on the opposite side from Isla Negra. As she approached the cul-de-sac, her heart quickened. Raymond's Range Rover was parked in the driveway. Yellow light glowed through the curtains pulled closed against the windows. Where before it was cast in dormancy, now it seemed to have warmed back to life, however feebly.

Emboldened, Emily clambered across the concrete culvert to the top tier of the bluff. The surf roared in her ears. She walked until she was opposite the sliding glass door where Raymond's writing desk was situated. In the murky light it was difficult to see inside, but she thought she could make out the husked silhouette of a man coming and going once from the desk.

Emily picked her way back across the culvert and skulked up on to the planked deck with quiet steps. A gust of wind rose up and the umbrella of palm fronds clattered in warning. Emily stood away at an angle, hands gripping the rough trunk of one of the palms, hiding behind it. Inside, Raymond could be seen sitting at his writing slope, but he was a different Raymond. Next to him was a fifth of tequila and a shot glass. He refilled and drank from it like someone playing a slot machine. Pen poised in hand, he seemed to be poring over pages staring back up at him.

Emily moved around the palm and edged closer, angling in from the side. She stopped when she reached the frame of the window and peered inside with prying eyes. A stack of pages rested on the writing slope. Raymond, it appeared, was scribbling marginalia like a possessed madman revising a manifesto or a lecture he had to deliver tomorrow, or . . . had he gone back to *The Archivist*? From Emily's vantage point she couldn't make out whether it was a screenplay or prose. From the lusty way he swung back and forth from the pen to the bottle she believed it must have been the screenplay. At one point, he lowered his forehead to the pages in what appeared to be a paroxysm of despair. Struck dumb by his presence, Emily almost thought she was hallucinating him bent over his writing slope.

Suddenly he pushed back the chair in a violent motion, stood bolt upright, and stepped forward to the sliding glass door. Emily quickly backed away into the hedges that ringed the decking and huddled out of sight. Over the tops of the prickly leaves Emily made out Raymond staggering out onto the patio. He staggered in place, facing the sound of a relentless surf beating against the cliffs and a moon traveling spookily through storm clouds. The unmistakable paced clanging of an approaching train rose in volume. Its headlight sprayed the train tracks below. At the moment it passed, as if Raymond had glimpsed something terrible in his mind, he screamed in unison with the roar of the passing train. He screamed in a primitive howl of pain like an animal that had been shot and was struggling mightily for its last few steps before toppling to the ground.

Emily knew whom the anguished cries were for. They were both trapped in what they couldn't bring to the surface: Nadia. He had tried. Then circumstances had conspired against him as if driven by some malevolent design to keep the two of them apart forever. Emily had tried. She had done everything she could, but no one believed her. Maybe Nadia had drowned. Maybe Nadia had committed suicide. Maybe Raymond didn't even know.

Driven half-mad by the darkness, Raymond hugged his chest, nothing on the horizon coming to pardon his grief. All alone on the planked deck, he looked like a man who had come to the end of a life wrecked by destiny, at the place where once his future burned with infinite hope. Peering into the darkness, he appeared to be charting where his love affair with Nadia had shipwrecked. Emily's instinct was to rush to him and console him, but she didn't want him to think she was spying on him. His anguished, unintelligible braying was palpable, and it rent her heart. The two of them, the only two who knew the real story, were here alone in the night with the pounding surf.

Seized with feeling, she impulsively decided to go to him—damn what he might think of her!—but was halted by car headlights coming down the alley. From the side of the house she could make out a car wheeling into the driveway and disappearing from view. Paralyzed with fear, Emily crouched lower.

Raymond jackknifed forward, hands planted on his knees, and screamed again. It was the howl of a man drunk out of his mind, oblivious of the world, dredging a pain he had kept bottled up inside him, but whose venting seemed to only inflame its anguish out of its quiescence.

Emily heard a woman's voice against the crashing surf. "Ray! Come inside."

Raymond whipped violently around and flung his head in the direction of the voice, loose-limbed like an animal mortally pierced by an arrow. "Leave me alone, Liz!"

The woman stepped out onto the deck. A beautiful woman in black slacks and a fuchsia blouse, her helmet of hair a blown tumbleweed on her head. "Ray. Come on."

"Leave me alone," he shrieked at her as if she were standing three times farther away than she was.

Elizabeth rested a hand on his shoulder to comfort him, but he brushed it aside. He staggered forward on uncertain legs to the edge of the deck. He teetered for a moment like he might fall.

"I'm tired of being your trained monkey," Raymond bellowed. "You've colonized my unconscious! You've infantilized me!"

"Come inside, Ray, you're drunk."

Emily backed away. To witness Elizabeth out on the patio, the wind whipping her hair, not all regal like at her home in La Jolla, her face lined with worry, trying to corral a brilliant, troubled, and wayward husband, it felt disjointed. Emily was eavesdropping on a marriage that had taken a fatal turn to dissolution.

When she reached the street, she could still hear the rise and fall of the viscerally personal quarrel. She strode up Little Orphan Alley, guilty that she, and she alone, had brought it all on. A gray tabby stopped in the middle of the street, a frog writhing in her jaws, her green eyes burning holes in the night. Emily shuddered. Then the cat darted off.

CHAPTER 24

Truth Is the Final Residue of All Beings

11/1/18

I have seen the truth, and it's engraved with lies.

Emily knew she had fallen into a state of black depression because the red badge on her Gmail app displayed double-digit unanswered emails. She wasn't ready to leave the hotel and return to her apartment. It was expensive, but she needed the anonymity, its refuge. Like Raymond and his Isla Negra, she rationalized.

Emily crossed the street and walked through throngs of university students in the direction of the looming Memorial Library. Billowy black-and-gray clouds burgeoned in the sky. The rain wasn't there yet, but it was coming.

An inexplicable quiet greeted Emily when she walked, with bowed head, into Special Collections. As she smiled a hi to Samantha at the reference desk, she noticed Helena's office door was closed and the blinds were drawn shut.

She settled into the desk chair in her cubicle. Nicola had done as he was instructed and had hauled away the empty West boxes and disposed of them, so her shelves were nearly empty. Ignoring her computer, she eyed in stupefaction her cubicle's emptiness. Raymond's demoralizing animalistic cries haunted her, and she could hear their suffering yowling echoing in her imagination. It comforted her to know he missed Nadia. Emily was sure he missed her more than life itself.

"Knock, knock."

Emily swiveled her head without dropping her feet from the desk where they were propped and threw Chloe a backward glance.

"Hi, stranger," Chloe said.

"Hi, Chloe."

"How're you feeling? Better?"

Emily didn't answer. She glanced away from Chloe, wanting to be left alone. "Is Helena out for the day?" she asked in an undertone.

"Out for the week." Chloe spun an imaginary lasso. "Traveling. Giving talks. New York. Chicago. Seattle. Won't be back until the day of the big gala."

Emily's eyes narrowed at the information. What she knew and what Chloe didn't, and never would, know remained unexpressed.

"Some of us here in the department would like to take you to lunch before you leave," Chloe offered. "Do you know where you're going next?"

Emily shook her head, as if she didn't care, as if life had no meaning anymore. Then, fearing the gossip in Chloe, Emily tossed her another backward look, this time accompanied with a forced smile. "Let me know when. Text me."

"Okay. Great." She lingered for a moment. "You okay?" Emily nodded, deep in thought, neurotically pinching lips with thumb and index finger. "You look sad." Emily didn't say anything. "End of a project blues, I guess," Chloe commiserated.

Emily could feel Chloe's eyes dawdling on her for a moment before she heard footsteps. Once they were out of earshot, she picked herself up from the desk and walked down the corridor to Joel's cubicle.

He tore his headphones off when he sensed her presence. "Emily?" He rose from his chair, an anxious look lengthening his face. "Are you all right? I've been trying to reach you."

"I'm fine."

"Where've you been?"

"How's Onyx?" Emily asked.

"Fine. I like him."

"Don't get too attached."

Joel smirked

"I took him to a vet and turns out he isn't microchipped. So, he's mine."

"That's nice. I'm glad. You could use an emotional support animal."

"Ha-ha."

"So, the big Gala is this weekend."

"Yeah," said Emily unenthusiastically.

"Have you seen the eighth floor?"

"Not recently, no," Emily replied.

"You should check it out."

Emily nodded detachedly.

"You look depressed?"

"Don't you get depressed when a project's done?" Emily asked.

"I try to stay emotionally uninvolved."

"There's never been one like this," Emily lamented.

Joel nodded understandingly. "Let's go surfing. Take your mind off everything."

"I'll think about it."

"Are you back in your apartment?" Emily shook her head. "It was probably a random break-in, but still . . ."

Emily gazed inward, wondering if Joel wasn't right after all. And Detective Taggart. And . . .

During her lunch break, Emily climbed the spiral stairs to the eighth floor. Her thighs were burning when she reached the upper landing. She stepped over yellow caution tape and opened the door to the eighth floor. She found herself in a large, cleared-out area that only twenty-five million dollars could have transformed so opulently. The floors were retiled in a gleaming polished terrazzo. Ceilings were hung with dazzling chandeliers. Brocaded curtains had replaced the cheap sun-yellowed blinds. The dated wooden study carrels had all been removed and refurnished with beautifully upholstered lounge chairs. The rows and rows of gray metal shelving that had stored books for over half a century had been hauled off and all four rectangular areas flowed in 90-degree angles into one another and seemed to broaden out to the infinitude of the vast university that stretched before Emily in a spectacular 360-degree view. The irony that she was on the top floor of one of the most recognizable and revered libraries in the world and it no longer held a single book wasn't lost on her. The symbolic meaning of the abandonment of books punched her in the gut in a visceral way. What was her future in this changing world?

Emily circumnavigated the transformed top floor of Memorial Library in a daze around the enormous concrete central tower shaft that housed the elevator and stairwell. A hurly-burly of construction workers came and went, banging ladders, pushing carts, lugging equipment, working frenetically to finish. Along the north-facing windows Emily came to a stop at a bank of archival display cases she had seen empty before, the panes of glass dancing with the sun's reflection. She gazed down into them, her face diaphanously superimposed over the items laid in the black-papered wells like a palimpsest. Beautifully mounted were manuscript pages and photographs and other memorabilia from the West Papers. In her absence, she realized with a pang of shock, Helena and Jean had wrested control of its finalization. Emily recognized several of the items she had pulled from the collection, but there were others—more maudlin, more celebratory of the West marriage—that made Emily realize that, with a bow to conservatism, Special Collections had succeeded in bowdlerizing Raymond West the artist.

"Hi, Emily," an older man's voice spoke.

Emily whirled around, relieved when she saw it was Verlander. He was attired professionally in a brown coat and yellow button-down shirt. His amiable smile suggested he bore no ill will toward her, was likely oblivious of the personal turmoil that had generated so much suffering and formed the cyclone that had brought everything, finally, to this eighth-floor exaltation of Memorial Library.

"Hello, David," Emily said.

"The display cases look nice, don't they?" he complimented. "You did a terrific job." He gazed around the remodeled north wing. "For four decades I've come up here and it looked one way. Now, look at it."

"Don't you miss the books?" Emily asked.

"I guess it's a sign of the times," he bemoaned. "Soon, it'll all be digital." He opened his arms histrionically like a Baptist preacher. "In the cloud!"

He dropped his eyes to hers. "Except in Special Collections. Some things will never change."

Emily nodded. Her eyes roamed the items in the display case absently. She realized her job had come to an end. It was as if *The Archivist*—and Nadia—had never existed. They had successfully whitewashed her from the library's memory, erased all traces of her. To Emily, her spirit still streamed like a fog through the campus buildings, but to history, the history of this magnificent library to which Nadia had sacrificed twelve years of her life, she had been coldly expunged. She had paid the ultimate price for love.

"Quite a career," Verlander said. "Too bad about the Nobel being postponed this year. Still, he's young. It'll come around again."

"Yeah." Emily was jolted back to the kiss with Raymond.

Verlander looked up from the display cases and said in a mischievous change of tone, "How was the Vindas, by the way?"

Emily frowned with a puzzled look.

"*Le Rêve d'un Flagellant.*"

Emily blushed. "Oh, pretty racy," she said. Then, remembering her lie, "I guess my friend really liked it."

Verlander started to turn. "Coming down?"

Emily shook her head with a bleak smile.

"I guess I'll see you at the Gala before you head off."

Emily kept nodding, a chasmal emptiness faulting inside her.

Verlander turned to go, stopped and gave her a backward look. "Whatever happened to that unfinished book of Raymond's you were looking for? *The . . .* ?"

"*The Archivist,*" Emily said.

"That's the one. Did you ever find it?"

"No," said Emily. "Must have been another one of his abandoned projects."

Emily listened to Verlander's leather-soled heels click against the new terrazzo flooring and retreat around the corner. She shut her eyes when the elevator signaled, *bing bing*, that the car had arrived to take him down. She opened them when quiet had taken possession of the vast eighth floor again and gazed out the windows at the sky. It was darkening ominously.

A yellow moon was climbing to the east. *Le Rêve d'un Flagellant,* reflected Emily, seemed like years ago. The string-tie envelope in the back of the Clarice Lispector photo. The library card catalog card. The letter.

Back at the hotel, Emily grew restless in the room all alone. She missed Onyx, but she knew she couldn't have him for the time being. Absently, she went to the Society of American Archivists website to begin the hunt for potential jobs in the event she didn't want to return to Austin. Torpor capsized her resolve and she drifted into reverie. She reread her copy of Nadia's final handwritten letter to Raymond. A part of her wanted to replace it back in Vindas's *Le Rêve d'un Flagellant,* return full circle back to the beginning as if nothing had happened, but the book of erotica was no longer there.

Emily cast her eyes at the window. Night had fallen. A menacing palm had sketched its shadow on the curtain like a giant, carnivorous starfish swimming in some Grimm's fairytale threatening to snatch her away and pull her deeper into the ocean than she ever wanted to sink. Emily had an idea. Maybe it would end the torture of what she knew but couldn't prove. She would go to Black's Beach and bury the letter, bury the thumb drive—Raymond had all the Moleskine originals, and the correspondence was still in the dark archives—and maybe put the whole business to rest. A final tribute. A kiss goodbye.

Galvanized by her inspiration, Emily suddenly felt the fervency of a motivation that hoisted her out of her malaise. She gathered up a few belongings and walked out to claim her car. The valet asked her how long she would be gone, and Emily shrugged.

Emily drove slowly south on Torrey Pines Road to nearby La Jolla Farms Road. At the metal swing gate to the private road that snaked down to Black's Beach, she idled her car in Park, clambered out, and for the first time ever used Nadia's key to unlock the gate. The heavy brass lock clicked open the first try. She unbolted it from the weighty, coiled chain, swung open the gate, rolled a nearby rock with her foot to hold it in place. She drove her car onto the private road, braked, got out, relocked the gate, and coasted down the single lane asphalt road, lit only by the headlights of her Mini. In her descent, she felt more alone than ever. In her descent, she imagined she was going to where Nadia was going. The sound of the surf, detonating in the silence, portentously beckoned.

At the terminus of the private road, Emily horseshoed around the lifeguard tower and parked where the road ended at the sand. She climbed slowly, dolefully, defeatedly, out of her car. The moon had regained its bluish light as it made its ascent into the immensity of the sky where, Emily believed, history was preserved for time immemorial. The waves snapped in the darkness and then formed like the grins of enormous marine monsters before they dissipated at the shore's edge and mourned their own ending.

The soft, fine sand felt cold on Emily's bare feet as she trudged her way to the water, kicking up little flurries with each footfall, pulled by the Pacific Ocean as if it were a powerful magnet, clutching Nadia's letter to Raymond in one hand, and the thumb drive in the other. The tide was resurgent, and it was a short walk to where the waves had spent themselves. Emily knelt in the cold sand, inches from the surging seawater. The ocean reeked of rotting kelp. She closed her eyes and images of Nadia's dead body on the news video were evoked in all their lurid horror. Maybe in a wandering daze Nadia *had* trekked all the way from Scripps Pier and walked into these dark waters of Black's. Maybe Emily, in her solitariness, had fabricated a narrative out of all proportion to reality. Crouched at the shore's edge where Nadia's body was discovered, Emily found herself drifting in doubt and self-lacerating equivocation. Taggart was right: pregnant women *did* end their lives because they didn't want their children to grow up in a world they had made a mess of.

At her feet, Emily clawed a hole in the sand with hooked fingers. She set the string-tie envelope with the catalog card in it first. Then the thumb drive, with all of Nadia's and Raymond's emails, Nadia's heartbreaking memoir, and personal photos on top in a kind of archivist's consecration in memoriam. With mortally wounded heart, she started to scoop the mound of loose sand over it. Remembering something, she paused and caressed the ouroboros necklace that dangled around her neck in Nadia's honor. She started to unclasp it, then decided against it. No, she wanted a keepsake to help her remember this tragic chapter in her life. She covered the thumb drive and envelope with sand and patted it down with the palm of her hand. Slowly, she stood. As if drawn by the mesmeric power of liberation in drowning, Emily started toward the waters, fueled by a fantasy that had been growing inside her ever since she checked into the hotel and given it her best shot with Taggart. She didn't want to return to the isolating alienation of the hotel. She couldn't go back to her apartment. A wave splashed at her knees. November now, the water was icy cold. It was numbing her feet, her calves. She stopped with the current midthigh, its force beckoning her to come with it, death the ultimate deliverer from all her suffering. She couldn't go through with it. Her suicide would be interpreted as an admission of both her guilt and her treacherous journey into Nadia's private world as conclusive proof to Taggart, and others, of her mental instability. Her suicide would empower them. She, Emily—the *temp*—would have died in ignominy. She wasn't going to give Helena, and with it the library, that false absolution.

Emily, shoulders slumped, feet freezing, turned and trudged across the sand back to her car. She climbed in. Her hand groped the passenger seat until she found the familiar shape of her cell. She tapped Voice Memos. She tapped the red button. The gray wave amplitude of the VU meter looked back at her, moving left to right in a flat line, waiting for her to speak. It jumped when she said, "The waters where you died"—she shut her eyes and tears leached from their corners—"are the waters where I'm going to redeem you." Emily bowed her head. The line went flat.

Emily sat there, eyes closed, tears quelled, lost and alone, not sure where to go, when she heard a hastening scuffling of feet. She whipped around, but not in time, it happened too fast. The back door opened and slammed shut and she felt something cold and hard pressed to the back of her head. A leather-gloved hand curled around the seat, clutched her throat, pulled her head violently back to the headrest, and stationed it immovably there with a man's strength. She struggled against the powerful hand throttling her windpipe, her legs convulsed ineffectually, but she was trapped in the intruder's grip. The cell now was between her thighs as a man's voice rasped in a threatening tone:

"Where are the notebooks? I know you have them." Emily fought the hand with both of hers, but the man had an unshakable grip on her, her neck was spasming and she was gasping for air. She could feel his arm over her shoulder, and it bulged with muscles. "You're going to take me to them. Or I'm going to put a bullet through the side of your head. And it's going to be the easiest sell of suicide to Homicide ever, given what you've done, what you've stolen, who you've been with, who you've told!"

The assailant loosened his grip on her throat, but he kept her head pinned to the backrest, immobilizing her. Emily's terrified and widened eyes shot to the rearview mirror. Her eyes had dilated to the full moon, and its light touched the tanned face of the man on the security video, the man Nadia had taken photos of, the man who had accepted the check for $30,000 from Helena: Richard Seymour. He might have been a former cop turned private investigator to Taggart, but he was also a cold-blooded contract killer.

"I don't have them," Emily wheezed, her heart beating wildly.

"Who does?" He pressed the gun into the back of her head. "I swear to fucking God I'm going to blow your head off if you don't take me to them."

"Nadia Fontaine's husband!" Emily blurted out. She wasn't sure if he believed her, if the explosion of a handgun was going to be the last sound she heard, or what lethal fate lay in store for her.

"I assume you know where that is," he growled. Emily nodded once. "Where?" he barked.

"Black Mountain Ranch," Emily uttered breathlessly.

"You've been there?" Her pulse racing, Emily nodded. "Drive me there. Now!"

Struggling for air, Emily pressed the starter. She shifted the car into reverse, backed out turning, stopped and shifted into first.

In a terrible silence, they labored up the steep incline of the private road in first gear. Glancing down, Emily noticed that Voice Memos was still recording. She knew it would go forever because one time she had fallen asleep and awakened to find that over an hour had elapsed on the timer.

When they reached the top of the private road, Seymour made her surrender the car keys and the key to the chain lock. With the muzzle of the handgun pressed to the back of her head, he forced her out of the car and told her to lie prone on the asphalt with her hands interlaced behind her head. He unlocked the gate and lurched the car through, Emily still on the ground. With a shock of her hair gripped in a callused hand, he dragged her back to the driver's-side door and roughhoused her back behind the wheel. He let go of her hair for a moment, but as soon as he was in the back seat behind her he clutched her throat in a viselike grip again and handed her the keys. She inserted them in the ignition.

"Drive," he ordered. "Let's get this over with."

She restarted the car and took off. The first parked car they passed was the gray Volvo SUV. Not having a key, he had followed her down to Black's on foot, she realized. Emily turned onto a quiet Torrey Pines Road through a green light and steered in the direction of the freeway. He relaxed his grip on her throat again, but kept the gun thrust painfully into the back of her head.

"Why do you want the notebooks?" Emily asked, the words dying in her throat.

"I don't. Someone else does. Just doing a job."

"Raymond West's wife, Elizabeth?"

He scoffed at the suggestion, but his derisive tone attested to the fact that he knew whom she was referring to.

"Helena Blackwell?"

"You know too much for a snoopy little librarian," he sneered. "Way too much." He arced the muzzle of the gun from the back of her head to her temple and then burrowed it in with a twisting motion. She audibly grimaced. "Why'd you go poking into this? Make my life a living hell. Go to the cops. What are you, psycho? You know who you're fucking with?" She could see him shake his head in disgust in the rearview mirror as the freeway lights illuminated his face intermittently.

"You followed her, didn't you?" said Emily. "You threatened her. Because she wouldn't give you the notebooks." She paused dramatically and then half turned to Seymour: "You killed Nadia Fontaine, didn't you?"

"It would have been less tragic had she just given them to me," he said. "I didn't kill anybody. She got in harm's way."

"You killed her over a work of literature," Emily accused, indignation locked in combat with fear.

"Is that what you call it?" Seymour snorted in contempt. "There were other issues," he reminded her.

"The pregnancy?"

"Shut up and keep driving. I get those notebooks, you drive out of town, I'm cool."

Emily glanced over at the glove compartment. If she closed her eyes, she could see the flashing green LED on the transponder attached to her Mini. She prayed the battery hadn't died on the tracking device Nathan had installed at Emily's behest. *If I come in your direction, there's something wrong.* And he had warily complied.

Emily angled off on the Carmel Valley Road exit and wended her way north to Vineyard Drive, the ache in the back of her skull from the pressure of the gun muzzle driving an intense fire of pain through her head.

Seymour seemed to sense they were growing closer. "If her husband is there—which I'm guessing he will be—you're going to knock and tell him you need to talk to him about something. I'll take care of it from there. If he's not there, we're going to go through that house until we find them. If you're lying to me and I don't find them, I'm going to be fucking pissed."

Emily turned into Nathan's two-car driveway. Under the house's outdoor amber floodlights, his BMW gleamed.

"I think he's here," Emily said tonelessly, shutting down her engine and switching off her headlamps.

"Get out," Seymour commanded, as he pushed down on the lever of his door.

As soon as she was out of the car, Seymour thrust the gun into the back of her head. This time he grabbed her by a shoulder with a strong, clawed grip. He half pushed Emily, as he led her to the door.

"If he panics, you're going to tell him I'm going to kill you, understand?" Seymour barked.

"Yes," answered Emily, trembling.

They scuffled to a stop at the front door. As Emily reached her hand up to touch the doorbell, a sudden rustling noise, as if a large animal had been spooked from its concealment in a bush, generated alarm. A man's voice shrieked a war cry in a rising blast at the top of his lungs. The pressure of the gun was released from the back of her head at the same moment the leather-gloved hand let go from her shoulder. Emily spun around, staggered in place, regained her balance, fought through the murky light, and tried to focus.

On the pavement, Seymour was lying with his back on top of Nathan, who had him in a paralyzing headlock. A muzzle flash of bright orange and a single gunshot rang out shrilly, reverberating loudly in the quiet neighborhood. Emily advanced on the two of them, kicked at the flailing weapon, which sailed from Seymour's outstretched hand and clattered all the way down the drive to the gutter.

"Call nine-one-one!" screamed Nathan, as he maintained his hold on Seymour, the two of them wrestling on the cement in a writhing clash of two equally matched men.

Emily quickly recovered her phone from her Mini and dialed 911. When the dispatcher came on, Emily spoke in urgent tones. "Guy with a gun! One twenty-five eleven Vineyard Drive. We've got him subdued." She listened. "No, we disarmed him. Come quickly!"

The gunshot had been heard by neighbors because lights flooded on in nearby windows, silhouetting their occupants, and Emily could already faintly hear the wail of approaching police sirens. Seymour struggled violently with Nathan, but Nadia's husband had him locked in a wrestler's half nelson, neutralizing the threat.

Two, then more, County Sheriff patrol cars converged on Nathan and Nadia's house with squealing tires. Brandishing weapons, officers disgorged from the cruisers over the neon-green lawn like military men in a video game. Emily looked at her cell. She touched the red button that ended Voice Memos. It asked her to save it as a file. She typed "Seymour Confession" and tapped Save. Tears sprang to her eyes. Everyone assumed she was crying because her life had been saved. No, because the truth had been preserved.

CHAPTER 25

Pride Goeth with the Fall

11/11/18

Back in my apartment. Onyx is here with me again. Someday I will write in more detail what happened. I gave my complete, and unadulterated, deposition to the police. The only thing I lied about was when I said I didn't know where The Archivist *Moleskines were. I don't trust the authorities with preserving the historical record. What happens next, I don't know.*

It felt strangely comforting to be back in her apartment, even if she had already started to pack. Standing at the picture window, she was confronted by storm clouds that had amassed over the ocean and were finally beginning to open up, squalling the skies and graying the view out of focus. Water began to streak the glass in downward-moving rivulets. A low-pressure system generating churning winds was bearing down over the ocean and pitching it into a fury of ragged whitecaps. Staring through the rain-blurred windows, Emily reflected on the fires and the fierce, hot Santa Ana winds that had greeted her upon her arrival at Regents Special Collections & Archives. She had come to do a job, and she had done it well, but it had left a hole widening in the pit of her stomach. Regardless of what the inquest proved, nothing would bring Nadia back. The opened-up skies seemed to be weeping for her, consoling her for the loss of someone close she had never met in person.

In the week leading up to the Eighth Floor Gala, Emily had busied herself with looking for new work. She had contacted Professor Erickson at Harry Ransom and wondered if the offer of a full-time position as an archivist in manuscripts processing when she left was still on the table. They had recently brought in the papers of a British writer of literary note and recognition, and Emily was eager to bury herself in the world of someone new.

The police and the press downplayed the arrest of Richard Seymour. The investigation of the assault of a university archivist was "ongoing," reported one local paper, but nothing definitive—no arrests, other than Seymour—had been announced. No bombshells had hit the news media. Either that, or someone wanted it handled quietly, discreetly. Then, after a few days, there appeared to ensue a news blackout of the assault on Emily.

Emily had turned over her Voice Memos recording of Seymour to the police, had given her statement in an intense interrogation with Taggart, but she didn't know where it would lead, how high up it would go, whether Seymour had acted on his own—highly unlikely—or if the investigation would end in a cul-de-sac to save the reputations of those whom it would damage most.

As the Gala neared and Emily heard nothing—not even a follow-up from Taggart—her hopes that justice would be served began to dim, then just flickered out, as if it were a fire that had never raged, leaving the bitter taste of ashes accumulating in her mouth. Nothing in the news about Seymour, Nadia Fontaine, the library, nothing. Emily tried both emailing and calling Taggart, but he had gone silent, perhaps fearing she compromised the investigation, or worse, fearing she was being deliberately kept away from it. Wanting university property back from Emily, and assaulting her at gunpoint to get it, wasn't automatically traceable back to Nadia's death, despite the evidence and powerful, if convoluted, deposition Emily had given to Taggart and the other investigators. In the ongoing inquest there was information Emily wouldn't disclose that Taggart needed for corroboration in gearing up an argument for reopening of the case: Raymond; the Moleskines; Joel's involvement . . . evidence that went to the indictment of Seymour for the murder of Nadia. Early on, Taggart threatened to subpoena Emily's testimony, but the threat was never carried out, probably for fear it would bring back to life the closed investigation into Nadia's death.

Memorial Library treated the whole incident with silence. Helena was still out of town on her lecture tour. Jean and Chloe had gone strangely silent, as if coached by someone not to talk to Emily. Even Joel, who had been brought in for questioning, not wanting to be implicated, had to lie and downplay his relationship with Emily. Emily understood. In the lead-up to the Gala, a blanket had been thrown over the investigation, and the cover-up was underway. Her remaining days, wandering Special Collections & Archives, were spent as if a ghost, a tacit persona non grata, much as Nadia had once been. Greetings were curt, smiles were forced. Emily experienced an omnipresent feeling of amiable shunning, as if her colleagues all feared for their jobs if they didn't distance themselves.

Maybe it *was* all about getting the Moleskines back in Elizabeth's and Helena's possession. Emily's biggest fear was that in the aftermath of the confrontation with Seymour, Raymond, in fear of the trail leading to his doorstep, had, to protect his wife and his own reputation, destroyed the Moleskines. After all, to Raymond, it was just another novel. The discovery of the Moleskines would open up another Pandora's Box for him. Emily took solace in the fact that she didn't give up Raymond or the location of the Moleskines. And, if in saving him from being hauled in as a potential suspect, along with his prominent wife, she had denied Nadia's finding justice, then so be it.

Maybe Nadia, in despair over the sudden, tragic, end of her relationship with Raymond, did walk into those dark waters. This was a question that continued to haunt Emily. It was out of her hands now though. In her heart, she knew she had exhausted the exhumation of the truth. As an archivist, she rationalized, that's all she could do.

On the day of the Eighth Floor Gala, Emily stood back from the bathroom mirror and looked at herself with head cocked to the side. For the A-list event she had picked out a black spaghetti strap dress that fell to her knees. She stood higher up on the only pair of heels she owned as she gazed at herself admiringly. Pursing out her lips, she applied an extra touch of lipstick until they burned two matching curves of vermillion into the mirror. All at once she felt nervous about seeing Raymond again. Elizabeth. And Helena, who was flying in from the East Coast hours before the event.

Emily drove alone to the university. The storm clouds were broken with patches of blue and their outlines limned with all the hues of the warm end of the color spectrum. The sky was spectacular, doming an ocean that churned furiously, a Turner painting come to life. The buffeting winds rocked her car as she passed the natural wind tunnel of the Los Peñasquitos Lagoon.

Emily parked in the Jameson parking structure for the last time. When she emerged out of the complex she gazed up, also for the last time, at the immensity of Memorial Library, a final marveling at its imperiousness. The top floor was resplendent in warm light, a nimbus of change, she thought to herself. With the lights deliberately banked on all the other floors for the celebratory event, the top floor floated in the sky like a massive corona, haloing this symbol of education, wealth, and hypocrisy.

People were converging on the library from the various parking options, as if Memorial Library pulled in the wealthy and the prominent of San Diego like an enormous magnet. Emily came to a stop at a new sign planted at the end of a pathway that broadened out to the third-floor mezzanine and the gigantic cement pedestal that supported the library's colossal diamond-shaped upper floors. The sign had been unveiled in a press conference televised on all the local news organizations. Planted in the ground on two sturdy posts, it was a simple rectangular panel of wood with white-painted lettering: Elizabeth West Library. Underneath this was painted Regents University. It was official. Helena Blackwell's years-long cultivation of Elizabeth West's friendship—and money—had led to this moment. Raymond West, doomed to a society marriage of convenience, had been properly embalmed and laid to rest in the catacombs, thanks to Nadia's and Emily's assiduous work on his papers. That's how Emily cynically viewed it now. Seymour would plead out, give up no one, retain the finest criminal defense attorneys the one who hired him could afford and spend a few years in jail. Yes, he had been hired to find the Moleskines, but murder was his own idea. The gears of wealth and power would bury it; they always did. True justice would not be served because the tributaries never flowed back to the headwaters of true power.

A gust of wind blustered out of the storm off the ocean and blew unimpeded across the mezzanine and Emily hugged her arms close to her chest. Thunder startled the sky with a low rumble out over the ocean. A delayed few seconds later, a silent jagged line of lightning fissured the sky. Raindrops spattered on the cement. Against the glowing eighth floor the rain fell like silver threads. The guests quickened their paces, spoking in from all directions. A few with foresight broke open umbrellas. Emily joined the vortex, massing now toward the library's lighted, beckoning entrance. READ WRITE THINK DREAM. It had once been so, thought Emily, as she passed through the automatic sliding glass doors.

Out of habit, Emily debated taking the stairwell, but the thought of climbing eight floors in high heels made her worry she would arrive at the top with blistered feet and busted heels.

Crammed together with tuxedoed men and women rustling in formal wear, Emily rode the elevator—*bing bing*—without even a scintilla of her former anxiety and dreaded misophonia. It was as if she were numb to it all now. She had lived through a death of one of her own, and she had nearly died herself in the process, and she feared nothing.

The elevator doors sprung open to a stunning sight. Chandeliered ceilings cast a warm glow on the Who's Who crowd of San Diego, as well as other literary and academic luminaries who had flown in for the rechristening of the library and the honoring of the Raymond West Papers and their official new home. Fresh-faced young waiters, uniformed in black and white, moved desultorily through the throng of guests holding up trays of champagne and canapés on inverted palms. Foldup chairs had been arranged in front of a movable stage where a large podium stood, with a microphone mounted on it.

Emily accepted a glass of champagne from a smiling waiter and drifted over to the display cases of the West Papers. She recognized a few famous literary faces in the crowd. A man about Raymond's age, with his signature blue-framed spectacles and short-cropped hair, introduced himself to a guest as Nick Peterson, Raymond's editor. When they had done exchanging congratulations and the like, Emily approached him.

"Hi, Mr. Peterson, I'm Emily Snow. I'm the archivist who finished the Raymond West Collection."

Peterson reached for her outstretched hand and took it in his. "So good to meet you, Ms. Snow." He swiveled his head all around, casing the crowd. "What an incredible night this is," he exclaimed over the collective voices. "A fitting tribute all around."

"Yes," said Emily. "You know, I've always wanted to ask you something—if you don't mind."

Peterson returned his gaze to her, beetled his brow. "Go ahead."

"Did you ever hear about an unfinished book of Raymond's with the working title *The Archivist*?"

A dark ray crossed Peterson's face. He smiled stoically without showing his teeth.

"In my archival duties I came across some correspondence between you and Mr. West where it was mentioned," Emily elaborated.

"The title sounds vaguely familiar," Peterson allowed. "I believe he abandoned it."

"I don't think he did," Emily asserted. "In fact . . . I know he didn't."

Peterson frowned at her, intrigued, but vaguely disconcerted too. In hushed tones he leaned down and inquired, "Did you . . . come across it somehow?"

Emily bore her eyes into his with deep, subterranean meaning. "I think you should ask him about it."

Peterson's head bent close to hers until their faces were almost touching, the publisher in him smelling a literary coup. "You've read it?"

Emily met his question with eyes of burning magnesium. "I'm not at liberty to say." Then Emily did something uncharacteristic for her: she winked.

Peterson seemed baffled by her words. He drew back his head. "I'll bring it up with Raymond. We're having brunch tomorrow. *The Archivist*, you say it was titled?"

Emily nodded. "Do that," she said, with that blue fire still glinting in her eyes. "The world is owed that book."

A woman tugged at Peterson's elbow. "Nick, darling, Salman Rushdie's here, let's go say hi."

Peterson held out a hand to Emily. "It was a pleasure to meet you."

He started off, pulled away by his wife. Peterson threw Emily a backward, fretfully knowing glance, as he blended into the crowd. Emily could tell from his expression she had sown a seed.

Emily lowered her eyes into the display cases. The glass reflected the twinkling light of the chandeliers and her young, but no longer callow, face. She had fantasized about the twelve Moleskines arrayed in an arc, but the money that bought the eighth floor didn't buy the truth. Art, too, erected its boundaries and bared its ramparts to the world.

Emily drifted away from the bowdlerized display. A sadness accumulated inside her. She had come to meet the one person she wanted to talk to, Nick Peterson. And she had said her peace in a final cry from the void that her predecessor had leaped into, unapologetically, unhesitatingly, fearlessly.

Emily toured the upper floor, circumnavigating for the last time the now four grand rectangular areas where books no longer existed. The library had been constructed entirely because of the existence of the printed word and the writers who sacrificed their lives for the expression of their own truth they were seeking, and now they had been replaced by an event center to raise money on the invisible husks of their deracinated works.

Emily roamed eastward, then north. A jazz combo maintained a steady beat in one of the corners, its music reverberating off the hard surfaces. The elegantly upholstered lounge chairs were now spilling out with the affluent guests, noshing on lox and sipping Moët. The collective, overlapping conversations were compressed into an indistinguishable hum of the elite.

"Knock knock," said a familiar voice.

Emily spun around to find a giggling Chloe. She was transformed in a blue satin dress. Next to her stood Jesse, tall and grinning. Remembering the drunken night with Jesse's business partner, Emily flashed an embarrassed grin.

"Hi, Emily. Nice to see you," said Jesse.

"I'm surprised they invited the staff," quipped Chloe, looking around at the star-studded crowd. "Did you see Ann Patchett?" she whispered. "I adore her work."

"Yeah, I heard she was here," Emily said.

Through the crowd, Joel came toward the three of them. "Hi, Emily. You look beautiful. Never seen you dressed up before."

Emily smiled at the compliment. "Nice to see you, Joel."

"Well, this is half of Special Collections," Chloe chirped, throwing her hands up in the air in a giddy moment of exultation.

"There's going to be a lot more once that gift endows those new positions," said Joel. "I, for one, am not looking forward to acquainting myself with new coworkers."

Everyone laughed.

"Has anyone seen the redoubtable Helena?" Emily asked.

Chloe shook her head.

"She's probably going to make one of her patented grand entrances," Joel said with barely disguised disdain.

Near them, the elevator doors slammed open, and they all turned at the thunderous noise. Off stepped Raymond West. He was attired in formal black and white, with the slight subversive touch of a cowboy's bolo tie. The cane, that symbol of so much, was gone, and it was grip-and-grin time for the famous honoree. In his expression, Emily could easily make out the wholesale resignation to obligation in his tight smile as guests converged on him, like moths to an incandescent light of fame.

"Excuse me," Emily said to her coworkers, breaking away and threading through the horde of guests in the direction of Raymond. Stopping a few steps short of him, she waited for his wife to be pulled away by the commanding magnetism of her own celebrity, now that she had officially announced her candidacy in the San Diego mayoral race.

When she was out of earshot, Emily surreptitiously knifed through the cluster of well-wishers and sidled up next to Raymond. He was shaking a bearded man's hand and kissing the cheek of the man's wife as they lauded his work in gushing hyperbole and congratulated him on the rechristening of the library, effusing praise from radiant, starstruck faces.

"Hi, Raymond," Emily said, edging her slender frame through the throng of bodies.

Raymond turned and dropped his eyes to her. He stood even taller in his cowboy boots. "Hi, Ms. Snow," he said with clipped formality, glancing around nervously, his height affording him a view of the entire gathering. Assured that his wife had been pulled far enough away, he held out his hand and Emily took it in hers. "Did you ever figure out where you're headed next?"

"University of Texas. Harry Ransom."

"Good place. Do you know something? Whenever I finish a work, I always launch my book tours in Austin."

"Seriously?"

"Superstition, I guess," he said in a distant voice.

"Didn't know that. Will there ever be another work, now that you're a hotshot screenwriter?"

Raymond studied her with keen eyes. He waited. He wasn't one for sentimental nostalgia, especially of the tragic variety. He smiled faintly.

"Don't want to end up like Ian McEwan," Emily said, trying to lighten the mood. "Just writing movies now."

Raymond's smile deepened. A cloud crossed his face and settled there, occluding the smile. An unspoken silence hung between them, a tacit understanding of a subterranean story that flowed like a dark river and, like the ouroboros Emily wore conspicuously around her neck—which she saw Raymond noticed—would keep flowing back to the source, forever regenerating, unable to die. Some hearts, like memories, pumped forever.

Their private understanding was interrupted by the elevator doors clanging open. Helena Blackwell stepped off with a goateed man on her arm, a tenured history professor she was rumored to be dating.

Emily started to make a remark to Raymond when she noticed he had furtively slipped away into the crowd. Did he not want to be seen in Emily's presence? Had the reality returned to fiction? A photographer was snapping pictures for the media and perhaps he didn't want to be photographed with her now that the news had broken that Nadia's death was being reinvestigated as a possible homicide.

Helena was greeted by well-wishers. Her black-and-silver mane was professionally styled. Her dress was Rent the Runway, but it looked "fabulous." Her face was a lopsided landscape of laughter, her arms and hands an octopus of greetings and introductions and congratulations on the opulent spectacle of the eighth-floor renovation. Her ultimate triumph, her dream made manifest, she basked in its unveiling, gushed a hundred thank-yous.

Emily slinked away and secreted herself into the crowd when she spotted Elizabeth approaching Helena with open arms. The two of them hugged, gripped each other's shoulders like old friends, and exchanged mutually flattering compliments. Emily heard Elizabeth ask Helena, "When did you get in?" but didn't hear Helena's answer.

After another tour of champagne and canapés by the bustling wait staff, someone tapped the front table's microphone and requested everyone be seated. As Emily came in from the east side of the floor with Joel, she recognized Verlander holding court at the podium. Except for the first few rows, where the seats were designated with paper name signs, the remaining chairs were open seating. Emily and Joel found seats near the front.

Finally, after some corralling by event coordinators, the some 150 guests settled into the folding chairs and the room quieted to a respectful silence.

Verlander, looking incongruously uncomfortable in a tuxedo, lowered his mouth to the microphone. He adjusted the glasses on the brow of his nose and rested his hands on the table. "Welcome, everyone. Thank you all for coming." Verlander waited a moment for the crowd to fully settle. A hush fell over the packed west wing of the eighth floor. "Tonight is a special night. Regents University opened for students in 1965. There was one college. Now there are six. Back then, there were fewer than two thousand students. Now, there are over thirty-five thousand. We are the second largest employer in all of San Diego."

Applause greeted his roll call of the university's growth and accomplishments.

Verlander beamed and held up his hand. "And this library is the center of the university. More people come here than any other building on campus. And our Special Collections is the glittering jewel. And that jewel has been polished and rubbed and polished . . . by one person over the span of thirty-five glorious years." With a penchant for the melodramatic, Verlander paused.

One of the interns swung a light from the stage to spotlight Helena Blackwell. It lit up the silver streaks in her hair like freeway lane dividers.

In a rising tone, Verlander introduced, "Our esteemed director. Please welcome Ms. Helena Blackwell." He opened an arm to the entire eighth-floor world and the castle she had created. She rose to thunderous applause on arthritic hips. Turning to the Who's Who of San Diego and the university, she waved to everybody in the crowd. Emily slowly, and unenthusiastically, clapped as Helena made her way to the podium. One of the young interns offered her an outstretched hand. Helena took it, and he helped her up the short flight of steps to the stage, the spotlight following her as if she were a movie star at a red-carpet premiere. At the podium, she and Verlander hugged collegially.

As Helena addressed the microphone, Verlander stepped backward, clapping along with the standing ovation that greeted Helena. "Thank you, David," she said. She turned to the audience and waited until they were all seated again and had quieted down.

She began, "Thirty-five years ago, I came to this library and was hired in, of all things, public relations. I had a degree in English literature. I loved books. I've always loved books. I'm sad to see them go. But as our Special Collections grew, as we lobbied and secured the acquisition of the archives of celebrated writers and artists and scholars, as we forged into the digital future, I envisioned this eighth floor to be an event center for the kind of fundraising we need to do if we're going to grow and prosper and remain current with the times."

Emily could see how filled with pride Helena was. This was her night, and she had been rehearsing for it for years. The ingratiation of the rich was over. This was her moment to bask in the limelight. This was her house on the hill that looked down on everybody else.

"Thirty-five years ago, I remember coming up to this floor late at night. I saw a young, handsome man, sitting all alone at a table, his nose buried in a book. Probably *War and Peace*." She paused to give way to a few scattered chuckles. "I informed him we were closing and he had to leave. He looked up at me as if he had lost all track of time. We spoke in the elevator on the way down. He was very intense, enthusing about what he had been reading . . ." She paused to clear her throat. "Who would have guessed he would have gone on to write a Pulitzer Prize–winning novel, become the youngest writer inducted into the American Academy and Institute of Arts and Letters, honored with countless awards, too many to list here. What *is* worth noting is that this library was where it all began for this budding young writer—this library and its trove of books inspired him. Of course, today, he wouldn't find an empty desk because we've grown so big!" she boasted. Helena waited for more applause. "If Special Collections is the jewel of this library, then his papers are the crown jewel. I am, of course, speaking about our esteemed Professor Raymond West, whose work and life we're celebrating tonight." Helena extended an arm.

Raymond West was encouraged to stand at the explosion of the deafening applause. He rose gingerly on a still-painful leg. As he straightened to a standing position, he seemed to rise higher than anyone else in the room. Emily saw him as someone who had reluctantly retreated into the world of academia, the man of arts and letters, the man married to the wealthy woman, now politely clapping at his side and looking up at him with pleased eyes. The horse she had risked her fortune on had won the Triple Crown. Soon they would move to the mansion they were building overlooking all of La Jolla. Elizabeth's mayoral victory was all but a foregone conclusion.

Raymond gave a backward glance, waved and sheepishly smiled in appreciation to the assembled illuminati. It was his moment too, and despite all the suffering that had underpinned its engenderment, he was a man who had learned how to assimilate everything and place it in its proper context, its segmented chronicle of his journey to this moment. Nadia Fontaine was now only one marker on that road to this illustrious occasion, and Raymond, burying the tragedy of her death, now reached down and exhibited the good form and manners his wife had always exacted of him. He luxuriated in the applause like the true court jester of the San Diego and literary elite he had become. He was officially one of them. He had shed the memory of Nadia, *The Archivist*, and it was time to move on. Elizabeth West, and her money, had triumphed.

Was Emily the only one on the eighth floor who, in the buzz of adulatory applause, heard the *bing bing* of the arriving elevator? She turned to her left the moment the doors clanged open. Off stepped Detective Taggart. Flanking him on his right was a badass-looking, impassive-faced female uniformed officer, a .357 bouncing heavily on her holstered hip. Their grim countenances and professional attire suggested to anyone who noticed that they weren't invited to this event. The elevator doors slammed shut behind them, punctuating their entrance with a bang, heightening the portent of their arrival to Emily. An intern approached Taggart and whispered something to him. Whatever Taggart said made the intern quail and back away.

Taggart's eyes found Emily's gazing back at him from the aisle. His, it seemed to her, were heavy and almost dolorous with apology. Taggart spoke in undertones to the female officer, and she nodded with a serious expression, then moved crabwise along the elevator shaft to assume a new position. Taggart returned his attention to the podium. Underneath his brown coat Emily could make out the menacing bulge of a weapon. Emily wasn't sure what was going to happen next, but in the meeting of their eyes was born, she dreamed, the seed of justice.

Helena prattled on. "A university library of this glorious magnitude would not be what it is without our donors . . . many of whom are here tonight. But when it comes to donors, there is one person who stands out above all the rest." A smiled widened out onto her face. "I am, of course, speaking about the wife of Raymond West: the fabulous philanthropist, Elizabeth West." Helena threw out a bejeweled arm and motioned her to come up.

Elizabeth West stood, magnificent in a royal blue pant ensemble and blouse, a triple-strand pearl necklace adorning her neck, fingers winking with glittering jewels. She was the stylish and beautiful twin of Catherine Deneuve, grace and confidence built into her small frame and leonine mane of hair.

Taking the podium to a standing ovation, Elizabeth and Helena demonstratively embraced on the stage, held each other back in girded arms, and beamed at each other victoriously.

Helena let go and moved her mouth back to the microphone and spoke in a rising, trilling voice. "Twenty-five million dollars to invest in state-of-the-art technology, hire the finest archivists to take us into the new digital frontier, build spectacular event spaces like this eighth floor, endow new positions like David Verlander's and others. Just as this great library of ours was designed with a futuristic look a half century ago, Elizabeth West's generous gift secures this library's future far into the twenty-first century." She turned and smiled radiantly at Elizabeth as the audience erupted into applause, the majority rising to their feet to pay their respects to this admired of all Regents donors. Helena waited and then continued, "The eighth floor will now forever be changed. During the day it will be a luxury reading lounge open to the public." Helena extended an arm to the west-facing windows with their brocaded curtains and row of luxury lounge chairs. "At night, for special occasions, it will be restruck and transformed into an all-purpose event center. And, in exchange for making this eighth-floor renovation possible, we are naming the top floor," she paused and finished on a triumphant note, "Liz's Lounge."

On cue, a curtain behind Helena dramatically parted to reveal a neon sign pulsing the words: "Liz's Lounge."

More applause greeted the unveiling. To Emily, the sign appeared tawdry. From a floor of timeless literature to a luxury lounge for rich students hypnotized by their devices.

Her chest swelling with pride, Helena shouted above the applause. "As of tonight, and forever more, we are now officially the Elizabeth West Library." She held out an outstretched arm to Elizabeth. "Elizabeth West, everyone, the next mayor of San Diego!"

Helena backed away clapping. The applause from the audience continued unabated. Helena reached the edge of the stage and paused for Elizabeth's opening words.

"Thank you, Helena," Elizabeth began. "Thank you, everyone, for coming out on this rainy night and honoring this majestic institution." She waited for the applause to subside. "And, yes, it is true, I've announced my candidacy for mayor." Scattered applause erupted again, which Elizabeth quickly silenced by holding up her hand. "But that's not why we're here tonight." She paused. A warm glow emanated from her as she gazed down on her husband. *Conferring on him forgiveness?* Emily wondered. "I met Raymond twenty-five years ago," she began, "In him, in his early works when I was a book editor in my early days, I recognized a unique talent, an original voice." She paused and smiled down at him again. "I guess I wasn't wrong," she said with deep emotion through adoring, pardoning eyes. As Elizabeth launched into her paean to her husband and their wonderful two and a half decades together in the literary firmament, Emily, nausea building in her at the hypocrisy of the whole rechristening of this famous edifice, looked off toward the elevator doors.

Taggart, with the bleak inevitability of the job at hand, stepped away from the elevator in the direction of the far side of the stage. As his coat shifted, his bronze law enforcement badge flashed over his heart with the glint of authority. Emily instinctively rose from her seat and shadowed him. She didn't know why, but she did, her legs discharged by a feeling, her heart seized by a dark thrill. This was her journey to justice too.

During Elizabeth's gracious paean to her husband and acceptance of the library's rededication, Helena had stepped down from the edge of the stage and was returning to her seat when Taggart intercepted her and blocked her from going farther. Helena, obliquely recognizing Taggart, regarded him with a pallid expression of utter shock, as if: *this can't be happening*. Emily sidled up next to Taggart as he said, "Helena Blackwell?"

"Yes?" Helena replied in a quavering voice, looking all around her, appearances being everything at this Himalayan high moment of hers.

In dignified undertones, Taggart said, "You are under arrest. You're charged with the murder of Nadia Fontaine. You have the right to remain silent. Anything you say can and will be used against you in a court of law." Helena drew a hand to her mouth and emitted a muffled shriek. She backed away. Taggart grabbed her wrist, clicked one end of a pair of handcuffs on it, and stopped her in her tracks.

At Taggart's words, at the flashing of those handcuffs, Emily blinked back rejoicing tears.

Taggart continued reading her Miranda rights, "You have the right to speak to an attorney, and to have an attorney present during any questioning. If you cannot afford a lawyer, one will be provided for you at government expense." He paused and pulled an aghast Helena toward him. "Please come with me, Ms. Blackwell."

Taggart started to escort her off. A commotion was brewing in the audience as attention was drawn away from the podium and to the rippling disturbance of Helena Blackwell's arrest. Awakening to what was happening, Helena broke free from Taggart's grasp and ran wildly, screaming at the top of her lungs.

Taggart raised a hand and signaled to the female officer, motioning for her to head her off. At Taggart's signal, his partner broke into a brisk walk to intercept Helena, who was heading for the stairwell doors on the north end of the center tower like a giant, flightless bird, chased by predators, fighting headwinds on broken wings.

Pandemonium seized the audience. Some stood, looked all around with disconcerted expressions. Elizabeth had paused in her speech, alarm utterly annihilating her earlier aplomb. Murmuring voices of puzzlement rose in volume from behind Emily.

Emily and Taggart reached the door to the stairwell. As if sucked in by a mortal force, they both went inside the vast cylindrical stairwell. The female officer was already inside, shouting over the railing at Helena, who was looking up at them from the seventh-floor landing, her face drawn in a rictus of doom, her whooping cries reverberating in the stairwell shaft.

Taggart took up the exhortation to Helena. "Ms. Blackwell! There are police waiting downstairs. There's nowhere to go! Give yourself up!"

Helena looked down, then back up at the two officers and Emily. Emily, who never had been able to look down over the railing from the eighth floor to the bottom without her acrophobia rearing its head, now leaned over the railing and stared into the frightened face of the director of Special Collections & Archives, the woman who had hired her.

Panicked, with nowhere to go, Helena, in a moment of madness, or appalling recognition that the remaining years of her life would be spent in public ignominy, clambered awkwardly, desperately, pathetically, over the railing and let go.

Her screams continued to echo in the stairwell as she plunged seven floors to the concrete below. Emily heard the horrifying impact of Helena's collision with the floor as flesh and cartilage met concrete in an unbroken fall.

Emily kicked off her heels and started down the spiral stairwell, one hand sliding along the railing all the way, unhesitating, unafraid, in her descent.

"Stop!" shouted Taggart. "Ms. Snow. Stop!"

Emily ignored him. She circumvoluted the eight floors in a fast-stepping, headlong pace until she reached the bottom. Uniformed officers were already closing in on the suicide scene, their walkie-talkies squawking with voices summoning ambulances.

Emily reached the bottom where Helena Blackwell's limp body lay splattered against the concrete in a twisted mass of warped limbs, blood puddling in a mottled circle and widening its radius in a spreading sea of red. Blood vermiculated from every orifice: nostrils, eyes, ears, and the corners of her grotesquely agape mouth. The limp arm with the handcuffs on her wrist seemed to speak volumes. Thirty-five years to get to the top floor, 3.5 seconds to perish in abject humiliation at its bottom. Where Special Collections held the secrets she couldn't abide, where conspiracy to murder seemed her only desperate recourse to get to the top floor and her dream of a reborn library. First, the truth had to be quashed.

CHAPTER 26

Becoming a Pelican

The night had been long, and chaos and confusion reigned. The news media reported on the developing story of Helena Blackwell's death. As the scandal bled into morning like a red tide into shallow waters, erupting on the local news, reverberating nationally, Emily followed it online. The police reported Helena Blackwell would have been arrested for conspiracy to murder of Nadia Fontaine. The actual murderer was Richard Seymour, who had pled guilty and testified Helena hired him to kill, or get rid of, Nadia, by whatever means necessary. As the university and Elizabeth West's LA attorneys plunged into damage control, the motivation for the murder fed to the media was that Ms. Fontaine had discovered a slush fund where Helena Blackwell had been embezzling thousands of dollars through a fictitious catering company. When Ms. Fontaine threatened to go to authorities, Seymour killed her after refusing to be extorted. In the end, the university and Elizabeth West had taken control of the narrative and refashioned it the way their sanctimonious editors had wanted. It didn't matter to Taggart that the love affair, the Moleskines, the pregnancy, were all buried under the now official story, that the real motive lay in a different kind of greed, one that had more to do with vanity. To Taggart, the case of an accidental drowning had simply been reopened, reinvestigated, and Nadia's death ruled and solved as a murder. Vindication exacted, perpetrators brought to justice.

Emily's name was kept out of the media. Taggart obliquely referred to her as an "inside source." There was no mention of the Moleskines or *The Archivist* or Emily Snow.

To Emily, it was a Pyrrhic victory. A sadness still engulfed her as she drove to the Gliderport to meet Joel a week later. The passing storm had washed the skies clean, and the ocean slipped away to a coral- and violet-streaked horizon.

After getting situated with all the gear, Joel held Emily in his arms from behind. They were both strapped into a paragliding harness. The wind filled their chute as Joel expertly operated the contraption like an accomplished marionette.

"Here we go," he said to Emily. "Are you ready?"

"Let's do it!" Emily said, with the confidence she once lacked.

Together, they stutter-stepped toward the precipice of the cliff and the thousand-foot drop-off. Emily screamed in exhilaration and nervous fear, but she didn't hold back. She wasn't afraid of dying; she wasn't afraid of the void.

When they left the ground and dropped into the abyss above Black's Beach, Emily was still screaming, but she experienced a freedom she had never felt before. The wind colliding with the cliff produced a powerful updraft, and soon they were rising skyward, as if borne by some supernatural force. Joel leaned back into the glider basket and Emily fell on top of him in a similarly supine position. Expertly maneuvering the various lines and risers, Joel banked their flying machine in a big arcing, swooping turn, and navigated it south. They soared along the cliffs in the direction of Black's Beach, with only the whooshing of the wind in their ears.

Emily, strapped against Joel's chest, reached out both arms to the world below her, liberated from everything. Free as a pelican. Tears of joy whipped backward to her temples by the rushing air.

EPILOGUE

18 Months Later

It was a beautiful spring evening in Austin, Texas, as Emily Snow strolled her way across campus toward the Harry Ransom Center, her new place of employment as its new head of Digital Archives and Manuscripts Processing. Her article "Ethics and the Dark Archives," where she wrote about a case similar to Nadia's and Raymond's at a fictitious Special Collections, was published in *The American Archivist* and had gained her a modicum of recognition in the field. Emily never told the true story. She had too much respect for the privacy of all those involved.

With a smile on her face, Emily strode proudly into the facility and navigated her way into the main reading room. She stopped at the threshold. A line had formed leading to a table where an author was signing books. The author looked up and saw Emily.

Raymond West, in his signature off-white muslin button-up shirt, raised his hand and motioned for her to come to the front of the line. He seemed to have regained his vigor. His hair was cut short, and it looked like he had been working out.

Emily paralleled the fans waiting in line. When she reached the table, she saw the pile of books, copies of Raymond's new novel. *The Archivist.* In book holders, both front and back covers were presented to the fans. The front cover image was taken from one of the black Moleskines with the silver handwritten lettering of Nadia spelling out the title and the names of the coauthors: Raymond West and Nadia Fontaine. The back cover was sheared into two triangles. The upper left triangle featured a wryly smiling Raymond West. The lower right triangle, slashed by a deliberately jagged diagonal line, displayed the fey-looking face of Nadia Fontaine, with that hauntingly decadent beauty of hers, that thick mane of sable-black hair and those penetrating brown eyes, the author she had aspired to become, with Raymond forever.

Emily, overcome with emotion, blinked back the onset of tears. She had gotten word about the imminent publication from Verlander, but seeing the book in person for the first time, picking one up and turning it over in her hands, evoked a deeper upwelling of feeling in her.

"Emily," greeted Raymond warmly. "What a lovely surprise."

"Hi, Raymond."

Their eyes met in an awkward embrace.

Almost in disbelief, Emily turned the book over and over in both hands with the care of a professional archivist, seized by an emotion she struggled to give voice to.

"She won't ever be forgotten, will she?" Emily finally said, tears springing to her eyes.

"No," said Raymond, pausing. "And neither will you. Now everyone will know the truth."

Emily croaked, "Yes."

Raymond leaned his head forward and lowered his voice so others crowded around couldn't hear. "She unlocked all my dreams of love. You resurrected them from the dead."

"Me and Nadia," Emily reminded him.

"Yes. You *and* Nadia."

A silence fell. The clamoring of Raymond's fans behind them sounded far away suddenly.

Raymond finally spoke. "I've always wanted to ask you—why did you do it? You risked so much."

Sniffling, Emily gathered herself and spoke to their conjoined pictures on the back cover, a couple in love. "I happened upon something extraordinary, beautiful, and extremely rare. How could I let someone destroy that?"

Biting his upper lip to hold back his own emotion, Raymond nodded thoughtfully. They could both sense the people around them growing restless. Emily hugged the book to her chest. "Thank you, Raymond."

"Come visit me at Regents anytime," he invited.

"It's all in the dark archives," Emily said.

"Yes," said Raymond. "And one day the restrictions will be lifted." He winked archly.

Emily smiled at his words. "I'm glad to hear that."

Looking at their authors' photos sheared together, Emily asked, "Do you still miss her?"

As if he had been holding himself together since Emily's approach, Raymond suddenly broke down and began to softly cry. He covered his face with his hands to staunch the tears. When he removed them, his eyes were bloodshot and sodden with grief. "Every fucking day of my life."

Emily reached out her hand. Raymond took it in both of his.

"It was a pleasure working on your collection, Raymond."

"Thank you for all your hard work, Emily. I'll miss you."

"And I'll miss you."

They shook hands, holding them clasped for a long moment.

"Come visit me," Raymond repeated.

"I promise." Emily started off, stopped, turned to Raymond. "Out of curiosity, what did your now ex-wife think?"

A wry smile curled his lips. "She thought it was art."

Emily smiled back.

Raymond pursed his lips and nodded, mourning a sadness too ineffable to even begin to voice. *The Archivist* was its awful, redemptive, truth.

Emily held out the copy she had picked up. "Would you autograph my book?"

Raymond took the book from her and smiled. He set her copy of *The Archivist* down on the table and opened it to the title page. He took meticulous care in signing his name as if he didn't want her to leave, as if he wanted to hold on to her forever. When he was finished, he looked up at her and held out the book for her to take.

Their eyes locked on a wavelength that was inexpressibly theirs, and theirs alone. "Will you please inscribe it?" Emily asked through eyes now blurred with tears, wanting to extend the moment too.

"I already did." Raymond slowly opened the book to the dedication page, turned it around 180 degrees and slid it across the desk so that it was directly beneath Emily's tearstained eyes. "Without you, all of this would have been lost forever. Don't you deserve to be remembered, too?"

Emily looked down and read the dedication burned in sans serif font into *The Archivist* for all eternity:

For Emily Snow, my Eavesdropping Angel . . .

The End